Bir
e

THE AMBLER
WARNING

ROBERT LUDLUM

THE AMBLER WARNING

ORION

First published in Great Britain in 2005 by Orion,
an imprint of Orion Books Ltd
Orion House, 5 Upper St Martin's Lane, London WC2H 9EA

1 3 5 7 9 10 8 6 4 2

ISBN 0 75285 749 5 (hardback)

ISBN 0 75286 788 1 (trade paperback)

A CIP catalogue record for this book is
available from the British Library

Printed and bound in Great Britain by
Clays Ltd, St Ives plc

www.orionbooks.co.uk

The unapparent connection is more powerful than the apparent one.

—Heraclitus, 500 B.C.

PART ONE

PART ONE

CHAPTER ONE

The building had the invisibility of the commonplace. It could have been a large public high school or a regional tax-processing center. A blocky structure of tan brick—four stories around an inner courtyard—the building looked like countless others erected in the 1950s and '60s. A casual passerby would not have given it a second look.

Yet there was no such thing as a casual passerby here. Not on this barrier island, six miles off the coast of Virginia. The island was, officially, part of America's National Wildlife Refuge System, and anyone who made inquiries learned that, owing to the extreme delicacy of its ecosystem, no visitors were permitted. Part of the island's leeward side was, indeed, a habitat for ospreys and mergansers: raptors and their prey, both endangered by the greatest predator of all, man. But the central part of the island was given over to a fifteen-acre campus of manicured green and carefully graded slopes, where the bland-looking facility was situated.

The boats that stopped at Parrish Island three times a day had NWRS markings, and from a distance it would not be apparent that the personnel ferried to the island looked nothing like park rangers. If a disabled fishing vessel tried to land on the island, it would be intercepted by khaki-clad men with genial smiles and hard, cold eyes. No one ever got close enough to see, and wonder about, the four guard towers, or the electrified fencing that surrounded the campus.

The Parrish Island Psychiatric Facility, as unremarkable in appearance as it was, contained a greater wilderness than any that surrounded it: that of the human mind. Few people in the government knew of the facility. Yet simple logic had decreed its existence: a psychiatric facility for patients who were in possession of highly classified information. A secure environment was needed to treat someone who was out of his mind when that mind was filled with secrets of state. At Parrish Island, potential security risks could be carefully managed. All staff members were thoroughly vetted, with high-level clearance, and round-the-clock audio and video surveillance systems offered further protection against breaches of security. As an additional safeguard, the facility's clinical staff was rotated every three months, thus minimizing the possibility that inappropriate attachments might develop. Security protocols even stipulated that patients be identified by number, never by name.

Rarely, there would be a patient who was deemed an especially high risk, either because of the nature of his psychiatric disorder or because of the particular sensitivity of what he knew. A patient so designated would be isolated from other patients and housed in a separate locked ward. In the western wing of the fourth floor was one such patient, No. 5312.

A staffer who had just rotated to Ward 4W and encountered Patient No. 5312 for the first time could be sure only of what could be seen: that he was six feet tall, perhaps forty years of age; that his close-cropped hair was brown, his eyes an unclouded blue. If their eyes met, the staffer would be the first to look away—the intensity of the patient's stare could be unnerving, almost physically penetrative. The rest of his profile was contained in his psychiatric records. As to the wilderness within him, one could only surmise.

Somewhere in Ward 4W were explosions and mayhem and screams, but they were soundless, confined to the patient's troubled dreams, which grew in vividness even as sleep itself began to ebb. These moments before consciousness—when the viewer is aware only of what he views, an eye without an I—were filled by a series of images, each of which buckled like a film strip stopped before an overheated projector bulb. A political rally on a steamy day in Taiwan: thousands of citizens assembled in a large square, cooled only by the very occasional breeze. A political candidate, struck down in midsentence by a blast—small, contained, deadly. Moments before, he had been speaking eloquently, ardently; now he was sprawled on the wooden rostrum, in a cowl of his own blood. He lifted up his head, gazing out at the crowd for the last time, and his eyes settled on one member of the crowd: a *chang bizi*—a Westerner. The one person who was not screaming, crying, fleeing. The one person who did not seem surprised, for he was, after all, in the presence of his own handiwork. The candidate died staring at the man who had come from across the world to kill him. Then the image buckled, shimmied, burned into a blinding white.

A far-off chime from an unseen speaker, a minor-key triad, and Hal Ambler opened his sleep-sticky eyes.

Was it truly morning? In his windowless room, he had no way of telling. But it was *his* morning. Recessed into the ceiling, soft fluorescent lights grew in intensity over a half-hour period: a technological dawn, made brighter by the whiteness of his surroundings. A pretend day, at least, was beginning. Ambler's room was nine feet by twelve feet; the floors were tiled with white vinyl, and the walls were covered with white PVC foam, a dense, rubbery material, lightly yielding to the touch, like a wrestling mat. Before long, the hatch-style door would slide open, making a hydraulic sigh as it did. He knew these details, and hundreds like them. It was the stuff of life in a high-security facility, if you could call it a life. He experienced stretches of grim lucidity, intervals of a fugue state. A larger sense that he had been abducted, not just his body but also his soul.

In the course of a nearly two-decade career as a clandestine operative, Ambler had occasionally been taken captive—it had happened in Chechnya and in Algeria—and he had been subjected to periods of solitary confinement. He knew that the circumstance wasn't conducive to deep thoughts, soul-searching, or philosophical inquiry. Rather, the mind filled with scraps of advertising jingles, pop songs with half-remembered lyrics, and an acute consciousness of small bodily discomforts. It eddied, drifted, and seldom went anywhere interesting, for it was ultimately tethered to the curious agony of isolation. Those who had trained him for the life of an operative had tried to prepare him for such eventualities. The challenge, they had always insisted, was to keep the mind from attacking itself, like a stomach digesting its own lining.

Yet on Parrish Island, he wasn't in the hands of his enemies; he was being held by his own government, the government in whose service he had spent his career.

And he did not know why.

Why *someone* might be interned here wasn't a mystery to him. As a member of the branch of U.S. intelligence known as Consular Operations, he had heard about the facility on Parrish Island. Ambler understood, too, why such a facility had to exist; everyone was susceptible to the frailties of the human mind, including those in possession of highly guarded secrets. But it was dangerous to allow just any psychiatrist access to such a patient. That was a lesson learned the hard way, during the Cold War, when a Berlin-born psychoanalyst in Alexandria whose clientele included several top government officials came to be exposed as a conduit to East Germany's notorious Ministerium für Staatssicherheit.

Yet none of this explained why Hal Ambler found himself here, ever since—but how long had it been? His training had stressed the importance of keeping track of time when in confinement. Somehow he had failed to do so, and his questions about duration went unanswered. Had it been six months, a year, more? There was so much he did not know. One thing he did know was that if he did not escape soon, he really would go mad.

Routine: Ambler could not decide whether the observance of it was his rescue or his ruin. Quietly and efficiently, he completed his personal calisthenics regimen, finishing with a hundred one-armed push-ups, alternating between left and right. Ambler was permitted to bathe every other day; this was not one of them. At a small white sink in a corner of his room, he brushed his teeth. The toothbrush handle, he noticed, was made of a soft, rubbery polymer, lest a piece of hard plastic be sharpened into a weapon. He pressed a touch latch, and a compact electric shaver slid from a compartment above the sink. He was permitted precisely 120 seconds of use before he had to return the sensor-tagged device to its security compartment; otherwise an alarm would chime. After he finished, Ambler splashed water on his face and ran his wet fingers through his hair, finger-combing it into some sort of order. There was no mirror; no reflective surface anywhere. Even the glass in the ward was treated with some antireflective coating. All to some therapeutic end, no doubt. He donned his "day suit," the white cotton smock and loose, elastic-waisted trousers that were the inmates' uniform.

He turned slowly when he heard the door slide open, and smelled the pine-scented disinfectant that always lingered around the hallway. It was, as usual, a heavyset man with a brush cut, dressed in a dove gray poplin uniform, a cloth tab carefully fastened over his pectoral nameplate: another precaution that the staff took on this ward. The man's flat vowels made it clear that he was a Midwesterner, but his boredom and incuriousness were contagious; Ambler took very little interest in him.

More routine: The orderly carried a thick nylon mesh belt in one hand. "Raise your arms" was the grunted instruction as he came over and placed the black nylon belt around Ambler's waist. Ambler was not permitted to leave his room without the special belt. Inside the thick nylon fabric were several flat lithium batteries; once the belt was in place, two metal prongs were positioned just above his left kidney.

The device—it was officially known as a REACT belt, the acronym standing for "Remote Electronically Activated Control Technology"—was typically used for the transport of maximum-security prisoners; in Ward 4W, it was an item of daily attire. The belt could be activated from as far away as three hundred feet and was set to deliver an eight-second charge of fifty thousand volts. The blast of electricity would knock even a sumo wrestler to the floor, where he would twitch uncontrollably for ten or fifteen minutes.

Once the belt was snap-locked in place, the orderly escorted him down the white-tiled hallway for his morning medications. Ambler walked slowly, lumberingly, as if he were wading through water. It was a gait that frequently resulted from high serum levels of antipsy-chotic medications—a gait that everyone who worked in the wards was familiar with. Ambler's movements were belied by the swift effi-ciency with which his gaze took in his surroundings. That was one of the many things the orderly failed to notice.

There were few things that Ambler failed to notice.

The building itself was decades old, but it had been regularly re-furbished with up-to-date security technology: doors were opened by chip cards—cards that contained transponder wafers—rather than keys, and major gateways required retinal scans to operate, so that only authorized personnel could pass. About a hundred feet down the hall from his cell was the so-called Evaluation Room, which had an internal window of gray polarized glass that allowed for observation of the subject within, while making it impossible to observe the observer. There Ambler would sit for regular "psychi-atric evaluations," the purpose of which seemed as elusive to the physician in attendance as it was to him. Ambler had known true de-spair in recent months, and not as a matter of psychiatric distur-bance; instead, his despair flowed from a realistic estimation of his prospects for release. Even in the course of their three-month rotations, the staff had, he sensed, come to regard him as a lifer, someone who would be interned at the facility long after they had left it.

Several weeks ago, however, everything had changed for him. It was nothing objective, nothing physical, nothing *observable*. Yet the plain fact was that he had *reached* someone, and that would make all the difference. More precisely, *she* would. She already had begun to. She was a young psychiatric nurse, and her name was Laurel Holland. And—it was as simple as this—she was on his side.

A few minutes later, the orderly arrived with his lead-footed patient at a large semicircular area of Ward 4W called the lounge. *Lounge:* neither the noun nor the verb was necessarily appropriate. More accurate was its technical designation: surveillance atrium. On one end was some rudimentary exercise equipment and a bookshelf with a fifteen-year-old edition of the *World Book Encyclopedia*. On the other was the dispensary: a long counter, a slat-like sliding window of wire-mesh glass, and, visible through it, a shelf of white plastic bottles with pastel-colored labels. As Ambler had come to learn, the contents of those bottles could be as incapacitating as manacles of steel. They produced torpor without peace, sluggishness without serenity.

But the institution's concern was not peace so much as pacification. Half a dozen orderlies had gathered in the area this morning. It was not unusual: only for the orderlies did the designation *lounge* make sense. The ward had been designed for a dozen patients; it served a population of one. As a result, the area became, informally, a sort of rest-and-recreation center for orderlies who worked in more demanding wards. Their tendency to congregate here, in turn, increased the security in this one.

As Ambler turned and nodded at a pair of orderlies seated at a low foam-cushioned bench, he allowed a slow rivulet of drool to roll down his chin; the gaze he turned toward them was unfocused and hazy. He had already registered the presence of six orderlies as well as the attending psychiatrist and—Ambler's one lifeline—the psychiatric nurse.

"Candy time," one of the orderlies said; the others snickered.

Ambler made his way slowly to the dispensary, where the auburn-haired nurse was waiting with his morning's pills. An imperceptible flicker—a fleeting glance, a fractional head nod—passed between them.

He had learned her name by accident; she'd spilled a cup of water on herself, and the fabric that was supposed to conceal her acetate nameplate became wet and translucent. Laurel Holland: the letters were ghosted beneath the fabric tab. He'd said her name aloud in a low voice; she seemed flustered yet somehow not displeased. With that, something was sparked between them. He studied her face, her posture, her voice, her manner. She was in her thirties, he figured, with hazel eyes flecked with green and a lithe frame. Smarter and prettier than she realized.

Conversations between them were murmured and brief, nothing that would attract notice from the surveillance systems. But a great deal was conveyed even through an exchange of glances and hovering smiles. As far as the system was concerned, he was Patient No. 5312. But by now, he knew that he was much more than a number to her.

He had cultivated her sympathy over the past six weeks not by acting—she would have been on to that, sooner rather than later—but by allowing himself to respond to her as she was, in a way that encouraged her to do the same. She recognized something about him—recognized his *sanity*.

Knowing this had bolstered his faith in himself, and his determination to escape. "I don't want to die in this place," he had murmured to her one morning. She made no reply, but her stricken look told him all he needed to know.

"Your meds," she had said brightly, the next morning, placing three pills on his palm that looked slightly different from the usual dulling neuroleptics. *Tylenol,* she mouthed. Clinical protocol required him to swallow the tablets under her direct supervision and open his mouth afterward to show that he had not secreted them anywhere. He did so, and within an hour he had proof that she had told him the truth. He was lighter on his feet, lighter, too, in spirit. Within a few days, he began to feel brighter eyed, more buoyant—more himself. He had to make an effort to appear medicated, to feign the heavy-gaited Compazine shuffle that the orderlies were accustomed to.

The Parrish Island Psychiatric Facility was a maximum-security center, well equipped with latest-generation technology. Yet no technology ever invented was wholly immune to the human factor. Now, with her body shielding her movements from the camera, she slipped her key card into the elastic waistband of his white-cotton uniform.

"I'm hearing there could be a Code Twelve this morning," she murmured. The code referred to a major medical emergency, requiring a patient's evacuation to an offsite medical center. Laurel Holland did not explain how she knew, but he could guess: the likeliest scenario was that a patient had been complaining of chest pains—early warning signs of a more serious cardiac event. They would be monitoring the situation, knowing that if there were further signs of sudden arrhythmia, the patient would have to be removed to an ICU on the mainland. Ambler remembered one previous Code Twelve—an older patient had suffered a hemorrhagic stroke—and recalled the security procedures that had been followed. As formidable as they were, they represented an irregularity: an irregularity he might be able to exploit.

"Listen," she whispered. "And be ready to act."

Two hours later—hours of glazed silence and immobility on Ambler's part—an electronic chime sounded, followed by an electronic voice: *Code Twelve, Ward Two East.* The prerecorded voice was of the sort heard in airport shuttle trains and modernized subway cars, unsettlingly pleasant. At once, the orderlies were on their feet. *Must be that old guy, in 2E. His second MI, right?* Most of them left for the second-floor ward. Both the chime and the message repeated at frequent intervals.

An elderly heart-attack victim, then, just as one would have predicted. Ambler felt a hand on his shoulder. The same thickset orderly who had been at his door earlier in the morning.

"Standard procedure," the man said. "Patients return to their room during all emergency protocols."

"What's going on?" Ambler asked, thick tongued and dull.

"Nothing you need to worry about. You'll be safe and sound in your room." Translation: *lockdown.* "Now come with me."

Long minutes later, the two men were in front of Ambler's room. The orderly presented his card to the reader, a gray plastic device mounted at waist level near the door, and the hatch-style door slid open.

"In you go," the thickset Midwesterner said.

"Need help to . . ." Ambler took a few steps toward the threshold and then turned back to the orderly, gesturing helplessly toward the porcelain commode.

"Oh hell," the orderly said, his nostrils flared in disgust, and followed Ambler into the room.

You only get one go. No mistakes.

As the orderly came over to him, Ambler stooped, keeping his legs slightly bent at the knees, as if he were starting to crumple. Suddenly he shot upward, ramming the man's jaw with his head. Panic and bewilderment showed in the orderly's face as the jarring force of impact was absorbed: the shuffling, narcotized inmate had turned into a whirlwind of activity—what had happened? Moments later, the orderly fell heavily to the vinyl-tiled floor, and Ambler was on him, going through his pockets.

No mistakes. He could not afford even one.

He collected the chip card and the ID badge and then swiftly changed into the man's dove-gray shirt and trousers. The fit was approximate but not absurd: it could withstand a casual glance. He quickly rolled the trouser cuffs up and inside, invisibly shortening the inseam. The waist of the trousers rode over the stun belt: he would have given almost anything to be rid of it, but this was physically impossible in the time he had. All he could do was cinch in the uniform's gray fabric belt and hope the black nylon mesh of the REACT device remained concealed.

Holding the orderly's chip card to the internal card reader, he opened the door to his room and glanced out. There was nobody in the hallway just now. All nonessential staff had been dispatched to the scene of the medical emergency.

Would the hatch close automatically? He couldn't afford to be wrong. Stepping into the hallway, Ambler held the card to the outside reader. After a couple of clicks, the door slid shut.

Now he raced a few yards to the wide push-bar-equipped door at the end of the hallway. One of the four-point Electrolatch doors. Locked, of course. He presented the same key card he had just used, heard a few clicks as a lock motor turned over. Then nothing. It remained locked.

This wasn't a passageway authorized for orderlies.

He realized why Laurel Holland had given him her chip card: the doorway had to open onto the same corridor by which the dispensary was stocked.

He tried her key card.

This time the door opened.

He found himself in a narrow service corridor, dimly lit by a strip of low-wattage fluorescents. He looked right, taking in the wheeled linen cart at the other end of the corridor, and crept toward it. It was obvious that the janitors hadn't visited the area yet today. There were cigarette butts on the floor, and cellophane wrappers, and then his shoe encountered something flat and metal: an empty can of Red Bull that someone had stomped on. Responding to an indistinct intuition, Ambler stuck it in his back pocket.

How much time did he have? More concretely, how long before the orderly's disappearance would be noted? Within a few minutes, the Code Twelve would be concluded and someone would be sent to retrieve Ambler from his room. He had to get out of the building as fast as possible.

His fingertips brushed against something projecting from the wall. He had found it: the metal lid of the laundry chute. He climbed inside, holding on to the entrance ledge with both hands and feeling around him with his legs. He had worried that the chute might be too small; it fact, it was too large, and there was no side-mounted scuttle ladder, as he'd dared hope. Instead, the chute was lined with smooth sheet steel. To stop from falling, he had to press against opposite sides of the chute with both his hands and his sneaker-clad feet.

He slowly lowered himself down the chute, repositioning each of his limbs in strenuous sequence; the muscular strain imposed was terrific and, before long, terrifically painful. Rest was not an option; muscles had to be exerted at all times, or else he would plunge, in what seemed to be a straight drop.

It seemed as if hours had passed by the time he had scuttle-rappelled to the bottom, though he knew the elapsed time was closer to two minutes. His muscles were shuddering, spasming in agony, even as he pushed through bags of soiled laundry, nearly gagging at the fetor of human sweat and excrement. He felt as if he were digging himself out of a grave, clawing, wriggling, *forcing* himself through a resistant substance. Every fiber of his musculature was screaming for rest, yet there was no time for rest.

He finally pushed his way onto a hard cement floor, and he was—where?—in a hot, low-ceilinged basement space, loud with the rumble and din of laundry machines. He craned his head. At the end of a long row of white-enameled industrial washers, two workers were loading a machine.

He stood up and stepped across the aisle of laundry machines, forcing discipline upon his quivering muscles: if he *was* seen, his steps had to be confident. Once he was out of the sight line of the laundry workers, he stood beside a row of wheeled canvas laundry carts and assessed his location.

He knew that medical evacuations were conducted using a high-speed boat and that the boat would be landing shortly, if it had not already arrived. Right now the heart-attack victim was being strapped onto a gurney. If Ambler's plans had any chance of succeeding, he could afford no delays.

He had to get himself on that boat.

Which meant finding his way onto the loading dock. *I don't want to die in this place:* he wasn't just playing on Laurel Holland's sympathies when he said it. He had spoken the truth, perhaps the most urgent truth he knew.

"Hey," a voice called out. "What the fuck are you doing here?"

The petty authority of a midlevel ward attendant, someone whose life consisted of taking shit from his bosses, and giving it to those he bossed.

Ambler forced an easygoing smile as he turned toward a small bald man with a cottage-cheese complexion and eyes that seemed to swivel like a surveillance camera.

"Take it easy, dude," Ambler said. "I swear I wasn't smoking."

"This is a joke to you?" The supervisor walked over to him. He glanced at the badge on Ambler's shirt. "How's your Spanish? Because I can have you busted down to ground maintenance, you—" He suddenly broke off, having realized that the face on the ID badge was not that of the man in the uniform. "Holy shit," he breathed.

Then he did something curious: he moved about twenty feet away and unhooked a device from his belt. It was the radio transmitter that activated the stun belt.

No! Ambler couldn't let it happen. If the belt was activated, he would be struck down by a tidal wave of pain and left twitching and spasming on the floor. All his plans would be for nothing. He would die in there. A nameless captive, pawn of forces he would never understand. As if of their own accord, Ambler's hands reached for the flattened soda can in his back pocket, his subconscious mind operating a split second before his conscious one.

It was impossible to remove the stun belt. But it was possible to slide the piece of flat metal *underneath* the belt—and that was what he did, shoving it against his skin with all his strength, hardly conscious of the way it scraped his flesh. The stun belt's two metal contacts now rested on the conductive metal.

"Welcome to a world of pain," the supervisor said in a level voice as he pressed the stun-belt activator.

From the rear of the belt Ambler heard a raspy buzzing. His body was no longer the path of least resistance between the stun prongs; the flattened metal can was. He smelled a wisp of smoke, and then the buzzing ceased.

The belt had been shorted out.

Ambler charged at the supervisor, swiftly overtaking him and tackling him to the floor. The man's head slammed against the concrete, and he let out a low, concussed moan. Ambler remembered what one of the training officers at Consular Operations always insisted: that bad luck was just the flip side of good luck. *There's opportunity in every mishap.* It didn't make logical sense, but to Ambler, often enough, it made intuitive sense. Glancing at the series of initials underneath the man's name, Ambler saw that he had inventory-management responsibilities. That meant overseeing how things entered and left the building—which meant regular use of the service entrances. The building's actual points of egress were far more demanding even than the internal gateways: they required biometric signatures from authorized personnel. Such as the man who lay limply at Ambler's feet. He replaced the orderly's badge he had been wearing with that of the superintendent. Even unconscious, the man would be his ticket out.

The steel gate at the west service exit bore a white-and-red sign that stated the policy bluntly: USE OF THIS PASSAGEWAY BY NONAUTHO-RIZED PERSONNEL STRICTLY PROHIBITED: ALARM WILL SOUND. There was no keyhole or card reader by the push bar. Instead, there was some-thing far more formidable: a wall-mounted device whose simple in-terface consisted of a horizontal glass rectangle and a push button. It was a retinal-scan device, and it was virtually infallible. The capillar-ies that emerge from the optic nerve and radiate through the retina had a unique configuration in every individual. Unlike fingerprint-based readers, which worked with only sixty indices of resemblance, retinal scans involved many hundreds of them. As a result, retinal-scan devices had a false-accept rate that was essentially zero.

Which wasn't the same as foolproof. *Say hello to your authorized personnel,* Ambler thought as he put his arms beneath those of the unconscious supervisor, hoisting him before the scanner and hold-ing his eyes open with his fingers. He pushed the button with his left elbow, and two bursts of red light came from the scanner glass. After a couple of long seconds, there was the sound of a whirring motor from inside the steel door, and it swung open. Ambler let the man drop to the floor, walked through the gate and then up a short flight of concrete steps.

He was at a loading dock at the west side of the building, breath-ing unfiltered air for the first time in a very long while. The day was overcast: cold, wet, dismal. But he was *outside.* A giddy, silly feeling rose in him, fleetingly, clamped down by a larger anxiety. He was in greater danger than ever before. From Laurel Holland he knew about the electrified perimeter fencing. The only way out was to be offi-cially escorted out—or to be one of the official escorts.

He heard the distant sound of a motorboat and then, closer by, another motorized sound. An electric vehicle, like an oversize golf cart, was driving up to the south side of the building. In short order, a gurney was wheeled up to the back. The electric cart would take the patient to the boat.

Ambler took a deep breath, strode around the building, and ran up to the vehicle, banging on the driver's side. The driver regarded him warily.

You're calm; you're bored. It's just a job. "They told me I was supposed to stick with the heart-attack guy all the way to the medical center," Ambler said, climbing aboard. Meaning: *I'm no happier with the assignment than you are.* "Newbies get all the shit jobs," he went on. The tone was of mild complaint, the message one of apology. He folded his arms on his chest, concealing his badge and its ill-matched photo ID. "This joint's the same as every place I ever worked."

"You with Barlowe's team?" the driver grunted.

Barlowe? "You know it."

"He's a real shitheel, isn't he?"

"You know it," Ambler repeated.

At the wharf, the men who were in the express cruiser—the boat's pilot, a paramedic, and an armed guard—grumbled when they were told that the body was to be accompanied by an attendant from the facility. They weren't trusted to do the job right? Was *that* the message? Besides, the paramedic pointed out, the patient was already dead. This was going to be a morgue run. But the combination of Ambler's blasé manner and the driver's shoulder shrugging reassured them, and nobody wanted to loiter in this weather. The crew members each grabbed one end of the aluminum-framed stretcher, shivering slightly in their navy windbreakers as they transported the body to a below-deck sleeping berth, toward the rear of the boat.

The forty-foot Culver Ultra Jet was smaller than the vessels that transported staff to and from the facility. It was also speedier: with its twin five-hundred-horsepower jet drives, it could complete the distance to the coastal medical center in ten minutes, faster than it would take to summon, land, and load a helicopter from either the Langley Air Force Base or the U.S. Naval Base. Ambler kept close to the pilot; the boat was a recent military model, and he wanted to make sure he understood the control panels. He watched as the pilot adjusted the stern and bow thrusters, then shifted the throttle to full. The boat was riding high in the water now, pressing past thirty-five knots.

It would be ten minutes to shore. Would the ruse survive that long? It wasn't hard to make sure that the photograph on his ID badge was flecked with shore mud, and Ambler knew that people took their cues from tone—from voice, from manner—rather than from documents. After a few minutes, Ambler joined the paramedic and the guard on a bench behind the helm.

The paramedic—late twenties, red-splotched cheeks, curly black hair—still seemed offended by Ambler's presence. Finally he turned to Ambler and said, "They didn't say anything about the body being accompanied. You realize the guy's dead, right?" A Southern accent, the speaker someone bored and irritable, probably resentful of having been sent to retrieve a patient who was already dead.

"Is he?" Ambler stifled a yawn, or pretended to. *Christ, would he let it go already?*

"Damn right he is. I checked myself. So it ain't like he's gonna escape, you know?"

Ambler remembered the officious air of the man who had worn his badge. *That* was the tone to take. "Until they got a notarized certificate, your say-so ain't shit to them. Nobody at Parrish has that authority. So the rules are the rules."

"It's such bullshit."

"Quit busting his balls, Olson," the guardsman said. It was not solidarity; it was sport. But that was not all it was. Ambler could tell that the two did not know each other well and were not comfortable around each other. Probably it was the classic problem of unresolved authority; the paramedic wanted to act like he was in charge, but it was the guardsman who carried the service weapon.

Ambler gave the guardsman a friendly glance. He was burly, in his mid-twenties, with a haircut that came from a military barber. He looked to be an ex–Army Ranger; certainly his hip-holstered HK P7 pistol, compact and deadly, was a piece long favored by the Rangers. He was the only armed man on the boat, but Ambler could tell he was no slouch.

"Whatever," the paramedic said after a pause. But he wasn't deferring to the guardsman; he was saying, *What's your problem?*

As the three resumed an uncompanionable silence, Ambler allowed himself to feel a tincture of relief.

The boat had gone only a few miles from Parrish Island when the pilot, wearing headphones, gesticulated to get the attention of the others and pressed a lever that brought the radio on the cabin speaker. "This is a Five-Oh-Five from Parrish Island." The radio dispatcher's voice sounded agitated. "We have an escaped-inmate situation. Repeat: an escaped-inmate situation."

Ambler felt his stomach clutch. He had to act, had to *use* the crisis. He jumped to his feet. "Christ on a raft," he grunted.

The speaker crackled again with the dispatcher's voice: "Cruiser 12-647-M, the inmate may have stowed himself on your vessel. Please confirm or disconfirm immediately. *Holding.*"

The guardsman gave Ambler a hard look; a thought was beginning to form. Ambler would have to get *ahead* of it, redirect it.

"Shit," Ambler said. "I guess now you know why I'm here." A beat. "You think it's an accident they've insisted on putting security reps on every vehicle leaving the island? We've been hearing static about some kind of escape attempt for the past twenty-four hours."

"Could've told us," the guardsman said sullenly.

"Not the kind of gossip the facility's looking to spread," Ambler said. "Gonna check that body right now." He scrambled to the rear below-deck berth. Inside, to the left, was a narrow tool closet, re-cessed into the cargo area of the inner hull. There were a few oily rags on the floor. On a platform of steel checker plate, the body was still bound to the stretcher with Velcro straps; it looked bloated, per-haps 250 pounds, and the gray pallor of death was unmistakable.

Now what? He would have to work fast, before the others decided to follow him.

Twenty seconds later, he raced back to the cabin.

"You!" Ambler said accusingly, thrusting his forefinger at the paramedic. "You said the patient was dead. What kind of bullshit was that? I just felt the guy's neck, and guess what. He had a pulse same as you and me."

"You don't know what you're talking about," the paramedic said indignantly. "That's a goddamn corpse down there."

Ambler was still breathing hard. "A corpse with a pulse rate of sev-enty? I don't think so."

The guardsman's head swiveled, and Ambler could tell what he was thinking: *This guy sounds like he knows what he's talking about.* Ambler had a momentary advantage; he had to press it.

"Are you part of it?" Ambler demanded, fixing the paramedic with an accusatory glare. "You *in* on it?"

"What the hell are you saying?" the paramedic replied, his splotchy cheeks reddening further. The way the guardsman was looking at him riled him even more, and the effect was to make him sound defensive, insecure. The paramedic turned to the guardsman. "Becker, you can't be taking this guy seriously. I know how to take a pulse, and that's a goddamn *stiff* we got on the stretcher."

"Show us," Ambler said grimly, leading the way back to the berth. The pronoun *us* was a powerful one, he knew: implicitly it drew a line between the man he was accusing and the rest of them. Ambler needed to keep everyone off balance, needed to foment dissension and suspicion. Otherwise the suspicion would gravitate toward him.

He glanced back and saw that the guardsman was bringing up the rear with his pistol out of its holster. The three men stepped around the transom platforms and proceeded to the rear berth. The medic swung open the door to it and then said, in a stunned voice, "What the hell . . . ?"

The two others peered inside. The stretcher lay askew, its Velcro straps undone. The body was gone.

"You lying sack of shit," Ambler exploded.

"I don't understand," the paramedic said, his voice unsteady.

"Well, I think the rest of us do," Ambler said in a freezing voice. The subtle sway of syntax: the more he used the first-person plural, the greater his authority. He glanced at the tool-closet door, hoping nobody would notice how the slide latch was bulging with the strain of keeping the door shut.

"You're telling me a *corpse* walked hisself out of here?" the buzz-cut guardsman demanded, turning toward the curly-haired Southerner. The guardsman gripped his pistol firmly.

"Probably just slipped over the side and went for a nice swim," Ambler sneered. *Push your scenario; prevent them from thinking of alternate ones.* "We'd never have heard, and in this fog, we'd never have seen. Three miles to shore, at this point, not too strenuous if you keep your blood flowing. Typical corpse behavior, right?"

"This is *crazy*," the paramedic protested. "I had nothing to do with it! You gotta believe me." The form of denial was automatic, but it effectively confirmed the crucial element of the allegation: that the man on the gurney was the escapee.

"Guess we know why he was so pissed off they made me tag along," Ambler said to the guardsman, just loudly enough to be heard over the engines. "Listen, you better call this in ASAP. I'll keep a watch on the suspect."

The guardsman looked confused, and Ambler could read the conflicting impulses on his face. Now Ambler leaned over and spoke confidingly into the guardsman's ear. "I know you had nothing to do with it," he said. "My report's gonna make that real clear. So you got nothing to worry about." The message relayed was not to be found in the content of the words. Ambler was perfectly aware he wasn't addressing the guardsman's concern: it hadn't yet occurred to the man that anyone might suspect him of being involved in an escape from a maximum-security facility. But in giving assurance on the matter—and speaking of his "report"—Ambler was subtly establishing his authority: the man in the dove-gray tunic now represented officialdom, procedure, the discipline of command.

"Understood," the guardsman said, and he turned to Ambler for reassurance.

"Give me your pistol and I'll keep an eye on this joker," Ambler said, his voice level. "But you need to radio this in *right now*."

"Will do," the guard said. Ambler could tell that he was feeling a pang of unease, even as events—bewildering and unaccustomed events—overrode his normal caution. Before handing the fully loaded Heckler & Koch P7 to the man in the gray tunic, he hesitated for a moment.

But only for a moment.

CHAPTER TWO

Langley, Virginia

Even after nearly three decades of service, Clayton Caston still relished the small details of the CIA complex—like the outdoor sculpture known as the *Kryptos,* an S-shaped copper screen perforated with letters, which had been a collaboration between a sculptor and an agency cryptographer. Or the bas-relief of Allen Dulles on the north wall, beneath which were incised the eloquent words: *His monument is around us.* Not all the more recent additions were as pleasing, however. The agency's main entrance was actually the lobby to what was now known as the Original Headquarters Building—it had become "original" when the New Headquarters Building was completed in 1991, and nomenclatural habits were such that there was no longer anything called just Headquarters Building. One had to choose between the Original and the New, an array of six-story office towers that were built into a hillside next to the OHB. To reach the main entrance of the NHB, then, you had to go to the fourth floor. It was all very irregular, which was never, in his view, a recommendation.

Caston's own office was in the OHB, of course, but nowhere near its brightly windowed exterior walls. It was, in fact, fairly hidden away—the sort of windowless interior space that usually housed copying machines and office supplies. It was a fine place if you didn't want to be disturbed, but few people saw it that way. Even agency veterans tended to assume that Caston had been the victim of internal exile. They looked at him and saw a mediocrity who had surely never accomplished much, a time-server in his fifties, gently pushing around pieces of paper while ticking off days until he could retire with a pension.

Anyone who saw him take his seat at his desk this morning, his eyes fixed on his desk clock, pens and pencils arrayed on his blotter like silverware on a table mat, would only have had such preconceptions confirmed. Eight fifty-four, the clock said: six minutes before the workday properly began, in Caston's opinion. He pulled out a copy of the *Financial Times* and turned to the crossword puzzle. His eyes flicked to his desk clock. Five minutes. Now he went to work. One across. *What's over the facade, after I am reduced? An obstacle.* One down. *An annoyance: sounds like someone's visiting the WC.* Four across. *A gamble about a short priest elevates you without a raise.* Two down. *Authentic British capital.* Soundlessly, his pencil filled in the boxes, seldom pausing for longer than a second or two. *Impediment. Inconvenience. Brevet. Sterling.*

And now he was done. Eight fifty-nine, the clock said. He heard a rattling by the door: his assistant, arriving just on time, breathless from having jogged down the hall. Punctuality had been the subject of a recent conversation between them. Adrian Choi opened his mouth, as if about to deliver an excuse, then he glanced at his watch and slid quietly into his seat before his smaller, lower workstation. There was a hint of slumber about his almond-shaped eyes, and his thick black hair was damp from the shower. Adrian Choi was all of twenty-one years old, with a discreet stud below his lower lip and still cutting it close.

At 9:00 A.M. on the dot, Caston put the *Financial Times* in the wastebasket and activated his secure e-mail list. Several e-mails were agency-wide notifications of little interest: a new Wellness Program, a minor emendation to the dental insurance, an intranet address whereby employees could check on the status of their 401(k) plans. One was from a clerk at an IRS office in St. Louis who, though mystified by getting a request from the CIA's Office of Internal Review, was happy to oblige with the details of the special-purpose entities formed by a light-industrial firm over the past seven years. Another was from a small company listed on the Toronto stock exchange and contained the list Caston had requested of the trading activities conducted, in the past six months, by its board members. The comptroller did not see why Caston had needed the actual time of day for each transaction but had duly complied with the request.

Caston realized how drab his activities seemed to most of his colleagues. The ex–jocks and frat boys who used to work in the field, or hadn't yet but still hoped to, treated him with genial condescension. "You gotta go if you wanna know" was their watchword. Caston never went anywhere, of course, but then he didn't subscribe to that dogma. Often, settling down with a sheaf of spreadsheets could tell someone everything he needed to know without his ever leaving his desk.

Then again, very few of his colleagues actually knew what Caston did. Wasn't he one of the guys who audited people's travel-and-entertainment accounts? Or was his oversight more to do with requisitions of paper and toner cartridges—wouldn't want anybody fiddling with the back office ledgers, right? Either way, it was a job just slightly above the custodial in prestige. There were a few of Caston's colleagues, however, who treated him with deference, even something close to awe. They tended to be the members of the CIA director's inner circle, or of the very top tier of the counterintelligence directorate. They knew how Aldrich Ames was really apprehended in 1994. And they knew about how a slight but persistent discrepancy between reported income and expenditures was the thread that led to the exposure of Gordon Blaine and the unraveling of a larger web of intrigue. They knew about dozens of other victories, some of comparable magnitude, that would never come to public attention.

It was a mixture of qualities and skills that enabled Caston to make inroads where whole bureaus failed. Without leaving his office, he burrowed deep through the twisting maze of human venality. The realm of emotion held little interest for him, though; rather, he had an accountant's preoccupation with columns of digits that did not add up. A trip booked but not taken; a receipt claimed for a conveyance that was at odds with a reported itinerary; a credit-card charge for a second, unreported cell phone: there were a thousand small slips to which the prevaricator was prone, and it only took one. Yet those who wouldn't brave the tedium of collation—of making sure that No. 1 across was consistent with No. 1 down—would never detect them.

Adrian, his hair starting to dry, came to his desk with his hands clutching various memos, animatedly explaining what he had sorted through and thrown out. Caston glanced up at him, taking in the young man's tattooed forearm and the occasional glimpse of a tongue stud, nothing that would have been allowed when he was starting out, but no doubt the agency had to change with the times.

"Be sure you send the quarterly I66 forms out for processing," Caston said.

"Super," said Adrian. He said *super* a lot, which had a midcentury ring to Caston but had apparently taken on a new life. It meant, so Caston inferred, something like *I've heard what you just said and have taken it to heart.* Perhaps it meant less; it certainly did not mean more.

"As for this morning's incoming: Anything out of the ordinary? Anything . . . irregular?"

"A voice mail came in from the Assistant Deputy Director of Intelligence, Caleb Norris?" A hint of Californian uptalk entered Adrian's voice—the questioning intonation in which young people so often sheathed their assertions.

"You're asking me or you're telling me?"

"Sorry. Telling you." Adrian stopped. "I have a feeling it's kind of urgent."

Caston leaned back in his chair. "You *feel* that?"

"Yes, sir."

Caston studied the young man, like an entomologist scrutinizing a gall wasp. "And you're . . . sharing your feelings. Interesting. Now, am I a member of your family, a parent or sibling? Are we *pals*? Am I a spouse or girlfriend of yours?"

"I guess—"

"No? Just checking. In that case—and here's a deal I'm proposing—please don't tell me what you *feel*. I only care about what you *think*. What you have reason to *believe*, even with only partial certainty. What you *know,* by observation or inference. As far as these nebulous things called *feelings* are concerned, keep them to yourself." He paused. "I'm sorry. Did I hurt your feelings?"

"Sir, I—"

"That was a trick question, Adrian. Don't answer it."

"Very enlightening, master," Adrian said, a smile hovering about his lips without actually settling on them. "Point taken."

"But you were saying. About nonstandard incoming messages."

"Well, there's this yellow interoffice thing from the deputy director's office."

"You should know the agency color codes by now. There's no 'yellow' at the CIA."

"Sorry," Adrian said. "*Canary.*"

"Which signifies what?"

"It's for . . ." He paused, his mind temporarily a blank. "It's for a stateside incident with security implications. Ergo non-CIA. Something to do with the other services. OGAs." OGAs: other governmental agencies. A convenient "wastebasket" term.

Caston nodded briskly and accepted the bright yellow envelope. It was distasteful to him, like a garish, shrieking tropical bird: a canary, in fact. He broke the security seal himself, put on his reading glasses, and quickly scanned the report. Potential security breach related to an inmate escape. A Patient No. 5312, resident at a high-security clandestine treatment center.

It was strange, Caston reflected, that the inpatient wasn't named. He reread the report to see where the incident had taken place.

The Parrish Island Psychiatric Facility.

It rang a bell. A warning bell.

———

Ambler pushed through the half-dormant coastal vegetation—yards of saltbush, switch grass, and bayberry, the sandpapery blades and thorny scrub scratching at his sodden clothing—and then through a stand of leafless, salt-stunted trees. He shivered as the cold wind gusted again, and tried to ignore the gritty sand that had spilled into his ill-fitting shoes, abrading his skin with every step. Given that the Langley Air Force Base was probably twenty or thirty miles to his north and the U.S. Naval Base about the same distance to his south, he expected, any moment now, to hear the low *whomp-whomp-whomp* of a military helicopter. Highway 64 was within half a mile of where he was. There was no time to rest. The longer Ambler was a lone man in the open, the greater the danger he was in.

He quickened his pace until he heard the thrumming of the highway. On the wide shoulder, he brushed off sand and leaves, put up a thumb, and smiled. He was wet and bedraggled and wearing a strange uniform. The smile would have to be pretty damned reassuring.

A minute later, a truck decorated with a Frito-Lay logo pulled over. The driver, a pug-featured man with an immense stomach and knockoff Ray·Bans, waved him in. Ambler had his ride.

The words of an old hymn came to him: *We have come this far by faith.*

A truck, a car, a bus: a few transfers later, he was in the asphalt penumbra of the capital. In a strip mall, he found a sporting goods store, where he hurriedly bought a few nondescript garments from the bulk bins, paying with cash that was in the pockets of his uniform and changing into the clothes behind a hedge of boxwood that adjoined the store. He hadn't had time even to glance at himself in a mirror, but he knew his current garb—the khakis, flannel shirt, zippered windbreaker—was close to the default wardrobe of the American male outside the office.

A five-minute wait at the bus stop: Rip van Winkle was coming home.

Watching the landscape grow denser as the bus moved closer to

Washington proper, Ambler found himself in a contemplative mood. There was always a point when the body's system of stress hormones depleted itself, and excitement, or fear, gave way to numbness. Ambler had reached that point now. His mind wandered. Faces and voices from the place he'd left swirled through his consciousness.

He had left his captors behind, but not his memories of them.

The last psychiatrist who had "evaluated" him had been a lean, tightly wound man in his early fifties with black-framed glasses. His hair was graying at the temples, and a long brown forelock fell across his forehead in a boyish manner that only emphasized how far from boyish he really was. But when Ambler looked at him, he saw other things, too.

He saw a man who, fidgeting protectively with his carefully tabbed folders and felt-tip pens (ballpoints, like pencils, were viewed as potential weapons), resented his job and his surroundings—resented the fact that he worked in a government facility where secrecy, not treatment, was the paramount concern. How had he ended up here? Ambler could readily conjecture: a career trajectory that began with a ROTC scholarship to college and med school, and a psychiatric residency at a military hospital. But it wasn't supposed to end up like this, was it? Alert to a thousand different expressions of wounded wariness, Ambler saw a man who had dreams of a different sort of life, perhaps the kind of life that used to figure in old novels and movies: a book-lined office on Manhattan's Upper West Side, a tufted leather couch and wing chair, a pipe, a clientele of writers, artists, and musicians, fascinating challenges. Now the hardest part was simply getting through his rounds at a place he despised, among patients and staff members he mistrusted. Frustrated, he would have looked for something else to make him feel alive, special, not just another government drone at an E9 pay grade. Maybe he was a world traveler, husbanding his vacation days and going off on special package ecotours through rain forests and deserts. Maybe he had put together a remarkable wine cellar or was a handball fanatic, an obses-sive golfer—*something*. It was always something with these burned-out cases. Every particular detail in Ambler's speculations might be wrong. Yet he was sure that he had the basic structure of sentiment right. He knew people: it was what he did.

It was what he *saw*.

The psychiatrist disliked him—was made uneasy by Ambler on a hindbrain level. The man's expertise was supposed to give him special insight into his patient, and with that, usually, went a sense of power, of authority: the authority of the teacher over the pupil, the physician over the patient. But this man did not experience that sense of authority around Ambler.

"Let me remind you that the purpose of these sessions is strictly evaluative," the man told his patient. "My job is to monitor progress, and keep an eye on any untoward side effects of the medications. So let's start with that. Any new side effects I should be aware of?"

"It would be easier to talk about side effects," Ambler said ponder-ously, "if I knew what the main effect was supposed to be."

"The meds are meant to control your psychiatric symptoms, as you know. Paranoid ideation, dissociative disorder, ego-dystonic syndromes . . ."

"Words," Ambler said. "Without meaning. Sounds without sense."

The psychiatrist typed a few notes on his laptop computer. His pale gray eyes were chilly behind his glasses.

"Several different psychiatric teams have wrestled with your dis-sociative identity disorders. We've been through this." The doctor pressed a button on a small remote control, and an audiotape played, the sound emerging bright and clear through recessed speak-ers. A voice—Ambler's voice—was audible, spewing conspiracy the-ories with an unhinged sense of urgency: "You're behind it. All of you. And all of them. The trail of the human serpent is over all." On and on the recording went. "The Trilateral Commission . . . Opus Dei . . . the Rockefellers . . ."

To Ambler, the sound of himself, recorded from a previous psychiatric session, was almost physically painful.

"Stop it," he said quietly, unable to tamp down an upwelling of emotion. "Please stop it."

The psychiatrist paused the tape. "Do you still believe those . . . theories?"

"They're paranoid fantasies," Ambler said, groggily but distinctly. "And the answer is no. I don't even have a memory of having held them."

"You deny that's you on the tape?"

"No," Ambler said. "I don't deny it. I just don't . . . remember it. That's not me, OK? I mean, that's not who I am."

"You're somebody else, then. Two different people. Or more?"

Ambler shrugged helplessly. "When I was a kid, I wanted to be a fireman. I don't want to be a fireman anymore. That kid isn't who I am."

"Last week you said that when you were a kid, you wanted to be a ballplayer when you grew up. Or was I speaking to someone else entirely?" The psychiatrist took his glasses off. "The question I'm putting to you is the question you need to put to yourself: Who are you?"

"The problem with the question," Ambler said after a long pause, "is that you think it's multiple-choice. You want me to choose from your little list of options."

"Is that the problem?" The psychiatrist looked up from his laptop. "I'd say the real problem is that you're checking off more than one answer."

It took Ambler a few moments to rouse himself when the bus came to the Cleveland Park stop, but he made it out in time. On the street, Ambler put on his cap and looked all around him—first alert to any departure from normality and then full-heartedly appreciative of normality itself.

He was back.

He wanted to leap into the air. He wanted to throw his arms up. He wanted to track down those responsible for his confinement and serve brutal justice to them: *Did you think I wouldn't get out? Is that what you thought?*

This was not the weather he would have chosen for a homecoming. The skies were still dark; drizzle kept the pavements slick and black. It was an ordinary day in an ordinary place, he realized, but after his long period of isolation, he was overwhelmed by the frenetic activity he saw everywhere around him.

He walked past lampposts of octagonal concrete, trussed with metal bands that held in place photocopied bills and posters. Poetry readings in coffeehouses. Concerts given by rock bands only recently graduated from garages. A new vegetarian restaurant. A comedy club with the unfortunate name Miles of Smiles. All the blooming, buzzing confusion of human activity, clamoring for attention on sodden pieces of paper. Life on the outside. No—he corrected himself—just life.

He craned his head, hyperalert. An ordinary street on a dismal day. There were dangers, yes. But if he could reach his apartment, he could retrieve the ordinary detritus of his existence; indeed, its very ordinariness was what made it so precious to him. The ordinary was what he craved; the ordinary was what he needed.

Would they really dare to come after him *here? Here*—one of the few places on earth where there were people who actually knew him. Surely it was the safest place of all. Even if they appeared, he had no fear of a public confrontation. Recklessly, he almost craved one. No, he would not fear those who had interned him; it was time for them to fear *him*. Evidently, a rogue element had abused the system, attempting to bury him alive, submerging him among lost souls, spies gone torpid with depression or frenzied with delusion. Now that he was out, his enemies should be on the run, going to ground. The one thing they could not afford was to confront him here, in the open, where the local police would inevitably get involved. For the more people who found out about him, the greater the threat to them of exposure.

At the corner of Connecticut Avenue and Ordway Street, Ambler saw the newsstand he used to pass every morning when he was in town. He saw the grizzled gap-toothed man behind the counter, still wearing his red knit wool cap, and smiled.

"Reggie," Ambler called out. "Reggie, my main man."

"Hey," the counterman said. But it was a reflex, not a greeting.

Ambler strode over to him. "Been a long time, right?"

The counterman looked at him again. There was not a flicker of recognition in his face.

Ambler glanced down at a stack of *Washington Posts*, the top copy dappled with rain, and, noticing the date, felt a pang. The third week of January—no wonder it was so cold. He blinked hard. *Nearly two years.* Nearly two years had been taken from him. Two years of oblivion and despair and anomie.

But now was not the time to dwell on loss.

"Come on, Reggie. How you been? Working hard, or hardly working?"

On Reggie's creased visage, puzzlement was hardening into suspicion. "I ain't got no change for you, bro. And I don't give out no free coffee, neither."

"Reggie, come on—you *know* me."

"Move along, big guy," Reggie said. "I don't want any trouble."

Ambler turned away, wordless, and walked the half block to the large Gothic Revival apartment block where he had been a tenant for the past decade, Baskerton Towers. Built in the 1920s, it was a six-story structure of red brick, adorned with light gray half-columns and pilasters of concrete. In the windows that let onto the hallways on each floor, the venetian blinds were lowered partway, like drooping eyelids.

Baskerton Towers. A sort-of home for a man who really had

none. To spend a career in a special-access program—the highest tier of operational security—was to spend a career under an alias. No division of Consular Operations was more secret than the Political Stabilization Unit, and none of its operatives ever knew one another except by a field name. It was not a way of life that lent itself to deep civilian ties: the job meant that most of your days were spent abroad, essentially unreachable, and for unpredictable stretches of time. Did he have any real friends? Still, the paltriness of his domestic existence had given special weight to his casual street acquaintances here. And for as little time as he spent in Baskerton Towers, the apartment was an authentic abode for him. It was not the sanctuary of his lake house, but it was a badge of normality. A place to drop anchor.

The apartment block was set in from the street, a shallow, oval drive permitting cars to come up to the lobby. Ambler looked around the streets and sidewalks, saw no sign of anybody taking a particular interest in him, and walked up to the building. Someone there would know him—one of the doormen, if not the building manager or superintendent—and would let him into his apartment.

He looked at the long tenant plaque, black plastic letters on a white board, rows of names in alphabetical order.

No Ambler. *Alston* was followed by *Ayer*.

Had they taken his apartment, then? It was a disappointment but something less than a surprise. "Can I help you, sir?" It was one of the doormen, emerging from the heated vestibule: Greg Denovich. His strong jaw was, as always, shadowed by a heavy, razor-resistant beard.

"Greg," Ambler said jovially. *Greg* was presumably for *Gregor*, he'd always assumed; the man was from the former Yugoslavia. "Been a real long time, huh?"

The expression on Denovich's face was becoming familiar to Ambler: it was the puzzlement of someone who has been greeted as a friend by a complete stranger.

Ambler removed his cap and smiled. "Take your time, now, Greg. Apartment 3C?"

"Do I know you?" Denovich asked. But it wasn't a question this time, either. It was a statement. A statement in the negative.

"I guess not," Ambler said softly. And then his perplexity gave way to panic.

From behind him, he heard the sound of tires braked hard on a rain-slick street. Ambler turned around quickly and saw a white van stopping too fast across the street. He heard doors opening and slamming shut and saw three men emerge, in the uniform of the facility's guards. One was carrying a carbine; the other two had drawn pistols. All three were running toward him.

The van. He recognized everything about it. It was part of an emergency "retrieval service" used by clandestine branches of the federal government for sensitive domestic "pickups." Whether involving rogue agents or foreign operatives on U.S. soil, such parcels had in common that they were not destined for any branch of the official justice system. And on this wet and cold January morning, Harrison Ambler was the parcel to be picked up. No explanations would need to be offered to the local police, because he would have vanished long before their arrival. This was no open confrontation; what they had orchestrated was a swift, unnoticed abduction.

In showing up here in the first place, Ambler realized, he had permitted wishful thinking to swamp his better judgment. He could afford no more mistakes.

Think—he had to *think*.

Or rather, he had to *feel*.

After two decades as a field operative, Ambler had been forced to master the requisites of escape and evasion. It was second nature to him. But he never approached it through grids of logic, "decision trees," and the other arid devices that trainers sometimes foisted upon the tyros. The challenge was to feel your way out of situations, improvising as seemed necessary. To do otherwise was to fall into a rut of routine, and anything that was routinized could be anticipated and countered by adversaries.

Ambler scanned the street in front of the Baskerton building. A three-point blockage would have been standard procedure: at either end of the block, a unit would have been in place *before* the van had pulled up opposite. Indeed, Ambler could see armed men, some uniformed, some not, moving toward the building from both directions with the purposeful stride of experienced retrieval agents. Now what? He could bolt into the lobby of the building and search out a rear exit. But the move would have been anticipated, precautions taken against it. He could wait for a passing crowd of pedestrians, join them, then try to outrace the men stationed at the far end of the block. There were dangers to that tack as well. *Stop thinking,* Ambler told himself. It was the only way to outsmart them.

Staring at the man with the short-barreled rifle who was hastening across the boulevard, Ambler willed himself to see all that he could of his face, even as the drizzle turned to showers. And then he decided to do the most dangerous thing of all.

He ran directly *toward* the man. "What *took* you so long?" Ambler bellowed at him. "Haul ass, goddammit! He's *getting away*!" He swiveled around and gestured vigorously with his thumb toward the lobby of the Baskerton Towers.

"We got here as soon as we could," the man with the carbine replied. The other two, Ambler could see now, as they hurried past him, carried tactical .45s, twelve rounds in the magazine. It was a lot of firepower to capture one man. Assuming that the orders were to capture.

Now Ambler walked heavily across the street to the idling retrieval van. Its passengers had fanned out around the area of the Baskerton lobby; it would be only moments before they realized their error.

Ambler approached the driver's door of the white van, flipped open the wallet that had belonged to the Parrish Island supervisor, and held it up to the driver for a brief moment, as if displaying a badge or certificate. He was too far away for the driver to make any-thing out; the authority of the gesture itself would have to convince. As the driver powered down the window, Ambler took his measure. The man's eyes were hard, watchful, and his neck was short and thickly muscled: a weight lifter.

"You guys get the change in orders?" Ambler demanded. "It's kill, not capture. And what took you so long? If you'd been in place a minute earlier, we'd be all done."

The driver said nothing for a moment. Then his gaze hardened. "That thing you showed me? I couldn't see it."

Suddenly Ambler felt the man's big, beefy hand grab his right wrist.

"I *said* I couldn't see it." The driver's voice was low, menacing. "Show me again."

With his left hand, Ambler reached into his jacket for the pistol he had taken from the guardsman on the boat, but the driver was su-perbly trained, with lightning fast reflexes; he smashed the heel of his free hand into the P7, sending the weapon flying into the air. Am-bler had to act immediately. He wrenched his wrist around, yanked it toward his body and up to the level of his shoulders, then, sharply, down, using his forearm like a crowbar, and slammed the driver's arm against the edge of the mostly lowered window.

The driver yelped, but he didn't let go. His grip was like steel. With his other hand, he was beginning to feel for an under-the-dashboard compartment, no doubt where a weapon of some sort was stored.

Ambler let his right arm go limp, let the driver pull him part of the way into the cab. Then, with his other hand, he spear-punched the man's larynx with a carefully aimed blow.

The driver released him and leaned forward, both hands tearing at his collar. He was struggling for breath, as the ruined cartilage im-peded his airflow. Ambler opened the door and pulled the driver from his seat. The man took a few steps away from the van before collapsing to the ground.

As Ambler climbed aboard, gunned the motor, and sped down the street, he could hear the cries of confusion among the men of the second unit. But it was too late for them to take action.

Ambler did not envy the team leader who had to explain how the parcel not only had escaped from under their noses but escaped in the team's own vehicle. Yet his maneuver involved no calculation or forethought. Reflecting upon it now, he realized that his actions sprang from the look on the first man's face: searching, wary—and uncertain. A hunter who was not sure whether he had found his quarry. The retrieval team had been dispatched too quickly to have been provided with photographs. Ambler was expected to do what fugitives almost invariably do in such situations: identify himself by attempting to flee. But how to give chase when the fox was running with the hounds?

The van was serving admirably as a getaway car; within minutes, though, it would become a glaring beacon, signaling his presence to his pursuers. A few miles farther down Connecticut Avenue, Ambler eased the van into a side street and left it idling once more, with the keys in the ignition. If he was very lucky, someone would steal it.

At this point, anonymity would be best secured by a populous area that was both a residential and a business neighborhood—a neighborhood that contained embassies, art museums, churches, bookstores, apartment buildings. A place with a brisk pedestrian traffic. A place like Dupont Circle, then. At the intersection of three of the city's major avenues, Dupont Circle had long been a thriving neighborhood, and even on this dismal winter morning the sidewalks were reasonably full. Ambler took a cab there, getting out at New Hampshire Avenue and Twentieth Street and swiftly losing himself among the day-trippers. He had a destination in mind but maintained an expression of bored aimlessness.

As he walked through the crowds, he tried to stay aware of his surroundings without making eye contact with anyone. Yet whenever his gaze alighted upon a passerby, the old feeling returned: especially in his hyperalert state, it was as if he were reading a page from someone's diary. It took only a glance to register the hurrying step of the sixtyish woman with peach-blond hair, a navy kick-pleat skirt showing beneath an open check-patterned coat, large gold-plated earrings, a plastic Ann Taylor shopping bag gripped too tightly by an age-spotted hand. She had spent hours getting ready to go out, and *out* meant shopping. A pouting loneliness flickered on her countenance; the raindrops on her cheeks might as well have been tears. She was childless, Ambler guessed, and maybe that, too, was a source of regret. In her past, no doubt, there was a husband who was going to make her whole and complete her life, a husband who—ten years ago? longer?—got restless and found someone younger, fresher, to make *him* whole and complete *his* life. Now she collected store-specific charge cards and met people for tea and played rubbers at bridge, but maybe not so often as she would have liked; Ambler sensed a larger disappointment with people. She probably suspected that her own sadness repelled them in some subliminal way; they were too busy for her, and her isolation only made her sadness deeper, her company all the less appealing to others. And so she shopped, bought clothing that was too youthful for her, pursuing "bargains" and "deep discounts" for apparel that looked no more expensive than it was. Was Ambler's every supposition correct? It hardly mattered: he knew the essential truth was in there.

His eyes took in a slouchy young black man, wearing low-slung jeans and a visored cap pulled down over a bandanna, a diamond stud in one ear, and a patch of beard below his lip. He was drenched in Aramis cologne and his gaze drifted across the street to another young man—proud and preppy looking, with an athlete's trouser-rubbing thighs, and long blond hair—then he shifted his gaze back, *wrested* it back, determined not to betray his interest. A full-breasted, cocoa-skinned girl with straightened hair and glossy dark lipstick on her pillowy lips, short despite her stilettos, was working hard to keep up with the young black man: her boyfriend, or so he let her imagine. Eventually she'd wonder why her boyfriend, preening and cocky on the street, was so chaste and hesitant when they were alone. Why their dates ended so early, and where he really went off afterward. But Ambler could tell she was still innocent of any such thoughts—any inkling that he could truly be who he was only with other young men like himself.

The cybercafe was where Ambler remembered it, near Seventeenth and Church, three blocks east of the circle. He identified a computer station that afforded him a good view of its storefront window; he would not be caught unaware again. With a few keystrokes, he brought up the Watchlist, a collective database coordinated by the Justice Department for use by multiple federal agencies involved in law enforcement. Dimly remembered pass codes still functioned, he was reassured to find. Now he typed his full name, Harrison Ambler, into the internal search engine; he wanted to see if there was any flag on his name. After a few moments, a message was displayed.

No records match HARRISON AMBLER.

It was an odd glitch; any federal employee, even one who was no longer on the payrolls, should have had at least a perfunctory listing. And though his Cons Ops identity was necessarily sequestered from such databases, his civilian cover job at the State Department was a matter of public record.

With a shrug of annoyance, he keyed his way to the State Department Web site and then went behind a firewall to a password-protected, albeit low-security, internal employee database. Verifying his civilian cover job should have been straightforward. For years, Hal Ambler could always explain, if anyone asked, that he was a mid-level staffer at the State Department, working at the Bureau of Educational and Cultural Affairs. It was a subject—"cultural diplomacy," "friendship through education," and so on—that he could hold forth upon at earnest and eye-glazing length, if required to. Never mind that it had nothing whatever to do with his real career.

He used to wonder what would happen if he gave a candid answer when someone at a cocktail party asked him what he did. *Me? I work for an ultraclandestine division of an already clandestine intelligence service called Consular Operations. A special-access program, with maybe twenty-five people in the government cleared for it. It's called the Political Stabilization Unit. What does it do? Well, a lot of things. Often enough, it involves killing people. People who, you hope, are worse than the people you save from them. But, of course, you can't always be sure. Can I get you another drink?*

Typing in his name into the State Department database, he clicked RETURN and waited a few long seconds for the results.

EMPLOYEE **HARRISON AMBLER** NOT FOUND. PLEASE VERIFY SPELLING AND TRY AGAIN.

His eyes swept across the window that overlooked the street, and though he saw no sign of unusual activity, he felt himself breaking out in a cold sweat. He keyed his way into the Social Security database and ran a search for his name.

HARRISON AMBLER not found.

It made no sense! Methodically, he summoned more databases, conducting search after search. One after another yielded a maddening refrain, variations on a theme of negation.

Your search did not match any documents.
No records were located for "Harrison Ambler."
HARRISON AMBLER not found.

Half an hour later, he had plumbed more than nineteen federal and state databases. All to no avail. It was as if he had never existed.

Madness!

Like a distant foghorn, the voices of various Parrish Island psychiatrists returned to him, with their spurious diagnoses. It was nonsense, of course—all nonsense. It had to be. He knew precisely who he was. Until the period of his institutionalization, his memory of his life was vivid, clear, and continuous. It was, to be sure, an unusual life—entangled in an unusual vocation—but it was the only one he had. There must have been some mix-up, some technical error: he was certain of it.

He typed in another rapid succession of keystrokes, rewarded only by another null response. And he began to wonder whether certainty had become a luxury. A luxury he could no longer afford.

A white car—no, a van, moving too fast, faster than the stream of traffic, suddenly came into view. And then another. And a third, pulling up directly in front of the café.

How had he been located so fast? If the cypercafe had registered the IP address of its private network and a digital trigger had been installed within the State Department database, his own probing would have activated a counterprobe—and the physical address of the TCP/IP network device he had been using.

Ambler sprang to his feet, pushed his way past an Employees Only door, and raced up the stairs—if he was fortunate, he would find his way to the roof and then to the roof of an adjoining building. . . . But he had to move fast, before the retrieval team was fully positioned. And while his muscles pumped and he began to gulp air, a fleeting thought passed through his mind. *If Hal Ambler doesn't exist, who are they after?*

CHAPTER THREE

Sanctuary was what it had always meant to him. It was a single-pen cabin, nothing but local timber from the ridgepole on top to the butting pole down below. As a shelter, it was almost as primeval as the nature that surrounded it. The ceiling and floor joists, the eaves beams, even the stick-and-mud chimney—he had done it all himself, in the course of one warm, buggy June, using little more than a pile of wood and a gas-powered chain saw. It was meant for one person, and he had only ever been there alone. He never spoke of it to anyone he knew. In violation of the rules, he had not told his employers about the acquisition of the lakeside parcel—an acquisition that, to further protect his privacy, he'd arranged through a hard-to-trace offshore business entity. The cabin was nobody else's. It was his alone. And there had been times when he'd arrived back at Dulles International Airport, unable to face the world, and would drive nonstop to the simple wood dwelling, covering the 180 miles in just three hours. He'd take his boat out and go fishing for smallmouth bass and try to save some part of his soul from the maze of deceit and subterfuge that was his vocation.

Lake Aswell hardly merited a spot of blue on any map, but it was a part of the world that made his heart swell. Located at the base of the Sourland Mountains, it was an area where farmland gave way to a thickly wooded terrain, and was surrounded by stands of willow, birch, and pignut hickory, above a sometimes thick underbrush. In the spring and summer, the grounds were dense with foliage, alive with flowers, berries. Now, in January, most of the trees were drab and leafless. Even so, there was a somber elegance to it all: the elegance of potential. Like him, the woodland needed a season of recuperation.

He was bone weary, the price of long hours of vigilance. The car he
started out with was an old blue Dodge Ram minivan, which he had
picked up a few blocks from the cybercafe. It was an awkward, boaty
ride; what recommended it was simply that its owner had affixed a
StorAKey box inside the wheel well. The box was a foolish contraption, used by drivers who valued the security of a spare key more
than the security of their vehicles. The twelve-year-old green Honda
Civic he was now driving came from the Trenton train station's
overnight parking area and had been protected from theft with similar vigilance, or lack thereof. It was as anonymous a model as he
could hope for, and, so far, it had done its job.

His mind churned as he drove north on Route 31. Who had done
this to him? It was the same question that had preyed on him for untold months. The legitimate, if clandestine, facilities of the United
States government had been mobilized against him. Which meant—
what? That someone had lied about him, had somehow set him up,
had persuaded higher authorities that he had gone mad, had become
a security threat. Or that someone or some group with *access* to the
powers of state had sought to make him vanish. Someone or some
group that considered him a threat but that nonetheless chose not to
kill him. His head began to throb; a headache was opening behind
his eyes, like a malignant flower. There were colleagues of his at the
Political Stabilization Unit who could help him—but how could he
find them? These were not men and women who reported for work
at desk jobs; they changed their location regularly, like pieces on a
chessboard. And he had somehow been locked out of every electronic forum he knew about. *Harrison Ambler not found*—it was
madness, yet there was method in it, too. He could *feel* it, feel the malignity like the pulsing headache that made conscious thought a kind
of agony. They had tried to lose him. They had tried to bury him.

They! The exasperating bare plural *They!* A word that said everything and nothing at all.

To survive, he needed to know more, yet he could not know more unless he survived. Barrington Falls, in Hunterdon County, New Jersey, was off a stretch of Route 31 that flowed through the central New Jersey countryside, crosshatched by unmarked intersections with small streets. Twice he pulled into one of those side streets, to make sure he wasn't being followed, but there was no sign of it. He glanced at the clock on the dashboard when he saw the small road sign for Barrington Falls; it was 3:30 P.M. Only this morning he was being held in a maximum-security psychiatric facility. Now he was nearly home.

A quarter of a mile south of the access road to the lake, he pulled the Honda Civic off the road and left it hidden in a copse of hemlock and cedar trees. The fiber-filled tan jacket he had picked up en route kept him warm. As he walked along the springy ground, his footfalls softly crunching on the carpet of leaves and pine needles, he felt the tension beginning to drain from him. Drawing nearer to the lake, he found that he recognized every tree. He heard the fluttering of an owl in the enormous bald cypress tree, its reddish trunk seemingly barkless, gnarled and grooved like an old crone's neck. He could just make out the rubblework chimney of old man McGruder's saddle-bag cabin, perilously close to the water on the far bank. It always looked as if one big storm could wash it right into the lake.

Just past a dense stand of spruce trees, he pushed through the wooded enclave and reached the magical glade where, seven years ago, he had decided to build his cabin. Curtained by magnificent old evergreens on three sides, it provided not only seclusion but tranquillity: a peaceful view of the lake framed by ancient trees.

He had returned, at last. Taking a deep, cleansing breath, he stepped through a gap in the line of firs and looked around at—

—a small, empty glade where his cabin should have been. The same clearing he had come upon seven years earlier, when he had decided to build there.

A wave of dizziness and disorientation overtook him; he felt as if the ground were rippling beneath his feet. *It was impossible.* There was no cabin. No cabin and no trace that a cabin had ever been built here. The vegetation was utterly undisturbed. His memory of where he had sited the single-pen structure was indelible—and yet all he could see were patches of moss, a ground-hugging sprawl of juniper, and a low, deer-cropped yew tree that looked to be at least twenty or thirty years old. He walked around the area, circling it, eyes alert to any sign of human habitation, past or present. Nothing. It was a virgin parcel of land, precisely in the state it had been when he had acquired it. Finally he could no longer fend off the daze of incomprehension, and he sank to his knees on the cold, mossy ground. Even to frame the question filled him with fear, and yet he had to: Could he trust his own memories? The past seven years of his life—start with those. Were his recollections real? Or was his current experience the illusion—would he awake any moment and discover himself to be in his white locked room in Ward 4W?

He remembered having once been told that, when dreaming, a person has no sense of smell. If so, he was not dreaming. He could smell the lake water, the subtle fragrances of organic decay, of leaf mold and earthworm castings, the faint resinous odor of conifers. No, it was—God help him—no dream.

Which is exactly what made it a nightmare.

He rose to his feet and let out a low guttural roar of fury and frustration. He had arrived at his soul's own home, and there was no home. A captive could at least nurture the hope of escape; the torture victim—he knew this firsthand—had at least the hope of easeful respite. But what hope had a creature that has lost its sanctuary?

Everything here was familiar, and nothing was. That was what was so maddening. He began to pace, listening to the chirps and whistles of winter birds. Then he heard a faint, whistling noise of a different kind and felt a sharp sensation—combining pain and a sense of percussive force—just below his neck.

Time slowed. His hand reached for the area, felt an object projecting from his body, and *yanked* it out. It was a long, pen-like dart, and it had hit the top part of his sternum, right below the throat. It had hit him there and stuck, like a knife thrown into a tree.

There was a word for this area of thick bone, Ambler recalled from a training manual: *manubrium.* In offensive combat, it was a well-protected area you wanted to avoid. Which meant that Ambler might have been very lucky. He dived into the low-draping branches of one of the great eastern hemlocks, and counting on the temporary invisibility conferred by his hiding place, he examined the metal projectile.

It was not merely a dart; it was a barbed syringe dart, made of stainless steel and molded plastic. On the syringe barrel, small black lettering identified its pressurized contents as carfentanyl—a synthetic opioid ten thousand times more powerful than morphine. A six-ton elephant could be completely immobilized with just ten milligrams; an effective human dosage would be measured in micrograms. The sternum was so close to the skin that the needle's barbs had no chance to anchor themselves in his flesh. But what about the contents of the syringe dart? It was empty, but that didn't tell him whether it had emptied itself before or after he pulled it out. His fingers returned to the hard bony ridge beneath his throat. He could feel an angry welt where the dart had struck him. So far, he still felt alert. *How long had it been in him?* His reflexes were fast; surely the elapsed time was less than two seconds. Yet a single droplet could do the task. And a syringe dart of this class was designed to disgorge its contents within moments.

Then why wasn't he already unconscious? The question might answer itself before long. For the first time, he became aware that his thinking was growing unfocused, woozy. It was a feeling he was all too accustomed to: he realized that he had been dosed with similar narcotics before, and perhaps many times, on Parrish Island. It was possible that he had built up a measure of tolerance.

There was a second protective factor. Because the hollow tip of the needle had buried itself in bone, it would have been blocked, the fluid prevented from squirting out freely. And, of course, the complete dosage contained in the dart syringe must have been designed to be sublethal; otherwise a bullet would have been less troublesome. A dart like this, though usually a prelude to abduction, was not itself intended to serve death.

He was meant to be unconscious by now; instead, he was merely slowed. Slowed at a moment when he could least afford any diminishment of his faculties. The carpet of pine needles beneath him now seemed like a good place to lie down and take a nap. *Just for a few minutes.* He would rest now and wake up refreshed. *Just for a few minutes.*

No! He could not succumb. He had to feel the fear. Carfentanyl, he recalled, had a half-life of ninety minutes. In event of overdose, the optimal treatment was to infuse the opiate-antagonist naloxone. But where that was not available, an injection of epinephrine could be resorted to. Epinephrine. Better known as adrenaline. Survival would come not from keeping terror at bay but from embracing it.

Feel the fear, he repeated to himself, crawling from beneath the apron of the great eastern hemlock and craning his neck around him. And suddenly he did feel it, as he heard a faint whistling sound again, the sound of rushing air on the rigid, stabilizing wings of a fast-moving projectile, missing him by inches. Adrenaline coursed through his bloodstream: his mouth went dry, his heart began to hammer wildly, and his stomach knotted. Someone was after him. Which meant someone must know who he really was. Self-consciousness evaporated, giving way to the deeply laid circuits of training and instinct.

Both darts had come from the same direction, from farther up the bank. But what distance? Standard procedure would be to avoid unnecessary close work; a man with a tranquilizer rifle could be effective while stationing himself at a safe remove. Given the limited range of the syringe darts, though, the distance could not be great. In his mind, Ambler walked to his southwest, trying to visualize every detail of the terrain. There was the large stand of hemlocks, their branches tipped with small brown cones; a procession of boulders that could be mounted like steps; a gulch where, during the summer, skunk cabbage and lady's slippers would flourish in the wet shade. And, securely lashed to an old, ailing elm, a tree stand for deer hunting.

But of course. A sturdy, portable stand that, like so many "temporary" things, had been put up years ago and never been dismantled. The seat was about three feet square; the heavy straps that held it up were secured around the tree and kept in place by a couple of eyebolts that had been threaded through the trunk. The deer stand was, he recalled, maybe twelve feet off the ground—ground that was maybe twelve feet higher than the ground that Ambler was on. Any professional would have taken advantage of it. How long had the man with the trank gun been studying him before he squeezed the trigger? And who the hell were these people anyway?

The uncertainties were beginning to tire Ambler, somehow reactivating the micrograms of carfentanyl in his blood: *I could rest here. Just for a few minutes.* It was almost as if the powerful opiate was whispering the suggestion. *No!* Ambler wrenched himself back to the present crisis, the *here* and the *now*. So long as he was free, he had a chance. That was all Ambler asked for. A chance.

A chance to make the hunter taste the fear he had inflicted. A chance to stalk the stalker.

The challenge would be to keep his form low while moving through the woods in a quiet, sure-footed manner. He would have to call on training he had seldom used. Rising from the dense, concealing undergrowth to a crouched position, Ambler slowly lifted his knee, relaxing his ankle and foot as he swung it forward while keeping his knee where it was. The toe of his foot touched down and pressed gently against the surface, making sure there were no twigs that might crackle underneath. The rest of his foot followed, toe to heel, in a smooth, continuous motion.

Keeping his weight evenly distributed across his foot maximized the surface area upon which the force was applied and so reduced the downward force exerted. *Slow and steady,* he told himself: but slow and steady was never how he worked. If it hadn't been for the traces of carfentanyl in his blood, he wasn't sure he could have stopped himself from bolting.

Finally, he completed an elliptical course that led him past the ailing elm tree and then back toward it. As he drew within thirty feet of the tree, he found a line of sight through the bramble, trunks, and branches and looked where he expected to find the stand.

But though the tree was as he had imagined, there was no stand on it. No stand and no sign of a stand. As cold as it was outside, he flushed hotly, seized with apprehension. If not the old deer stand—

The wind gusted, and he heard a sound, faint but distinct, of wood scraping against wood. He turned toward it and finally made it out. A deer stand. Another deer stand—bigger, higher, and newer, it seemed, secured to the vast trunk of an old plane tree. As quietly as he could, Ambler moved toward it. Mounded around the base of the tree was a thicket of multiflora rose. If only they lost their razor-sharp thorns in winter as well as their leaves! An invasive species from Asia, it tended to form itself into something like natural concertina wire. And for practical purposes, concertina wire was what it might as well have been, coiled around the trunk of the ninety-foot-tall plane tree.

Ambler peered through branches—past the small bristly seed-pods that were outlined against the sky, like pendant sea urchins—and finally made out the figure. He was a big man, dressed in camouflage fatigues and, luckily, facing the opposite direction. That meant that Ambler's movements had not been detected; the rifleman assumed that he was still somewhere on the terrain that sloped down toward the lake. Ambler peered again, straining to see in the late-afternoon gloom. The rifleman was holding up to his eyes a pair of Steiner autofocus binoculars—again, a military model, with low-glare coated lenses and a green, rubberized waterproof casing—scanning the distance intently, methodically.

Dangling around his shoulders from a strap was a long rifle. It had to have been the dart gun. But the man also had a small sidearm—from its outline, it was probably a Beretta M92. A 9mm U.S. military issue, but usually reserved for members of Special Operations units.

Was the man alone?

He *seemed* to be: he had no walkie-talkie, no visible communicator, no earphone, as you would expect if he was part of a team. But assumptions could not be made.

Ambler looked around himself one more time. His view of the gunman was partly blocked by a thick branch of the old plane tree, its bark dappled but smooth. *The branch*—if Ambler moved to his left and jumped straight up, his hands would grasp it, at a point where it was probably thick enough to support his weight. The branch projected straight out from the trunk, just about horizontally, for maybe twenty-five straight feet, and for fifteen feet of that it was thicker than his thigh. Which, he guessed, meant it was thick enough and strong enough for his purposes. If he could swing himself up on it, he could propel himself over the brambles and within a yard or two of the deer stand.

Now he waited for the next gust in the right direction—away from the gunman, toward him—and sprang upward as hard as he could. His hands grasped the branch, not slapping against it but encircling it swiftly and silently. Another surge from his adrenals enabled him to swing himself up and onto the branch in a single motion.

A low groaning noise came from the wood itself, as the thick bough flexed a little under his weight. But it was not so loud as Ambler had feared, and the gunman on the deer stand—Ambler was able to see him now—gave no sign that he noticed. The wind had gusted; a tree had groaned: the sequence made sense. It did not attract the hunter's attention.

Ambler inched his way down the bough, using his hands and feet in rippling sequence, until at last the stand's heavy nylon strap was within his grasp. He had hoped to release the nylon webbing, sending the platform crashing to the ground. That would not be possible. The strap's latch had been positioned on the other side of the trunk, toward the stand. In fact, he could not get much closer without making some small sound that would give him away. Ambler clenched his jaw, willing himself to focus. *Nothing ever goes according to plan. Revise, and improvise.*

Ambler raised himself to another branch, squeezed his eyes shut for a moment, filled his lungs with air, and *pushed* off, throwing himself at the gunman. It was a flying tackle of the sort Ambler hadn't attempted since his high school gridiron.

It was also a mistake. Alerted by the noise of Ambler's exertion, the man turned around. Ambler, for his part, hit the man too low— at knee level, rather than waist level—and instead of being knocked out of the stand the man fell forward and grabbed hold of Ambler with a grip of steel. It was the most Ambler could do to get his hands on the Beretta.

With a powerful blow, the man knocked the pistol from Ambler's hand and into the brambles below. As the two men faced off on the small stand, Ambler could tell he would have the worst of it. The man was six foot five, heavily muscled, and yet astonishingly agile. His head was smooth-shaven, a stump-like extension of his thick, powerful neck. He landed blows like a trained boxer: each punch carefully aimed and powered by his entire torso, the arm immediately retracting to a defensive position. It was the most Ambler could do to protect his head; his body was left exposed and the crushing blows, he knew, would soon cause him to double over.

Now Ambler stepped out of position, slammed himself against the tree trunk, and dropped his hands. He couldn't have said why.

The big man looked more pleased than puzzled as he moved in for the kill.

CHAPTER FOUR

As Ambler gulped air, his entire body quaking with muscular fatigue, a flicker of the big man's eye told Ambler what he needed to know: the man was going for the coup de grâce—a single roundhouse punch to the jaw, with all the immense upper-body strength he possessed.

Except that Ambler did the one thing he was capable of doing, the one thing no professional would think of doing: he dropped to the ground, with exquisite timing. And the bare-knuckled punch connected with the trunk.

As the man howled in pain, Ambler sprang upward, butting his head into his opponent's solar plexus, and then, before he even heard the reflexive expulsion of breath, he grasped the man's ankles and heaved. At long last, the gunman spilled out of the stand, and Ambler plunged down after him. On top of him. Ambler, at least, had something soft to break his fall.

With fast, deft movements, Ambler yanked off the man's Kevlar-lined camouflage jacket and combat vest. Then he detached the long-barreled rifle from its sling and used the sling to tie the gunman's hands behind his back. The center two knuckles of his right hand were red, bloodied, and beginning to swell, obviously broken. The man moaned in agony.

Ambler looked around for the Beretta. It glinted from beneath the thorny coils of the multiflora rose, and Ambler decided to put off retrieving it.

"Kneel, GI Joe," Ambler said. "You know the position. Cross your ankles."

The man did so, moving with reluctance but without uncertainty, like someone who had forced others into the same position. He had obviously had standard U.S. combat training. Undoubtedly he had had a great deal more.

"I think something's broken, man," the man said in a low, strangled voice, clutching his ribs. Deep South—Mississippi, Ambler would have guessed.

"You'll live," Ambler said shortly. "Or not. That's really for us to decide, isn't it?"

"I don't think you understand the situation," the man said.

"Which is exactly where you come in," Ambler replied. He started patting the man's trouser pockets and extracted a military-style pocketknife. "Now we're going to play a little game of truth or dare." He swung out the pocketknife's fish scaler and held it to very close to the man's face. "See, I don't have a lot of time. So I'm going to have to go straight to the meat of the matter." Ambler worked to control his breathing. He needed to seem calm and in command. And he needed to focus on the kneeling man's face, even as he menaced it with the fish scaler. "First question. Are you working alone?"

"No way. A bunch of us here."

He was lying. Even dulled by the carfentanyl, Ambler knew it, the way he always knew it. When colleagues would ask how, he found himself giving different answers in different cases. A tremble in the voice in one case. A tone of voice that was too assertively smooth and insouciant in another. Something around the mouth. Something around the eyes. There was always something.

Consular Operations had once assigned people to study his peculiar faculty; to the best of his knowledge, nobody had ever managed to duplicate it. Intuition was what he called it. *Intuition* meant: he didn't know. Sometimes he even wondered whether his gift wasn't so much a capacity as an incapacity: he wasn't able *not* to see. Most people filtered what they saw when they looked at someone's face: they operated by the rule of inference-to-the-best-explanation, meaning that whatever didn't sync with the explanation that made the most sense to them they ignored. Ambler lacked that ability to tune out what did not sync.

"So you're alone," Ambler told the kneeling operative. "As I would have expected."

The man protested, but without conviction.

Even without knowing who they were or what they wanted, Ambler realized that they must have figured it was a long shot that he'd show up here. There were fifty other places he might have gone to, and, he guessed, there were people positioned at those other places, too. Given the odds and the short notice, strategy would dictate a single watcher at each. It was a question of manpower.

"Next question. What's my name?"

"I wasn't informed," the man said in an almost resentful tone.

The claim seemed incredible, but the man was telling him the truth.

"I don't see a subject photograph in your pockets. How were you going to identify me?"

"No photo. Assignment arrived a few hours ago. They said you were forty years old, six foot tall, brown hair, blue eyes. To me, you're just January man. Basically, if anybody showed up in this godforsaken place today, it was going to be you. That's how they explained it. It wasn't like I was being sent to an NRA convention, OK?"

"Well done," Ambler said. The account given was strange; it was not deceptive. "You told me the truth. You see, I can always tell."

"Whatever you say," the man said. He was not a believer.

Ambler needed to *make* him a believer. The interrogation would go more smoothly that way. "Try me. I'll ask you a few harmless questions; you answer truthfully or not, as you prefer. See if I can tell. For starters, did you have a dog when you were a kid?"

"Nope."

"See, now you're lying. What was the dog's name?"

"Elmer."

"An honest answer. What was your mother's first name?"

"Marie."

"Wrong. How about your father's?"

"Jim."

"Wrong," Ambler said, and he saw that the kneeling man was visibly spooked by the ease with which his responses were assessed. "How did Elmer die?"

"Run over by a car."

"Right," Ambler said encouragingly. "A truthful answer. Now hold that idea tight. Because from now on, only truthful answers will do." A beat. "Next section of the exam. Who are you working for?"

"My goddamn ribs are broken."

"That's nonresponsive. I warned you that I have no time to waste."

"They'll explain. It's not for me to say." Confidence was starting to return to the man's voice; Ambler would have to undermine that confidence or lose his chance to learn what he needed to know.

"Explain? *You* don't seem to understand. They're not in charge of you right now. I am." He pressed the serrated edge of the fish scaler to the gunman's right cheek.

"Please," the Southerner moaned.

Small pinpricks of blood were visible at the projecting edges of the jagged implement. "A word of advice. If you're going to take a gun to a knife fight, make sure you win." Ambler's voice was arctic and assured. That was part of the craft of interrogation: the aura of utter determination and ruthlessness.

He focused on the long-barreled rifle. A Paxarms MK24B. A .509-caliber syringe projection rifle.

"A pretty fancy piece of equipment," Ambler said. "Not part of GI Joe's usual kit bag. What's the deal?" He pressed down again with the fish scaler.

"*Please,*" the man said, and it was as if all the air had come out of him.

"You were tasked to an abduction detail. Instructions were to knock me out—and then what?"

"Those weren't exactly the instructions." The man sounded almost sheepish. "Seems the people I work for have taken a real interest in you."

"The people you work for," Ambler repeated. "The government, you mean."

"Huh?" A puzzled look, as if he thought Ambler might be teasing him but wasn't sure. "We're talking about a strictly private outfit, OK? I don't work for a government pay grade, that's for damn sure. They said you might show up, and if so, I was to make an approach."

Ambler head-pointed to the Paxarms rifle. "That's what you mean by an 'approach'?"

"They said to use my discretion if I thought you might be dangerous." He shrugged. "So I took the trank gun just in case."

"And?"

He shrugged again. "I thought you might be dangerous."

Ambler's gaze was unblinking. "Was there a drop-off point in the scenario?"

"I wasn't told ahead of time. They were going to radio that info to me once I reported in that you were either on board or in custody. Assuming you showed. I don't know how likely they thought that was."

"*They?* I have to tell you, that's not my favorite word."

"Look, these people hire me to do jobs, but they do it at a remove. It's not like we play mah-jong on Sundays, OK? The sense I got was, they just learned you were on the market, and they want to sign you up before someone else does."

"Nice to be in demand." Ambler struggled to process what he was hearing. Meanwhile, it was important that he not let the rhythm of questioning falter. "Method of contact?"

"We've got a kind of long-distance relationship. This morning I got an encrypted e-mail with the instruction. Partial payment was wired into an account. The deal was on." The words came out in a rush. "No meetings. Total breakaway security."

The man was telling him the truth—and his words told Ambler even more than their explicit content. *Breakaway security*. Jargon from U.S. intelligence. "You're an American operative," Ambler said.

"Retired, like I said. Used to be MI." Military intelligence, then. "Special Forces for seven years."

"So now you're freelance."

"You got it."

Ambler unzipped a pouch attached to the man's camouflage vest. There was a slightly battered-looking Nokia cell phone, probably for personal use, and Ambler pocketed it. He also found, as he expected, a military version of a BlackBerry text-messaging device. End-to-end RASP data security. Both the gunman and the outfit that had recruited him were accustomed to using U.S. clandestine-service equipment.

"So here's the barter," Ambler said. "You tell me the e-mail protocol and your pass codes."

There was a pause. Then, with a new look of resolve, the man slowly shook his head. "Dream on."

Ambler felt a twinge; once again, he had to regain the dominant position. He knew, studying the emotions on the man's countenance, that he wasn't dealing with a fanatic, a true believer. The man before him really was play-for-pay. His objective was to maintain his reputation for reliability; future jobs depended on it. What Ambler needed to impress upon him was that his having a future at all depended upon his cooperation. At times like this, an air of calm reasonableness wasn't effective. Rather, the air to be projected was that of a resolute sadist, happy to be provided with any opportunity to ply his craft.

"Do you know what a man's face looks like when it's flayed?" Ambler said evenly. "I do. The dermal matrix is surprisingly tough, but it adheres only loosely to the layers of lipid and muscle underneath it. Once you cut a flap, in other words, the skin separates quite easily from the fascia beneath. It's like stripping sod from a lawn. And once you lift up the skin, you can see the incredibly intricate striation of the facial muscles. The fish scaler isn't the ideal tool for it—it's very messy, makes very ragged cuts. Still, it gets the job done. You won't be in a position to look, I'm afraid, but I'll describe what I see. That way you won't miss anything. Now then. Shall we begin? You might feel a little pinch. Well, more than a pinch. It'll feel more like—well, like someone's tearing your face off."

The kneeling man's eyes constricted in fear. "You said a barter," the man said. "What do I get?"

"Oh, that. You get to—how shall I put it? Save face."

The man swallowed hard. "Pass code is 1345GD," he said hoarsely. "Repeat: 1345GD."

"A friendly reminder. If you lie, I'll know immediately," Ambler said. "Get a single detail wrong, and we'll return to our anatomy lesson. You need to understand this."

"I'm not lying."

A wintry smile. "I know."

"E-mail encryption is automatic with the hardware. Subject line must say: 'Seeking Ulysses.' Capitalizing doesn't matter. Sign-off is 'Cyclop.'" The man continued to detail the communication protocols that had been established, and Ambler committed them to memory.

"You got to let me go, man," the Southerner said after Ambler had made him repeat everything three times.

Ambler took off his tan jacket and put on the man's combat vest and camouflage jacket; they seemed like articles that were likely to come in handy. He fished out the man's belt wallet and strapped it on himself; most off-the-books operatives carried substantial sums of cash on them, and that, too, might come in handy. The Beretta remained lost somewhere in the thorny underbrush.

As for the rifle, its bulk would make it more of an impediment to Ambler than an advantage, at least in the short term—and right now the short term stretched before him like a dozen lifetimes. He field-stripped it and tossed the six remaining tranquilizer darts into the thickets. Only then did he untie the man's hands and toss him his tan jacket. "So you don't freeze," he said.

Ambler felt a slight stinging sensation at the side of his neck—a gnat, a mosquito?—and absently slapped at it with a hand. It was a few moments before he realized that there would be no such insects around at this time of the year, and by then, he had noticed that his fingertips were wet with his own blood. Not an insect. Not a dart.

A bullet.

He whirled around. The man he had just untied crumpled to the ground, bright red blood spilling from his mouth, the fixed stare of death on his face. A sniper's bullet—the same bullet that grazed Ambler's neck—must have entered his mouth and penetrated the back of his head. Ambler had decided to spare the man's life. Someone else had not.

Or was the bullet meant for Ambler?

He had to run. Ambler plunged through the woods at top speed. His gift of the tan coat might well have been a death sentence, flagging the man for execution. A distant sniper would have keyed to the color. But why send someone to "make an approach" if the plan was to kill him?

Ambler had to leave the Sourlands. The Honda had no doubt already been located. What other vehicles were in the area? He remembered seeing a tarp-covered Gator, a quarter of a mile up the hill. It was a low green off-road utility vehicle, capable of traversing almost any terrain—swamps, streams, hills.

When he reached it, he wasn't surprised to find that the keys were in it. This was still a part of the world where nobody locked his front door. The Gator started up easily, and Ambler drove through the woods as fast as it would go, holding on to the steering wheel when the vehicle bounced over rocks, ducking his head down when low branches threatened. It lurched easily over brambles and thickets; as long as he had room to maneuver between trees, the underbrush would not stop him. Nor would the rocky gulches and streams. The ride was bumpy and lurching, like mounting a horse that hadn't quite been broken; but its grip of the terrain was never less than secure.

The windshield of the Gator suddenly exploded, turned opaque with spiderwebbing.

A second bullet had finally arrived.

He steered crazily, randomly, hoping that the bouncing of the vehicle on rough terrain would make him harder to keep in the crosshairs of the sniper scope. Meanwhile, his mind reeled, in a wilderness of uncertainties. The line of fire told him that the shot had to have been fired from somewhere across the lake—somewhere in the area of McGruder's old house. Or the pylon farther up the hill. Or—he scanned the horizon in his mind—the grain silo at the Steptoe farm, a little up the hill. Yes, that's where he would set up if he was running an op. Safety lay *up*—up the slopes to where the incline gave way to an indented area. A paved road ran along it, and if he could reach it, he'd be protected from the sniper by the earth itself.

Gunning the engine, he found the vehicle was able to move up the steepest slopes of the Sourland Mountains with ease; ten minutes later, he reached the road. The Gator was too slow to keep up with regular automotive traffic, and the gunshot-shattered windshield would attract the wrong kind of notice. So he drove the Gator behind a dense stand of eastern red cedars and turned off the engine.

There was no sound of any pursuer, no sound of anything but the ticking of the Gator's stilled engine and the rushing of cars on the nearby mountain road.

He took out the slain man's PDA. *They want to sign you up.* The man had believed it, but was it a ruse? Clearly, whatever outfit had recruited the American ex-operative intended to keep itself at a remove: breakaway security. Yet Ambler had to learn what they knew. Now it was up to him to make an "approach," but on his terms and as someone other than who he was. To overcome the mechanisms of caution, the message needed to promise something—threaten something? The imagination was a powerful thing: the less specific the message, the better.

After a few moments' thought, he thumb-typed a message, one that was terse but carefully crafted.

An encounter with the subject, he explained, had not gone as planned, but he now found himself in possession of some "interesting documents." A meeting would be necessary. He kept the explanation minimal, without elaboration of any sort.

Awaiting instructions, he typed. Then he sent the message off to whoever was at the other end of the cryptosystem.

Now he made his way to the side of the road. In the camouflage jacket, he would look like an out-of-season hunter. Few people from the area were likely to disapprove. A couple of minutes later, a middle-aged woman driving a GMC with an overflowing cigarette tray picked him up. She had a lot on her mind and talked nonstop before dropping him off at the Motel 6 near Route 173. Ambler was certain he had made polite noises as she spoke, but he barely heard a word.

Seventy-five dollars for a room. For a brief moment he worried that he wouldn't have enough, but then he remembered the belt wallet. Checking in—under a randomly confected name—he struggled to keep at bay the utter exhaustion that threatened to engulf him at any moment and probably would have even without whatever carfentanyl remained in his system. He needed a room. He needed a rest.

The room was as utterly nondescript as he could have hoped: the style of no style. Hurriedly he went through the contents of the slain man's belt wallet. There were two sets of identification cards; most useful would be the driver's license from Georgia, where the computer systems were particularly unevolved. The license looked unremarkable, but as Ambler flexed it, he could tell that it was actually designed to make alteration easy. Ambler would have no difficulty getting a postage-size photograph of himself at a shopping mall and adapting a license that had been spurious to begin with. The operative's height and eye color were different from his, but not dramatically enough to arouse notice. Tomorrow—but there were so many things he would have to deal with tomorrow. So many things that he was too exhausted to contemplate right now.

Indeed, he felt on the verge of blacking out: the combination of physical and emotional stress was nearly overwhelming. Instead, he force-marched himself into the shower, made the water as hot as he could tolerate, and remained there for a long time, sudsing the sweat, blood, and grime off his body until nothing remained of the small motel-issue bar of soap. Only then did he stagger out of the shower and begin to dry himself with the white cotton towels.

There was so much he needed to ponder—and yet he somehow felt that he could not allow himself to do so. Not now. Not today.

He towel-dried his hair vigorously and stepped over to the mirror above the sink. It was fogged with steam, and he heated it with the hair dryer until an oval was cleared. He could not remember the last time he had seen his own face—how many months had it been?—and he braced himself for a haggard countenance.

When he finally saw himself in the mirror, vertigo overcame him completely.

It was the face of a stranger.

Ambler could feel his knees buckling beneath him, and, the next thing he knew, he was on the floor.

The man in the mirror was unrecognizable to him. It wasn't a gaunter or harrowed version of him. It wasn't him with an age-etched brow or dark hollows beneath his eyes. It wasn't him at all.

The high, angular cheekbones, the aquiline nose: it was a perfectly handsome face—a face most would consider more handsome than his own—save for a certain cruelty to the visage. His own nose had been more rounded, broad and slightly fleshy at the tip; his cheeks had been more convex, the chin cleft. *He is not me,* Ambler thought, and the illogic battered him like a powerful wave.

Who was the man he saw in the mirror?

It was a face that he could not recognize but that he could read. And what he read in it was the same emotion that filled his own breast: terror. No, something beyond terror. Dread.

The cataract of psychiatric jargon to which he had been subjected during his months of captivity—*dissociative identity disorder, personality fragmentation,* and on and on—suddenly filled his mind. He could hear, as if in a chorus of murmured voices, the doctors' insistence that he had suffered a psychotic break and was drifting through fictive identities.

Could they have been right?

Was he mad after all?

PART TWO

CHAPTER FIVE

Sleep, fitful sleep, finally overtook him, but even unconsciousness provided no sanctuary. His dreams were captive to memories of a far-off land. Once again, an image buckled and shimmered like a celluloid frame paused before an overheated projector bulb—and then he knew where he was.

Changhua, Taiwan. The centuries-old town was surrounded by mountains on three sides; to the west, it faced the Taiwan Strait—the fraught hundred miles of salt water that separates the island from the mainland. Fukien emigrants first settled there in the seventeenth century, during the Ching dynasty; many waves of settlers followed. Each successive wave added its distinctive imprint, but the town itself, like some intelligent organism, decided which additions would be preserved, which lost to history. At a park at the base of the Bagua Mountains stood a massive black Buddha, guarded by two massive stone lions. Visitors gaped at the Buddha; the townsmen had almost equal regard for the lions—emblems of defense, with coiled muscles and sharp fangs. Years ago, Changhua was a major fort. Now a populous city, it had become a garrison of another sort. A garrison of democracy.

On the outskirts of town, near a paper factory and flower farm, a makeshift platform had been assembled. The man many believed would be the next president of Taiwan, Wai-Chan Leung, was about to appear before a crowd of thousands. Supporters had flocked from the Tianwei and Yungjing townships along the provincial Route 1, and small, dusty cars filled every side street and alley. Never in memory had a political candidate inspired such excitement among the ordinary people of Taiwan.

He was, in many ways, an unlikely figure. For one thing, he was much younger than most candidates: just thirty-seven years of age. He was the scion of a wealthy family, one that had merchant lineage, and yet he was a genuine populist, with a charisma that stirred the spirits of the least well off. He had founded the fastest-growing new political party in Taiwan and was personally responsible for its re-markably broad appeal. The island republic had no shortage of po-litical parties and organizations, but Wai-Chan Leung's party had immediately set itself apart by its clear-eyed commitment to reform. Having led successful anticorruption campaigns on the local level, Leung now asked to be given the authority to cleanse national poli-tics, national commerce, of corruption and cronyism. Nor did his political vision end there. Whereas other candidates exploited the long-standing fear and resentment toward the "Chinese empire" rep-resented by the mainland, Leung spoke, rather, of a "new policy toward the new China"—a policy centered on conciliation, trade, and an ideal of shared sovereignty.

To many old China hands in the State Department, the young man sounded too good to be true. According to a dossier painstak-ingly compiled by Consular Operations' Political Stabilization Unit, he was.

That was why Ambler had been deployed at Changhua, as part of an "action team" dispatched by the Political Stabilization Unit—one of the Stab boys, in the sardonic shorthand. Which meant he was there not as Hal Ambler but as Tarquin, the field name he had been assigned since the beginning of his career in covert ops. Tarquin, he sometimes felt, was not just a persona but a person in his own right. When Ambler was in the field, he *became* Tarquin. It was a form of psychic compartmentalization that enabled him to do what had to be done.

One of the very few Westerners in a sea of Asian faces—by auto-

matic presumption, therefore, a member of the foreign media—
Tarquin moved through the dense crowd, keeping his eyes peeled on
the platform. At any moment, the man would appear. The great hope
of Taiwan's new generation. The youthful idealist. The charismatic
visionary.

The monster.

The facts were carefully detailed in the PSU dossier. It revealed the
murderous fanaticism that lay beneath the candidate's fifth-
columnist pose of moderation and sweet reasonableness. It exposed
his ideological ties with the Khmer Rouge. His personal involvement
with the "Golden Triangle" drug trade—and with a string of political murders throughout Taiwan.

There was no way to unmask him without compromising dozens
of assets, leaving them to face torture and death at the hands of Leung's secret confederates. Yet he could not be allowed to succeed—to
take his place at the helm of Taiwan's National Congress. It was to
ensure the survival of democracy itself that the poisoned populist
had to be removed from the democratic arena.

That was the kind of job that the Stab unit specialized in. The
ruthlessness of some of its operations earned it the disapproval of
those State Department intelligence analysts with soft hearts and
softer heads. In truth, unpalatable action was sometimes necessary
to fend off even more unpalatable consequences. Undersecretary
Ellen Whitfield, Stab's director, was devoted to that principle with a
single-mindedness that made her peculiarly effective. Where other
unit directors were content to analyze and assess, Whitfield would
act—and do so early. "Remove the cancer before it spreads" was
both her motto and her record when it came to political threats.
Ellen Whitfield did not believe in endless diplomatic temporizing
when the peace could be kept by means of a swift, surgical intervention. Seldom, though, had the stakes been so great.

Tarquin's earpiece crackled softly. "Alpha One in position," a voice
murmured. Translation: the team's explosive-ordnance technician

had established himself at a safe distance from where he had secreted his device, ready to activate the radio-controlled detonator at Tarquin's signal. The operation was complex because it had to be. Leung's family, fearing for his safety and distrustful of the state police, had provided him with an elaborate security team. All the obvious sniper's nests would have already been checked out and cleared. Other guards, expert in both the ancient traditions of the martial arts and the newer ones of contemporary combat, would scan the crowd, and some would be planted within it at regular intervals: any sign of a weapon would be met with force. Leung traveled in an armored car, stayed at hotel rooms carefully guarded by loyalists. None would imagine that the threat lurked within the ordinary-looking podium.

Now it was showtime.

From the growing rustle of the crowd Tarquin knew that the candidate had made his appearance. Tarquin looked up as Leung stepped smartly onto the dais.

Applause began and grew, and the candidate beamed. He was not yet positioned directly in front of the podium, however, which was crucial. To avoid collateral injuries, the small explosive device had been designed to have a precise directionality. Tarquin waited, holding the props of a journalist's narrow notepad and ballpoint pen.

Awaiting your signal, a metallic voice was prompting him from his earpiece. A signal that meant death.

Awaiting your signal.

The sound changed to another, as the air temperature seemed to drop, and he heard a faint noise again—the very noise that, he now realized, had awakened him into the here and now, thousands of miles across the world and more than two years later.

Ambler tossed in his motel bed, the sheets knotted and clammy with sweat. The noise—a rattling from the bedside table. The slain man's BlackBerry was vibrating, indicating the arrival of a text message. Ambler reached for it and, after pressing a few buttons, confirmed that a reply to his e-mail had arrived. The message was brief but conveyed precise instructions. A rendezvous had been arranged for two-thirty that afternoon, at the Philadelphia International Airport. Gate C19.

They were clever. They were effectively using the airport's security staff and metal detectors for their own purposes, ensuring that he would arrive unarmed. The public nature of the arena provided further protection against any violent moves on his part. Yet the hour selected was when the fewest people would actually be waiting for flights. In a largely vacant part of the terminal—and Ambler was certain that they had selected the specific gate with this in mind, too—they would have some measure of seclusion. Isolated enough for privacy, public enough for security. Well done. They knew what they were doing. It was not an entirely comforting thought.

Clayton Caston sat at the breakfast table, dressed, as usual, in one of his dozen nearly interchangeable gray suits. When he had bought them, mail-order, from the Jos. A. Bank clothiers catalog, they had been marked 50 percent off, so the price point seemed very reasonable to him, and the wool/polyester blend minimized wrinkling, which was very practical. "Year-round executive three-button suit," the catalog said: an "all-season blend." Caston took the clothiers at their word; he wore the same suits all year round. So, too, with the repp ties, red with green stripes or blue with red stripes. He realized some of his colleagues considered his nearly unvarying attire eccentric. But what was the point of variety for its own sake? You found something that did what it was supposed to do, and you stuck with it.

It was the same with his breakfast. He liked cornflakes. Cornflakes were what he had in the morning; cornflakes were what he was having now.

"That is such *bull!*" his sixteen-year-old daughter, Andrea, exploded. She wasn't talking to him, of course; she was talking to her brother, Max, older by one year. "Chip is *gross*. Anyway, he's into Jennifer, not me—thank God!"

"You are *so* transparent," Max said implacably.

"Use one of the grapefruit knives if you're cutting grapefruit," their mother said, mildly reproving. "That's why we've got them." She was dressed in a terry-cloth bathrobe, her feet in terry-cloth slippers, her hair held back in a terry-cloth headband. To Clay Caston, she was still a vision of loveliness.

Max accepted the curved grapefruit knife without a word; he was still needling his sister. "Chip hates Jennifer and Jennifer hates Chip, and you made sure of it when you told Chip what Jennifer said about him to T.J. And, by the way, I hope you let Mom know about what happened in your French class yesterday."

"Don't you dare!" Andrea jumped up from her seat, in a towering sixteen-year-old rage. "Why don't we talk about the little *scratch* on the side of the Volvo? It wasn't there before you went out with it last night. Think Mom's noticed yet?"

"What kind of a scratch?" Linda Caston asked, putting down her pond-sized mug of black coffee.

Max gave his sister a smoldering look, as if he was trying to come up with some regimen of torture that would begin to serve justice.

"Let's just say Mad Max hasn't mastered the subtleties of parallel parking yet."

"You know something?" Max said, not taking his eyes from his sister. "I think it's time your friend Chip and I had a talk."

Caston looked up from his *Washington Post.* He was acutely aware that he did not figure large in the consciousness of his two children right now, and he minded not at all. That they were his own children in the first place was something of a mystery to him, so little did they take after him.

"You wouldn't dare, you little toad."

"What kind of a scratch?" Linda repeated.

The others at the table were going at one another as if he didn't exist. Caston was used to it. Even at the breakfast table, he was the world's most nondescript bureaucrat, and Andrea and Max were slightly absurd and self-absorbed, as adolescents always were. Andrea, with her raspberry-scented lip gloss and her marker-decorated jeans; Max, budding star of the high school gridiron who never remembered to shave his neck properly and wore too much Aqua Velva. Caston mentally corrected himself: *any* amount of Aqua Velva would be too much.

They were an undisciplined, rambunctious couple of brats, who would start squabbling over the slightest scrap. And Clayton Caston loved them like life itself.

"Is there any orange juice left?" Caston's first words at the breakfast table.

Max handed him the carton. The inner life of his son was largely opaque to Caston, but every once in a while, he saw something close to pity in Max's expression: a young man trying to categorize his dad according to the anthropological categories of high school—jock, stud, geek, dweeb, loser—and realizing that if they were classmates they *definitely* wouldn't hang out together. "There's a swallow or two left, Dad," he said.

"One swallow does not make a spring," Caston replied.

Max shot him an uneasy look. "Whatever."

"We need to talk about the scratch," said Linda.

There was less shouting in Caleb Norris's office at the CIA two hours later, but the hushed voices only emphasized the heightened tension. Norris was an Assistant Deputy Director of Intelligence, and when he had summoned Caston for a 9:30 A.M. meeting, he did not tell him what it was about. He did not have to. Since the Parrish Island bulletin had arrived the previous morning, further signals—most of them conflicting and maddeningly vague—had come in, suggesting that there had been additional disturbances related to the incident.

Norris had the broad face of a Russian peasant, with a lumpy complexion and small, wide-spaced eyes. He was barrel-chested and hirsute; wisps of black hair emerged from his shirt cuffs and, whenever he removed his tie, from his shirt collar. Although he was the agency's senior-most officer in intelligence analysis and a member of the director's inner circle, someone who had only seen Norris in a photograph would place him in an entirely different profession— that of a bouncer, say, or a mobster's bodyguard. Nor did his shop-steward manners give any inkling of his curriculum vitae: an undergraduate degree in physics at the Catholic University of America; a National Science Foundation fellowship to work on the military applications of game theory; stints at civilian organizations such as the Institute for Defense Analyses and the Lambda Corporation. Norris was too impatient for a traditional career, he recognized early on, yet at the agency his impatience became a virtue. He pushed through the logjams and bottlenecks that left others behind. He realized the extent to which power in an organization is the power you assume, not the power formally accorded to your position. It was a matter of not taking "we're still working on it" for an answer. Caston admired that about him.

When Caston appeared at the door, Norris was in a characteristic posture of agitation—pacing his office, his stout arms folded on his chest. Norris was not so much worried by the Parrish Island incident as he was annoyed by it. It annoyed him because it reminded him how much of the intelligence establishment was outside the purview of its titular director. That was the larger problem, and a perennial one. Every division of the military—the Army, Navy, Air Force, and Marine Corps—had its internal intelligence units, while, along different lines, the Department of Defense lavished its resources on the Defense Intelligence Agency. The White House's National Security Council retained a separate staff of intelligence analysts. The National Security Agency, in Fort Meade, had its own vast infrastructure, largely devoted to "signals intelligence"; additional signals work was done by the National Reconnaissance Office and the National Geospatial-Intelligence Agency. The State Department supported a bureau of intelligence and research, in addition to its clandestine-service division, Consular Operations. And every organization was further partitioned internally. The fissures and fault lines were numerous, and each represented the potential for catastrophic failure.

Hence a seemingly minor annoyance like this bulletin bothered Norris like an ingrown hair. It was one thing not to know what was happening on the steppes of Uzbekistan; it was another to be in the dark when it came to your own backyard. How was it that nobody seemed to know who it was who had escaped from Parrish Island?

The facility was used on a "joint resource" basis by all branches of America's clandestine services. A man who was not only detained at Parrish Island but, so it appeared, was kept isolated in a locked ward was presumably a very dangerous man indeed, either because of what he was capable of disclosing or what he was capable of *doing*.

But when the office of the CIA's director had inquired as to the identity of the escaped man, nobody had an answer. That was either madness, of a kind untreated in Parrish Island, or something like insubordination.

"Here's the thing," the ADDI said to Caston, blurting it out when Caston entered, as if they were already in the midst of conversation. "Every patient in that facility goes with a—whaddaya call it?—a requisition signature, a billing code. 'Joint resource' means every agency contributes to the extent they use it. If Langley checks in a loony-tunes analyst, Langley foots his bill, or some chunk of it. If it's someone at Fort Meade, Ford Meade gets billed. Meaning, every patient comes with a billing code. Twelve-digit. For security reasons, the payment procedure is kept separate from the operations files, but the records are supposed to give the name of the officer who authorized the custodial detention. Only not this time. I'm hoping you can figure out what's gone wrong. The Parrish Island account records tell us that the billing code for the patient worked—the financials were always just fine. But now the accounts guys at Consular say they can't find the billing code in their database. Ergo, we haven't even figured out who authorized his detention."

"I've never known that to happen."

Another gust of indignation returned to fill Norris's sails. "Either they're telling us the truth, in which case they're screwed, or they're stonewalling, in which case they're screwing us. And if so, I'd like to figure out a way to screw them back." Norris tended to speak in disjunctions—either-ors—when he was agitated. The ADDI's light blue shirt was growing wetly dark beneath his arms. "But that's my fight, not yours. What I want from you, Clay, is a lantern in the darkness. My usual request, right?"

Caston bowed his head. "If they're stonewalling, Cal, it's on a very high level. I can tell you that already."

The ADDI turned an expectant gaze toward him and made a summoning gesture with his hand. "More" was all Norris said.

"It's pretty clear that the fugitive is a former high-value agent."

"An HVA who went off his rocker."

"That's what we're told. Best I can figure, Consular Operations has given us 'file front' info on Patient 5312. And we got a psych profile zapped over from Parrish Island. Dozens of database fields, filled with terms from the *Diagnostic and Statistical Manual* of the American Psychiatric Association. Basically, he's a severe dissociative."

"Meaning?"

"Meaning he thinks he's someone he isn't."

"Then who is he?"

"That's the question of the hour, isn't it?"

"Goddammit," Norris said, nearly crying out in exasperation. "How can you just lose somebody's identity, like a goddamn sock in the dryer?" His eyes flashed with anger. After a moment, he reached out and patted Caston on the side of his shoulder, and a wheedling smile appeared on his face. Caston, he knew, could be prickly: one enlisted his efforts, one did not presume them. If Caston felt bullied, he reacted badly, could retract into the ordinary bureaucrat he affected to be. Caleb Norris had learned that lesson early on. Now the ADDI focused his charm on the stoop-shouldered numbers cruncher. "Did I ever tell you how much I like your tie? It's you."

Caston acknowledged the affectionate japery with a wince of a smile. "Don't try to get on my good side, Caleb. I don't *have* a good side." He shrugged. "Here's the situation. Like I say, psychiatric files we've got, all indexed under the patient number, 5312. But the information they've got doesn't retrieve any Cons Ops personnel files— no matter what root you probe in the system. The personnel details don't come up."

"Meaning they've been erased."

"Meaning, more likely, that they've been disconnected. In all probability, the data exists somewhere, but it isn't linked to a digital ID anybody has access to. It's the digital equivalent of a severed spinal cord."

"Sounds like you've spent time roaming through the computer system there."

"The major systems at State aren't integrated internally, and there are major-league platform incompatibilities with our systems. But they use the same comma-delimited back-office program we do for payroll, deductibilities, costing information, and procurement." Caston rattled off these accounting categories like a waiter speeding through the daily specials. "If you know your way around back-office accounts management, you get the equivalent of a plank you might use to board one ship from another."

"Like Captain Kidd chasing Bluebeard."

"Hate to break it to you, but I'm not sure there really was a Bluebeard. So I seriously doubt he makes any appearance on Captain Kidd's résumé."

"No Bluebeard? Next you're gonna be telling me there's no Santa, either?"

"Sounds like you got fed some bad intel from your parents, there," Caston said, straight-faced. "Holiday disinformation. May need to scrub your tooth-fairy files, too, while you're at it." He scanned Norris's desk, looking slightly disapprovingly at the messy piles of unsorted memos. "But I think you've got the general idea. A person would rather be escorted onto a ship the proper way. When there's no alternative, though, a long plank can be surprisingly effective."

"So what did you learn once you got that plank out and galloped across it?"

"Not a lot so far. We're still combing through the patient records. And there's a partial ops record, under his field alias, Tarquin."

"Tarquin," Norris repeated. "A field alias but no name. Curious and curiouser. Anyway, what do we know about this guy?"

"The main thing we know is that Agent Tarquin wasn't just Cons Ops. He was a member of the Political Stabilization Unit."

"If he's a Stab guy, he's probably a wet-work expert."

Wet work. Caston despised such euphemisms. The evidence all suggested the agent was a dangerous sociopath. That seemed to be a job requirement for a successful career at PSU. "We only know scraps about his ops record. The PSU connection I was able to make by the coding system. Their staff has a 7588 suffix to their ID numbers, and we pulled that from the 5312 records at the facility. But when we turn to the State databases, things get grim: the rest has been delinked from the Tarquin folder."

"So what's your gut tell you?"

"My *gut*?"

"Yeah, what do your instincts say?"

It took Caston a moment to realize that Norris was putting him on.

Early in their working relationship, Caston had made his scorn for the notion of "gut instinct" abundantly clear. It was, in fact, something of a hobbyhorse with him. He was deeply annoyed when people asked for him to provide a "gut response" before the data had provided any real direction: as far as Caston was concerned, to go on hunches was to go off half-cocked. It prevented one from analyzing things logically; it impeded the workings of reason and the rigorous techniques of probabilistic analysis.

Caston watched as Norris's face split into a grin; the ADDI enjoyed goading Caston into delivering his firmly held convictions on the subject.

"I'm just busting your balls," Norris said. "But tell me, what are we supposed to make of this guy? What does your, ah, decision matrix say?"

Caston responded with a thin smile. "It's all highly preliminary. But, again, there are several data points that suggest he's a bad egg. I guess you know my views about agents who color outside the lines. If you're on the payroll, you're supposed to comply with the parameters established by federal decrees. There's a reason for that. You can talk about 'wet work.' The way I see it, either a practice is authorized or it isn't. There's no middle path. I want to know why we have people like this 'Tarquin' in the employ of the federal government. When will our intelligence services learn that it never works?"

"*Never* works?" Norris raised an eyebrow.

"Never works as planned."

"Nothing in creation ever does. Including creation itself. And God had seven days to get it right. I can only give you three."

"What's the rush?"

"Just a feeling I have." Norris raised a hand, preempting Caston's reproval. "Truth is, the intelligence directorate has been getting signals—they're nonspecific, but they're persistent enough that we can't ignore them—about some sort of off-the-books activity that's going on. By us? Against us? I don't know yet, and neither does the DCI. We think it involves highly placed members of the government—and that whatever it is, it's been fast-tracked. So we're all on alert. Anything irregular—well, we can't know whether it's connected or not, but it's dangerous to presume otherwise. So we need a definitive report from you in three days. Find out who this Tarquin really is. Help us bring him in. Or bring him down."

Caston nodded stonily. He did not need encouragement. Caston detested anomalies, and the man who escaped from Parrish Island was an anomaly of the worst kind. Nothing could bring Caston greater satisfaction than identifying this anomaly—and eliminating it.

CHAPTER SIX

At the Motel 6 near Flemington, New Jersey, Hal Ambler used the slain man's Nokia to place a number of phone calls. First was to the U.S. Department of State. He could make no assumptions, at this point: he could not know whether his relation to the intelligence unit in which he had spent his career was one of friend or foe. He could not use the emergency numbers he had memorized as an operative, in case that triggered a tracing mechanism. Instead, it would be safer to knock on the front door. Accordingly, the first call he made was to the State Department communications office. Pretending to be a reporter from Reuters International, he requested that he be connected to the office of Undersecretary Ellen Whitfield. Could she confirm a statement that had been attributed to her? Her assistant, to whom he was connected after a number of intermediate relays, was apologetic. The undersecretary was traveling, part of an overseas delegation.

Was it possible to be more specific? the Reuters correspondent asked. The assistant was sorry, but she could not.

An overseas delegation: no doubt the information was accurate. It was also essentially useless.

Ellen Whitfield's official designation as an "undersecretary" in the Department of State blandly concealed her real administrative charge as the director of the Political Stabilization Unit. His boss, in short.

Did his colleagues think he was dead? Mad? Vanished? What did Ellen Whitfield know about what had happened to him?

The questions eddied in his mind. If she did not know, she would *want* to know, wouldn't she? He struggled to recall the period of time just before he had found himself a captive in a psychiatric penal colony. Yet those last memories remained opaque, encased, inaccessible—hidden within the fog that had eclipsed his existence. He tried to inventory what he could recall before that fog settled in. He recalled the few days he spent in Nepal, visiting with the leaders of a group of self-identified Tibetan dissidents who were seeking American assistance. They were dissembling, Ambler swiftly concluded: in fact, they were representatives of a Maoist insurgency that had been repudiated by China and banished by Nepal's own struggling government. The Stab operation at Changhua commenced thereafter—preparing for the "removal" of Wai-Chan Leung—and then? His mind was like a torn page: there was no sharp line separating recollection from oblivion; rather, it feathered irregularly to an end.

It was the same when he tried to push back his memories of Parrish Island to before the final months. So many of his earlier memories were fractured moments, stripped of any sense of time or sequence.

Perhaps he needed to go further back—before the weeks surrounding his abduction, to the time when his memories of his life were vivid, continuous, were as real as the ground beneath his feet. If only he could find someone who would share those memories. Someone whose reminiscences would provide the corroboration he desperately needed: the assurance that he was who he was.

On impulse, Ambler called directory assistance for Dylan Sutcliffe in Providence, Rhode Island.

Dylan Sutcliffe was someone he had scarcely thought about for years, someone he'd met half a lifetime ago. He had met Dylan when they were both freshmen at Carlyle College, a small liberal arts school in Connecticut, and they hit it off at once. Dylan was a cutup, with a gift for gab and a great store of tales about growing up in Pepper Pike, Ohio. He also had a pronounced weakness for pranks.

One morning in late October—it was their sophomore year—the campus woke up to discover that an enormous pumpkin had appeared on the spire of McIntyre Tower. The pumpkin had to have weighed nearly seventy pounds, and how it materialized there was a mystery. It was a source of merriment among the students and consternation among the administrators: no maintenance worker would agree to risk his neck in order to bring it down, so the pumpkin was left to make its way down by itself. The next morning, a cluster of small jack-o'-lanterns appeared at the base of McIntyre Tower, positioned as if looking up at the big pumpkin overhead; some of them bore signs saying JUMP! The undergraduate glee only heightened the ill humor of the college officials. A few months before graduation, two years later, when the administration was no longer so exercised, the word finally went around that the class had Dylan Sutcliffe, an expert and well-equipped rock climber, to thank. Sutcliffe was a prankster but a prudent one; he never directly owned up to it and had always appreciated Ambler's discretion. For Ambler, having noticed something in Sutcliffe's face when the matter was discussed, was the first to guess that he was behind it, and though he let Sutcliffe know that he knew, he never told anyone else.

Ambler remembered the Charlie Brown–style shirts Sutcliffe favored, with their broad, colorful horizontal stripes, and his collection of clay pipes, seldom used, but more interesting than the usual undergraduate collection of beer bottles or Grateful Dead basement tapes. Ambler recalled attending his wedding just a year after graduation, knew that he had a good job at a Providence community bank, once independent, now part of a national chain.

"This is Dylan Sutcliffe," a voice now said. Ambler did not immediately recognize it, but he was overcome with warmth all the same.

"Dylan!" Ambler said. "It's Hal Ambler. Remember me?"

There was a long pause. "I'm sorry," the man said, sounding confused. "I'm not sure I caught your name."

"Hal Ambler. We were at Carlyle together two decades ago. You were in my suite, freshman year. *I was at your wedding.* Coming back now? Been a long time between drinks, huh?"

"Listen, I don't buy things from strangers over the phone," the man said curtly. "I suggest you try this on somebody else."

Could this be the wrong Dylan Sutcliffe? Nothing about him *sounded* like the Sutcliffe he remembered. "Whoa," he said. "Maybe I got the wrong guy. You didn't go to Carlyle, then?"

"I did. It's just that nobody in my class was named Hal Ambler." There was a click as the man hung up on him.

Roiled by a mixture of anger and fear, he now called Carlyle College and got himself transferred to the registrar's office. To the young man who answered, Ambler explained that he was a human-resources officer for a major corporation, prospective employer of one Harrison Ambler. As a matter of corporate policy, they were verifying certain items on the applicant's résumé. All he had to do was confirm that Harrison Ambler had indeed graduated from Carlyle College.

"Certainly, sir," the man from the registrar's office said. He asked for the spelling and entered the name; Ambler could hear quiet, swift clicking from a keyboard. "Sorry," the voice said. "Could you give me the spelling one more time?"

With a growing sense of apprehension, Ambler did so.

"I guess it's a good thing you called," said the voice on the phone.

"He didn't graduate?"

"Nobody by that name has ever matriculated here, let alone graduated."

"Is it possible that your database doesn't go back far enough?"

"Nope. We're a real small college, so that's one problem we don't have. Believe me, sir, if this guy was enrolled here at any time during the twentieth century, I'd know."

"Thank you," Ambler said, his voice hollow. "Thank you for your time." His hand was trembling as he pressed the OFF button on the cell phone.

It was madness!

His entire sense of who he was—could it be a phantasm? Was that possible? He shuttered his eyes briefly and allowed the countless memories of his four decades to surge and spill and swirl in his mind, yielding to a free and unstructured flood of association. There were memories beyond counting, and they were the memories of Hal Ambler, unless he truly was mad. The time, exploring his own backyard as a young child, that he stumbled on a subterranean nest of yellow jackets—how they spurted from the ground, like a black and yellow geyser!—and he wound up in the emergency room with thirty stings. The hot July in summer camp, learning to do the butterfly stroke in Lake Candaiga, and catching a glimpse of breast when one of the camp counselors, Wendy Sullivan, was changing in a Portosan with a broken door. The August he spent, age fifteen, working in the barbecue restaurant of a fairground ten miles south of Camden, Delaware, learning to ask customers, "Would you like some of our fresh corn on the cob with that?" when they'd only asked for the plate of spare ribs and mashed potatoes. His earnest after-work conversations with frizzy-haired Julianne Daiches, who was stationed at the Frialator, about the difference between heavy petting and light. There were less comfortable memories as well, some having to do with his father's departure, when he was six, and the weakness both his parents had for the solace of the bottle. He remembered an all-night poker game he'd played during his freshman year—how the upperclassmen, especially, grew uneasy with his steadily growing pile of chips, as if he had found some undetectable method of cheating. He remembered, too, a sophomore-year crush at Carlyle—God, the breathlessness of their early encounters, and then the tears, the stormy recriminations and reconciliations, the lemon-verbena fragrance of her shampoo, which had seemed so exotic and which, for years afterward, could still leave him stricken with nostalgia and yearning.

He remembered his recruitment and training at Consular Operations, his trainers' growing fascination with his peculiar gift. His cover job at the State Department's Bureau of Educational and

Cultural Affairs, as a cultural exchange officer, someone who was regularly stationed abroad. All these things he remembered with clarity and precision. His had been a double life. Or was it simply a double delusion? A throbbing was building in his head as he left his room.

In a corner of what passed for the motel's lobby, an Internet-enabled computer was available, as a minor amenity for guests. Ambler sat down in front of it and, using a pass code held by the State Department's analytic bureau, logged on to the newspaper database LexisNexis. The local newspaper at Camden, where Ambler grew up, once ran a small item about him when, as a sixth grader, he won the county spelling bee. *Enthalpy. Dithyramb. Hellebore.* Ambler spelled them all, fluently and correctly, establishing himself as the best speller not only in Simpson Elementary School but in Kent County. When he made a mistake, he always knew it immediately—knew it from the judge's expression. His mother—who was by then raising him by herself—had been inordinately pleased, he recalled. But more than a child's egotism was involved now.

He ran the Nexis search.

Nothing. Nothing matched the description. He remembered the *Dover Post* item so clearly—remembered how his mother cut it out and kept it on the refrigerator door with a magnet designed to resemble a slice of watermelon. Kept it there until it yellowed and started to crumble from the light. Decades' worth of the *Dover Post* was on LexisNexis, an archive of all sorts of local news, about who won and who lost in the city council elections, about layoffs at the Seabury Hosier Company, about capital renovations at city hall. But as far as Nexis was concerned, Harrison Ambler did not exist. He did not exist then. He did not exist now.

Insanity!

———

The airport was the familiar jungle of terrazzo, steel, and glass, with the familiar air of a fully staffed facility. Wherever one turned, one saw airline employees, airport security officers, and baggage handlers, all wearing badges and uniforms of various sorts. The milieu, Ambler decided, was a cross between a federal mail-handling facility and a resort town.

He bought a ticket to Wilmington, one-way, a hundred and fifty dollars: the cover charge, so to speak, of the rendezvous. He looked as bored as the woman at the ticket counter, who stifled a yawn as she stamped his boarding card. The photo ID he submitted—the Georgia license, altered to display a photograph of its current bearer—would not withstand close scrutiny, but it received none.

Gate D14 was at the very end of a long walkway and adjoined two others in a radial array. He glanced around; fewer than a dozen travelers were visible. It was half past two. The next flight at any of these gates would not be for another ninety minutes. Within half an hour, more people would arrive for a flight to Pittsburgh, but for the moment it was, indeed, a dead period.

Had the person he was to meet already arrived? That seemed likely. But who was it? *You'll know who I am,* the message had said.

Ambler walked around the various seating areas, taking in the stragglers and early birds. The plump woman feeding candy to her plump daughter; the man in the ill-fitting suit, thumbing through a PowerPoint presentation; the young woman with piercings and jeans she had marked up with different-colored felt tip pens—none of them were contenders. Ambler's sense of frustration began to mount. *You'll know who I am.*

Finally, his eyes alighted on someone who was seated by himself, near a window.

It was a turbaned Sikh gentleman, moving his lips as he read *USA Today.* As Ambler walked over to him, he noticed that there was no evidence of any hair underneath the turban—not a single stray strand could be seen. A faint gleam of adhesive on the man's cheek suggested that the full beard was recently applied. Was the man really moving his lips as he read, or was he communicating on a fiber-optic microphone?

To anyone else, the man would have seemed perfectly settled, bored, and still. To Ambler, he seemed anything but. On instinct, Ambler swiveled and stepped *behind* the seated figure. Now, with a lightning-swift movement, he grabbed the man's turban and lifted it up. Beneath it, he saw the man's pale, smooth-shaven pate—and, taped to it with a fabric bandage, a small Glock.

The gun was in Ambler's hand now, and he let the turban drop back into place. The seated man remained stock-still, with the tactical immobility and silence of a highly trained professional who knew when the prudent response was *not* to respond. Only his raised eyebrows registered surprise. The whole soundless maneuver had taken no more than two seconds and had been concealed from anyone's view by Ambler's own body.

The pistol was oddly light in his hand, and he recognized the model at once. The body was made of plastic and ceramic; the slide contained less metal than was found in a typical belt buckle. The odds that it would set off a metal detector were low; the odds that the security guards would interfere with a Sikh's religious headdress were even lower. A tube of bronzer and a yard of muslin cloth: a cheap, efficient costume. Once again, the skill and efficiency of the rendezvous inspired both admiration and anxiety.

"Bravo," the fake Sikh said in a low voice, a faint smile pulling at the corners of his mouth. "A fine defensive move. Not that it changes anything." He spoke English with the perfectly enunciated consonants of someone who had received instruction in it abroad, albeit from an early age.

"I'm the one with the weapon. That doesn't change anything? In my experience it does."

"Sometimes you make best use of a weapon by giving it up," the man said, his eyes almost twinkling. "Tell me, do you see the guy in the airline uniform, standing at the gate counter? He's just arrived."

Ambler glanced over. "I see him."

"He's with us. He stands ready to shoot you, if that proves necessary." The seated man looked up at Ambler, who was still standing. "Do you believe me?" The question wasn't a taunt but a point of inquiry.

"I believe he'll try," Ambler responded. "For your sake, you'd better hope he doesn't miss."

The fake Sikh nodded, with approval. "But then, unlike you, I'm wearing Kevlar, just in case." Again he looked up at Ambler. "Do you believe me?"

"No," Ambler said, after a beat. "I don't."

The man's smile widened. "You are Tarquin, aren't you? The package, not the deliveryman. You see, your reputation precedes you. They say you're devilish good at reading people. I needed to be sure."

Now Ambler took the seat next to him; the meeting would be less conspicuous that way. Whatever the man had in store for him, it wasn't a quick death.

"Why don't you explain yourself?" Ambler asked.

The other man extended a hand in greeting. "The name's Arkady. You see, I'd been told that quite a legendary field agent, alias Tarquin, might now be 'available.'"

"Available?"

"For recruitment. And no, I don't know your real name. I am aware that you seek information. I do not have that information. What I have is access to that information. Or rather, access to those who possess the information." Arkady cracked his knuckles. "Or access to those with access to those who possess the information. You will not be surprised to learn that the organization to which I belong is carefully partitioned. Information flows only where it must."

As he spoke, Ambler watched him intently, concentrating. Hopefulness sometimes obscured perception, he knew, and so did despair.

As he had regularly explained to colleagues who were bewildered by his gift, *We don't see what we don't want to see.* Cease wanting. Cease projecting. Just receive the signals that, willy-nilly, are being sent. That was the key.

The Sikh before him was a lie. But he was not lying to him.

"I have to say the speed of the invitation is puzzling," Ambler said.

"We don't like to waste time. That's something we have in common, I'd guess. One punctual stitch obviates nine such, as you Americans say. In the event, the squawk went out yesterday morning." *The squawk*—trade jargon. An alert that had been radioed to all the country's intelligence services had gone out on "the squawk." The channel was used when urgency overrode secrecy; it was a leaky form of communication. A message sent to that many ears was liable to reach a few eavesdroppers as well.

"Even so," Ambler said.

"I think you can connect the dots. Clearly, your admirers have been waiting for this moment. Quite likely, they had hoped to recruit you even before you disappeared from view. And, no doubt, they think they have competition for your services. They don't want to let the moment pass."

Clearly . . . quite likely . . . no doubt. "You're speculating, you're not stating for a fact."

"As I told you, information is strictly partitioned in the organization. I know what I have to know. I can surmise a certain amount beyond that. And, of course, there is a great deal I must be content not to know. The system works for us all. It keeps them safe. It keeps me safe."

"But it doesn't keep me safe. One of your guys tried to kill me."

"I very much doubt that."

"The large-caliber bullet that grazed my neck would beg to differ."

Arkady looked bemused. "That doesn't make any sense."

"Yeah, well, the Southern guy looked pretty surprised, too, the moment before the bullet traveled on through the back of his head."

Ambler's voice was a low rasp. "What kind of a crazy goddamn game are you guys running?"

"Not us," Arkady said. Almost to himself, he murmured, "This sounds like a case of interference. It just means we weren't the only people to hear the squawk and respond."

"Then you're telling me there was a second party involved."

"There had to have been," Arkady said, after a long pause. "We'll do the analysis, make sure there's been no breach. But it very much sounds like a parasitic visitation, so to speak. It won't happen again. Not once you're with us."

"Is that a promise or a threat?"

Arkady winced. "Oh dear. We really have gotten off on the incorrect foot, haven't we? But I tell you this. My employers would very much like to keep you safe—so long as they can be assured that you will do the same for them. Trust must run in both directions."

"That they can trust me," Ambler said steadily, "is something they'll have to take on trust."

"But that's the one thing they never do, you see." Arkady sounded apologetic. "Such a bore, I know. They have another idea. In fact, they want to kill two fowl with one rock. They have a little job for you." For the first time, Ambler could hear the diphthongs of the man's native tongue, which was obviously Slavic.

"Like an audition."

"Exactly!" Arkady's eyes lit up. "And it's all terribly 'win-win,' as my employers like to say. The job we have for you is small, but . . . ticklish."

"Ticklish?"

"I won't lie to you—what would be the point?" He beamed. "It's a small job, but it has defeated others. Yet it must be done. You see, my employers have a problem. They are careful people—you'll see, and you'll be grateful of it. As the maxim has it, birds of same plumage seek out one another's company. But maybe not all their friends are quite so careful as they are. And maybe a penetration agent made some inroads with some of their confreres. All that coruscates is not gold, alas. Maybe such an agent, having collected some evidence, is about to testify in a legal proceeding. All very messy."

"A penetration agent? Let's be clear. You're talking about an under-cover federal agent."

"It's awkward, isn't it?" Arkady said. "ATF, in fact."

If the investigator was with the Bureau of Alcohol, Tobacco and Firearms, the investigation quite likely involved gun smuggling of some sort. That did not mean the organization Arkady worked for was involved in the trade; *confreres* was the word Arkady used. The obvious assumption was that gunrunners who supplied the organi-zation had been ensnared.

"One day this man will die," the fake Sikh went on contempla-tively. "A stroke. A heart attack. Cancer. Who can say? But like all of us he is mortal, and one day he will die. We simply wish to place a rush order on that eventuality. That is all."

"Why me?"

The Sikh made a face. "This is so embarrassing, really."

Ambler just stared.

"Well, the truth is, we don't exactly know what he looks like. Oc-cupational hazard, right? The person he had direct dealings with isn't in a position to help us out."

"Because he's dead?"

"The reason is irrelevant—let's not get distracted from the big picture here. We've got a venue, we're got a time, but we don't want to take out the wrong person. We don't want to make a mistake. You see how scrupulous we are? Some people would just machine-gun everyone in the vicinity. But that's not our way."

"Mother Teresa, watch your back."

"I'm not saying we're in competition for sainthood, Tarquin. But then you aren't, either." His dark eyes flashed. "To return to my point: you'll be able to tell at a glance who the mark is. Because, being the mark, he *knows* he's marked. That's the sort of thing you'll be able to pick up on."

"I see," Ambler said, and he did, or was beginning to. Some sort of rogue outfit wanted his services. The job discussed was indeed an audition—but what they needed to establish was not his ability to read people. No, by killing a federal agent, he would be proving his bona fides—proving that he had severed all loyalties to his former employers, not to mention conventional morality. They must have had reason to believe that he was sufficiently embittered and disaffected to entertain the assignment.

Perhaps they were misinformed. Perhaps, though, they simply knew more than he did—perhaps they knew, as he did not, exactly why he had been committed to Parrish Island. Perhaps he had cause for grievance far beyond that of which he was aware.

"Then do we have a deal?"

Ambler thought for a moment. "If I say no?"

"You'll never know, will you?" Arkady smiled. "Maybe you *should* say no. And resign yourself to ignorance. There are worse things. They say that curiosity proved fatal to the feline."

"And that satisfaction brought it back." Not to know was the one thing he could not survive. He needed to know, and he needed to serve justice on those who had tried to destroy his life. Ambler glanced at the blue-jacketed man behind the gate counter. "I think we can do business."

It was madness, and it was the one thing that might save him from madness. Ambler recalled, from some long-ago classroom, the Greek legend about the labyrinth of Crete, the lair of the Minotaur. The labyrinth was so intricately twisted that those imprisoned within could never find their way out. But Theseus had been aided by Ariadne, who gave him a ball of thread, and tied one end to the door of the maze. By following the thread, he had made his escape. At the moment, this man was the closest thing Ambler had to a thread. What he could not know was which end of the maze it would lead to—to freedom, or to death. He would chance either rather than remaining lost in the maze.

Finally, Arkady began to speak in the tone of someone who had committed precise instructions to memory. "At ten A.M. tomorrow, the undercover agent has a meeting scheduled with the U.S. Attorney for the southern district of New York. We believe that an armored limousine will bring him to the corner of 1 St. Andrew's Plaza near Foley Square in lower Manhattan. He may be accompanied, part of a group; he may be alone. Either way, it will be a rare interval of vulnerability: the agent will have to traverse an extended pedestrian area on foot. You must be there."

"No backup?"

"One of our people will be there to help. At the appropriate time, our person will pass you a weapon. The rest is in your hands. All we insist is that you follow the instructions exactly. I realize this is like asking a jazz musician to follow the notes on a score rather than improvise, but in this instance, there can be no improvisation. How does that American expression go? 'It's my way or the thoroughfare,' right?" Yet another English idiom he had obviously learned in his native tongue; the double translation was exacting a considerable toll. "The plan must be respected in its particulars."

"It's highly exposed," Ambler protested. "A lousy plan."

"As much as we value your particular expertise," Arkady said, "you must grant us ours. You don't know the facts on the ground. My employers do, and they've studied them. The target is a cautious man. He isn't skulking under bridges for your convenience. This is actually an extraordinary opportunity. We may not get another for a long time, and then it will be too late."

"There are dozens of potential problems," Ambler persisted.

"You're free to walk away," Arkady said, a glint of steel in his voice. "But if you do complete the assignment, as per instructions, you will be introduced to someone up my line of command. He's someone you know. Someone who has worked beside you."

Someone, then, who might well know the whole story of what had happened to Harrison Ambler.

"I'll do it," Ambler said. He was not thinking ahead—was not thinking about what he was agreeing to. He knew that if he let this thread drop, he might never find it again. *Ariadne's thread—yet which way did it lead?*

Arkady leaned forward and patted Ambler's wrist. From a distance, the gesture would look affectionate. "Really, we don't ask so very much. Only that you should succeed where others have failed. It wouldn't be the first time."

No, Ambler mused, *but it might be the last.*

CHAPTER SEVEN

Langley, Virginia

Clayton Caston was looking thoughtful when he returned to his windowless office. Not *lost* in thought, Adrian Choi decided; *found* in thought was more like it. Caston looked as if he had his hooks in something. *Probably something to do with a very long spreadsheet,* Adrian thought gloomily.

So many things around Caston seemed to involve spreadsheets. Not that Adrian thought he really had this fellow figured out. His very blandness was mystifying. It was hard to imagine he was even in the same profession as, say, Derek St. John, the swashbuckling hero of those Clive McCarthy novels Adrian treasured. Caston would give him a hard time if he ever found out, but Adrian actually had the latest paperback from the Derek St. John series in his backpack, had read most of a chapter over breakfast. It involved a nuclear warhead hidden in the wreckage of the *Lusitania.* Adrian had left off during an exciting sequence: Derek St. John, scuba-diving through the wreckage, had just narrowly avoided a harpoon grenade launched by an enemy agent. Adrian would try to sneak in another chapter or two during his lunch hour. Caston would probably be reading the latest *Journal of Accounting, Auditing and Finance.*

Maybe it was a form of comeuppance, his having been parceled off to someone who had to be the most boring man in the whole entire Central Intelligence Agency. Adrian realized he had come on a little strong in his job interview. This was no doubt someone's idea of a joke; probably someone in Human Resources was thinking of him right now and blowing soup through his nose.

So maybe the joke was on Adrian now. Every day, the man he

worked for showed up in an identical Perma-Prest white shirt, a near identical tie, and a Jos. A. Bank suit that ranged in hue from an exciting *medium* gray to a wild and crazy *charcoal* gray. Adrian knew he wasn't working for *GQ*, but wasn't this taking routine a little far? Caston not only looked bland, he *ate* bland: his unvarying lunch was a soft-cooked egg and lightly toasted white bread, washed down by a glass of tomato juice, with a swig of Maalox on the side. Just in case. Once, when he had asked Adrian to fetch him his lunch, Adrian had brought him a V8 instead of plain tomato juice and Caston had looked betrayed. *Hey, live dangerously once in a while,* Adrian had thought of telling him. The guy never seemed to use any weapon more dangerous than a sharpened No. 2 pencil.

Still, there were moments—moments when Adrian wondered whether he had the full measure of the man, wondered whether there might, in fact, be another side to him.

"Anything I can do?" Adrian said to Caston now, eternally hopeful.

"Yes," Caston said. "As a matter of fact, there is. When we put in the request for Consular Operations files pertaining to the special-access alias 'Tarquin,' we were only given partials. I'll need anything they can scrounge. DCI-level clearance. Tell them to verify clearance conditions with the DCI's office, and expedite this." There was the faintest trace of Brooklyn in Caston's voice—it took Adrian a while to pick up on this—and he spoke technical jargon and billingsgate with equal fluency.

"Wait a minute," Adrian said. "You're cleared to the DCI level?"

"Those clearances are allocated on a project-by-project basis. But yes, as a general rule."

Adrian tried to conceal his surprise. He had heard it said that fewer than a dozen people in the entire agency were ever cleared to that level. Was Caston really one of them?

But if Caston was cleared way up, then he, being Caston's assistant, must have been vetted pretty heavily, too. Adrian flushed. He had heard it said that there was automatic surveillance for newer people exposed to high-level secrets. Could they have bugged his apartment? Adrian had signed endless documents before his appointment had been finalized; he had no doubt that he had signed away any privacy rights he might have enjoyed as a citizen. But could he really be the subject of operational surveillance? Adrian turned over the possibility in his mind. He found it—well, if he was honest with himself, he found it delightful.

"Also, I need more from Parrish Island," Caston said. He blinked a few times. "I want their personnel records for everyone who was working at Ward 4W over the past twenty months: doctors, nurses, orderlies, guards, everyone."

"If the records are digital, they should be able to send them via secure e-mail," Adrian said. "Should be automatic."

"Given the patchwork quilt that is the U.S. government's complex of operating platforms, nothing automatic is really automatic. The FBI, the INS, even the goddamn Department of Agriculture all have their proprietary systems. The inefficiencies are staggering."

"Plus some of this stuff might still be paper. Could take even longer."

"Time is of the essence. You need to make sure everybody's clear on that."

Adrian was silent for a moment. "Permission to speak freely, sir."

Caston rolled his eyes. "Adrian, if you want to be granted 'permission to speak freely,' you should have joined the Army. You're in the CIA. We don't do that."

"Meaning I can always speak freely?"

A quick shake of the head. "You seem to have confused us with the Culinary Institute of America. It happens."

Sometimes Adrian was convinced that Caston's sense of humor was nonexistent; at other times, he decided it was just extremely dry—Death Valley dry.

"Right, well, I got the sense that they were dragging their feet at

Consular Operations," Adrian said. "They didn't seem too happy with the request."

"Of course not. Then they'd have to acknowledge that the Central Intelligence Agency is, in fact, this country's central intelligence agency. It offends their sense of pride. But I can't solve the entire organizational mess today. The fact remains that I need them to cooperate. Which means I need you to get them to cooperate. In fact, I'm counting on it."

Adrian nodded soberly, hairs pleasantly raised on the back of his neck. *I'm counting on it.* That sounded almost like *I'm counting on you.*

An hour later, a large, compressed digital file arrived from the system at Parrish Island. After decompressing and decrypting, the main component turned out to be some sort of audio file.

"You know how this thing works?" Caston grunted.

He did. "This bad boy is a twenty-four-bit data file, formatted into the professional audio-recording integrated system. That's PARIS format. Looks to be a five-minute-long audio clip." Adrian shrugged, modestly disavowing praise that didn't actually come. "Hey, I was president of the audiovisual club in high school. I'm an ace at anything to do with this kind of thing. You ever decide you want to host your own TV show, I'm your guy."

"I'll try to remember that."

After making a few software adjustments, Adrian set the PARIS file to play on Caston's computer. Apparently it had been recorded at a psychiatric session with Patient No. 5312 and represented his current state of mind.

Patient No. 5312, they knew, was a trained government operative. An HVA of two decades' standing and therefore in possession of two decades' worth of operational secrets—procedures, ciphers, assets, informants, sources, networks.

He was also—the recording made plain—stark raving mad.

"I've got a bad feeling about this guy," Adrian ventured.

Caston scowled. "How many times have I got to tell you? You want to talk to me about logic, information, evidence, I'm all ears. When you've got a considered judgment, please let me know. *Degrees of belief* is our stock-in-trade. But don't talk to me about 'feelings.' I'm happy you've got feelings. It's possible I've got 'em, too, though that's disputed. It's just that they don't belong in the office. We've been through this."

"Sorry," Adrian said. "But having a piece of work like that on the loose . . ."

"Not for long," Caston said, mostly to himself. Then he repeated, in a still quieter voice, "Not for long."

Beijing, China

As chief of the Second Bureau of the Ministry of State Security—the bureau devoted to foreign operations—Chao Tang visited Zhongnanhai on a regular basis. And yet his heart always raced a little when he arrived. So much history was concentrated in this place: such hopes and such disappointment; such achievement and such failure. It was a history Chao knew well, and that seemed to shadow his every step.

Zhongnanhai, sometimes known as the Sea Palaces, was a capital within the capital. The immense, heavily guarded complex where China's top leaders lived and ruled had been a symbol of empire ever since the Mongol overlords had walled it in during the Yuan dynasty of the fourteenth century. Subsequent dynasts rebuilt the area over the centuries, razing and raising mighty edifices; some were dedicated to the pursuit of power, others to the pursuit of pleasure. All the edifices were arrayed among vast man-made lakes in the sylvan splendor of an artificial arcadia. In 1949, the year that Mao attained absolute control over the country, the complex, which had fallen into disrepair, was once more rebuilt. In short order, the country's new rulers had a new home.

What was once a carefully landscaped simulacrum of nature had to yield to the practical requirements of pavement and parking lots; the extravagant finery of yore gave way to a grim and graceless Eastern bloc décor. But those were cosmetic matters merely; the revolutionaries proved entirely faithful to the older and deeper traditions of secrecy and seclusion. The question, in Chao's view, was whether the sway of those traditions would give way before a man who was intent on overturning them: China's youthful president, Liu Ang.

It had been, as Chao recalled, the president's decision to reside here. His immediate predecessor had lived not in Zhongnanhai proper but on a nearby guarded estate. Yet Liu Ang had reasons of his own to live in the same complex as the rest of the leadership. He believed in his powers of personal suasion, put much stock in his ability to win over pockets of resistance by means of informal visits, strolls through the ornamental copses, unscheduled teas.

The meeting tonight, however, was neither informal nor unscheduled. It had, indeed, been foisted upon Liu, and not by his opponents but by his loyalists. For what was at stake was nothing less than Liu's own survival and the future of the world's most populous nation.

Fear galvanized five of the six men gathered around the black lacquered table on the second floor of Liu's residence. Yet the president himself refused to take the threats seriously. Chao could read Liu's clear gaze: *frightened old men* was what he took them for. Here, in a small granite compound in the shadow of the Palace Steeped in Compassion, it was hard for Liu Ang to grasp his extreme vulnerability. He had to be *made* to grasp it.

The intelligence reports were shadowy, yes, and still indistinct, but when reports from Chao's colleagues in the First Bureau, which specialized in domestic intelligence, were combined with those from Chao's own bureau, the shadows deepened into something black indeed.

A narrow-shouldered, soft-spoken man, seated to Liu Ang's right, exchanged glances with Comrade Chao and began to address the president. "Forgive me for speaking forthrightly, but what good are all your plans for reform if you are not alive to carry them out!" the man said. He was Liu's advisor on security matters and, like Chao, had a background in the MSS, though with the domestic bureau. "One must remove the snapping turtles from the pool if one hopes to swim unmolested. One must dredge the koi pond if one wishes to clarify the waters. One must uproot the poison ivy from the chrysanthemum garden if one wishes to pluck the flowers. One must—"

"One must scythe the thickets of metaphor if one wishes to harvest the grain of reason," Liu interrupted with a small smile. "But I know what you are trying to say. You have made the case before. And my answer remains what it was." His tone grew resolute. "I refused to be paralyzed by fear. And I refuse to take action against people based solely on suspicion, not evidence. To do so would make me indistinguishable from my enemies."

"Your enemies will destroy you while you sit perorating about your high-minded ideals!" Chao interjected. "And then you will be easily distinguished from them indeed—*they* will be the victors, and *you* will be the vanquished." He spoke with candor and with heat. Ang had always insisted upon the candor; the heat came with it.

"Some of those who oppose me are men and women of principle," Liu Ang said, without raising his voice. "Men and women who cherish stability and regard me as a threat to it. When they see that they have been in error, their opposition will subside." Here, he had often insisted, time was on his side. He could win his argument about the pace of reform by going ahead with his plans and showing that no social chaos had resulted.

"You mistake a knife fight for an exchange of analects!" Chao countered. "There are powerful men—even within the inner councils of state—for whom the real enemy is change, *any* kind of change." He scarcely had to elaborate. Everyone knew about hardliners who were opposed to any movement toward transparency, fairness, and efficiency, having prospered from their absence. These hard-liners were the ones who had made the Palace Steeped in Compassion a mockery of its name. Especially dangerous were the hard-liners on the governing committee—all too well represented in the People's Liberation Army and the bureaus of state security— who had grudgingly acquiesced to his appointment in the belief that he could be *controlled*. It was said that Liu's patron, the vice chairman of the Communist Party, had given such assurances. As they discovered that Liu was nobody's puppet, their discontent flared into a sense of betrayal. So far, none had dared to move publicly against him; to take on someone so popular really could stir up seismic forces of social rebellion. But they had watched, and they had waited, and they had bided their time, and they were growing impatient. A small cadre of hard-liners had decided that Liu was only growing more powerful over time—that they had to act soon, before it was too late.

"You who proclaim your loyalty to me—why would you turn me into the very thing I despise!" Liu Ang protested. "They say that power corrupts, but they don't say how. Now I know: *this* is how. The reformer starts to listen to the counsel of fear. Well, I *refuse* to do so."

It was all Chao could do not to pound the table. "Are you *invulnerable*?" he demanded, his eyes flashing. "If someone fires a bullet at your reformist brain, does the bullet bounce off? If someone takes a sword to your reformist throat, does the blade give way? The *counsel of fear*, you say? How about the *counsel of sanity*!"

Chao's devotion to the young president was as personal as it was professional, and there were many who were perplexed by both elements of it. As someone who had spent decades deep within China's bureaus of intelligence, Chao did not fit the usual profile of Liu's fervent supporters. But even before Liu's elevation two years ago as general secretary of the National People's Congress and chairman of the Standing Committee of the NPC, Chao respected the man's combination of agility and integrity. In Chao's view, it embodied the very best of the Chinese character. Nor had a career dealing with the party cadres left Chao with any illusions about the apparatus that Liu had hoped to dismantle. It did not merely foster idleness, self-dealing, and insularity; it fostered self-deception, and to Chao there was no greater sin.

Hence his heated words at this evening's meeting. Despite the president's protests, he did not want Liu Ang to transform himself; he simply wanted Liu Ang to survive. Aggressive preemption might strike the president as despotism, but it would be despotism in the service of a larger good.

"You know that Comrade Chao and I have disagreed about many things," said a fifty-year-old man named Wan Tsai, his large eyes further magnified by his wire-rimmed glasses. "Yet about this we are in agreement. The precautionary principle must be upheld." Wan Tsai was an economist by training and one of Liu's oldest friends. It was Tsai who had first persuaded Liu, as a young man, to work within the system; a blow against the status quo would be all the more powerful if it came from inside. Unlike other members of Liu's personal council, Wan Tsai had never worried about the speed of the young president's reforms—had, in fact, been impatient to do even more, even faster.

"Let us drop the euphemisms," Liu reproached. "You want me to launch a purge."

"Just weed out the disloyal!" cried Wan Tsai. "It is a matter of self-defense!"

The president gave his mentor a sharp look. "As the sage Mencius asks, what good is self-defense if it comes at the expense of the self?"

"You wish to keep your hands clean," Chao said, coloring slightly. "I say, soon everyone will admire those clean hands of yours—at your funeral!" Chao took pride in his self-control, but now he was breathing hard. "I claim no expertise about law, economics, philosophy. But I do know about *security*. I've spent my career at MSS. As Mencius also said, when a donkey speaks about donkeys the prudent man listens."

"You're not a donkey," Liu Ang tossed off with a half smile.

"You're not a prudent man," Chao returned flintily.

Like the others at the table, Chao had not only recognized Liu's extraordinary potential early on; he had helped Ang to realize it. They had a personal stake in his welfare. There had been men like Liu before in Chinese history, but none had ever succeeded.

It was a mixed blessing that the youthful president—at forty-three, he was far younger than any others who had occupied the position, and he looked even younger than his years—was so beloved by the multitudes beyond the Zhongnanhai's gates. For their adoration, like the Western media's enthusiastic coverage, only heightened the hardliners' reflexive suspicion toward him. Yet Liu's actions would have earned their enmity anyway. After only two years in his position, he had already established himself as a vigorous force of liberalization, variously confirming the fears and hopes of those around him. It made him a deeply inspiring figure. But among many hard-liners, what he mainly inspired was loathing and apprehension.

Members of the Western media, of course, were quick to ascribe his policies to his background. They made much of the fact that he had been a onetime Tiananmen Square protester, the first of that cohort to rise within the Party ranks. They noted that he was the first Chinese head of state to have studied abroad, ascribing exaggerated significance to the year he spent taking engineering classes at MIT. They further conjectured that his pro-Western sentiments had been reinforced by friendships he made during that time. His resentful comrades, in turn, worried that his judgment had been clouded by the same factors. Chinese people who had spent time in the West were nicknamed *hai gui*—a term that meant "sea turtle" but also punned on "returner from the sea." Suspicious Chinese who were hostile to the *hai gui*'s cosmopolitanism defiantly called themselves the *tu bie*, the local turtles. For many *tu bie*, the struggle against the influence of the *hai gui* would be a struggle to the death.

"Do not mistake me," Liu said gravely. "I'm not discounting the worries you raise." He gestured toward the window, toward an ornamental island on the South Lake, now a drab acre of snow, glowing with artificial illumination. "Every day I look out there, and I see where my forerunner, the emperor, Kuang-hsü, was imprisoned. His punishment for launching the Hundred Days of Reform. Like me, the imprisoned emperor was motivated by both idealism and realism. What befell him a century ago may befall me. There isn't a moment when I forget this."

It had happened in 1898, a legendary reversal, and one that had ultimately paved the way for the massive upheavals in the century that followed. The emperor, inspired by national setbacks and by the counsel of the great scholar and governor Kang Yu Wei, had done something as bold as any of his predecessors had ever done. In the course of a hundred days, a series of decrees was issued that would have transformed China into a modern constitutional state. The grand hopes and lofty aspirations were soon dashed. After three months, the dowager empress, backed by the governors-general, had the emperor, her nephew, imprisoned within the ornamental island on the South Lake and restored the old order. Entrenched interests found the reforms all too threatening, and those interests had prevailed—at least until the shortsighted conservative restoration was displaced by forces of revolution far more sweeping and ruthless than anything envisioned by the deposed emperor and counselor.

"But Kang was a scholar without popular support," a weedy-looking man toward the end of the table said, his eyes downcast. "You have both intellectual and political credibility. Which makes you that much more threatening."

"Enough of this!" said the youthful president. "I cannot do what you want me to do. You say that this is a way to protect my own position. Yet if I resort to purges—destroying my opponents because they *are* my opponents—my administration will not be *worthy* of protection. People may go down this road for the loftiest of reasons.

Yet this road has no branches—it leads to one place only. It leads to tyranny." He paused. "Those who oppose me for reasons of principle I shall endeavor to persuade. Those whose motives are less wholesome, well, they are opportunists. And if my policies succeed, they will do what opportunists always do. They will see which way the wind is blowing, and realign themselves accordingly. Just you see."

"Is this the voice of humility or hubris?" asked a man at the other end of the table. The man, Li Pei, had white hair and a face as wrinkled and veined as a walnut shell. He was a generation older than the others and in some ways was the most incongruous of Liu's allies. Li Pei came from hardscrabble origins in the provinces and was known by the not unadmiring sobriquet *jiaohua de nongmin,* or "wily peasant." A consummate survivor, he had kept a place in the Zhongnanhai compound, either in the State Council or in the Party itself, through Mao and Mao's various successors—through the Cultural Revolution and its dismantling, through massacres and crackdowns and reforms and a thousand ideological course corrections. Many assumed Li Pei was simply a cynic who adjusted to whoever was in charge. That was only part of the story. Like many of the most corrosive cynics, he was a wounded idealist.

At the head of the black lacquered table, President Liu Ang took a sip of green tea. "Maybe I am guilty of both hubris and humility. But not ignorance. I know the risks."

Another voice at the table spoke quietly. "We should not only look within. It was Napoléon who said, 'Let China sleep. For when she awakes, let the nations tremble.' Among your enemies are foreigners who do not wish the Middle Kingdom well. They fear that under your watch, China will indeed slumber no more."

"These are not theoretical concerns," Chao Tang said, exasperated. "The intelligence reports I refer to are *deeply* worrying. Have you forgotten about what happened to Wai-Chan Leung in Taiwan? Many viewed the young man as a kindred spirit of yours, and you see what became of him. You may be facing some of the same enemies: the kind who fear peace more than war. The dangers you confront are real. Indeed, as I say, it would appear that some sort of conspiracy is already in motion."

"'Some sort'?" Liu echoed. "You warn me of an international conspiracy, and yet the truth is that you have no idea who the principals are or what their aims may be. To speak of a conspiracy without knowing its nature is to bandy words only."

"Is it certainty you want?" Chao asked. "Certainty is what one has only when it is too late. A plot whose details we knew would be a plot we had already foiled. But there are too many whispers, hints, oblique references to ignore any longer—"

"The merest conjecture!"

"Plainly, members of your own government are involved," Chao said. It took an effort to keep his voice level. "Nor can we disregard evidence suggesting that certain elements in the U.S. government may be involved as well."

"Your intelligence is not *actionable*," Liu protested. "I appreciate your concern, but I do not see what I can do that is consistent with the example I wish to set."

"Please consider—" Wan started.

"Feel free to continue your discussion," the youthful president said, rising to his feet. "But if you'll excuse me, I have a wife upstairs who is beginning to think she has been widowed by the People's Republic of China. Or so she has recently hinted. At least in this particular, partial information *shall* suffice for action." The laughter that followed was perfunctory, hardly leavening the atmosphere of anxiety.

Perhaps the young president did not *want* to know the threats against him; he seemed to fear those threats less than he feared the consequences of political paranoia. The others could not afford to be as sanguine. What Liu Ang did not know could kill him.

CHAPTER EIGHT

St. Andrew's Plaza, Lower Manhattan

Ambler's eyes felt sandy, inflamed; his muscles ached. He was seated on a bench upon a large concrete platform between three looming federal buildings, each stone-faced and gray. As in much of lower Manhattan, the giant structures were crowded together, like trees in a dense forest competing for light and air. In most cities in the world, any one of the buildings would have been regarded as a grand edifice indeed. In lower Manhattan, none left any individual impression at all. Ambler shifted again in his seat, not so much to get comfortable as to get less uncomfortable. The jackhammer of a Con Ed street repair crew, somewhere nearby, was beginning to prompt a headache. He checked his watch; he had already read the *New York Post* from cover to cover. A vendor across the plaza was selling sugared nuts from his four-wheeled cart; Ambler was thinking about buying a bag, simply to give himself something to do, when he noticed a middle-aged man in a Yankees jacket emerging from the back of a black Town Car.

The mark had arrived.

The man was paunchy and sweating despite the cold. He looked around agitatedly as, unaccompanied, he climbed the steps that led from the sidewalk to the plaza. This was someone who knew himself to be acutely vulnerable and was filled with a sense of foreboding.

Ambler stood up slowly. Now what? He had figured that he would play out Arkady's scenario as long as he could—that something would come to him when it had to. It seemed entirely possible that the whole thing would prove a dry run.

Walking toward Ambler rapidly was a woman in heels and a green vinyl raincoat. She had a full mane of tendrilly blond hair, full lips, gray-green eyes. The eyes put Ambler in mind of a cat, perhaps because, like a cat, she never seemed to blink. Incongruously, she was carrying a brown lunch sack. As she approached, her attention seemed distracted by the revolving door to the federal building on the north side of the plaza and she stumbled into him.

"Aw, cripes, I'm sorry," she murmured in a raspy voice.

Ambler found that his hands were now clutching the paper sack, which, his fingers quickly confirmed, did not hold lunch.

The man in the Yankees jacket had reached the plaza and was starting to walk toward the building. Perhaps twelve seconds remained.

Ambler opened his tan raincoat—on every block of the city, one would see a dozen just like it—and pulled the weapon from the sack. It was a blued-steel Ruger .44, a Redhawk. More powerful than the job required and certainly too loud.

He turned and saw that the blonde was seated at another bench, near the building. She had given herself a ringside view.

Now what? Ambler's heart was pounding. This was no dry run. This was madness.

It was madness to have agreed to do this. It had been madness to have asked him in the first place.

The mark stopped abruptly, looked around, and started to walk again. He was no more than thirty feet away from Ambler.

An intuition glinted and then flared in Ambler's mind, like the sun passing from under a cloud. Now he understood what he had previously only vaguely, subconsciously surmised. *They never would have asked him.*

No doubt Arkady believed what he had been told, but sincerity was no guarantee of truth. In fact, the story made no sense: a risk-averse organization would never give someone of uncertain loyalties an assignment of this nature. He could have easily tipped off the authorities and ensured the mark's safety. *Ergo . . .*

Ergo the whole arrangement was a test. Ergo the gun was empty.

The mark was twenty feet away, walking steadily to the building on the east side of the plaza. Now Ambler strode rapidly toward him, withdrew the Redhawk from his coat, and, aiming at the back of the man's baseball jacket, squeezed the trigger.

There was the quiet, dry click of an empty gun, a sound largely swallowed by the traffic noises and the jackhammering of the Con Ed crew. Feigning dismay, he squeezed again and again, until all six chambers had been hammered.

He was sure that the blond woman had seen the cylinder rotate, the firing pin twitch without effect.

Detecting sudden movement in his peripheral vision, Ambler turned his head. A security guard across the plaza had seen him! The guard pulled out his own gun from his short navy coat and crouched in a two-handed firing position.

The guard's gun, of course, was loaded. Ambler heard the hard, popping sound of a .38 pistol and the higher-pitched *twang* as a bullet zinged by his ear. The guard was either lucky or skilled; Ambler could well be killed before he decided which.

Even as Ambler started to run toward the stairway on the south side of the plaza, he noticed another sudden movement; the vendor, as if panicked, had pushed his wheeled cart into the guard, knocking him over. Ambler heard a pained grunt from the fallen guard and the metallic skittering of the pistol that had been knocked from his hand.

Yet what had just happened made no sense: no mere bystander would ever move *toward* gunfire. The man posing as a vendor was surely part of a team.

Ambler heard the roar of the motorcycle before he saw it, seconds later: a powerful black Ducati Monster, seemingly emerging from nowhere, the face of its driver hidden behind his helmet's visor. *Friend or foe?*

"Jump on!" the driver bellowed at him, slowing down without coming to a full stop.

Ambler threw himself on the large rear section of the motorcycle's seat, and the Ducati roared off again. There had been no time to reason through the odds; he had had to follow his instinct. He could feel the power of the engine thrumming against his thighs.

"Hold on tight!" the driver bellowed again. Moments later, the motorcycle was bounding down the steps at the opposite side of the plaza, the back half-torquing upward wildly.

Pedestrians on the sidewalk had already scattered in dismay. The driver knew what he was doing, however, and soon the bike had zipped into traffic, maneuvering around a dump truck, a taxicab, a UPS van. The driver seemed to be monitoring the double rearview mirrors for any sign of police. Two blocks north, he turned onto Duane Street and pulled over, beside a standing limousine.

The limousine was a burgundy-colored Bentley; its driver, Ambler noticed, was attired in olive-drab livery. The passenger door opened for Ambler, and he got inside, settling back on the light tan leather seat. The Bentley was beautifully soundproofed; when the rear door was closed with a solid *thunk,* the city noises disappeared. The rear cabin was spacious; it was also carefully recessed away from the sight lines of pedestrians or other motorists.

Despite the immediate sense of seclusion, Ambler was not alone. Another man was already seated in the back, and now he opened a window in the glass partition and spoke to the driver in a soft guttural tongue: *"Ndiq hartën. Mos ki frikë. Paç fat të mbarë. Falemnderit."*

Ambler took another look at the driver: dirty blond hair, a face that was all angles and planes. Now the driver sent the limousine off gently into the city traffic. Ambler's fellow passenger then turned and greeted him with a cheerful "Hello."

Ambler felt a jolt of recognition. He knew this man. It was the man Arkady had promised Ambler he would meet. *He's someone you know. Someone who has worked beside you.* A man he had known only as Osiris and who had known him only as Tarquin.

Osiris was a large man in his sixties, bald save for a fringe of red hair around his ears and nape. He had been soft around the middle when they'd worked together in the Political Stabilization Unit but was always surprisingly fast on his feet. Especially considering his other incapacity.

"It's been a while," Ambler said.

Osiris moved his head slightly as Ambler spoke, and smiled, his blue, filmy eyes almost but not quite meeting Ambler's eyes. "Long time no see," he agreed. Osiris was skilled at making people forget that he was blind, had been since birth.

Osiris spoke in visual terms, alert to the sun, to the texture of someone's jacket, and continually translated tactile or auditory information into its visual counterpart. But then translation was always his forte. Consular Operations had had no more brilliant linguist. It was not just that he could speak and understand all the major languages; he was expert at creoles, minor dialects, regional accents—the languages people actually spoke, not the idealized versions of them taught at language schools. He knew whether a German came from Dresden or Leipzig, Hessen or Thuringen; he could tell the vowels of one Hanseatic province from another, could differentiate thirty strains of "street" Arabic. In third-world regions where multiple languages were found in a single neighborhood—in Nigeria, say, where Igbo, Hausa, Yoruba, and strange creoles and pidgins of English and Arabic might be spoken within one extended household—Osiris's skills could be invaluable. He could listen to recordings that would cause experts at the State Department's Africa Desk to throw up their hands or ask for a three-month study period, and provide an instantaneous rendition of the rapid-fire palaver.

"Our driver doesn't have any English, I'm afraid," the man known as Osiris told Ambler. "But he speaks Albanian like a prince. In fact, I'm sure most of his fellow expats find him a bit *prissy*." He pressed a button and a drinks compartment slid out from the partition; his hands betrayed almost no trace of groping as he removed a bottle of water and poured some into two glasses. He waited for Ambler to take one before he took the other. A man alleviating the natural suspicions of another man.

"Apologies for all the monkey business," Osiris went on. "I'm sure you've figured out the score. My employers needed to confirm that you weren't a sawbuck on a string. And it wasn't as if they could exactly check references."

Ambler nodded. It was as he had thought. The setup at the plaza had been a means to verify his bona fides: they had just watched him pull the trigger at a man he had been told was a government agent. Had he still been in the employ of the United States, he would never have done so.

"What happens to the mark? The guy in the Yankees jacket?"

"Who knows? Nothing to do with us, really. Apparently, the Feds launched an investigation into price fixing in the construction industry, and that guy got flipped, turned state's evidence. If you sensed he was running scared, you were right. Lots of scary people would like to see him go down. Just not us."

"But Arkady didn't know."

"What Arkady told you is what we told him. He thought he was on the level, because he didn't know we put him on the slant." Osiris laughed. "I lied to him, he lied to you, but it got purified in the pass-along, because he believed what he was saying."

"A useful reminder," Ambler said. "How do I know you haven't been lied to as well—about other things?" He glanced up at the driver's rearview mirror, experienced a surge of vertigo: the fleshy, balding Osiris was seated next to another man, someone Ambler could not immediately place. Short brown hair, blue eyes, and a face—

—a face that was symmetrical, almost cruelly handsome. A face it took Ambler a moment to recognize.

A face that was and was not his own. A face that he had seen for the first time in a Motel 6 and that still had the power to chill his blood.

"The premise of the question would negate my ability to answer it," Osiris said, in a deliberative tone. His filmy blue eyes stared sightlessly at Ambler. "So trust your instincts. Isn't that what you always do?"

Ambler swallowed hard, took a deep breath, and turned toward the blind operative. "A pop quiz, then. Do you know my name?"

"How many jobs did we work on together? Three, four? After having known you for all these years, you'd think I would have picked up a thing or two. Tarquin. Real name Henry Nyberg—"

"Nyberg's another cover name," Ambler interrupted. "Used a few times and discarded. *What's my name?*"

"Now you sound like a Ninth Avenue pimp," Osiris drawled, trying to maintain a jocular tone. " 'What's my name?' 'Who's your daddy?' Look, I understood you'd have questions. But I'm not the information desk. I may have some answers. I don't have *all* the answers."

"And why is that?"

Osiris's opaque blue eyes looked curiously alert beneath his faint, almost porcine eyebrows. "Because some answers are, well, above my pay grade."

"I'll take what I can get."

"A little learning is a dangerous thing, my friend. Words to take to heart. You may not want to know what you think you want to know."

"Try me."

Osiris's sightless eyes fixed him with a long, considering look. "I know a better place to talk," he said.

CHAPTER NINE

Beijing

Though President Liu Ang had retired to his private quarters in another wing of the compound, the conversation continued.

"What of the photographic evidence you mentioned?" the soft-spoken MSS veteran prompted, turning to Chao.

The Second Bureau chief, Chao Tang, nodded and removed a dossier from his black portfolio. He spread several photographs across the middle of the table. "Of course, I have already shown this to Ang, with predictable results, which is to say none at all. I have asked him at least to cancel his foreign appearances for the sake of security. He refuses. But the rest of you should see."

He tapped one of the photographs: a crowd before a wooden platform.

"Taken a few minutes before the assassination in Changhua," said the spymaster Chao. "You'll recall the event. It was a little more than two years ago. Please notice the Caucasian in the crowd."

He distributed another photograph, a digitally enhanced close-up of the same man.

"The assassin. The man whose bloody handiwork this is. In other photographs, you'll see him at the location of other killings. A monster indeed. Our spies have learned a thing or two about him."

"What's the monster's name?" the elderly Li Pei demanded, in his harsh country accent.

Chao looked distressed by Li Pei's question. "We have only a field alias," Chao admitted. "Tarquin."

"Tarquin," Pei repeated, his dewlaps quivering like an old sharpei's. "An American?"

"We believe so, though we are not certain who controls him. It has been difficult to filter signal from noise. Yet we have reason to think he may be a capstone actor in the plot against Liu Ang."

"Then he must be eliminated," said the white-haired man, slapping the table. *Indeed wily,* Chao thought, *but indeed a peasant, too.*

"We think alike," the spymaster said. "Sometimes I worry that Liu Ang is too good for this world." He paused. "Fortunately, I am not."

There were grim nods around the table.

"In the event, precautions have already been taken. We've had a team from the Second Bureau's signals intelligence unit working the matter. Yesterday, when we gained credible information about his possible whereabouts, we were able to take immediate action. Trust me, the finest this country has to offer is on the case."

It sounded like empty rhetoric, Chao reflected, yet in a strictly technical sense he believed it to be true. Chao had found Joe Li when he was still in his adolescence and had taken first prize in a regional shooting competition, run by the local branch of the People's Liberation Army. Test scores indicated that the boy, despite his rural background, had unusual aptitudes. Chao was always alert for the hidden prodigy; he believed that China's ultimate asset was to be found in its numbers—and not merely the brute muscle of cheap labor but the occasional prodigy that sheer numbers were bound to yield. If you shucked a billion oysters, you would find more than a handful of pearls, Comrade Chao liked to say. He had been convinced that young Joe Li was such a pearl and took it upon himself to see that he was prepared for an extraordinary career. Intensive language training began early. Joe Li would become adept not only in the major Western languages but also in the folkways of the Western nations; he would have a mastery of what was common knowledge there. He would also receive extensive training in weaponry, camouflage, Western-style hand-to-hand combat, and Shaolin-style martial arts.

Joe Li had never disappointed Chao. He had not become a large man, and yet his small size proved an advantage; it made him especially unthreatening and inconspicuous, his extraordinary skills concealed by a carapace of the commonplace. He was, Chao had once told him, a battleship disguised as a skiff.

There was more to him, however. Though Joe Li did his work with professional dispatch and dispassion, his personal loyalty to his country and to Chao himself was beyond question. Chao had made sure of it. Partly for reasons of security, partly because Chao was mindful of the constant squabbling for resources at the highest levels of government, he had kept Joe Li's operational controls strictly sequestered. Not to put too fine a point on it, China's most formidable operative reported to Chao and to no one else.

"But this Tarquin—he is dead?" asked the economist Tsai, drumming his fingers on the black lacquered table.

"Not yet," Chao said. "But soon."

"How soon?" Tsai pressed.

"An operation of this sort on foreign soil is always delicate," Chao cautioned. "But as I have assured you, we have our very best in place. This is a man who has never failed me yet, and we are supplying him with a steady stream of real-time intelligence. Death and life have their determined appointments, as the great sage has it. Suffice it to say that Tarquin's appointment is coming up momentarily."

"How soon?" Tsai repeated.

Chao glanced at his watch and allowed himself a tight smile. "What time do you have?"

New York

The Plaza Hotel, at Fifth Avenue and Central Park South, had been erected at the start of the twentieth century and was a mainstay of Manhattan elegance ever since. With its copper-edged cornices and gilt-and-brocade interiors, it suggested a grand French château on the corner of Central Park. Its Oak Room and Palm Court, along with its upscale galleries and boutiques, provided countless opportunities for people to help pay for its upkeep, even those who had not rented one of its eight hundred bedrooms.

But it was the hotel's Olympic-sized swimming pool, on the fifteenth floor, where, at Osiris's insistence, the two men continued their conversation.

Another clever rendezvous, Ambler judged, as the men disrobed and changed into Plaza-provided swim trunks. It would be hard to conceal a listening device under these conditions—and nearly impossible to make an audible recording over the ambient noise of splashing water.

"So who are you working for these days?" Ambler had prompted, treading water in the deep end beside Osiris. An elderly woman toward the shallow end was lazily swimming laps along the pool's narrower dimension. Otherwise the pool was vacant. A few dowager types, dressed in one-piece swimsuits, were sipping coffee or tea as they reclined on poolside chaise lounges, doubtless summoning energy for some postponed exertion.

"They're people like us is who they arc," Osiris replied. "Really, just organized differently."

"I'm intrigued," Ambler said. "But not enlightened. What the hell are you talking about?"

"It's really about unleashing talent. You've got all these former covert-ops people, lots of old Stab hands, in fact, who might not have been using their skills to full advantage. Now they're still serving American interests, but they're paid for and deployed by means of a private concern." Osiris's avoirdupois kept him buoyant; treading water cost him minimal effort.

"Private enterprise. An old story in this country. Old as the Hessian mercenaries who helped spice things up during the American Revolution."

"A little different, maybe," Osiris said, breathing easily. "We're organized as a private-sector network of associates. Network's the key idea."

"More like Avon or Tupperware than Union Carbide, then. The multilevel marketing model."

Following the sound of Ambler's voice, Osiris repositioned his face slightly; his sightless eyes seemed almost to peer. "Not how I'd put it, but yes, that's the general idea. Independent agents, working independently, but coordinated and deployed by their 'upline.' So you can understand why the team is so eager to have you aboard. They want you for the same reason they wanted me. I have a unique skill set. So do you. And these people are intent on bringing in unique talent. Puts you in a good bargaining position. You know, you're something of a mythic figure among the Stab boys. The bosses figure if only half the stories they tell about you are true . . . and I've seen you work, so I know the score. I mean, Christ, what you did in Kuala Lumpur—now *that's* the stuff of legend. And I was there, you'll recall. Not a lot of Malay speakers in the Political Stabilization Unit."

"That was a long time ago," said Ambler, arching himself into a back float.

Kuala Lumpur. It had been many years since he thought about it, but the memories came back swiftly enough. A convention complex at the Putra World Center, in the city's financial district, by the Golden Triangle Area and the Petronas Twin Towers. It was an international trade convention, and Tarquin was officially a representative of a New York law firm specializing in intellectual property: Henry Nyberg had been the field legend on that occasion. A member of one of the foreign delegations, Tarquin's bosses had learned, was a terrorist plant—but which? Tarquin had been dispatched as a walking lie detector. They thought it might take him the full length of the four-day conference. Instead, it took him less than half an hour. He had strolled into the lobby of the convention center on the first morning, wandering around clusters of people, with their conference-provided blue binders, watched the marketing reps exchange cards, watched entrepreneurs stalk potential investors, and the thousand other dances conducted among business executives. The air in the lobby had been heavy with coffee and warm breakfast pastries. Tarquin allowed his mind to wander aimlessly as he circled the lobby, nodding, from time to time, as if to someone just past the sight line of anyone who was looking at him. Twenty-five minutes later, he knew.

It wasn't one person but two, both of whom had attached themselves to a banking delegation from Dubai. How had he known? Tarquin did not bother to parse the subliminal signs of furtiveness and fear; he saw them, and he knew, the way he always did. That was all. An intel team from the Political Stabilization Unit spent the rest of the day confirming what he had detected at a glance. The two young men were nephews of the bank's chairman; they had also been inducted into a *jihadi* brotherhood while studying at the University of Cairo. The brotherhood had instructed them to procure certain pieces of industrial equipment—hardware that, while harmless in itself, could, in combination with more commonplace materials, be used in the manufacture of munitions.

Ambler allowed himself to float peacefully in the water for a few long moments. *These people know what you can do,* he reflected. *How will that change the equation?*

"In Kuala Lumpur, everyone asked you how you knew, and you said it was obvious, that those guys were sweating bullets. But it wasn't obvious, not to anyone else. And they weren't sweating bullets. The Stab analysts reviewed the video later. The fact is, to everyone else, they were doing a damn impressive job of blending in. They looked bored and dutiful, exactly as they wanted to look. Only, you saw them differently."

"I saw them the way they were."

"Exactly. Something nobody else could. We never really talked about this. It's an amazing skill. A *gift.*"

"Then I wish I could exchange it."

"Why—is it too big for you?" Osiris chuckled. "So what's the deal? Some witch doctor give you an amulet one day?"

"I'm not the best person to ask," said Ambler soberly. "But I think it has to do with this: Most people see what they want to see. They simplify things, engage in hypothesis confirmation. I don't. I can't. It isn't something I can turn on or off."

"I don't know whether that's a blessing or a curse," Osiris said. "Or a little of both. *Comme d'habitude.* The condition of knowing too much."

"Right now my problem is knowing too little. You know what I'm after. Enlightenment." Indeed, for him it was a matter of life or death. He needed to know the *truth,* or he would be dragged into an undertow of the unconscious from which he would never emerge.

"But enlightenment comes in steps," Osiris said. "As I said, what I've really got to offer is judgment, rather than information. Tell me the relevant facts, and I may be able to help you make sense of them."

Ambler looked at Osiris, who was still treading water almost effortlessly. Water beaded on his broad shoulders, but his fringe of red hair remained dry. The man's blue sightless eyes were welcoming, even fond; what tension Ambler could detect was not the result of stratagem or deception. His misgivings were automatic, and he would have to set them aside. The opportunity, if it was real, could not be passed on.

The Chinese man in the well-tailored suit—a subtle glen-plaid pattern, in a superfine merino—attracted hardly any notice as he came through the revolving doors and into the front lobby of the Plaza Hotel, on Fifth. He was slight of build, handsome, with delicate features and bright, friendly eyes. He nodded at one of the clerks at the front counter, and she returned his nod, assuming that the man had confused her with whatever girl had checked him in. He nodded at the concierge, who flashed his if-I-can-be-of-service grin, and did not break stride as he made his way past the elevator bank. If he had looked uncertain, if he had stopped to orient himself, one of the underoccupied staffers might have stepped in with a *May I help you, sir?* But at an eight-hundred-room hotel, it was a safe bet that someone who looked like he belonged did indeed belong.

Within a few minutes, he had ascertained that his quarry was in none of the lobby or dining spaces of the hotel; within a few minutes more, he had determined that they were in none of the other public spaces of the lower levels—the art galleries, shops, styling salons, or spa.

Joe Li had already ruled out the possibility that the quarry had taken a hotel room here: an upscale establishment like this made an inconvenient number of demands—IDs, impressions taken of credit cards, and so forth. These did not look like people who wished to leave such a record of their visit. Their absence from the main public spaces left two other possibilities. One was the hotel fitness center.

None of the hotel's many official greeters saw him turn down a carpeted corridor between two elevator banks and through a discreetly marked service entrance. They did not see him open his briefcase and assemble the pieces of equipment it had carried. They did not see him step into a janitor's slate gray coveralls, which completely concealed his lightweight suit, and board a service elevator, accompanied now by a wheeled mop-and-bucket assembly.

If they had encountered him now, they would not have recognized him. Simply by muscular changes and postural adjustments, he had aged himself by twenty years; he was now a stooped man, tending to his bucket and an endless list of chores, the hovering custodial presence that few people really notice.

Osiris was beginning to sound a little breathless, and not because of any physical exertion. "Don't you see," he was saying. "There's an al-

ternate hypothesis." He treaded water with small graceful movements, as if he were conducting a small chamber orchestra. The blue
of his eyes matched the blue of the pool water.

"Consistent with my experiences over the past twenty-four
hours?"

"Yes," said his old colleague. "Your account has been admirably
clear. You've been baffled by the fact that your memory of who you
are doesn't square with the world you inhabit, and you assume it's
the world that has been manipulated. What if that assumption is
wrong? What if it's your *mind* that has been manipulated?"

Ambler listened with a rising sense of dread as the big-bellied operative began to explain.

"It's Occam's razor: What's the simplest explanation?" Osiris went
on. "It's easier to alter the contents of your head than it is to change
the whole world."

"What are you trying to tell me?" Ambler felt numb.

"You know about Bluebird, Artichoke, MKULTRA—all those
behavioral-science programs from the fifties—right? They've been
declassified, hashed over. Funny little episode in the history of the
spy agencies is what people think."

"And rightly so," Ambler scoffed. "You're naming Cold War follies,
fantasies from a bygone era. Discontinued long ago."

"Well, that's the thing. The program names changed, but the research never was discontinued. And the history isn't irrelevant. Really, it started with Josef Cardinal Mindszenty—name ring a bell?"

"Another midcentury victim of the Communist regimes, early in
the postwar era. Hungary had a show trial, got him to confess on
camera to charges of treason and corruption. But it was bogus."

"Sure it was. But the CIA was curious. It had this audiovisual feed
of him confessing, and it ran the feed through all these stress-test in-
dicators and tried to find evidence that he was lying. And the strange
thing was, they failed. All the tests said he was telling the stone truth.
Yet the charges really were trumped up—they knew that, too. Which

got them thinking. Could the prelate really have *believed* what he was testifying? If so, how had they convinced him of this . . . alternate reality? If he'd been drugged, what drugs were they using? And so forth. All of which kick-started our own mind-control experiments. For the first couple of decades, most of it was bullshit, all right. They'd put someone into a coma with pentothal, then inject him with enough Dexedrine to make him bug-eyed. What would that do to someone—would it make them receptive to narcohypnotic suggestions? The best and the brightest became fascinated by the possibilities. Pretty soon, the Technical Services Staff was commandeered to the cause. But they needed even more resources, so they figured out a way to bring in the Army's Special Operations Division at Fort Detrick in Maryland, where they had a biological research center."

"How do you know so much about it?" asked Ambler. A shiver ran down his spine.

"Why do you think they put us together in the first place?" Osiris shrugged. "My background is in psy-ops. Like a lot of linguists. Language used to be a major sticking point for the mind benders. In the good old days, psy-ops would interrogate a Russian defector in a German safe house, or a North Korean in an apartment in Seoul, and they'd drug the guy up with some complicated protocol. Soon then these guys would have regressed, be blabbering away in the language of their home village, and these Berlitz monkeys at the agency would have no idea what was being said, and no ability to talk to them in their native dialect. That's when they decided they needed people like me. They'd turn over a lot of rocks to find us and bring us in. So we'd pay our dues in one of the psy-ops projects. Then, by and by, we'd be loaned out to OGAs. 'Collegiality,' they called it. Actually, it was a matter of resource distribution, spreading the budget lines around."

"OGAs—other governmental agencies. Like Consular Operations. Or its Political Stabilization Unit."

"You know the routine. I finally asked for an official transfer to State because I thought it would be more stimulating on the language front. At Cons Ops, though, they were intrigued by the psych training I'd received. Back then, they still worried about you. Worried about how reliable you were. They liked the thought of my being around you on a couple of jobs."

"So you were filing reports on me."

"You got it. You'd be filing reports on the bad guy, I'd be filing reports on the good guy who was helping us get the bad guy. But you knew it at the time, I've no doubt. Business as usual, right?"

"I seem to recall that *I* was asked to file a report on *you*," Ambler said. "They were still trying to grapple with the idea of a sightless operative. Wanted reassurance, again."

Osiris smiled merrily. "Talk about the blind leading the blind. You must have known my brief, as I say. My sense was, you were too well mannered to call me on it."

"I guess I knew you didn't mean me any harm."

"I didn't," Osiris said. "Actually, I've always liked you. Ever since Kuala Lumpur."

"Really, that episode got way overblown."

"Catching the *jihadi* puppies? Not what I'm talking about."

"Then what?"

"Cast your mind back to just before that happened."

"You were supposed to be working the door at the Putra World Center. Meaning you were sitting at the end of the bar, drinking some sort of apple fizz. Looked like beer. Had an earbud in an ear, so the tech could rotate microphone feeds from around the lobby. Idea was, if you heard something interesting or anomalous, you'd be able to signal me about it."

"I never did, never had to. But what I'm talking about happened a little earlier. We were marching over there together, with our conference badges. And those Kilgour, French & Stanbury business suits that said 'billable hours' down to the very cuff buttons."

Ambler grunted. "I'll take your word for it."

"These fingertips never lie. A very nice worsted, perfectly draped around the neck and shoulders." Osiris lifted his hands and waggled his fingers. "So we're on the sidewalk, not far from our destination, and this peasant from the provinces has been trying to get directions to the nearest train station, and nobody's been giving him the time of day. From his accent, I can tell he's a Dyak, you know, one of the fairly primitive ethnic minorities who live in villages scattered around what's left of rural Malaysia—and this is the heart of the financial district, mind you. People are busy, and nobody has time for a Dyak, so of course they ignore him, like he's made of air. In desperation, this little guy—he's probably in sandals and funny robes—turns to *you* for directions."

"If you say so," said Ambler.

"Now, you weren't from there; you had no idea. But instead of telling the guy, 'Sorry, can't help you,' you stop one of those fast-striding businessmen. Of course they're happy to stop for a prosperous-looking Westerner like you. Then, with the little Dyak by your side, you say, 'Can you tell us where the nearest train station is?' and you stand there while the suit explains exactly how you get there. Meanwhile I'm cracking my knuckles in my trouser pockets, because we've got a big-deal piece of business ahead of us, and you're taking the time to help some tribesman find his way home."

"So?"

"It's nothing that would stick in your mind, because it didn't mean anything to you. It meant something to me, though. I had you figured as a major-league asshole like most of the Stab boys, and suddenly I'm thinking maybe you're not."

"Not even triple-A?"

"Strictly farm team." Osiris laughed again. Ambler remembered that he was a big laugher. "It's funny the things you remember. And funny the things you don't. Which brings us to next phase of the psych experiments. Vietnam is still going strong. Nixon hasn't been to China yet. And what happens next is that a very brilliant, very dangerous, very powerful man finally gets on board."

"You giving me a goddamn history lesson?"

"You know what they say. Those who forget the past—"

"Flunk their history exams," Ambler said. "Big deal. Sometimes I think only those who *remember* the past are condemned to repeat it."

"I hear you. You're talking about people who nourish grudges and grievances over shit that happened centuries ago. But what if I plant something nasty in your fruit patch—put some nightshade among your blueberries? Wouldn't you want to know?"

"What are you saying?"

"I'm talking about James Jesus Angleton, and one of his legacy's many victims."

"*Who*, goddammit?"

"Maybe you."

It was not the fitness center, then. Joe Li had checked the area carefully, including the locker room. It was remarkable how little attention he attracted; it was as if he had donned some magic invisibility garment when he put on the janitor's coveralls. Now he had pushed his bucket through the locker rooms of the swimming pool. No sign of his quarry. The last place to look was the pool itself. Indeed, it had distinct advantages as a meeting site.

Walking with the shambling gait he had adopted for the role, Joe Li made his way into the area of the swimming pool. Nobody had given him a second look; nobody had given the long handle of the squeeze mop a second look, either. The fact that its diameter was too great for its ostensible job was too complicated a thought to have presented itself to anyone's consciousness. As Joe Li wheeled his bucket assembly along the floor of small ceramic tiles, he casually glanced around him. The man he was after had narrowly evaded him in the Sourlands. It would not happen twice.

If his quarry was here, his work would soon be finished.

Ambler closed his eyes and dived to the floor of the pool, then let himself ascend quickly. He needed a break. Angleton, the CIA's great mastermind of Cold War counterespionage, was a genius whose paranoid obsessions almost destroyed the agency he served.

"There weren't many pies that Angleton didn't have a finger in," Osiris went on. "Upshot is that when the Church Committee is starting up and the CIA has to mothball MKULTRA, in the early seventies, Angleton makes sure the program wasn't shut down. It really just migrates to the Pentagon. Soon Angleton is on the outs, but his true believers keep the faith. Year after year, they're spending millions on research, inside and outside the government. They've got scientists in pharmaceutical firms and academic labs on retainer. And they're doing their own work, without any bullshit from some bioethics committee. Working with scopolamine, bufontenine, corynanthine. Uppers and downers and in-betweeners. They're developing modified versions of the old Wilcox-Reiter machines, for electroconvulsive therapy. Building on breakthroughs in the area of 'depatterning,' where you'd mess with someone's mind so hard that they started to lose all sense of space and time, all their usual neural patterns, basically their sense of self. You'd combine that with a technique they called 'psychic driving,' where they'd put a patient in a stupor and bombard him with messages on a tape loop—sixteen hours a day for weeks on end. All very crude in those days. But Angleton thought there was a practical application for it. He was obsessed with Sov mind-control techniques, naturally. He knew that our agents could be, had been, captured by the enemy, the contents of their minds plumbed by means of stress, trauma, and psychopharmacology. But what if you could alter the contents of human memory?"

"That's impossible."

"Angleton didn't think so. The call was to adapt the old research on depatterning and psychic driving, and bring it to a whole new level.

Now we're in the Pentagon's Strategic Neuropsychology Division, where they developed a technique known as *mnemonic overlay*. Forget about the old tape loops. We're way beyond that now. It involved 'rich feed'—video, audio, olfactory stimuli—and the manufacture of hundreds of discrete memory vignettes. Subjects would be put under the influence of all sorts of infused psychotomimetic chemicals, and then exposed to the *feed,* a stream of vivid episodes, presented in jumbled, constantly changing order, from defecating, as a toddler, on a plastic potty to heavy petting with a thirteen-year-old girl next door . . . a high-school graduation scene . . . a college keg party. . . . A name, that of the overlaid identity, would be repeated again and again. The result was an alternate self that an agent would, automatically, retreat to under conditions of extreme stress or altered consciousness. The idea was that you'd produce an interrogation-proof agent. But you know how the clandestine services work. Once you've developed a technique, it's anyone's guess how they'll put it to use."

"And you're suggesting . . ."

"Yeah," said the sightless operative. "I'm suggesting. Not stating like I know, because I don't. I'm just putting it to you. What makes most sense of what you know?"

Ambler was beginning to feel prickly heat, despite the cool water. *Identity fragmentation . . . abreactive ego dystonia . . .* the psychiatric jargon returned to him in sharp, lacerating shards.

Madness!

Trying to affirm the immediacy of his senses—to anchor himself in the real—he felt the chill of the water around him, the ache in his muscles. He craned his head, taking in all the tiny particulars of his surroundings. The old lady swimming her short, side-to-side laps, she had to be eighty. The girl—she had to be her granddaughter—in the lacy red suit. The plump coffee drinkers seated on poolside chaise lounges, in their modest one-piece outfits, no doubt discussing diets and exercise routines. On the other side of the tiled deck, a stooped custodian with a bucket and mop. Chinese guy, indeterminate age . . . except there was something off, wasn't there?

Ambler blinked. The stoop was not quite convincing—and, as he studied the scene before him, neither was the mop.

Oh Christ!

Was he hallucinating? Succumbing to paranoid delusions?

No—he could not allow himself to think like that.

"Osiris," Ambler said suddenly. "There's a janitor. Chinese. One of yours?"

"Not remotely possible," Osiris said. "This was a spur-of-the-moment decision, coming here. Nobody was notified."

"There's something odd about him. Something . . . I just don't know. But we can't stay here." Ambler dived underwater, intending to resurface a few yards away, so that he could take another look at the janitor without being obvious about it. Ambler couldn't shake the feeling that there was something *wrong* about that man.

Moments later, the water nearby had grown clouded, dark.

On instinct, Ambler stopped himself from resurfacing, dived deep into the pool before looking up.

Blood was gouting from Osiris's body—the speed and pressure indicating that a bullet must have severed a carotid artery—and it spread through the chlorinated water like billowing clouds.

Kevin McConnelly was trying to be patient with the middle-aged blowhard in what the Plaza insisted on calling the changing area. *Locker room* was too low-class, McConnelly guessed. *Locker room* said athlete's foot and jockstraps; the Plaza was all about cosseted rich people who liked to think the world was designed just for them, as if some Savile Row tailor had taken his scissors and pins over the whole goddamn Western Hemisphere and nipped and tucked everything to their liking. Is Cincinnati in the way, sir? We'll move it. Lake

Michigan not big enough? We'll let it out some more, sir. That was how they talked. That was how they *thought*. And if there was any bubble on the planet where they could indulge the fantasy, it had to be the Plaza Hotel.

"Not at all," McConnelly told the blowhard, a red-faced man with no neck. "If you think someone stole your wallet, we have to take that seriously. All I'm saying is that we've very seldom had a problem with property theft in the changing area."

"Always a first, though," the red-faced man grumbled.

"Did you check your jacket pocket?" McConnelly asked, gesturing toward the lump in the lower left pocket of the man's navy blazer.

The man glowered but patted the pocket. Then he pulled out the wallet and actually opened it up, as if to verify that it was really his.

Like whose wallet were you expecting to find, you fat fuck? Mc-Connelly refrained from smiling; it might have been taken the wrong way. "All right, then," he said.

"I never keep my wallet here," the man said petulantly. "Strange." He gave McConnelly a suspicious look, as if McConnelly were the culprit. As if it were his idea of a goof. A slash-like smile: "Sorry to waste your time, then." But the tone somehow said that McConnelly was to blame.

A real class act. McConnelly just shrugged. "No worries. Happens a lot." *Especially with arrogant bastards like you who won't admit when you screw up.* This was one problem he never had to deal with when he was an MP. Military police dealt with people who had no need to establish their place. Their place was specified precisely on their shoulder board.

He was about to fetch a clipboard and file an "incident" report— except that they should be called nonincident reports, since most of the time that's all they were, complaints without a cause—when he heard screams coming from the pool area.

———

Another bullet pierced the water, trailing a shaft of bubbles like a string of pearl beads, missing Ambler by just a few feet. The index of refraction had put the gunman off his target. But he would not make the same mistake again. What was the angle of fire   how far was the "janitor" from the side of the pool? Staying well below the surface, pulling himself with powerful strokes of his arms and legs, Ambler raced to the side nearest the gunman: closer was actually safer. The gunman would have to reposition himself to have an angle on Ambler now.

Ambler glanced toward the red-billowing mass in the center of the deep end: Osiris was already dead, he could see, hovering near the surface with his limbs spread out.

Oh dear Christ no!

Where was safety? Ambler had been underwater for perhaps fifteen seconds. He could hold his breath for perhaps fifty or sixty seconds. In the crystalline blue water, there was no place to hide. Except—the blood, the hemorrhaging cloud a few yards away . . . Osiris's own lifeless body offered the only protection he had. It would hardly last long, and Ambler, clad only in the hotel-provided swimming trunks, was utterly vulnerable. He shot to the surface, along the side of the pool nearest the assailant, and took a few deep breaths, opening his mouth wide to minimize the sound. The air was filled with shrieks. The others in the pool and on the tiled deck were screaming and fleeing. Hotel security would soon arrive, but it would be too late for Ambler, and besides, he suspected they would be no match for the Chinese gunman.

Without protection—that wasn't quite right, was it? The water itself was a kind of armor. Fourteen feet of it at the deep end. Water was a thousand times as dense as air, producing a thousand times as much drag as air. Bullets could travel no more than a few feet in it without losing speed and direction.

He dived deep and when he moved toward the surface he hid himself in the spreading cloud of blood beneath the lifeless operative. Then he dragged the body toward the diving boards. Another shot zipped into the water, missing Ambler's shoulder by a few inches. A rifle that could be easily disassembled and reassembled, and whose barrel could pass as a mop, was a compromised weapon. Most likely, it was of a stripped-down single-bolt design that had to be reloaded before each shot. Hence the four-or five-second lag between bullets.

Through the bloodied water, he glimpsed the high-diving board, now overhead. The concrete stanchion that supported it would provide some protection.

The Chinese man was holding the long, dowel-like rifle with its stock to his cheek. It looked to be a narrow-bore weapon, perhaps modified from an AMT Lightning, one of those folding-stock models designed for stealth sniping.

Another *crack* as he squeezed off a bullet; Ambler, who could tell that he was about to squeeze the trigger moments before he did so, had thrashed violently to reposition himself and evade its path. Now he plunged deep into the water again.

Timing was all. It would be another five or six seconds before he could fire again. Could Ambler make it to the concrete stanchion in time? And if he did, what would he do next?

Yet there was no time to plan. He had to live in the moment or he would die in the moment. He had no choice. *Now!*

Not pain screams, Kevin McConnelly decided, *panic* screams. He was slouchy and out of shape—the mirror never lied—but the fifteen years he had spent as an MP gave him survival instincts. He ducked his head into *Le Centre Nautique*, as the sign pretentiously called the swimming-pool area, and then stepped back. What he had seen was a professional, firing from an odd-looking paramilitary rifle; he knew this was not someone to take on with a handgun. He charged into the locker area and looked around desperately. He was sweating, his stomach furled, and he remembered why he had left the military police. Still, something had to be done, and he would have to do it.

Something. But what?

He did not consider himself much of a brain, but the next thing he did, he decided later, was very, very smart. He found the circuit breaker for the hall and turned off all the lights. An inky darkness shrouded everything, and a curious silence, too, as fans and motors stopped running, the kind one wasn't aware of until they cut out. He realized that it might help the gunman to escape, but that was not his main problem. He had to stop the shooting. Nobody went shooting in the dark, did they? Now, there had to be a flashlight around somewhere.

He heard the sound of someone streaking toward him. He stuck out a leg and tripped the man.

The runner crashed into a stand of lockers. As McConnelly turned the lights on again, he saw a six-foot-tall man in swim trunks. Short brown hair, a smoothly muscled body—late thirties, early forties, the sort of age where, if someone had kept in shape, it was hard to say.

"What the hell'd you do that for?" The man glared as he massaged a bruised shoulder.

Not the shooter. The shot-at, more likely.

McConnelly took a quick look around; no sign of the gunman. No sign of the gun.

The bad guy had fled the scene: they both knew it. McConnelly, anyway, was relieved.

"Here's the deal." McConnelly liked to say those words. It was the voice of authority, and it was amazing how persuasive it was even to the real muckety-mucks. "I'm going to get the police to come right now and secure the area. Then you're going to explain to me and to them exactly what went down." He stood with his hands on his hips, spreading open his sports jacket and exposing his belt holster.

"Is that what you think?" The man went straight to his locker, where he scrubbed at his head with a towel and started to change into his street clothes.

"That's what I know," McConnelly said levelly, following him.

Then a curious thing happened; the man caught a glimpse of himself in the wall-mounted mirror and suddenly blanched, like he'd seen a ghost. After a moment, the man turned away and took a deep breath.

"Call one of the tabloids," the man said harshly. "I'd like to tell them about what happened. 'Plaza Pool Shoot-out'—the headline practically writes itself."

"That's not necessary," McConnelly said, with a sinking feeling. What had happened was not something he looked forward to explaining to the hotel management. In fact, it was more than his job was worth. And they would probably blame him for it, same as that red-faced asshole, and with as much logic.

"How come you get to decide what's necessary?"

"I'm just saying that we can have a police investigation without a lot of distracting publicity."

"I think the tabloids can do better. Maybe 'Plaza Pool of Blood.'"

"It's real important that you stay here," McConnelly said. But he did not say it as if he meant it, because deep down he didn't.

"Here's the deal," the man said over his shoulder as he walked away. "You never saw me."

Langley, Virginia

Caston was staring unhappily at a list of State Department civilian covers.

The trouble, of course, was that it almost certainly did not contain the name he was after. That name had been deleted. How was he supposed to find something that did not exist?

His eyes drifted over to that morning's *Financial Times,* which reposed in the wastepaper basket by his desk. It went to show how damned distracted he was that, for the first time he could remember, he made a mistake in filling out the crossword puzzle. *Nothing important; thrice before the transport begins* was the clue. He'd written down *trivia* and he had to erase it; *trifle* was plainly the right answer. He pulled the furled newspaper out of the bin and glared at the puzzle. Tiny eraser crumbs still adhered to the page.

Caston dropped the paper, but the cogs in his head were starting to turn. To erase was to take something away. But when we did so, didn't we always end up *adding* something, too?

"Adrian," he called out.

"Master," Adrian said, bowing his head with lighthearted irony. If it were less affectionate, it would be just shy of insubordination.

"Prepare a Requisition 1133A, would you?"

Adrian pursed his lips. "That's, like, an iron-mountain search, right? For offline archival retrieval."

"Very good, Adrian." The young man had been doing his homework.

"The clerks hate like hell to do those. A major pain in the ass."

Which was no doubt why they always took an inordinately long time. To Adrian, Caston was glacial: "Is that what the manual says?"

Adrian Choi colored. "I know somebody who works there."

"And who would that be?"

"Just some girl," Adrian mumbled, regretting that he had said anything about it.

"Girl, meaning a female of your approximate generation?"

"I guess so," Adrian said, his eyes downcast.

"Well, Adrian, I really am in a great hurry for my Requisition 1133A."

"OK."

"Would you call me a charming man?"

Adrian gave him a doe-frozen-in-the-headlights look. "Um, no?" he finally said, obviously having realized he could not say yes and maintain a straight face.

"Correct, Adrian. I am happy to know that you haven't lost touch with reality. The advantage of being a newcomer. Someone here once described me, accurately, as having a 'charm deficit,' and that was someone who actually *liked* me. Now, I have very careful instructions for you. I want you to call your young friend in Archives and"—he cleared his throat—"charm the panties off the little heifer. Can you manage that?"

Adrian tilted his head, looking startled. "I—I think I can, yeah." He swallowed: his country was calling on him! With greater conviction, he added, "Definitely."

"And then get my Req. 1133A processed faster than any Req. 1133A has ever been processed in agency history." He smiled. "Consider it a challenge."

"Super," said Adrian.

Then Caston reached for the telephone; he needed to have a word with the ADDI. He had not moved from his seat in hours. But he was closing in.

CHAPTER TEN

Gaithersburg, Maryland

It was a one-story ranch-style house, generic looking, distinguished from its neighbors only by the well-pruned holly bushes that grew around its foundations, a moat of spiny-leafed greenery, even in winter. It seemed an unlikely place of safety, and maybe it was not one. But Ambler had to find out.

He rang the doorbell and waited. Would she even be home?

He heard footsteps, and another question formed in his mind: Would she be alone? There was just one car in the garage, an old Corolla, and none in the driveway. He had heard no noises of cohabitation. But that was not proof.

The front door was opened a few inches, a chain stretched across the opening.

A pair of eyes met his and widened.

"Please don't hurt me," Laurel Holland said in a quiet, frightened voice. *"Please, just go away."*

And the nurse who had helped free Ambler from Parrish Island shut the door on him.

He was prepared to hear her footsteps rush away, a phone being dialed. The door was cheap brown-painted fiberboard with glued-on detailing. The chain was a joke. One shove and it would have broken off the latch. Yet that was not an option. Ambler had only one chance; he had to play it right.

She had stepped away from the door but, he could tell, was still standing near it, as if frozen by uncertainty, indecision.

He rang the bell again. "Laurel," he said.

There was quiet in the house; she was listening. The words he spoke next would be critical.

"Laurel, I *will* go if you want me to. I'll go, and you'll never see me again. I promise you that. You saved my life, Laurel. You saw something nobody else saw. You had the courage to listen to me, to risk your career—to do what no one else did. And I'll never forget it." He paused briefly. "But I *need* you, Laurel. I need your help again." He waited several long moments. "Please forgive me, Laurel. I won't bother you anymore."

He turned away from the door, his heart sinking, and walked down the two-step porch, scanning the street. It seemed impossible that he could have been followed—and surely there was no reason for people to think he would be paying a call on anyone from the Parrish Island rotation—but he would reassure himself yet again. He had made the trip down from New York using a cab and two rented cars, and, throughout his journey, he had monitored the traffic for any sign of a tail. He had carefully scouted out the entire subdivision where she lived before making his approach. And there was nothing awry. At midafternoon, the street was nearly deserted. A few cars of people who, like Laurel Holland, worked an early shift and were home, awaiting the return of their children from school. Game shows spilled from the windows of some of the ranches; elsewhere soft-rock radio stations played as housewives—a hardy species, despite bulletins warning of their endangered status—did ironing or sprayed polish on department-store furniture.

He heard the door opening behind him before he reached the drive, and he turned around.

Laurel Holland was shaking her head in self-reproach. "Come inside quickly," she said. "Before I come to my senses."

Wordlessly, Ambler entered the modest house and looked around. Lace curtains. A cheap imported rug on the mass-produced oak flooring. A generic sofa, but covered with an interesting Oriental-looking piece of embroidered fabric. The kitchen had not been changed since the house was built. The counters were linoleum, the appliances harvest gold; the floor was the kind of harlequin-patterned vinyl that was cut from a roll.

Laurel Holland looked scared, angry at him but angrier at herself. She also looked beautiful. In Parrish Island, she had been the brusque, pretty nurse; at home, with her hair down, dressed in a sweater top and jeans, she was more than just pretty, he could see. She was lovely, even elegant, her strong features softened by her wavy auburn hair; she moved with natural grace. Under her loose-fitting sweater top, she was hard and soft, supple and yielding. Her waist was narrow, and yet there was something almost maternal to the swell of her breasts. Ambler realized he was staring, and he averted his eyes.

With a pang, he saw the small revolver—a Smith & Wesson .22—mounted on a bracket near the spice rack. Its presence was significant. More significant was the fact that Laurel Holland had made no move toward it.

"Why are you here?" she demanded, looking at him with wounded eyes. "Do you realize what can happen to me?"

"Laurel—"

"If you're grateful, get out! Leave me alone."

Ambler flinched, as if he had been slapped, and bowed his head. "I'll go," he said in a voice like a whisper.

"No," she said. "I don't want—I don't know what I want." There was anguish in her voice—embarrassment, too, that he was witness to it.

"I brought you trouble, didn't I? Because of what you did. I want to say thank you, and I want to say I'm sorry."

Absently she ran an anxious hand through her lustrous hair. "The key card? It wasn't actually mine. The night-shift nurse always leaves hers in the dispensary drawer."

"So they figured I'd palmed it from her somehow."

"You got it. The video made it pretty obvious what happened, or so they thought. Everyone got a reprimand, and that was the end of it, aside from the two guys on medical. So. You left. And now you're back."

"Not *back* back," Ambler corrected.

"They told us you were a dangerous man. Psychotic."

Ambler's eyes flickered toward the wall-mounted revolver. Why hadn't she grabbed it, armed herself? Somehow he doubted that she was the one who put it there. Someone must have mounted the gun for her. A husband, a boyfriend. It wasn't a man's gun. But it was the gun a man would have obtained for a girl. A certain kind of man, anyway.

"They told you those things, and you didn't believe them," Ambler said. "Otherwise you wouldn't have let the dangerous psycho in your house. Especially since you live alone."

"Don't be so sure," she said.

"You didn't used to," Ambler said. "Tell me about your ex."

"You seem to know so much, why don't you?"

"He is, or was, a double-ex. Ex-you. Ex-military."

She nodded, looking slightly startled.

"A veteran, in fact."

She nodded again, the color beginning to drain from her face.

"Maybe a little paranoid," Ambler said, tilting his head toward the gun bracket. "So let's think this through. You're a psychiatric nurse, in a secure facility belonging to the Walter Reed complex. Now why would that be? Maybe because your man came back home from a tour of duty—from Somalia, Desert Storm?—a little messed up in the head."

"Post-traumatic stress disorder," she said quietly.

"And so you tried to heal him, make him whole."

"Tried," she said. There was a tremor in her voice.

"And failed," Ambler said. "But not for lack of effort. So you go to school, maybe at one of the military professional schools, and they encourage you to specialize, and you throw yourself into the subject, and you're smart, so you do well. A psychiatric nurse, military background. Walter Reed. Parrish Island."

"You're good," she snapped, resentful of being reduced to a case study.

"*You're* good—that's what got you in trouble. Like they say, no good deed goes unpunished."

"Is that why you're here?" she said, stiffening. "To see that punishment is served?"

"*Christ*, no."

"Then why the *hell*—"

"Because . . ." Thoughts swirled in Ambler's head. "Maybe because I'm worried that I *am* mad. And because you're the one person I know who looks at me as if I'm *not*."

Laurel shook her head slowly, but he could tell that the fear was ebbing from her. "You want me to say you're not psychotic? I don't think you're psychotic. But what I think doesn't mean diddly."

"To me it does."

"Want some coffee?"

"If you're making it," said Ambler.

"Instant OK?"

"You don't have anything faster?"

She gave him a long, level look. Once again, it was as if she were looking through him, to some core selfhood, some essential sanity.

They sat together, drinking coffee, and suddenly he knew exactly why he had come. There was a warmth and a humanity to her that he desperately craved right now, the way he craved oxygen. Osiris's discussion of *mnemonic overlay*—of the armamentarium of mind-control techniques—had been profoundly harrowing: it was as if the ground beneath his feet had vanished. The spectacle of the man's violent death, harrowing, too, only added to the authority of his voice.

Where others, it seemed, sought him as an operative for hire, Laurel Holland was the one person in the world he could find who, for whatever reason, believed in him, as he wanted to believe in himself. The irony was painful: a psychiatric nurse, who had seen him at his very nadir, was the sole witness to his sanity.

"I see you," she said slowly, "and it's like I see myself. I know we're as different as can be." She closed her eyes for a moment. "But there's something we've got in common. I don't know what."

"You're my port in a storm."

"Sometimes I think ports welcome storms," said the nurse.

"A virtue of necessity?"

"Something like that," she said. "Speaking of which, it was Desert Storm."

"Your ex."

"Ex-husband. Ex-Marine. It's kind of an identity in itself, being ex-Marine. It never really leaves you. Any more than what happened to him in Desert Storm ever really left him. So what does it all mean? Am I just attracted to trouble?"

"He wasn't post-traumatic when you met, was he?"

"No, not then. That was a long time ago. But he got shipped out, did two back-to-back tours, and came back different."

"And not in a good way."

"Started to drink, a lot. Started to hit me, a little."

"A little is too much."

"I kept trying to reach him, like there was a broken little boy inside him and I could somehow make him all better if only I could *love* him enough. I did love him. And he loved me, too. He wanted to protect me was the thing. He got paranoid, started to imagine enemies everywhere. But he was afraid for me, not just for him. Only thing that never occurred to him was that, for me, *he* was what there was to be afraid of. That gun on the wall—he put it there for me, insisted I learn how to use it. Most of the time, I forget it's there. But sometimes I thought about using it to protect myself—"

"—against him."

She closed her eyes, nodded, embarrassed. She was silent for a while. "I should be terrified of you. I don't know why I'm not. It almost scares me that I'm not scared of you."

"You're like me. You go by your instincts."

She gestured around her. "And see where it's got me."

"You're a good person." Ambler spoke simply. Without thinking about it, he reached over and placed a hand on hers.

"That what your instincts say?"

"Yeah."

The woman with the green-flecked hazel eyes just shook her head. "So tell me, is there a shell-shocked vet in your background?"

"My lifestyle wasn't conducive to deep relationships. Or shallow relationships, for that matter. Hard to keep a lover if you're going to be disappearing for seven months in Sri Lanka, or Madagascar, or Chechnya, or Bosnia. Hard to have civilian friends when you know you're dooming them to an intensive period of surveillance. Just protocol, but when you're in a special-access program, a civilian contact is either somebody you're using or—the fear is—somebody who's using *you*. It's a good life for a loner. A good life if you don't mind relationships that come stamped with an expiration date, like a quart of milk. It was a sacrifice. A big one. But it was supposed to make you less vulnerable."

"And did it?"

"I've come to think it had the opposite effect."

"I don't know," Laurel said, the recessed overhead lights burnishing her wavy hair. "With my luck, I would have been better off if I'd always been alone."

Ambler shrugged. "I know what it's like to have people change on you. I had a dad who drank. He was really good at holding it, and then he wasn't."

"An angry drunk?"

"At the end of the day, most of them are."

"He beat you?"

"Not much," Ambler said.

"Not much is too much."

Ambler looked off. "I got good at reading his mood. With drunks, it's tricky, because they can turn on a dime. Giddy, laughing, then suddenly it's *smack,* with an open hand or a closed fist, depending, and the expression on his face blackens into a kid-you-got-a-smart-mouth-on-you scowl."

"Christ."

"He was always sorry afterward. Really, really sorry. You know what it's like—the guy says he's going to change this time, and you believe him because you want to."

She nodded. "You have to believe him. Like you believe that some-day the rain's got to stop. So much for instincts."

"I'd call it self-deception. *Ignoring* your instincts. See, if you're that little boy, you get real good at watching your old man's face. You learn to recognize when he seems to be in a bad mood, but it's only because he's down on himself. You ask him then if you can have your allowance, if he can buy you a new action figure, and he looks at you like you did him a favor. Hands you a fiver, maybe a ten, and says, 'Make yourself happy.' Says you're a good kid. Other times he seems giddy, happy, and you look at him cross-eyed and suddenly it's a cloudburst and he's going to belt you for sure."

"So you never knew how it was going to play out. He was totally unpredictable."

"No, that's the thing," Ambler said. "I *learned.* I learned to tell the difference, learned the subtleties. Learned to tell apart the weather systems. By the time I turned six, I knew his moods like I knew the alphabet. Knew when to get the hell out of his sight. Knew when he was in a generous mood. Knew when he was angry and aggressive, knew when he was passive and self-pitying. Knew when he was lying to me or to my mom."

"A heavy thing for a kid."

"He left by my seventh birthday."

"Were you and your mom relieved?"

"It was more complicated than that." He stopped.

Laurel was quiet for a while, as they sipped bad coffee. "You ever had another job? Other than being a spook, I mean."

"A couple of summer jobs. Serving up barbecue at a fairground place outside of town. You hoped people would eat their spare ribs *after* they went on the roller coaster. I used to be pretty good at drawing. I did a junior-year-abroad in Paris, tried to make money as a street artist. You know, you'd sketch portraits of passersby, try to get a few francs from them."

"Your road to riches, huh?"

"I had to take the first exit. People got incredibly upset when they saw what I drew."

"Bad at resemblances?"

"It wasn't that." He broke off. "God, I haven't thought about this for years. It took me a while to realize what the problem was. Basically, the way I saw these people wasn't necessarily the way they wanted to be seen. Somehow on my sketch pad people ended up looking scared, or eaten by self-doubt, or despairing—and maybe it was the truth. But it wasn't a truth they wanted to see. A lot of the time, it freaked them out, or pissed them off. I'd hand them the sketch, and they'd go crazy—crumple it up, then rip it into pieces before putting it in the trash. It was almost a superstitious thing. Like they didn't want anyone else to see it, to glimpse their soul. At the time, as I say, I didn't fully understand what was happening."

"Do you understand what's happening now?"

He stared at her. "You ever get the sense you don't really know who you are?"

"Try all the time," she replied, her lynx eyes drawing him in. "What did they do to you?"

He responded with a miserable half smile. "You don't want to know."

"What did they do to you?" she repeated. Now she put a hand on his, and the warmth from the contact seemed to travel up his arm.

Slowly, he began to tell her about his disappearance from the databases and electronic archives, and then, in broad strokes, the essentials of what Osiris had told him. She listened contemplatively, and her calm was contagious.

Finally, she said, "You want to know what I think?"

He nodded.

"I think they tried to mess with your mind when you were on the inside. In fact, I'm sure of it. With drugs and electroshock and Lord only knows what else. But I don't believe you can ever really change who a person is."

Quietly he said, "When I was . . . inside . . . I heard a recording. Of myself." He described it bloodlessly.

"How do you know it was really you?"

"I just . . . know," he said, flailing.

Laurel's focus was razor-sharp. "That can all be explained."

"Explained? *How?*"

"I did a unit on pharmacology in nursing school," Laurel said. "Let me get my textbook, and I'll show you."

When she returned a few minutes later, she was carrying a thick textbook with a maroon and gold-embossed cover. "The sort of psychosis you were talking about? It could be drug induced." She turned the pages to a chapter on anticholinergic drugs. "Look here, in the discussion of overdose symptoms. It says anticholinergics can result in psychosis."

"But I don't remember any of it. I don't remember the psychosis. Don't remember getting doped up."

"They could have combined the anticholinergic with another drug like Versed." She flipped through the onionskin pages. "Look here." She tapped a bulleted passage with a finger. "Drugs like Versed interfere with memory formation. There's a whole warning about 'anterograde amnesia'—meaning, amnesia of events following the injection. What I'm saying is, with the right drug cocktail, you could have been plunged into an episode of madness, but you'd have no memory of it. You'd be a raving lunatic for a few hours . . ."

Ambler nodded slowly. The hairs on the back of his neck were prickling with excitement.

"And then they record you while you're in this state," she went on. "And make believe that you're crazy. Try to persuade *you* that you're crazy. For whatever reasons of their own."

Reasons of their own.

The larger questions—*Who? Why?*—yawned like an abyss that would repay those who gazed too deeply into it with destruction. Grappling with the elementary question of *What?* was exhausting enough.

Reasons of their own.

To ascribe reason to madness was only a seeming paradox. The artificial induction of dementia was, in fact, in the counterespionage arsenal of dirty tricks. A method of discrediting someone. A tape could be quietly circulated, which would persuade any interested parties that the subject was indeed stark raving mad. Inquiries would be swiftly put to rest.

The prospect was horrifying. Then why did Hal Ambler feel oddly exhilarated? Because he was not alone. Because he was putting the pieces together with somebody else.

Somebody who believed him. Who believed *in* him. And whose belief helped him to regain his own belief in himself. He might still have been lost in a labyrinth, but Theseus had found his Ariadne.

"How do you explain about the databases?" Ambler pressed. "It's as if I never lived."

"You know about the things that powerful people can do. So do I. I hear gossip at work, the stuff people aren't supposed to talk about but do anyway. About creating records for people who never existed. Not that much harder to erase the records of someone who actually did exist."

"You know how crazy that sounds?"

"Less crazy than the alternative," Laurel said firmly. There was certainty in her voice, a certainty that dismissed Osiris's hypothesis out of hand. "They're burying you in the psych system. So they want to put off any casual inquiries. Kind of like kicking away the ladder after you've climbed through the window."

"What about what I saw in the Sourlands? There was no sign of my cabin, no sign that it ever really existed."

"And you think that's beyond the landscaping skills of somebody able to enlist a powerful government agency."

"Laurel, listen to me," he said, his voice almost breaking. "I look in the mirror and *I don't recognize myself.*"

She reached over and touched his cheek. "Then they changed you."

"How is that possible?"

"I'm not a surgeon," she said. "But I've heard rumors about plastic surgery techniques, about how they can change people so the person himself couldn't even tell he'd ever been operated on. I know that you can keep people anesthetized for weeks at a time. They do it in burn wards, sometimes, to spare patients from a period of agony. There are all sorts of 'minimally invasive' surgery they do now. They could have changed your face, then kept you under until you'd healed up. Even if you had conscious intervals, Versed therapy, again, could stop memories from forming. How would you ever know?"

"That's crazy," Ambler repeated.

She came over to him, stood very close, and placed her hands on his face. She examined the skin along his jaw, his ears, and then felt for scars that might be concealed behind his hairline. She peered closely at his eyelids, cheeks, nose. He could feel the warmth of her own face near his, and then, as she ran her fingertips over his features, something stirred within him. *God, she was beautiful.*

"See anything?" the operative asked.

Laurel shook her head. "Haven't found any entry scars—but that doesn't mean anything," she insisted. "There are techniques I wouldn't even know about. The scalpel could enter through the mucosa of the nose, the reverse of the eyelids, all sorts of possible surgical portals. It isn't my field."

"You don't have any evidence for this. You just think it." Although the words were of skepticism, Ambler was momentarily buoyed by her stalwart conviction.

"It's the only thing that makes sense," she said heatedly. "It's the only thing that makes sense of what you've experienced."

"That's assuming, of course, that my experience—my memory—makes sense." He fell silent. "Christ, I feel like such a goddamn *victim*."

"Maybe that's how they want you to feel. Look, the people who did this to you—they're not good people. They're *manipulators*. I don't think they put you on Parrish Island because you're weak. Probably they put you on Parrish Island because you were too strong. Because you'd started to see through something you weren't meant to see through."

"You're starting to sound as crazy as me." He smiled.

"Can I ask you a personal question?" she said, almost shyly.

"Bring it on," he said.

"What's your name?"

For the first time that day he laughed—a loud, explosive laugh from his belly, from his soul. He extended a hand, mock-formally. "Pleased to meet you, Laurel Holland," he said. "My name is Harrison Ambler. But you can call me Hal."

"I like that better than Patient Number 5312," she said. She placed both her hands in his short brown hair and then, once more, brushed them lightly over his face. She turned his head in one direction and another, as if playing with a mannequin. Then she leaned forward and caressed his cheek.

It took him a few moments to respond at all. When he did, it was the way a desert traveler who had been dying of thirst arrives at an oasis. With both arms, he clasped her to him, and she was firm and she was soft and she was all he had in the world and she was enough.

When they broke off, there were tears in both their eyes.

"*I believe you,*" she said, her voice trembling but resolute. "I believe you're *you.*"

"You may be the only one," he said quietly.

"What about your friends?"

"I told you—for the past twenty years, I've been pretty much an *isolato.* Professional protocol. My friends were my colleagues, and there's no way to track them down—at the moment, they could be at any latitude and longitude you name, depending on the assignment. None of us operatives knew one another's real names, anyway. That was a basic rule."

"Forget that—what about friends from childhood, college?"

Shivering with the sudden recollection, he told her about his call to Dylan Sutcliffe.

She was stopped by that, but only for a few seconds. "Maybe he's got early Alzheimer's. Maybe he was in a car crash, scrambled his brains. Maybe he always hated you. Or maybe he thought you were trying to borrow money. Who knows?" She stood up, fetched a pencil and a piece of paper, and placed them in front of him. "Write down the names of people you can remember and who'd remember you. A kid from the neighborhood when you were growing up. A roommate at college. Whatever. Go for the less common names, so we don't get too many false hits."

"I'd have no idea of how to reach these people now—"

"Write," she charged, with a brush-off gesture.

Ambler wrote. A dozen random names—from his Camden neighborhood, from high school, from summer camp, from Carlyle. She took the sheet from him, and together they walked to a small nook off the kitchen, where she had a slightly battered-looking computer; it looked as if it had been purchased from an Army surplus store.

"It's a dial-up connection," she apologized, "but it's amazing what you can find out online."

"Listen," he said cautiously. "I'm not sure you really want to do this." He had already brought her more deeply into his own nightmare than he had meant to; he dreaded entangling her further.

"It's my house. I'll do what I want."

As he watched over her shoulder, she seated herself before the computer and typed the names into a "people finder" search engine. Five minutes later, she had got half a dozen phone numbers from the dozen names, and she transcribed the phone numbers in neat handwriting.

Then she handed him the handset of a nearby telephone. "Reach out and touch someone," she told him. There was certainty in her eyes.

"No," he said. "Not from your phone."

"Worries about the long-distance charges? That's sweet. You can leave a quarter on my bureau, like Sidney Poitier in *Guess Who's Coming to Dinner.*"

"It isn't that." Ambler paused; he didn't want to sound paranoid, but he knew that precautions that were second nature to an operative could seem strange to a civilian. "It's just that I don't know for sure whether—"

"Whether my phone's tapped?" She seemed unfazed by the prospect. "Isn't there a way to check?"

"Not really."

She shook her head. "What a world you live in." He watched as she idly typed his name into her search engine. The result now had the aura of inevitability:

Your search—HARRISON AMBLER—did not match any documents.

"I'll use a cell phone," Ambler said, taking out the Nokia. "Safer that way." He took a deep breath and called the first number on the list.

"Is there an Elaine Lassiter there?" he asked, keeping his voice even.

"My wife passed away last year," a whispery voice replied.

"I'm sorry to hear that," Ambler said hastily. The phone at the second number, for Gregson Burns, was picked up immediately.

"I'm looking for a Gregson Burns," Ambler began.

"Speaking," the voice cut in.

"Greg! It's Hal Ambler. It's been a long time, I know—"

"If this is a courtesy call, please put me on the 'do not call' list," the voice—a tenor, reedy with annoyance—instructed.

"Did you grow up on Hawthorn Street, in Camden?" Ambler persisted.

Warily: "Yes." Ambler made out a woman's querulous voice in the background: "Who's that calling?"

"And you don't remember Hal Ambler, from across the street? Or *anybody* named Ambler?"

"Eric Ambler, the writer, I've heard of. He's dead. Feel free to join him, because you're wasting my time." The man clicked off.

The floor seemed to sway beneath Ambler's feet. Swiftly he called the next number on the list. Julianne Daiches—or Julianne Daiches Murchison, as she was now listed, still resident in Delaware. Yet there was not a flicker of recognition when the woman by that name finally came to the phone. Unlike Gregson Burns, she was cordial, unhurried, and unsuspicious, seemingly baffled by her caller's confusion. "Now, you didn't say your name was *Sandler,* did you?" she asked, trying to be helpful. "Because I definitely knew a boy named *Sandler.*"

By the time Ambler was halfway through the list of numbers, he was having a hard time getting his eyes to focus; cold sweat had broken out on his face. Now he stared at the sheet for a long time and crumpled it into a ball, crushing it in his fist. Presently he sank to his knees and closed his eyes.

When he opened then, he saw Laurel Holland standing over him, her face drawn.

"Don't you see? It's no use." The words came from Ambler like a groan from deep within him. "I can't do this anymore."

"Screw it," she said. "Everybody's in on it. Or—or I don't know what. It doesn't matter. We don't need to deal with this right now. I shouldn't have pushed you to."

"No." His voice was husky. "But I'm sorry, I just can't—"

"And you're not going to. Not anymore. Don't apologize. You're not going to give them the satisfaction."

"*Them.*" That empty, unpalatable word again.

"Yes, *them.* Whoever's responsible for the whole goddamn charade. You're not going to give them the satisfaction. Maybe they're trying to drive you around the bend. Well, screw it. We're not playing their game. Deal?"

Ambler shakily rose to his feet. "Deal," he said, his voice thick with emotions he could no longer control.

She took him into her arms, and he seemed to grow stronger in her embrace.

"Look, maybe we're all an idea in the mind of God. I once had a boyfriend who used to say that our best chance of immortality was the realization that we do not exist. Granted, he was stoned at the time." She pressed her forehead to his, and he could feel her smile. "I'm just saying, we have to *choose* what to believe, sometimes. And—oh hell—I choose you. Instincts, right?"

"But Laurel—"

"Shut up, OK? I believe *you*, Harrison Ambler. I believe you."

Ambler felt as if the sun, warming and radiant, had suddenly appeared in a midnight sky.

CHAPTER ELEVEN

As he drove his rented Pontiac from her subdivision and made a left onto the busy two-lane road it adjoined, he felt oddly buoyed, a damaged vessel dancing on a wave. The relief was real; it was also precarious. Yet he felt uneasy prolonging his visit, as desperately as he wanted to. Laurel Holland had already done so much for him: he could not let her make any further sacrifice.

At the next intersection, a few miles later, he waited patiently at a red light, adjusting his high beams to low as a van approached the intersection opposite. As the light turned green and he drove through the intersection, he felt a sudden chill and confirmed with his left hand, that warm air was blowing from the vents even as he glanced at his rearview mirror and—

Oh Christ oh Christ oh Christ—the van! The hatchet-faced driver. A retrieval team.

Or worse.

He wanted to veer around immediately in a U-turn, but a procession of cars was now clogging the opposing lane of traffic. He was losing time and had none to lose.

How had it happened? *It's my house. I'll do what I want.* Laurel Holland's computer. Her goddamn computer: her searches must have triggered something. Various government agencies had trap-and-trace programs—the FBI's Carnivore was only the best known—that monitored Internet traffic. These systems used so-called "packet sniffer" techniques to monitor specific nodes and data loci on the Internet. As with the computer he had used at the Dupont Circle cybercafe, Laurel's machine would have a unique digital address, which could be used to retrieve its registration information—and its owner's address.

There was a break in the oncoming traffic, and tires squealing, Ambler made a 180-degree turn. He heard the blaring horn of the car he had cut in front of, heard its tires skid as it slowed enough to avoid a collision. The light at the intersection was red, which would not have stopped him, but cars were whizzing by from the transverse road. If they had been traveling more slowly, he would have tried to nose through, but with cars sweeping through in both directions, the likelihood of an accident was too great. Better to accept a delay of a minute or two than not to arrive at all. Yet every *second* seemed to pass with agonizing slowness. Finally, there was a letup in the traffic, and—*now now now,* a traffic gap, perhaps three seconds' worth—Ambler shot through the red light, gunning across the intersection while tires squealed and horns blared.

Moments later, Ambler found himself behind a laggard station wagon, traveling at thirty miles per hour in a forty-five-mile-per-hour zone. He leaned on his horn—*Dammit, there was no time!*—but the wagon maintained its speed, almost defiantly. Ambler veered abruptly across a double yellow line and into the opposing lane, overtaking the wagon with an immense *vroom* of acceleration. By the time Ambler swerved onto Orchard Lane, he noticed that his shirt was soaked with sweat. Tearing through the quiet subdivision street at autobahn speeds, he brought the sedan juddering to a halt in front of Laurel Holland's ranch house, where—

oh Christ oh Christ oh Christ—the van had already pulled up to her house, in a hasty diagonal to the driveway, the rear double doors ajar and facing her porch. He heard screams—Laurel's—and heard her front door crash open. Two large men, muscles stretching their knit black shirts, had somehow trapped her into a canvas stretcher and were *hoisting* her, a pale, thrashing bundle, into the back of the van. *No! Dear God no!*

Just two of them, but—*dear God no!*—one of them was pulling out a large hypodermic, the needle glinting in the streetlights, preparing to render her insensate with it. What terrified Ambler as much as anything was the look of resolute, professional calm on the men's faces.

He knew what would follow. Ambler was never meant to have surfaced from his prison of blinding white, the sterile psychiatric *hole* where they had buried him. Now that same fate was being prepared for Laurel. She knew too much now. She would never be released to tell her tale. If they were merciful, they would kill her; if they were not, she would spend the rest of her existence as they had intended Ambler to spend his. Not interned so much as *interred*. Buried alive. Experimented upon. Then left to languish, as the traces of her existence were erased from the world of the living.

No—dear God no! He could not let it happen.

One of the men, the hatchet-faced driver, started to run toward Ambler.

Ambler floored the accelerator while in neutral and then, as the engine revved and roared, suddenly engaged the clutch and shifted into gear. The car *leaped* up, all its power abruptly harnessed by the transmission, and shot toward the van, just forty feet away. The hatchet-faced man was now at Ambler's left, as if preparing to grab him from the vehicle. At the last moment, Ambler threw out the driver's side door, heard it *smash* into the man, walloping him unconscious. Then he ground the brakes and turned the steering wheel all the way to the left. The back of the car abruptly slewed in the opposite direction, slamming into the van, absorbing the impact while leaving Ambler unharmed.

The screams were still audible when Ambler scrambled out of the car, and he felt a curious sense of relief: it meant she was still breathing, still safe from the glistening syringe. He charged to the rear of the van where Laurel, trussed up in canvas straps, was kicking and thrashing with all her might, struggling with her hugely muscled captor. Now Ambler stepped behind the front door of the van, which had opened from the force of the collision.

"Step away from her or you *die,* you son of a bitch," Ambler bellowed. "One head shot, one gut shot." The specificity would cinch it, he knew. In these shadows, a weapon would be assumed, even without visual verification. These men were professionals, but they were not zealots: they were doing a job for pay. "Now!" Ambler roared.

The man did as instructed. Holding his hands up in a posture of submission, he began to walk slowly around the van. As he rounded the front, he did what Ambler expected: he suddenly dived inside and, keeping his head ducked down, gunned the motor. Survival was his sole concern now. Ambler vaulted around the van and made sure that Laurel was safely outside of it as the man raced the engine of the powerful van, nosing aside the sideways Pontiac and lurching across the lawn and to the safety of the street.

He had fled the scene, but there would soon be others.

"Laurel," Ambler called out as, with swift, deft movements, he undid the canvas straps that bound her.

"Are they gone?" she asked in voice tremulous with fear.

"We need to get out of here" was all he said.

Suddenly she fell on him, clutching him with quivering arms. "I knew you'd come for me," she kept repeating, her breath warm against his throat. "I knew you'd come for me."

"We've got to get out of here" Ambler interjected urgently. "Is there someplace you can stay—someplace you'd be safe?"

"My brother lives in Richmond."

"No! They'll have a record of it, they'll track you down in an instant. Someone else, someone they won't have on file."

Laurel's face was drawn. "There's a woman who's like an aunt to me—was my mom's best friend when I was growing up. She lives in West Virginia now. A place outside Clarksburg."

"That'll do," Ambler said.

"Please . . ." she began, and he saw the desperation and fear etched on her face. She did not want to be left alone.

"I'll take you there," Ambler said.

The ride to Clarksburg took a few hours, mainly on the interstates 68 and 79; they were driving her car, an old Mercury, and Ambler remained alert to any sign of pursuit or surveillance. Laurel spent some of the time weeping, some of the time in stony silence. She was processing something that was alien to her range of experience, was responding to trauma, ultimately, with rage and resolve. Ambler, meanwhile, was silently berating himself. In a moment of weakness, a nurse had helped him: now her life was imperiled because of it— would, perhaps, never be the same. The woman seated beside him looked at him, he could tell, as if he were her savior, a bulwark of safety. If anything, the opposite was true. But she would never be persuaded of that. It was a logical truth that held no emotional truth for her.

When they parted—he had arranged for a taxicab to wait by an intersection near Laurel's destination—she almost flinched, as if a bandage was being ripped from a wound. He felt something of the same.

"I brought this on you," Ambler murmured, as much to himself as to her. "*I'm* to blame."

"No," she said fiercely. "Don't you *ever* say that. They're the ones, dammit. *They're* the ones. People like that—" She broke off.

"Will you be all right?"

She nodded slowly. "You get the bastards," she told him through gritted teeth, before she turned and walked toward "Aunt Jill's" gingerbready Victorian. A porch light cast a warm yellow glow. It seemed like another world that Laurel was entering—one of safety. A world he did not inhabit.

He dare not expose her further to his own dire predicament.

Somewhere in the maze, the monster lurked. Theseus had to slay the Minotaur, or neither of them would ever be safe.

That night, in an inexpensive motel near Morgantown, West Virginia, sleep came only with difficulty. Old memories began to seep through the chambers of his mind like basement radon. His father, appearing to him in shards and splinters: a handsome, square face, less handsome on close inspection, for the years of boozing took a price in broken capillaries and coarsened skin. The licorice scent of Sen-Sen, the candy he would dissolve in his mouth to try to conceal the alcohol on his breath. His mother's characteristic expression of wounded passivity—it took him a while to detect the anger that underlay it like an organ bass line. Her face was always powdery with foundation makeup; it was part of her daily maquillage, so that nobody would look twice when that foundation served to cover a bruise.

It was a few weeks shy of his seventh birthday. "Why is Daddy leaving?" Hal was asking. He and his mother were in the darkened space off the kitchen that they called the family room, despite the fact that they had seldom gathered there as a family. She had been seated, knitting a muffler she must have known nobody would ever wear, heavy needles clacking through a ball of bloodred yarn. Now she looked up and paled beneath her heavy foundation. "What are you *talking* about?" There was pain and bewilderment in her voice.

"Isn't Daddy leaving?"

"Did Daddy tell you that? Did he say he was leaving?"

"No," said the almost-seven-year-old boy. "He didn't *say* anything."

"Then—I just don't understand what's gotten into you." Anger bloomed in her voice.

"I'm sorry, Mommy," the boy said quickly.

"I swear the Devil's in you. Why would you *say* such a thing?"

But isn't it obvious? he wanted to tell her. *Don't you see it, too?*

"I'm sorry," the boy repeated.

But sorry wasn't good enough—not when, a week later, Daddy had indeed decamped. His closets were cleaned out, his little knickknacks—tie tacks, brass lighter, cigars—gone from the cupboards, his Chevy gone from the garage: Daddy gone from their lives.

Hal's mother had picked him up from some after-school event, having been out in the Camden mall to shop for birthday presents. When they got home and realized what had happened, Hal's mother started to keen.

Despite his own tears, he had tried, fumblingly, to comfort her, and she had recoiled, shuddering, from his childish touch. He would always remember the look she gave him. She was calling to mind what he had said a few days earlier, and her countenance was stretched tight with horror.

In time she tried to put on a bright face, as she did during his birthday. But things were never the same between them. She felt herself unnerved by his gaze and started to avoid it. For Hal, it was the first in a long series of such moments. All of which bore the same lesson: that it was better to be alone than to be abandoned.

Then the seven-year-old was a thirty-seven-year-old, and this time the penetrative gaze belonged to another. To a Taiwanese candidate—from another time, another place.

You'd started to see through something you weren't meant to see through.

He was in Changhua again, positioned in the dense crowd of supporters, waiting for the candidate to reach the optimal position before signaling the munitions tech to detonate the explosive device.

Such neutral diction for an act of carnage. Perhaps it was what enabled them to do what they did.

Wai-Chan Leung was smaller than he had expected, slender in build and rather short. Yet to the crowd there was nothing diminutive about his stature and, as he started to speak, Tarquin, too, could not longer experience him as small.

"My friends," the politician began. He had a wireless lavalier microphone clipped to his lapel and walked freely, not reading from a printed speech. "May I call you my friends? I think I may. And my greatest hope is that you may call *me* your friend. For too many years, in the Republic of China, our leaders have not truly been our friends. They have been the friends of foreign capital, perhaps. The friends of wealthy dynasts. The friends of other rulers. The friends of the International Monetary Fund. But I do not feel that they have always been *your* friends."

He paused as a round of applause momentarily interrupted his words. "You know the old Chinese story about the three abstemious fellows walking past the wine house. The first one says, 'I'm so sensitive, if I have just one glass of wine, my face turns red and I pass out.' The second one says, 'That's nothing. If I even smell wine, I turn red and stagger about until I collapse.' And the third one says, 'As for me, if I even *see* someone who has smelled wine . . .'" The crowded responded to the familiar anecdote with appreciative chuckles. "In an era of globalization, there are some countries that are more vulnerable than others. Taiwan is that third man. When there is capital flight, when the American dollar spirals up or down, when we witness such things happening elsewhere in the world, our economic and our political systems grow red-faced and begin to stagger." He paused and moved toward the podium.

Tarquin—he *was* Tarquin now—watched him intently, mesmerized. Nothing about the human being twenty yards in front of him matched the Stab dossier given to him and his team. Tarquin had no facts on his side, merely intuition, but for him the intuition had the force of truth. The dossier described someone who was furled with cunning and calculation, prone to vengeful, deadly wrath, hollowed out with cynicism and resentments. Someone whose public display of compassion was a disingenuous performance. Tarquin detected none of these traits: not a trace of artifice or cynicism, not a flicker of the deceiver's self-consciousness. The man who was speaking took satisfaction in his eloquence, but he also believed what he was saying—in its import, in its urgency.

You'd started to see through something you weren't meant to see through.

"They call Taiwan the little tiger," Wai-Chan Leung was saying, in an almost prayerful voice. "What worries me is not that we are little. What worries me is that tigers are an endangered species." He paused once more. "Self-sufficiency is a fine ideal. But is it a realistic ideal? We need both things—we need ideals, and we need realism. Some people will tell you that you must choose between them. Yet they are the same people who insist that you can enjoy democracy so long as you let them tell you what to do. Do you know who they remind me of? Recall the man, of ancient times, who set up shop in a village selling both a spear he said would penetrate anything and a shield he claimed nothing could penetrate."

A rumble of applause and laughter.

"The people of Taiwan—*all* the Chinese people—have a wonderful future ahead of them, if they choose it. A future that we ourselves will create. So let us choose wisely. The mainland is changing. Shall we alone stand still?" He was now just a foot or two from the dark-stained wooden podium. A foot or two from death, and Tarquin felt his heart speeding. Every nerve in his body told him that the operation was *wrong*. Wrongly conceived. Wrongly initiated. Wrongly targeted. Wai-Chan Leung was not their enemy.

The candidate held his forearms before him, at right angles to his body, his hands forming fists. He moved them together, knuckles pressing against knuckles. "Do you see? Simply to *oppose*—like this—leads to immobility. Paralysis. Should this really be our relation to our cousins across the strait?" Now he interlaced the fingers of both hands, illustrating his vision of how sovereignty might coexist with regional integration. "In cooperation—in togetherness—we can find our strength. In integration, we can regain our integrity."

Tarquin's earbud crackled: "I don't have your sight line, but seems to me that the target's in position, no? Awaiting your signal."

Tarquin did not speak. It was time to activate the device, to bring the young man's role in the world to an end—but Tarquin's every instinct fought against it. He was in a condition of total awareness, standing in a crowd of thousands of Taiwanese citizens, wearing polo shirts or button-down shirts, invariably with a white T-shirt beneath, in the national manner. If he saw the faintest clue that the dossier was correct . . . But nothing.

The cricket-like noise in the earbud: "Tarquin, you dozing? Homeroom period's over. I'm going to click—"

"No," Tarquin whispered into the fiber-optic mike concealed in his collar. *"Don't do it."*

But the ordnance tech was impatient, fed up, and he would not be deterred. When the tech replied, Tarquin could hear the jaundiced cynicism of a man who had been in the field a few years too long: *"One for the money, two for the show, three to get ready, now go, cat, go. . . ."*

The explosion, when it came, was far softer than Tarquin had been expecting. It was the sound of a paper bag that a child had inflated with air and eagerly popped. The inner sides of the podium had been reinforced with steel in order to minimize collateral injuries, and the cladding helped both to muffle the sound and to focus the force of the explosion toward the figure standing behind it.

As if in slow motion, Tarquin watched Wai-Chan Leung, the great hope of so many Taiwanese—reform-minded urbanites and peasant farmers, college students and shopkeepers—stiffen abruptly and then topple forward on the dais, his body outlined with the spray of his own viscera. The blackened wreckage of the podium now lay in a heap to his left, a small wisp of smoke rising from it.

For a few moments, the man's prone body was still. And then Tarquin could see him lifting his head from the floor and looking at the crowd before him. What happened next transfixed Tarquin and changed him: the eyes of the dying man, in his agonized final throes, came to rest on Tarquin's.

It was a warm, humid day in subtropical Taiwan, and Tarquin's skin felt arid and chilled; he somehow knew that every moment of what he saw would be forever etched in his memory and in his dreams.

He had come to Changhua to kill a man, and the man had duly been killed. A man who, through the intensity of his gaze, was, in a spell of eerie intimacy, *sharing* with Tarquin the remaining moments of his life.

Even now, the dying man's face was devoid of hatred or anger. There was bewilderment in it, and sadness. It was the face of a man suffused with gentle idealism. A man who knew he was dying and wondered why.

As Tarquin, too, now wondered why.

The crowd was roaring, wailing, screaming, and, amid it all, he somehow made out the sound of a bird. He wrenched his eyes from the human destruction before him toward a palm tree, where an oriole was trilling loudly. Ceaselessly.

Across the earth, across the years, Ambler now stirred in his bed, suddenly conscious of the stale motel air. He opened his eyes: the trilling continued.

The Nokia he had taken from the stalker in the Sourlands.

He pressed the ON button and brought it to his ear. "Yes?"

"Tarquin," a hearty voice brayed.

"Who is this?" said Ambler, suddenly wary. A cold fear washed over him.

"I'm Osiris's controller," said the hearty voice.

"That's not much of a recommendation," Ambler replied.

"You're telling me. We've been terribly concerned about the security breach."

"Someone opens your mail, that's a breach. Somebody shoots your operatives dead, that's something a little more serious."

"Damn straight. And we've got some ideas about what happened. Point being, we need you, and we need you now."

"I don't know who the hell you are," Ambler said. "You say Osiris worked for you. For all I know, the guy who works for you is the one who killed him."

"Tarquin, listen to me. Osiris was an extraordinary asset. I mourn his loss—we all do."

"And you expect me to take your word for it."

"Yes, I do," the man said. "I know your abilities."

Ambler paused. Like Arkady, like Osiris, the man had confidence in Ambler's ability to detect deception. Honesty was no guarantee of ultimate truth, he reminded himself. The man himself could be deceived. But Tarquin—Ambler—had no choice but to play along. The further he could burrow into the organization, the greater his chance of reaching the truth about what had happened to him—and who he truly was.

A thought nagged at him. During his career Ambler had sometimes been involved in what was known as a sequence operation: one piece of information leading to another, each more critical than the one before, designed to draw in and ensnare an adversary. Every sequence operation, he knew, depended on the utmost air of credibility; the more skilled the adversary, the higher the level of credibility required. The more sophisticated subjects, however, were wary; they would employ blind intermediaries, equipping them with questions that had to be answered on the spot. The answers did not have to be faultless—the subject of the operation might be suspicious if they were—but they had to pass a gut check; a single misstep, and the game was blown.

The wiliest subjects of all, however, would set about *reversing* the sequence operation, like a tail wagging the dog. Decoys would be programmed with information specially crafted to tantalize U.S. intelligence; the sequence operation would work, but backward. A newfound zeal for an unexpected windfall would obscure original objectives; the hunter would become the quarry.

What Ambler could not determine was whether he was, in fact, being ensnared within a sequence operation and, if so, whether he would be able to exploit it for his own ends. There was no more dangerous game. Yet what was his alternative?

"All right," Ambler said. "I'm listening."

"We're going to meet tomorrow in Montreal," the man said. "Use whatever ID you've got—the one Osiris gave you should work fine. But your choice." The man went on to give him more detailed instructions: he was to fly to Montréal Dorval that very morning.

Shortly before he set out, the phone rang in his motel room: Laurel. She sounded calmer, more whole, and yet there was concern in her voice—concern for *him,* not for herself. He explained quickly that he had an appointment to keep, that he had received a call from Osiris's controller.

"I don't want you going," she said, and he could hear both her fear and her determination.

"You're afraid for me. I'm afraid, too. But I'm more afraid *not* to go." He paused. "I'm like a fisherman in a yawl, with something tugging on the line. A sailfish? A great white shark? I don't know, can't know, and I don't dare let go."

There was a long pause before she spoke again. "Even if it sinks your boat?"

"Can't let go," Ambler said. "Even if."

Discovery Bay, New Territories

The luxurious Hong Kong villa had twelve rooms, all beautifully appointed in a manner consistent with its 1920s construction—much fine French furniture of giltwood and damask; walls upholstered with shot silk—but its true glory was its flower-decked terrace, with its view of the calm waters of Discovery Bay. Especially now, as the waters shimmered with the rosy sun of the early evening. On one end of the terrace, two diners sat at a table, its white linen cloth covered with a dozen dishes, rare delicacies prepared by expert hands. As the aromas mingled in the faint breeze, a silver-haired American with a prominent forehead inhaled and reflected that in previous centuries such a banquet would be available to few outside China's royal courts.

Ashton Palmer sampled a dish made from hatchlings of the mountain bulbul; the bones of the tiny songbird were as undeveloped as those of a sardine, providing only a pleasing texture. As with the ortolan dish perfected by Escoffier—another tiny songbird, which French gourmands knew to hold by the beak and eat whole, behind a napkin—one ate the bulbul hatchling in a single bite, crunching on its near-embryonic bones, relishing the slight resistance as one did the yielding exoskeleton of a soft-shelled crab. It was a dish whose Mandarin name was *chao niao ge*—literally, stir-fried birdsong.

"Extraordinary, don't you agree," Palmer said to his only dining companion, a Chinese man with broad, weathered features and hard, gimlet eyes.

The man, a longtime general of the People's Liberation Army, smiled, his leathery skin forming grooved striations from cheek to mouth. "Extraordinary," the man agreed. "But from you, one has grown to expect nothing less."

"You are too kind," Palmer said, noting the uncomprehending faces of the serving staff. For Palmer was speaking to General Lam in neither Mandarin nor Cantonese but in the dialect of Hakka spoken in the general's native village. "Still, I know that you, like me, appreciate attention to details. This dish, *chao niao ge,* was last served, so far as anyone knows, in the final decades of the Qing dynasty. I fear

that your friends in Wanshoulu"—he referred to a heavily guarded
suburb of Beijing where many of China's top officials made their
homes—"or Zhongnanhai would find it *decadent*."

"They prefer Burger King," General Lam grunted. "Pepsi-Cola
served in silver goblets."

"Obscene," the American scholar said. "But all too true."

"Not that I have been spending so much time at Zhongnanhai,"
the general said.

"If Liu Ang had his way, all the warriors would be exiled to the
provinces. He regards the PLA as an enemy, and so has turned it into
one. But then, as Chinese history shows, in exile lies opportunity."

"That has been the case for you," the general said.

Palmer smiled but did not deny it. His career trajectory was not
one he would have chosen when he had started out in life, but then
the mistake would have been his. When he was still a young Ph.D. in
the State Department's Policy Planning Staff, the smart money had
him pegged as the next Henry Kissinger—and the most promising
policy intellectual of his generation. But, as it emerged, he had a fatal
flaw for a career in Foggy Bottom: he had, he believed, a zeal for the
truth. With startling abruptness, the lionized wunderkind came to be
the shunned enfant terrible. Thus had the mediocrities upheld their
rule, expelling the one who threatened their comfortable assumptions. In some ways, Palmer reflected, his own exile had indeed been
the best thing that ever happened to him. The rise-and-fall story
about him that ran in *The New Republic* asserted that, having been
drummed out of the corridors of power, he had "retreated" to the
groves of academe. If so, it was a strategic retreat: a regrouping as
much as anything. For his disciples—Palmerites, in his enemies'
sneering term—gradually took policy positions in the Defense Department and the State Department, including the Foreign Service,
as well as the more connected Washington-based think tanks. He
had drilled into them hard lessons of discretion, and the lessons were

learned. His protégés were now in the most sensitive of positions. As years passed by, their guru, retired like a Cincinnatus on the Charles, had been patiently biding his time.

Now, however, he was counting the days.

"As for the Zhongnanhai," Palmer said, "I am pleased that we still share the same perspective on these matters."

The general touched one cheek and then another as he intoned a Hakka idiom: "Right eye, left eye." It meant that two people were as close in their views as were a man's two eyes.

"Right eye, left eye," Palmer echoed in a murmur. "Of course, to *see* is one thing. To *act* is another."

"Very true."

"You have not developed second thoughts," Palmer said quickly, alert to any sign of faltering resolve.

The general responded with a Hakka proverb. "The wind does not move the mountain."

"I am pleased to hear you say so," Palmer replied. "For what lies ahead will test everyone's resolve. There *will* be winds, and they will be of gale force."

"What is to be done," the general said, "is what *must* be done."

"Sometimes great disruption is necessary," Palmer said, "to ensure a greater stability."

"Exactly so." The general raised the well-spiced bulbul hatchling to his lips. His eyes narrowed as he savored its crispy perfection.

"One must fell a tree to heat the rice pot," Palmer said: another Hakka saying.

The general was no longer surprised at the professor's intimate knowledge of his native region. "This is no ordinary tree, the one to be felled."

"Nor an ordinary rice pot," said the scholar. "Your people know their roles. They must know when to act, and do so unfailingly."

"Certainly," General Lam said.

But the silver-haired scholar's gaze was unwavering. *"Six days remain,"* he said, with understated emphasis. "Everyone must play his part to perfection."

"Without fail," the general said, his weathered face tightening in resolve. "After all, the course of history is at stake."

"And, we can agree, the course of history is far too important a thing to be left to chance."

The general nodded gravely and raised his finger again. "Right eye, left eye," he said quietly.

CHAPTER TWELVE

Montreal

The man on the cell phone told Ambler to be at the northwestern corner of Dorchester Square at 11:00 A.M. Arriving early, Ambler took a cab to the corner of rue Cypress and rue Stanley, a block away, and did reconnaissance. The Sun Life Building on Dorchester, a beaux arts behemoth, had once been the largest building in the entire British empire. Now it was dwarfed by modern skyscrapers, many of which were clustered around Dorchester Square. Indeed, that was why Dorchester Square made Ambler nervous; it was overlooked by too many buildings.

He was carrying shopping bags from Place Montreal Trust, had a camera around his shoulder—and looked, he hoped, like just another tourist. After loitering in the side streets, he satisfied himself that he saw nobody suspicious in Dorchester Square proper, and he ventured into it. The square's walkways were perfectly cleared of snow—several straight paths intersecting with a central circle, where a statue of one Sir John A. Macdonald, the country's first prime minister, looked out. Another monument honored Canada's role in the Boer War, and not far from it was a Catholic graveyard, for victims of some early-nineteenth-century cholera epidemic. The stones were weathered, their lichen-darkened hues set off by the white snow. Towering over it all was a steel-and-slate erection of the Imperial Bank. In front of the Dominion Square Building, a massive structure in the Renaissance revival style, a red bus marked LE TRAM DU MONTREAL had come to a stop.

However much he reconnoitered, it was clear, the critical elements could change at any moment. Was that why Osiris's controller had chosen it? Peering through the camera lens, Ambler scanned the hundreds of windows visible from the various office towers. Most were designed not to open; those that could open were closed, given the weather. Though he had dressed warmly, the temperature was in the lower twenties, and his ears were beginning to freeze. He heard footsteps coming toward him, purposeful ones, and whipped around.

"Excuse me, mister."

Ambler saw an elderly couple dressed in bright down-filled jackets, their white hair tousled by the wind.

"Yes?" Ambler replied, trying to keep his voice bland, incurious.

"Would you mind taking a picture of us?" The man handed him a yellow disposable camera, the sort sold at any drugstore. "With Sir John Macdonald in the background, OK?"

"All right," Ambler said, embarrassed by his suspicion. "You American?"

"From Sacramento. But we were here on our honeymoon. Guess when that was?"

"Can't guess." Ambler tried not to sound distracted.

"Forty years ago!" the wife squealed.

"Well, congratulations," Ambler said, squeezing the button on the top right of the camera. As he stepped forward to frame the picture, he noticed something—a person stepping behind the statue, a bit too quickly, as if he did not want to be seen. Ambler was perplexed; it was an amateur's mistake, and surely he was not dealing with amateurs.

He handed the disposable camera back to the elderly couple and suddenly took a few long strides toward the statue's pediment.

A young man—no, a boy, probably fourteen or fifteen—shrank away.

"Hey," Ambler said, as neutrally as possible.

"Hey," the boy said.

"So what's the deal?"

"I think I screwed up," the boy said, speaking with a slight Québécois accent. He had a pronounced nose that he might one day grow into and short spiky blond hair that was obviously bleached.

"Nothing you can't make right, I bet." Ambler's eyes did not leave the boy's face; he was attuned to every shifting expression.

"You weren't supposed to see me yet. Not until eleven A.M.," the boy said.

"Who has to know?"

The youth brightened. "So you won't tell?"

"Why would I? Don't you think I already know?"

"It's just that your friend told me it was a birthday surprise. Like some sort of treasure hunt, maybe?"

"Tell me what you were supposed to tell me. I'll act surprised. Promise."

"You gotta," the boy said anxiously.

"How much is he paying you? I'll pay you the same."

Now the boy was grinning. "How much is he paying me?" he repeated, stalling.

"Right."

"Forty." The boy was a clumsy liar.

Ambler raised an eyebrow.

"Thirty?"

Ambler maintained a look of skepticism.

"Twenty," the boy finally corrected himself.

Ambler peeled off a twenty and gave it to him. "Now, then, what were the instructions?"

"Instructions were the rendezvous has changed. You're supposed to meet in the Underground City."

"Where?"

"Les promenades de la Cathédrale," the boy said. "But if there's a surprise for you, you got to remember to act surprised."

Someone with a mind for metaphor would find it either apt or ironic that beneath Christ Church Cathedral was a vast upscale shopping mall, the promenades de la Cathédrale. Famously, the cash-strapped

Anglican diocese had bailed itself out by selling the land underneath. *Upon this rock thou shall build a church* had been translated into the language of a commercial era, when a church had to support itself by selling the rock on which it stood.

Ambler had just taken the escalators down to the promenades and was trying to orient himself in the cavernous mall when he felt a pair of hands on his shoulders, spinning him around.

A burly ginger-haired man smiled cheerfully at him. "Face-to-face at last," the man said.

Ambler did a double take. He knew this man—not personally but by reputation. Many people did. His name was Paul Fenton, and his reputation was as murky as his gaze was clear.

Paul Fenton. A prominent American industrialist, who first made his name as the founder of a Texas-based electronics firm with major defense contracts. But his business concerns had expanded a great deal since then, and by the late eighties he had earned notoriety in certain circles for funding right-wing insurgencies and counterinsurgencies around the world. Among the beneficiaries of his patronage were the Contras in El Salvador, Renamo in Mozambique, and Unita in Angola.

To some, he was a patriot, a man whose loyalty was to his country, rather than the almighty dollar. To others, he was a dangerous zealot who played fast and loose with the laws governing the foreign export of munitions, reminiscent of the businessmen who had backed the disastrous Bay of Pigs invasion of the early sixties. That Fenton was a savvy and aggressive entrepreneur was disputed by no one.

"You *are* Tarquin, aren't you?" Fenton asked. He took Ambler's silence for assent and extended a hand. Yet the question had not been rhetorical—there was a measure of uncertainty. *Fenton had not known what he looked like.*

Ambler took Fenton's hand and stepped forward, speaking in a low, harsh voice. "It's idiotic to meet me in public this way. You're too goddamn recognizable."

Fenton just winked. "I find people don't see what they don't expect to see. And I'm not exactly a Hollywood celebrity. Besides, sometimes the best place to hide is in a crowd, don't you find?" He took a step back, gestured around him. "Welcome to the world's largest underground pedestrian network." Fenton's voice was a honeyed baritone. His skin was ruddy, weathered, large-pored, yet oddly smooth, possibly the result of dermabrasion. His hairline was recessed into a widow's peak, though the areas of recession were dotted with tiny clumps of hair arranged almost geometrically, like doll hair. A man with a passion for self-improvement, then.

He looked athletic, rugged. He also looked rich. There was a sleekness to him, a warrior who would spend one weekend playing polo in the Argentines, another running Abrams tanks through Chad, and the next getting mineral-salt scrubs at a Parrot Cay spa. Rugged, weathered, but . . . moisturized. The visage of the billionaire tough guy.

"The Underground City," Ambler said. "Perfect place for the underground man."

Fenton, he knew, had not been exaggerating: the so-called Underground City consisted of twenty miles of passageways and included sixteen hundred boutiques, a couple of hundred eateries, dozens of cinemas. Despite the freezing temperatures above, the Underground City was pleasantly warm and brightly lit. He looked around. Long arched skylights, several tiers of escalators, and balconies that overlooked the enormous volume all contributed to a sense of spaciousness. The Underground City linked the upscale shopping galleries of Cours Mont-Royal to the Eaton Centre and extended through the arcades-filled Complexe Desjardines and even to the Palais des Congrès, the hulking convention center that straddled the Ville Marie Expressway like some gargantuan of steel, glass, and concrete.

Ambler realized why Fenton had chosen the venue: it was to provide Ambler himself with reassurance—the risks of violence would seem small in such a public place.

"Tell me something," Ambler went on. "Are you actually here by yourself? A man of your . . . stature?"

"Why don't you tell me?"

Ambler glanced around him, sweeping across dozens of faces. A square-faced man in a drab wax duffle coat, midforties, short hair. Another, twenty feet to his left, looking much less comfortable in much more costly apparel—a double-breasted camel's hair topcoat, the slacks of a dark flannel suit. "I see just two. And one of them's not used to this sort of posting."

Fenton nodded. "Gillespie's basically a secretary. Good with the maître-d's and such." Fenton nodded at the man in the camel's hair topcoat, who nodded back, coloring slightly.

"But you were going to tell me about Osiris. And this doesn't seem the ideal setting for a tête-á-tête."

"I know just the place," Fenton purred, and led Ambler to an extremely exclusive-looking clothing boutique, a little farther down the terrazzo walkway. In the window was a single dress, mainly iridescent purple shot-silk with the seams showing and basting threads visible in sloppy green loops. It looked as if it were a garment that was still being made, the sort of thing that tailors sometimes display in their shops, but Ambler realized it was the finished garment: some high-style "deconstructed" look that no doubt wowed the fashion press when worn by a slinkily anorexic model on a runway. A small sign of etched copper gave its name: SYSTÈME DE LA MODE.

Again, Ambler was impressed with Fenton's choice of venue: this one was cunningly designed to offer both reassurance and privacy. The store, with its intimidating and recherché offerings, was visible to passersby, but not one in a thousand would actually dare to come in.

At the entrance there was the usual antitheft portal, the two plastic-clad towers, though placed a little farther from the door than was usual. A low beep started when Ambler approached.

"Sorry about that," Fenton said. "Probably doesn't like your camera."

Which meant it wasn't an inventory-control portal at all. Ambler removed his camera and stepped through.

"Actually, if you could just stand there for a moment longer," Fenton said apologetically.

Ambler did so. The door sucked closed behind him.

"You're good to go," the burly industrialist said. "Welcome to my humble little shop. You might not think it's my speed, but if you were a fashionista you'd be damned impressed. There isn't a single price tag in this place that doesn't have a comma."

"Get a lot of customers?"

"Nary a one," Fenton said, his cheeks broadening in a moisturized smile. "We're almost never open. And when we are, I've got the world's scariest shopgirl—Brigitte's her name—and she specializes in making people feel like they've got shit on their shoes. She's out to lunch at the moment, and I'm sorry you won't get to meet her. Because she's something, Brigitte is. She doesn't exactly tell folks that they're not worthy to be shopping here, but they get the message."

"I get the picture. If you're trying to set up a safe house, I guess it's more discreet than a big sign saying KEEP OUT! And let me guess— the door tower isn't really for inventory control. It's bug repellent."

"Total wide spectrum. Real powerful. We test it all the time— never been able to sneak a listening device through it. More pleasant than having to strip people naked and do a cavity search. More effective, too. Not that it would even matter if they did. Go check out the window glass."

Ambler walked over to the storefront glass; peering closely, he made out a fine-mesh metal screen within the glazing. It looked ornamental; it was in fact functional. "This whole place is a screen room," he marveled. A screen room was a space enclosed by a grounded ferromagnetic mesh or gauze; the shielding blocked the transmission of any radiofrequency signals.

"You got it. See that shiny back wall? Twelve layers of lacquer—twelve—with each layer polished before the next layer is applied, all done by real artisans. And underneath those twelve layers? Plaster and metal gauze."

"You're a careful man."

"Which is why we're meeting face-to-face. You talk to someone on the phone, you can never know whether you're just talking to him, or to him and his tape recorder, or to him and whoever might have a digital intercept. I'm a big believer in compartmentalization, see. Do whatever I can to keep the information partitions in place, like the trays of a TV dinner." The mogul chuckled contentedly. It was important to him that Ambler be impressed with his precautions.

Keep him on the defensive. "In that case, how do you explain what happened to Osiris?" Anger flared in Ambler's voice.

Fenton's ruddy face paled a little. "I guess I was hoping we wouldn't focus on that." Ambler saw a salesman put off his stride—but what was he selling? "Listen, what happened to Osiris was a goddamn *tragedy*. I've got a crack team looking into it, and though we don't have answers yet, we'll have them soon. The man was a prodigy, one of the most remarkable operatives I've had the privilege of knowing."

"Save your eulogies for the funeral," Ambler sneered.

"And he was a big-time admirer of yours—you should know that. Soon as it went on the squawk that Tarquin was out and about, Osiris was the first one who said I needed to reach out and bring you in. He knew that where I'm concerned, 'on the loose' just means 'on the market.'"

Ariadne's thread—find out where it leads.

"You seem to know a lot about me," Ambler said, the comment a prod. Exactly what *did* Paul Fenton know?

"Everything and nothing, it seems. Tarquin's the only name anybody has for you. You're exactly six feet tall, plus whatever your shoe heels add. Weight a hundred and ninety pounds. Age forty. Brown hair, blue eyes." He smiled. "But those are just facts. Data. Neither you nor I is likely to be overimpressed with data."

Keep him talking. Ambler thought about the long afternoons he used to spend fishing—the alternating rhythms of letting out the line and reeling it in, tiring the big fish by letting it swim against the drag. "You're too modest." Ambler prodded further. "I think you know a lot more than you're saying."

"I've heard tales from the field, all right."

"From Osiris."

"Others, too. I got a lot of contacts. You'll learn that about me. Not many people I don't know—among people who count, I mean." Fenton paused. "Obviously you had some powerful enemies—and some powerful friends. I'd like to be one of them." Fenton grinned again, shaking his head. "You impress the hell out of me, and not a lot of people do. In my book, you're a goddamn wizard. A magician. *Poof*—the elephant vanishes from the stage. *Poof*—the magician's gone, cape and wand and everything. How the hell did you manage that?"

Ambler sat down on a brushed-steel stool, studying the industrialist's smooth, ruddy face. *Are you my enemy? Or will you lead me to my enemy?* "How do you mean?" Ambler kept his voice low-key, bored.

"Professional secret, huh? They told me that Tarquin was a man of many gifts, but I had no idea. *Incognito ergo sum*, huh? You realize we ran your prints?"

Ambler flashed on the water tumbler that Osiris had given him in the back of the Bentley.

"And?"

"And *nothing*. Nada. Bubkes. Zip. You got yourself deleted from every single database in existence. We ran the standard biometrics—all the usual digital identifiers—and nothing comes up." He broke off, started reciting: " 'As I was going up the stair I met a man who wasn't there. . . .' "

"He wasn't there again today," Ambler put in.

"I wish, I wish he'd come to play!" The ginger-haired man grinned as he misquoted the old nursery rhyme. "It won't surprise you to learn that we've got access to *all* the State Department personnel files. Remember Horus?"

Ambler nodded. Horus was a giant of a man who worked out too much—his arms dangled away from his torso when he walked, ape-like, and his acne-dappled back indicated steroid abuse—but he could be useful for rough stuff in less-than-finely-tuned Stab operations. Ambler had worked with him three or four times. They were not friends, but they got along fine.

"Know his real name?"

"Of course not. Those were the rules. We never bent them."

"I do. Harold Neiderman. Wrestling champ at his high school in South Bend. Did a stint with a SOLIC unit"—special-operations, light-intensity combat—"got married, got a business degree at a two-year school in Florida, got divorced, reenlisted . . . but the details don't matter. Point is, I can go on about Harold Neiderman. Remember Triton?"

Coppery hair, freckles, oddly narrow wrists and ankles, yet remarkably dexterous at silent kills: he was superb at garroting sentries, slicing throats—the kind of measures resorted to where even a silenced firearm would have been too noisy. Ambler nodded.

"Triton would be Ferrell W. Simmons, the *W.* standing for *Wyeth.* Army brat, spent most of his early years in Wiesbaden, and most of his teens at the Lawton public high school, near Fort Sill, Oklahoma. This personnel info is all deep-down hidden stuff, by the way, not what you'd get from a casual trawl. But I've got insider privileges. I guess that's clear enough. So it should be easy for me to get the four-one-one on Tarquin, right? But I got nada. Because you're a magician." The tone of wonderment in his voice was genuine. "Which, of course, makes you all the more valuable as an operative. If you're captured—not that you would be, but if it happened—you'd be nothing more than a cipher. A smoke ring. A floater in your eye. Blink and it's gone. Voilà—the Man Who Wasn't There. Absolutely nothing would connect you to anyone else. Genius!"

Ambler paused; he would not disabuse Fenton. Fenton himself was no small game. *I got a lot of contacts:* an understatement if anything.

"Of course, a good magician can make things reappear, too," Ambler said carefully. He turned and peered outside: shoppers tramping past, soundlessly, unseeing. He could *use* Fenton—but had others used him, too? If members of the retrieval team had somehow learned of the meeting . . . but so far there was no sign of it.

"And you *have*—you're here, aren't you? But do you have any idea what you're worth to me? According to your former colleagues, you're the closest thing they've ever met to a mind reader. And you officially don't exist!"

"So that's why I feel so empty inside," said Ambler dryly.

"I'm all about getting the best," Fenton said. "I don't know just what you did to get yourself in trouble. Don't know what kind of jam you were in. Don't much care, either."

"I find that hard to believe." Yet Ambler did believe it.

"You see, Tarquin, I like to surround myself with people who are truly, truly excellent at whatever they do. And you, my friend, are off the charts. I don't know how you managed to do what you did, but you are a man after my own heart."

"You think I'm a rule breaker."

"I *know* you are. Greatness consists in knowing when to break the rules. And knowing how."

"Sounds like you've been putting together the Dirty Dozen."

"We're bigger than that. You've heard of the Strategic Services Group?"

Ambler nodded. *Ariadne's thread—find where it leads.* Alongside McKinsey, Bain, KPMG, Accenture, and dozens of others, it was one of those management-consulting firms that seemed to offer spurious solutions to spurious problems. He could remember the occasional billboard stationed in the major airports. The initials were big: *SSG*, the words *Strategic Services Group* much smaller beneath them. Emblazoned over a scene of perplexed-looking business executives was the slogan IT'S NO USE HAVING THE RIGHT ANSWERS IF YOU AREN'T ASKING THE RIGHT QUESTIONS.

"Glad to hear it, because I'm thinking it's your future."

"I'm not exactly the MBA type."

"I'm not going to beat around the bush with you. Here we are, in a specially soundproofed space, privacy guaranteed by Faraday shielding and wide-frequency RF intercepts. Could not be more private if we were on the moon."

"And the atmosphere's better."

Fenton nodded impatiently. "SSG is kind of like this place. It provides one kind of service publicly, but that isn't why it exists. Maybe Osiris started to explain. See, what I am is the showrunner. That's what they call me."

"Then what's the show?"

"An international management-consulting firm—what's that, really? A bunch of people in suits and ties who travel all around the world, racking up the frequent-flier miles. Every major airport in the world is flooded with these guys. Any customs or border control official can recognize a business consultant a mile away: they're pros, look like people who have learned how to live on airplanes. But you know how the ads talk about the 'SSG difference'?"

" 'Asking the right questions, not just providing the right answers,' " Ambler recited the advertising slogan.

"The real difference, though, is that our core team is actually composed of former covert operatives. And not the bottom-of-the-barrel types, either. I've been creaming off the best. I've hired the Stab boys en masse."

"So it's like a retirement perk?" The provocation was deliberate.

"They're not retired, Tarquin," the ginger-haired man replied.

"They're doing what they used to do. *Better.* Difference is, now they're free to do their jobs—their *real* jobs."

"Which is working for you."

"Which is working for freedom. For truth, justice, and the goddamn American way."

"Just checking," Ambler interjected.

"But *really* working. Not filling out paperwork in triplicate and falling on their sword every time they stub the toe of a goddamn foreign national—the way the Washington bureaucrats would have it. When things need to get rough, they get rough. No apologies required. You got a problem with that?"

"Why would I?" *Let the line out.*

"I never met an operative who did," Fenton said. "My point is, I'm a true-blue patriot. But what's always driven me crazy is the way we've let ourselves get shackled by regulation and federal oversight and UN accords and international treaties and what have you. The cautiousness, the timidity, of U.S. covert ops is *obscene.* A form of treason, almost. Our people are the best in the business—then the bureaucrats put leg irons on them! My thing is, I'm taking those leg irons *off;* now let's see what you can do."

Reel it in. "Which should make you an enemy of the very government you're trying to protect." Ambler's words were pointed, his voice level.

"You asking whether I'm stepping on government toes?" Fenton raised his eyebrows, his weathered forehead sporting four amazingly regular creases, as straight as the creases on a boxed shirt just back from the laundry. "The answer is yes and no. Plenty of pencil-necks disapprove, no doubt about it. But there are good men and women in Washington, too. The people who really count, right?"

"The people who count on you."

"You got it." Fenton glanced at his watch. He had been worried about the time, had assured himself that he remained on schedule. But *what* schedule? "Listen, there's a well-established model for this sort of relationship. I think you know how crucial private military firms—PMFs—have been over the past couple of decades."

"For auxiliary purposes, backup stuff, sure," Ambler started.

"Balls!" Fenton slapped the incongruously delicate table at the side of his chair. "Not sure how long you've been away, but it sounds like you haven't kept up. Because it's a brave new world out there. Things got global when Defense Service Limited—Brits, you know, mostly SAS—merged with Armor Holdings, which was an American company. They were guarding embassies, mines, and oil installations in southern Africa, doing Special Forces training in Indonesia, Jordan, the Philippines. Then it acquires Intersec and Falconstar. It acquires DSL, moves into risk-management services big-time, everything from mine clearance to intelligence. Then Armor buys the Russian firm Alpha."

Alpha, Ambler knew, was staffed by former members of an elite Soviet division, a Russian counterpart to the U.S. Delta Force. "The Spetsnaz of Spetsnaz," Ambler said.

Fenton nodded. "They buy Defense Systems Colombia, mostly ex–military people from South America. Pretty soon, they're one of the fastest-growing companies around. Then you've got Group 4 Flack, a Danish corporation, which owns Wackenhut. You've got Levdan and Vinnell. And, in the L-3 Communications group, you've got MPRI, which gave me my original inspiration. Military Professional Resources, Incorporated—just that one firm, based in Virginia—is what kept peace and stability in Bosnia. You think the blue-helmets were doing it? Nope, it was MPRI. One day the Department of Defense's Special Advisor to the Bosnian-Croat Federation retires. Next day he's working the Balkans again—but for MPRI. It's 1995, and all of a sudden the Croats are kicking Serbian butt up and down the block. How's that happen? How did this ragtag bunch of incompetents suddenly learn how to execute a textbook-perfect series of assaults against Serbian troop positions? Can you spell MPRI? That's what drove the Serbs to the bargaining table, as much as the NATO air raids. It isn't just about privatizing the war, it's about privatizing the peace. Men of the private sector working for the public good."

"I think we used to call 'em 'mercenaries.' "

"So what's new? Hell, when Ramses II was fighting the Hittites, he brought in special military advisors from the Numidians. Or what about Xenophon's Ten Thousand? Basically, a bunch of retired Greek warriors who hired themselves out to kick Persian ass. Even the Peloponnesian War involved a lot of subcontracting to the Phoenicians."

"You're telling me it was *outsourced*?"

"You'll forgive an old war buff for going on about these things. But how can you believe in the genius of the marketplace *and* the importance of security without wanting to put the two things together?"

Ambler shrugged. "I get the demand. What about the supply?" Again, his eyes swept along the terrazzo walkway outside the boutique, then back to the industrialist in front of him. Why was Fenton looking so intently at his watch?

"Ever wonder what happened to the 'peace deficit'? The American military has a third as many soldiers as it had during the height of the Cold War. We're talking about vast demobilization. Elsewhere, too—South Africa, Britain, especially. Whole regiments got cashiered out. What's left? The UN? The UN's a joke. It's like the medieval pope: lots of papal writs, not a whole lot of bayonets."

"So we get an army of exes."

"It's more complicated than that, boyo. I'm not in the military sector anymore—that marketplace got too crowded for my taste. Paul Fenton likes to feel he's making a unique contribution."

"And you're doing that now?"

"Well sure. Because SSG isn't competing with the PMFs. They do overt. We do *covert*. That's the beauty part, see? Ops, not combat. What we're up to is something even more important. We're about covert operations. Think of us as Consular Operations, Incorporated."

"Spies for hire."

"We're doing God's work, Tarquin. We're making the U.S. of A. as strong as she ought to be."

"So you are and aren't part of the U.S. government."

"We can do what the U.S. can't." Fenton's eyes sparkled. At first, those eyes seemed to be no particular color; peering more closely, Ambler noticed that one eye was gray and the other green. "Oh sure, plenty of bureaucrats in Fort Meade and Langley, not to mention Foggy Bottom, are happy to denounce me, like I say. But deep down they're *glad* I do what I do."

"With some, I'd imagine, it's not very deep down at all. You must have close ties with some pretty high-ranking officers." *High-ranking officers: including those who know what was done to me—and why.*

"Absolutely. Officers that actively enlist our services. It's a matter of outsourcing covert ops to Strategic Services."

"All the flavor, none of the calories," Ambler said, forcing down a gorge of revulsion. Zealots like Paul Fenton were all the more dangerous because they viewed themselves in a heroic light. Even as their lofty rhetoric could justify every kind of inhumanity, they quickly lost the ability to distinguish between self-interest and the Great Cause to which they devoted themselves. They suckled their corporate entities on public funds while sermonizing about the virtues of private enterprise. True believers like Fenton placed themselves above the laws of men, above justice itself—which made them a threat to the very security they prized.

"Everybody knows that the enemies of freedom—including the free market—are the enemies of Paul Fenton." The industrialist looked grave for a moment. "A lot of our operations may seem small. But we're after bigger game now." There was excitement in Fenton's voice. "Now we've been given a truly major commission."

"Is that so?" Ambler had to play Fenton carefully: he could not appear overly interested, but he could not be too cool, either. A studied dispassion was what he was aiming for. Let the fish swim against the drag.

"Which is why we need you."

"What have you heard about me?" Ambler asked him, intently studying his face.

"Lots. Even heard some people think you're a dangerous lunatic," Fenton replied candidly.

"Then why would you want anything to do with me?"

"Maybe because the government's idea of a dangerous lunatic isn't necessarily mine. Or maybe because only a dangerous lunatic would take on the assignment I got for you. And only a dangerous lunatic with your skill set has a chance of completing it." Fenton stopped. "So where do I stand with you? Can we do business? Can we help fix this rattletrap world together? What do you make of my enterprise? Be honest!"

Ariadne's thread—where would it lead?

"Before we met," Ambler said, fingering one of the dresses on a rack, "I had no idea what could be done with pleated voile."

Fenton's laughter was nasal and high-pitched, almost a cackle. Then he stared at Ambler for a long moment.

"Tarquin, I'd like you to come with me now. Would you do that? I got something to show you."

"Glad to hear it," Ambler said, looking around the icy chic of the brushed-steel and gray-carpeted boutique. "Because there's nothing here in my size."

The two men left the boutique and reentered the bustling, cavernous world of the Underground City. As they made their way down a triple-tiered bank of escalators, Ambler thought about Fenton's curious combination of zeal, craft, and openness. Few people of his wealth walked around without a sizable entourage; Fenton seemed to pride himself on his self-reliance. It was the same odd mixture of rugged individualism and cosseted self-regard he had displayed in other ways. Maybe it was what made him a mogul in the first place.

An enormous poster for the Gap hung below the light well over-head. Everywhere one looked there were kiosks and shops and lights and shoppers. Through the throngs, Fenton and Ambler pushed through several blocks' worth of passageways. Finally, they reached the exit for the Palais des Congrès at the Ville Marie Expressway. When they rode up a couple of flights of escalators and reached the surface, it was as if they had returned to a cold and icy planet. The Palais des Congrès convention center was itself a chilly structure, a leviathan of glass and steel and concrete.

Fenton brought Ambler to the sidewalk in front of it. Ambler could see that there were extensive security cordons around the building.

"What's going on?"

"A meeting of the G7," Fenton said. "G7 plus one, really. Trade ministers from all over. The United States, Canada, France, Britain, Italy, Germany, and Japan, plus special guests. A big deal. They never announce the location, to head off antiglobalization protesters. But it's never exactly a big secret, either."

"I don't recall having been invited."

"You're with me," Fenton said, twinkling. "Come along. It's going to be something special to watch."

High up in the office tower attached to the glass-sheathed Complexe Guy-Favreau, Joe Li adjusted his power binoculars. He had received an intelligence warning that his quarry might try to penetrate the international meeting. Next to him was a Chinese sniper rifle, a Type 95 7.62mm rifle. It had been carefully zeroed that very morning. At the moment, the man known as Tarquin was visible, exposed; save for the irregularly gusting wind, Joe Li had a reasonably good shot.

But who was Tarquin with? Joe Li adjusted his binoculars as he brought into focus the ruddy-faced, powerfully built man who was Tarquin's companion.

Act or analyze? It was the ancient dilemma: one could easily perish, or allow others to perish, while analyzing the options. Yet in this case, Joe Li wondered whether further intelligence would be required before taking further action. It went against the fiber of his being, the grain of his consciousness: he had been built—selected and trained—to *act*. A human weapon, Comrade Chao had once called him. Yet effective action was never impetuous; timing was crucial, and so was the ability to adapt and respond to changing circumstances.

He removed his finger from within the trigger guard of the rifle and picked up a digital camera, fine-tuning its focus until the image of the ruddy-faced man was centered and sharp. He would send in the image for analysis.

Joe Li seldom experienced fear, but he did feel a faint ping of concern. Liu Ang's enemies, it seemed reasonable to worry, might have found themselves a formidable new asset.

He glanced again at the rifle, his misgivings growing by the second. Analyze—or act?

CHAPTER THIRTEEN

As Ambler followed Fenton into the conference center, the man's entire frame seemed to be vibrating with anticipation.

The hall of the Palais was a several-story atrium of mitred glass above hexagonal granite tile, and the lobby and three balconies overhead were bathed in the dull silver glow of the winter sky. A sign—charmingly, the old-fashioned kind of Peg-Board, white letters laboriously affixed onto the slotted black plastic—indicated which spaces had been allocated for the various meetings.

"Any moment now," Fenton murmured, "you're going to see proof of what our operation can do."

From the adjoining hall Ambler heard the rustle and rumble of rejoined conversation—the sound of a meeting that was breaking up. People were standing up; chairs were moved slightly, some attendees rushing forward to introduce or reintroduce themselves to others. Some went for coffee or headed outside for a smoke.

"What time do you make it, Tarquin?"

"Eleven fifty-nine." A beat. "Twelve noon."

Abruptly, loud shrieks echoed through the granite-and-glass atrium. The conversational rumble ceased at once, replaced by a tattoo of terror: *Oh my God! Oh my God! Oh my God!* The screams and keening swelled. Fenton stood by a carpeted staircase, an arm hooked around Ambler's shoulders.

Black-jacketed security guards started to hustle in, paramedics a few minutes later. Somebody at the meeting had been killed.

Controlling his emotions, Ambler turned to Fenton. "What just went down?"

Fenton spoke briefly into a cell phone, then nodded. "The dead guy's name was Kurt Sollinger," he told Ambler in a low voice. "A Brussels-based European trade negotiator."

"And?"

"According to our intel, he is—was—a real menace. Guy fell in with some Baader-Meinhof remnants when he was in grad school, started living a double life after that. An economist of the first water, and an incredibly engaging fellow—everybody would tell you. Meanwhile he was exploiting his EU position to set up IBCs, international business companies, around the world, laundering money from rogue nations and diverting significant sums to hand-picked terrorist cells. They called him the Paymaster. And what he paid for was bombings and, especially, assassinations."

"But why would you—"

"Today's a special day, did you know that?" Fenton's eyes were hard. "An anniversary, of sorts. Do you recall when the U.S. Deputy Treasury Secretary was murdered?"

Ambler nodded slowly. Several years ago, at a grand São Paolo hotel, the deputy treasury secretary—once the youngest tenured member of the Harvard economics department, and the architect behind two Latin American currency bailouts—had been gunned down before a crowd. He had been among the brightest lights in the American government. Yet the assassin had never been apprehended. Though authorities suspected the involvement of antiglobalization extremists, an extensive international investigation had gone nowhere.

"It happened exactly five years ago today. At *exactly* twelve noon. In a hotel ballroom. In public. His killers were hirelings who prided themselves on their ability to time it with precision, and to carry out the deed brazenly. Kurt Sollinger was the Paymaster. Working through former affiliates of the Rote Armee Fraktion, he paid for the hit. We learned this not long ago. Not the kind of evidence you can use in court, you understand, but the real deal."

"Jesus Christ," Ambler breathed.

"Exactly five years ago today, at twelve noon. Trust me, the message won't be lost on those bastards. We've just sent a signal on their radio frequency. They'll know they've been rumbled, and they'll panic—they'll disperse and try to regroup later. Existing operations will be disrupted. Their existing network of contacts will come under suspicion. And their own paranoia will do them more damage than we'd be able to. Those shrieks, those screams—exactly the same sound track as in São Paolo. Poetic fucking *justice*." Fenton lit up a cigarette.

Ambler swallowed hard. That Fenton was simply hanging around an assassination that he had orchestrated struck him as close to showing off.

Fenton anticipated his thoughts. "You're wondering why I'm here? *Because I can be.*" His gaze was unwavering. "We don't run scared at SSG. I need to impress that on you. Our work may be clandestine, but we're not fucking *outlaws*. We *are* the law."

No doubt that was Fenton's way. The industrialist knew that nobody would ever trace him to the lethal incident just yards away.

"But we've got a much bigger fish for you." Fenton handed him a sheet of paper, an oddly filmy sheet, like a cross between onionskin and old-style thermal fax paper. The scent told Ambler that it was highly combustible security paper, designed to be consumed by flame within a matter of seconds. "Or shark, I should really say."

"This the guy you want me to take out?" Ambler's stomach churned, but he fought to keep his voice even. *Ariadne's thread—find where it leads.*

Fenton nodded gravely.

Ambler read the sheet quickly. The target's name was Benoit Deschesnes. Ambler knew the name. The director-general of the International Atomic Energy. Agency. A very big deal indeed. Other occupational and residential details were provided, along with a description of his daily habits.

"What's the situation with this guy?" Ambler asked, struggling to sound casual.

"Deschesnes used to work on nuclear weaponry for the French government. Now he's been taking advantage of his position as head of the IAEA to transfer nuclear expertise to countries like Iran, Syria, Libya, Algeria, even Sudan. Maybe he thinks a level playing field is only fair. Maybe he wants to make himself a fortune. Doesn't matter. Point is, he's dirty. He's dangerous. And he's got to go." Fenton took another puff on the cigarette. "You've absorbed what's on the data sheet?"

Ambler nodded.

Fenton took the sheet back and touched it with the tip of his cigarette. For a brief moment the sheet blossomed into pink-white flame—it was like a magician conjuring a rose into his palm—and then it all vanished. Ambler looked around; nobody had noticed.

"Remember, Tarquin, we're the good guys," Fenton said. The cold made his breath visible. "You believe me, don't you?"

"I believe *you* believe you," Ambler answered smoothly.

"Trust me, this is going to be the start of something very special. You take care of Benoit, and you'll be the equivalent of a made man. Then we'll talk. Then you go to the head of the class."

Ambler closed his eyes for a moment. His predicament was exquisite. He could alert the government about Deschesnes, but what would be the point? Government officials were the ones who had "outsourced" the task to Fenton in the first place. Besides, his words would carry no credibility. His former bosses believed that Tarquin was insane, and there was no evidence that Harrison Ambler had ever lived. His enemies would not have gone to all the trouble of inducing a psychotic episode like that if they hadn't intended to use it. The recording of Ambler's paranoid ravings would surely have been screened to key members of the intelligence community. Then, too, if Ambler passed on the assignment, Fenton would find somebody else for it.

Suddenly a police officer strode toward them. "You, sir!" the thick-necked uniformed man barked at Fenton.

"Me?"

"You!" The policeman came over with an affronted look. "You think you're above the law? That what you think?"

Fenton looked like a picture of innocence. "I'm sorry?"

The policeman put his face close to Fenton's and curled his lips. "There's no smoking in the conference center. No smoking in any municipal building, by city statute. Don't act like you didn't know. There are signs *everywhere*."

Ambler turned to Fenton, shaking his head. "Man, you are so busted."

A few minutes later, the two walked outside along a cleared bluestone path in front of the conference center. Snow lay heavily on the ground, frosting rows of boxy shrubs to either side of the bluestone.

"So have we got a deal?" Fenton asked.

It was *madness*—there was no sense, no logic, in his joining an enterprise whose basic legitimacy he rejected. Yet to refuse would be like dropping the thread—and that was one thing he could not do. Not while he remained in the labyrinth. To lose the thread was to lose himself.

"You'll pay me in *knowledge,* showrunner," Ambler heard himself say.

Fenton nodded. "It's the usual story, isn't it? Somebody messed with you. You want me to find out who, find out why. Like that, right?"

There's nothing usual about this story, Ambler almost replied. "Like that," Ambler said softly.

The skies had grown darker; it was now the sort of definitive, conclusive gray that made it impossible to think that the sky had ever been or could ever be any other hue.

"With your skill set, you should have no trouble," Fenton said steadfastly. "And if you do—if you're captured?—well, you're the Man Who Wasn't There, aren't you? You officially don't exist! Nobody will be the wiser."

"Sounds like a good deal," Ambler said leadenly. "Unless you *are* the Man Who Wasn't There."

Langley, Virginia

Clay Caston was looking disapprovingly at the oatmeal carpeting in the ADDI's office; there was a coffee stain a few feet from the tan leather sofa. It had been there on his last visit. He suspected it would be there on his next visit. Caleb Norris had no doubt ceased to see it. Many things were like that. One failed to see them not because they were hidden but because one was accustomed to them.

"I think I'm following you so far," Norris was saying. "You find the patient's intake date, and then you do a . . ."

"A variance analysis."

"Right. A variance analysis. You're looking at subtle patterns in expenditures. Like a fiduciary plume around the event. Good thinking." An expectant pause. "So what did you find?"

"Nothing."

"Nothing," Norris repeated, downcast. "Oh well."

"Which I found pretty fascinating."

Norris gave him an uncertain look.

"It's like the dog that didn't bark, Cal. A special low-level operation means a lot of paperwork for authorization, and all sorts of special requisitions, even if it's a few dollars from petty cash. If a junior-grade staffer does anything that involves agency resources, he's filling out requisition forms. Spoors in the forest—a trail. The higher up you go, the less there is of that. Because you've already got the resources at your command. What I'm trying to tell you, Cal, is that the absence of any irregularities at all suggests the presence of a high-level mover. Nobody drives up to Parrish Island and checks himself in. You're bundled in by men in white coats. That means the redeployment of vehicles, the possibility of overtime, and on and on. But when I went looking for the *reverb,* I couldn't find anything."

"How high, do you think?"

"At least an E17 level," Caston said. "Someone your rank, or higher."

"That should narrow things down."

"Oh? Did the government suddenly shrink while I was at the men's room?"

"*Humph.* Reminds me of the way you nabbed that guy from the Directorate of Operations who'd made that secret trip to Algeria. Used a fake passport and everything—covered his tracks perfectly. So far as we knew, he'd spent the week in the Adirondacks. I love the thing that tipped you off: abnormal rate of toilet-paper usage in the men's room outside his office!"

"Please, it wasn't exactly subtle. He was going through a full roll every day."

"Traveler's diarrhea, you figured. Giardiasis—an intestinal bug endemic in Algiers, you said. We got a confession two days later. God, you were on a . . . roll." The hirsute administrator chuckled to himself. "But what about the career coverage? Learn anything more about the escape artist?"

"A thing or two," Caston said.

"Because I'm thinking we've got to figure out a way to lure him in, make approaches."

"That won't be so easy," Caston said. "We're dealing with an unusual customer. I'll tell you one detail I found suggestive. Seems that, in the field, nobody would play cards with the guy."

"He cheated?" Caleb Norris unknotted his tie but left it in place, in the manner of a tabloid newspaper editor. Tendrils of black hair curled over his unbuttoned collar.

Caston shook his head. "You know the German word *Menschenkenner?*"

Norris squinted. "A person knower? Someone who knows a lot of people?"

"Not exactly. A *Menschenkenner* is someone with a knack for figuring people out, for taking their measure."

"He can read people, then."

"Like a book. You wouldn't want to get near this guy when you've got something to hide."

"A walking lie detector. I'd like to get me some of that."

"The people I spoke to doubt Tarquin himself knows how he does it. But, no surprise, they've done research in the area."

"And?" Norris plopped himself down on the sofa.

"There are a lot of variables at play. But the research indicates that people like Tarquin are particularly attuned to things like 'microexpressions'—facial expressions that last no more than thirty milliseconds. The kind of subtleties most of us would never notice. Specialists talk about 'leakage' and 'emblems.' Seems there are all kinds of ways that hidden emotion spills out. In terms of the human face, there's lots of information that we simply tune out. Probably we couldn't get through the day otherwise."

"You've lost me, Clay." Norris put his legs up on a battered coffee table. Caston guessed that it was not battered when the Department of Office Supplies & Services delivered it. Everything in Norris's office looked a little more shopworn and scuffed than mere age would account for.

"Again, this is all stuff I've just found out. Apparently, though, various psychologists have been making a study of this. You videotape someone speaking, then you slow it down, go through it frame by frame, and sometimes you see another expression that's at odds with what's being said. The subject's looking mournful—then, for a fleeting instant, they look triumphant. But it's so fast that we mostly aren't aware of it. There's nothing mystical about what he does. It's just that he's responding to things that are so fleeting that on most of us, they don't register."

"So he sees more. But what does he see?"

"It's an interesting question. People who study faces have worked out certain combinations of muscles that are involved in squelched emotions. Someone starts to smile, and immediately forces down the corners of their mouth. But when you're doing that consciously, you're going to move your chin muscle, too. When the corners of your mouth are pulled down involuntarily—because of sincere feeling—the chin muscle doesn't change. Or if you're putting on a fake smile, there are certain muscles in the forehead that don't change the way they should. Then there are involuntary muscles in the eyebrow and eyelid that convey anger or surprise. Unless you're a Method actor—unless you're genuinely experiencing these emotions—there are going to be subtle muscular discrepancies when you're simulating. In most cases, we don't see them. They're too subtle for us. There are hundreds of ways in which the facial muscles can interact, and it's like we're looking at a rich canvas, but we're color-blind—we see in shades of gray. Whereas a guy like Tarquin sees all the colors."

"Makes him a damned formidable weapon." Norris's heavy eyebrows became a pair of circumflexes. He wasn't pleased with what he was learning.

"No question," Caston said. He did not voice a suspicion that was still inchoate in his mind: that there was a connection between Tarquin's uncanny gifts and his hospitalization—indeed, the erasure of his civilian existence. Caston hadn't worked out the logic yet. But the day was young.

"For twenty years, he was working for us."

"That's right."

"And now, we've got to assume, he's working against us." Norris shook his head hard, as if erasing some internal Etch-A-Sketch. "This isn't a man you want to have on the other side."

"Whatever side that is," Caston said grimly.

CHAPTER FOURTEEN

The gloom of the Montreal afternoon brightened momentarily when Laurel called him on his cell phone.

"Are you all right?" Ambler asked urgently.

"I'm fine, Hal, I'm *fine*," she said, forcing herself to sound casual for his sake. "*Everything's* fine. Aunt Jill's fine. I'm fine. Her sixty Mason jars filled with peach preserves are fine, too, not that you asked, and not that anybody will actually be eating them." She muffled the phone with her hand for a moment, having an exchange with someone nearby, and then said, "Aunt Jill wants to know whether you like peach preserves."

Ambler tensed. "What did you tell her about—"

"You? Not a thing." She lowered her voice. "She assumes I'm talking to a boyfriend. A 'beau,' as she would say. Imagine."

"And you're sure you haven't noticed anything off. Anything at all."

"Nothing," she said. "*Nothing,*" she repeated, too quickly.

"Tell me about this 'nothing,' " Ambler said.

"Just—oh, it really *is* nothing. Some guy from the oil company called a little while ago. They were updating their customer records, asked me all sorts of silly little questions, then when they got into stuff about oil usage and the type of oil burner equipment we use, and I went and checked and saw Aunt Jill uses natural gas, not oil, and I came back to the phone, they'd hung up. Must have been some sort of mix-up."

"What was the name of the company?"

"The name?" She paused. "You know, they actually didn't say."

Ambler felt encased in ice. He recognized the hallmarks of the approach: the innocent-seeming confusion, the pleasant professional phone call, probably one of dozens they had been placing—with a voiceprint analyzer on the other end.

It was a probe.

He was silent for a few moments, not wanting to speak until he could speak *calmly*. "Laurel," he said. "When was this?"

"Maybe . . . twenty minutes ago?" The sangfroid had left her voice.

Twelve layers of lacquer. Twelve layers of dread. "Listen to me very carefully. You need to leave *now*."

"But—"

"You need to leave *right now*." He went on to give her precise instructions. She was to drive her car to a car repair shop, tell them that the steering alignment needed to be fine-tuned, and drive off with whatever "loaner" car they'd have for her. It was a cheap, easy way of getting a vehicle that could not readily be traced to her.

Then she was to drive off somewhere—anywhere she had no connections to.

She listened, repeated the odd detail: he could tell she was taking it all in, calming herself by translating the threat into a set of procedures to be implemented.

"I'll do this," she said, taking a deep breath. "But I need to see you."

"That won't be possible," he said, as gently as he could.

"I can't *do* this otherwise," she said: stating a fact, not making an entreaty. "I just . . ." she faltered. "I just can't."

"I'm leaving the country tomorrow," he explained.

"I'll see you tonight, then."

"Laurel, I don't think that's a good idea."

"I need to see you tonight," Laurel repeated with grim finality.

Late that night, at a motel near Kennedy Airport, Ambler stood in his twentieth-floor room—he had insisted on a high, north-facing floor—studying the traffic on 140th Street in Jamaica, Queens, through a scrim of bad weather. The rain was coming down in sheets, had been for an hour, flooding culverts and forming layers of slick on all the roads. Though not as cold as Montreal, it was decidedly chilly, in the lower forties, and it felt cooler because of the damp. Laurel said she would be driving, and it was no weather to drive in. Yet his spirits leaped at the prospect of seeing her. To be truly cold was to doubt whether you would ever feel warm. Right now, he felt that she was the only thing that could warm him up again.

At 11:00 P.M., squinting through binoculars, he saw the sedan drive up, a Chevrolet Cavalier, pummeled by the downpour. Somehow he knew it was Laurel even before he caught a glimpse of her tousled auburn hair through the windshield. Now she did as he had instructed: waiting for a minute in front of the hotel, then rejoining traffic, driving until the next exit appeared, and reversing direction. From his high floor he was able to peer at the patterns of traffic surrounding her. If she was being tailed, he should be able to tell.

Ten minutes later, she had returned to the hotel's concrete porte cochère. Once he called her cell phone to reassure her that she had no visible tail, she emerged from the car, holding a bundle wrapped in plastic, holding it as if it were a precious thing. She knocked on his door just a few minutes after that. As soon as the door was closed, she dropped her blue nylon parka to the floor—as sodden as only supposedly waterproof garments can get—and laid her bundle on the carpet nearby. Wordlessly she stepped toward him, in to him, and they held each other close, feeling each other's beating hearts. He was clutching her the way a drowning man clutches a lifesaver. For a long moment, the two stood together, nearly stationary, holding each other tightly. Then she pressed her lips to his.

He pulled back after a few moments. "Laurel, all that's happened—you need to step back. You need to be careful. This isn't—what you want." The words came out in a rush.

She looked at him, her eyes imploring.

"Laurel," he said thickly. "I'm not sure that we . . ."

He knew that trauma could produce forms of dependency—could distort perceptions, emotions. She still saw him as the man who had rescued her; could not accept that it was he who had imperiled her in the first place. He also knew that she needed desperately to be comforted: to be possessed, even. He could not push her away without wounding her, and the truth was that he did not want to.

Guilt mixed with aching desire washed over him, and soon the two tumbled onto the bed, two naked bodies, flexing and shuddering and flushing and, together, creating the warmth each desperately craved. When their bodies finally parted—spent, out of breath, glazed with perspiration—their hands sought out each other, and they interlaced fingers, as if neither could bear to be wholly separated. Not just now. Not just yet.

After several minutes of being quiet together, Laurel turned to him. "I made a stop on the way," she whispered. She rolled from the bed, got to her feet, and retrieved the package she had arrived with. His heart quickened as he watched her naked form, silhouetted against the drawn curtains. *God, she was beautiful.*

She removed something from a plastic bag and handed it to him. A large, heavy volume.

"What is it?" Ambler asked.

She was trying not to smile. "Take a look."

He switched on the bedside lamp. It was a clothbound yearbook, the Carlyle College logo embossed on a tan cover and still in its original shrink-wrap, now looking slightly brittle. His eyes widened.

"Pristine," she said. "Untouched, unaltered, untampered with." She handed it to him. "This is your past. This is what they could never get to."

Carlyle College was where she had stopped. "Laurel," he whispered. He felt a surge of gratitude and of something else, as well, something even stronger. "You did this for me."

She looked at him hard, and there was pain in her eyes and something like love, too. "I did it for us."

He took the book into his hands. It was substantial, a bound volume meant to last for decades. Laurel's faith in him was evident in the fact that she had not even felt the need to open the yearbook herself.

His mouth felt dry. She had found a way to punch through the lies—to expose a cunning charade for what it was. Laurel Holland. *My Ariadne.*

"Dear God," he said. There was wonder in his voice.

"You told me where you went to school, you told me what class you were in, and so I got to thinking. The way they'd tried to erase your past—I figured they'd done enough to put off a casual investigator. But they couldn't do more than that."

The vaporous plume of the third-person plural: *they.* A verbal placard over a chasm of uncertainty. Ambler nodded encouragingly.

"There's just too much *stuff,* right? I was thinking about that. It's like when you rush through the house with a vacuum because company's coming. Maybe everything looks really tidy. But there's always stuff—dust under the rug, a take-out carton under the sofa. You just have to look. So maybe they could have altered the computer records at the provost's. But I went to the alumni office, you see, and I bought a copy of your yearbook. The real, physical object. Paid sixty dollars for it."

"Dear God," Ambler repeated, his heart in his throat. Now he slit open the age-stiffened shrink-wrap with a fingernail and sat back, leaning against the headboard of the bed. The yearbook emitted the plastic smell of expensive printing—of ink and heavy coated stock. He paged through, smiling as he saw images of old hijinks: the infamous pumpkin prank; the full-grown Guernsey cow that had been led into the library, her tail flicking the card catalogs. What struck him most was how skinny most of the kids looked. As he must have.

"Brings back memories, huh?" Laurel snuggled beside him.

Ambler's heart began to pound as he continued to flip slowly through the book. There was something comforting about its very weight and solidity. He thought back to his open-faced twenty-one-year-old visage and the quote he had run beneath his photograph, a quote from Margaret Mead that had somehow impressed him deeply at the time. He still knew the words by heart: "Never doubt that a small group of thoughtful, committed citizens can change the world. Indeed, it is the only thing that ever has."

Ambler reached the A's of the regular face pages, and he ran a finger down the column of small rectangular black-and-white images, an array of bushy hair and braces. ALLEN, ALGREN, AMATO, ANDERSON, ANDERSON, AZARIA. His smile faded.

The photographs were displayed in five rows per page, four faces across. There was no question where the HARRISON AMBLER photograph should have appeared.

Nothing. Not a blank space. Not a PHOTOGRAPH UNAVAILABLE notice. Just the face of another student, one he vaguely remembered.

Ambler felt light-headed and a little sick.

"What's wrong?" Laurel asked. When she looked where his finger rested, she, too, seemed stricken.

"I got the wrong yearbook," she said. "I got the year wrong, didn't I? I'm so stupid."

"No," Ambler husked. "The year isn't wrong—*I'm* wrong." He exhaled heavily, shut his eyes, and opened them again, *willing* himself to see something he had not seen before. Something that was not there to be seen.

It couldn't be.

Hurriedly, desperately, he flipped to the index. ALLEN. ALGREN. AMATO. ANDERSON.

No AMBLER.

He riffled through the book until he found a group photograph of the Carlyle crew team. He remembered the uniforms, remembered the goddamn boat—the slightly beaten-up Donoratico eight—that was visible in the background. Yet when he searched the group shot, he was nowhere to be found. Young men in yellow Carlyle Ts and shorts. His teammates were all assembled, young men with confident looks, shoulders thrown back and chests puffed up for the photographer. A team of—he counted them—twenty-three undergraduates. Familiar faces all. Hal Ambler was not one of them.

On autopilot, he continued to page through the book, finding other group shots—teams, moments, activities—where he expected himself to appear. He was nowhere.

Osiris's words returned to him. *It's Occam's razor: What's the simplest explanation? It's easier to change the contents of your head than it is to change the whole world.*

Harrison Ambler was . . . a lie. A brilliant interpolation. It was a life concocted from a lacuna, assembled from a thousand real-world fragments, and funneled into the mind of someone else. *Rich feed.* An artificial life supplanting an authentic one. *A stream of vivid episodes, presented in jumbled, constantly changing order.* A slate erased and then rewritten.

Ambler cradled his head in his arms, seized by terror and bewilderment, by a sense that something had been taken from him that he would never recover: his very identity.

When he looked up, he saw Laurel staring at him, her own face tearstained.

"Don't give in to them," she said in a hushed voice.

"Laurel," he started.

"Don't do this to yourself," she said, steel in her voice.

He felt himself collapsing in on himself, like some astral body crushed by its own gravity.

Laurel put her arms around him, spoke in a low voice. "How's that poem go? 'I'm Nobody! Who are you? Are you Nobody, too?' We can be nobodies together."

"Laurel," he began. "I can't do this to you."

"You can't do this to yourself," she replied. "Because then they *win*." She slipped her hands around his shoulders, grabbing hold of them, as if to bring him back from whatever distant place he had drifted to. "I don't know how to put this. It's a matter of *instincts*, right? Sometimes we *know* what's true even if we can't prove it. Well, let me tell you what I know is true. I look at you, and I don't feel alone anymore—and I can't tell you how rare a feeling that is for me. I feel *safe* when I'm with you. I know you're a good man. I know it because, trust me, I know the other kind all too well. I have an ex-husband who turned my life into a living hell—I had to get a restraining order against him, which didn't do shit. Those men last night—I saw how they looked at me, like a piece of meat. Didn't care if I lived or died. One of them said something about 'having a slice of that ass' as soon as I was put under. The other said he'd 'have a helping,' too. Nobody would ever know, they agreed. That's the *first* thing that was going to happen to me. Only, they didn't count on *you*."

"But if it wasn't for me—"

"*Stop it!* Saying that is like saying *they're* not to blame. But they are, and they're going to pay, too. Listen to your instincts, and you'll get to what's true."

"What's true," he echoed. The words sounded hollow in his mouth.

"*You're* true," she said. "Let's start with that." She pulled him close. "I believe. You need to believe, too. You need to do that for me."

The warmth of her body strengthened him, like armor. She was strong—*God, she was strong*. He had to recover his strength as well.

For a long while, neither spoke.

"I have to go to Paris, Laurel," he finally said.

"Flight or pursuit?" It was both a question and a challenge.

"I'm not sure. Burrowing in, maybe. I've got to follow the thread wherever it goes."

"I accept that."

"But, Laurel, we need to be prepared. At the end of it, maybe I find out that I'm not who I think I am. That I'm someone else. Someone who's a stranger to us both."

"You're frightening me," Laurel said quietly.

"Maybe you should be frightened," Ambler said. He held both her hands in his, gently. "Maybe we both should be."

Sleep was a long time coming, and when it came, it brought unbidden images of a past he still believed to be his own.

His mother's face, foundation covering the livid bruises, pain and confusion in her voice.

"Did Daddy tell you that? Did he say he was leaving?"

"No. He didn't say anything. . . ."

"I swear the Devil's in you. Why would you say such a thing?"

His unspoken reply: *But isn't it obvious? Don't you see it, too?*

The pain and bewilderment in his mother's face dissolved into the intense look of awe and calculation on Paul Fenton's.

You're a goddamn wizard. A magician. . . . Poof—the magician's gone, cape and wand and everything. How the hell did you manage that?

How indeed?

Another face came into focus—first just the eyes, eyes of comprehension and serenity. They belonged to Wai-Chan Leung.

Recall the man, of ancient times, who set up shop in a village selling both a spear he said would penetrate anything and a shield he claimed nothing could penetrate.

He had returned to Changhua, hurtled back to the innermost recesses of his mind. Memories that had disappeared from his awareness now flooded him, like a geyser from a hidden spring.

He did not know why he couldn't remember before; he did not know why he could remember now. The memories seared as they returned, the pain awakening earlier memories of pain. . . .

He had witnessed carnage and, holding the gaze of the dying man, experienced none of his spiritual serenity. Instead, what possessed him was rage, a rage greater than any he had ever experienced. He and his colleagues had been *manipulated*—that was plain to him. The dossier: a tapestry of lies, hundreds of weak threads that became strong when woven together.

You'd started to see through something you weren't meant to see through.

By the day's end, the Taiwan government announced that it had taken into custody members of a left-wing radical cell, which, it claimed, was behind the assassination; the cell was placed on an official list of terrorist organizations. Tarquin was familiar with the so-called cell: a dozen or so superannuated graduate students who got up to little more than distributing photocopies of Maoist pamphlets from the 1950s and debating obscure doctrinal points over cups of weak green tea.

For the next four days, as the others in his team had dispersed to be redeployed to their next assignments, Tarquin went on a controlled rampage, determined to expose the truth. The pieces of the puzzle were not difficult to locate. As he raced among the island's various power centers, Taiwan itself was reduced to a blur of pagodas, intricately painted and incised temple roofs, and densely sprawling cityscapes, cramped with markets and shops. The island was dense, most of all, with *people,* on family-sized motorbikes and in tiny cars and buses, and betel-nut chewers noisily expectorating bloody-looking spit onto the sidewalk. He met with "assets" in the Taiwanese military who scarcely disguised their glee at Leung's murder. He paid a visit to the henchmen and confederates of the corrupt politicos, courtiers, and businessmen who held the true reins of power, sometimes inveigling information by means of feigned sympathy—sometimes extracting it by sheer terror and a measure of brutality he had not realized he possessed. He knew their type, too well. Even when their words were carefully chosen, their faces expressed their furtive agendas plainly. Yes, he knew these people.

Now they were coming to know him.

On the third day, the Metropolitan Rapid Transit system took him to Peitou. Ten miles north of central Taipei, Peitou was once a hot-springs resort. Later it became a seedy red-light district. Now it was something in between. Past a teahouse and a hostel, he found a hot-springs "museum," a sort of upscale bathhouse. On the fourth floor, he caught up with the chubby young man he was looking for—a nephew of a powerful general who was involved in the drug trade, helping to arrange transshipments of heroin from Burma to Thailand, to Taiwan, and thereupon to Tokyo, Honolulu, Los Angeles. A year earlier, the chubby young man had decided to run for a seat in Parliament, and though the playboy was better acquainted with the varieties of cognac than with the political issues of his prospective constituents, the seat had looked safe for a KMT-backed candidate. Then he learned that Leung had been in talks with another candidate for the seat. He did not take the news well: if Leung endorsed his rival, his political fortunes would be imperiled. For that matter, if Leung's anticorruption campaign succeeded on a national level—or even inspired another government to adopt one in defensive emulation—his uncle was in danger of being destroyed.

The man was lounging in steamy water up to his nipples, watching KTV—karaoke television—with a narcotized expression. He grew more alert when Tarquin walked over to him, fully dressed, and pulled a six-inch titanium serrated-edge combat knife from its Hytrel sheath. The nephew proved more communicative after a few incisions were made along his scalp and blood from that highly vascular region began to drench his face. Tarquin knew the peculiar terror induced when a man was blinded by his own blood running into his eyes.

It was as Tarquin had begun to suspect. The "intelligence" in the dossier had been manufactured by Leung's political rivals—cunningly weaving enough accurate detail about *other* malefactors to garner a superficial plausibility. But that left a larger mystery. How did this crude disinformation find its way into the Consular Operations intelligence network? How had the Political Stabilization Unit been tricked into vetting this farrago of deception?

No intelligence pitfall was more familiar to professionals: a man's enemies were always willing to say anything that would bring misfortune upon him. In the absence of confirmation from disinterested parties, no such claim had a claim to truth. It was almost to be expected that those threatened by a reformist political figure should seek to undermine him by spreading lies. What was not expected—what was not explicable—was the Stab unit's analytic failure.

The emotions he was experiencing were molten and dangerous. Dangerous to others, dangerous, he dimly realized, to himself.

When Ambler awoke, he felt, if anything, even less rested than when he lay down, and it had nothing to do with the muffled roar of jet planes from the nearby airport. He felt he had come close to uncovering something, something of great portent; the thought hovered in his mind like morning fog and then dissipated just as quickly. His eyes were inflamed, and his head pulsed as if he were suffering a hangover, although he had had nothing to drink.

Laurel was already up and dressed; she was wearing khaki trousers and a softly pleated pale blue shirt. He looked at the bedside clock, reassuring himself that he remained on schedule.

"You've got plenty of time—we won't miss our flight," she said when he finally staggered to the bathroom.

"*Our* flight?"

"I'm going with you."

"I can't let you," he said. "I don't know what the dangers are, and I can't expose you to—"

"I accept that there are dangers," Laurel interjected. "That's why I need you. That's why you need me. I can help. I can watch your back. Be an extra pair of eyes."

"It's out of the question, Laurel."

"I'm an amateur, I get that. But that makes me the one thing they won't be looking for. Besides, you're not frightened of them. You're frightened of yourself. And that's where maybe I can make things easier, not harder."

"How would I live with myself if anything were to happen to you over there?"

"How would you feel if something were to happen to me here and you weren't around?"

He gave her a sharp look. "I did this to you," Ambler said once more, with muted horror. He did not voice the silently insistent question within him: *When will it stop?*

Laurel spoke quietly but with steel. "Don't leave me, OK?"

Ambler cupped her face with his hands. It was madness, what she was proposing. But it might well save him from another form of madness. And what she said was true: on another continent, he would not be able to protect her from those who threatened her on this one.

"If anything should happen to you . . ." he began. It wasn't a sentence he had to finish.

Her gaze was steady and unafraid. "I'll pick up another toothbrush at the airport," she said.

CHAPTER FIFTEEN

Paris

As the train pulled into the Gare du Nord, Ambler felt both a pulsing current of anxious vigilance and a wave of nostalgia. The smell of the place—he remembered every city by its distinctive odors—brought him back with full force to the nine months he had spent there as a youth, nine months in which he had matured faster, so it seemed, than in the preceding five years. He deposited his suitcase at the left-luggage office and entered the City of Light through the grand portals of the railroad station.

As a safety precaution, they had traveled separately. He had flown to Brussels, using identity papers Fenton provided in the name of one "Robert Mulvaney," and arrived here via the hourly Thalys train. She was using a passport he had altered from one he'd hurriedly purchased on Tremont Avenue in the Bronx: the name, Lourdes Esquivel, wasn't the perfect match for the amber-eyed American, but he knew it would pass muster in a busy airport. Now he glanced at his watch and walked through the crowd at the station. Laurel was seated in a waiting area, just as they had arranged, and her eyes lit up when she saw him.

His heart swelled. She was obviously tired from the trip and yet as beautiful as he had ever seen her.

As they walked together out into the Place Napoléon III, he watched as Laurel stared in wonder at the magnificent facade with its Corinthian columns.

"Those nine statues represent the major cities of northern France," Ambler said in his best tourist-guide mode. "This station was built to be the gateway to the North: northern France, Belgium, Holland, even Scandinavia."

"It's amazing," Laurel breathed. Such words were often spoken. Yet in her mouth they were not formulaic or perfunctory; they expressed her heart. As he saw the familiar sights through her own fresh eyes, they became new again.

The symbolic gateways before him—they were the perfect distillation of human history. There were always those who sought to open the gates; there were always those who sought to shut them tight. Ambler, in his day, had done both.

An hour later, he left Laurel at his favorite café, the Deux Magots, with a large cappuccino, a *Blue Guide,* and a view, as he told her, of the oldest church in Paris. He explained that he had some business to do and would return before long.

Ambler walked west at a steady pace into the Seventh Arrondissement. He made a few detours, checking in windows to see if he could identify anyone following him, scanned the faces he encountered. There was no sign of surveillance. Until he made his contact with Fenton's people in Paris, he could hope that no one would know he and Laurel were here. Finally, he made his way to an elegant nineteenth-century building on the rue St. Dominique and rang the bell.

The Strategic Services Group logo was incised on a rectangular brass plaque on the door. He caught a momentary glimpse of a strange man reflected in it and felt a squirt of adrenaline; the next moment, he realized that the man was himself.

He straightened himself and took a second look at the door. Mounted on the door frame was a glass square that had the glazed, dark look of an unpowered television screen. Ambler knew it was part of a new-generation audiovisual entry system; embedded in the silicate plane were hundreds of microlenses that captured fractional light feeds from a radial array of nearly 180 degrees. The result was a sort of compound eye, like that formed by the ommatidia of an insect. The feeds from hundreds of separate visual receptors were integrated by computer into a single mobile image, one that could be rotated and viewed from a wide range of angles.

"*Est-ce que vous avez un rendezvous?*" A man's voice sounded from the speaker.

"My name is Robert Mulvaney," Ambler said. It was almost more comforting to have a name he knew was fake than one he could only hope was real.

After a few moments, during which a computer no doubt compared his image to the digital image with which Fenton would have supplied them, Ambler was buzzed into a bland institutional-looking foyer. A large plastic display, at eye level, was emblazoned with the Strategic Services Group logo, a larger version of what had been incised on the brass plaque. To a balding factotum Ambler itemized the equipment and documents he would need—including a passport, dated from a year ago, with the appropriate stamps, in the name of Mary Mulvaney. The page with the photograph would be left blank, with the security film unattached. Ambler would provide the photograph himself and heat-seal it in place. Half an hour later, he was presented with a hard-sided briefcase. Ambler did not bother to inspect its contents. He had no doubts about the efficiency of Fenton's outfit. While his "order" was being filled, he had studied the updated dossier on Benoit Deschesnes. He mulled over its contents as he walked back to the Deux Magots.

Three high-resolution pictures showed a grizzled, sharp-featured man in his midfifties. His hair was long and lustrous, and in one of the pictures he was wearing pince-nez that made him look mildly pretentious. There were also a few pages that summarized the man's life.

Deschesnes, whose current address was an apartment on rue Rambuteau, was clearly a brilliant man. He had studied nuclear physics at the Ecole Polytechnique, the most elite scientific university in this most elitist of countries, and gone on to work at a nuclear research lab at CERN, the European nuclear research center in Geneva. Then, in his early thirties, about fifteen years ago, he had moved back to France and joined the faculty at Paris VII, where he became increasingly interested in nuclear policy. When a slot opened for a nuclear arms inspector at the UN's International Atomic Energy Agency, he applied and was immediately accepted. Soon he showed himself to be unusually savvy at navigating a course through the UN's bureaucratic shoals and to have a genuine gift for administration and internal diplomacy. His rise was swift, and when he was proposed for the director-general of the IAEA, he worked hard to make sure that the members of the French mission were solidly behind him.

There had been some concerns, especially among senior members of the French Ministry of Defense, arising from Deschesnes' youthful involvement with the Actions des Français pour le Désarmement Nucléaire, an NGO that argued for the total abolition of nuclear weapons. When he had first joined the IAEA, the French Ministry of Foreign Affairs had questioned what they called the "objectivity of his judgment." It was, evidently, a storm that Deschesnes had weathered. Without the backing of his country, Deschesnes would not have been considered for so illustrious and powerful a position.

He was generally deemed a success. Though the IAEA Secretariat was headquartered at the Vienna International Center, on Wagramer Strasse, where the agency's top career staffers were clustered, few were surprised that the Frenchman spent nearly half the year at the IAEA's Paris offices. That was the way with Frenchmen; everyone at the UN knew that. His trips to Vienna were frequent, and he even took care to make regular appearances at the IAEA laboratories in Seibersdorf, Austria, and in Trieste, Italy. In his three years as director-general, Deschesnes had shown a gift for sidestepping unnecessary controversy while carefully husbanding the agency's prestige and credibility. A brief article in *Time,* reproduced in the dossier, called him "Dr. Watchdog." According to the newsmagazine, he was "no mere Brie-eating bureaucrat" but rather a "cerebral Frenchman with a heart as big as his brains," who was "bringing new brio to bear on the most important threat to global security: loose nukes."

Yet the public had no idea about the real story: that about a year ago the CIA had observed the IAEA director-general meeting secretly with a renegade Libyan nuclear scientist. The agency had captured enough of the conversation to deduce that Deschesnes' high-profile role as the world's leading antiproliferation officer seemed to be a cover for a profitable sideline in helping nonnuclear states acquire nuclear weapons technologies. Deschesnes' antiproliferation work was a front; the anti-American invective in his early AFDN speeches was not.

From Fenton, Ambler knew that the source of the information was someone senior in the American intelligence community. Certainly the analysis had all the hallmarks of a CIA analytical report, down to the starchy phrasings, the careful qualifications and weasel words. Evidence never "proved" that a conclusion was true. Rather, it "raised the concern that," "made plausible the supposition that," or "provided additional support for" the hypothesis advanced. None of that worried Fenton. The CIA, captive to the legalistic culture of Washington, was not defending the country, but that was where Fenton figured he came in. He could do for his country what its official defenders were too cautious to do.

Three-quarters of an hour after he had left, Ambler was back at the Deux Magots. Inside, the warm air was fragrant with coffee and cigarettes, the café's kitchen not yet geared up for the evening meal. Laurel was visibly relieved when she caught sight of him. She summoned a waiter and smiled at Ambler. He seated himself at her table, stood his briefcase by his chair, and took her hand in his, feeling its warmth.

He explained about the document work. Laminating her photograph into the passport would be the work of a minute. "Now that Mr. and Mrs. Mulvaney have their papers in order, we can behave like a married couple."

"In France? Doesn't that mean you have to take a lover?"

Ambler smiled. "Sometimes, even in France, your wife *is* your lover."

As the two walked down the block toward a taxi stand at the corner, Ambler had a distinct sense that they were being followed. Abruptly he turned around the corner and up an adjoining street; Laurel kept pace with him, unquestioning. The presence of a patrol was not itself a cause for alarm. No doubt Fenton's people wanted to make sure that he didn't disappear again. In the next five minutes, Ambler and Laurel turned down several streets, at random, only to find the same broad-shouldered man traipsing behind them, across the street, lagging by approximately a third of a block.

Increasingly, something bothered Ambler about the tail, and now he realized what it was: the man was making it too easy. He was failing to keep an appropriate distance between himself and his putative subject; moreover, he was dressed like an American, in what looked like a dark Brooks Brothers suit and a candy-striped tie, like a local assemblyman from Cos Cobb. The man *wanted* to be seen. That meant that he was a decoy—meant to provide spurious reassurance when he was eluded—and that Ambler had not yet identified the real tail. Doing so took several minutes longer. It was a stylish brunette in a dark midlength coat. There was no point in losing either of them. If the tail wanted to be seen, Ambler himself wanted Fenton's people to know where he was going; he had even gone so far as to call the Hotel Debord at the SSG branch office, ostensibly confirming his reservation.

Finally, he and Laurel grabbed a taxi, collected their cases from the left-luggage office at the Gare du Nord, and checked into a room on the third floor of the Hotel Debord.

The hotel was a little dank; a slight mildewy smell emanated from the carpets. But Laurel voiced no misgivings. Ambler had to stop her before she set about unpacking.

He opened the hard-sided briefcase that the balding factotum had provided him. The pieces of the TL 7 rifle he'd asked for—a collapsible CIA sniper weapon—were securely lodged in compartments slotted into stiff black foam. The Glock 26—a subcompact pistol that fired 9mm rounds—was secured in place as well. The documents he had asked for were in a side compartment.

What Ambler was looking for was exactly what wasn't visible. It would take him a while to find it. First he examined the exterior of the case carefully, making sure that there was no nonfunctioning appliqué. Then he removed the black packing foam, and with his fingertips, he felt along every square inch of the case's lining. He detected nothing out of the ordinary. He tapped the handle with his fingernails and examined every inch of the stitching along the top, for any sign of tampering. Finally, he turned to the black foam itself, squeezing it with his fingertips until he detected a small lump. Using a pocketknife, he prized the two layers apart until he finally uncovered what he had been searching for. The object was shiny and oval, like a vitamin pill wrapped in foil. In fact, it was a miniature GPS transponder. The tiny device was designed to signal its location, pulsing radio signals on a special frequency.

As Laurel Holland stared at him in perplexity, Ambler studied the hotel room. There was a small green-floral patterned sofa beneath the window, with a seat cushion above its curved ball-and-claw legs. He lifted the cushion and secreted the transponder beneath it. He was probably the first person to lift the cushion in a year, to judge from the scattering of coins and dust; he doubted it would be lifted for another year.

Now he took the hard-sided briefcase along with his garment bag and gestured to Laurel to take her own luggage. Wordlessly they walked out of the room. Laurel followed him as he walked past the bank of passenger elevators and around a corner, to a cavernous service elevator, where the flooring was grip-textured steel instead of carpeting. At the ground floor, they found themselves near a rear loading dock. It was vacant at this hour. He led the way through a wide steel push-bar door and onto a ramp that brought them to an alley.

A few minutes later, they settled into another taxicab for a short ride to the Hotel Beaubourg, on the rue Simon Lefranc, a stone's throw from the Pompidou Center. It was the perfect place for American visitors interested in modern art, and just around the corner from Deschesnes' apartment. Once again, there was no problem getting a room—it *was* January—and, once again, Ambler paid with cash, hard currency taken from the operative in the Sourlands; to use the Mulvaney credit cards would be to send up a flare. The hotel was not grand. It had no restaurant, only a small breakfast area in the basement. But the bedroom had exposed oak beams on the ceiling and a comfortable bathroom with a large claw-footed tub. He felt a measure of safety, the safety that came with anonymity. He could tell that Laurel felt it, too.

She broke the silence first. "I was going to ask you what *that* was all about. But I guess I kind of know."

"A needless precaution, let's hope."

"I have a feeling that there's a lot you're not telling me. And I should probably be grateful for it."

In an easy silence, they settled in. It was early evening after a long day, but Laurel wanted to go out for dinner. As she took a quick bath, Ambler heated the small iron that the hotel had provided and carefully laminated her photograph onto the passport. What made U.S. passports difficult to forge was simply the material with which they were made—the paper, the film, the holographic metallic strip, all of which were tightly controlled. Most likely, then, Fenton's supply was courtesy of his governmental collaborators.

Laurel came out of the bathroom, covering herself shyly with her towel, and Ambler kissed her lightly on the neck.

"We'll have dinner and get an early night. Tomorrow we can have breakfast in one of the cafés round the corner. The man I'm looking for lives a few blocks away."

She turned around and looked at him, wondering, Ambler thought, if she could ask him something. Something that was important to her. He gave her a reassuring look. "Come on. You can ask me. Anything to get that worried expression off your face."

"You've killed people, haven't you?" Laurel asked. "I mean, when you were working for the government."

He nodded gravely, his own face mask-like.

"Is it . . . hard to do?"

Was it hard to kill? That was not a question Ambler had asked himself for years. But there were related questions that did haunt him. What did it *cost* to kill—what did it cost in the currency of the human soul? What had it cost *him*? "I'm not sure how to answer that," he said softly.

Laurel looked abashed. "I'm sorry. It's just that I've dealt with patients who seemed, well, *damaged,* damaged because of the damage they inflicted on others. They didn't *seem* vulnerable—most of these people had to pass extensive psych workups before they were hired in the kind of jobs they had. But it's like a piece of ceramic with a hairline crack. Nothing could seem tougher, until it suddenly shatters."

"Is that what the Parrish Island facility was like—a box filled with shattered ceramic soldiers?"

She did not answer right away. "Sometimes that's how it seemed."

"Was I one of them?"

"Shattered? No, not shattered. Bruised, maybe. Like they tried to crush you, but you just wouldn't crush. It's hard to put in words." She looked into his eyes. "But in your career, you've had to . . . do things that must have been hard to do."

"I had a Cons Ops instructor who used to say that there are really two worlds," he began slowly, softly. "There's the world of the operative, and it's a world of murder and mayhem and all the skulduggery you could imagine. It's a world of boredom, too—the endless tedium of waiting and planning, of contingencies that never come into play, of traps that never spring. But the brutality is real, too. Not less real for being so casual."

"It all seems so heartless. So cold." There was a catch in her voice.

"And there's another world, Laurel. It's the normal world, the everyday world. It's the place where people get up in the morning to do an honest day's work, and angle for their promotions, or go shopping for a son's birthday present, and change long-distance plans so they can call their daughter at college for less. That's the world where you sniff the fruits in the supermarket to see whether they're ripe, and look up a recipe for orange roughy, because they had that on special, and worry about arriving late for a grandchild's Communion." He paused. "And the thing is that sometimes these worlds intersect. Suppose a man is prepared to sell technology that can be used to kill hundreds of thousands, maybe millions, of people. The safety of the normal world, the world of everyday people, depends on making sure the bad guys don't succeed. Sometimes, that means taking extraordinary measures."

"Extraordinary measures," she said. "You make it sound like medicine."

"Maybe it *is* a kind of medicine. It's more like medicine than it is like police work, anyway. Because at the shop I worked for, there was a simple creed: if we operated by the policeman's rules, we would lose ground we can't afford to lose. We'd lose the war. And there *was* a war. Beneath the surface of every major city in the world—Moscow, Istanbul, Tehran, Seoul, Paris, London, Beijing—there were battles going on every minute of every day. If things work the way they're supposed to, people like me spend their lives working for people like you, by keeping that battle from erupting into view." Ambler stopped.

So many other questions remained unanswered, perhaps unanswerable. Was Benoit Deschesnes a part of this war? Could he, in fact, kill this man? *Should* he? If Fenton's intelligence was correct, Benoit Deschesnes was betraying not just his own country, not just the United Nations, but all the people whose lives would be threatened by nuclear weapons in the hands of tin-pot dictators.

Laurel broke the silence. "And if they *don't*? If they *don't* work the way they're supposed to?"

"Then the great game becomes just that, another game, only a game played with human lives."

"You still believe this," Laurel prodded.

"I don't know what I believe anymore," he said. "At this point, I feel like a cartoon animal who's run off a cliff, and if he doesn't keep pumping his legs in midair, he'll plunge to the bottom."

"You feel angry," she said, "and lost."

He nodded.

"That's how I feel," she said, and it was almost as if she were thinking aloud. "Except I feel something else, too. I feel like I've got a sense of *purpose* now. Absolutely nothing makes sense, and, for the first time in my life, it's like everything makes sense. Because stuff's broken, and it has to get fixed, and if we don't do it, nobody will." She broke off. "Don't listen to me—I don't even know what I'm *saying*."

"And I don't even know who I *am*. We're a swell pair." He sought out her eyes with his, and, together, they shared a small smile.

"Pump those legs," Laurel said. "Don't look down—look forward. You came here for a reason. Don't forget it."

For a reason. The right one, he hoped to God.

After a while they decided to go out for fresh air and walked into the open plaza of the Pompidou Center. Laurel was delighted by the building, a great glass monster, with its innards on the outside. As they moved toward it, with people bustling by in the winter cold, her mood seemed to lift.

"It's like a giant box of light, floating over the square. A huge kid's toy, with all those brightly colored tubes around it." She paused. "It's not like anything I've ever seen before. Let's walk around it."

"Sure." Ambler took pleasure in her delight. But he was grateful, too, for the opportunity to use the endless windows to search for any reflections of the man in the Brooks Brothers suit and the woman in the midlength coat. This time, though, they were nowhere to be seen. There was only one moment when Ambler heard the belling of an internal tocsin: the reflection of a man, fleetingly glimpsed—short-haired, features that were handsome but almost cruel, eyes that searched too hard, too insistently, too desperately.

It was not entirely reassuring when he realized that the man he had glimpsed was himself.

At seven-thirty the next morning, the American couple greeted the desk clerk with a cheerful "*Bonjour.*" The clerk tried to direct them to the breakfast room in the basement, but Ambler begged off, explaining that they were going to have "*un vrai petit déjeuner améri-cain.*" They set off for the café around the corner on the rue Rambuteau that he had identified the previous evening. Once they had settled in at a table with a view onto the street, Ambler made sure he could see the entrance to the apartment building at 120. Then the watching began.

They had slept well. Now she looked lively and refreshed, ready for whatever awaited them.

They ordered a large meal at the Café Saint Jean. Croissants, a couple of poached eggs, orange juice, coffee. Ambler stepped out for a moment to grab a copy of the *International Herald Tribune* from a news vendor.

"We may be here awhile," Ambler said quietly. "No need to rush."

Laurel nodded and opened the front section of the *Tribune* on the wrought-iron table.

"The news of the world," she said. "But which world, I wonder. Which of those two worlds you told me about?"

He glanced at the headlines. Various business and political leaders were addressing the annual meeting of the World Economic Forum at Davos, Switzerland, their platforms and entreaties dutifully noted and analyzed. A strike had hit Fiat, crippling production at the automaker's Turin plants. A bomb had gone off during a religious festival in Kashmir, Hindu extremists blamed. Talks failed in Cypress.

The more things change, Ambler reflected mordantly.

As it turned out, they did not have to stay long. Deschesnes appeared at about eight o'clock, briefcase in hand, and scanned the street for a few moments before he entered a black limousine that had arrived for him.

Ambler, obscured by the sun's glare on the café window, stared intently at that face. Yet it had told him little.

"Sorry, honey," Ambler said loudly. "I guess I left my guidebook at the hotel. You go ahead and eat your breakfast and I'll go get it."

Laurel, who had not seen the pictures of Deschesnes, looked puzzled for a moment—but just a moment. Then she beamed at him. "Why, thank you, honey; that is so sweet." She was almost enjoying this, Ambler thought. He handed her a shopping list—items of clothing that would come in handy—and he was off.

A couple of minutes later, Ambler went into the Rambuteau metro station; Deschesnes had to be headed for the office—nothing in his expression indicated that this day would be out of the ordinary—and Ambler took the metro to the Ecole Militaire station. He got out near the regional office of the IAEA, which was located in a hulking modernist building on the Place de Fontenoy, a demilune of a street off the avenue de Lowendal, at the opposite end of the Parc du Champ de Mars from the Eiffel Tower. The surroundings were scenic; the building itself was not. Largely given over to the office requirements of UNESCO, the building was ringed by a steel fence and had the forbidding aura of midcentury modernism: a configuration of girders, stone, and glass designed not to welcome but to intimidate.

Ambler turned himself into a bird-watcher at the Square Combronne, gazing about with compact field glasses, occasionally feeding pigeons with the crumbs of a pastry acquired from a street vendor. Despite his idle and distrait air, not one person left 7 Place de Fontenoy without his noticing.

At one o'clock Deschesnes strode out of the building, a purposeful look on his face. Was he off to have lunch at one of the restaurants nearby? In fact, he entered the Ecole Militaire metro station: a peculiar move for the director-general of a powerful international agency. Deschesnes, Ambler suspected, was someone who was usually accompanied by an entourage—visiting dignitaries, staffers, colleagues in need of a moment of his time—and who usually traveled in style. His UN office made him a personage as well as a person. When someone of that eminence disappeared into the subway system, it carried a suggestion of subterfuge.

Ambler thought back to the man's face across the street that morning; there was no evidence of particular stress, of his being mindful of a hazardous rendezvous.

Ambler trailed him as the UN administrator made his way south to Boucicaut, trailed him as he emerged at Boucicaut Station, strode to the end of the block, made a left, and, in the middle of a quiet residential street lined with classic *Parisien* manses, took out his key ring and let himself in to one.

It was, then, a rather early version of that classic form of French liaison, the *cinq à sept*. What Deschesnes was up to involved both subterfuge and routine. He was conducting an assignation, an affair, doubtless one of long standing. Across the street, Ambler took out his field glasses and peered at the windows of the drab building of weather-stained limestone. A flicker of light at a curtained window on the fourth floor told him that it was the apartment Deschesnes had entered. He glanced at his watch. It was twenty after one. He saw Deschesnes' figure shadowed against the unlined curtains. He was alone; his mistress was probably a professional woman and had not yet arrived. Maybe she would arrive at half past and Deschesnes would busy himself with his ablutions until then. There were too many *maybes*. Ambler's instincts told him to intercept Deschenes now. He felt the small Glock 26, which fit comfortably and invisibly in a waistband holster. He had noticed a florist at the corner; a few minutes later, he buzzed the fourth-floor apartment, a bouquet of elegantly wrapped flowers in hand.

"*Oui?*" a voice said a moment or two later. Even through the crackly interference on the loudspeaker Ambler could hear the wariness in Deschesnes' tone.

"*Livraison.*"

"*De quoi?*" Deschesnes demanded.

"*Des fleurs.*"

"*De qui?*"

Ambler kept his voice bored, impassive. "*Monsieur. J'ai des fleurs pour Monsieur Benoit Deschesnes. Si vous n'en voulez pas—*"

"*Non, non.*" The buzzer sounded. "*Troisième étage. A droit.*" Ambler was in.

The building was in poor repair, the steps worn smooth from decades of hard-soled shoes, the banister broken in a couple of places. It was not the kind of building that either Deschesnes or his lover would have chosen as a residence, Ambler was sure, but it was easily afforded, a pied-à-terre whose expense would not noticeably affect the household budget of either.

When Deschesnes came to the door, he saw a man in a respectable winter coat holding out a bunch of flowers with his left hand. Ambler hardly looked like a deliveryman, but his open, pleasant smile reassured the Frenchman, and he opened the door wider to take the bouquet.

Ambler dropped the bouquet and extended his right foot into the door. His right hand was holding the Glock, aimed at the Frenchman's abdomen.

The Frenchman cried out and, rearing back, tried to slam the heavy wooden door. At the same time, Ambler lunged forward, shoulder first, and the door slammed futilely against the doorstop.

The Frenchman had been hurled back several feet, his face drained of color. Ambler could see him desperately scanning the room behind him for some potential weapon or shield. Moving swiftly, Ambler closed the door behind him, securing the door chain and dead bolt with his free hand; they would not be disturbed.

Now he stepped toward Deschesnes, forcing him back into the sitting room. "Be quiet or I *will* use this," Ambler said in English. He had to project an aura of overwhelming force.

As he had thought, Deschesnes was alone. The winter sunlight was beaming through the large window opposite the door and casting a silvery glow onto a sparsely furnished living room. There was a bookshelf with a few books, a coffee table covered with newspapers, typescripts, and magazines. It had been an advantage before that the whole room was visible from the street; now it was a disadvantage.

"Bedroom?" Ambler asked.

Deschesnes jerked his head to the left toward a doorway and Ambler marched him across to it.

"You're alone?" Ambler asked as he scanned the bedroom.

Deschesnes nodded. He was telling the truth.

The man before Ambler was large framed but soft, with the expanding girth of too many expensive meals, too little exercise. Fenton's workup had described a man who was truly a force for evil in the world. *Take care of Benoit and you'll be the equivalent of a made man. Then we'll talk.* If Fenton was correct, the UN dignitary *deserved* death, and by arranging that death Ambler could infiltrate into the very heart of Fenton's enterprise. He would obtain the knowledge he sought. He would learn who he really was—and was not.

The bedroom had opaque roller shades, and Ambler, keeping the physicist within his sights, pulled the blinds down. He sat on the arm of a sofa by the window, piled up untidily with clothes. "Sit," he said, pointing the gun at the bed. Then he sat still for a moment, staring intently at Deschesnes.

With slow movements, the Frenchman withdrew his billfold from his pocket.

"Put that away," Ambler said.

Deschesnes froze, his fear compounded with confusion.

"I'm told your English is pretty good," Ambler went on, "but if you don't understand anything I say, just tell me."

"Why are you here?" These were Deschesnes' first words.

"Didn't you know this day would come?" Ambler said quietly.

"I see," Deschesnes said. A sorrowful look came over him. He sat down as if winded. "Then you are Gilbert. It's funny, but I always assumed you were French. She never told me you were not. Not that we ever talked about you. I do know that she loves you, that she has always loved you. Joelle, she was always up-front about this. What we have—what we have is a different thing. It is not *sérieuse*. I don't expect you to excuse or forgive, but I must tell you—"

"Monsieur Deschesnes," Ambler broke in, "I have no connection to Joelle. This has nothing to do with your personal life."

"But then—"

"It has everything to do with your professional life. Your *covert* professional life. Those are the true *liaisons dangereuses.* I refer to your connections with those whose hearts are set on nuclear weaponry. Those you are too eager to please."

A look of pure bewilderment appeared on Deschesnes' face—the kind of bewilderment it was extremely difficult to fake. Was it that his English was limited? It seemed utterly fluent, but perhaps his comprehension was imperfect.

"*Je voudrais connaître votre rôle dans la prolifération nucléaire,*" Ambler said, enunciating clearly.

Deschesnes replied in English. "My role in nuclear proliferation is a matter of public record. I have spent a career working against it."

He broke off, suddenly wary. "A ruffian invades a residence of mine and holds me at gunpoint, and I am supposed to talk about my vocation? Who sent you? What in God's name is this about?"

"Call it a performance review. Speak to the point or you'll never speak again. No games. No second-guessing."

Deschesnes' eyes narrowed. "Did Actions des Français send you?" he asked, referring to the organization of antinuclear activists. "Do you people realize how incredibly counterproductive this is—acting as if *I* am the enemy?"

"Speak to the point," Ambler barked. "Tell me about your meeting with Dr. Abdullah Alamoudi in Geneva last spring."

The UN eminence looked bewildered. "What are you talking about?"

"I'm asking the questions here, goddammit. Are you pretending you don't know who Dr. Alamoudi is?"

"Certainly I know who he is," the Frenchman returned, with wounded dignity. "You refer to a Libyan physicist who is on our watchlist. We believe him to be involved in a secret weapons programs involving various Arab League nations."

"Then why would the director-general of the International Atomic Energy Agency be meeting with such a person?"

"Why indeed?" Deschesnes spluttered. "Alamoudi would no more be caught in the same room as me than a mouse would curl up with a cat." Ambler detected no trace of deception.

"And how do you explain your trip to Harare last year?"

"I cannot," the UN eminence said simply.

"Now we're getting somewhere."

"Because I have never *been* to Harare."

Ambler stared at him intently. "Never?"

"Never," the man said stoutly. "Where are you *getting* this information? Who has supplied you with such *lies*? I should like to know." He paused. "It was Actions des Français, wasn't it?" A crafty look crept over his face. "They served a useful role once. Now they consider me a turncoat. They doubt everything they see, everything they hear. The truth is, if they wanted to know where I stood, what I did, they could read the newspapers or turn on the radio."

"Words and deeds do not always match."

"*Exactement,*" Deschesnes said. "You tell your friends at Actions des Français that they would do more good if they put honest pressure on our elected officials."

"I'm not with Actions des Français," Ambler returned steadily.

Deschesnes' gaze returned to Ambler's handgun. "No," he said after a while. "Of course not. Those xenophobes would never entrust anything important to an American. Then you are . . . CIA? I suppose their intelligence is just bad enough to explain such a blunder." Ambler could tell Deschesnes was struggling between his indignation and his desire to calm an intruder who was holding him at gunpoint in his pied-à-terre. Volubility, and indignation, seemed to gain the upper hand. "Perhaps you should give your employers a message directly from me. Fill their intelligence dossiers with the truth, for a change. Because the *truth* is that the great nations of the West have been criminally negligent on the greatest threat the world now faces. And America isn't the exception: it's the prime culprit."

"I don't recall your speaking with such candor before the members of the UN Security Council," Ambler taunted.

"My UN reports spell out the facts. I leave the rhetoric for others. But the bare facts are shaming enough. North Korea has enough plutonium for several nuclear warheads. Iran does as well. More than twenty other states have so-called research reactors with ample highly enriched uranium to build their own nuclear bombs. And of those bombs that already exist, hundreds are stored in conditions of *risible* security. A silk blouse at a Samaritaine department store is better secured than many Russian nuclear warheads. It's a moral *obscenity.* The world should be terrified, and yet you people could care less!" The UN eminence was breathing hard, voicing the fury that had driven his career, his early fear and confusion almost forgotten as he spoke.

Ambler was shaken; he could no longer doubt the man's sincerity—not without doubting his own perceptions.

Someone had set Deschesnes up.

Yet at what remove? Fenton betrayed not the slightest doubt about the "source integrity" behind the assignment. How far up—or down—did the intrigue go? And what motivated it?

Ambler needed to know who, and he needed to know why. But the Frenchman was little help here.

Now, from the window, Ambler saw a small black-haired woman approach the entrance from the street. Joelle, no doubt.

"Is there anyone home in the apartment upstairs?" Ambler demanded.

"The neighbors all work," Deschesnes said. "There is never anyone home before six. But what does that matter? I do not have the key. And Joelle—"

"I'm afraid we haven't finished our conversation," Ambler said. "I would prefer not to involve Joelle. If you agree . . ."

Deschesnes nodded, ashen.

Pistol still in hand, Ambler followed the Frenchman as he made his way to the floor above. The door was indeed locked, but that was hardly more than a formality. Ambler had observed how flimsy the knob latches were in the building, shallow brass tongues mounted in decaying wood. With a sudden movement, he slammed his hip into the door. It gave in, with a small explosion of splintered wood, and the two walked inside. Below, Joelle would have been approaching the bottom landing. She would be puzzled that Deschesnes had failed to show, but there were many possible explanations. Ambler would leave it to Deschesnes to settle on one.

The fifth-floor apartment looked scarcely inhabited—there was an oval rug of jute, a few battered items of furniture that would not have made the grade at a flea market—but it would suffice. At Ambler's insistence, the two spoke in hushed voices.

"Let's stipulate," Ambler said, "that I have indeed been supplied with false information. That you have enemies who mean to set you up. Then the question for us is *why*."

"The question for me is why you don't get the hell out of my life," Deschesnes replied, in a gust of cold fury. He had decided that he was no longer in immediate danger of being shot. "The question for me is why you insist on waving that gun in my face. You want to know who my enemies are? Then look in the mirror, you American cowboy! *You* are my enemy."

"I'll put the gun away," Ambler said. As he did so, he added, "But it won't make you any safer."

"I don't understand."

"Because there are many more where I come from."

Deschesnes blenched. "And you are from . . . where?"

"It's not important. What's important is that powerful officials have been assured that you pose a major risk to international security. Again, why would that be?"

Deschesnes shook his head. "I can't think of any reason why," he finally said. "As the director-general of the IAEA, I am something of a symbol of international resolve on this issue—leaving aside the fact that this resolve is, too often, *merely* symbolic. My views about the nuclear menace are common sense, shared by millions of people and thousands of physicists."

"But surely some of your work isn't public. Surely some of it involves confidential dealings."

"We do not release provisional findings, as a rule. But almost all of it is destined to become public, when the time is right." He paused. "The main unreleased work I am doing now is on a report on the Chinese role in proliferation."

"What have you found?"

"Nothing."

"What do you mean, nothing?" Ambler walked over to the window, watched as the petite brunette walked hesitantly from the building and back to the sidewalk. She would have questions; they would be answered later.

"Despite what the American government says and the French government says and NATO says, there is no evidence at all that China is currently involved in proliferation. Liu Ang has, from everything we have been able to determine, strongly abjured the spread of atomic technology. The only question is whether he will be able to keep the Chinese military under control."

"How many people are working on this report?"

"Just a handful of staffers, in Paris and Vienna, though we are processing information from a large team of arms inspectors and analysts. But I am the principal author. I alone am in a position to confer on it the complete credibility of my office."

Ambler felt his frustration rising. Deschesnes may have been an innocent man, but he was also, and by the same token, an irrelevant man. He was just another aging Frenchman, one of dubious private morality, perhaps, but undoubted public probity.

Yet there had to be a reason for someone—or some group—to have ordered his death. And if Ambler did not fulfill the assignment, others would not hesitate to do so.

Ambler squeezed his eyes shut for a moment and then saw what he had to do.

"Vous êtes fou! Absolument fou" was Deschesnes' first response when Ambler explained the situation.

"Perhaps," Ambler replied placidly. He knew he had to get the Frenchman's confidence. "But consider. The people who sent me are serious. They have the resources. If I don't kill you, they'll send someone else. But if we can persuade them you're dead, and you can disappear for a while, I have a chance of finding out who's set you up. It's the only way you'll be safe."

Deschesnes stared at him. "Insanity!" He stopped. "And exactly how could such a thing be done?"

"I'll contact you in a few hours when I've worked out the details," Ambler replied. "Is there a place you can retreat to for a week or so, a place you won't be found?"

"My wife and I have a place in the country."

"Near Cahors," Ambler broke in impatiently. "They know that. You can't go there."

"Joelle's family has a place near Dreux. They never go there in the winter. . . ." He stopped. "No. No, I can't involve her. I *won't* involve her."

"Listen to me," Ambler said, after a long pause. "It shouldn't take me more than a week or two to deal with this. I suggest you rent a car—don't use your own. Drive south and stay somewhere in Provence for a couple of weeks. If the plan works, they won't be looking for you. Send me a phone number at this e-mail address." Ambler wrote it on a piece of paper for him. "I'll call you when it's safe."

"And what if you don't call?"

Then I'll be dead, Ambler thought. "I'll call," he said. He smiled coolly. "You have my word."

CHAPTER SIXTEEN

Langley, Virginia

Clayton Caston could not stop himself; he found his gaze drifting toward the coffee stain on Caleb Norris's oatmeal carpeting. Perhaps it would never come out. Perhaps the solution was to wait until the rest of the carpet was stained with coffee, rendering the whole thing a uniform hue. That was *one* way to hide something: change the nature of its surroundings. There was an idea lurking in that.

Norris's voice interrupted his musings. "So what happened?"

Caston blinked. Dust motes were visible in the morning light that filtered through Norris's window. "Well, as you know, we've got a bunch of people who were teamed with him in one place or another. So I tried to figure out what our man's last assignment was in the field. Turned out to be in Taiwan. The question is, who was the OIC—the officer in charge? Because the final report should have had the authorizing signature of the OIC. I figure the OIC is going to know who Tarquin was before he was Tarquin. Maybe he was the person who recruited Tarquin in the first place."

"And who signed at the X?"

"No signature. Authorization was coded. OIC alias was Transience."

"So who's Transience?"

"Couldn't get that."

"Our jobs would be a lot easier if the CIA was entrusted with the identity of Cons Ops agents," Norris said grumpily. "Their precious 'partition principle'—all too often it means you end up pinning the donkey tail to your own goddamn ass."

The auditor turned to face him squarely. "Like I say, I couldn't get it. So you're going to get it. I want you to call the person who runs the Political Stabilization Unit, Ellen Whitfield, and ask the undersecretary directly. You're an ADDI; she has to pay attention."

"Transience," Caleb Norris repeated. "I'm starting to get a bad feeling about this. . . ." He stopped at Caston's pointed scowl. "I just mean that there are a lot of unknowns. Like you're always saying, there's a difference between risk and uncertainty, right?"

"Well, sure. Risk is quantifiable. Uncertainty isn't. It's one thing to know there's a fifty-fifty chance of something going wrong. It's another not to know what the chances are at all."

"So it's a matter of knowing what you don't know. And not knowing." Norris took a deep breath and turned to Caston. "My worry is that we're in a situation where we don't even know how much we don't know."

As Caston returned to his office, he felt a growing sense of—well, uncertainty, he supposed. Adrian was looking inappropriately buoyant, as he usually did, but there was something restful about Caston's own tidy desk: the pen and pencil close together but not touching, the thin manila folder two inches to their left, the screen of his computer exactly aligned with the edge of his desk.

Caston sat down heavily, his fingers pausing over that computer keyboard. Risk, uncertainty, ignorance: the concepts sprouted in his mind like weeds in a seedbed.

"Adrian," he said abruptly. "I have a ceramic urn filled with black balls and white balls."

"You do?" The young man looked around Caston's office cautiously.

"Pretend I do," the auditor groused.

"Super."

"You know that precisely half the balls are black and half of them are white. There are a thousand balls. Five hundred black, five hundred white. You're going to draw a ball at random. What odds will you give me that it's black?"

"Fifty-fifty, right?"

"Now, let's say I've got another urn, filled at the same ball factory. In this case, you know it contains black balls or white balls or both. But that's it. You have no idea whether most of the balls are white or black. Maybe all the balls are black. Maybe all of them are white. Maybe they're evenly divided. Maybe there's only one ball in the urn. Maybe there's a thousand. You just don't know."

"So this time I'm pig ignorant," Adrian said. "Beyond the fact that there are black and/or white balls in the urn, I don't know anything. That the deal?"

"Exactly. Give me odds that you'll draw a black one."

Adrian furrowed his unlined brow. "But how can I know what the odds are? They could be a hundred percent. They could be zero percent. They could be anywhere in between." He ran a hand through his mop of thick black hair.

"Right. And if you *had* to lay odds? Would you give me ten-to-one odds that the ball you draw is black? A hundred to one? A hundred *against*? What?"

The young man shrugged. "I'd have to say . . . fifty-fifty again."

Caston nodded. "That's what any expert would say. You ought to behave the same way in the second case, where you know almost nothing, as you do in the first case, where you know a great deal. Back in the 1920s, an economist named Frank Knight distinguished between 'risk' and 'uncertainty.' With risk, he said, you could tame randomness with probabilities. With uncertainty, he said, you don't even have knowledge of probabilities. But here's the thing. As von Neumann and Morgenstern saw, even ignorance gets quantified. Our systems couldn't work otherwise."

"This have anything to do with an urn called 'Tarquin,' master?" Adrian's labret stud twinkled in the fluorescent light.

Caston made a noise that was somewhere between a grunt and a laugh. He picked up a photocopy of a Taiwanese newspaper that was included in the manila file that had arrived that morning. Caston could not read it, and no translation had been provided. "I don't suppose you know Chinese?" he asked hopefully.

"Let me think. Does *dim sum* count?"

"Sorry, it's Korean that you speak, right?" Caston faltered.

"Not a word," Adrian said serenely.

"Your parents *were* Korean immigrants, weren't they?"

"That's why." A slow grin. "They had to learn to say 'Clean your room' in English. I bought a *lot* of time that way."

"I see."

"Sorry to disappoint. I don't even like kimchi. Hard to believe, I know."

"So we have at least one thing in common," Caston said dryly.

Paris

There was a great deal to do and little time within which to do it. Ambler could no longer turn to Fenton's people for supplies—not when executing a double play on them. Ingenuity and opportunism would have to replace the well-supplied stockroom.

By late afternoon, Ambler had begun to collect the items he would need. He decided to appropriate Director-General Deschesnes' pièd-à-terre near Boucicaut Station; it would serve as well as any for a rudimentary workshop. Using a can opener on three containers of bouilion, he produced three circular pieces of steel. He backed these with rubber cement and a thin layer of foam—packaging material that accompanied a cheap clock radio. He fashioned the blood packs out of extra-thin latex prophylactics and a bottle of viscous FX blood that he bought at a costume shop, Les Ateliers du Costume, in the Ninth Arrondissement.

Finally he laboriously removed the primer charge from a couple of the 0.284-inch centerfire rifle cartridges that had been supplied by Fenton's armorer. It was harder than he had expected. The Lazzeroni cases made it difficult to decap the primer, which was just below, flush with the cartridge base. He had to work without proper tools, making do with the kind of wrenches and pliers he could get at the nearest *quincaillerie,* or hardware store. If he twisted the rim with too much pressure, he risked detonating the factory-loaded primer compound and injuring himself. The work was slow, painstaking. The centerfire primer contained less than a grain of priming compound; he would need to collect the primers from four cartridges in order to produce one workable squib.

It was another hour and a half before he completed the ensemble: the latex-wrapped blood pack glued on top of the primer charge; the small wire that would run to a 9-volt battery.

When Ambler met up with Laurel in the gallery on the top floor of the Pompidou Center, he had been away for hours, assembling the props for the drama—a theater of death meant to substitute for death itself.

Laurel's response to his careful explanation began with incredulity, but before long her remarkable self-possession came to the fore. Yet there was a problem with the plan, as become increasingly clear when he talked it through with her. She saw it, too.

"If people see a man shot," she said, "they're going to summon an ambulance."

Ambler frowned; he kept going over the sticking point in his mind. "It would take a medical tech two seconds to discover what was going on. The whole ruse would be blown. And that can't happen." He had to think of a solution, or the whole plan would have to be abandoned. "*Damn,*" he said under his breath. "We've got to use an ambulance of our own. Set the whole thing up ahead of time. Hire a driver somehow."

" 'Somehow'?" Laurel echoed. "Is that one of those special spycraft terms?"

"You're not helping, Laurel," he said, in a tone midway between entreaty and complaint.

"That's the problem," she said. "Or maybe the solution. You need to let me help. *I'll* drive it."

His hard stare melted into one of admiration. He did not bother to argue. She was right. It was the only way. The two discussed the details further as they ambled, arm-in-arm, southward toward the Seine. The man in the Brooks Brothers suit had reappeared. It was important that they not look hurried; Fenton must not suspect what he was planning. Laurel may have entered a funhouse, as she said, but she had come to realize that for her, just then, there was no other reality. She would make a home of it, as he had.

He turned toward her, taking in her lithe frame, her wavy auburn hair, her warm hazel eyes, flecked with green like inclusions on a cut stone of topaz. Every look she gave him, every question she asked, every gentle pressure on his arm told him that she trusted him and was ready to do whatever he asked.

"OK," she said. "So now all we need to do is to commandeer an ambulance."

Ambler gazed at her in fond admiration. "Did anyone ever tell you that you were a quick study?"

The Clinique du Louvre was in an elegant building that filled most of a city block—wide arching windows on the ground floor, an array of smaller double-hung windows above, large beige stones giving way to small beige bricks—and was situated between the Louvre, Paris's premiere museum, and Les Grands-Magasins de la Samaritaine, the city's premiere department store. Opposite it, to the north, was the church of Saint-Germain l'Auxerrois; a block south was the Quai du Louvre, a few hundred yards from the Pont Neuf, which crossed the river. It was central and easily approached from many directions. It was also the perfect place to go looking for an ambulance. Municipal rules had ensured that it had a large fleet of emergency medical vehicles—and not to mention a pool of emergency medical technicians—far in excess of its actual needs.

Ambler stood by himself near the hospital, willing himself into a condition of glacial calm. He inhaled the violet-tar aroma of damp pavement, the metallic fug of exhaust, and, more faintly, the organic stench of dog excrement, for Paris was a city of dog lovers and innocent of laws regulating their leavings. Now it was time for the tableau to begin.

At Ambler's signal, Laurel walked over to the guard who sat in a glass booth at the entrance to the circular parking garage. She was a tourist seeking directions. The guard—an unprepossessing man with a parrot nose and some sort of port-wine birthmark on his balding scalp—was alone but for the telephone, an outmoded computer, and a spiral notebook in which he marked vehicular comings and goings. He gave her a look that was wary but not hostile. To a man confined to a guard's booth, a pretty woman was scarcely an unwelcome sight. Her French was scant, as was his English. Soon she was unfolding an enormous map of the city and holding it up to him.

As the parrot-nosed guard's view was blocked by what seemed an acre of Michelin street map, Ambler silently vaulted over the low, swinging safety gate and strode up the curved concrete ramp to the parking level above and over to a small fleet of Renault ambulances—painted a stark, sanitary white, with an orange stripe and blue lettering. Most of them were boxy, with foreshortened hoods and low-to-the-ground chassis. These were backup vehicles, seldom used, but they clearly had been regularly washed and maintained, and they gleamed whitely in the dim light. He chose a mini-ambulance that seemed to be the most elderly vehicle on the lot. The key cylinder was quickly dismantled. Slower work was filing a key blank with a corresponding pattern of indentation. But ten minutes later, the work was done. He tested the key more than once, confi-

dent that the sound of the motor would be lost amid the noisier rat-
tlings of other vehicles both within the garage and outside of it.

Yet his sense of satisfaction quickly paled before his recognition of
the difficulties ahead. Too many things could go wrong.

Two hours later, at the Hotel Beaubourg, Ambler broke down and
stripped the TL 7 rifle, making sure that all the parts were properly
lubricated and clean. Then he reassembled it, except for the muzzle.
With the hinged stock in collapsed position, the object was inconspicuous in an athletic bag. He changed into a sweat suit and sneak-
ers, as if he were going off to a gym. At the lobby, he waved toward
the concierge at the hotel desk. "*Le* jogging," he said, smiling.

The concierge laughed, shrugging his shoulders. It was obvious
what he was thinking. *Americans—obsessed with fitness.* "See you
later, Monsieur Mulvaney."

Laurel joined him a few minutes later at the plaza outside of the
Pompidou Center, and they quietly, hurriedly, reviewed the step sequence ahead of them, as Ambler's eyes swept the arena repeatedly,
with a ratcheted-up sense of awareness. Nothing seemed out of
place—nothing he could detect, anyway. The operational sequence
had been established; it could not be safely interrupted.

At a quarter to five, Benoit Deschesnes appeared, as he did most
evenings, for a walk in the Luxembourg Gardens, that sixty-acre re-
doubt of tranquillity and play in the Sixth Arrondissement. Ambler
watched him through his pair of field glasses, relieved that the dignitary's movements were unself-conscious and fluid. He seemed lost in
thought, and perhaps he was.

Decades ago, Ambler had once been told, members of the Lost
Generation snatched doves at the Luxembourg Gardens in order to
fend off hunger. These days there were more children than artists
about. The gardens, in the best French manner, were formally arrayed, the trees in geometric patterns. Even in the winter, children

could ride on an aging carousel or watch a display of Grand Guignol puppetry.

Such scenes flitted through Ambler's head but left little impression; he was intent on mounting his own work of Grand Guignol theater. He had already ascertained that he had picked up his followers, as he had hoped; the Brooks Brothers–clad American affected to be reading the plaques at the bases of various statues. A few hundred feet away, a small group of jeans-wearing Frenchmen busied themselves in a game of *petanque,* while others huddled over chess tables. Still, the park was relatively vacant.

Deschesnes, as another glance verified, was walking as instructed, his coat open to the breeze, displaying his white shirt. He sat for a moment on a bench in the park, apparently admiring the fountain, still pulsing even in winter. The day was cloudless and the evening sun cast shadows across the empty flower beds. The physicist shivered.

Ambler hoped that Deschesnes had remembered all of his instructions. Directly over the bloodpacks, his white shirt was invisibly scored with a razor blade, to ensure that when the tiny explosive charges were detonated the fabric was punctured.

"Remember," Ambler had cautioned the physicist, "when the squibs go off, don't try anything overly dramatic. Forget about what you've seen onstage or on screen. Don't throw yourself backward; don't fall forward; don't fold your hands together on your chest. Just slump, gently, to the ground, as if you were hit by an immense wave of drowsiness." Ambler knew that though the metal would protect Deschesnes from injury, the man would be genuinely startled by the squib explosions; they were bound to be somewhat painful, whatever precautions were taken. That was a good thing: it would make his reaction to the "gunshots" all the more convincing.

It took Ambler several minutes to locate the man with binoculars who was watching the scene from a window in one of the elegant apartment buildings overlooking the gardens. The man would be able to see only Deschesnes' back, at the moment, but that would suffice. Only another professional could tell that Ambler was anything more than an exercise enthusiast in a sweat suit, returning from his exercise, his gym bag slung over his shoulder. Ambler continued to scan the area until he found the brunette in the midlength coat. Then he waited for events to unfold.

They were his audience, though he could not swear there were no others. When Ambler was sure that none of the civilians were watching, he disappeared silently into the evergreen bushes sixty yards from the fountain and set up the rifle. He had Deschesnes plainly in view once more. Ambler activated the small walkie-talkie he had stowed in his bag. Holding the microphone close to his mouth, he spoke quietly.

"Deschesnes. If you can hear me, scratch your ear."

A moment later the physicist did so.

"I'm going to count down from five. When I reach one, squeeze the device in your pocket and close the circuit. Don't worry. This'll all be over soon." He looked around. A young woman passed close to the bench and moved on. Another group of people was approaching from thirty yards away. They would make good witnesses. He raised the rifle and let the barrel emerge a couple of inches from the bushes. He wanted Fenton's brunette to see it. "Five, four, three, two, one—" He fired twice, then a third time. A distinct spitting sound punctuated each squeeze of the trigger, the sound of a silenced rifle. A faint plume of gas would have been visible from the muzzle; the human eye would not be able to detect the fact that no actual projectile came from it.

In perfect sequence, a spurt of red fluid burst through the front of Deschesnes' shirt, and then two more. Deschesnes made a loud grunt—Ambler could see, through the scope, the startled look in his eyes—and slumped from the bench to the cold ground. Red stains were visible on his stiff white shirt, seeping and spreading.

The men playing *petanque* saw what had happened and ran first toward the body and then, as one of them realized the dangers, away. Ambler swiftly dismantled the rifle and put it back in his bag. Then he waited. For a long minute, nothing happened. Then he heard the sound of an ambulance. He took a white coat from the athletic bag and put it on. Laurel stopped the ambulance, as they had arranged, and ran toward the body.

Now Ambler ran to the ambulance, his white coat flapping, and grabbed a stretcher. It took him about thirty seconds. When he got there, Laurel, white-coated like him, was standing mute and pale, staring down at Benoit Deschesnes. "He's dead," she said in a quavering voice.

"Right," Ambler said, and heaved the body onto the gurney. *Something was wrong.*

"No, I mean he's really dead." Laurel gave him a stricken look.

Ambler felt as if he had swallowed ice. *It was impossible.*

Yet the body had the limpness, the heaviness, of death.

"We need to get him out of here," Ambler murmured, his eyes only now focusing on the fallen man. Then he saw it.

A tiny trickle of blood falling from the man's hairline, a tiny, circular area of matted hair above. Ambler felt the man's scalp with his fingertips and was overcome by a roiling wave of vertigo. There was a small-caliber bullet hole a few inches above his forehead. It was the kind of shot that bled very little and caused instantaneous death. A shot that could have come from above—from too many potential sniper nests to count. Someone, somewhere in the park or the adjoining buildings, had shot the UN's chief arms inspector through the head.

Numbly, the two moved the body as quickly as they could to the ambulance. It could not be left behind or the squibs would give away Ambler's failed intrigue. Yet too much time had elapsed. The vehicle had by now attracted a group of curious onlookers. Ambler closed the rear door and began to remove Deschesnes' clothes. He took off the makeshift squib vest and wiped the fluids off Deschesnes' chest.

Now Ambler heard pounding on the door of the ambulance. He looked up.

"*Ouvrez la porte! C'est la police!*"

Why? Did one of the policemen want to ride with them to the hospital? Was that standard procedure? It could not be permitted. They were two Americans in a stolen ambulance, with a dead body. Ambler moved swiftly to the front of the vehicle and climbed into the driver's seat. The engine was still running. They had been planning to drive out of Paris to the Bois de Boulogne, where Deschesnes had parked a rented car. Now there was no point. But they needed to go *somewhere.* He put the vehicle in gear. This was not the moment for a conversation with the gendarmerie.

Ambler glanced at the scene behind him in the rearview mirror. A policeman was shouting angrily into his walkie-talkie. At the edge of the park, a little set off from the rest, the brunette in the midlength coat was talking on her cell phone. Ambler hoped she was reporting only that he had accomplished his mission. But then he noticed something over her shoulder that sent a chill running through his body.

There, ten yards behind Fenton's agent and mingling with a crowd of curious bystanders, was a face he wished he did not recognize. A Chinese face. A handsome, slightly built man.

The gunman at the Plaza Hotel.

CHAPTER SEVENTEEN

Washington, D.C.

The main building of the United States Department of State, 2201 C Street, was really two adjoining structures, one completed in 1939, the other in 1961—one, that is, at the advent of a world war, the other at the nadir of the Cold War. Every organization has a local history, an institutional memory that is cherished within its hallowed walls, if forgotten outside them. At the Department of State, there were auditoriums and meeting rooms for public events that bore the names of deceased dignitaries—there was, for example, the Loy Henderson Room, honoring a revered Director of Near Eastern and African Affairs from the forties; and a large hall named for John Foster Dulles, the Secretary of State during the crucial years of the Cold War. Deep within the bowels of the newer building, however, were secure conference rooms that were not even dignified with names but known only by numeric and alphabetic designations. The most secure such conference room was designated 0002A, and a casual visitor to the basement might have assumed that it was given over to maintenance and janitorial equipment, like those to either side. The room was along a subterranean corridor of gray-painted cinder block, copper pipes, aluminum ductwork, and exposed fluorescent tubes. Meetings there were never "catered"; one did not go to any of the triple-zero rooms expecting pastries or cookies or sandwiches. The meetings were to be endured, not enjoyed, and anything that might prolong them was to be shunned.

Certainly the subject of this morning's conference afforded no one any gratification.

Ethan Zackheim, the leader of the freshly assembled team, scanned the eight people at the table for signs of unspoken dissent. He was wary of "groupthink"—of the tendency of groups to fall into step, to agree on a unitary interpretation where the evidence itself was equivocal, open textured, ambiguous.

"Does everyone here feel confident of the appraisals we've been hearing so far?" he asked. Only noises of agreement were voiced.

"Abigail," Zackheim said, turning to a large-boned woman in a high-collared blouse. "Are you confident of your read of the signals intelligence?"

She nodded, her brown bangs lacquered and immobile. "It's confirmatory," she cautioned, "not conclusive. But in combination with the other data streams, it raises the confidence level of the assessment."

"What about your team at Imaging, Randall?" He turned to a slender, chalky-faced young man in a blue blazer, who sat at the table with his shoulders hunched.

"They've verified it twenty different ways," Randall Denning, the imaging expert, replied. "It's authentic. We're seeing a subject whom Chandler's people have identified as Tarquin, arriving at the Montréal Dorval just hours before the Sollinger assassination. We've confirmed the authenticity of the security video. We don't see a significant margin of uncertainty here." He slid the Montreal photographs to Zackheim, who looked them over, though fully aware that his unaided eyes would see nothing that had eluded the imaging experts with their computer-assisted methods of analysis.

"Likewise this picture, from the Luxembourg Gardens, about four hours ago," the imaging expert went on.

"Pictures can be misleading, no?" Zackheim gave him a questioning look.

"It's not just about the picture, it's about our ability to interpret them, which has become immeasurably more sophisticated in recent years. Our computers can look at 'thresholding,' border analysis, saturation gradients of all kinds, and detect variances that even most experts would never notice."

"Plain English, dammit!" Zackheim interjected.

Denning shrugged. "Consider that this one image is an enormously rich package of information. The twig patterns of a tree, the sap spills, the algae growth—all these things change day by day. A simple tree is never the same object two days in a row. Here you've got a complex field of objects, terrain with a very particular contour, patterns of shadows, which not only identify the time of day but also provide information about the configuration of thousands of discrete objects." He tapped at the lower quadrant of the photograph with a black stylus. "Under magnification, we can see that there's a bottle cap approximately three centimeters from the gravel path. An Orangina bottle cap. It wasn't there the day before."

Zackheim found himself drumming his fingers. "That seems a pretty slender reed—"

"*Diurnal detritus* is the trade jargon in my department for this sort of detail. It's exactly what makes real-time archaeology possible."

Zackheim fixed him with a hard stare. "We're about to do something that's as serious as a coronary, and every bit as irreversible. I need to be sure we have everything nailed down. Before Tarquin is declared 'beyond salvage,' we need to be sure we're not heading off half-cocked."

"Certainty is possible in high school arithmetic textbooks." The speaker was a round-bellied man with a spherical head and heavy black-framed glasses. His name was Matthew Wexler, and he was a twenty-year veteran of the Department of State's Bureau of Intelligence and Research. He was a homely man with a slovenly appearance. He was also in possession of a formidable intellect, compared by one Secretary of State to a combine harvester: he had the uncanny ability to assimilate vast quantities of complex information and turn them into clear bullet-point distillations. He could translate data into action items, and he was not afraid to make a decision. In Washington, it was a quality of mind that was in scarce supply and great demand and valued accordingly. "Certainty does not exist in the real world of decision making. If we were to wait for complete certainty, action would be so delayed as to be irrelevant, and as the painful old saw reminds us, 'Not to decide is to decide.' One cannot decide with no information. But one can't wait until one has complete information. There's a gradient between the two termini, and procedural integrity consists in the ability to choose the right point of partial knowledge."

Zackheim struggled to conceal his annoyance. Ever since someone had dubbed this credo the Wexler principle, the analyst missed no opportunity to recite it. "In your view, have we reached it?"

"In my view," Wexler said, "we're a safe distance beyond it." He stretched his arms in a stifled yawn. "I'd also draw people's attention to the question marks that hover over previous assignments of his. This is someone who must be stopped. Discreetly. Before he brings his employers into disrepute."

"I trust you mean his *former* employers." Zackheim turned again to the chalky-faced young man in the blue blazer. "And the identification is good?"

"Very," Randall Denning said. "As we've discussed, Tarquin has changed his physiognomy, by surgical means—"

"The typical resort of an agent gone rogue," Wexler put in.

"But the basic facial indices are constant," Denning went on. "You can't alter the distance between the orbital cavities—the eye sockets—or the slope of the supraorbital foramen. You can't change the curve of the mandible and maxilla without destroying dentition."

"What the hell's *that* supposed to mean?" Zackheim barked.

The imaging expert glanced around him. "The point's just that plastic surgery can't touch the basic bone structure of the skull. The nose, cheeks, chin—these are superficial protuberances. Computer-assisted facial identification systems can be set to ignore them and zero in on what can't be changed." He handed Zackheim yet another photograph. "If *that* is Tarquin"—the image showed a man in his thirties, a distinctively Western face in a crowd of Asians—"then so is *this*." He tapped his hard rubber stylus at the surveillance photograph of the man at the Montreal airport.

The deputy director of Consular Operations, Franklin Runciman, had said little at the meeting. He was a rugged-looking man, with piercing blue eyes, a heavy brow, strong features. His suit looked expensive, a blue-gray worsted with a subtle windowpane pattern. Now he sat glowering. "I see no reason to postpone a decision," he said at last.

Zackheim had been perplexed, even annoyed, by Runciman's decision to attend the meeting; Zackheim had been tasked with leading the team, but the presence of a more senior officer could not but undermine his authority. Now he gave the deputy director an expectant look.

"Alerts will be relayed to all of our stations and posts," the Cons Ops man said in a rumbling voice. "And a 'retrieval' team"—he pronounced the euphemism with vague distaste—"must be tasked and deployed. Capture or terminate."

"I say we bring in the other agencies," Zackheim said, clenching his jaw. "The FBI, the CIA."

A slow head shake from Runciman. "We'll outsource if we need to, but we don't drag in our American colleagues. I'm old-school. I've always believed in the principle of self-correction." He paused and turned his piercing gaze on Ethan Zackheim. "At Cons Ops, we clean our own litter box."

CHAPTER EIGHTEEN

Paris

When had it happened—and what, exactly, had happened? There were surprises everywhere. One of them was Laurel herself. Once again, she had undergone a shattering experience—yet remained unshattered. Her resilience was remarkable and heartening. The proximity of death had only heightened emotions already latent within them. Fear was one of them, but there were others, too. More and more, he found, he had started to think in the first-person plural: there was an *us* where there had once been merely a *me*. It was a thing compounded of words and looks, of shared emotions—both exhilaration and despondency. Of pain and respite from pain. And quiet laughter. It was a thing of gossamer, and he knew of nothing stronger.

It seemed a small miracle. They created a normalcy where none had existed; they conversed as if they had known each other for years. Asleep in bed—he grew aware of this last night—their bodies cupped each other's naturally, limbs gently interlaced, as if they had been made for it. When their bodies coupled in lovemaking, there was bliss, and, at moments, there was something even more elusive—something very like serenity.

"You make me feel safe," Laurel said after a while as they lay together beneath the sheets. "Is it insulting to be told that?"

"No, though it might be tempting fate," Ambler replied with a small smile. He had, in fact, thought about changing hotels and decided against it; the risks of a new registration at a new establishment exceeded the risks of maintaining the old.

"But then you already knew that's how I felt, didn't you?"

Ambler did not reply.

"It's funny," she said. "I feel like you know everything there is to know about me, even though that can't really be."

My Ariadne, he thought. *My beautiful Ariadne.* "There are facts, and there are truths. I don't know the facts. Maybe, though, I know a few truths."

"Because of the way you see," she said. "It must make some people uncomfortable. That sense of being seen through." She paused. "I guess I ought to feel that way, too. Like my slip is showing, only a thousand times worse. But I don't. Never have. It's the darnedest thing. Maybe I don't care if my slip is showing around you. Maybe I want you to see me for what I am. Maybe I'm tired of being looked at by men who just see what they want to see. Being seen through is almost a treat."

"There's a lot to look *at,*" Ambler said, smiling and pulling her close.

She interlaced her fingers with his again. "It reminds me of what kids say, sometimes: 'I know that you know that I know that you know . . .'" A slow smile appeared on her face, as if the smile on Ambler's face had spread to hers. "Tell me something about myself."

"I think you're one of the most sensitive people I've ever met," Ambler said steadily.

"You should get out more." She grinned.

"When you were a girl, you were different from the others, weren't you? Maybe a little bit on the outside of things. Not an outsider, exactly, but you maybe had an ability to see things that others didn't, including yourself. The ability to, you know, pull the camera back a little bit."

Laurel was not smiling any longer. She was looking at him now, transfixed.

"You're a caring person, an honest one, too, but you have a hard time letting people in, letting people know the real Laurel Holland. Once you finally do let somebody in, though, it's pretty much for keeps, as far as you're concerned. You're loyal that way. You don't form friendships fast, but when you form them, they *are* fast—fast and strong, because they're for real, not for show. And sometimes, maybe, you wish that you could form personal relationships more easily, that you could slip in and out of them the way other people do." Ambler paused. "Is this making sense to you?"

She nodded silently.

"I think you're a deeply trustworthy person. Not a saint—you can be selfish; you can have a temper, too, sometimes, and lash out at people close to you. But when it really counts, you're *there*. You understand the importance of being a good friend. It's important to you that you seem in control, but often you don't *feel* that way. It's almost an act of will, of discipline, to keep yourself calm and in command of situations, which also means being in command of yourself."

She blinked slowly but remained silent.

"There have been times in the past when you've been too honest with your feelings," Ambler went on. "When you felt that you revealed too much of yourself. And that's made you a little cautious sometimes, even a little reserved."

Laurel took a deep breath, let it out unsteadily. "There's just one thing you missed—or maybe you were too polite to mention," she said quietly. There was a catch in her voice. Her eyes were inches from his, and he could see her pupils widen.

Ambler pressed his mouth to hers and took her in his arms, a long, slow embrace that was almost an act of lovemaking in itself. "There are some things that don't need to be put in words," he whispered after a while, and he sensed—he *knew*—that the glow that suffused him also suffused her: brightening, warming, like a dawn within them.

Later, as they lay together, bodies slick with sweat and sheets almost randomly intertwined with limbs, she gazed at the ceiling and spoke. "My dad was a Vietnam vet," she said, sounding far away. "A good man, I think, but damaged, almost like my husband got to be. You might think I was drawn to that type, but I don't think so. It was just my lot in life."

"He hit your mom?"

"Never," she said sharply. "*Never*. He would have lost her forever if he raised a hand to her even once, and he knew it, too. People talk about uncontrollable rages. Very few of 'em are really uncontrollable all the way. The tide sweeps up the beach, but it won't go past the sandbags. Most people have sandbags of a sort in their lives. The things you won't say, the things you won't do. My dad grew up on a dairy farm, and if he had his druthers, he'd have had me raised with a milk pail in my hands. But he had a family to support. And there were certain economic realities to be faced. So I grew up in a subdivision in Virginia, outside of Norfolk. He worked in an electrical equipment plant; Mom worked as a receptionist at a doctor's office."

"Maybe something else that drew you to the medical profession."

"The suburbs of the medical profession, anyway." Laurel closed her eyes for a moment. "The place where I grew up wasn't much of anything, but it had a good school district, and that's something they cared about. Good arts program, I guess. They thought I'd do well there. Mom cared a lot about that. Maybe too much. You could tell she used to think Dad was going to make more of himself than he ever did. She kept telling him to ask for a raise, a promotion. Then one day she ended up talking to some people at the plant—it might have been a bake sale at the school, some event like that—and, well, I didn't put it together right away, but I guess she was led to understand that the plant was only keeping Dad on the payroll in the first place out of kindness. His Vietnam service and all. So a promotion wasn't really in the cards. Mom changed a little after that. I think she was sad at first, and then business-like. Like she'd just given up on him, but she'd made her bed and had to lie in it."

"Which left you."

"As a vehicle for hoping? Yeah." A trace of bitterness entered her voice. "And when I won my first Oscar and thanked her in front of a billion television viewers, well, you can see how all her dreams came true."

"She's dead, isn't she?" Ambler said gently. "They both are."

"I guess she was never prouder than when they saw me play Maria in the high-school production of *West Side Story*," Laurel said, her voice thickening. Ambler saw that her eyes had grown moist. She turned to him, but in her voice was the distance of something old newly recollected. "I can still hear my dad hooting and whistling when the curtain came down, and stamping his foot. But it was when they were driving home that it happened."

"You don't have to say it, Laurel."

Tears were rolling down her cheeks, dampening the pillow beneath her head. "There was an icy patch on some intersection and a municipal trash hauler fishtailed there, and Dad just wasn't paying attention, he'd had a couple of beers and they were both happy, and he was driving a company truck when he plowed into the van, and it was filled with electrical equipment. The truck stopped; the equipment kept flying forward. Crushed them both. They were in the hospital, in a coma, for another two days, and then they both gave out, died within the very same hour."

She squeezed her eyes shut, trying to clear the wetness from them, striving to regain control. "Maybe it changed me. Maybe it didn't. But it became part of me, you know? A drop of dioxin in the watershed."

The wound had been bandaged and healed by time, Ambler knew, but it was not the kind of wound that could ever heal fully. Ambler knew, too, exactly why it was important to her that he know. She wanted him to know her—*needed* him to know her, not just who she was but how she became who she was. Her very *identity* was what she sought to share with him. It was an identity that was composed of a hundred thousand mosaic tiles, a hundred thousand incidents and memories, and yet was unitary all the same, a single, un-questioned thing. An entity that was *hers*—no, an entity that was *her*.

Ambler felt a churning sense of something he did not immediately recognize as envy.

Beijing

Was it possible to enjoy protection without suffering isolation? It was something of a koan, thought President Liu Ang. Certainly the city within a city that was the Zhongnanhai often seemed isolated to him. Like the emperor Kuang-hsü, in his splendid captivity, the president wondered whether he was not dwelling in a gilded or, any-way, lacquered, cage. Yet it would be selfish not to take some ele-mentary precautions: the stakes were great, greater than his individual life. By the same token, however, he could never consent to the crippling suggestion that he demur from overseas appear-ances, such as his upcoming presentation at the World Economic Forum. If he were to heed the counsel of fear, he would lose the mo-mentum that was necessary for his reforms to succeed. The presi-dent's gaze drifted out the window. In winter the North Lake and the South Lake looked glazed, dull—like the eyes of a slain giant, Liu Ang thought. They made him shiver; familiarity could not dull the ominous pulse of history.

Yes, his greatest concern had to be the security of his agenda—his legacy—rather than of his life. It would be a fool's compact to sacri-fice the first on the altar of the second. If his death could usher in the new era of freedom and democracy he so ardently wished for, he hoped he would have the physical courage to accept it. At the mo-ment, however, it appeared that his continued existence was more likely to secure such an arrangement: he hoped this belief was not mere vanity. Besides, if he were to succumb to vanity, there was always the *jiaohua de nongmin* to correct him. Everyone feared the wily peasant's sharp tongue—particularly sharp, some wags said, because of the long years he spent having bitten it—but the *jiaohua de nongmin* no longer feared anyone.

The youthful president looked at the familiar faces who had gathered around the black lacquered table—familiar faces with familiar-looking worry lines.

Chao Tang, of the Ministry of State Security, Second Bureau, was looking especially sobersided this morning.

"We have new intelligence," he was saying.

"True or just new?" Liu Ang asked lightly.

"Both, I fear." Comrade Chao was not in a joking mood, but then he seldom was. From a slender leather portfolio he withdrew a number of photographs, showing them to Liu Ang before passing them to the others.

"Here is the man they call Tarquin," Comrade Chao said. "In Canada, at the meeting of the G7 a couple of days ago. You will notice the time stamp on this photograph. Just a few minutes previously, a member of the European delegation was assassinated. Kurt Sollinger. A friend of ours, economically speaking—someone who was working hard on an economic agreement that would have facilitated trade between this country and the European Union."

The soft-spoken man who sat to Liu Ang's left, his special advisor on domestic security matters, shook his head glumly. "When the wood owl kills the chicken, the good farmer must take up arms against the wood owl."

"I thought wood owls were extinct," the president said wryly.

"Not yet, but soon, if precautions aren't taken. You have *that* in common," snorted Wan Tsai, the president's aging, peppery mentor, his large eyes blinking through his wire-rimmed glasses.

"And here is another photograph of Tarquin," Comrade Chao resumed, "taken in the Luxembourg Gardens in Paris minutes before the IAEA director-general, Benoit Deschesnes, was shot dead. Dr. Deschesnes, as it happens, was preparing an arms-inspection report that would have cleared this regime of the canard that we have been contributing to nuclear proliferation."

The soft-spoken security advisor looked even more distressed. "Here is an assassin who has the future security of China itself in his sights."

"The vital question," Liu Ang said, "is *why*."

"That is optimistic. The vital question may be *when*." Comrade Chao laid two photographs of Tarquin side by side. "Here is a magnification of Tarquin, taken at the Changhua incident. Here he is again in Canada."

"Why, they are different men," the president said.

"No," Comrade Chao said. "Our analysts have scrutinized the images for those aspects of physiognomy that cannot be altered—such as the distance between the eyes, the distance from eye to mouth, and so forth—and they have concluded that this is the same man. He changed his appearance, obviously in an attempt to elude his enemies. Some reports say he had plastic surgery and has gone rogue. Other reports insist that he remains in the employ of his government."

"There are many ways of working for one's government," said the *jiaohua de nongmin* grimly.

President Liu Ang glanced at his watch. "I appreciate the update, gentlemen," he said. "But I cannot be late for my meeting with the PLA Industrial Committee. They will take it poorly." He stood and, with a quick bow, excused himself.

The meeting, however, did not adjourn.

"Let's return to the president's question," Wan Tsai said. "It is not to be brushed aside. Quite simply: Why?"

"*Why* is indeed an important question," said the white-haired man known as the wily peasant, turning to Comrade Chao. "In particular, why is the assassin still alive? When we last met, you said you had taken measures."

"Perhaps he is even wilier than you," Comrade Chao said softly.

Paris

The Fourteenth Arrondissement, which extends from the boulevard du Montparnasse, was once favored by the American community in Paris. Yet Ambler doubted that this was why Fenton had chosen the area for his safe house—or at least one of his safe houses, for Ambler suspected he owned many. Through the usual maze of one-way streets, the arteries conveyed a steady stream of traffic bound to Orly and the industrial districts farther to the south. Protesters, a genus as defining of Paris as the homeless are of New York, had long favored Denfert Rochereau, at the intersection of the major arteries. But even the less trafficked streets offer an array of Breton crêperies, night-clubs, and cafés. One had to go farther into the arrondissement be-fore one reached the quiet, residential neighborhoods. Forty-five rue Poulenc was in one such. Fenton had given Ambler the address when they spoke in Montreal. It was where Ambler was to report in, fol-lowing the Deschesnes assignment. After his one visit, the Strategic Services branch office was declared strictly out-of-bounds.

Forty-five rue Poulenc was striking only in its drabness. It might have been taken for the office of a local professional—an optician or a dentist. Dusty venetian blinds were visible in the stoop-level win-dow; in other windows, one could see spider plants hanging from planters, cheerless attempts to establish good cheer.

Ambler buzzed and then waited for nearly a minute, during which his visage was doubtless being scrutinized, either through the peep-hole or by means of a hidden camera. A low thrumming indicated that the door was opened. He turned the knob and walked into the carpeted foyer. There was no one visible in the hallway. A narrow staircase on the right was covered with an expensive-looking runner held in place with brass rods at the corner of each tread and riser. He heard a voice through an intercom near the base of the staircase, Fenton's voice, his baritone sounding tinny through the small speakers: "I'm downstairs. End of the hall."

Ambler made his way through an unlocked door and down another narrow staircase. At the landing, he saw a closed pair of double doors and knocked.

Paul Fenton opened the door and brought him into what looked like a scholar's study. Every available surface was lined with books. Not the kind bought for decor but the kind that had been put to serious use: books with fraying spines, many faded by the years.

"Have a seat," Paul Fenton said bluffly. He gestured toward a wheeled office stool and then sat down on a metal folding chair nearby.

"Love what you've done to the place," Ambler said. He was oddly calm. The ambulance had been stowed in an automatic parking garage; nobody at Hotel Beaubourg glanced at them twice when they returned. Just like that, they had been immersed in utter normality again. Now, entering the billionaire's quietly bizarre empire, Ambler just felt numb.

"You laugh," Fenton replied, "but it's a nearly exact replica of Pierre du Pré's office at the Collège de France. Upstairs—it's an almost perfect replica of the office of a Montparnasse *dentiste*. Could be a film set. I had two of our technicians do it, just to see whether it could be done. Wasn't easy, I can tell you."

"They say two heads are better than one," Ambler said, swiveling slowly on his vinyl-topped stool. "I suppose you figure that two pairs of hands are better than one."

"How's that?"

With studied nonchalance, Ambler turned to face the mogul fully. "I was just surprised that you'd decided to post a second gunman at the Luxembourg Gardens—without telling me, I mean. You may have considered it a backup feature, but in my opinion it's operationally unsound. I might have taken out your guy by mistake. Misidentified him as a hostile."

"Not following," Fenton said with a mildly quizzical expression.

Ambler bore down on him. "I'm just saying I don't work with backups if I don't know about them."

"What backups?"

Ambler studied Fenton's features for any flicker of dissembling, for the faintest twitch of tension. There was none whatever. "And as for the Chinese gentleman . . ."

"What Chinese gentleman?" Fenton interjected blandly.

Ambler paused. "You have no idea what I'm talking about, do you?" he said at last.

"Afraid not," Fenton said. "Was there someone else at your rendezvous, Tarquin? Something I need to be worried about? If you've got any reason to suspect a security lapse, I need to know."

"Believe you, if I had, you'd be the first to hear," the American operative replied smoothly. "No, nothing like that. I appreciate your need to have observers in position."

"But that's standard protocol," Fenton protested.

"Not a problem. In Stab operations, I usually knew the full complement, but that was then. Forgive an old jungle cat for being on edge. Really, it's nothing to be concerned about."

"Good," Fenton said. His success had come from his capacity for narrow-bore focus—which meant he would not be distracted by details he could deem irrelevant. "I was worried about you for a moment. But you've lived up to your reputation. I'm very pleased. You did the job, did it swiftly and cleanly. Showed resourcefulness, swiftness, top-notch decision-making skills. Executive caliber. Fact is, I think you've got a future in my inner circle. Top of the org chart. Mind you, there are no desk jockeys at SSG. The people who have a bird's-eye view of everything have got to be raptors themselves. That's my philosophy." He stopped, raised a hand. "But I haven't forgotten our conversation outside the Palais des Congrès. There was stuff you wanted to find out. I'd told you that you had powerful enemies and powerful friends, and it seems I was right. I spoke to my principal partner at State."

"And?"

"Clearly there's a story to be told, but they won't tell it to me. A matter of information partition—which is fine, I can respect that. Good news is, the principal has agreed to a face-to-face meeting with you, promises to fill you in completely. We'll schedule it soon as we can. Maybe even here."

"Who's the principal?"

"I promised not to say. Not yet. One thing you'll learn about me, Tarquin, is that I'm a man of my word."

"And I'm holding you to it," Ambler snapped. "Dammit, Fenton— I told you I was to be paid with *knowledge*. You think you can fob off a check's-in-the-mail excuse like that?"

Fenton's ruddy face colored further. "It's not like that, Tarquin," he said steadily. "My partner very much wants to meet you. All the more now. That's going to happen within a matter of days. And it's not like you're going to be cooling your heels in the meantime. I know that an operative like you must be eager to get back to work. At this point, there's no assignment I wouldn't entrust you with. Not a lot in this world that's good as advertised. But you are, Tarquin. You are."

"What can I say?" Ambler replied neutrally. *Ariadne's thread— find where it leads.*

"Got a *real* exciting project for you coming up. But don't pack your skis just yet. There's just one more assignment we've got for you here."

"One more?"

"A man who really needs killing," Fenton said. "Apologies for being so plainspoken. But this one's going to be tricky."

"Tricky," the operative echoed.

"Tell you what else, a Cons Ops 'beyond salvage' order has already gone out on this guy. They're put their in-house best on it. But when the rubber hits the road, they still come to me. Because they can't leave anything to chance. You bring in Fenton, you're guaranteed of results. So now I'm putting *my* best on it—and that means you."

"Tel me more about the target."

"We're talking about somebody with top-notch skills and training. A high-flying covert-ops ace gone bad."

"Sounds like trouble."

"You bet. About the worst thing that can happen."

"Who?" Ambler asked simply.

"A sociopath who happens to have reams of government intel in his head, because of his experience in the field and in the office." Fenton had a look of grave concern. "Firsthand knowledge of all kinds of government secrets, pass codes, operational procedures, you name it. And he's *out of his mind.* Every day this guy draws breath is a day his country is at risk."

"Thanks for narrowing it down. But I'll need to start with a name."

"Of course," Fenton said. "The target's name is Harrison Ambler."

The operative blanched.

Fenton raised an eyebrow. "You know him?"

Ambler struggled to breathe normally. "Let's just say we have a history."

PART THREE

CHAPTER NINETEEN

Langley, Virginia

Clayton Caston returned to the patient file "jacket," which had just arrived this morning, and briefly scrutinized the color copy of the small photograph. A handsome but unremarkable face, though with something almost cruel about the sharp regularity of its features. Caston did not dwell on the image long. There were some investigators who liked putting a "face" on their quarry; he was not among them. Digital signatures, patterns of expenditures—those were far more revealing than the contingent details of what one already knew: that the person in question had two eyes, a nose, and a mouth.

"Adrian?" he called.

"Yes, *Shifu*," Adrian replied, pressing his flattened hands against each other, in a prayerful gesture of mock homage. *Shifu*, Caston had learned, meant "instructor" and was an honorific used in martial-arts movies. The young had a curious sense of humor, Caston reflected.

"Any progress with the personnel list for Ward 4W?"

"No," Adrian said. "But you got the 1133A, right?"

"I did indeed. Impressively expedited."

"Plus you saw I got an actual copy of the patient file 'jacket,' with his actual photograph."

"I did," Caston said.

"As for the personnel lists, though—well, they're saying that the lists are being updated."

"We'll take whatever they have."

"That's what *I* said. No-go." Adrian bit his lower lip contemplatively, and his gold labret stud glinted in the overhead fluorescents. "I gotta say, it's been tough. I swear, they're literally battening the hatches."

Caston arched an eyebrow, mock censorious. "*Literally* literally or figuratively literally?"

"Don't worry. I haven't given up."

Caston shook his head with a fading smile and leaned back in his chair. His unease was growing. The data he had received felt predigested somehow. Prepared. As if it had been meant for eyes like his. More and more information about Tarquin had been furnished— concerning his assignments as a member of the Political Stabilization Unit of Consular Operations. But there was not a molecule more about Tarquin's civilian identity. And nothing at all about how he had been committed to the Parrish Island facility. Normally, that was a paperwork-intensive process. Yet somehow the paperwork pertaining to Tarquin's confinement there was unavailable. Parrish Island was a secure government facility; there had been extensive records of each employee. Yet Caston's every attempt to get personnel records from Tarquin's ward had been stymied. Caston doubted that the clerks were complicit; he even doubted whether his counterparts at the Department of State would dare to circumscribe his investigation. But that meant that the blocking agent or agents were at another level: either lower, beneath the radar, or higher, above scrutiny.

It was *galling*, really.

Caston's phone chirped with the double tones of an internal call. Caleb Norris was on the other line. He did not sound happy. Caston was to come see him immediately.

When Caston arrived at the office of the Assistant Deputy Director of Intelligence, Norris appeared as morose as he had sounded.

He folded his ropy arms on his chest, tufts of curly black hair protruding from his cuffs; his broad face wore a look of distraction.

"Word from the top. We've got to bring this investigation to an end."
Norris's eyes did not meet Caston's as he spoke. "There it is."

"What are you talking about?" Caston controlled his surprise.

"Thing is, there have been some high-level communications between State and the DCI," Norris said. His forehead was gleaming with sweat and flashed in the slanting late-afternoon sun. "The message we're getting is, the investigation is interfering with a live special-access operation."

"And what are the details of that operation?"

Norris shrugged with his whole upper body. His face was darkened with a mixture of annoyance and repugnance, neither directed at Caston. "Special-access, right? We haven't been entrusted with that information," he said, sounding flustered. "They say Tarquin's in Paris. They'll pick him up there."

"Pick him up or pick him off?"

"Who the hell knows? It's like a gate has slammed down. Beyond what I've said, we know bupkes."

"The proper response to an outrage," Caston said, "is to be outraged."

"Goddammit, Clay. We've got no choice on this. This isn't a game. The DCI himself is saying hands off or heads off. You hearing me? The DCI himself."

"That son of a bitch wouldn't know a polynomial from a polyp," Caston snapped. "It's *wrong.*"

"I know it's wrong," Norris flared. "A goddamn institutional power play. Nobody in the intel community wants to acknowledge the primacy of Central Intelligence. And until we've got the backing of the commander in chief and the Senate, it isn't going to happen, either."

"I really don't like to be interrupted," Caston persisted. "Once I begin an investigation . . ."

Norris shot him an exasperated look. "What you think, or I think—that's really the least of it. There are procedural principles at stake. But the fact is, the deputy director caved on this, the DCI has made his decision, and it's our job to fall into line."

Caston was silent for a long moment. "Don't you find this whole thing *irregular*?"

"Well, sure." Norris began to pace unhappily.

"It's *damned* irregular," Caston said. "Doesn't sit well with me."

"Me, neither. And it doesn't make a bit of difference. You're closing the books, and so am I. Then we're burning the books. And we're forgetting we ever opened them. That's our marching orders."

"Damned irregular," Caston repeated.

"Clay, you gotta choose your battles," Norris said in a defeated tone.

"Don't you find," the auditor replied, "that it's always your battles that choose you?" He turned on his heel and started to walk out of the ADDI's office. Who the devil was calling the shots, anyway?

Caston continued to brood as he returned to his desk. Perhaps one irregularity deserved another. His eyes darted from the files on his desk to those in Adrian's less tidy work space, and the wheels in his head kept turning.

They say Tarquin's in Paris. They'll pick him up there.

Finally, he took out a yellow pad of paper and began to make a list. Pepto-Bismol. Ibuprofen. Maalox. Imodium. It wouldn't do to travel without such medicinal precautions. He'd heard about "traveler's tummy." He shivered as he contemplated the prospect of getting into an airplane. It wasn't about heights, the fear of crashing, or the sense of enclosure. It was the prospect of breathing in the endlessly recycled breath of his fellow passengers . . . some of whom could well have tuberculosis or some other airborne mycobacterial infection. The whole affair was so *unsanitary*. He would be assigned a seat from which some flight attendant had sponged up vomit earlier in the day. Intestinal parasites could lurk in every crevice. Blankets would be distributed and with them long spirochete-ridden *hairs* clinging to them by static.

He had a *Merck Manual* in a lower desk drawer, and it was all he could do to keep himself from starting to flip through the index.

He exhaled noisily, his sense of dread deepening, and put down his pen.

Once he arrived, there would be the repugnance of foreign food to cope with. France would have its own parade of horrors; there was no getting around it. Snails. Frogs' legs. Mold-veined cheeses. The distended livers of force-fed geese. He didn't know the language; communication problems would be a constant peril. He might order chicken and get, instead, the flesh of some revolting creature that tasted just like chicken. In a tuberculoid-weakened state, such mishaps could extract an even greater toll.

He shuddered. It was a very heavy burden he was taking on. He would not do so if he had not been sure that the stakes were very high.

He picked up his pen again and began making further notes.

Finally, after filling most of the front sheet with his neat script, he looked up and swallowed hard. "Adrian, I'm going to be traveling. To Paris. On vacation." He tried to keep the dread out of his voice.

"That's *super*," said Adrian with inappropriate enthusiasm. "A week or two?"

"I'd think so," Caston said. "What does a person normally pack on such a trip?"

"Is this a trick question?" Adrian asked.

"If so, the trick's not on you."

Adrian pursed his lips contemplatively. "What do you *usually* take on vacations?"

"I don't go on vacations," Caston replied with wounded dignity.

"Well, when you travel."

"I hate traveling. Never do it. Well, except to pick up the kids from camp, if that counts."

"No," Adrian said. "I don't think that does count. Paris will be great, though. You'll have an incredible time."

"I very much doubt that."

"Then why are you going?"

"I told you, Adrian." A rictus-like display of teeth. "Vacation. Nothing to do with work at all. Nothing to do with our investigation, which, I have just been officially instructed, is to be discontinued."

Comprehension dawned on Adrian's face. "You must find that . . . *irregular*."

"Highly."

"Verging on the *anomalous*."

"Quite."

"Got any instructions for me?" Adrian brandished a ballpoint pen. "*Shifu*?" There was a glint of excitement in his eyes.

"I do have a few, now that you mention it." Caston allowed himself a small smile as he leaned back in his chair. "Listen well, Little Grasshopper."

CHAPTER TWENTY

Paris

Within a few hundred yards of the Place de la Concord, the rue St. Florentin was an elegant Haussmann-style block, with spindly wrought-iron balconies adorning tall, multipaned windows. Red awnings sheltered the storefront windows of upscale libraries and perfumeries, which alternated with the offices of foreign bureaucracies. Including the one on 2 rue St. Florentin. It was the Consular Section of the U.S. embassy and the last place Ambler should show himself. Yet in that seeming recklessness lay the rationale of his decision.

After what had happened at the Luxembourg Gardens, there was little doubt in Ambler's mind that Consular Operations stations, here and around the world, would be on alert for Tarquin. Paradoxically, it was an anxiety he could exploit.

It was partly a matter of knowing what one was looking for, and Ambler did. He knew that the clerical services offered by the "consular section" at 2 rue St. Florentin were a perfect cover for the Cons Ops station. On the ground floor, hapless tourists with lost passports lined up and filled out forms given out by a clerk who had all the animation of a funeral director. When it came to non-citizens in particular, it would not do to get anyone's hopes up. Visa applications were processed at the pace of a snail with Parkinson's.

None of the visitors or regular employees ever thought to wonder what took place on the upper floors; to wonder why they insisted on a separate cleaning service from that employed by the visa and passport processors and used different exits and entrances. The upper floors: Paris Sector, Cons Ops. A realm that, as Fenton's new request had proved, had decided that a former HVA known as Tarquin was beyond salvage.

He would try to enter the lion's den—but only if he could be certain that the lion had left it.

The lion in question was one Keith Lewalski, a corpulent man of sixty who ran the Consular Operations' Paris Sector with an iron fist and a level of paranoia that was more suited to midcentury Moscow than to contemporary Western Europe. The resentment, even scorn, that he inspired among his underlings was a matter of indifference to him; those to whom he reported viewed him as a solid manager, with a record free of any notable failures. He had risen as far he had wished to, had never harbored any further ambitions. Ambler knew him only by reputation, but the reputation was a formidable one, and Ambler had no intention of putting it to the test.

It was all in Laurel's hands.

Had that been a mistake? Was he placing her in jeopardy? Yet he could think of no other means to accomplish what he needed to accomplish.

He took a chair at a nearby café and glanced at his watch. If Laurel had succeeded, he should see the results at any moment now.

And if she failed? A cold fear washed over him.

His instructions for her had been detailed, and she had memorized them thoroughly. But she was not a professional; would she be able to improvise, to deal with the unexpected?

If all had gone according to their schedule, she would already have placed a phone call from the American embassy at 2 avenue Gabriel; he would have done so himself, but he could not take the chance that the consulate switchboards hadn't been equipped with voiceprint analyzers. Yet had she been able to do it?

They had discussed various scenarios, various pretexts, various eventualities. She was to have presented herself to the public affairs section as the personal assistant of a well-known museum curator, one who was involved in the International Partnerships Among Museums program and who had dispatched her to retrieve an agenda for an upcoming meeting. The pretext was as simple and vague as that. It had been easy enough to gather enough plausible details from the embassy's Web site. Ambler was also counting on the fact that the embassy's cultural affairs department was disorganized to the point of dysfunction. Its staffers were continually tripping over one another's shoes, variously duplicating or dropping administrative tasks. The curator's assistant would have been sent up to the fourth floor, while the apparent error or miscommunication was sorted through. While there, she would have asked to use a private telephone to call her boss and explain the mix-up.

Then her instructions were to dial the number he had given her, using the particular argot he had prepared her with, and so convey an urgent summons to Keith Lewalski. A State Department dignitary from Washington had arrived at the embassy; a debriefing with Mr. Lewalski was sought, immediately. The consulate switchboard would have authenticated the call as originating from the U.S. embassy; the special words and phrases employed would convey the urgency.

Laurel's assignment required little by way of acting but a great deal by way of precision. Could she do it? *Had* she done it?

Ambler glanced at his watch again, trying not to think of all that could have gone wrong. Five minutes later, as he watched an aging, obese bureaucrat emerge from 2 rue St. Florentine with a harried air and get into a limousine, he felt a pulse of relief. She had done it.

Could *he*?

As soon as the limousine turned the corner, Ambler strode into the building with an air of someone jaded but resolute. "Passport applications to the left, visa applications to the right," said a bored-looking man in a uniform. He sat at what looked like a schoolroom's chair desk. On it was a cup filled with golf pencils—presharpened three-and-a-half-inch eraser-less pencils. They probably went through a couple of dozen a day.

"Official business," Ambler grunted to the uniformed man, who directed him to the back with a brusque nod. Ignoring the lines at the other counters, Ambler walked up to the "Official Inquiries" desk. A heavyset young woman sat at the counter, a preprinted list of office supplies spread out before her. She was ticking off boxes.

"Arnie Cantor around?" Ambler said.

"Just a sec," the woman said. He watched her wander back through a door. An efficient-looking young man trotted back to the counter moments later.

"You wanted Arnie Cantor?" he asked. "Who can I say was asking for him?"

Ambler rolled his eyes. "Either he's here or he's not here," he said, exuding a sense of supreme boredom. "Start with that."

"He's not here at the moment," the young man said carefully. He wore his hair short—corporate short, not military short—and had the open-faced look that junior clandestine types made a point of cultivating.

"Meaning he's in Milan, shtupping the *principessa*? No, don't answer that."

The young man cracked a smile despite himself. "Never heard her called that," he murmured. He gave Ambler a slightly overrehearsed look of complete candor. "Maybe I can help you."

"It's above your pay grade, trust me," Ambler replied testily. He glanced at his watch. "Aw, shit. You guys are a complete joke, aren't you?"

"I'm sorry?"

"Not half as sorry as you're gonna be."

"If you'll tell me who you are . . ."

"You don't know who I am?"

"I'm afraid not."

"Then the assumption you should make is that you're not *supposed* to know who I am. You smell to me like you're a couple of weeks out of the incubator. Do yourself a favor. When you're over your head, call for a lifeguard."

The incubator—Cons Ops slang for the special training program that all field agents had to undergo. The young man gave Ambler a crooked smile. "What do you want me to do?"

"You got a couple of choices, don't you? You can get Arnie on the phone—I'll give you Francesca's number if you don't have it. Or you can rustle up one of your desk cowboys upstairs. I'm the bearer of news, *comprenez-vouz*? And the sooner you get me out of the sight lines of the civvies out here, the better. In fact, let's go now." He glanced at his watch again, dramatizing his impatience. "Because I really don't have any more time. And if you fuckups were on the ball, I wouldn't have had to drag my sorry ass here in the first place."

"But I'll need to see some identification?" The request turned into a query; the young agent felt wrong-footed, uncertain.

"Man, you are going down for the third time. I got no shortage of identification—for five different identities. I told you I got dragged in here from the field. You think I got my real papers on me?" Ambler broke off. "Hey, don't let me give you a hard time. I was once standing exactly where you are now, you know that? I remember what it's like."

Ambler stepped behind the counter and pressed the button to the accordion-doored elevator a few yards away.

"You can't go up there by yourself," the young man said.

"I'm not," Ambler replied breezily. "You're coming with me."

The young man looked bemused but followed Ambler inside the elevator. The authority and assurance in the stranger's voice were far more effective than any certificate or form of identification could have been. Ambler pressed the button for the third floor. Despite the antique-looking fixtures—the accordion gate, the leather-clad door with the small window—the machinery itself was new, as Ambler expected, and when the elevator opened again, he stepped into what looked like an entirely different building.

Not an unfamiliar one, however. It looked like any number of divisions at the State Department's Bureau of Intelligence and Research. Rows of desks, flat-screen computers, telephone units. Rows of pails with shredders affixed to their top—standard State Department protocol after the 1979 takeover of the U.S. embassy in Tehran. Most of all it was the personnel who looked familiar: not as individuals but as types. White shirts, repp ties: with small adjustments, they could be employees of IBM from the early sixties, the heyday of the American engineer.

Ambler quickly scanned the room, identifying the senior-most officer moments before the man—pigeon-chested, wide-hipped, a narrow, priggish face with heavy black eyebrows, hair that flopped over his forehead in a manner that must once have been collegiate-cool—rose to his feet. Keith Lewalski's second-in-command. He had been seated at a corner desk in a room that had no private offices.

Ambler did not wait for his approach. "You," he called brusquely to the pigeon-chested man. "Come over here. We need to talk."

The man walked over with a look of perplexity.

"How long you been stationed here?" Ambler demanded.

A brief pause before he spoke. "Who are you, exactly?"

"How *long*, goddammit."

"Six months," he replied cautiously.

Ambler spoke to him in a low voice. "You get the Tarquin alert?"

A fractional nod.

"Then you know who I am—who *we* are. And you know better than to ask any more questions."

"You're with the retrieval team?" The man spoke in a hushed voice. There was anxiety in his expression, and a measure of envy, too—a bureaucrat speaking to a professional assassin.

"There is no retrieval team, and you never met me," Ambler said, his voice like gravel, even as he assented to the query with a fractional nod of his own. "That's how we're going to play it, you understand? Any problems with that—any problems with *us*—you take it up with the undersecretary, you got that? Though if you're interested in career longevity, I'd think twice about it. People are putting their asses on the line out there, so you can keep your fat asses on the chairs in here. I lost a man today. If our investigation reveals that you've been slacking on the job, I'm going to be ripshit. And so's everyone in my chain of command. Let me remind you: time *is* of the essence."

The pigeon-chested man extended a hand. "I'm Sampson. What do you need?"

"It's mop-up at this point," Ambler said.

"You mean . . . ?"

"Target's been eliminated, as of 0900 hours."

"Fast work."

"Faster than we feared. Messier than we'd hoped."

"I understand."

"I very much doubt that, Sampson." Ambler's voice was imperious, authoritative. "We're concerned about your little boat over here. Worried you may have sprung a leak."

"*What?* You can't be serious."

"As a goddamn aneurysm. It's only one possibility—but we have to check it out. Tarquin knew too much. Like I said, it got messy. I'm going to need a secure communications hookup to Washington. I'm talking end-to-end security. No little pink ears pressed to the wall."

"We should really discuss this with—"

"*Now*, goddammit."

"Then you want the keep—the secure datasphere chamber, upstairs. Swept every morning. Designed for acoustic, visual, and electronic privacy, all according to department specs."

"I helped write those specs," Ambler said witheringly. "Specs are one things. Their execution is another."

"I guarantee its security personally."

"I've got a report to transmit. Which means I'm going to need to do some fast research, too. And let the chips fall where they may."

"Of course," Sampson said.

Ambler gave him a hard look. "Let's go."

Most major consular buildings contained some version of the "keep," where intelligence was stored, processed, and transmitted. In the past few decades, U.S. Central Command facilities had become especially important to the projection of American power, the State Department less so, bowing to the ascent of military over diplomatic resources in the post–Cold War conjuncture. That was the world, but it was not the world people like Sampson lived in; they dutifully filed their analytical reports and regarded themselves as in the thick of the action, even though the action had long since passed them by.

The secure datasphere was situated behind two separate doors, and the ventilation system was designed to give the chamber a slightly positive pressure relative to the rooms outside, so that one would be immediately aware if either of the doors was opened. The doors themselves were blast resistant, of thick steel with a rubberized flange that ensured a tight, soundproof seal. Specs called for walls made of alternating layers of fiberglass and concrete.

Ambler stepped into the chamber and pressed the button that magnetically clamped the doors closed. For a moment, there was silence; the room was unpleasantly hot and dimly lit. Then there was the low sibilance of a ventilation system kicking into gear, and the halogen lighting system blinked on. Ambler was in a space that was approximately four hundred square feet. There were two workstations, arranged side by side, surfaced with some sort of white laminate, and a pair of "task" chairs with oval seats and backs, clad in black synthetic fabric. At the workstations were flat-panel screens like they had downstairs and black keyboards; beige computer towers rested on a rack overhead. By means of a continuous high-speed fiber-optic connection, highly encrypted data was exchanged with the digital storage complex in Washington; remote data facilities like this one were updated—synchronized—on an hourly basis.

The triple-bay configuration held an eighty-four-terabyte storage system, equipped with proactive monitoring, along with error detection and correction software. It was also programmed, Ambler knew, with automatic erase features in case of disturbance. Every precaution had been taken to ensure that this vast data storehouse would never end up in the wrong hands.

Ambler turned on the monitor and waited a few moments for it to flicker to life; the connection was already live, already on. Now he began to type the keywords of his search. He had brazened his way into the most sensitive place in the Cons Ops station; his ruse could be exposed at any moment. He was assuming that Lewalski's trip to avenue Gabriel would take twenty minutes, but if traffic was light, it could be less. He would have to make use of his time wisely.

Wai-Chan Leung, he typed. A few seconds later, a standard biography appeared, prepared by the Department of State's Bureau of Intelligence and Research, the INR. Underlined hyperlinks led to separate files on the man's parents, their commercial interests, origins, political ties. The appraisal of the parents' business concerns revealed little of interest. Their dealings were not squeaky clean—friendly assemblymen duly received donations; minor payoffs to foreign officials in a position to expedite certain transactions were assumed, if not documented—but by the standards of the time and place conducted with a certain measure of probity. Impatiently he scanned the biography of Wai-Chan Leung himself, recognizing the familiar points on a familiar public time line.

There was no hint of the allegations that had been in the dossier prepared by the Political Stabilization Unit—and he was well acquainted with the methods of hinting, the techniques of indirection employed by professional intelligence analysts. They typically consisted of tepid disavowals preceded by "Despite rumors of contacts

with . . ." Or "Although some have conjectured that . . ." Yet there was
nothing of the sort here. The analysts were mainly interested in how
his prospects as a national political figure had been affected by his
"determinedly nonbelligerent rhetoric" on the subject of relations
with China. Ambler's eyes skittered and bounced from paragraph to
paragraph, like a racing coupe on a bumpy mountain road. Occasionally, he paused, at passages of potential significance.

> *Wai-Chan Leung had great confidence in a future of*
> *"convergent liberalization." He believed that the emergence*
> *of a more democratic mainland China would lead to more*
> *intimate political relations. His opponents, by contrast,*
> *maintained the older, inflexible posture of stalwart hostility*
> *and suspicion—a posture that doubtless reinforced the hos-*
> *tility and suspicion rampant among their counterparts in the*
> *Chinese Communist Party and People's Liberation Army.*
> *Wai-Chan Leung's position on this issue would probably*
> *have been politically untenable for any politician who lacked*
> *his enormous* personal *appeal.*

The words were dry, carefully parsed, but they referred to the ide-
alistic young candidate Ambler had seen—someone who had spoken
up for his ideals, regardless of political expedience, and been respected for it all the more.

Kurt Sollinger's file was far more cursory. A trade negotiator, he
had spent fifteen years on economic affairs for Europe, under various designations—the European Common Market, the European
Community, the European Union. He had been born in 1953 and
grew up in Deurne, Belgium, a middle-class suburb of Antwerp. Father a Lausanne-trained osteopath; mother a librarian. There were
the usual leftist affiliations from his years in high school and
college—spent at the Lyceum van Deurne, Katholieke Universiteit

Leuven—but nothing generationally unusual. He had been photographed with a group protesting the deployment of intermediate-range missiles in Germany during the early eighties, had been a signatory of various petitions circulated by Greenpeace types and other environmental activists. But such activism did not survive his twenties. Instead, he had taken to the groves of academe with a certain single-mindedness, working on an economics doctorate with a Professor Lambrecht, something to do with local economies and European integration. Ambler's eyes swept across the dry write-up, looking for—well, what? He couldn't be sure. But if there was a pattern to be uncovered, this was the only way to do it. He had to leave himself open and receptive. He would see it. Or he would not.

Ambler continued to scroll down, skimming a mind-numbing list of the various bureaucratic promotions and preferments that the multilingual Dr. Kurt Sollinger had attained. His progress was steady, if unspectacular, but in a field of highly trained technocrats like himself, he had slowly developed a reputation for integrity and intelligence. The next section of Sollinger's biosketch was headed "The East Team"; this report concerned his chairmanship of a special committee tasked with East-West trade issues. Ambler read more slowly. The group had been making notable strides in hammering out a special trade accord between Europe and China, an accord that, however, had been derailed by the death of the principal European negotiator, Kurt Sollinger.

His heart beginning to pound, Ambler keyed in the name of Benoit Deschesnes. He skimmed over the details of Deschesnes' lycée and university training, the fellowships and faculty appointments, the bureaucratic details of the Frenchman's consulting work for the United Nations Monitoring, Verification and Inspection Commission, and then his rapid rise to the helm of the International Atomic Energy Agency.

He found what he was looking for toward the end of the file. Deschesnes had appointed a special commission, tasked with investigating charges that the Chinese government had been engaging in nuclear proliferation. Many felt the charges had been made for political purposes; others worried that there could be fire where smoke had been detected. As director-general of the IAEA, Deschesnes had a reputation for rectitude and independence. The State Department's own analysts had concluded, based on its all-source intelligence review, that the report, a year in the making, would exonerate the Chinese government. The latest update, submitted and posted only several hours earlier, stated that the release of the special commission's findings would be postponed indefinitely due to the violent death of the principal investigator.

China.

The orb of the web was centered over China. The word told him everything and nothing. What was crystal-clear was that the assassination of Wai-Chan Leung did not arise from inadvertence; it was not the result of credulousness toward misinformation spread by his opponents. On the contrary, that misinformation was deliberately made use of. From every indication, Wai-Chan Leung's death was part of a pattern. Part of a larger effort to eliminate various influential personages who seemed well disposed toward China's new leadership. But *why*?

More questions, more conclusions. If he had been turned into a catspaw by cunning indirection, the same technique had no doubt been employed on others. Fenton's very zealotry would make it all the easier for someone to use him. Zealots like him were always in danger of being misdirected when their fanaticism overrode their instinctive wariness. It would be easy to appeal to his patriotism and feed him fake intel—then sit back to watch the results.

But again, *why*?

Ambler glanced at his watch. He had already stayed too long;

every passing moment escalated the risks. Before he switched off the monitor, however, he keyed in one final name.

Ten long seconds passed, as the eighty-four-terabyte array of hard disks whirled futilely before admitting failure.

No record for HARRISON AMBLER found.

CHAPTER TWENTY-ONE

The Daimler limousine that took Ellen Whitfield to the estate waited in a graveled parking area as the undersecretary herself strode into the magnificent building.

The Château de Gournay, just forty minutes to the northwest of Paris, was a treasure of seventeenth-century architecture that, if far less ostentatious than nearby Versailles, was no less impressive in its details. Designed by François Mansart for a duke in Louis XIV's court, the château was among the most noteworthy of its kind in France, from a foyer that was the apotheosis of the period's classicism to its much-photographed buffet of carved stone. The eleven bedrooms were intact from its original construction; the tennis court and pools were more recent additions. Over the past half-century, it had been used by international conferences of governmental and non-governmental organizations, by high-level conclaves of industrialists and their information-age successors. At the moment, it had been rented by a lavishly funded conservative think tank based out of Washington, at the behest of Professor Ashton Palmer, who chaired its Pacific Rim program and who always preferred settings that expressed the very finest of what civilization had to offer.

A liveried manservant greeted Undersecretary Whitfield in the foyer.

"Monsieur Palmer is waiting for you in the blue room, madame," the French servant told her. He was a man in his late fifties, with a broken nose, a square jaw, and a wiry build—a man who, one suspected, had a range of experiences and expertise that was greater than was strictly required by his ostensible position. Whitfield would not have been surprised if Palmer had hired a former member of the French Foreign Legion; he was a great believer in "dual-purpose" employees—the valet who was also a translator, the butler who was also a bodyguard. Palmer's penchant for multiplicity was related to an aesthetics of efficiency: he recognized that a person could play more than one role on the stage of history, that the best-chosen action would achieve more than one effect. Palmer's doctrine of multiplicity was, indeed, key to the scenario that was even now being played out.

The blue room turned out to be an octagonal bay overlooking the stables. The vaulted ceiling was at least sixteen feet high, the carpets the finest broadlooms of the period, the chandeliers easily of museum quality. The undersecretary stepped over to the window, taking in the beautifully contoured landscape. The stables themselves, elegantly built of brick and wood, could have been converted into an elegant manse.

"They understood craftsmanship, didn't they?"

Ashton Palmer's voice.

Ellen Whitfield turned and saw Palmer entering from a discreet set of pocket doors. She smiled. "As you always say, 'It is not the skill, it is the degree of skill.'"

"That was the striking thing about the Sun King's court: the very highest level of civility, the greatest appreciation for accomplishments in literary, artistic, natural-scientific, and architectural realms. At the same time, there was much they were oblivious to—the seismic instabilities of the social order they battened upon. The basis for the revolution that would consume their children a century later. Theirs was a spurious sort of peace, which contained the seeds of its own destruction. People are quick to forget what Heraclitus taught us: 'War is common, strife is customary, and all things happen because of strife and necessity.'"

"It's good to see you, Ashton," Whitfield said warmly. "These are—dare I invoke the old Chinese curse?—interesting times."

Ashton Palmer smiled. His silver hair was thinner than it had been when Whitfield was his student, but no less tidy, his forehead high and impressive; sheer intelligence radiated from his slate eyes. There was something ageless about him, something that transcended the day-to-day. Whitfield had, in the course of her career, encountered many figures deemed historic, but she believed that he was the one truly great man she had ever met, a visionary in every sense. It had been a privilege when she first made his acquaintance—she was conscious of it even then, when she was in her early twenties. She was equally conscious of it now.

"What have you to tell me?" the sage asked. Whitfield knew he had just flown straight from Hong Kong, but he looked remarkably rested.

"So far, everything has been happening exactly as you've predicted." There was a gleam in the undersecretary's eye. "As you *envisioned,* I should say." She glanced at herself in the elegant Venetian mirror. The pewter light of a French winter shafted through the leaded glass, accentuating her high cheekbones and strong features. Her chestnut hair, parted on one side, was carefully coiffed; she wore a cerise skirt suit and a single strand of pearls around her neck. Subtle eye shadow brought out the blue of her irises. "Quite a place you've got here."

"The Center for Policy Studies is about to hold a conference here. 'Currency Regulation: An East/West Perspective.' What did you tell your people?"

"The Château de Gournay is on the itinerary, no worries. Meeting with scholars on currency liberalization."

"Because precautions must still be taken."

"I'm well aware of this," the undersecretary said. She sat down at the giltwood table, and Palmer joined her there.

"I remember the first time I heard you lecture," she said, looking off through the leaded glass. "I was a Radcliffe undergraduate, you were teaching a survey course on 'global dominion' held at Sanders

Theatre, and you wrote three German words on the board: *Macht-politik*, *Geopolitik*, and *Realpolitik*. Someone in the back of the lecture hall called out, 'Are we going to have to speak German?' And you said no, but that there *was* a language we'd need to learn, and that only a few of us here would gain fluency in it: the language of politics."

Palmer's eyes crinkled in recollection. "I thought it fair to warn people."

"That's right," she said. "You announced that most of us just wouldn't ever have the knack. That only a few of us would master it on a high level, while the rest would fall into the clichés of the historically insignificant—the local alderman's view of the universe, I think you called it. Strong stuff for young minds."

"You had the mental sinews, even then," Palmer said. "The sort of tough-mindedness you either have or you don't."

"I remember when you talked about Genghis Khan, and how, in modern terms, one would have to say that he was devoted to trade liberalization and freedom of religion, because that was how he ran his empire."

"Which was precisely what made him so dangerous." He spread his hands out upon the pearwood marquetry.

"Exactly. And on the map, you showed the extent of the Khan empire, how by 1241 his son and heir, Ogodei, had taken Kiev, destroyed a German army in the East, pushed through Hungary, and reached the gates of Vienna. Then the hordes stopped. The Mongol empire was almost exactly coterminous with the Eastern Bloc. That was the mindblower. You showed us the two areas, one of the Mongol dominion, the other the Communist empire, from North Korea and China all the way to Eastern Europe. It was the same area—the 'footprint of history,' you called it. And it was mere fortuity that the Mongols stopped at Vienna."

"Mere fortuity," Palmer repeated. "Ogodei had died, and the army leaders wanted to return to help select his successor."

"You showed us that there was a pattern to the great empires. In the sixteenth century, Suleiman the Magnificent was the most powerful Ottoman sultan, and he was also the most committed to basic principles of equal justice, procedural fairness, free trade. As a historical proposition, you proved that the Eastern empires were always dangerous to the West in proportion to how liberal they were internally."

"A good many people have been unable to read the writing on the wall," Palmer said. "Especially when it's in Chinese."

"And you explained to these sleepy-eyed kids how for the past several centuries, China—the Middle Empire—had never posed a threat to Western hegemony, even though, in principle, it could have been its greatest rival. Chairman Mao was the real paper tiger. In China, the more totalitarian the regime, the more cautious, purely defensive, and inward looking its military posture. It was powerful material, powerfully delivered. The smart kids weren't sleepy eyed anymore, once they realized the implications of what you were saying. I remember getting goose bumps."

"Yet some things don't change. Your colleagues in the State Department still refuse to see the plain truth: that as China has become more Western in its governance, it has also become more of a menace—militarily as well as economically. The president of China has a pleasant face, and that face has blinded our government to the reality: that he, more than anyone, is determined to awake a slumbering dragon." He glanced at his slim, elegant Patek Philippe wristwatch. Whitfield noticed that it displayed sidereal time as well as the Eastern Standard and Beijing times.

"Even when I was a student, you seemed to understand so much more than anyone else. The seminar on international relations I took in my first year of graduate school—there was a sense of being one of the illuminati."

"Fifty students applied; I admitted only twelve."

"An amazing bunch. I couldn't have been the most brilliant of them."

"No," he allowed, "but you were the most . . . *capable*."

She remembered the first day of the grad seminar. Professor Palmer had talked about how the world looked from the perspective of the British prime minister Benjamin Disraeli in the late nineteenth century, at the helm of a mighty Pax Britannica. Disraeli must have assumed that his empire was imperishable, that the next century would belong to the British and their powerful navy. A few decades into the next century, Britain had been reduced to a second-rate power. It was a transformation, Palmer said, akin to the Roman Empire turning into Italy.

The twentieth century was the American century; America's industrial and economic supremacy was unchallenged in the aftermath of the Second World War, and the elaborate mechanisms of its military command posts projected its power to the farthest reaches of the globe. But it would be a mistake to assume, Palmer warned, that the next century was America's by right. Indeed, if the Middle Kingdom was fully to rouse itself, the next century could belong to *it*; the center of global preeminence could move east. And policies of "constructive engagement" were exactly the sort of thing that would strengthen the Chinese and speed their ascendancy.

Echoing Marx's repudiation of the French "Marxists" of the 1870s, Ashton Palmer had once quipped that he was "not a Palmerite." He was disavowing vulgar misconceptions of his core doctrines—the people who inferred historical inevitabilities from his work. Palmer's method brought together the grand history of *long duree*—the history of centuries-long epochs—with the microhistory of the very near term. It could not be reduced to slogans, saws, formulas. And *nothing* was inevitable: that was a crucial point. To believe in historical determinism was to embrace passivity. The history of the world was a history of actions taken by human beings. Such actions *made* human history. Such actions could remake it.

The liveried manservant cleared his throat.

"Professor Palmer," he said. "You've received a transmission."

Palmer turned to Whitfield with an apologetic look. "If you'll excuse me."

He disappeared down a long hallway. When he returned, a few minutes later, he looked both anxious and energized.

"Everything is falling into place," he told Whitfield. "Which raises the pressure."

"I understand."

"What about Tarquin?"

"As I said, everything is falling into place."

"And his newfound 'companion'—any concerns on that front?"

"No cause for concern. We're keeping an eye on things."

"I can't impress this upon you enough: seventy-two hours remain. Everyone must play his role to perfection."

"So far," Undersecretary Whitfield assured him, "everybody has."

"Including Tarquin?" Palmer demanded, his slate eyes flashing.

Whitfield nodded, with a trace of a smile. "Especially Tarquin."

Ambler's eyes were fixed straight ahead as he left 2 rue St. Florentin; he wanted to look like a man with no time to waste. That was not a great challenge, for he *was* a man with no time to waste. Once he was out on the street and away from the consulate, he adjusted his gait, adopting the air of an aimless stroller as he walked past the red awnings and glittering shop windows. He was walking away from the Place de la Concord, toward the rue Saint Honoré—from peace to honor, he supposed—acutely aware of his surroundings while affecting to be lost in his own world.

Environmental alertness was more than a matter of seeing. It was also a matter of listening: one always had to listen for the footfalls of someone, out of view, hurrying and then slowing down in an effort to maintain a constant distance from the one he was following.

Someone *was* following him, Ambler realized—but not in accordance with any clandestine mode of operating. Ambler heard the sound of someone hurrying in his direction, someone with legs significantly shorter than his and, to judge from the faint panting sounds, someone in poor physical condition.

Ambler knew he should feel alarm, yet the man scurrying after him was moving with all the subtlety of a waiter chasing a customer who had forgotten to pay his check. Perhaps that was the very point of the ruse—to overcome a seasoned operative's suspicions by an excess of obviousness?

Ambler lengthened his stride and turned left at the end of the block, onto the narrower rue Cambon, and then, after a short jaunt, onto the rue du Mont Thabor. Fifty feet ahead of him was an alleyway, serving some of the adjoining boutiques. He paused before it and pretended to check his wristwatch. Reflected on its dial he saw the man who had been pursuing him. With a swift, sudden movement, he whirled around and grabbed the stranger, wresting him into the alley and against a graffiti-strewn cinder-block wall.

The man was a singularly unimpressive specimen of humanity: pasty-faced, out of breath, with thinning black hair, faint hollows beneath his eyes, and a bit of a paunch. His forehead was gleaming with sweat. He was perhaps five foot six and looked entirely out of his element. His clothing—a cheap tan raincoat, a poly-blend white shirt, some sort of non-descript, boxy gray suit—was American, sold there if not manufactured there. Ambler watched his hands to see whether he would make a move toward a concealed weapon or device.

"You're Tarquin, right?" the pallid stranger asked, breathing hard.

Ambler slammed him against the wall—"*Ow*," the man protested—and ran his hands over his clothes, his fingertips alert to any kind of weapon: the pen that was a little too thick, a little too long, the wallet that seemed just a bit too bulky for a payload of paper and plastic.

Nothing.

Now Ambler stared at him hard, searchingly, looking for any flicker of guile. "Who wants to know?"

"Take your hands off me, you piece of shit," the man spit. There was a trace of Brooklyn in his voice, though just a trace.

"I said, who wants to know?"

The man drew himself up, a look of affronted dignity on his face. "The name's Clayton Caston." He did not offer to shake hands.

CHAPTER TWENTY-TWO

"Don't tell me," Ambler said with unconcealed scorn and suspicion. "You're a *friend*. You're here to *help me*."

"You've got to be kidding," the pallid man replied testily. "I'm no friend of yours. And I'm here to help myself."

"Who are you with?" Ambler demanded. The man was hopeless: his ineptness at basic field maneuvers was not the kind that could be faked. But he could be useful indeed as a part of a team, drawing Ambler out, lulling him into a sense of false confidence while others moved in for the kill.

"You mean my place of employment?"

"I mean right now, right here. Who else is out there? And *where*, goddammit? Tell me now, or I can promise that you'll never speak again."

"And I was wondering why you don't seem to have any friends."

Ambler formed a rigid-fingered spear hand and cocked his arm back. He wanted it to be clear that he could deliver a crushing blow to the man's neck at any moment.

"Who else is out there?" the man went on. "About eleven million Frenchmen, if you're counting the whole metropolitan area."

"You're telling me you're operating alone?"

"Well, for the moment," the man said, reluctance in his voice.

Ambler found himself starting to relax; there was no hint of dissembling in the man's face. He *was* operating alone. In saying so, he was not reassuring an anxious subject, Ambler sensed; he was admitting an awkward truth.

"But you should know I'm with the CIA," the man cautioned,

sounding nettled. "So don't get any ideas. If you hurt me, it would be bad for you. The Company hates paying medical bills. They wouldn't take it sitting down. So just put that . . . *hand* away. That's a real bad move for you. Could be bad for *me,* come to think of it. Definitely a lose-lose scenario."

"You're joking."

"A frequent surmise, and frequently erroneous," he said. "Listen, there's a McDonald's near the Paris Opéra. Maybe we could talk there."

Ambler stared at him.

"What?"

"*McDonald's?*" Ambler shook his head. "This some new agency rendezvous point?"

"I really wouldn't know. It's just that I'm not sure I can stomach the local grub. If you haven't guessed already, I'm not really into the"—he wriggled his fingers—" 'cloak-and-dagger' stuff. That's not my thing."

Ambler's eyes darted regularly to scan the streetscape. So far he had detected none of the subtle alterations in foot traffic that indicated that a pedestrian patrol—a squad of "walkers"—was in place. "Fine, we'll talk at a McDonald's." *You never agree to a rendezvous chosen by the other party.* "But not that one." Tarquin plunged his hand in the suited man's breast pocket and pulled out his cell phone. An Ericksson multistandard cell phone. A cursory inspection revealed that it had a prepaid French SIM card. Probably he had rented the device at Charles de Gaulle. Tarquin pressed a few keys, and the phone displayed its number, which he promptly committed to memory.

"I'll give you a call in fifteen minutes with an address."

The man glanced at his watch, a digital-display Casio. "Fine," he said, with a slight harrumphing sound.

Twelve minutes later, Ambler got out of the Pigalle metro. The

McDonald's was opposite the station; the milling crowds would make it easy for Ambler to maintain a discreet scrutiny of the venue. He phoned the man who called himself Caston and gave him the address.

Then Ambler waited. There were hundreds of methods by which walkers could discreetly insert themselves in position. The laughing couple by the newspaper kiosk, the solitary, sallow man looking dourly at the windows of a store for erotic "aids" of latex and leather, the young, apple-cheeked man clad in a fleece-collared denim jacket, with a camera hanging from a strap around his neck—all would move along momentarily, and all could be replaced by people of a similar profile, who would avoid eye contact with one another but would be invisibly connected by a common coordinator.

Yet such an insertion always produced subtle disturbances, which an alert observer could detect. Human beings spaced themselves from one another in accordance with laws they were unconscious of but that patterned their behavior all the same.

Two people in an elevator divided the space between then; if there were more than three, eye contact would be scrupulously avoided. When an additional passenger entered the cabin, the current occupants would reposition themselves to maximize the distances among them. It was a small dance, repeated hour after hour, day after day, in elevators around the world: people acting as if they had been trained in the maneuver yet entirely unconscious of what impelled them to move a little farther to the back, a little farther to the left, a little farther to the right, a little farther to the front. Yet the patterns were obvious once you were attuned to them. There were similar patterns—elastic and amorphous but real—to be found on the sidewalk, in the way people clustered around a shop window or lined up at a newsstand. The presence of someone who was *stationed* at a position where one usually stood out of mere human velleity subtly upset the natural order. A sufficiently receptive observer would be aware of disturbances just on the verge of consciousness. To spell out what was wrong, Ambler knew, was more difficult than simply, instantaneously, to *feel* it. Conscious thought was logical and slow. Intuition was fleet, unreflective, and usually more accurate. Within a few minutes, Ambler had satisfied himself that no surveillance team, no patrol, had arrived.

The pasty-faced man arrived via taxicab, stopping at the corner just before the McDonald's. When he got out, he swiftly craned his head around, squinting above him, a useless gesture that was more likely to identify himself to anyone following him than it was to identify the followers.

After the CIA man entered the restaurant, Ambler watched until the cab had disappeared down the road and around the corner. Then he waited another five minutes. Still nothing.

Now he crossed the busy street and walked into the McDonald's. It was dark inside and illuminated with reddish lights, which struck Ambler as apt for a red-light district. Caston was seated at a corner booth, nursing a coffee.

Ambler bought a couple of Royals with bacon and sat down at a table that was in the rear third of the restaurant but afforded a clear view of the door. Then he caught Caston's eye and gestured for him to join him. Caston had evidently selected his booth because it was the least visible. It was the sort of defensive mistake that no field agent would have made. If hostiles entered your arena, it was because they knew you were present. Far better to be aware of *their* presence as soon as possible—to maximize your own state of awareness. Only amateurs blinded themselves to stay out of sight.

Caston sat down opposite Ambler at the small blond-wood table. He looked unhappy.

Ambler kept scanning the room. He could not eliminate the possibility that Caston was an inadvertent cat's-paw; if there were a transponder in the heel of his shoe, for example, it would be easy to assemble a team out of sight; visual surveillance would be unnecessary.

"You're bigger than your photograph," Caston said. "Then again, your photograph was only three by five inches."

Ambler ignored him. "Who knows you're here with me?" he asked impatiently.

"Just you," the man replied. There was a grumble in his voice but, again, not a trace of dissembling or guile. Liars frequently looked at you attentively after they spoke; they wanted to see whether you went for the lie or they needed to do more in order to persuade you. Those who told the truth, in ordinary conversation, just assumed they would be believed. Caston's eyes settled on the hamburgers on the tray in front of Ambler. "You going to eat both of those?"

Tarquin shook his head.

The American picked up a hamburger and started to wolf it down. "Sorry," he said after a while. "Haven't eaten for a while."

"Hard to get a good meal in France, huh?"

"Tell me about it," the man said earnestly, oblivious to Tarquin's sarcasm.

"No, you tell me. Who are you really? You don't look like a CIA agent. You don't look like any kind of field agent or law enforcement officer." He regarded the stoop-shouldered, soft-bellied man before him. The man was obviously out of shape. And out of place. "You look like an accountant."

"That's right," the man said. He took out a mechanical pencil and pointed it at Ambler. "So don't mess with me." He smiled. "Actually, I was a CIA before I joined the CIA. Certified Internal Auditor, you know. But I've been with the agency for thirty years. It's just that I'm the kind who don't usually get out."

"Back office?"

"That's what you front-office types would say."

"How did you end up at the Company?"

"Do we really have time for this?"

"Tell me," Ambler said, an insistent note in his tone that was not far from a threat.

The man nodded; he understood that the man he knew as Tarquin was not asking out of idle curiosity but as a measure of verification. "The quick story is that I started out working on corporate fraud at the SEC. Then I did a stint at Ernst & Young, except somehow that seemed too much like *doing* corporate fraud. Meantime, some bright spark in Washington figured that the Company really *was* a company, on some basic level. Decided they needed to bring in someone with my peculiar skill set." He drained his coffee. "And they did mean peculiar."

Ambler studied the man as he spoke and, again, detected no deceit. "So I was found by a rank amateur in the field," Ambler said. "A complete desk jockey. I don't know whether to be amused or mortified."

"I may be a complete desk jockey, Tarquin. That doesn't make me a complete idiot."

"Quite the contrary, I'm sure," the operative said. "Tell me how you found me, and tell me *why*."

A smile flicked at the corner of the man's mouth, a moment of suppressed vanity. "It was simple, really—once I heard you were Paris bound."

"As you pointed out, that's an area with a population of eleven million."

"Well, I started to think about the probabilities. Paris isn't a good place to hide out: it's still a major sector for the intelligence communities of several nations. In fact, it's pretty much the last place you should be. So you weren't here to go to ground. Maybe you had a job to do—but then why wouldn't you decamp as your earliest opportunity? Left decent odds that you were here because you were in pursuit of something—of information. Now, what would be the last place in the world that a former Consular Operations employee, one now classified as 'rogue,' should make an appearance? Obviously, the Paris offices of Consular Operations—at least, that's the way my colleagues would figure it. Last place you should be."

"So you promptly made your way there and kept a vigil on the bench across the street."

"Because the information you needed had to involve Consular Operations in some way, and the world of Consular Operations was the one you were most at home with."

"So it was just a feeling you had, huh?"

Caston's eyes flashed. "A 'feeling'?" He was majestic in his scorn. "A 'feeling'? Clay Caston does not proceed by *feelings*. He does not traffic in hunches or intuitions or instincts or—"

"You want to keep your voice down?"

"Sorry." Caston flushed. "I'm afraid you touched a nerve."

"Anyway, by your wonderful succession of logical inferences—"

"Well, it's more a matter of a probabilistic matrix than strict syllogistic logic—"

"By whatever screwy juju you rely upon, you decided to stake out one particular doorway. And you got lucky."

"*Lucky?* Obviously you haven't heard anything I've said. It was a matter of applying Bayes' Theorem to estimate the conditional probabilities, giving due weight to the *prior* probabilities and thus avoiding the fallacy of—"

"But the harder question is *why*. Why were you looking for me?"

"A *lot* of people are looking for you. I can only answer for myself." Caston paused. "And that's hard enough. A few days ago, all I was interested in was finding you so that you could be put out of business—an irregularity eliminated. But now, I've come to think that there's a *larger* irregularity to contend with. I'm in possession of certain data points. I believe you are in possession of a somewhat different set of data points. By pooling the information—establishing a larger *sample space,* to use the technical term—we may be able to make progress."

"I still don't understand why you aren't in your office sharpening pencils."

Caston snorted. "I was being *stonewalled* is what it comes down to. There are some bad actors who want to find you. I want to find *them*. That might give us a shared interest."

"Let me see if I've got this straight," Ambler said. He kept his voice quiet and conversational, knowing it would be lost in the general hubbub at any distance greater than three feet. His eyes continued to scan his surroundings. "You wanted to track me down to take me out. Now you want to track down others who want to track me down."

"Exactly."

"Then what?"

"Then? Well, then it will be your turn. After I turn them in, I'll want to turn you in. After that, it's back to sharpening those Number Two pencils."

"You're telling me that *eventually* you hope to 'turn me in'? Put me 'out of business'? Why would you *tell* me a thing like that?"

"Because it's the truth. See, you represent everything I *detest*."

"Flattery will get you nowhere."

"Fact is, people like you are a blight. You're a cowboy, and you're deployed by other cowboys, by people who have no consideration for rules and regs, people who will take the shortcut every time. But that's not all I know about you. I also know that you pretty much always know when someone is lying to you. So why should I bother?"

"What you heard is right. It doesn't spook you?"

"Makes life easier, the way I figure. Prevarication was never my strong suit."

"Let me ask you something one more time: Have you told anyone where I am?"

"No," Caston replied.

"Then tell me why I shouldn't kill you."

"Because it's like I said. In the short run, we have certain shared interests. In the long run—well, as Keynes said, in the long run we're all dead. I figure you'll take your chances on a temporary alliance."

"The enemy of your enemy is your friend?"

"Christ, no," Caston said. "That's *hateful* philosophy." He started to fold up the paper wrappings into an origami crane. "Let's be clear. You're not my friend. And I'm sure as hell not yours."

Washington, D.C.

Ethan Zackheim gazed at the faces of the analysts and technical specialists assembled around the table at conference room 0002A and idly wondered how many tons of stone and concrete lay above him—six stories of 1961-era construction, the hulking mass of 2201 C Street. Just now, the weight on his own shoulders felt oppressive enough.

"All right, people, we obviously haven't achieved our objectives, so please tell me that we've at least *learned* a thing or two. Abigail?"

"Well, we've analyzed his consulate downloads," said the signals-intelligence specialist, her eyes darting uneasily beneath her brown bangs. Tarquin's penetration of a supposedly secure data facility in Paris remained a sore spot among them—a coup both stunning and mortifying, and the occasion for recriminations in all directions—and that was not a discussion any of them wanted to revive. "Three of his searches were for info pertaining to Wai-Chan Leung, Kurt Sollinger, and Benoit Deschesnes."

"His victims," grunted Matthew Wexler. As a twenty-year veteran of the State Department's Intelligence and Research Bureau, the INR, the policy analyst claimed the prerogative to interject freely. "The criminal revisiting his crimes."

Zackheim loosened his tie. *Is it hot in here or is it just me?* he wondered but decided not to ask it out loud. He had a feeling it was just him. "What sense does that make?"

"It makes the connection between him and these victims pretty damn clear if it wasn't already." Wexler leaned forward, his round belly pressed against the table. "I mean, we had strong circumstantial evidence before, but now there can't be any doubt at all."

"I don't think the image analysis can be dismissed as *circumstantial*," Randall Denning, the imaging expert, said quietly, as if only to put his demurral on the record. His blue blazer sagged around his slight frame. "It places him at the scene. Definitively."

"Matthew, you're proceeding under the assumption that we all agreed to make," said Zackheim. "But something about these downloads gives me pause. Why would someone be investigating the backgrounds of the people he killed? I mean, isn't that the kind of thing a guy does *before* taking someone out?"

At the opposite end of the table, Franklin Runciman, the deputy director of Consular Operations, looked uneasy with the direction Zackheim was taking. He cleared his throat. "Ethan, you're right that there are multiple interpretations available to us." His eyes seemed especially piercing beneath his heavy brow. "There always are. But we can't pursue multiple courses of action. We have to pick one, based on our best read of the evidence—*all* the evidence. We don't have time to entertain counterfactuals."

Zackheim clenched his jaw. Runciman's question-begging summary exasperated him: what was factual and what was contrary to fact was exactly the issue to be resolved. But it was pointless to remonstrate. Runciman was correct, anyway, that multiple interpretations were possible. Still, Abigail's findings disturbed Zackheim for reasons he found difficult to articulate. Tarquin, whoever he was, appeared to be doing what *they* were doing—he was acting as if he was conducting an investigation, not as if he was the target of an investigation. Zackheim swallowed hard. It didn't sit well with him.

"The real kick-in-the-pants is Fenton," Wexler said. Zackheim noticed that the analyst had not remembered to button his button-down collar. Given Wexler's brilliantly well-organized mind, of course, nobody cared about his personal dishabille.

"It's a definite ID," Denning put in. "That's the man accompanying Tarquin in the immediate arena of the Sollinger assassination. Paul Fenton."

"Nobody's disputing that," Wexler said, as if speaking to a slow student. "We know he was there. Question is what that signifies." He turned to the others. "What's the latest on that?"

"There have been some clearance issues here," Abigail said in a gingerly tone.

"Clearance issues?" Zackheim was incredulous. "What are we, the editorial board of *The Washington Post*? There shouldn't be any internal impediments here. Clearance? That's bullshit!" He turned to Wexler. "What about you—you pick over Fenton's files here?"

Wexler turned his beefy palms up. "Sequestered," he said. "The special-access protocol is inviolate, it seems." His eyes darted toward Runciman.

"Explain." Zackheim spoke directly to Runciman. Bureaucratic logic told him that the deputy director of Consular Operations had either acquiesced to the barriers or actively implemented them.

"It's not relevant to the purposes of this team," Runciman said, unfazed. Even under the cheap fluorescent lights, his dark suit—some sort of charcoal flannel with a subdued pattern—looked sleek and expensive.

"*Not relevant?*" Zackheim was almost spluttering. "Isn't that something for the team to decide? Dammit, Frank! You asked me to spearhead this thing, we've got all your aces here from Imaging, Sigintel, Analysis—and you're not going to let us do our jobs?"

Runciman's rugged features betrayed not a trace of tension, but his eyes bore down on Zackheim. "We've moved past the fact-finding part of the assignment. Now the *job* is to execute the mission we agreed on. Not to convene a bull session, not to speculate about hypotheticals, not to do archival research or indulge your idle curiosity. When a mission is established, your job is to make sure it succeeds. To provide operational support and *actionable* intelligence to our deputized agents so they can do what we've tasked them to do."

"But the picture we're getting—"

"The picture?" Runciman cut him off, with undisguised scorn. "Our *job*, Ethan, is to take the bastard *out* of the picture."

Paris

Half an hour later, the two men, operative and auditor, arrived separately at the hotel where Caston was staying, a curious, cramped place called the Hotel Sturbridge, part of an American-based chain. Caston was obviously trying to insulate himself from the local environs as much as possible, and his room was large, by Parisian standards, albeit boxy and institutional in feel. It could have been a hotel in Fort Worth. Caston invited Ambler to sit on a cabriolet-legged armchair, upholstered in mustard velveteen, as Caston set about arraying papers on a small, glossily veneered desk, the sort of object that proclaimed its cheapness by its failed attempt to look posh.

Caston asked Ambler a few dry, pointed questions about experiences since leaving Parrish Island; Ambler's responses were equally matter-of-fact.

"A bizarre . . . condition," Caston said after a while. "Yours, I mean. This whole erasure thing. If I weren't in the bottom decile for empathy, I'd have to think that the experience would be kind of *unsettling*. It's like some strange identity crisis or whatnot."

"*An identity crisis?*" Ambler scoffed. "Please. That's when a software engineer holes up in a small adobe house in New Mexico and reads a lot of Carlos Castaneda. That's when a Fortune 500 marketing exec decides to quit his job and start a business selling vegan muffins to organic food stores. We're way beyond that—can we agree on this?"

Caston gave a half-apologetic shrug. "Listen, I've spent the past few days assembling all the data points I could, with the help of my assistant. I've retrieved a good deal of your performance record at the Political Stabilization Unit, or, anyway, what purports to be a performance record." He handed a stapled sheaf of pages to Ambler.

Ambler thumbed through it. It was a curious sensation, to see, in a desiccated and abbreviated form, the product of blood, sweat, and tears. It filled him with a sense of bleakness. His career, like that of so many others, was one devoid of any public profile; its utter obscurity was to be redeemed by the covert heroism of his actions. That was the promise, the covenant: Your deeds, albeit hidden, may change history. You will be history's hidden hand.

But what if that was all an illusion? What if a life of obscurity—a life that had forced him to sacrifice the close human ties that gave meaning to so many lives—was without any real and enduring consequences, or at least any good ones?

Caston caught his gaze. "Focus, OK? You see anything that looks faked, you let me know."

Ambler nodded.

"So a profile emerges: you've got an extraordinary facility at 'affective inference.' A walking polygraph. Gives you a lot of value in the field. The Stab team snaps you up early on in your Cons Ops career. You're in the rough-and-tumble. Engaged in the kind of assignments that the unit likes to get up to." He was not trying to hide his distaste. "Then we've got the job at Changhua. Successfully completed, according to the files. Next thing, you drop off the map. Why? What happened?"

Ambler told him briskly, keeping his eyes on Caston's face all the while.

Caston didn't speak immediately, but after a while, his gaze sharpened. "Tell me exactly what happened the evening when you were taken away. Everything you said, everything that was said. Everything—and everyone—you remember seeing."

"I'm sorry, but I don't . . ." His voice trailed off. "It just isn't there. Laurel says it's something to do with drug-induced retrograde amnesia."

"It has to be in your head somewhere," Caston said. "Doesn't it?"

"I don't know," Ambler said. "There's my life, and then it sort of rags off into nothing for a while."

"A lost weekend."

"To another order of magnitude."

"Maybe you're not trying hard enough," Caston growled.

"Dammit, Caston. I lost *two years* of my life. Two years of mind games. Two years of desolation. Two years of hopelessness."

Caston blinked. "That's six years."

"If you ever get to thinking about entering the helping professions, Caston, don't. You have no idea what I've been through—"

"Neither do you. That's what I'm trying to find out, right? So save your whining for somebody who'll pretend to give a damn."

"You don't get it. I cast my mind back then, and there's nothing, OK? Nothing but fuzz on the screen. No picture." A wave of exhaustion swept over him. He was tired. Too tired to talk. Too tired to think.

He walked over to the bed and lay down, staring miserably at the ceiling.

Caston snorted. "Screw the picture. Start with the small facts. How did you get back from Taiwan?"

"No idea."

"What means of conveyance?"

"God*dammit,* I told you *I don't know,*" Ambler exploded.

Caston was undeterred, seemingly blind to Ambler's emotions, to the agony caused by his proddings. "Did you swim? Take a steamer?"

The operative's head was pounding; he struggled to control himself, to moderate his breathing. "Fuck you," he said, more quietly. "Did you hear a word I said?"

"What means of conveyance?" Caston repeated. There was no tenderness in his voice, only impatience.

"Obviously, I must have flown."

"So you *do* have some idea, you self-pitying bastard. Where would you have flown from, exactly?"

Ambler shrugged. "I guess Chang Kai-shek Airport, outside Taipei."

"What flight?"

"I don't . . ." He blinked. "Cathay Pacific," he heard himself say.

"A commercial flight, then." Caston evinced no surprise. "A commercial flight. Twelve hours. You have a drink on board?"

"Must have."

"What would you have had?"

"A Wild Turkey, I guess."

Caston picked up the telephone and dialed room service. Five minutes later, a bottle of Wild Turkey arrived at the door.

He poured a couple of fingers into a tumbler, handed it to Ambler. "Relax, have a drink," the auditor said stiffly. His brows were knit darkly, and the offer was an order: the auditor had turned into the bartender from hell.

"I don't drink," Ambler protested.

"Since when?"

"Since . . ." Ambler faltered.

"Since Parrish Island. You used to drink, though, and you're going to drink now. Bottoms up!"

"What's this about?"

"A science experiment. Just do it."

Ambler drank, the bourbon burning slightly as it went down his gullet. He felt no euphoria, only a sense of dizziness, confusion, a growing queasiness.

Caston poured him another drink, and Ambler downed it.

"What time did the plane get in?" the auditor demanded. "Evening arrival or morning?"

"Morning arrival." An eel of unease squirmed in his bowels. Knowledge was coming to him, as if from another dimension. It was not at his beck and call; he could not summon it. Yet it *had* been summoned, and it *had* appeared.

"Did you do a debrief with the operation's OIC?"

Ambler felt frozen. He must have done one.

"Next question," Caston asked relentlessly. It was as if he was proceeding through a vast inventory of tiny questions, like a bird pecking away at a cliff. "Who's Transience?"

Ambler felt as if the room was spinning around him, and when he shut his eyes, the room spun faster still. For a long time he was silent. Like a gunshot in the Alps, the question triggered a small cascade that turned into an avalanche. Blackness overcame him.

And then, out of the blackness, a glimmering.

CHAPTER TWENTY-THREE

Once more, he was in Changhua. A past that shadowed his present. In a frenetic blur of images, he grew aware of a whirlwind of activity, a rampage through the island. He had found what he had feared. Then, a series of fleeting, aleatory pictures. The flight attendant on the Cathay Pacific flight, a geisha of the airways; another bourbon was a hand gesture away, and she kept him well supplied. The taxi driver at Dulles, a Trinidadian with sunken cheeks and strong views about the quickest route. Ambler's apartment, at Baskerton Towers, which seemed, that day, so small, so sterile. Little more than a place to bathe and dress and prepare himself, so it seemed, for battle.

For battle.

What battle? An odd sort of fog swept over his memories again, a hovering opacity. But Ambler . . . no, *Tarquin*—he was Tarquin— had felt a glinting emotion. If he could retrieve the emotion, he could retrieve the memories that came with it. The emotion was a particular, and a particularly potent, compound: partly guilt, mostly rage.

The fog thinned. Buildings and people came into view; voices, at first dissolved into a stream of white noise, became audible and distinct. The urgency that drove him became vivid, real, *present*. Tarquin lacked the moral narcissism to suppose that his hands were ever clean, but he was outraged to discover that they had just been made bloody by an unfathomable lapse of professionalism. *Transience had to be told.*

Still seething with fury and disbelief, Tarquin returned to headquarters in Washington, D.C. A man with a tie, like countless others,

He felt a surge of the fury he had known in Changhua. A fury at betrayal. It was now Friday afternoon, the end of a Washington workweek, but not the end of his. *I'm sorry, but Undersecretary Whitfield is in a meeting. You can leave another message, if you like.* When he phoned an hour later, the assistant's reply was equally impassive, an underling requested to fend off a pest. *I'm sorry, Undersecretary Whitfield has left for the day.*

Insanity! Did she really think she could avoid him—avoid the *truth*—forever? Livid, he got into a car and drove to Whitfield's home, in the outskirts of Fox Hollow, a village west of Washington. He knew where she lived, and there would be no evading him there.

A half hour later he nosed his car past a white post-and-rail fence into the long drive, a graceful, gently curving allée lined with pear trees. The house itself was a tall, stately, Monticello-style structure, with elegantly corniced and quoined facades of weathered red brick, and large bay windows. It was surrounded by artfully pruned magnolias and high-mounded rhododendrons. Broad stone steps led from the circular drive to the carved oak entrance door.

The Whitfield family, he recalled, had made several industrial fortunes during the nineteenth century, some involving steel smelting and railroad ties, some involving not the manufacture but the export of such products. The family fortune ebbed somewhat in the postwar years, as the family scions moved into sectors more notable for cultural or intellectual prestige than for the generation of wealth—there was a Whitfield at the Metropolitan Museum, at the National Gallery, at the Hudson Institute, as well as a few who had drifted to the more sanitized realms of international banking. But well-managed trust funds ensured that no Whitfield needed to worry overmuch about the brutish business of getting and spending, and, as with the Rockefellers, a family ethic of service had somehow persisted over the decades. The fact that service did not require the repudiation of earthly pelf was clear from the Virginian grandeur of

Whitfield's house. It was stately, rather than showy, but definitely nothing that a government salary would swing.

Ambler pulled up to the large double doors at the center of the house and got out of his car. He rang the doorbell. Moments later, a woman in a maid's uniform of worsted black and a frilly white front—a Filipina?—came to the door.

"I'm Hal Ambler, and I'm here for Ellen Whitfield," he said, biting off his words.

"Madame not seeing anybody," the uniformed woman said. Then, more stiffly, she added, "Madame not here."

She was lying, of course. If Ambler hadn't already known, Whitfield's voice could be heard from an adjoining room. Ambler pushed past the protesting Filipina, strode down the tiled foyer, and barged into a wood-paneled library, with a large bay window and double-height bookshelves.

There was Ellen Whitfield, sitting in front of an array of documents with an older man. Ambler stared. The man looked familiar somehow. He was silver-haired, scholarly looking, with a prominent forehead; his red silk tie was tightly knotted and disappeared into a buttoned sweater-vest under a tweed jacket. Both of them were absorbed in the papers before them.

"Madame, I *tol'* him you no—" As the silence was broken by the noisily protesting Filipina, both Whitfield and the silver-haired man looked up suddenly, startled and dismayed.

"God*dammit,* Ambler!" Whitfield yelled, surprise now surging into a towering rage of indignation. "What the *hell* are you doing here?" The older gentleman had turned away from him, as if he had developed a sudden interest in the books on the shelves.

"You know goddamn well what I'm doing here, *Undersecretary* Whitfield," he returned, uttering her title with withering scorn. "I want answers. I'm fed up with your delaying tactics. You think you can dodge me? What are you trying to hide?"

Whitfield's face was mottled with fury. "You paranoid son of a bitch! Get out of my house! Get out *now*! How *dare* you violate my privacy like this! How *dare* you!" An outstretched arm pointed to the door. Ambler noticed it was trembling. With rage? Fear? Both, it seemed.

"You got my memorandum," Ambler replied icily. "It contains the truth. You think you can bury that truth? You think you can bury me? Well, forget about it. Believe me, I've taken precautions."

"Look at yourself. *Listen* to yourself. Your conduct is totally unprofessional. Verging upon the *unhinged*. Don't you hear how *crazy* you sound? In my job, I've got to deal with more things than you can *possibly* imagine. If you want a conference, we can conference first thing Monday. But listen to me, and listen to me hard. If you're not out of this house immediately, I *will* have you banished from the services of this country—permanently and irrevocably. Now get the *hell* out of my sight."

Ambler stood, breathing hard, his own anger somewhat preempted by her stormy ire. "Monday," he said heavily, and he turned to go.

A few miles outside of Fox Hollow, an EMT box van, with pulsing red lights and siren, suddenly appeared behind him, and he steered to the side of the road. Swiftly the ambulance pulled over in front of him, and another car, a heavy Buick, pulled over behind him, blocking him in. Several men—emergency medical technicians? but something was *off*—poured out of the ambulance. Others emerged from the sedan behind him. As they pulled him from his car, a hypodermic jabbed gracelessly into his arm, he tried to make sense of what was happening. The men were acting in an official capacity, following orders, behaving with the practiced efficiency of professionals. Yet who were they—and what did they want from him?

The fog in his mind had not burned off entirely; it hovered over what came after, as it had been over what had come before. As he was strapped onto a gurney, he heard quiet, tense exchanges among the team of medics. Then his consciousness began to waver and dim. It was the beginning of a long twilight.

It was twilight, too, when Ambler opened his eyes again.

A few days ago, he had been an "inpatient" at a maximum-security facility. Now he was an ocean away. And he was still not free.

CHAPTER TWENTY-FOUR

Ambler opened his eyes, focused on the pallid auditor, and began to speak, providing as detailed a recounting of his movements and observations as he could. Time had fogged thousands of details, and yet the lineaments of the episode were now vivid to him.

"I was afraid you'd blacked out there for a while," Caston said after Ambler had spoken for five minutes without pausing. "Glad to have you back among the living." He put down the publication he had been reading, *The Journal of Applied Mathematics and Stochastic Analysis.* "Now will you get the hell off my bed?"

"Sorry." Ambler stretched, got up, and sat down on the mustard-colored chair. He must have nodded off. According to his watch, four hours had passed.

"So Transience was Ellen Whitfield herself?"

"It was the alias she used back when she was in the field. When the files went digital, all that stuff was lost. No official records were to be retained. Especially when it came to her own records—she wanted a total scrub. She said it was a security precaution."

"Explains why the name didn't pull anything," Caston said. He regarded the operative silently for a moment. "You want another drink?"

Ambler shrugged. "They got some mineral water in the minibar?"

"Oh sure, they got some Evian. With the current exchange rate, it comes out to $9.25 for five hundred milliliters. That's, what, 16.9 ounces. So it's like fifty-five cents an ounce. Fifty-five cents for an ounce of *water?* Enough to make me throw up."

Ambler sighed. "I guess I should admire your precision."

"What are you talking about? I'm rounding like crazy."

"Please tell me you don't have a family."

Caston reddened.

"You must drive them crazy."

"Not at all," the auditor said, almost smiling. "Because, you see, they don't listen to a word I say."

"That must drive *you* crazy."

"Actually, it suits me just fine." There was a funny look on the auditor's face for a moment, and Ambler caught a glimpse of an attitude that was almost worshipful; the dry-as-dust auditor was a doting father, Ambler realized with surprise. Then Caston returned to the matter at hand, abruptly business-like. "The man who was with Undersecretary Whitfield, seated in her library—describe him to me in as much detail as you can."

Ambler now looked off into the distance and brought the image to mind. A man in his sixties. Silver hair, carefully groomed, above a high forehead. The forehead was remarkably unlined, the face fine featured and studious looking, the cheekbones high, the chin strong. Ambler started to describe the figure he recalled.

Caston listened and again lapsed into silence. Then he stood up, agitated; a vein was pulsing on his forehead. "It can't be," he breathed.

"It's what I remember," Ambler said.

"You're describing . . . but it's impossible."

"Out with it."

Caston fiddled with his laptop computer, which he had plugged into the phone jack. After typing in a few commands into a search engine, he stepped aside and gestured for Ambler to take a look. The screen was filled with the image of a man. The very man Ambler had seen at Whitfield's house.

"That's him," Ambler confirmed, his voice hard with tension.

"Do you know who that man is?"

Ambler shook his head.

"His name is Ashton Palmer. Whitfield studied with him when she was a graduate student."

Ambler shrugged. "So?"

"Later she repudiated him and everything he stood for. Had no contact with him whatever. She wouldn't have had a career otherwise."

"I don't understand."

"Ashton Palmer—the name doesn't ring any bells?"

"Only vaguely," Ambler said.

"Maybe you're too young. There was a time, twenty, twenty-five years ago, when he was the brightest light of the foreign policy establishment. Wrote some widely reprinted articles in *Foreign Affairs*. Both political parties were wooing him. He gave seminars in the Old Executive Office Building, in the West Wing, in the goddamn Oval Office. People hung on his every word. He was given an honorary appointment in the State Department, but he was bigger than that. He was destined to be the next Kissinger: one of those men whose vision leaves an imprint on history, for good or bad."

"So what happened?"

"A lot of people would say he self-destructed. Or maybe he just miscalculated. He came to be recognized as an extremist—a dangerous fanatic. He may have figured that his political and intellectual authority had reached the level where he could express his views frankly, and win people over to them by the simple fact that it was he who was making the arguments. If so, he was wrong. The views he expressed were dangerous, and would have put this country on a collision course with history. He gave a particularly incendiary speech at the Macmillan Institute for Foreign Policy, in D.C., and afterward a number of countries, thinking that he represented the government, or some faction of the government, actually threatened to recall their ambassadors. Can you imagine?"

"Hard to."

"The Secretary of State spent all night working the phones. Practically overnight, Palmer became persona non grata. He took up a teaching position in the Ivy Leagues, built an academic center of his own, was appointed to the board of directors of a somewhat fringe think tank in Washington. This image is taken from the Harvard Web site. But anyone at State who was too closely associated with him became an object of suspicion."

"So none of his people got anywhere."

"Actually, there are lots of Palmerites, all throughout government. Brilliant students, graduates of Harvard's Kennedy School or its graduate program in government. But if you want to have a career, anyway, you can't admit to being a Palmerite. And you certainly can't maintain any connection to the old rogue."

"Makes sense."

"Yet you saw the two of them together—and that doesn't."

"Slow down."

"We're talking about a major player of the State Department in the company of Professor Ashton Palmer. Do you realize how explosive that is? Do you realize how utterly ruinous that could have been to her? As a great American jurist once said, 'sunlight is the best disinfectant.' And it was the one thing they couldn't afford."

Ambler narrowed his eyes, brought back Ellen Whitfield's rage-mottled countenance: now he understood the fear that he sensed in her. "So this is what it was all about."

"I wouldn't hazard that it was *all* about that." Caston was precise, as ever. "But for a high-ranking member of the State Department, maintaining ties with Palmer was career suicide. As the head of the Political Stabilization Unit, especially, Whitfield simply couldn't afford to have any ongoing association with Palmer."

Ambler leaned back and reflected. Whitfield, a glib and fluent liar, could probably have explained away Palmer's presence to anybody else. But Ambler was the one person she could never hope to deceive.

That's why he was railroaded. *That* was the intelligence she couldn't afford to have leaked. The tape of his paranoid ravings, then, was an insurance policy, establishing that nothing he said could be taken at face value.

She must have panicked that night and activated a 918PSE, the rarely used protocol for a psychiatric emergency involving a clandestine officer. Because he had spoken of having *taken precautions*—implying that damaging information would be released in the event of his death—she must have concluded that the only solution was to lock him away. And then try to make him disappear.

Ambler felt his heart hammering as he tried to make sense of how such a small incident had precipitated such a major upheaval in his existence. Yet what was she covering up? Just a personal relationship—or something more?

He excused himself and used his cell phone to call Laurel. He gave her the names of the two principals; at the mammoth Bibliothèque nationale de France, in the Eighth Arrondissement, they agreed, she would be able to search the scholarly archives for relevant materials, materials that would not easily be accessible through other means. He felt a little calmer by the time he'd rung off, and he realized why he had really called her. He needed to hear her voice. It was as simple as that. Laurel Holland had stood between him and complete despair; she remained a beacon of sanity in a world that indeed seemed mad.

After a while, Caston turned to him. Something was on his mind. "Can I ask you a personal question?"

Ambler nodded distantly.

"What's your name?"

Nothing but the best for Paul Fenton, Undersecretary Whitfield reflected as he invited her into his rooms, the Empire Suite at the elegant hotel Georges V. The eight-floor hotel, located midway between the Arc de Triomphe and the Seine, was perhaps the most celebrated in the city, and with reason. Most rooms were elegantly appointed in a light and airy version of Louis XVI style. Not the Empire Suite, which made the others look Bauhaus-austere. At the Empire Suite, a grand entrance foyer opened onto a spacious salon and an adjoining seating and dining area. There was even a powder room off the salon for visitors—guests of the guest. The suite was densely decorated with paintings and sculptures rendering homage to Napoléon and Josephine. Aside from the walls, which were upholstered in a yellow-gold fabric, the early Empire theme was rendered in green hues and dark woods. Bronzes and flower vases cropped up everywhere, in arboreal profusion. From the window, one could see a breathtaking skyline of the City of Light, with les Invalides, Montparnasse Tower, and, of course, the Eiffel Tower clearly visible.

Ellen Whitfield appreciated the view. The suite itself struck her as appalling. To her discriminating eye, it was terribly overdone, cluttered, garish—the worst kind of fustian. Yet Fenton's whole career was a testament to the idea that nothing succeeded like excess.

Fenton—ruddy, ginger-haired, bear-like—led her into the salon, where they sat on green-striped chairs across a small glass table. She ran her fingertips down the arms of the chair, which were of wood adorned with gilded bronze ornaments in some sort of Egyptian motif.

"I don't know whether I've ever fully told you how grateful I am—how grateful we all are—for everything you've done for us over the years." Whitfield spoke in full-hearted tones, her eyes widening almost sensually. She leaned forward confidingly. Up close, she noticed how plumped, pink, and smooth Fenton's skin was, as if he had spent the morning having a mud wrap. He had the overdeveloped pectorals and thickened arms of someone who spent hours pumping iron. Fenton was a man of many projects; one of them, obviously, was his own body.

He shrugged modestly. "Would you like some coffee?"

The undersecretary turned her head toward an ebony sideboard. "I noticed you had a tray of coffee all ready—so thoughtful. But let *me* get it." She stood up and returned with the tray. There was a pot—polished silver, glass lined—of freshly brewed coffee, a small ceramic pitcher of milk, and a bowl of sugar. "I'll be Mother," Whitfield said, pouring coffee into two delicate Limoges cups.

She reclined in the Empire chair and took a sip of the perfectly brewed coffee; she liked her coffee black. Fenton, she knew, preferred it heavily sweetened, and she watched him as he shoveled spoonful after spoonful of sugar into his cup, the way he always did.

"All that sugar," she murmured in a tone of maternal reproval. "It'll kill you."

Fenton took a sip and grinned. "Exciting times, right? You know I've always been honored to provide whatever help I could. It's a pleasure to work with someone who sees the world the way I do. We both understand that America deserves a safer tomorrow. We both understand one has to combat tomorrow's threat today. Early detection, right?"

"Early detection, early treatment," she agreed. "And nobody does it better than your people. Without your operatives and your intelligence systems, we'd never have been able to make so many crucial advances. You're not just a private contractor, in our view. You're really a full partner in the mission of preserving the American ascendancy."

"We're similar in a lot of ways," Fenton said. "We both like to win. And that's what we've been doing: winning. Winning one for a team that we both believe in."

Whitfield watched Fenton as he finished his coffee and returned the empty cup to its saucer. "It's easier to win," she said, "when your opponents don't even know you're playing the game." Her look of gratitude was unwavering.

Fenton nodded vaguely; he closed his eyes and opened them

again, as if having a hard time keeping them focused. "But I know you didn't want to meet me here just to congratulate me," he said, slurring his words slightly.

"You were going to give me a progress report on Tarquin," she said. "He doesn't know you're at this hotel, I assume. You've taken precautions?"

Fenton nodded sleepily. "I met him at a safe house. But he did real good." He yawned. "Excuse me," he said. "I guess jet lag is catching up with me."

She refilled his cup. "You must be *exhausted,* with everything that's gone on over the past several days," Whitfield said, her eyes alert. She noticed his mush-mouthed consonants, the way his head was starting to bow.

Fenton yawned and sluggishly shifted on the sofa. "This is so strange," he murmured. "I just can't keep my eyes open."

"Don't fight it," Whitfield said. "Just let it come." Her agents had had no difficulty in lacing the sugar with a fast-acting CNS depressant—a crystalline derivative of gamma hydroxybutyrate—that, in levels great enough to produce unconsciousness, would elude forensic detection, because its metabolites were naturally present in mammalian serum.

Fenton's eyes opened for a moment, perhaps responding to the arctic chill that had entered her tone. He made a sound like a sleeper's muted groan.

"I really am sorry." She glanced at her watch. "It was a difficult decision for Ashton and me to make. It's not that we doubt your loyalty. We don't. It's just that, well, you know who I am. You'd be able to connect the dots—and we weren't sure you'd like the picture that results." She glanced at Fenton, now slumped in a position that suggested unconsciousness. Was he even able to hear her words?

What she said, however, was no more than the truth. There was a risk that Fenton would feel betrayed if he learned the true nature of the operation he had been enlisted in—and betrayal too often begot betrayal. The upcoming event was too important to allow anything to go wrong. Everyone had to play his part to perfection.

As she stared at the motionless body before her, she reflected that Paul Fenton already had.

CHAPTER TWENTY-FIVE

"I don't have a good feeling about this," Ambler said. The two men were walking down boulevard de Bonne Nouvelle, the auditor holding both his hands together under his overcoat for warmth. Ambler would never do that—no operative would—but then Caston's hands were good for very little outside of an office. Caston's eyes were downcast, monitoring the sidewalk in front of him for dog feces; Ambler's gaze casually swept the street, alert to any signs of surveillance.

"You *what*?" The auditor gave him a withering look.

"You heard me."

"Did your horoscope say your stars were in a bad alignment? Did an entrail-reading priest find something nasty in the offal? I mean, look, if you know something I should know, let's talk about it. If you've got a rationally justified belief, more power to you. But how many times do we have to go through this? We're grown-ups. We should be responsive to facts. Not *feelings*."

"Reality check: You don't have the home field advantage here. We're not in spreadsheet land. Those are real glass-and-stone buildings around you, not columns of digits. And if somebody takes a shot at one of us, it'll be with a real bullet, not a goddamn bell curve of possible bullets. Anyway, how would somebody like you even know about an agency safe house? On the principle of need-to-know, it should be off your radar screen. Because it sure isn't info a pencil-neck like you needs to have."

"You still don't get it. Who pays the rent? Who sees the bills? Nothing that costs the agency money is off my radar screen. I'm an audi-tor. Nothing auditable is alien to me."

Ambler was silent for a moment. "How do you know the place isn't going to be occupied?"

"Because the lease comes up at the end of this month and we're letting it expire. And because we've got a budget item for the cleanup crew that's slated to arrive next week. Ergo, it's empty, but it's still equipped. I reviewed requisition items related to Paris before I left. So I can tell you that the average monthly cost of the rue Bouchardon residence for the past forty-eight months was, in ad-justed dollars, twenty-eight hundred and thirty dollars. Additional variable charges include, in descending order of magnitude, telecom expenses, which, in turn, range from—"

"OK, stop. You've made your point."

The building on rue Bouchardon looked oddly desolate, the stone facade dappled with lichen and soot, the windows grimy, and, at the doorway, the black metal grille battered and chipped. A nearby mer-cury street lamp sparked and buzzed.

"How do we get in?" Ambler asked Caston.

"Not my department." Caston looked affronted. "What, you expect me to do everything? You're the goddamn operative. So operate."

"Shit." This wasn't like the parking garage at the Clinique du Lou-vre; the site was exposed, which meant he'd have to try something that worked fast. Ambler knelt down and untied one of his shoes. When he stood up again, he was holding a thin key, flat but for five small elevations between the cuts. It was called a bump key, and get-ting it to work required both skill and luck; he doubted he had enough of either. "Stay here," he told Caston.

Ambler loped over to a Dumpster at the end of the short street and returned a few minutes later with a soiled paperback novel someone had thrown out. Still, it was thick, and the spine was hard. It would work as well as a mallet.

A bump key was designed to hit the bottom pin in the keyway column hard enough that the top pin bounced clear of it for an instant, high enough to go past the shear line. In that same instant, before the spring pushed the top pin down again, the key would turn.

In theory.

The reality seldom measured up. If the pin columns did not bounce high enough, it would not work. If the button pin bounced too high, it would not work. If the key was twisted an instant too late, it would not work.

Now he positioned the bump key right in front of the hole and banged it with the spine of the paperback, shooting it through the keyway as hard as he could and then twisting it the instant it was in.

Ambler could not believe it. It worked—the first time! That almost never happened. The key turned, retracted the latch, and he pushed the door open. He felt a surge of pride at his handiwork and, smiling, turned to Caston.

The auditor was stifling a yawn.

"Finally," Caston groused. "I can't believe it took you so long."

With great effort, Ambler remained silent.

Once they were inside the building, Ambler would be able to work on the apartment door without fear of being observed; the building seemed entirely vacant. But the CIA team that had equipped the apartment had also taken care to give it a proper mortise lock.

Ambler scrutinized the strike plate for a few minutes before giving up. With a proper tension wrench, he might have been able to make progress, but he lacked the tools for the job.

Caston was openly scornful. "Can't you do anything right? You're supposed to be the hotshot operative. Twenty years at the PSU. And now—"

Ambler cut him off. "Caston? Put a sock in it."

Finally, Ambler walked to the building's cramped courtyard. The ground floor apartment had a couple of windows that faced the desolate courtyard. It would be an inelegant mode of entry, but it would do.

Hammering, again, with the spine of the paperback book, Ambler smashed a rectangular pane of glass and methodically removed all the remaining shards. He stood stock-still for a moment, listening. But there was nothing to be heard. No sign of any habitation. No sign that anyone had heard the broken glass.

"You just cost the United States of America four hundred dollars," Caston said softly. "At *least*. Never mind the replacement costs. The labor costs for a glazier in Paris are astronomical."

Ambler placed both hands on the stone ledge and, with a sudden jerk, pulled himself up and then over, through the glassless window. A sturdy-looking bookcase projected beneath it, and he was able to somersault over it gently and land on his feet.

Walking carefully in the gloom, he made his way to the door, turned on some lights, and then retracted the dead bolt.

At last he opened the front door, where Caston, arms folded on his chest, was standing—slouching—impatiently.

"Plus it's freezing outdoors," Caston said. "And you had to break a goddamn window."

"Just get in." He closed the door behind Caston and, reflexively, locked it again. A safe house would not have an alarm system; the possible arrival of the police represented a greater threat than any random burglary.

The two men wandered through the apartment until they found a small room with a large television in it. Beneath it was what looked, on a casual glance, like a regular cable box. Ambler knew better. The roof of the building would have satellite equipment, connected to the ground floor with a noninterceptible fiber-optic cable; the box contained complex decryption equipment.

It was not a high-security device and was not designed for the reception of sensitive information. But then the material they would be accessing was technically unclassified, if not widely available.

Caston pulled at drawers in the monitor stand until he found a keyboard. He smiled at it, as if he had come across a friend. Now he turned on the monitor and busied himself with the keyboard for a few minutes.

The screen blinked to life, but it only displayed snow. "Let's see if I can remember how this is done," Caston said, mainly to himself, as he fidgeted with the remote. Abruptly the screen filled with digits, displaying size and times for a series of large-file downloads.

Caston no longer looked peevish; now he looked grave.

"I'm taking these from Open Source sector," he explained to the operative. "Nonclassified, public-domain materials, for the most part. I just want you to see Ashton Palmer in his element. You're the face expert, OK? I want you to see that face full-sized, in color, and at maximum resolution." He fussed with the keyboard for another minute, adjusting various settings. Suddenly the screen was vibrant and animated with the image of Palmer speaking at a lectern.

"This is from the mid-nineties," Caston went on. "A speech he gave at a conference sponsored by the Center for Policy Studies. There was a reference to it in one of the journal articles that your friend found in the BnF. Palmer's polite, but I doubt you'll have to listen very hard to figure out what he's really saying."

On the screen, Ashton Palmer looked confident, magisterial, almost serene. Dark curtains were visible behind him. He looked elegant in a navy suit, dark red tie, and pale blue shirt.

"The traditional form of Chinese housing in cities was the *siheyuan*—literally, 'four-side enclosed courtyards.' They were composed of inward-facing dwellings on all sides, a tableau of complete enclosure. In other civilizations, the metropolitan centers were centers, too, of the cosmopolitan urge—the urge to look outward whether in conquest or discovery. This has never been the Chinese way. Rather, the very architecture of the *siheyuan* has proved an apt symbol of the national character." Ashton Palmer looked up from the lectern, his slate-gray eyes glittering. "The Middle Kingdom was, for a millennium—and for dynasty after dynasty—a profoundly inward-looking realm. A pervasive xenophobia was perhaps the deepest and most constant element of that multifarious array of customs and habits of thought we call Chinese culture. Chinese history contains no Peter the Great, no Empress Catherine, no Napoléon, no Queen Victoria, no Kaiser Wilhelm, no Tojo. Since the collapse of the Tatar yoke, there has been nothing we can call a Chinese empire: there has only been China. Vast, yes. Powerful, without question. But ultimately a four-sided enclosure. Ultimately an enormous *siheyuan*. One may debate whether this ingrained xenophobia served the Chinese people well. What should be beyond debate is that it has served the rest of us well."

Ambler moved nearer to the fifty-six-inch high-density screen, riveted by the image of the eloquent scholar, the burning intelligence he seemed to radiate.

"Some political scholars believed that China would change once the Communists seized control," Palmer said, after taking a sip of water from a glass at the lectern. "Surely international Communism was just that—international in its orientation. Surely its expansionist horizons would turn China outward, open it at least to its Eastern bloc brethren. So students of politics supposed. Of course, that is not what happened. Chairman Mao maintained the tightest control over his countrymen of any leader in history; he made himself into a godhead. And for all the bellicosity of his rhetoric, he not only insulated his countrymen from the strong winds of modernity, but he was deeply conservative, indeed reactive, in his projection of military force. A few very minor skirmishes aside, there are only two instances of note. One was the conflict in the Korean peninsula in the early fifties, where—nota bene—the Chinese actually believed that the United States was planning to launch an invasion. The Korean standoff resulted from a defensive, not an offensive, posture. The fact is that Chairman Mao was truly the last emperor—one whose obsessions were inward, having to do with the purity of his followers."

Palmer's expression remained dispassionate as he elaborated his vision, but his words were spoken with mesmerizing fluency. "It is only in recent years that we have begun to see a seismic shift within China—a genuine turning outward, fueled by its incredibly swift insertion into the system of global capitalism. It was the very development that one American administration after another fervently hoped for, and sought to promote. But as the Chinese would say, one should be careful what one wishes for. We have awoken the tiger, hoping to ride it." He paused, and his mouth formed a thin smile. "And, dreaming as we have of riding the tiger, we have forgotten what happens when you fall off it. The political strategists convinced themselves that economic convergence would lead to political convergence, a harmonization of interests. Something like the opposite is true. Two men in love with the same woman—a recipe for peaceable coexistence? I think not." The sound of scattered laughter from the audience could be heard. "Likewise when two entities share the same competitive goal, whether economic domination in some realm or political dominion over the Pacific region. It seems to have escaped the attention of our myopic political masterminds that, as China has become increasingly market driven, she has become increasingly war-like as well. A decade after Mao's death, China sank three Vietnamese ships in the area of the Spratly islands. By 1994 you see the clash between American ships and a Chinese submarine in the Yellow Sea, and in subsequent years the seizure of Mischief Reef from the Philippines, the missiles fired by the coast of Taiwan, in an international waterway, and so on. The Chinese navy has acquired an aircraft carrier from the French and a series of surveillance radar systems from the British, while China has constructed a passage from the Yunnan Province to the Bay of Bengal, thus securing access to the Indian Ocean. The actions we have seen so far can be easily dismissed, for they are deceptively small in scale. In fact, these are *probes,* nothing less, attempts to assess the resolve of the international community. Time and again, they have learned of the toothlessness of their competitors, their rivals. And make no mistake, we are—for the first time in history—rivals."

Palmer's gaze grew eerily intent as he pressed his point. "China is on fire, and it is the West that has provided the fuel. By its moves toward economic liberalization, China has gained hundred of billions of dollars in foreign capital. We're seeing a GDP growth rate upward of ten percent a quarter—faster than any nation has grown without massive upheaval. We're seeing gigantic increases in consumption, as well: the awakening tiger will, within a few years, be consuming ten percent of the world's petroleum production, a third of its steel production. Simply as a consumer, it has a disproportionate influence over the nations of Southeast Asia, as well as Korea, Japan, and, indeed, Taiwan. Our conglomerates increasingly depend upon the Chinese dynamo for their own growth. Does any of this sound familiar, ladies and gentlemen?"

Again, Palmer fell silent, his eyes scanning the unseen audience before him. His sense of cadence was masterly. "Let me break it down for you. Consider a country that has experienced what could be called a second industrial revolution. A country where labor was cheap, capital and resources abundant—a country that was able to transform its economy into the most efficient and swiftest growing in the world. I refer"—he raised his voice subtly—"to the United States of America, as it appeared in the early years of the twentieth century. We all know what ensued. A period of unquestioned military, industrial, economic, and cultural supremacy—a period of power and prosperity we designate, in shorthand, as the American century." He glanced down at the lectern before resuming. "The American century was a redoubtable thing. But nobody ever promised it would be permanent. Indeed, there is every reason to believe that it will not be—every reason to believe that the twenty-first century will, in retrospect, be identified as the Chinese century."

Murmurs from the audience were audible.

"Whether this is a condition to be celebrated or bemoaned, it is not my place, as an impartial scholar, to say. I will only note the irony that this development will have been the fruits of our own labor.

Well-meaning Americans, dominant within our foreign-policy establishment, have ceaselessly worked to awaken the tiger. To turn an inward-facing kingdom outward. Our children will live with the results." In a soft voice he added, "Or die from them."

Ambler shuddered; he tried to remember other times when he had seen faces that exuded such self-certainty and zeal. The visages that presented themselves were not reassuring: Dr. Abimael Guzman, the murderous founder of Peru's Shining Path terrorists, was one. David Koresh, the self-styled messiah of the Branch Davidian, was another. Yet Ashton Palmer had a quality of urbanity, of spurious civility, that distinguished him from such obvious fanatics—and made him, potentially, even more dangerous.

"Again and again, our soi-disant 'China hands' misread the green tea leaves. Everyone here will recall the widespread unrest in China when her embassy in Belgrade was bombed in the course of an American air strike. Millions of Chinese citizens refused to believe that it could have been an accident. Hand-wringing could be seen throughout Washington. The resurgence of anti-Americanism was widely taken to be a bad thing. These experts have not learned the wisdom of what the Chinese sage Chung-wen Han called, simply, *shuangxing,* or 'doubleness.' In fact, the efflorescence of xenophobia might actually have been good for America. Anything that slows China's integration into the community of nations, we know, will also serve as a drag on the engines of her growth. A skeptic might hold that any such development was a good thing for America, and a good thing for the world. Since I am an impartial and dispassionate scholar, of course, it is not my place to root for one outcome or another. But if, as I believe, we have reached a fork in the road, perhaps I can help direct our attention at what lies at the end of each path. Conflict with China is inevitable. What is not inevitable is whether we lose. That will depend on our choices—on choices we make today."

Clay Caston knelt down and typed a series of commands on the keyboard again, until another video clip began to play. This feed was fuzzier, apparently copied from a C-SPAN broadcast, from just a couple of years ago.

"Here, you'll hear him singing a different tune," Caston said. "Of course, the Center for Strategic Studies conference was a closed event—it was Palmer speaking mainly to acolytes. The C-SPAN broadcast was of a panel assembled in Washington by another think tank, representing a diversity of opinions. He may have decided to assume a different face."

Among a panel of five sinologists, Ashton Palmer stood out; his expression was of icy imperturbability; his high forehead and clear gray gaze exuded intelligence and thoughtfulness.

The clip began with a question asked by a young, gangly man in the audience, with a thick beard and thicker glasses. "Do you feel, Professor Palmer, that America's policy toward China is insufficiently skeptical, insufficiently attuned to our own national interests? Because many people in the State Department today would look at the rise of President Liu Ang and call that a great success, and a tribute to their policy of 'constructive engagement.'"

Palmer smiled as the camera returned to him. "And that's fair enough," he said. "Liu Ang is a marvelously appealing politician. I have only the greatest hopes that he represents the future."

Palmer smiled again, showing white, even teeth. Despite the smooth avowal and easy manner, Ambler felt a chill: as he studied Palmer's face, he detected—no, he simply *saw*—a profound and seething contempt and hostility toward the statesman of whom he spoke. At the very moment he uttered Liu Ang's name, a fleeting expression passed over Palmer's face that utterly belied his words.

". . . So I can only say that I truly hope the State Department triumphalists are correct," Palmer concluded. "Anyway, we have to work with him."

Caston grunted. "The guy sounds totally plausible here, too. He's a hard cat to figure."

Now it was Ambler's turn to work the keyboard. The video software had an icon that enabled one to move the video display forward or back, and he reversed the clip until it reached the moment when Ashton Palmer said the name of the Chinese president. Now Ambler advanced the video frame by frame. *There.* In a micropause between the two parts of the Chinese name, Palmer's face settled into a radically different expression. The eyes were drawn, the corners of his mouth pulled down, the nostrils flared: it was a face expressive of both outrage and disgust. By another frame or two, it had vanished, replaced by an artificial look of smiling approval.

"Jesus *Christ*," Caston said.

Ambler said nothing.

Caston shook his head. "I would never have picked up on that."

"There are a lot of things on heaven and earth that don't show up on your almighty spreadsheets," Ambler said.

"Don't underestimate me," Caston said. "I get there in the end."

"Just in time to pick up the shells after the shoot-out is over, I'm sure. I've known a few analysts and number crunchers. You work with paper, computers, pore over printouts—charts, graphs, scatter plots—but you don't deal with people. You're more comfortable with bits and bytes."

Caston tilted his head. "John Henry did beat the steam drill— once. Maybe you were sleeping in when the information age dawned. Today, technology spans borders. It watches. It hears. It registers patterns, small statistical perturbations, and if we're willing to pay attention—"

"It can hear, but it can't *listen*. It can watch, but it can't *observe*. And it sure as hell can't converse with the men and women we've got to deal with. There's no substitute for that, goddammit."

"I find the money trail tends to be a lot more voluble and revealing than most people are."

"You *would*," Ambler snapped. He stood up and started to pace. The room felt enclosed, stifling. "OK, you want to talk about logic and 'probabilistic inference'? What's happening in China these days, what does it all mean for a guy like Ashton Palmer? Why does he hate Liu Ang so much?"

"I'm a numbers man, Ambler. I don't do geopolitics." He shrugged. "But I read the papers. And we've both heard Palmer's rap at that Strategic Studies meeting. Since you ask, the main thing about Liu Ang seems to be that he's enormously popular among his own people, and an incredible force of liberalization. He's opened markets, established fair trading systems, even cracked down on media piracy, knockoff manufacturing, and the like."

"But it's gradualism, right? That's the Chinese way."

"Gradualism, yes, but on an accelerated schedule."

"That's a contradiction in terms."

"Liu Ang is a paradoxical figure in a lot of ways. What was that word Palmer referred to? *Doubleness*. Follow the logic of Palmer's argument, all that stuff about the Chinese century, about what could happen if an inward-looking kingdom starts to become gregarious, starts to become integrated in the community of nations. If you're Palmer, Liu Ang is your worst nightmare."

"If you're Palmer," Ambler interjected, "you'd want to do something about it."

"I read somewhere that Liu Ang's making some big state visit to America next month," Caston said. He fell silent for a long moment. "I'm going to have to make some calls."

Ambler's gaze returned to the frozen image of the scholar, trying to extract everything he could from his visage. *Who are you? What do you want?* He lowered his head, lost in thought.

Then the image vanished.

Ambler saw the monitor explode—blossoming into a cloud of glass fragments—even before he heard the *popping* sound that accompanied it.

Time slowed.

What had happened? A bullet. Large-caliber. Rifle. Silenced.

He whirled around and saw a black-clad gunman, crouched commando style, at the end of the hallway outside the room. The man was holding a military assault rifle, a model Ambler recognized. The Heckler & Koch G36. A curved magazine mounted in front of the trigger guard held thirty rounds of 5.56×45mm NATO rounds; the optical sights used a red-dot reticle. Its casing was a high-strength, lightweight black polymer. Highly portable, highly lethal.

Standard issue for the Consular Operations armory.

CHAPTER TWENTY-SIX

Ambler threw himself down a split second before a triple burst drove more bullets in his direction. Caston, he saw, had hurtled himself toward the far side of the room, away from the commando's sight line.

For now.

The commando was not alone; Ambler could see it in his eyes. He had the confidence of a member of a team.

A team using special-ops-issue weaponry. How many? Four to six would be standard for a special-ops squad with a civilian target. If this was rapid response, however, it could be as few as two or three. They would have arrived using different routes of entrance—some through the door, some through the window. With a heat scope, it would have been a cinch to determine their exact position in the safe house.

The question was why Ambler wasn't already dead.

As the first commando remained seated, a second black-clad gunman ran past him: a standard flanking maneuver.

With a sudden movement, Ambler kicked the study's door closed.

"I know what you're thinking," Caston breathed. He was cowering, his usually pallid face now sheet white. "But believe me, I had nothing to do with this."

"You don't, and you didn't," Ambler said. "I know that. One of the downloads must have triggered an alarm. The I/O identifier would have given away the location. Like you said, this place was supposed to be unoccupied."

"So what now?"

"It isn't good. We're dealing with pros. Armed with H&K G36 rifles. You have any idea what that means?"

"The H&K G36," Caston repeated, blinking rapidly. "On orders over a thousand, we pay a negotiated unit price of eight hundred forty-five dollars. However, the nonamortizable cost of cartridges—"

"*Silenced* G36s," Ambler cut him off. "These guys are a goddamn mop-up team."

A blast of bullets tore away at the upper half of the door, filling the air with splinters and the smell of carbonized wood. The door would not last much longer.

Ambler leaped up and switched off the lights in the room before throwing himself on the floor again.

Why was he alive?

Because there were two of them. The infrared scopes would have told them as much. They had not shot Ambler because they had not been able to verify that it *was* Ambler. Identify, then kill: that would be the order of business. Their instructions did not cover the presence of a second party.

"We don't have anything to hold them off," Caston said. "We've got to surrender."

Another triple burst had punched a large hole in the door—noisy damage from a silenced assault rifle.

Ambler knew what would come next. The commandos would approach the aperture they had blasted into the door and then train their rifles on the two men; it would enable them to take as much time as they needed to verify the identity of their target.

He had just seconds to put them off their game plan.

Ambler's only weapon was the small Glock 26—utterly useless against an assault rifle, a squirt gun to their water cannon. It had no sights, was inaccurate at any real distance, and its small-caliber bullets would not penetrate a commando's lightweight Monocrys body armor. In this situation, it had essentially no offensive value at all.

Revise and improvise.

"Actually, you do have something you can use." Ambler spoke to the harrowed auditor in a low voice.

"I don't think so. The remote control doesn't work against these guys. I've already tried the 'Pause' button."

"What you've got," the operative said, "is a hostage."

"You're mad."

"Shut up and listen," Ambler whispered. "You need to shout, loud as you can, that you've got a hostage and you're going to shoot him if they take another step. *Now*."

"I can't do that."

"You can, and you *will*." Ambler mouthed the word, *Now*.

Caston looked deathly, but he nodded and took a deep breath. "I have a hostage," he bellowed to the gunmen, in a surprisingly steady voice. "You take another step and I'll shoot him."

A few seconds of silence were followed by a barely audible exchange between the gunmen.

Ambler removed the small Glock 26 from his back holster and pressed it into the auditor's hand. "You hold it to the back of my head, OK?"

"Easy for you to say," Caston whispered. "I'm the one they're going to shoot dead."

"You're just going to have to trust me on this. You've done well so far."

Caston's anxiety and confusion were visible, yet Ambler could tell that he was also pleased by the reassurance.

"You're going to use my body as a shield," Ambler said. "That means you don't let them see you, if you can avoid it. It means keeping me between you and them at all times. I'll help with that, but you need to understand the maneuver."

"Except *you're* the one they're after, right? It doesn't make any sense."

"Just go with me on this," Ambler repeated. It would take too long to explain the method in the madness. Hostages always made missions like this one messy. In the midst of a tension-fueled operation, nobody would think to second-guess the identity of hostage and hostage taker. It did not matter whether the gunmen had been given good photographs with their orders; they were not calmly studying images on a light table. They were men with guns, pumped with adrenaline, trying to complete their orders without a career-destroying mistake. Letting the hostage die could be that mistake. The active, enacted position of hostage and hostage taker would present itself to them as a vivid, present *fact*, and it would swamp other considerations, details like hair color and height.

Ambler whispered further instructions in Caston's ear.

Finally, Caston took another deep breath. "Let me speak to your commanding officer," he roared. At a normal, conversational volume, his voice might have trembled; forced to shout, however, he sounded bold and authoritative.

No response came.

Arranging his countenance into a look of sheer terror, Ambler hurtled himself toward the ravaged door, as if he had been shoved, Caston concealed behind him. "Don't let him kill me," he whimpered, pressing his face into the large, jagged hole. "Please don't let him kill me. Please don't let him kill me." His eyes were wide, staring, darting wildly with the hysteria of a civilian caught in a nightmare beyond his imagining.

He saw the same two commandos as before: square-jawed, dark-haired, muscular men, obviously highly trained. They were trying to look *past* him, into the darkened room, oblivious of the fact that their quarry was, literally, staring them in the face.

"I want to speak to the commanding officer," Caston repeated in a loud, confident voice. *"Now."*

The two men exchanged glances, and Ambler felt his pulse quicken. *There was no commanding officer present.* Not yet. The two gunmen were alone. Rapid response came at the expense of team staffing. No doubt others would arrive shortly, but for the moment, the duo was operating without backup.

"Please don't let him kill me," Ambler repeated, in a sniveling mantra of terror.

"You're going to be OK," one of the commandos, the larger of the two, said in a low voice.

"Let the hostage go," the other commando shouted. "And we'll talk."

"Do you think I'm a moron?" Caston immediately shouted. Ambler was astonished: the auditor was extemporizing.

"If you hurt him, it's all over for you," the second commando yelled back. Hostage negotiations would have been covered in the operative's early training, but cursorily. He was obviously trying to remember the basic tactics.

Suddenly Ambler sank to his feet, out of the commandos' view. "Ow!" he bellowed, as if he had just been struck.

Now he and Caston conferred quietly, hurriedly. What followed had to be flawlessly executed. Precision was something Caston valued; his look of intense concentration showed that he would honor it even now, even here.

Once more, Ambler showed his face through the jagged hole, his head jerking forward as if being prodded with a gun. "Please let me out of here," he wailed. "I don't know who you people are. I don't want to know. Just don't let him kill me." He contorted his features into a place beyond terror and let his eyes become moist. "He has a really long rifle with lots of bullets. He says he'll blow me to shreds. I got a wife, kids. I'm an American." He was jabbering, speaking in short, breathless sentences, a picture of panic. "You guys like movies? I'm in the movie business. I came here to scout locations. Plus the ambassador's a real good friend. And then this guy told me; he told me, oh *Christ* oh *Christ*—"

"Here's the plan," Caston boomed, unseen in the darkened room. "One of you can come to within five feet of the threshold. A foot nearer, and he dies. I'm going to let the civilian walk toward you so you can see that he's fine. But I'll have a red-bead on him all the time, understand? You make a wrong move, and my .338 Lapua Magnum gets to show you what it can do."

Ambler flung open the door and, walking stiffly and unsteadily, took a few steps into the hallway. Again, his face was a study in terror. The commandos would assume that their target was situated in a darkened corner of the room, out of their sight line, holding a sophisticated long-range rifle. The angle would permit him to kill his hostage without exposing himself to danger. Yet the two commandos had no choice but to go along. Time was on their side; their plan, now, was to stall as long as possible, to allow the other members of the team to assemble. Ambler could see it in their faces. Perhaps the hostage's death was an acceptable cost for completing the Tarquin sanction—but that call could only be made by their commanding officer.

Ambler took another step toward the second, larger commando, saw the man's sea-green eyes, dark hair, and second day's growth of beard. The commando considered the hostage to be little more than an impediment and a nuisance—an unknown that could not yet be removed from the equation. He was no longer holding his G36 in firing position; there seemed no point.

Now Ambler allowed himself to quiver with ostensible fear. He glanced back into the darkened room, pretended he could see a rifle trained at his head, conveyed this with a sharp intake of breath. Then he turned beseechingly back to the black-clad operative.

"He's going to kill me," Ambler repeated. "I know it, I know. I can see it in his eyes." As he spoke, words rushed out with mounting hysteria, Ambler began to flail his arms around, with corresponding agitation. "You need to help me. God, please help me. Call the U.S.

ambassador, Sam Hurlbut will vouch for me. I'm good people, I am. But please don't leave me with that, that *maniac*." As he spoke, he leaned forward, toward the commando, as if to try to speak to him in confidence.

"You need to calm down," the commando said in a hushed bark, scarcely concealing his distaste for the jabbering, panicking civilian, who was coming too close and talking too much as he continued to flail his hands wildly, until—

The opportunities will come. Take them.

"And you need to help me you need to help me you need to help me—" The panicked-sounding words rushed out independent of any sense. Ambler pitched himself forward, even closer to the commando; he could smell the operative's rancid stress sweat.

Grab the weapon by the buttstock, not the magazine. The magazine could snap off, leaving the bullets already chambered in the rifle. His grip on the trigger guard is loose. Grab it now—

With cobra-strike swiftness, Ambler wrested the G36 from the commando and *slammed* the silencer-cuffed barrel against his head. As the large man slumped to the ground, Ambler trained the assault rifle at the man's startled partner.

He saw a man trying to reassess all his assumptions, utterly bewildered. Ambler flicked the G36 on full fire.

"Drop yours now," he ordered.

The man did so, backing up slowly.

Ambler knew what the man was preparing to do. "Freeze," he shouted.

But the man kept backing away, his hands raised. When an operation had gone wrong, you evacuated. That was the rule you followed before any other rule came into play.

Ambler just watched as the man suddenly turned and ran out of the apartment, raced down the street, and disappeared, no doubt to rejoin his squad and regroup. Ambler and Caston, too, would need to evacuate immediately and regroup in their own way. In the event, killing the gunman would have been pointless.

There were too many operatives waiting to take his place.

Beijing

Chao Tang was an early riser and, like many early risers in a position of authority, compelled those who worked for him to become early risers, too, by the simple expedient of scheduling meetings at dawn. Members of his support staff at the Ministry of State Security had grown accustomed to his ways; little by little, they discontinued the late evenings of drinking rice wine, the sportive nightlife that senior members of the government could afford. The indulgences were not worth the pounding 6:00 A.M. headaches. Little by little, the bleary eyes cleared up to a look of calm alertness; the early-morning meetings no longer seemed like such a terrible imposition.

But the morning's meeting—a review of objectives accomplished and still pending—was now the furthest thing from his mind. He was in the secure communication room, poring over a communiqué that had arrived for him overnight, his eyes only, and what he had learned was profoundly disturbing. If Joe Li's dispatch was correct, the situation they confronted was even more dire than he had imagined. For Comrade Li's description of the incident in the Luxembourg Gardens violated their operating assumptions; new ones had to be arrived at, and swiftly. The question of *why* weighed upon Chao Tang greatly.

Could Joe Li have been mistaken? Chao Tang could not credit it. The report could not be dismissed. There were many enemies to contend with, but their greatest enemy, at the moment, was time. Chao could not wait any longer for Liu Ang to come to his senses.

Chao had to take a further, direct action on his own. Some would regard it as treason, an unconscionable and unpardonable transgression.

Yet Liu Ang's recalcitrance had given Chao no choice.

Chao took a deep breath. The message had to be delivered with both celerity and secrecy. And it had to be of a nature that would ensure that it would be accepted for what it was and acted upon. Normal rules of operating had to be suspended. The stakes were too great for *normal*.

As he transmitted his encoded instructions, he tried to reassure himself that he had taken the desperate measures that the situation required. If he had miscalculated, however, he had just made the biggest mistake of his life. Anxieties and apprehensions sluiced through his mind.

And so did the words of Joe Li's dispatch. Who else knew about it? The young man who delivered it to him, Shen Wang, was as bright eyed and bushy tailed this morning as he was every morning. At first Comrade Chao had been wary of him. He was effectively "on loan" from the People's Liberation Army—that was the terminology, but it was misleading. In order to promote the development of a common government culture—or, equally, to discourage the development of departmental division—the PLA had taken to "seconding" junior officers to the civilian branches of government. The catch was that one could not refuse such an assigned person, at least not without incurring grave displeasure. Thus a young factotum from the PLA was to spend a year as an intern at the central office of the Ministry of State Security. The MSS, in turn, placed one of its own at the PLA, but the consensus was that the PLA had the better of the deal.

At the MSS, the suspicion, of course, was that the PLA intern would report back to his PLA masters. Shen Wang was known to be a protégé of General Lam, a stiff-necked figure whom Chao regarded with a measure of distaste. Yet despite Chao's initial suspicions, the fresh-faced young man had steadily grown on him. Shen Wang was tireless, industrious, wholly devoid of cynicism. Chao had to admit that the young man—he could not be any older than twenty-five—seemed to be a true idealist, the sort of young man that Chao had once been.

Now Shen Wang appeared at the doorway, clearing his throat discreetly.

"If you will excuse my presumption, sir," he said, "you seem concerned."

Chao looked up at the hardworking intern. Had he looked at the communiqué himself? But his expression was so unclouded it seemed impossible he was guilty of any such thing.

"Matters have long been complicated," Chao replied. "This morning they grow more so."

Shen Wang bowed his head and was silent for a moment. "You work so hard," he said. "I think you are the hardest-working man I know."

Chao smiled wanly. "You're well on the way to outshining your elder."

"I cannot know the complexities of the state matters that burden you," Shen Wang said. "But I know that your shoulders are broader than any burden." He was alluding to an old proverb, his reassurance stopping just short of flattery.

"Let us hope so."

"Comrade Chao recalls his lunch appointment?"

Chao smiled distractedly. "You'll have to remind me."

Shen Wang glanced down at Chao's daily schedule. "A luncheon celebration of the People's Heroes. At the Peninsula Palace."

"I suppose I'd better get going then," Comrade Chao said. Neither needed to bemoan aloud the city's impossible traffic. Even a short trip involved an inordinate amount of time. Nor could someone in Comrade Chao's position travel without the protection of an armored car and a specially trained driver.

A few minutes later, as Chao climbed into the back of his black limousine, he reflected on Shen Wang's perceptiveness and graceful manner. Chao prided himself on recognizing potential, and he believed that this young man had a considerable future.

After ten minutes of sludge-like traffic, the sedan finally roared over an overpass at a reasonable speed.

A few hundred feet away, in the lane opposite, an enormous yellow bulldozer was visible. Roadwork of some sort, Chao thought, further ensnarling traffic. It was unfortunate that it could not have been postponed until a more reasonable hour of the day. At least it was in the opposite lane.

"Traffic's not so bad going our way, eh?" Comrade Chao's driver said.

The MSS director never replied. Instead, a scream exploded from his throat as the crushing impact came—so suddenly and unexpectedly. The enormous bulldozer, with its shovel blade low to the ground, had veered into their lane, and the sedan had been boxed in by the cars to either side. The windshield was smashed into pebbled shrapnel, piercing eyes and arteries; metal screamed against metal, twisting and crushing upon itself as the car lunged off the ground, lifted up by the shovel blade. Now the bulldozer crushed the sedan against the guardrail until the buckling vehicle catapulted over it and plunged onto a vast concrete basin below, where it burst into flames.

High in the unseen cab, the bulldozer's driver spoke into a cell phone. "The cleanup is completed," the driver said, in the rough dialect of the northern countryside.

"Thank you," Shen Wang told him. Given the soaring number of traffic accidents in Beijing these days, the death on the overpass would be dismaying but perhaps not altogether surprising. "The general will be very pleased."

Paris

"What's this?" Laurel asked, eyes widening in alarm. She and Ambler were in the hotel room, and he had just removed his shirt. Now she came over to him, running her fingers along a purplish bruise on the side of Ambler's shoulder.

"Caston's safe house wasn't all that safe, it turned out," Ambler admitted.

"Can you really trust that man?" Laurel asked, with a sharp look. She seemed uneasy, frightened for him.

"I have to think so."

"Why, Hal? How can you be so *sure?*"

"Because if I can't trust him, I can't trust myself." He stopped. "It's hard to explain."

She nodded slowly. "You don't have to. I understand. . . ." She trailed off. "I don't know why I'm worrying about it. The world stopped making sense a long time ago."

"A few days ago," Ambler corrected.

"Longer."

"Since *I* came into it." Acid splashed the back of his throat. "A stranger. A stranger to *myself.*"

Warningly: "Don't." Now she ran her fingertips over his chest, his shoulders, his arms, as if confirming that he was real, a person of flesh and blood, not a phantasm. When she met his gaze again, her eyes were moist. "I've never met anyone like you."

"Count your blessings."

She shook her head. "You're a good person." She tapped the center of his chest. "With a good heart."

"And someone else's head."

"Piss on that," she said in a mock snarl. "They tried to erase you, but you know what? You're realer than any man I've ever met."

"Laurel," he said, stopping when he heard the catch in his own voice.

"When I'm with you, it's like . . . it's like discovering I'd been all by myself my whole life long without fully realizing it, because I never knew what it was like to be *together* with someone—*really* together. That's how I feel when I'm with you. Like I'd always been alone and now I'm not. I can't go back to the way it was before. I can't go back to that." Her voice thickened with emotion. "You want to talk about what you've done to me, what you've put me through? *That's* what you've done to me. And I don't ever want it to come undone."

His mouth was dry. "Nothing frightens me more than losing you."

"I'm not lost anymore." Her amber eyes seemed lit from within; the green flecks glittered. "You've saved my life in more ways than one."

"You're the one, Laurel. Nothing makes sense without you. Not for me. I'm just—"

"Harrison Ambler," she said, smiling as she spoke the name aloud. "Harrison Ambler."

CHAPTER TWENTY-SEVEN

The Musée Armandier did not "mérite le détour," in Michelin-speak; it scarcely qualified as being worth a visit. But Ambler remembered it well from the year he spent in Paris as a youth and doubted it had changed much. It was one of the few private art museums in Paris and, to maintain its fiscal status as a museum, dutifully kept regular hours of admission. Yet it was largely deserted; it probably had less traffic than it did when it had been a private residence in the late nineteenth and early twentieth centuries. As a house—a neo-Italian villa, in style, with grandly arching windows deeply set in Purbeck limestone, and a partially enclosed courtyard—it was not unimpressive. Built by a Protestant banker who profited enormously from deals during the Second Empire, it was situated in the Plaine Marceau section of the Eighth Arrondissement, then a neighborhood favored by Bonapartist noblemen and a newer class of financiers and notably quiet even now. From time to time, the Musée Armandier would be rented by film crews working on costume dramas. Otherwise it was among the least visited public spaces in Paris. A fine place for a youthful assignation, perhaps—Ambler smiled at a long-ago memory—but of little interest to the museum-going public. The trouble was the collection. Marcel Armandier's wife, Jacqueline Armandier, had a taste for rococo art from the early eighteenth century, a school of work that had been decidedly out of fashion for the past half century. Worse still, she had a penchant for second-rate rococo art—canvases by such minor talents as François Boucher, Nicolas de Largillière, Francesco Trevisani, and Giacomo Amiconi. She liked her cupids to be plump and beaming, cavorting in a perfectly turquoise sky, and her Arcadian shepherds to be as Arcadian as possible. She sized up the landscapes as if it were the property depicted, not the picture itself, that she were acquiring.

In deeding the mansion to be a museum, Jacqueline, who survived her husband by a decade, must have hoped she was ensuring that her possessions would be celebrated through the succeeding generations. Instead, the odd art historian who paid a visit generally greeted Jacqueline's collection with muted catcalls or, worse, the mockery of campy adoration.

Ambler appreciated the museum for other reasons: unpopular as it was, it was a good place for a private encounter, and the combination of plentiful windows and a quiet street would enable him to detect any stalker patrols. At the same time, the Armandier foundation, charged with husbanding a limited budget, hired only a single guard for the whole museum, and the guard seldom wandered farther up than the second floor.

Now Ambler mounted the stairs to the fourth floor and turned down a hallway with gilt moldings and a long painting of lyre-strumming goddesses cavorting on what looked like a golf course and made his way to the large room at the end, where he and Caston had agreed to meet.

His footsteps were muffled by the peach-colored carpeting, and he could hear Caston's voice as he approached.

Ambler froze, felt a prickle of apprehension running down his neck. Was Caston with someone?

Silently he came closer, until he could make out the words.

"Good," Caston was saying. And: "Is that right?" And: "So they're doing OK?" A man talking on a cell phone. There was a long moment of silence. "Good night, hugglebunny," Caston said. "Love you, too." He closed the flip phone and pocketed it as Ambler entered the room.

"Glad you made it," Caston said.

" 'Hugglebunny'?" Ambler asked.

Flushing, the auditor turned and looked out the window. "I had my office check the Border Control database," the auditor said after a while. "Dr. Ashton Palmer arrived in Roissy yesterday. He's here."

"Your office—can you trust their discretion?"

"I say 'my office,' but it's really one person. My assistant. And yes, I trust him."

"What else did you learn?"

"I didn't say I learned anything else."

"You did," Ambler corrected him. "Just not in words."

Caston glanced around at the canvas-crowded walls and scowled. "The thing is, it's messy, and I'm not sure what to make of it yet. It's what they call 'chatter'—small interceptions, some fragmentary in nature, each inconclusive on its own."

"But added together?"

"Something's going on—or maybe I should say that something's about to happen. Something involving—"

"China," Ambler broke in.

"Well, that's the easier part of the conundrum."

"You're talking in riddles yourself."

"The harder part is *you*. Approaching matters logically, that's the place to start. Call it a variant of the anthropic principle. What we call observation selection effects."

"Look, Caston, would you try speaking English?"

Caston glared. "Observation selection effects are totally commonplace. At the supermarket, have you ever noticed how often you find yourself in the longer checkout line? Why is that? *Because those are the lines with the most people in them.* Let's say I told you that Mr. Smith, about whom you knew nothing at all, was standing on one of the checkout lines, and you had to predict which one, based only on knowing how many people were in each line."

"There'd be no way to know."

"But inference is about probabilities. And the most probable outcome, obviously, is that he's in the line with the most people in it.

Once you step back and consider yourself from an outsider's perspective, it becomes self-evident. The slowest traffic lane is the one with the most cars in it. The laws of probability say that any given driver is most likely to be in that lane. That means you. It's not bad luck or delusion that makes you think the other lanes of traffic are going faster. More often than not, they *are* going faster."

"Right," Ambler said. "It's obvious."

"It *is* obvious," Caston said. "Once it's pointed out. Just as if you knew nothing more about a person except that he or she lived on this planet today, and you were asked to guess the person's country of origin, you should guess that the person is Chinese. You'd be wrong less often than if you named any other country of origin, simply because China is the world's most populous nation."

"News flash," Ambler said. "I'm not Chinese."

"No, but you've become entangled in something that involves Chinese politics. And the question is: Why you? In the case of the checkout line, not much distinguishes you from any other shopper. But in this case, the population—the list of eligible candidates—is a lot more rarefied."

"I didn't choose this thing. I was chosen."

"Again, the question is why?" the auditor pressed. "What information did they have about you? Which data points were pertinent?"

Ambler remembered what various people involved in the Strategic Services Group had told him. He *was* special, from their perspective. "Paul Fenton told me they decided I was a magician because I'd 'erased' myself."

"When, in point of fact, you'd been 'erased,' if you want to put it that way. But this suggests that they had a particular need for an agent who can't be identified. And not just any agent, either. An agent with special skills—an agent with fantastically honed skills at inferring emotion. A walking polygraph."

"Fenton had my Stab records, or some of them. He didn't know my name, my real name, but he knew my assignments, what I'd done, where I'd been."

"So consider that factor, too. There are your inherent characteristics, and there are these historical ones: who you are and what you've done. Either or both could be relevant."

"Wouldn't want to leap to conclusions, huh?"

Caston smiled wanly. His eyes lingered on a painting of a verdant expanse of rolling green with a picturesque scattering of dappled cows and a flaxen-haired milkmaid with a beatific glow carrying a pail. "You know the old story about an economist, a physicist, and a mathematician driving through Scotland? They see a brown cow out of the window, and the economist says, 'Fascinating that the cows in Scotland are brown.' The physicist says, 'I'm afraid you're overgeneralizing from the evidence. All we know is that some cows in Scotland are brown.' Finally, the mathematician shakes his head at both of them. 'Wrong again. Completely unwarranted by the evidence. All we can infer, logically, is that there exists at least one cow in this country, at least one side of which is brown.' "

Ambler rolled his eyes. "I was wrong when I said you were the guy gets to the shoot-out in time to pick up the shell casings. Actually, you're the guy who, a thousand years later, picks the shell casings out of an archaeological dig."

Caston just looked at him. "I'm simply trying to get you to look for patterns. Because the fact is that there's a pattern here. Changhua. Montreal. And now Paris—the Deschesnes incident."

"Changhua . . . I tried to stop it. Too late, but I tried."

"But you failed. And you were there."

"Meaning?"

"Meaning there's very likely photographic evidence of your presence. You can't infer much from a single brown cow. But three brown cows in a row? That's where the laws of probability come into play. The question is why they wanted you. And what they really wanted you for. Changhua. Montreal. Paris. It's not just a string of events, Ambler. It's a *sequence*."

"Fine," Ambler said testily. The overheated museum was causing him to perspire. "It's a sequence. What's that mean?"

"Meaning we need to do the math. Zero, one, one, two, three, five, eight, thirteen, twenty-one, thirty-four, fifty-five—that's the Fibonacci sequence. A child might look at those numbers and not see the pattern. But the pattern is staring him in the face. Each number in the series is the sum of the preceding two. Every series is like that, however random it might appear. There's a pattern, a rule, an algorithm, and it makes order out of seeming chaos. That's what we need here. We need to see how each event is connected to the one before, because then we'll know what the next event is going to be." Caston looked grave. "Then again, we can just wait for the next event to happen. That might make everything clear. From every indication we've got, we're about to see what it's all leading up to."

"In which case it's probably too late," Ambler grunted. "So it's a progression. Meaning, basically, you have no idea what the logic is."

"Meaning we need to find out." Caston gave him a look that was both wry and wintry. "If I were superstitious, I'd say you were bad luck."

"Luck can change."

The auditor winced. "True sequences *don't* change. Not unless you change them."

Langley

Adrian Choi fidgeted with his ear stud as he sat at his boss's desk. It felt good, sitting there, and there couldn't be any harm in it. Besides, it wasn't as if anybody ever passed by—the hallway where Caston had his office wasn't out-of-bounds, but it was out of the way. Office space Siberia. Adrian made another phone call.

Caston had been dogged about trying to get those Parrish Island personnel files, and when Adrian asked how he could hope to succeed where Caston had failed, he said that thing about *charm*. Adrian didn't have Caston's authority, but there were informal routes. He smiled his sunniest smile as he called an assistant at the Joint Facilities Center, someone at his level. Caston had spoken to her boss to no avail. He'd grumbled and protested and blustered. Adrian would try another approach.

The woman who answered would need a lot of warming up. She sounded immediately wary.

"PIPF Ward 4W—yes, I know," she said. "I'll have to process the request forms."

"No, see, you guys already gave us a copy of the files," Adrian lied.

"Joint Facilities did?"

"Yup," Adrian said breezily. "I'm just asking for *another* copy."

"Oh," the young woman said, a little less frostily. "Sorry. Bureaucracy, right?"

"Tell me about it," Adrian said, making his voice as silkily confiding as he could. "I'd like to say it was a matter of national security. But it's really a matter of saving my own ass."

"How do you mean?"

"Well, Caitlin—it's Caitlin, right?"

"That's right," she said. Was he imagining it, or was she warming up, ever so subtly?

"You sound like the kind of person who never messes up, so I don't expect much sympathy from you."

"Me?" She giggled. "Are you *kidding*?"

"Nah, I know your type. You've got everything under control. Every scrap of paper's in order in *your* office."

"No comment," she said, and he could hear the smile in her voice.

"Hey, it's important to have somebody to look up to," Adrian said. "I've got this whole image of you in my mind—you got to let me cherish that."

"You're a funny guy."

"Then I must have been clowning when I forwarded the file directly to the DDI's office without keeping a copy for my boss." Adrian's voice was wheedling but a little flirtatious, too. "Which means my boss is totally going to pitch a fit. And my Stanford-educated ass is grass." He paused. "Listen, that's my problem, not yours. I didn't mean to lay this on you. Never mind. Really."

The young woman on the other end of the line sighed. "It's just that they've been really uptight about the whole thing, God knows why. Everything's in some Omega-level sequestered database."

"Intramural rivalries are always the fiercest, right?"

"I guess," she said doubtfully. "Listen, I'll see what I can do, OK?"

"You're a lifesaver, Caitlin," said Adrian. "I mean that."

Paris

Burton Lasker looked at his watch yet again and prowled the Air France lounge. It wasn't like Fenton to be late. Yet the flight had already started to board, and Fenton had still not appeared. Lasker checked with the attendants at the gate. They replied to his questioning gaze with a simple shake of the head; he had already asked them two or three times whether Fenton had appeared. A wave of annoyance swept through Lasker. There were any number of circumstances that could delay a passenger, but Fenton was the sort of person who prepared for the usual exigencies and inconveniences of travel. He had a well-developed sense of the tolerances of daily life and knew how far to test them. So where was he now? Why wasn't he answering his cell phone?

Lasker had been in Fenton's employ for a decade and, at least for the past several years, could style himself Fenton's staunchest lieutenant. Every visionary required someone who devoted himself to the tightly focused task of *execution*—of *follow-through*. Lasker excelled at that. He was a veteran of the Special Forces, but he never felt the contempt that some military men had for the civilian: Fenton was a patron of the operatives, as some people were patrons of artists. And Fenton truly was a visionary—truly understood how a private-public partnership could transform America's strengths in clandestine operations. Fenton, in turn, respected Lasker for his firsthand knowledge of ops and combat and the subtler operations of the counterterrorism squadrons he had helped train. Lasker considered his years with Fenton the most valuable and gratifying of his entire adult life.

Where was the man? As the Air France attendants, with an apologetic shrug, closed the ramp doors, Lasker felt an icicle of fear within his gut. Something was wrong. He phoned the front desk of the hotel where he and Fenton had both been staying. "No, Monsieur Fenton has not checked out." Something was very wrong.

Laurel Holland finally joined the other two men at the still-deserted fourth floor of the Musée Armandier a few minutes later than they had planned—her errands had taken her longer than she had expected, she explained.

"You must be Clayton Caston," she said to the auditor, and extended a hand. Her posture, as well as her words, was slightly formal. She still seemed to fear what he was, what he represented as a senior CIA official. At the same time, she trusted Ambler's judgment implicitly. He had made the decision to deal with Caston; she would follow suit. Ambler had to hope that he was not mistaken.

"I'm Clay," the auditor replied, "in your hands, anyway. Nice to meet you, Laurel."

"Your first time in France, Hal tells me. Mine, too, if you can believe it."

"My first time, and, if I'm lucky, my last time," Caston groused. "I hate this country. At the hotel I turned on the shower knob marked *C* and practically scalded myself. I swear I could hear fifty million Frenchmen laughing."

"Fifty million Frenchmen can't be wrong," Laurel told him solemnly. "Isn't that what they say?"

"Fifty million Frenchmen," Caston replied with a reproving stare, "can be wrong in fifty million ways."

"But who's counting?" Ambler said lightly, scanning the faces of the few pedestrians in the area. He glanced down at the newspaper Laurel had taken with her for cover. *Le Monde diplomatique.* On the front page was an article by one Bertrand Louis-Cohn, apparently an intellectual of note. Ambler skimmed it; the occasion was a conference of the World Economic Forum at Davos, but the content seemed to be gaseous generalizations about the current economic conjuncture. Something about *"la pensée unique,"* which, Louis-Cohn wrote, could be defined by its enemies as *"la projection idéologique des intérêts financiers de la capitale mondiale"*—the ideological projection of the financial interests of global capital—or *"l'hégémonie des riches,"* the hegemony of the rich. On and on it went, recycling leftist criticisms of *l'orthodoxie libérale* without either endorsing them or rejecting them. The whole essay seemed like some sort of weirdly stylized activity, intellectual kabuki.

"What's that say?" Laurel asked, pointing to the article.

"It's about some meeting of global titans in Davos. The World Economic Forum."

"Oh," she said. "Is the guy for it or against it?"

"Beats the hell out of me," Ambler said.

"I was there once," the auditor said. "The World Economic Forum wanted my expertise for some panel on money laundering. They like a scattering of people who actually know what they're talking about. It's like the greenery in a floral arrangement."

Ambler peered through the window to the street again, confirming that nobody suspicious had entered the vicinity. "Here's the thing. I'm tired of playing blindman's bluff. We know there's a pattern here—a progression or sequence, like you say. But this time I need to know the next step ahead of time."

"My assistant is working on getting more information from Joint Intel Resources," Caston said. "I think we should wait to see what he finds out."

Ambler gave the back-office man a flinty look. "You're along for the ride, Caston. Nothing more. Like I say, *this isn't your world.*"

Wu Jingu was a soft-spoken man, but he found he seldom had difficulty making himself heard. His career in the Ministry of State Security had established his reputation as a sober analyst, someone who was neither a Pollyanna nor an alarmist. He was someone people listened to. Yet President Liu Ang was frustratingly unmoved by his counsel. Little wonder that the muscles in Wu's narrow shoulders were bunched with tension.

He lay facedown and motionless on the narrow cushioned table as he readied himself for his twice-weekly massage, trying to banish the stress from his mind.

"Your muscles are so very tight," the masseuse said, her strong fingers manipulating the flesh around his shoulders.

It was not a voice he recognized—not his usual masseuse. He craned his head and looked at the substitute. "Where's Mei?"

"Mei felt under the weather today, sir. I'm Zhen. It is OK?"

Zhen was even more beautiful than Mei, and her grip was stong and confident. Wu nodded contentedly. The elite and exclusive Caspara spa, newly opened in Beijing, hired only the very best: that was clear. He turned back, placing his head on the open headrest, and listened to the soothing piped-in sounds of bubbling water and softly plucked *guzheng.* He felt as if Zhen's fingers were dissolving tension wherever they roamed.

"Excellent," he murmured. "For the welfare of the ship, one must calm the turbulent seas."

"That is our specialty, sir," Zhen said softly. "Such tight muscles— you must have many burdens and responsibilities placed upon you."

"Many," Wu murmured.

"But I know just the thing, sir."

"I am in your hands."

The beautiful masseuse began to apply acupressure to the soles of his feet, and he felt a growing lightness suffuse his body. So dozy was the security advisor that he did not respond at once when a hypodermic needle was inserted just beneath the toenail of his left foot—the sharp sensation was so incongruous that, at least at first, it did not register. And then, moments later, a wave of utter relaxation suffused his body like a tide of numbness. In the next few moments, he could only foggily contemplate the difference between relaxation and paralysis. He felt dead to the world.

And then, as Zhen matter-of-factly confirmed, he was just dead.

Burton Lasker boarded the Georges V elevator with the smooth-faced young manager on duty. When they reached the seventh floor, the young man knocked on the heavy oak door, then unlocked it with a special key card. The two men strode through the rooms, seeing no sign of habitation. Then the hotelier stepped into the bathroom; his face was ashen as he stepped out. Lasker immediately rushed over and saw what the other man had seen. He gasped. It felt as if there were a balloon inside his chest, making it hard to breathe.

"You were a friend of his?" the hotelier asked.

"A friend and business associate," Lasker confirmed.

"I am sorry." The man paused awkwardly. "Help will arrive shortly. I will make the calls."

Lasker stood rooted to the spot, trying to calm himself. Paul Fenton. His reddened, blistered body was slumped in the bathtub, naked. Lasker noticed the still-steaming bathwater, the emptied bottle of vodka propped by the basin—stage dressing that might confuse the gendarmerie but did not fool Lasker for a moment.

A remarkable man—a great man—had been murdered.

Lasker had a strong suspicion who was behind it, and when he went through Paul Fenton's PDA, his suspicions were confirmed. It was the man Fenton had called Tarquin. A man Lasker knew all too well.

Tarquin had served in the Political Stabilization Unit, and Lasker—field name Cronus—had had the misfortune of serving with him on a couple of assignments. Tarquin had somehow imagined himself superior to his colleagues and was oblivious to how much support they selflessly gave him. Tarquin was known for his peculiar gift of reading people, a gift that some of the strategists at Consular Operations were overly impressed with. They couldn't grasp what seasoned operatives like Cronus knew, as a matter of second nature: that operational success always came down to firepower and muscle.

Now Tarquin had killed the greatest man Lasker had ever known, and he would pay. He would pay with the only currency that Lasker would accept: his life.

What sickened Lasker was that he had once saved Tarquin's life—not that Tarquin could be bothered to display anything akin to gratitude. Lasker recalled a humid, mosquito-ridden night nearly ten years ago, in the jungles of Jaffra, Sri Lanka. That night, he had risked his own life to charge in, guns blazing, and save Tarquin from a group of terrorists who were planning to kill him. Mordantly, Lasker remembered the bitter old adage: *No good deed goes unpunished.* He had saved the life of a monster—an error for which he would now make amends.

Fenton did not explain everything that he was up to—no visionary could be expected to. Once, when he had asked Fenton about the rationale of a particular deployment, Fenton had said to him lightly, "Yours is but to do and kill."

It was no longer a laughing matter.

Lasker whisked through the transmission log of Fenton's wireless PDA. He would send a message to the condemned man. First, though, calls would be made to the dozen or so "associates" that SSG had on the ground in Paris. They would be put on alert at once, precise mobilization orders to follow shortly.

A spasm of profound grief passed over Lasker—and yet he could not allow himself grief until he had experienced vengeance. He summoned the discipline of his rarefied profession. A rendezvous with the condemned man would be established for sunset.

It would be, Lasker resolved, the last sunset Tarquin would ever see.

Caleb Norris pressed the OFF button of his cell phone. It was foolish that the CIA permitted the use of cell phones in headquarters at all, he reflected. Their presence nullified a great deal of the elaborate security precautions that were taken—like waterproofing a sieve. But at the moment, the circumstance suited him very well.

He fed various papers into the shredder beside his desk, retrieved his coat, and, finally, unlocked a steel-lined case secreted in his credenza. The long-barreled handgun fitted neatly into his briefcase.

"Have a *great* trip, Mr. Norris," Brenda Wallenstein said in her familiar nasal voice. She had been Norris's secretary for the past five years and devotedly followed the fashions of workplace injuries. When news stories started to appear about repetitive-motion disorder, she started showing up with special wrist braces and pressure bandages. More recently, she had taken to wearing special headphones, like a telephone operator, in order to spare her neck the perils of cinching up a handset. There had been a time, Norris vaguely recalled, when she started to develop scent allergies; that those allergies had failed to develop was only a function of her somewhat limited attention span.

Norris had long ago concluded that she simply preferred to imagine her job—which largely involved sitting at a keyboard and answering the phone—as being, in its way, every bit as hazardous as a tour of duty in the Marines. In her mind, anyway, she was obviously awarding herself as many "injuries sustained" badges.

"Thank you, Brenda," the ADDI replied heartily. "I intend to."

"Don't get sunburned," his secretary cautioned, with her unfailing instinct for identifying the dark sides of all situations. "See, down there they even have these little umbrellas so the *drinks* don't get sunburned. Those rays are *strong*. I went online and looked up the weather forecast for St. John and the Virgin Islands, and it's supposed to be nothing but clear skies."

"Just what we like to hear."

"Joshua and I went to St. Croix one year." She pronounced the word to rhyme with *stoics*. "He got such a sunburn on the first day, he was smearing spearmint toothpaste on his face just to get cool. Can you picture it?"

"I'd rather not, if it's all the same to you." Norris briefly debated whether to take additional ammunition but decided against. It was a little-known fact about him that he was an excellent shot.

Brenda cackled. "Forewarned is forearmed, right? But St. John has gotta be just what the doctor ordered. Blue skies, blue sea, white sand. And I just checked—your car is here, waiting at the 2A bay with your luggage. Dulles shouldn't even take half an hour at this time of day. Should be smooth sailing."

She was right—for all her garrulity and self-imposed mortifications, she was actually quite efficient—but Cal Norris had left himself plenty of time at the airport. Even with all the right paperwork, checking a weapon could take some time. In the event, the line at Business Class moved fast.

"Good afternoon," the airline clerk behind the counter said, in his programmed greeting. "And where are you headed for today?"

Norris slid his ticket across the counter. "Zurich," he said.

"Skiing, I bet." The clerk glanced at Norris's passport and ticket invoice before stamping his board card.

Norris stole a glance at his watch. "What else?"

As he watched a gust sweep through the street outside the Musée Armandier, Ambler felt the BlackBerry vibrating in an inside coat pocket. It had to be a message from Fenton or one of his people, who had given him the device in the first place. He scanned its small screen quickly. A deputy of Fenton's had called to arrange a meeting this evening—an outdoor rendezvous this time. As Ambler returned the device to his pocket, he felt a faint sense of unease.

"Where?" asked Laurel.

"Père-Lachaise," the operative replied. "Not the most imaginative venue, but I can see its advantages. And Fenton never likes to meet in the same place twice."

"Worries me," Laurel said. "I don't like the sound of it."

"Because it's a cemetery? It might as well be an amusement park—it's a pretty heavily trafficked area. Trust me, I know what I'm doing."

"I wish I shared your confidence," Caston said. "Fenton's a goddamn wild card. His whole arrangement with the federal government is a can of worms. Had my office look into it a bit, and it seems they buried it under black box appropriations. A high-level shroud—nothing I can penetrate while I'm here. But I'd love to have a chance to review those numbers. Damned irregular, I'd bet." He blinked. "As for a rendezvous at Père-Lachaise with people like that? That goes beyond the category of risk and into the dark realm of uncertainty."

"Caston, dammit, I already live in the dark realm of uncertainty," Ambler said, flaring. "Or haven't you noticed?"

Laurel reached a hand over to his. "I'm just saying be careful," she said. "You still don't know what these people are really up to."

"I'll be careful. But we're getting close."

"Close to finding out what they did to you?"

"Yes," Ambler said. "And close to finding out what they may have planned for the rest of the world."

"Take care of yourself, Hal," she said. With a side-glance at Caston, she leaned forward and whispered in Ambler's ear, "I *really* don't have a good feeling about this."

Beijing

"We must get the message to President Liu," Wan Tsai said, the horror in his gaze further magnified by his convex wire-rimmed glasses.

"But what if Comrade Chao's death really was an accident?" Li Pei asked. The two had convened in Wan Tsai's office, in the Hall of Diligent Government. "What if it *was*?"

"Do you believe that?" Wan Tsai demanded.

A faint chest rattle was audible as the older man exhaled. "No," he said. "I don't." Li Pei was in his late seventies but suddenly looked older still.

"We have all gone through the proper channels," Wan Tsai said, not for the first time. "We have all raised the alarm. Yet I find that he is already in the air, halfway there. We must get him to come back."

"Except he will *not* come back," Li Pei wheezed. "We both know that about him. He is as wise as an owl—and as stubborn as a mule." A mournful look passed over his age-etched countenance. "And who knows whether he might confront even greater dangers at home."

"Have you spoken to Wu Jingu, Chao's colleague?"

"Nobody seems to know where he is at the moment." The economist swallowed hard.

"How can that be?"

Wan Tsai shook his head in a shuddering motion. "Nobody knows. I've spoken to everyone else, though. We all want to think what happened to Chao was an accident. None of us truly can." The economist ran a hand through his thick, graying hair.

"It's not too soon to start wondering about Wu Jingu as well," the old man said.

A harrowed look threatened what remained of Wan Tsai's composure. "Who is in charge of Liu Ang's security retinue?"

"You *know* who," the wily peasant said.

Wan Tsai closed his eyes briefly. "The PLA, you mean."

"A unit under PLA control. It comes to the same thing."

Wan Tsai looked around him, at his own sprawling office, at the grand Hall of Diligent Government, at the facades of the Zhongnanhai that were visible from his outer window. The doors, the walls, the gates, the bars—every implement of security struck him as an tool of imprisonment.

"I will speak to the general in charge," Wan Tsai said abruptly. "I will appeal to him personally. Many of these generals are men of honor, on a personal level, whatever their political views may be."

A few minutes later, he had secured a connection to the man in whose safekeeping President Liu Ang currently was. Wan Tsai made no secret of his anxieties, admitted that they were not yet founded upon evidentiary certainty, and implored the man to have his retinue convey to Liu Ang an urgent message.

"Have no worries on that score," said the PLA official in a harsh, Hakka-inflected Mandarin. "Nothing could be of greater importance to me than the state of Liu Ang's security."

"Because I cannot stress enough that all of us who work with Liu Ang are *extremely* concerned," the economist said, not for the first time.

"We are in complete agreement," the PLA official, General Lam, said reassuringly. "As people from my village say, 'Right eye, left eye.' Trust that our beloved leader's safety will be my personal priority."

At least Wan Tsai *thought* that was what the general said. The man's heavy accent made the word "priority" sound almost like another, seldom-used Mandarin word, which meant "plaything."

CHAPTER TWENTY-EIGHT

Le Cimetière du Père-Lachaise was established, at the beginning of the nineteenth century, on the hill of the old Champ l'Évêque and was named for Louis XIV's confessor, Father Lachaise. Now, it was the resting place for legendary figures—Colette, Jim Morrison, Marcel Proust, Oscar Wilde, Sarah Bernhardt, Edith Piaf, Chopin, Balzac, Corot, Gertrude Stein, Modigliani, Stephane Grappelli, Delacroix, Isadora Duncan, and so many others. *Deathstyles of the rich and famous,* Ambler mused as he entered.

The cemetery was vast—well over a hundred acres—and webbed with cobbled walkways. Especially in winter, it could resemble an arboretum of stone.

He glanced at his watch. The meeting was to take place at 5:10. In Paris, during this time of the year, the sun set at around half past five. Already the light was fading rapidly. He shivered, only partly because of the cold.

You never agree to a rendezvous chosen by the other party. Basic protocol. But in this case he had no choice. He could not drop the thread.

On the map, Père-Lachaise was sectioned off into ninety-seven "divisions," like miniature counties, but the main routes had names and the instructions had been quite specific about which to take. Carrying a black backpack, Ambler dutifully went from the avenue Circulaire, the ring road along the outer periphery of the cemetery, to the avenue de la Chapelle and made a left on the avenue Feuillant. All the roads and walkways—each lined with mausoleums and tombstones like little houses—made it seem like a village. A village of the dead. Some of the tombs were in red granite, but most were carved slabs of pale limestone and travertine and marble. The grayness of the early evening added to the sepulchral air.

He did not visit the specified rendezvous immediately; instead, he walked the pathways surrounding it. The trees were plentiful but largely leafless, of little use for concealment. Still, Fenton could have positioned security guards behind the larger edifices. They could also have been interspersed, in plainclothes, among the tourists and visitors, also plentiful.

Ambler approached a nearby bench, a structure of green enameled steel slats, and, with a casual inconspicuous motion, left a black backpack underneath it. He strolled away and took up an observation post across a diagonal path and behind one of the larger stone memorials. Then he ducked into a kiosk marked WC, removed his jacket, and put on a sweatshirt. He exited swiftly, stepping around the kiosk and behind a ten-foot stone memorial for one Gabriel Lully, where he could observe without being observed.

A little over sixty seconds later, a denim-clad young man in a brown leather jacket and black T-shirt stumbled past, sat down on the bench and yawned, and then resumed a seemingly aimless walk—but as he walked away, Ambler could see that the backpack was gone.

The young man with the leather jacket was one of the Watchers and had done what Ambler had predicted, albeit with surprising fluidity and economy of movement. They had observed Ambler leaving the backpack in place and, intent on learning why, had dispatched someone to retrieve it.

The item was, in fact, filled with birdseed. It was a play on a tradecraft term: *birdseed* referred to anything of no actual value that might be used to attract the attention of enemy agents. They would understand the ruse as soon as the pack was opened and the bag of sunflower seeds and millet examined.

Meanwhile, however, Ambler had identified one of the sentries—

one of the Watchers. He would follow the young man and see whether he led him to others.

Walking down another cobbled path, Ambler was now wearing jeans, a gray sweatshirt, and horn rimmed glasses with clear glass lenses. His other clothes were folded tightly in the small nylon zip-bag he carried on a shoulder strap. He was utterly inconspicuous.

Or so he hoped.

He kept pace with the black-shirted Watcher, twelve yards behind him and to the left, and followed him through another square, a space where all manner of visitors—day trippers, tourists, art historians, even locals—congregated. The young man with the leather jacket and the black T-shirt was walking with a studiedly casual saunter. He glanced to his left and to his right; few people, however professional, would have registered the nearly imperceptible looks of recognition and acknowledgment, from a large woman to his left and a small, weedy-looking man on his right. But Ambler did. They were Watchers, too; then Ambler stole another glance at the large woman. She had mouse brown hair, cut short, and wore a lined denim jacket. Like many in the cemetery, she had a large pad of paper and a charcoal pastille, equipped to take "rubbings" of tombstone inscriptions. Yet he could tell at a glance that she was faking it; her eyes darted rapidly, attentive to her surroundings but not to the carved stone before her.

It was the same with the weedy-looking man, with his long dark hair combed in a part down the center, the ends looking greasy, almost matted. He, too, was a Watcher. He had earphones on and bobbed his head, as if to a beat. Ambler knew that the audio transmission he was listening to was anything but musical. Instructions could be transmitted to him at any time, via a concealed radio device, and the woman with mouse-brown hair would follow his lead. As Ambler proceeded to the next memorial square, the back of his neck began to tingle unpleasantly.

There were more of them.

He *felt* it as much as anything. It was in the gaze too intent on passersby—the gaze too quickly averted. The ostensibly casual glance that lingered too long or ended too swiftly. It was in the fleeting exchange of glances between two people who were, from all appearances, of different walks of life, people who were or should have been unacquainted with each other.

There was the sense of walking through a social *organism*—a seemingly unstructured collection of people who were connected by unseen strings, even as those strings were manipulated by an unseen puppet master.

Ambler's skin began to crawl. He had not been surprised to find a small number of plainclothes security operatives; some precautions would have been standard with a government official as senior as Undersecretary Whitfield was.

But the configuration of personnel he had come across was *all wrong:* all wrong for the sort of rendezvous he had been promised. There were far too many in place, for one thing. The netting was far too elaborate. People were situated in nondefensive positions, deployed as for rapid action. The patterns he was seeing were all too familiar to him; as a Stab operative, he had sometimes had to set up such a deployment, invariably in preparation for aggressive actions—abduction or assassination.

Ambler's blood ran cold. He reeled in his mind, forcing himself to focus. Ahead of him, the man in the leather jacket and black T-shirt was passing the nylon backpack to two stone-faced men in dark woolen topcoats. They received the package and hurried off, no doubt toward some sort of containment vehicle.

Two possibilities presented themselves. One was that the meeting had been compromised—that mutual enemies had learned of it and were organizing an interception. The second—and Ambler had to admit, the more likely—possibility was that the rendezvous had been a setup from the beginning.

Had Fenton been lying to him all along? Contemplating the

prospect was a grievous blow to Ambler's sense of himself, but he could not rule out the possibility. Perhaps Fenton was a spectacular actor—the sort of Method actor who had disciplined himself to *experience* the very emotions he displayed. Ambler's powers of affective perception may have been, as a life's experience suggested, unusual and uncanny; he had no illusions that they were infallible. He was not incapable of being fooled. Perhaps, though, Fenton himself had been misinformed. That seemed a likelier prospect. It would have been vastly easier to lie to Fenton than it would have been to lie to him.

Whatever the circumstances were, Ambler knew that an immediate retreat was the only safe move. It pained him: Any member of the team that had been mobilized here might know something that Ambler needed to know. Every enemy was a potential source. Yet knowledge could do him no good if he was dead. He had, at least, to accept that truth.

Ambler quickened his stride and took an immediate right; it would lead him to the Père-Lachaise metro station. Now, on the straight, cobbled pathway, he strode even faster, like a businessman who had realized he was going to be late for a meeting.

He saw what was happening to him too late: the two bulky men who had received the backpack, both dressed in similar dark topcoats, were closing in on him from opposite directions and now *stepping* into him, their broad shoulders catching Ambler's, spinning him around in a fluid, well-choreographed movement.

"*Je m'excuse, monsieur. Je m'excuse,*" they kept repeating loudly. A bystander would have made nothing of it, a minor collision among hurrying, distracted businessmen. Meanwhile, Ambler thrashed furiously and in vain. The two operatives were tall and broad—taller and broader than Ambler—and their enrobed bulk helped conceal the disciplined ferocity with which they propelled Ambler off the cobblestone and toward the back of an adjoining mausoleum. Moments later, concealed from view by an elaborate stone edifice, they stood to either side, hands gripping his upper arms, immobilizing him. The man on his right had an object in his other hand, a thing of plastic and a small glimmer of steel. A hypodermic, in fact, with an amber fluid visible in the calibrated tube.

"Not one word," the man said in a hushed voice, "or I sink this in your arm." He was an American, stocky-framed and broad-faced, and his breath had the bouillon stink of a bodybuilder's all-protein diet.

Now a third man sprang into view, and it was a few seconds before Ambler recognized him. His hair was curly, thinning, graying; his eyes were narrow set, his forehead deeply creased. When Ambler knew him, his face was smooth, his head of hair full and unruly. Unchanged was his long, straight, broad nose and flaring nostrils, which gave his face a certain equine cast. There was no mistaking the man he had known as Cronus.

Now Cronus smiled, a smile so devoid of warmth as to be a beacon of menace. "It has been a while, hasn't it?" he said in a conversational tone that was anything but conversational in intent. "Too long, Tarquin."

"Maybe not long enough," Ambler replied neutrally. His eyes flickered among all three men. Already it was obvious that Cronus was the figure of authority here; the others were looking to him for a signal to act.

"Ten years ago, I gave you a gift. Now I'm afraid I'll have to take it back. Does that make me an Indian giver?"

"I don't know what you're talking about."

"Don't you?" Cronus's eyes gleamed with pure hatred.

"Though it's an odd expression, don't you think?" Ambler needed more time—more time to figure out the situation he was in. "Odd, I mean, that we talk about 'Indian giving,' when you think about all those hundreds of treaties the white man made with the red man, all those promises and guarantees, all of which were broken. You'd think the expression should be 'Indian taker'—meaning, to accept something that will only be taken back. Wouldn't that make more sense?"

Cronus looked at him. "Did you really think you could get away with it?"

"With what?"

"You miserable fuck." The words came out in a quiet explosion. "Killing a great man doesn't make you any less insignificant. You're still a worm. And you'll be stepped on like a worm."

Ambler peered into the black depths of Cronus's eyes. Rage glinted there, but something else did, too: Sorrow. Grief.

"Cronus, what happened?" Ambler said softly, intently.

"You murdered Paul Fenton," Cronus said. "The question is why."

Fenton—*dead*? Ambler's mind began to cycle rapidly. "Listen to me, Cronus," he began. "You're making a big mistake. . . ." This whole rendezvous, he saw now, had never been anything other than a death trap. The revenge plotted by a faithful lieutenant half-crazed with grief.

"No, goddamn it, you listen to *me*," Cronus said, cutting him off. "You'll tell me what I want to know. I'll find out the hard way or the easy way. And I'm kind of hoping it'll be the hard way." Vengeful sadism fueled and twisted his face into a dark scowl.

The grand four-columned tomb of the Napoleonic general and statesmen Maximilien Sebastien Foy had a massive base and a finely wrought statue of its inhabitant. For Joe Li's purposes, however, its main point of attraction was the pitched stone roof above the pediment and entablature. Resting on the roof, concealed from view by the decorative parapet, Joe Li stretched like a cat and gazed through his binoculars. The view was extensive: the tomb was one of the highest elevations in the immediate vicinity, and the season had turned many of the trees and bushes into leafless skeletons. His rifle, a modified version of the QBZ-95 sniper rifle, was of Chinese design and manufacture; the 5.8×42mm ammunition it chambered was a kind exclusively made for China's special-operations forces. The Norinco model—developed by China North Industries Corporation—had been not merely reverse engineered from Russian prototypes but improved in the process; the bullets had greater penetration power, retained their energy over a longer portion of their trajectory. Joe Li himself had further modified the rifle, to make it more mobile, easier to collapse and conceal.

Through his powerful binoculars, he studied the tight knot of men around Tarquin. Tarquin had demonstrated a remarkable ability to escape difficult situations—with professional dispassion, Joe Li had to grant him that. But he was mortal. Only flesh and blood. In all likelihood, there would be a great deal of both flesh and blood on display, and before the sun had set.

Joe Li's last communication with Beijing had been unsatisfactory. His controller was growing impatient; in the past, Joe Li had always achieved results with considerable dispatch. He was not used to having to explain delays. He was even less accustomed to the sorts of complications that his assignment had presented him with. But Joe Li was not mere muscle, executing the commands of another; he had a head of his own. He collected and purveyed information. He had a highly developed faculty of judgment. He was no mere *shashou*—no mere triggerman. Tarquin was too formidable a target for a mere target shooter, and the stakes were too great to allow mistakes.

And yet the meaning of success, in this assignment, was proving to be less straightforward than Joe Li had first supposed.

He peered through the scope again, the focus electronically perfected to maximal sharpness at the precise point where the crosshairs met.

"Just curious. How many 'associates' do you have here?" Ambler asked.

"A baker's dozen," Cronus replied.

"Reticular placement," Ambler said, partly to himself. It was a standard configuration at Stab, one with which both he and Cronus had plenty of experience. Each operative had a connection—either visual, auditory, or electronic—with at least two others. A small number of operatives had a connection with a distant unit. The redundant pathways ensured a coordinated response even if any of participants were taken out of action. The old-fashioned top-down command-and-control structure had proven vulnerability to decapitation. The reticular system made that impossible.

"Not bad for something so last-minute," Ambler said, genuinely impressed.

"The Strategic Services Group has resources everywhere," Cronus said. "Fenton's legacy. We'd all give our lives for him. That's what people like you could never grasp."

"People like me?" Carefully, casually, Ambler took a step back. His best chance of escape was to be the apex of a triangle—to get the other three to align themselves in a single level. He composed his face into an expression of resignation and glanced at the man to his left. The man was looking at Cronus, getting his signals from the leader. Cronus's very authority would have to be used against him.

Now Ambler started speaking heatedly, testily—the sort of verbal protest that was normally inconsistent with physical aggression. "You're making a lot of assumptions, Cronus. You always did. You're wrong about Fenton, but you're too blind or too stupid to admit your mistake."

"Biggest mistake *I* ever made was saving your life, back in Vanni." He was referring to the region in northern Sri Lanka that was a heartland of the Tamil Tigers—the LTTE terrorists.

"You think you saved my life? That what you think? You almost got me *killed*, you goddamned cowboy."

"Bullshit!" Cronus spoke in a low voice, but his indignation was audible. "The meet was a setup. There were half a dozen Tamil Tigers present, armed to kill. Armed to kill *you*, Tarquin."

Ambler remembered the scene well. After many weeks of negotiations, he had finally arranged a meeting with select members of the so-called Black Tigers, guerrillas who had pledged to be suicide bombers, a technique that the Tamils had pioneered. Tarquin believed that a hiving off of factions could be engineered, much as happened with Sinn Fein, that the die-hard terrorists could eventually be isolated from the broader civil struggle. The particular rebel leader he was meeting with, Arvalan, had come to recognize the futility of terror. He and his circle thought they could bring others along with them, so long as certain resources were made available to them. Tarquin thought he knew a way to assist with that.

Cronus was part of a small backup team that Tarquin's superiors at the Political Stabilization Unit had insisted on. Tarquin's combat vest was equipped with a fiber-optic microphone system that would provide them an auditory feed. Several minutes into the meeting, as Tarquin expected, Arvalan started to berate the American. An eavesdropper ignorant of the situation might have thought that Tarquin was being threatened. But Tarquin could see from the man's oddly immobile expression that he was merely putting on an act, for the sake of his associates. Those were his lines. Tarquin knew his.

Then, suddenly, the thatched door to the jungle hut was pushed open, and Cronus barged in, his automatic weapon on full-fire. Another assault rifle—wielded by someone under Cronus's direct command—was jammed through the opposite doorway, blasting away at the assembled LTTE officials. Within a few seconds, the bloodshed was complete. Arvalan and most of his circle lay dead; one member of his retinue had escaped through the jungle.

Tarquin had been livid. All his efforts had been destroyed by the actions of one headstrong, heedless Stab operative. In fact, it was worse than undone; word of the massacre would spread swiftly among the LTTE. The prospects for any further Western mediation or intervention had now dimmed, precipitously. No Tiger would ever agree to such a meeting again; the consequences were now all too clear.

Yet there Cronus stood, among the carnage, glowing with pride and smirkily declining what he imagined to be Tarquin's gratitude. Afterward, Tarquin did something he rarely did. He cabled Whitfield and, explaining what had happened, told her that Cronus was a menace, someone who had to be removed from the field immediately, forcibly retired. Whitfield had, instead, relegated Cronus to a desk job among the analysts, on the grounds that his considerable experience in the field was too valuable simply to throw away. Tarquin understood the rationale, but he never forgave Cronus his blunderbuss impulses and self-satisfied manner.

"You were too full of yourself to know what the hell you did, back there in Jaffna," Tarquin said. "You were a goddamn menace. That's why they took you out of the field."

"You're demented," Cronus said. "I should have left you to die, in the Tigers' den. Like I said, my bad. But it won't happen twice."

"You think you saved my ass. The truth is, you nearly got me killed, and you destroyed an entire operation while you were at it. If it wouldn't have jeopardized operational clandestinity, you would have faced judicial proceedings. And these poor guys are taking orders from *you*?" The trick, Tarquin knew, was to keep talking even as he attacked.

"You think you earned"—Tarquin fluidly swiveled back—"my gratitude? That just goes to show"—*now*, with explosive force, he slammed a spear hand into the throat of the square-jawed giant to his left—"how oblivious you are." Despite the exertion, Tarquin did his best to maintain an ordinary speaking tone. The mismatch between his voice and his actions would confuse his assailants, gaining him a crucial few moments. He could feel the impact of his knuckles against cartilage. The damaged tissues surrounding the trachea would start to constrict his airway, but in the meantime, Tarquin would need to use the stricken man as a shield against the other two. Even as the syringe dropped to the ground, Tarquin lashed out at the other muscleman, but the man dodged the blow and reached into his jacket for a handgun. A second blow, to the temple, landed, and the impact shot a bolt of pain through Tarquin's arm. Even so, the man was only temporarily stunned. Now he and Cronus dived out of the way, racing in opposite directions—a reprieve that was no reprieve at all, Tarquin realized. It meant that he was in the field of fire.

As Tarquin dived to the ground, he heard four muted reports— from where?—and marble and dirt exploded all around him. He forced himself to survey the terrain opposite and saw a mound of dense rhododendrons, their heavy leathery leaves immune to the cold—and, fleetingly, a glimpse of a hunched, khaki-clad shoulder.

Time slowed. He yanked the long-barreled pistol from the downed man's shoulder holster, took careful aim, and fired a tight, rapid cluster of three shots.

He was surprised at the quiet spitting sound that came from the gun and realized that what he had taken to be a long-barreled pistol was, in fact, a Beretta 92 Centurion—a compact 9mm with a short-ened slide and barrel. A silencer was what had elongated the barrel.

Now, from the rhododendron hedge, he saw a bloodied arm flail into the air, and, moments later, a wounded man lurched from the foliage to the safety of adjoining statuary.

Yet there was no safety for Tarquin. He had to *move*—every mo-ment at rest was a moment he was in someone's crosshairs. He sprang off in the direction where Cronus had run, felt the stinging spray of marble against his ear. Another bullet had been aimed at him, this one, he sensed, from a sniper operating from an elevated location. Tarquin glanced around him as he ran: there were all too many places where such a sniper could be secreted.

A baker's dozen, Cronus had said, and he had not been bluffing.

All were seasoned killers, all programmed to take Tarquin down. He needed to shift the odds; he needed to use the peculiarity of the terrain against them. But how?

He was way past the irony of having to fight for his life on the grounds of a cemetery. Père-Lachaise was more than that: it was a giant game board, a fretwork of paths and lanes and monuments that could serve as obstacles or as points of attack. His enemies were arrayed in a network upon a network.

He needed to gain access to that network. Racing from one tomb to another, he was attracting less attention than he would have expected.

He had to think—no, he had to *feel*, to let his instincts guide him. How would *he* have arranged the team, if it were up to him? He'd have some of the SSG team in offensive positions, others merely taking up observation posts, to be deployed offensively only as a last resort. He had to use his peculiar skills—his comparative advantage—in his own defense, or he would die here. And he had come too far for that. Overwhelming his fear was the one emotion that was even more powerful: *rage.*

He felt rage at what had been done to him, starting in Changhua. Rage at the attempt to rob him of his very soul in the sterile environs of Parrish Island. Rage at the arrogance of the strategists who deployed human beings like so many pawns on a chessboard of geopolitics.

He would not die here. Not now. Not tonight. Others would die. For those who would kill him would be shown no mercy.

He raced down a lane signposted CHEMIN DU QUINCONCE, over an area of sodden turf to another cobbled walkway, the avenue Aguado. He was now nearing the northwestern section of the vast cemetery, approaching a large chapel in a Moorish style, with a round dome over a huge portico. In fact, it was a columbarium, a building erected to house cinerary urns. In front of the main entrance was a steep staircase leading to an open subterranean vault, like a dark, rectangular chasm.

Here was a place of refuge that could equally serve as a lethal snare. It was impossible that the SSG team would have left it unattended. Perhaps sixty feet away was what looked like a semi-enclosed arcade, a pillared walkway of limestone and slate. Tarquin darted into it, his eyes swiveling rapidly. To his left, he saw a Japanese man with a pocket-sized digital camera and a malevolent gaze. Tarquin did not give him a second thought; the tourist was annoyed because Tarquin had just ruined his shot. A young blond woman and an older man, olive skinned and graying at the temples, were standing in the next alcove, in something less than a full embrace; she was gazing soulfully at him, while his eyes darted toward Tarquin anxiously. Yet it was not the anxiety of someone determined to see; it was the anxiety of someone determined not to be seen. Perhaps the man was cheating on his wife or—this being France—cheating on his mistress, worse still. The adjoining pair of alcoves was vacant. In the next one, a broad-faced woman was reading what looked like a book of poetry. She glanced up at Tarquin briefly, registering no obvious interest, and returned to her reading.

It was a ruse that would have been more persuasive ten or fifteen minutes ago, when the light was still adequate to read comfortably. The woman had a broad, masculine face, and her thick legs were planted with a bend in the knee, in the manner of a trained operative. He saw her slip a hand into her nylon parka, as if for warmth. Any doubts Tarquin might have had vanished.

For the moment, however, he could not reveal that he knew. Instead, he deliberately kept his gaze straight ahead as he turned into her alcove. He moved as if he had noticed something through the bay and was straining to see. As he passed her, he suddenly veered, crashing his body into hers, and the two of them tumbled heavily to the stone flooring. He twisted her body as they fell, and thrust the muzzle of the silenced Beretta against her throat.

"Not one word," he said.

"Fuck you," she hissed, drawing in breath through her clenched teeth. Another native speaker, then. Her broad face was distended like that of a snake preparing to strike.

He rammed his knee into her stomach, and she gasped. There was fury on her face, much of it directed toward herself, toward her own failure to have anticipated his move. Tarquin grabbed her book—*Les fleurs du mal,* the cover said in maroon type—and opened it. As he expected, a miniaturized radio transmitter was lodged in a rectangular space carved out of the pages. "Tell them you have seen me," Tarquin whispered. "Tell them I have ducked down into the underground vault of the columbarium here."

Uncertainty flickered in her eyes, and he pressed ahead: "Otherwise I will leave your corpse there to join the others." He jammed the muzzle of the Beretta harder against her throat, and he saw her break. "You try anything, I'll know," he warned her.

Pressing a button on the transmitter, she said, "Constellation. Constellation Eighty-seven." The cemetery was divided into ninety-some areas; the chapel was in the middle of Division Eighty-seven. Tarquin was relieved that she did not identify herself as 87A or 87E—a complication that would mean others, too, had been positioned in his division.

He grabbed the small wireless earbud in her right ear and placed the flesh-colored piece of plastic in his own.

"What's your report?" the metallic voice crackled through the earbud. He nodded to the woman.

"He's hiding in the underground vault," she said.

He whispered into her ear, "And he's armed."

"And he's armed," she added.

They already knew that; her volunteering the detail would make it even more likely that her report would be credible. Now he yanked down the woman's nylon coat, trapping her arms.

A loud voice from the central walkway: *"Mam'selle. Il vous ennuie, ce mec-ci?"* Is that guy bothering you? A well-meaning question from an uninvolved passerby. Tarquin stole a quick glance at the man. He was thin, gangly, with an officious expression and a scholarly air—a student at a local university, perhaps. Impressions were formed in a split second, Tarquin knew, and could be erased in another. He pressed his face to the woman operative, mashing his mouth against hers. "My darling," he called out in English. "So the answer is yes! You'll marry me? You've made me the happiest man!" He pitched his voice in the tones of exaltation and joy, clutching her passionately. It did not matter whether the Frenchman spoke English; the import would be clear enough.

"*Excusez-moi,*" the man said quietly, reddening and turning on his heel.

Tarquin wiped his mouth on his sleeve and turned to what looked like a small tool case clipped to her belt. He unhooked it, knocking away her hands as she grabbed for it.

He recognized it at once: a *Kleinmaschinenpistole*—a folding machine gun known as "the businessman's subgun." The deadly device was based on a stamped-metal weapon developed by the KGB design bureau in Tula, the PP-90, and could discharge its entire load in a near instantaneous burst, like a death ray of lead. It was a marvel of miniaturization: the trigger guard was hinged; a spring-loaded catch controlled the folding of the weapon. It was just ten and a half inches, with a magazine that held thirty rounds of 9mm parabellums. On a corner of the metal oblong object was a spring-loaded button. When Tarquin pressed it, one part of the metal case swung to the rear and became a buttstock.

Then, without warning, he whipped his arm back against her neck and forced her head forward into the crushing vice. She would be unconscious for several minutes. He propped her body on the marble bench, letting her head loll back against the wall, as if she were napping. Now he removed her shoelaces and made a loop that encircled her left ankle, ran twice around the steel unguarded trigger of the subgun and then around both wrists. As soon as she attempted to stand or straighten herself, the loop would tauten.

He moved to another alcove, a few hundred feet away, that was now darkly shadowed but permitted a view of the steps that led down to the columbarium.

He did not have long to wait.

The first on the scene was the same leather-jacketed youth who had retrieved his backpack. Now he was racing down the steps into the columbarium, a hand inside his jacket, as if clutching his stomach. A bald middle-aged man with a pitted face and a large belly was next on the scene. He did not descend but rather stationed himself near the chapel, at the far end of the staircase. He could look down and see the landing below. A sensible backup position.

A third man arrived two minutes later. It was the second of the two men who had grabbed Tarquin as he tried to leave the cemetery. His face was reddened and glazed with sweat, from anxiety or the physical exertion of running or both.

Tarquin heard a low tone from the small, rubberized earbud and then the metallic voice again. "Constellation Eighty-seven, confirm subject remains in position." Tarquin, his eyes peeled on the sweat-slicked man, saw that his lips were moving as the voice was transmitted; obviously it was his voice, transmitted by means of a hidden fiber-optic lip mike.

A look of perplexity traveled across his face. "Constellation Eighty-seven, come in," he said.

Tarquin leveled the silenced Beretta on the stone ledge of the nearest bay, peering through the deepening gloom with a sinking feeling. Even if he had been a champion shooter—and he was not—the distance was too great for an accurate hit using a handgun. The odds were greater that he would give his own position away than that he would bring down a member of the assault team.

He waited for one more member of the team to appear in Division Eighty-seven—that was almost half of them, now—and then stealthily made his retreat, sliding through a low bay and then through a bramble-ridden area of the quadrant to his north. He could see a guardhouse, the large map for tourists, the tall dark green gates that let onto the city proper. If he squinted, he could see the faded green and white awnings of a Paris street. Its seeming proximity was deceptive.

From a distance, he heard a clattering burst of automatic fire and startled shrieks of alarm. The poetry lover had roused herself; the thirty rounds would have been harmlessly discharged into the stone depression beneath the marble bench. To the operatives in the area, however, it would act as a homing beacon, drawing them toward an apse-like space he had long abandoned.

Moving faster, he hurried past countless tombs and statues, leafless trees and rustling evergreen bushes, even as shadows lengthened and the setting sun's rosy glow began to ebb, like an expiring flame. His muscles were coiled, his senses on full alert. His ploy had, in the tradecraft jargon, "reduced the pressure" of the hostile forces, yet others would remain in position, scouting the terrain with binoculars. The danger was especially acute at the points of egress, such as the one he was approaching. It would be natural to place sentries at such locations.

He put on another burst of speed. He stumbled briefly on the uneven ground, cursing inwardly, and then he felt, rather than heard, the double tap: another spray of stone, sharp stinging fragments. Had his stride been steady—had he not stumbled—one of those bullets would have struck him in the upper body.

Tarquin rolled to the ground and ducked around a six-foot-tall obelisk. Where was the shooter? Again, there were too many possibilities.

Another silenced spray of stone—this time from the opposite side. The side where he had sought refuge. *Where was safety?*

He whipped his head around; given the obstacles that surrounded him, the angle of the shot was too low to have come from any distance.

"Stand up like a man, why don't you?"

Cronus's voice.

The burly operative stepped out of a shadowed space behind a large memorial stone.

Tarquin desperately scanned the area in front of him. He saw the back of an oblivious green-uniformed maintenance worker, *Père-Lachaise Équipe d'Entretien* stenciled in white along the shoulder area and on the back of the visored cap. Through the tall green gates—so close and yet a million miles away, it seemed—Tarquin could hear the faint bustle of a Paris street in the evening. A thinning array of tourists—the light was too dim to take good photographs—were unaware of the lethal game of possum that was in progress.

Cronus's pistol was trained on him; Tarquin could try to grab for his Beretta, yet the long silenced muzzle would add a fatal split second to the time needed to remove and deploy it.

All around him, the business of everyday life proceeded as usual. The groundskeeper or sanitation worker, or whatever he was, kept at his trash picker, his face shadowed behind the visored cap. The tourists started to flow through the gates, looking for taxis or figuring out where the metro station was, chatting among themselves in jaded end-of-day voices.

Cronus signaled to someone across the way—the sniper, Tarquin inferred. "Don't worry about our marksmen friend," Cronus said, in a voice of freezing malevolence. "He's just playing backstop. The kill is mine. Everyone knows that."

The sanitation man was steadily working his way along the ground, moving closer, and Tarquin found himself worrying that his movement could be restricted by his presence. The groundsman was uninvolved, a bystander, though Tarquin very much doubted whether the distinction made much of an impression on the likes of Cronus. For a moment, Tarquin had a hovering sense of danger—something about the way the man walked.

Suddenly a shaft of light from the setting sun dazzled off the windshield of a passing car, and for an instant the groundsman's face was illuminated. Tarquin felt another jolt of terror. He remembered the Plaza swimming pool. The face he had glimpsed at the Luxembourg Gardens.

The Chinese assassin.

His odds of survival had plummeted further.

"The thing you'll never understand, Cronus," said Tarquin, desperately trying to buy time, "is that—"

"I've heard enough out of you," the burly man said, his finger curling around the silenced pistol. Abruptly the expression of hostility left his face, replaced by an oddly vacant look.

At that same instant, Tarquin became aware of a plume of red droplets that had erupted from Cronus's left ear. The Chinese man had dropped to one knee, the trash picker in his hands replaced by a long silenced rifle. It had happened so rapidly that Tarquin could only make sense of the events retrospectively.

The Chinese man whirled around, toward Tarquin, and squeezed off a shot—and for a moment Tarquin wondered whether this was the last thing he would ever see . . . except that the man was peering through the scope and a professional did not peer through a scope to fire at a target fifteen feet away. Tarquin heard the *plink* of an ejected cartridge.

The assassin was not firing at him but at the sniper.

Tarquin's mind reeled. *It made no sense.*

The man before him aimed his rifle again, peering through the scope. Only someone extraordinarily skilled would attempt to hit a concealed sniper from a free-form firing position, matching the stability of a bipod with the frame of a squatting human being.

A double tap: two *plinks*—two more cartridges ejected. From some distance, Tarquin heard a moan of an injured man.

The green-uniformed marksman rose from his crouching position and folded the stock of his rifle.

Tarquin was dumbfounded, dazed with incomprehension and disbelief.

The assassin was letting him live.

"I don't understand," Tarquin said to him numbly.

He turned to Tarquin, his brown eyes solemn. "I know that now. It is why you are still alive."

Tarquin looked at him anew and saw a man who was doing what

he believed duty demanded, a man who took pride in his formidable skills but no pleasure in their deadly consequences. The man was, in his sense of himself, not so much warrior as *guardian;* he knew that throughout human history there had had always been men like him—whether praetorian prefect, Knight Templar, or samurai—who turned themselves into implements of steel so that others would not need to. Men who were hard so that others could be soft. Men who killed so that others could live safely. *Protection* was his watchword; *protection* was his creed.

A split second later, the Chinese man's throat exploded into a cloud of blood. The unseen sniper, however badly wounded, had at least one more shot in him, and he had trained it on the man who posed the greatest threat to him.

Tarquin sprang to his feet. For a brief interval—and *only* for a brief interval—the other assailants would be a safe distance away, impeded by the stones and sepulchers of this garden of death: he had to seize the opportunity or lose it forever. He charged toward the double green gates adjoining the street, not stopping until he found the rental car he had left on a nearby block. As he veered through the clamorous Paris traffic, taking pains to be sure that he had not been followed, he tried to process what he had learned.

The elements jostled and collided, tearing at his consciousness. Someone had killed Fenton. Was it a member of Fenton's organization—a mole of some sort? Was it someone Fenton worked with—someone in the United States government?

And the Chinese assassin: an adversary who had become an ally—indeed, someone who had given up his life to protect Ambler.

Why?

Who—who was he working for?

There were too many possibilities, too many impossibilities that had become possibilities. Tarquin—no, he had to become Ambler now—had reached a point where conjecture could be actively misleading.

Something else, too, frightened him: the wash of adrenaline had not been a wholly unpleasant sensation. What kind of man was he, after all? He shuddered, contemplating his own character. He had killed and nearly been killed this evening. Why, then, did he feel so alive?

"I don't understand," Laurel repeated. All three of them were gathered in Andrew's oatmeal-bland hotel room.

"I don't, either," Ambler said. "None of this *feels* right."

"It doesn't add up," Caston put in.

"Wait a minute," Laurel said. "You said the killings were all linked to China. You said it looked like a progression, a sequence, like it was leading up to something imminent. You figured that Liu Ang was the probable target."

"He's supposed to be visiting the White House next month," Caston said. "Big history-making thing, with dinners of state and all that. Plenty of opportunities. But . . ."

"But what?"

"Timing seems wrong. There's too much of a delay given the previous specifications of event density."

"There's no delay," Laurel said. She opened her large handbag and pulled out a furled copy of the *International Herald Tribune*. "Something you were saying about that *Le Monde* story made me think of it."

"Come again?"

"Tomorrow night," Laurel said. "President Liu Ang's big night."

"What are you talking about?" Ambler said.

"I'm talking about the World Economic Forum," she said. "I'm talking about what's happening in Davos this week."

Ambler began to pace as he thought out loud. "Liu Ang leaves the security of the Beijing cocoon for the first time since taking office. He comes to the West, makes his big speech, designed to make everybody feel warm and fuzzy toward the great tiger."

"Palmer couldn't have put it better himself," Caston said acerbically.

"In the midst of which, he's gunned down."

"Removed from the equation." Caston looked contemplative. "But by whom?"

Fenton's voice: *Got* a real *exciting project for you coming up. But don't pack your skis just yet.*

Ambler did not speak for a long moment. "Could Fenton have thought *I* would do it?"

"Is that possible?"

"Here's the thing. I'm been wrapping my mind around Fenton's death. To me, that killing is *evidence* of something. It's exactly the kind of loose end that you snip off when an operation is about to reach a climax."

"You speak so bloodlessly," Caston said. "You sure you've never been an accountant?"

"Chalk it up to a career spent in the service of the Political Stabilization Unit," Ambler said. "That's an important signpost. Another is that the assassin may well be someone I know. Someone I worked with on a previous Stab operation."

"That makes no sense," Laurel said.

"Stab prided itself on hiring the best of the best. Fenton prided himself on hiring the best of Stab. If you were entrusting someone with the assassination of the Chinese president, wouldn't you get the best-trained person you could?"

"And if it were a Stab operative," Laurel said slowly, "the odds are that you'd have had some dealings with the person."

"Absolutely," Ambler said.

"Well, fuck a duck," Caston said. "Do either of you have any idea what we're looking at? If it's Davos, then we're too late."

"We've got to figure out—"

"We've got to figure out what happens *after*," Caston said glumly. "Because the consequences . . . my God. The consequences. President Liu Ang is an incredibly beloved figure in China—he's like JFK and the pope and John Lennon all wrapped into one. When he's killed, a country of one-point-four billion people is going to be roiled by outrage. I mean, goddamn keening hysteria of the kind that'll deafen you halfway around the globe, and that hysteria is going to turn into wrath in a heartbeat, if anything—and I mean *anything*—should connect the assassination to members of the U.S. government. Do you have any idea what kind of safety valve you need for one-point-four billion outraged citizens? It could plunge the nations into war, OK? The belligerents could take over Zhongnanhai overnight."

"To risk that you'd have to be a fanatic," Laurel said.

"Like Ashton Palmer and his disciples." Ambler felt the blood drain from his face.

Laurel looked off in the middle distance as she repeated the words that once expressed Ambler's youthful yearnings. *"Never doubt that a small group of thoughtful, committed citizens can change the world. Indeed, it is the only thing that ever has."*

"Dammit, it's not over until it's over," Ambler said. Fury surged into his voice. "I'm not going to let them get away with this."

Now Caston leaped from his chair and started to walk back and forth. "They'll have thought this through. From every angle. Who knows how long they've been working on this? An operation like this, there will be a deep cover agent in place, and a backup, too. I've audited enough operations to know that operational redundancies are standard. An operation like this has got to have a hidden fail-safe mechanism. A call-off code. And some strategy of misdirection. There's always got to be a fall guy." His gaze sharpened. "It would simplify matters if that was also the gunman, of course. But we've got to assume they've done a thorough assessment of the parameters. All the parameters."

"An operation always involves human beings," Ambler said, a hint of defiance in his voice. "And human beings never quite behave like integers in a matrix, Caston. You can't quantify the human factor—not with any precision. That's what people like you never understand."

"And what people like *you* never understand is that—"

"Guys," Laurel interjected impatiently, tapping on the newspaper. "*Guys.* It says here that he's speaking at Davos at five tomorrow afternoon. That's less than twenty-four hours from now."

"Oh dear Christ," Ambler breathed.

Laurel's eyes shifted from Ambler to Caston and back again. "Can't we just alert everyone?"

"Trust me, they're already operating on top alert," Ambler said. "That's how they do business. The trouble is, there have been so many death threats against this guy that there's a serious boy-who-cried-wolf problem at this point. They know about the threats. There's nothing new there. And Liu Ang refuses to be immobilized by them."

Laurel looked bewildered, desperate. "Can you explain that this time the threat's really, really serious?"

Caston shot her a glance. "I'll do that," he said. "I'm sure it'll make all the difference." Now he turned to Ambler. "You really think there's a chance you'd recognize the assassin?"

"Yes," Ambler said simply. "I think they'd meant to recruit me for the job. But you're right, of course: Fenton doesn't work without a 'backstop.' An understudy has the job now. And he's bound to be from the same talent pool."

For a while, the three were silent.

"Even if he wasn't," Laurel said hesitantly, "you'd still be able to pick up on him. You've done it before—you have that gift of seeing."

"I've done it before," Ambler acknowledged. "It's just that the stakes were never nearly this high. Still, what choice is there?"

Laurel flushed. "You don't owe anyone anything, Hal," she said, suddenly agitated. "Don't be a hero. Let's just *disappear,* all right?"

"Is that what you really want?"

"Yes," she said, and then she murmured, "No." Tears welled up in her eyes. "I don't know," she said in a muffled voice. "All I know is— if that's where *you're* going, that's where I'm going. There's no other place I feel safe. You *know* that."

Ambler pulled her close, pressed his forehead to hers, and squeezed her tightly. "OK," he whispered, and he did not know whether the catch in his voice was of laughter or sorrow. "OK."

After a while, Caston turned around. "You have any idea how you might accomplish this?"

"Sure," Ambler said, his voice hollow.

Caston sat down in the mustard-colored armchair and looked at Ambler stonily. "Just so you're clear about this. You've got less than twenty-four hours to elude whatever lethal operatives Strategic Services and/or your own beloved Consular Operations have on the lookout, make your way into Switzerland, infiltrate a heavily guarded conclave of the global elite, and identify the assassin before he strikes."

Ambler nodded.

"Well, let me tell you something." Caston arched an eyebrow. "It's not going to be as easy as it sounds."

PART FOUR

CHAPTER TWENTY-NINE

When a roadside sign indicated that the Swiss border lay thirty kilometers ahead, Ambler impulsively veered off the thoroughfare and onto a small rural road. Had he been followed? Though he had detected no obvious signs, elementary prudence told him he could not afford to drive the rented Opal coupe through the border checkpoint.

Laurel Holland and Clayton Caston were traveling to Zurich by high-speed rail, the TGV, which would take just over six hours, the bus to Davos-Klosters adding perhaps another couple of hours at the end. The train route was a popular one; they would board separately and would likely experience little trouble. But they were not the targets of a Cons-Ops-authorized "beyond salvage" operation, of a no less lethal SSG sanction, of adversaries without name and beyond number. Mass transportation would land him into a dragnet. He had no choice but to drive, seek anonymity among the hundreds of thousands of cars on the Autoroute du Soleil. So far so good. But the border checkpoint would be the most hazardous part of the trip. Switzerland had held itself aloof from European integration; there would be no relaxation of its border controls.

At the Haute-Rhin town of Colmar, he found a cabdriver, who, once Ambler flashed a peacock's fan of hard currency at him, agreed to drive him through Samoëns to the hamlet of St. Martin, on the other side of the border. The driver, first name Luc, was a pudgy man with the shoulders of a bowling pin, greasy, limp hair, and that smell—redolent of pencil shavings, rancid butter, manure—that was peculiar to the unbathed, and that a drenching with Pinaud Lilac Vegetal aftershave did little to conceal. Yet he was also guileless and direct, even in his avarice. Ambler knew he could trust him.

Ambler cracked the window as they set off, letting the chill mountain air blow on his face. His travel bag lay on the seat beside him.

"You're sure you want the window down?" the driver asked, oblivious to the stifling fug within his car. "It's freezing, *mon frère*. As you Americans say, colder than a well digger's ass."

"That's OK," Ambler replied politely. "A little cool air helps keeps me awake." He zipped up his microfleece-lined winter jacket. The garment had been carefully chosen; there was little chance he would get too cold.

It was seven miles from the border town of St. Morency when Ambler again felt twinges of unease, began to pick up signs—equivocal, ambiguous, far from conclusive—that he might have been detected. Mere paranoia? There was a tarp-covered Jeep, maintaining a constant distance behind them. There was a helicopter, in a place and a time when no helicopter would normally be present. Yet a hypervigilant mind could always identify incongruities in even the most innocent of circumstances. Which, if any, of these things was truly significant?

A few miles from the Swiss border, Ambler noticed an aqua-blue van with a familiar license plate; he had seen it before. Again he wondered: Was he being paranoid? The slanting angle of the just-predawn light made it impossible to see the driver. Ambler asked Luc to slow down; the blue van slowed down at almost the same time, keeping a constant distance between them—a distance far greater than a trucker's professional caution would have dictated. Unease congealed into anxiety. Ambler had to follow his instincts. *We have come this far by faith.* The faith that had preserved Ambler's life so far was the most austere variety of all: faith in himself. He would not waver now. He had to accept a profoundly disturbing truth.

He had been found.

The sun was glimmering over the horizon, a ribbon of red; the air was the temperature of a meat locker. Ambler told Luc that he had had a change of heart, that he felt like going on an early-morning hike; yes, right here, what spot could be lovelier?

The transfer of more hard currency softened Luc's look of open suspicion to one of wryly amused skepticism. The driver knew he was not expected to believe the subterfuge, but if the story was counterfeit, the money was genuine. Luc did not protest. If anything, he seemed to enjoy the game. There were countless reasons someone might wish to avoid the border control, many having to do with the payment of luxury duties. So long as Luc's vehicle was not used for the conveyance of unreported goods, he himself was at no risk.

Ambler tightened the laces of his heavy leather climbing boots, grabbed his bag, and got out of the car. A crossing on foot was not an unexpected eventuality. Within minutes he had disappeared among the snow-laden firs, stone pines, and larches, traveling parallel to the road but a good two hundred yards to the side. After half a mile, he glimpsed two lampposts, situated at either side of the road: powerful lights within balloon-shaped frosted glass. The customhouse—dark brown wood with forest-green shutters and gingerbread latticework on a second story cinched in by an outsized, steeply raked roof— looked like a modified A-frame. Through the trees he could see both the French tricolor—blue, white, and red—and Switzerland's own distinctive flag, a white cross on a red shield. Along the roadside, rough-hewn boulders sat near white lines, barely visible on the snow-littered pavement, adding a physical obstacle to a legal one. A low, bright orange barrier was meant to control the flow of vehicles. Doorless booths sat to either side of the road. A little past the customshouse, the driver of a food-service *camion* had obviously taken advantage of the large paved shoulder to pull over a malfunctioning vehicle. Ambler could just make out the belly and legs of a short, paunchy mechanic who was bent over its engine, his head lost in its innards. Various engine parts were strewn on the cleared pavement alongside the truck. From time to time, a muttered French curse could be heard.

At the other side of the customshouse was a parking area, set lower than the road. Ambler strained to see: a cloud had passed over the once glimmering sunrise; he saw a match flare from a distance, a patrol guard lighting a cigarette. That was the kind of thing that the gloom actually made more visible. He glanced at his watch. It was a little past eight o'clock; sunrise came late in January, and the mountainous terrain postponed the sunrise even further.

He saw the canvas-topped Jeep, now stationed at the lower, snow-strewn parking lot, its canvas shuddering in the chill breeze. It must have ferried over the French border guards for the eight o'clock shift. Their Swiss counterparts would have arrived from the opposite direction. Ambler positioned himself behind a low copse of young spruce trees. Most of the mountain pines were "limbed up": though dense at the center, they had shed the branches that once grew at the bases of their trunks. By contrast, the spruce trees maintained a low apron of dense branches, providing cover that started close to the ground. Ambler raised his compact field glasses to his eyes and peered through an aperture between two interlaced spruce trees. The border-patrol guard who had just lit a cigarette now took a deep drag, stretched himself, and looked around unwarily. He was, Ambler could tell, a man expecting nothing other than an ordinary day's tedium at the checkpoint.

Through the windows of the customhouse, Ambler could see a number of the other guards drinking coffee and, to judge from their expressions, trading idle gossip. Seated among them, contentedly, was a man in a bright red flannel shirt and a pear-shaped body that told of a sedentary existence: the truck driver, Ambler guessed.

Traffic was sporadic; whatever the rulebook might say, it was hard to persuade men to stand outside in the freezing cold when the roadway remained empty save for the wind. Even without hearing the banter, Ambler could tell from the men's faces that a spirit of truculent joviality reigned.

One man, though, remained apart from the others, his body language indicating that he was not part of the community. Ambler turned his field glasses toward the man. He wore the uniform of a senior officer in the French customs authority: this was an official visitor, someone whose job was to make sporadic inspections of such checkpoints. If the others were at ease around him, it must have been because he had signaled his own indifference toward what could only have been an onerous and thankless chore. Perhaps the bureaucracy had dispatched him here as part of a regular rotation of oversight, but who would oversee the overseer?

As Ambler fine-tuned the focus of his field glasses, the man's face came into sharper view, and Ambler saw how wrong he was.

The man was not an officer with the customs authority at all. A cascade of images flashed through Ambler's mind: this was a face he recognized. After a few long moments, the sense of recognition resolved into identification. The man's name—but it did not matter what his name was; he used innumerable aliases. He had grown up in Marseilles, served, while still an adolescent, as a henchman for one of the drug mobs there. He was a seasoned killer by the time he drifted into employment as a mercenary in southern Africa and the Senegambia region. Now he worked freelance, used mainly in circumstances requiring great delicacy—and lethality. He was an efficient killer, skilled with a firearm, a knife, a garrote: a most useful man for the nonattributable kill. In the profession, this sort of man was known, blandly, as a *specialist*. The last time Ambler had seen him he had been blond; now he was dark haired. The hollowed cheeks beneath high, ridge-like cheekbones and slash-like mouth remained the same, if somewhat more weathered. Suddenly the man's eyes met Ambler's. Ambler felt a pulse of adrenaline—had he been seen? But it was impossible. The viewing angle, the circumstances of illumination: all ensured his concealment. The killer was merely surveying the scene out of the window; the apparent eye contact was momentary and accidental.

It should have been reassuring that the killer remained inside. It was not. The specialist would not have been dispatched alone. If he was inside, it meant that others had been deployed in the surrounding woods. Any sense of advantage Ambler had enjoyed evaporated at once. He was being stalked by others in his trade; they would anticipate his maneuvers and counter them. The specialist might be in command, but others were nearby. The specialist would be summoned when needed.

The gauntlet was beautifully conceived, taking advantage of the natural terrain as well as the official checkpoint. Ambler had to admire the professionalism. Yet whose was it—the Strategic Services team or one assembled by Consular Operations?

Now two border guards from the Swiss side emerged; a small white Renault van was pulling up to the checkpoint, idling before the low orange barrier. One of the guards bent down to speak to the driver, asking him the standardized questions. A face was matched with a passport photograph. It was a matter of professional discretion whether further actions would be taken. The French guard stood nearby, and the two glanced at each other. The driver had been sized up, a decision made. The orange barrier pivoted flat, and, with an indifferent hand gesture, the white van was waved on.

At the booth, the two men sat down on plastic chairs, adjusting their ear mufflers, their padded jackets.

"The woman in that Renault was so fat, she reminded me of your wife," one said to the other in French. He spoke loudly so he could be heard over the wind and through the other's ear mufflers.

The other scowled in mock outrage. "My wife, or your mother?"

It was the kind of japery, however monotonous and uninventive, that sufficed to fill the long days of boredom. Now the killer from Marseilles emerged from the customhouse and looked around. *Follow the eyes.*

Ambler traced his line of sight: the man was peering at a rocky outcropping on the far side of the road. Another member of the unit was surely stationed there. There had to be a third member, too. One dispatched as an observer, to be a participant only in extremis.

The specialist walked over to the lamppost and then to the lower parking lot, where he disappeared behind a low brick structure—the kind of place where maintenance equipment was stored. Was he conferring with someone?

There was no time to analyze the options; Ambler had to act. The growing daylight would only help his enemies. *We have come this far by faith.* He could get to the gray rocky outcropping along a diagonal, zigzagging path. Danger was often lessened by proximity. Now he scuttled from the spruce-tree copse to a distance several hundred yards up the road and stowed his bag under another copse, covering it with a mound of snow. He then clambered onto a narrow ridge, which the wind had denuded of snow. With long strides, he loped along the upward-sloping ridge. Then he grabbed hold of a bough from a stunted tree to pull himself up to a higher level and thus to another ridge that would serve him as a footpath. With a loud *snap,* the tree bough broke under his weight, and Ambler tumbled backward, stopping himself from sliding farther downward with his outstretched arms. He tried to scramble to his feet, but plush layers of fresh, fluffy snow defeated the grooves and cleats of his soles. Simply finding traction was a struggle. With one wrong footfall, he knew, he could easily tumble fifty feet down the hill, even farther. He used the stunted trees like a balustrade, leaped over rocks, forced his legs to pump harder when a frictionless snowdrift threatened his stride. He would not be shot here like a rabbit in the countryside. He remembered Laurel's heartfelt parting words, and they gave him strength. *Take care of yourself,* she had said. *For me.*

Caleb Norris never had troubled dreams; under pressure he seemed to sleep more deeply and peacefully, if anything. An hour before the plane made its landing at Zurich, he awoke and made his way to the airplane lavatory, where he splashed water on his face and brushed his teeth. When he disembarked and made his way into the bright expanses of the airport, he looked no more rumpled than he did on any other day.

Ironically, his weapon actually made luggage retrieval faster than it would have been otherwise. He reported to a special Swiss Air office that handled just such matters and marveled, not for the first time, at Swiss efficiency. He affixed his signature to two sheets and was given both his firearm and his overnight bag. A few other government types had also assembled in the office: a few Secret Service types, someone he vaguely recognized from joint conferences with FBI counterterrorism. From behind, he recognized a man—dressed in a dark gray striped suit but with a distinctive mop of hair dyed a shade that verged, implausibly, on orange. The man turned around and smiled at Norris, too cool to acknowledge surprise. Stanley Grafton was his name, and he was a member of the National Security Council. Norris remembered him from various security briefings he'd attended at the White House. Grafton was a better listener than most of the Council members, though Norris suspected he also had more to say.

"Caleb," Grafton said, extending a hand. "I didn't see your name on the agenda."

"And I didn't see yours," Norris replied smoothly.

"Last-minute substitution," Grafton said. "Ora Suleiman broke something." Suleiman was the current chairman of the Council and had a weakness for ponderous statements, as if she were always imagining herself as a character in a made-for-TV "historical reenactment."

"Couldn't be her funny bone. She hasn't got one of those."

Grafton smiled involuntarily. "So, anyway, they wheeled out the understudy."

"Same here," Norris said. "Last-minute cancellations, last-minute substitutions. What can you do? We've all come to mouth sonorous nothings."

"It's what we do best, right?" Laughter crinkled Grafton's eyes. "Hey, you want to hitch a ride with me?"

"Sure. You got a limo?"

The other man emitted a dismissive puff. "A copter, baby. A whirlybird. I'm NSC, we gotta travel in style."

"Glad to see our tax dollars at work," Norris jested. "Lead the way, Stan." He hefted his briefcase as he followed the NSC man. It actually felt better balanced with the long-barreled 9mm pistol back inside it.

"Got to hand it to you, Cal. For someone who's just stepped off a plane, you look fresh as a daisy. Or, anyway, as fresh as you ever look."

"Hey, like the poet says, I got miles to go before I sleep." Norris shrugged. "Not to mention promises to keep."

When Ambler reached a perch that gave him a good view of the checkpoint, he took a minute to peer through snowy branches and take inventory. The specialist from Marseilles had stationed himself in the middle of the road, scanning the road for traffic, the adjacent terrain for any sign of activity. The guards in the booth were still looking bored, their fellow officers in the customhouse less so; since the *camion* was being serviced, its driver was still around to regale them with stories.

The way down was easier than the way up. Where the terrain was too steep, he would slide or roll, controlling the rate of speed with his hands and feet but enlisting gravity to propel his descent. Finally, he returned to the low copse of spruce trees.

From a position only a few yards away he heard a man's low voice. "This is Beta Lambda Epsilon. Have you located the subject?" He was an American, spoke with a Texan accent. "Because, for Chrissakes, I didn't get out of bed to freeze my goddamned johnson off."

The response was inaudible, no doubt piped through earbuds. He was speaking on an electronic communicator, then, some sort of walkie-talkie. The Texan yawned and started to pace on the shoulder of the road, not for any purpose save to keep his feet from getting cold.

There were sounds of shouting—but from farther away, from the checkpoint itself. Ambler looked out at the car idling before the orange security barrier. An irate passenger—bald, pink faced, expensively dressed—had been ordered to step out of a chauffeured Town Car while the vehicle was inspected. "Bureaucratic madness," the rich man charged. It was a trip he made daily, and he had never been subject to such *harassment* before.

The guards were apologetic but firm. There had been reports. They were required to take special precautions today. He could take it up with the customs authorities—in fact, there was a visiting supervisor today. The man could take it up with *him.*

The pink-faced businessman turned toward the uniformed supervisor and felt the stony eyes of indifference and disdain. He sighed, his protests subsiding into a general air of peevishness. Moments later, the orange barrier angled down and the engine growled as the luxury car went on its way, wounded dignity almost sketched across its grille.

Yet the man's noisy protests had provided Ambler with cover.

Though he could not change the odds to favor him, he could lessen the odds against him. He crept along a path toward the road, until he spied a burly man with an expensive wristwatch, its gold band gleaming as the early-morning sun emerged from a cloud. The Texan in the flesh. The watch was inappropriate garb for such a posting; it suggesting an overprivileged agent with a loosely monitored expense account, someone whose field days were long behind him and who had been conscripted into a last-minute operation because of sheer proximity. Stepping from behind a bank of snow, Ambler sprang toward him, encircled his neck with his right arm, and hooked his hands together on the man's left shoulder. Then he squeezed the man's neck just below the jaw between his bicep and forearm, clamping down the man's carotid arteries and inducing a swift loss of consciousness. The man—doubtless posted as an agent of record—coughed once and went limp. Swiftly, Ambler patted the man down, looking for his communicator.

He found it in the lower pocket of the man's black leather coat— an expensive garment, with its fur lining, but hardly suited to an extended outdoor vigil in an Alpine winter. If the garment was a bad match with the assignment, it was a good match with the gold-banded Audemars Piguet on his wrist. The communicator, on the other hand, had clearly been assigned to him when he was tasked this morning; it was a small model, in a hard black plastic shell, with a limited range but a powerful signal. Ambler placed the tiny ear-buds into his own cars, took a deep breath, and called to mind the way the agent of record had spoken. Then he pressed SPEAK, and, in a plausible Texan drawl, he said, "This is Beta Lambda Epsilon, reporting in "

A thickly accented voice—the harsh French of the Savoyard province—cut him off. "We told you to cease communications. You jeopardize operational security. We are not dealing with an amateur here! Or if we are, the only amateur is *you*."

The voice was not that of the Marseilles assassin. It had to have been another man—a man who seemed to be running the operation.

"Shut the fuck up and *listen*," Ambler drawled angrily. The micro-com equipment provided a crisp, tinny rendering of voices, putting a premium on audibility but erasing the differences of timbre between one voice and another. "I *seen* the bastard. On the other side of the road. Saw him dart across the parking lot like a goddamn red fox. The pisser's *taunting* us."

There was silence on the other end. Then, cautiously, urgently, the voice returned: "Precisely where is he at this moment?"

What should he say now? Ambler had not thought this through and momentarily drew a blank. "He crawled inside the Jeep," he blurted. "Yanked up the canvas and crawled inside."

"And he's still there?"

"I'd have seen him if he wasn't."

"OK." There was a pause. "Good work."

If Ambler's cheeks weren't numbed with cold, he would have smiled. The members of the killing team were in his trade; they'd think of anything he would think of. Ambler could only outmaneuver them by *not* thinking—by proceeding on blind instinct, moment-to-moment improvisation. *Nothing ever goes according to plan. Revise and improvise.*

The killer from Marseilles strode from the booth toward the lower parking lot, where the canvas-topped personnel carrier was stationed. A powerful-looking, silenced firearm was in his hand. Another howling gust of wind swept down the ravines and roadway, slamming against Ambler's back.

What now? The assassin would be in a state of hyperawareness, of hair-trigger consciousness. Ambler had to take advantage of it, had to trigger an overreaction. He looked around for a rock, for something he could throw hard, something that would arc up and land on the other side of the road. Yet an icy glaze had cemented everything loose to the ground: pebbles, gravel, rocks. Ambler retrieved the Texan's Magnum pistol and removed a heavy lead bullet from the firing chamber. Now he whipped it high into the air. The gust of wind propelled it farther and, as the gust subsided, the bullet fell to earth, landing upon the vehicle's canvas top. The sound it made was disappointingly faint, nothing more ominous than a tap, yet the specialist's reaction was extreme. Without warning, the man dropped to his knees and, supporting his right arm with his left, fired repeatedly into the truck, perforating the canvas, the cushions, with a fusillade of silenced, high energy bullets.

Ambler watched through his field glasses as the flurry of violence was visited upon the empty vehicle. Yet where was the other man— the Savoyard? Of him there was no sign. The mechanic, sheltered from the wind by the raised hood of the *camion,* continued his feckless wrenchings, doubtless knowing that his fee increased the more time elapsed. In the outdoor booth, the Swiss guard and his French counterpart sat glowering on their plastic chairs, sipping coffee and exchanging insults with the practiced ennui of two old men playing checkers.

Ambler swallowed hard. Everything came down to timing. For a few seconds he would be able to cross the road without being glimpsed, and, impetuously, Ambler decided to do so. The Marseilles killer was ruthless, remorseless, relentless: if his quarry managed to escape the gauntlet, he would hunt him with renewed doggedness. Pride of ownership was at stake; it was the specialist, Ambler realized, who had devised the ambush for him.

Ambler would return the favor.

He rushed behind the low brick storage building and then approached the parking lot. The specialist had reduced the canvas tarp to tatters, had ascertained that nobody was in it after all. He was now backing away from the vehicle, swiveling his head, and turning around, toward Ambler. Ambler had the man in the sights of the .44 he'd taken off the Texan but, knowing that the loud report of the gun would rouse the others, hesitated. Instead of squeezing off a round, he would use the gun as a threat.

"Don't make a move," Ambler said.

"Whatever you say," the specialist lied in passable English.

Shoot him now: Ambler's instincts were practically crying out to him.

"You're in charge now," the specialist said soothingly. Yet Ambler knew he was lying, would have known it even if he had not simultaneously been raising his gun arm in a fluid motion.

"What the hell is going on here?" A booming voice came from behind them. One of the Swiss border guards had wandered over to the parking lot, perhaps having heard the slapping sound made by the impact of the bullets on the Jeep. The specialist turned around, almost out of curiosity.

"What the hell is this?" the Swiss guard demanded in French.

A small circle of red suddenly bloomed on the guard's forehead like a *bindi,* and he crumpled to the ground.

An instant later—an instant too late—Ambler squeezed the trigger . . .

And nothing happened. He remembered the bullet he had thrown, remembered too late that the firing chamber had been left empty. By then the specialist had swiveled back to Ambler, his long-barreled pistol held perfectly level, perfectly still, and aimed at his target's face. It was a shot a novice could have made, and the specialist from Marseilles was nothing if not a professional.

CHAPTER THIRTY

Ambler's nerves shrieked at him, now in reproach rather than in warning. Had he only listened to his instincts, the Swiss guard would not have been dead and Ambler would not be staring death in the face. He shuttered his eyes briefly. When he opened them again, he forced himself to *see*, with what felt like the physical exertion of a clean-and-jerk. He would see; he would speak. His mien—his voice, his gaze—would be his weapon. These were the crucial seconds.

"How much are they paying you?" Ambler demanded.

"Enough," the specialist replied impassively.

"Wrong," Ambler said. "They're playing you for a fool, *un con*."

Ambler tossed the heavy .44 pistol to the ground—did so before he was even aware of having decided to. Ironically, he felt much safer now. The fact that he was unarmed would lessen the pressure for an immediate kill. *Sometimes you make best use of a weapon by giving it up.*

"Don't talk," the specialist said. But he was vain about his financial savvy, Ambler knew; the taunt had bought him another few moments of life.

"Because after you kill me, they're going to kill you. This operation—it's an SCO. You understand what this means?"

The specialist took a step toward him, his reptilian eyes unblinking, displaying all the warmth of a cobra toward a rodent.

"A self-cleaning oven," Ambler said. "That's when we design an operation so that all the operational participants kill each other off. It's just a precaution, an SCO—a sort of auto-erase feature."

The killer from Marseilles stared dully, betraying only a modicum of interest.

Ambler let out a short, bark-like laugh. "That's why you're perfect—for their purposes. Cunning enough to kill. Too stupid to live. Ideal casting for an SCO."

"You bore me with your lies." Yet he would hear Ambler out, impressed by his victim's very effrontery.

"Trust me, I've helped design enough of 'em. I remember the time we sent a specialist like you to take out a mullah in one of the Malaysian islands—guy had been doing money laundering for some of the *jihadis,* but he had a cult following among the locals, so we couldn't afford to leave a trail. Sent another guy, a munitions tech, to put a Semtex pack on the little Cessna turboprop that the specialist was set to use for exfiltration, a Semtex pack with an altitude trigger. Then the specialist got instructions to terminate the munitions tech. Which he did, just before he took off in the Cessna. Three minus three equals zero. The math worked out beautifully. Always does. Same equation here. And you'll never see the minus sign until it's too late."

"You would say anything," the specialist said, testing him. "Men in your position always do."

"Men facing death? That describes both of us, my friend—and I can *prove* it." The look Ambler gave the assassin was disdainful rather than fearful.

A microflicker of confusion and interest: "How?"

"First, let me show you a copy of the Sigma A23-44D transmission. I've got a copy in my inside jacket pocket."

"Don't make a move." The specialist's deep-set eyes turned into slits, his knife-thin mouth into a sneer. "You must think I'm an amateur. You'll do nothing at all."

Ambler shrugged and held his hands up, at shoulder level. "Take it out of my pocket yourself, then," Ambler said evenly. "It's in the top right inside pocket—yank down the zipper. I'll keep my hands in view. Point is, you don't have to take my word for any of this. But if you want to keep your miserable goddamn life, you're going to need my help."

"I doubt that very much."

"Believe me, I don't give a shit whether you live or die. It's just that the only way I can save *my* ass is by saving yours."

"More nonsense."

"Fine," Ambler replied. "You know what an American president used to say: 'Trust, but verify.' Let's try a variant: Distrust, but verify. Or are you afraid to find out the truth?"

"You fucking *move* and I blow your brains out," the specialist barked as he grimly approached, holding up the gun in his right hand, reaching for the zipper puller with his left. The metal pull tag lay concealed within the zipper plaquet, just under the collar of Ambler's microfleece-lined winter jacket. It took two tries before the slider moved down the zipper chain. Now the man stepped closer to Ambler, groping around inside his jacket, feeling for the inside pocket. The flesh of the man's face seemed to cover his skull like a coating of hard rubber. Ambler could smell the man's meaty, slightly sour breath. His seemingly lidless eyes were colder than the mountain air.

Timing was everything. Ambler composed himself into a state of willed serenity, a state of pure waiting. To make his move too early or too late would be easy, and fatal. Rational thought would provide no reliable guide. He had to be mindful while banishing reflection, cognition, calculation—the encumbering leg irons of conscious thought. The world was gone now: the mountains, the air, the ground beneath his feet, and the sky above his head had vanished. Reality consisted of two pairs of eyes, two pairs of hands. Reality consisted of anything that moved.

Now the specialist had discovered that the inner pocket was itself zippered, horizontally, and the assassin's left hand was insufficiently dexterous to move the slider; when he tugged at the pull tag, it tugged the fabric tape into which it was sewn, impeding the slider's movement. As he fumbled, Ambler bent his knees slightly, an exhausted man diminishing himself further.

Then he closed his eyes, with the slow resignation of a migraine sufferer. The specialist was dealing with someone who had not only shed his pistol but was no longer even watching him. *Sometimes you make best use of a weapon by giving it up.* There was reassurance there, at once profound and subliminal—a mammalian gesture of surrender, like a dog exposing its throat to mollify a more aggressive dog.

Timing—frustrated, the specialist removed his hand, his awkward left hand. Ambler, bending his knees farther, lowered himself a little more. *Timing*—the specialist would have no choice but to shift his gun from his right hand to his left, an operation that would take no longer than a second. Even with his eyes shut, Ambler *felt* and *heard* the assassin start to make the quick switch. Time was metered out in milliseconds. The gun was being passed to the man's left hand; his left index finger would be extending toward the trigger guard, feeling for the curved apostrophe of steel within it, even while Ambler was bending his knees just a little farther, hanging his head down, like a bashful child. He was no longer thinking, just giving himself over to instinct altogether, and—*now now now now*—

Ambler surged forward, forward and *upward,* the coiled strength in his legs immense, his lowered head ramming into the other man's jaw. He felt and heard the man's teeth slamming together, the bone-jarring vibration traveling upward through his cranium, and then, moments later, the neck snapping back, the startled reflex causing the man's hand to spring open. Ambler heard the sound of a gun clattering to the pavement, and—*now now now now*—

Ambler's head smashed *downward* in a powerful reverse arc, the top of his forehead shattering the specialist's nose.

The man from Marseilles collapsed to the pavement, a rictus of shock on his face giving way to the slackness of insentience. Ambler collected the silenced gun, snaked his way through the woods behind the customhouse, with snow-muffled steps, and then crept back to the shoulder of the road. Technically, he supposed, he had just crossed the border between France and Switzerland. Along the paved shoulder, the assortment of engine parts by the food-service truck was even larger than it had been. But the big-bellied, thickset mechanic was no longer bent over the engine. He was some distance away from it, one finger pressed to his ear, walking calmly toward Ambler, his paunch straining at his grease-smudged overalls.

The man's face was jowly and unshaven, his expression the familiar mixture of boredom and resentment found among the French *hommes à tout faire.* He was whistling a Serge Gainsbourg tune, off-key. He looked up, as if he had just noticed Ambler, and gave him a wry nod.

A wave of dread swept over Ambler. In situations of extremity, he found himself acting, time and again, before he had consciously decided to act; this was one of those times. He yanked the silenced pistol from his jacket and leveled it . . . even as he found himself staring into the bore end of a large-caliber gun that—with the legerdemain of a magician finding nickels in thin air—had materialized in the other man's beefy hand.

"*Salut,*" the man in the *garagiste* overalls said. He spoke with the slightly Teutonic vowels of Savoyard French.

"*Salut,*" Ambler replied as—*now now now now*—he kicked out his legs from under himself and, in free fall, squeezed the trigger not once but three times, the quiet, spitting sound of each round accompanied by an incongruously forceful recoil. With near simultaneity, the Savoyard's long-barreled Magnum blasted away exactly where Ambler's head had been an instant before he had dropped himself to the ground.

Ambler landed rockily, but with more grace than the gunman in overalls. As blood gouted from the man's chest, wisps of steam formed in the cold air above it. After a few spastic coughs, the man fell still.

Now Ambler detached the Savoyard's key ring from his belt and found the key to his van. It had been parked thirty yards to the east of the checkpoint, decorated with a logo in both French and German: GARAGISTE/AUTOMECHANIKER. Seconds later, Ambler headed down the road into Switzerland, toward the town of St. Martin, stopping only briefly to retrieve his travel bag from beneath a roadside mound of snow. The checkpoint—France itself—had soon vanished from his rearview mirror.

The van was, he discovered, surprisingly powerful—its original engine must have been modified or replaced with one of greater horsepower. If he knew how these professionals worked, the mechanics firm existed in name only; the plates would be innocuously registered, while the markings on the vehicle would ensure that it could appear anywhere and at any time without prompting suspicion. Wherever there were automobiles, there could be an automotive breakdown. Nor would the police be inclined to stop such a vehicle for breaking speed limits. Though it was not exactly an ambulance, such repair vans were typically dispatched for automotive emergencies, including crashes. The vehicle's guise was well chosen.

He would be safe in this vehicle, at least for a while. As he tore through the countryside, time was a blooming montage of sunlight and shadow, of streets filled with people and roads filled with motorists. Veering one way and then another, he navigated around small, officious cars and big, pavement-rumbling tractor-trailers. Everything seemed a conspiracy to impede his progress—or, rather, his consciousness registered little except for such impediments. Meanwhile, the van itself gulped down the steepest grades with ease, its snow tires and four-wheel drive gripping the pavement with assurance. The gears never strained, no matter how hard he stressed them; the engine never whined, no matter how hard he pushed the limits of its capacity.

There were moments when he dimly recognized the dazzling beauty of his surroundings—the towering pines ahead of him that winter had turned into a castle of snow, a Neuschwanstein built from branches; the mountain peaks that punctuated the horizon like the sails of distant ships; the roadside freshets, fed by mountain streams, that continued to gush even while all around them was frozen. Yet his mind was consumed with the imperative of motion— of *speed*. He had decided that he could safely drive this vehicle for two hours, and in those two hours he had to consume as much of the distance between him and his destination as he possibly could. At the end of the line, there was danger—dangers to be confronted, dangers to be averted—but there was hope as well.

And there was Laurel. She was there, would have arrived already. His heart swelled and ached as he thought of her, his Ariadne. *Oh God, he loved her so.* Laurel, the woman who had saved first his life and then his soul. It did not matter how beautiful the landscape was; anything that separated him from Laurel was, simply by virtue of this, detestable.

He looked at his watch, as he had been doing obsessively since he had entered Switzerland. Time was running out. Another steep ascent of the Alpine road, followed by a shallower descent. He kept the accelerator pedal at or near the floor, grazed the brake pedal only when absolutely necessary. So close and yet so far: so many gulfs behind, so many gulfs ahead.

CHAPTER THIRTY-ONE

Davos

Few places on earth were at once so vast in the popular imagination and so diminutive in physical scale—essentially a mile or so of houses and buildings clustered mostly along a single road. Hulking snow-laden conifers surrounded it like frosted sentries. Geographers knew it as the highest-altitude resort town in Europe, but this was not merely a truth about its physical elevation. For a few days every year, it represented the pinnacle of financial and political power as well. Indeed, the town had become synonymous with the annual meeting of the World Economic Forum—a gathering of the world's global elite that took place there in the last week of January, when the seasonal gloom ensured that the visiting illuminati would sparkle and shine even more brightly. Although the forum was dedicated to the free movement of capital and labor and ideas, it was itself a heavily guarded encampment. Surrounding a sprawling compound of semi-spheres and blocks—the Congress Center, where the conference was actually held—were hundreds of Swiss military policemen; temporary steel fences blocked off all points of informal entrance.

Now he left the van in a parking lot behind an old, bleak church with a steeple like a witch's hat and trudged up a narrow street, Reginaweg, to the town's main street, the Promenade. The sidewalks had been carefully cleared of snow, the result of ceaseless efforts; wind continually swept in snow from the slopes even when none was falling from the skies. The Promenade was an arcade of sorts, with one shop after another, interrupted only by the occasional hotel and restaurant. Nor was there anything quaint about the storefronts. Here were upscale outlets of international brands like Bally,

Chopard, Rolex, Paul & Shark, Prada. He passed a store selling linens called Bette und Besser and a tall modern building that displayed three flags as if it were a consulate; in fact, it was a UBS branch office, displaying the flags of the state, the canton, and the company. Ambler had no doubt which of those commanded the bank's true fealty. Only the hotels—the Posthotel, with an iconic horn above its giant block letters, or the Morosani Schweizerhof, with a green and black image of traditional Alpine boots above its marquee—suggested any local character.

Davos might have been one of the most remote places in the world, but the world was here, in full metallic plumage. Cars with well-studded tires and headlights on high beam—he saw a dark blue Honda, a silvery Mercedes, a boxy Opal SUV, a Ford minivan—drove through the streets at ridiculously fast speeds. Otherwise, the battery of storefronts put him in mind of a Hollywood set, a back-lot Dodge City: one was continually reminded of how *narrow* the town was, because the enfolding vastness of mountain slopes was nearly always visible, a frozen cataract of trees spilling from an unseen summit. The folds of the earth itself—a looming, incomprehensible pattern of ridges, whorls, and arches like God's own fingerprints—made everything else appear inauthentic, impermanent. The oldest building he passed was a sparely elegant stone structure marked KANTONSPOLIZEI, an office of the regional police. But its residents, too, were only guests, policing what could not be policed—the immovable snow-clad mountains, the ungovernable human soul.

And what of his own soul? Ambler was exhausted, that was the truth, deluged by information that might mean anything or nothing. His spirits were as dim and chilled as the day was. He felt insignificant, impotent, isolated. *The man who wasn't there.* Not even to himself. Soft, sardonic voices began to clamor within his skull, berating and questioning. Here he was, near the top of a mountain, and he had never felt so at sea.

The ground beneath his feet seemed to rock and sway, gently but perceptibly. *What was happening to him?* Hypoxia, surely—mountain sickness—the effects of high altitude on those unacclimated to it, which could sometimes diminish blood oxygenation and cause mental confusion. He took deep breaths of the thin mountain air, tried to orient himself to the world around him. As he craned his head and took in the wall-like mountain peaks that seemed to rise up inches away from him, claustrophobia overtook him, casting him back to the rubber-coated enclosures of Parrish Island; and suddenly eddying through his mind was that stream of jargon to which he had been subjected: *dissociative identity disorder, personality fragmentation, paranoia, abreactive ego dystonia.* It was madness—*theirs,* not his—and he would overcome it, had overcome it, for his search for himself was what had led him here.

Unless that odyssey itself was the madness.

Joining the shadows that surrounded him were the shadows he had tried too hard to banish from his mind.

A booming, exultant voice of a burly industrialist: *You're the Man Who Wasn't There. . . . You officially don't exist!*

The gingerly tones of the brilliant, blind Osiris: *It's Occam's razor: What's the simplest explanation? It's easier to alter the contents of your head than it is to change the whole world. . . . You know about . . . all those behavioral-science programs from the fifties, right? . . . The program names changed, but the research never was discontinued.*

The psychiatrist with the rectangular, black-framed glasses, the long brown forelock, the felt-tipped pens—and the words that burned like an electrocautery. *The question I'm putting to you is the question you need to put to yourself: Who are you?*

Ambler staggered into an alleyway and then behind a Dumpster, leaning against the wall and trying, with a low groan, to drive away the clamoring, overlapping voices, the hellish din. He could not fail. He would not fail. He filled his lungs with another deep breath and another and squeezed his eyes shut, telling himself that it was the stinging wind that was making them water. In the brief interval of blackness he would pull himself together. Except that his mind now filled with the image of a computer screen—no, a whole series of screens, impossible to bring into focus except for a blinking cursor in the center of each one, a cursor pulsing like a warning beacon at the end of a single, short line:

HARRISON AMBLER NOT FOUND.

He doubled over and retched, the first wave followed by a second, even more powerful. Now he stood, bent, almost crouching, his hands on his knees, oblivious to the cold, to everything, panting like a dog in August. Another voice, another face, entered his mind, and it was as if the sun itself had appeared, burning away the darkness of his misery and despair. *I believe in you,* Laurel Holland was saying, pulling him close. *I believe. You need to believe, too.*

Moments later, the sickness passed. Ambler straightened up and felt his strength and resolve returning. He had swum free from the inky depths of his own psyche and shot to the surface—had emerged from a nightmare that was peculiarly his own.

Now he had to enter another nightmare, knowing that if he failed, the world itself would be entering it and might never emerge.

Checking his watch to verify that he remained on schedule, Ambler made his way toward the largest of the Davos hotels, the Steigenberger Hotel Belvedere, on Promenade 89, catty-corner from the main entrance to the Congresszentrum. The giant structure was a former sanitorium, built in 1875. Its pink exterior was fenestrated with narrow, arching windows, mimicking the embrasures of the battle-ready castles of the feudal era. But the only visible clashes, in the week of the forum's annual conference, were between corporate sponsorships. KPMG had a large blue and white banner mounted over the hotel's porte cochere, jostling for attention with a nearby sign for shuttle services that was emblazoned with the four inter-locked rings of the Audi logo. His pulse quickened as he approached the entrance; lining the hotel's circular drive, alongside the usual luxury cars, were military transport vehicles and a large-tired SUV with a blue rectangular police light on top and a Day-Glo red band along the side, against which the words MILITÄR POLIZEI were lettered in white. Across the street, the sidewalk was barricaded with a ten-foot-tall steel grating topped with sharpened points; laced through the grate was a candy-striped banner printed with a firm advisory to KEEP OUT in the three major Swiss languages: SPERRZONE, ZONE INTER-DICTE, ZONA SBARRATA.

Caston, he knew from a voice mail he'd listened to en route, had succeeded in joining the conference center officially: he had used his pull as a senior CIA officer to have himself added to the roster of guests. For Ambler, however, that would not be possible; and Caston had so far learned nothing. The task, after all, required perception, not ratiocination.

Or perhaps it required a miracle.

Inside the Belvedere's vestibule was a large sisal entrance mat for stamping out the snow from one's feet; beyond the double doors, sisal gave way to elegant Wilton-style carpeting in a subtle floral pat-tern. A brisk walk-through revealed several parlors that flowed one into another, as well as a dining area roped off with red velvet ropes and stanchions topped with ornamental brass pineapples. Ambler returned to a parlor not far from the hotel's front desk, where, from a discreet angle, he could watch people entering the hotel, and took a seat on a tufted leather chair; above mahogany dadoes, the walls were covered in black and burgundy striped silk and decorated with arcading. He glanced at himself in a mirror across the wall, satisfied that, dressed as he now was in an expensive-looking charcoal-gray nailhead suit, he looked the part he was playing. He would be taken for one of the many businessmen who, not so illustrious as the "par-ticipants," had paid very significant amounts to attend—those, that is, whose applications were accepted in the first place. In the rarefied realm of the World Economic Forum, the paying guest was regarded with the sort of condescension a penniless scholarship boy would have met with at an exclusive boardingschool. At home, such men, heads of local businesses or mayors of midsized cities, could imagine themselves to be masters of the universe; at Davos, they were its minions.

Ambler ordered a coffee, black, from one of the harried but pleasant attendants and lingered over the various business publications on the small table nearby: the *Financial Times, The Wall Street Journal, Forbes,* the *Far Eastern Economic Review, Newsweek International,* and *The Economist.* When he picked up *The Economist,* he felt a small twinge: on the cover was a photograph of Liu Ang looking cheerful, above the sprightly legend BRINGING THE PEOPLE'S REPUBLIC BACK TO THE PEOPLE.

He quickly flipped through the cover story, his eyes skimming through the copy, pausing at the bold subheads. THE SEA TURTLE RE-TURNS, ran one; AMERICAN INFLUENCE DEBATED was another. At frequent intervals, his eyes flicked up, watching the hotel guests come and go. Before long, he found a promising candidate: an Englishman in his early forties, with graying blond hair, someone in banking, to judge by his spread collar, his finely patterned yellow tie. He had just entered the hotel and looked slightly annoyed with himself, as if he had foolishly left behind an item that he needed. His round cheeks were still pink from the cold, and his black cashmere topcoat bore a few flakes of snow.

Ambler hurriedly left a few francs by his coffee cup and caught up with the businessman just as he was striding into a waiting elevator; Ambler stepped into the car moments before the door closed. The businessman had pressed the fourth-floor button. Ambler pressed the button again, as if he had not realized it was already lit. He glanced at the man's conference badge: *Martin Hibbard,* it read. Moments later, Ambler followed the businessman out of the elevator and down the hall, noting the number of the room where the businessman stopped but taking care to walk past him with a steady gait, vanishing at the turn at the end of the hall. Just out of sight, Ambler stopped, listened as the door shut behind the Englishman and then, half a minute later, opened again. The Englishman emerged clutching a leather portfolio and returned to the elevator bank. Given the time of day and his late-for-a-meeting air, it was a safe assumption that he had a lunch appointment and had a need of whatever documents were in the portfolio. In all likelihood, he would then head to the Congress Center for one of the two-thirty sessions and would not be back to his hotel room for hours.

Ambler returned to the lobby and scanned the various clerks at the front desk, an elegant station of mahogany and marble. One of them, a woman in her late twenties with slightly too much lipstick and eye shadow, would be his best chance, he decided. He would not take his chances with the shaven-headed man in his forties, although he was free, nor with the older, graying woman with the fixed smile and an underslept look about her eyes.

When the younger woman had finished up with the guest she had been dealing with—an African frustrated by his inability to exchange nairas for Swiss francs—Ambler stepped forward with a sheepish expression.

"I'm such a moron," he said. "Can you tell?"

"I'm sorry?" Her English was only lightly accented.

"I'm sorrier. Left my key card in my room."

"Not to worry, sir," the woman said pleasantly. "That happens all the time."

"Not to me it doesn't. The name's Marty Hibbard. Martin Hibbard, I should say."

"And the room number."

"What is it now?" Ambler pretended that he was racking his memory. "Oh, I remember—four seventeen."

The woman behind the marble counter rewarded him with a

commending smile, keyed in a few codes into her computer. Moments later, a new key card emerged from a machine behind her, and she handed it to him. "Hope you're enjoying your stay," she said.

"You know, I am, actually," Ambler said. "Thanks to you."

She smiled gratefully at the rare compliment.

Room 417 turned out to be spacious and grandly appointed, with light, airy colors and delicate furniture: a Sheridan-style highboy, a wing chair, a small desk and hard-backed wooden chair in the far corner. There was not a room for rent in the whole Davos-Klosters area, not during the last week of January, but the one he had taken momentary possession of would serve, at least for a while.

He made the phone call, turned off the lights, drew the curtains shut, including the inner, room-darkening ones, and waited.

The knock at the door came ten minutes later. Ambler pressed himself against the wall adjacent to the unhinged side of the door. That was standard placement, something that he had learned in training. Something that was second nature to an operative like Harrison Ambler.

If Harrison Ambler was really who he was.

An effluent of black anxiety arose in him like a toxic plume from a smokestack. He unlatched the door, opened it a crack.

The room was dark. But he did not have to see; he could smell her—smell her shampoo, the fabric softener on her clothes, the honeyed scent of her skin.

"Hal?" Her voice, barely more than a whisper. She closed the door behind her.

He spoke quietly, too, in order not to startle her. "Over here," he said, and his mouth formed a smile as involuntary as a sneeze, a sob, a laugh. It almost seemed to light the room by itself.

She stepped toward Ambler's voice, reached a hand out to his face like a blind person, found his cheek, caressed it, and now stood very near him. He felt her warmth, could feel her lips brushing his—and the contact was electric. He put his arms around her and drew her close, feeling her cheek against the top of his chest, and now he kissed her hair, her ear, her neck, inhaling deeply. He had to savor every moment he had with her. Though he knew he might not survive the day, a curious radiance swelled within him—the assurance that whatever happened to him, he would not die unloved.

"Laurel," he breathed, "I—"

She pressed her mouth to his, silencing him and seeming to draw courage from his kiss. "I know," she said after a pause.

He cradled her face in both his hands and gently moved his thumbs across her cheeks, along the tender skin beneath her eyes; they were wet, had just become so.

"You don't have to say the words," she said, her voice thickened by emotion but still hushed.

She stepped into his embrace again, on her tippy-toes, he realized, pressing her mouth to his once more. For a long moment, he was aware of nothing else but her: her warmth, her smell, her firm, soft, trembling flesh pressed against his, even the slow beating of his— her?—heart. The rest of the world vanished for him, the hotel room, the town, the mission, the world itself. Nothing else existed but the two of them, a twoness that was somehow no longer a twoness at all. He felt her clutching him, no longer desperately but with an odd serenity that had somehow suffused them both.

Now they both relaxed and stepped back, a twoness again. He flipped the switch near the door. With illumination, the space they were in changed, too; it became smaller, cozier, rendered more intimate by the opulent textures and colors. Laurel somehow did not change; she was exactly as he had pictured her, as if the image in his mind had materialized before his eyes: the large green-flecked hazel eyes, filled with yearning, love, concern; the porcelain skin and full, slightly parted lips. It was a look that radiated utter devotion, a look of the sort one rarely saw outside the movies—only it was *real;* it was here, within arms' reach. It was the realest thing there was.

"Thank God you're safe, my darling, my love," she said quietly. "Thank God you're safe."

"You're so beautiful." He spoke the thought aloud without consciously intending to. *My Ariadne.*

"Let's just *leave*," she said, a sudden wild sense of hope transforming her features. "Let's ski down that mountain and never look back."

"Laurel," he said.

"Just us," she said. "What happens will happen. We'll have each other."

"Soon," he said. "In just a few hours."

Laurel blinked slowly; she had been trying to keep her fear at bay, but it was spilling over now, unstoppable. "Oh, my darling," she said. "I have a bad feeling about this. I can't shake it." There was a quaver in her voice; her eyes glistened moistly.

The fear that ran through him now was fear for *her*—for her own safety. "Did you talk to Caston about it?"

She smiled ruefully through her tears. "Talk to Caston about *feelings*? He just started talking about *odds* and *probabilities*."

"Sounds like Caston."

"*Long* odds, and *slim* probabilities." She was no longer smiling. "I think he has a bad feeling, too. Only he doesn't admit to *having* feelings."

"Some people find it easier that way."

"He says you're going to do what you're going to do, no matter how long the odds of success are."

"Did his handheld calculator tell him that?" Ambler shook his head. "But he's not wrong."

"I don't want to lose you, Hal." She closed her eyes briefly. "I *can't* lose you." She spoke louder than she had meant to.

"My God, Laurel," he said. "I don't want to lose you, either. And then, somehow, there's a strange way that . . ." He shook his head, for there were words he could not speak, could not expect anyone to understand. His life had been cheap before—cheap to himself. He had never thought of it that way, was only now in a position to recognize it. Because it was no longer cheap. It contained something of infinite value. It contained Laurel.

Yet it was *because* of Laurel that he was here; it was *because* of Laurel that he would do what had to be done. He could not go to ground, disappear within some sprawling South American metropolis, living out an anonymous existence while warfare broke out among the great powers. A world that contained Laurel was a world that suddenly and intensely *mattered* to him. These were the things Ambler thought and could not say. He just gazed at her for a few moments, both of them gathering their fortitude for what lay ahead of them.

Never doubt that a small group of thoughtful, committed citizens can change the world. Indeed, it is the only thing that ever has.

The words returned to him like acid splashing in his throat. He could not begin to fathom the sort of global upheaval that would occur if the Palmerite conspiracy succeeded.

Ambler moved to the window, peered out toward the low-slung complex of buildings across the street: the Congress Center. Military policemen stood in clusters, almost entirely clad in midnight blue—it was the color of their zippered trousers, nylon-shelled jackets, and woolen caps—save for a turquoise stripe on the inside of their flipped-up jacket collars and their black high lace-up boots. When they stood close together, it was as if they brought the night with them. Tall fences of tubular steel, partly buried in snow, funneled visitors to a precisely indicated point of egress. Ambler had seen maximum-security prisons that were more inviting than this.

"Maybe Caston will figure out a way," Laurel said. "He got *me* in. Not that I learned a damned thing."

"He got you in?" Ambler was astonished.

She nodded. "He figured out that, technically, I've got an intel-service classification. High-level clearance, right? The WEF office was able to get official confirmation of that. Fact is, the groundskeepers at Parrish Island have high-level clearance, too—them's the rules at a facility like that—but how were they to know? It's all about these letters and numbers that go after your name, and Caston's a whiz at working the system."

"Where *is* he, by the way?"

"Should be here any minute," Laurel said. "I came early." She did not have to explain why. "But maybe he's hit on something—found one of those 'anomalies' of his."

"Listen, Caston is a good man, but he's an analyst, a numbers guy. What we're dealing with is people, not the electronic vapor trail they leave."

Someone rapped on the door three times; Laurel recognized the tattoo and let Clayton Caston in. His tan raincoat bore epaulets of snow, which were dissolving into rivulets down the front. Caston himself looked exhausted, even more pallid than usual. He had a black tote bag in one hand, silk-screened with the logo of the World Economic Forum. He looked at Ambler without a flicker of surprise.

"You find out anything?" Ambler asked him.

"Not a whole lot," the auditor said soberly. "I was inside the conference center for an hour and a half. Like I said, I was here once before, on a panel to do with offshore financial institutions and international money laundering. They've always got a lot of technical seminars, along with the glitzier events. This morning I wandered around the place, went in and out of the seminars. I ought to have a button that says 'Ask Me About Transnational Capital Flows.' Laurel got around, too, but it sounds like she didn't strike gold, either."

"The whole place kinda gave me the willies," Laurel admitted. "So many faces you recognize from magazines and the TV news. Makes you dizzy. It's just a reflex, but at first you keep nodding at people, because they look familiar and you somehow think you must know each other. Then you realize they just look familiar because they're famous."

Caston nodded. "Davos makes Bilderberg look like the Muncie Chamber of Commerce."

"Kept feeling that I stood out somehow, that everybody could tell I didn't belong," Laurel went on. "And the thought that one of them—just one of them—might be this *maniac . . .* "

"We're not dealing with a maniac," Ambler said carefully. "We're dealing with a professional. Far worse." He paused. "But there's good news, too—the simple fact that both of you were able to gain entrance," Ambler said. "That was your doing, Caston, and I'm still not sure how you pulled it off."

"You forget that I'm a senior officer of the Central Intelligence Agency," the auditor said. "I had my assistant call the office of the executive chairman, get my name added to the D.C. retinue. An official-sounding call from Langley, with lots of callback info, security assurances. They didn't argue."

"They don't mind having spooks at the table here?"

"*Mind?* They love it. You still don't get it—Davos is all about power. Power of every kind. They'd be *delighted* to have the DCI himself—he was here a couple of years ago—but they're quite pleased to have a senior CIA official, too."

"And you got Laurel on the books the same way?"

"My assistant swung it, actually. We described her as a psychiatric specialist with the Joint Intelligence Services—which happens to be her technical designation. She's also got a 12A-56J level of clearance, which happens to be mandatory for Parrish Island personnel. The last-minute nature of the request was slightly irregular, but not remarkably so, especially given their dealings with U.S. intel folks. The rest was a matter of *elision*, shall we say."

"But the WEF security people wouldn't just take your word for it, would they?"

"Of course not. They called Langley, reached my office through the switchboard—that's standard, as I say, the callback procedure—and had a second discussion with my assistant. I gather he intimated things about how it would be a 'special favor' to the DCI and the Secretary of State, that sort of thing. Then he provides them a zero-knowledge pass code for purposes of verification. See, there's a system for limited-access intranet verification, developed for collaborative operations with other nations. Upshot is that they can get an abbreviated personnel listing—a *stub* is the term—which provides C-level confirmation of what they've been told. My office then transmits a digital photograph for the security card—there's a JIS pic on file—and we're in like Flynn."

"You know, I almost understand what you just said." Ambler tilted his head. "But hang on. You agreed the security system here was foolproof."

"Pretty much foolproof, yeah. Do I look like a fool?"

"So can you do the same for me?"

"Um, let me think. Are you on the employee rolls at the CIA?" Caston's lids fluttered with a suppressed eye roll. "Do you have a personnel record with the Joint Intelligence Services division? If they call the switchboard at Langley to verify your employment and rank, what are they going to be told?"

"But—"

"*Harrison Ambler* does not *exist*," Caston snapped. "Or have you forgotten? Hate to be the one to break the news, but they *erased* you, all right? The World Economic Forum traffics in data, bits and bytes. It's a world of digital signatures, digital records, digital confirmation. I'd have an easier time getting a WEF security badge issued to Bigfoot or Yeti or the goddamn Loch Ness Monster. They don't exist, either, but at least you can find them on the Internet."

"You finished?"

"My fear is, we're *all* finished." Caston's eyes blazed. "All this time I figured you were holding back some grand scheme you had. The hell of it is, you're even more reckless than I'd imagined. You race pell-mell into a potential disaster area without a *plan*! You don't think ahead—hell, you don't *think*, period. From the outset, our chances were between slim and none. Well, slim's just left the house."

Ambler felt as if the force of gravity had suddenly doubled; his limbs felt like lead. "Just break it down for me—tell me how the badge system is organized physically."

"You can't bullshit your way in, if that's what you're thinking," Caston grumbled. "And you can't get in by doing whatever the opposite of bullshitting is, that peephole-to-the-brain trick you do. The system is very simple, and damn near impossible to spoof." He unbuttoned his gray wool-and-polyester suit jacket—Ambler noticed a faint smell of mothballs about it—and showed them the identification badge he was wearing on a white nylon string around his neck. It was deceptively simple: a white plastic rectangle, with a photograph of Caston to the left of his name; there was a silvery square hologram below, a blue color stripe above. He turned it around, exposing the magnetic stripe on the back.

"Mine's the same," Laurel put in. "Doesn't look like much. Couldn't you just steal one and alter it?"

Caston shook his head. "When you enter, you swipe the card through a reader. The card encodes a digital signature that calls up a guest record from the computer. Now, that computer at the door has the most powerful kind of cybersecurity you can ask for: it's 'airgapped.' In other words, it's a stand-alone, not connected to the Internet, so you can't hack into it. And there's a guard stationed at a monitor, and every time a card is read, the name and photograph from the computer record get displayed on the screen. Point is, if you're not already in the computer, you're shit out of luck."

"That the technical term?"

"And then there's a metal detector you've got to pass through, like at the airport," Caston went on. "Jackets, keys, and such go through a conveyor belt."

"Enough to keep out an assassin?" Laurel asked.

"We're talking about someone who has been planning this for

months, maybe longer," Caston replied. He glanced at Ambler. "You've got about two hours."

Ambler wandered over where Laurel had been standing and peered out the window into the gloomy afternoon again. Snow was drifting down, lazily but steadily.

What were his options? He felt a rising sense of panic, knew he must keep that emotion at bay: it could freeze him up, cause him to choke, to lose touch with his instincts.

Laurel's voice: "What if you say you've lost your card?"

"Then they apologize and escort you to the exit," Caston replied. "I saw that happen when I was here a few years back. And they don't care if you're the king of Morocco. Everyone inside that place has a card around his neck."

"Even heads of states?" Laurel pressed.

"I just saw the vice president of the United States. He was wearing a slate blue suit and a yellow tie. And a Davos ID card about five inches below the knot. It's simple, and it's ironclad. These people don't play. They've never had a security breach in some three decades, and there's a reason for that."

When Ambler turned back to the others, Laurel was looking at him expectantly. "There's got to be something, right? The human factor—like you always say."

Ambler heard her words as if they had been spoken from a long distance away. Scenarios flitted by in his mind—entertained, considered, explored, and rejected, all within seconds. Almost every organization had the porosity of human discretion, because day-to-day practicalities demanded some measure of flexibility. But the annual meeting of the World Economic Forum was not a day-to-day institution. It was a special event, lasting just one week. Here rules really could be infinitely stringent. Not enough time ever elapsed for the security officers to start taking much for granted.

Ambler's eyes fell on the black WEF tote bag that Caston had been carrying, filled with the material that people were given at check-in.

He picked it up and spilled its contents on the bed. There was a copy of *Global Agenda*, the WEF magazine that was prepared for the occasion, and a white binder with the schedule of events. Ambler flipped through it: page after page listed panels with such stultifying titles as "Whither Water Management?" "Securing the Global Health System," "The Future of U.S. Foreign Policy," "Human Security and National Security: Friends or Foes?," "Toward a New Bretton Woods." There was the schedule of addresses by the UN secretary-general, the United States vice president, the president of Pakistan, and others; Liu Ang's address was clearly the culminating and keynote event. Ambler closed the binder and picked up a short, thick, almost cubical book, listing all the "participants" in the WEF annual meeting— nearly fifteen hundred pages featuring photographs of each followed by a career biography crammed in small sans-serif type.

"Look at all the faces here," Ambler said. He rolled a thumb across its width, like a riffle animation.

"Make a hell of a police lineup," Laurel put in. Frustration began to fill the air like a stench.

Suddenly Caston sat bolt upright. "A police lineup," he echoed.

Ambler looked at him, saw something in Caston's eyes that almost scared him—his eyes were practically swiveling in their sockets. "What are you on about?" he prompted in a low voice.

"They ought to be outlawed," Caston said. "Lineups, I mean. They're responsible for a god-awful number of false convictions. The error rates are insupportable."

"You're exhausted," Laurel said quickly. She turned to Ambler anxiously. "He didn't sleep on the train at all."

"Let him talk," Ambler said softly.

"Because eyewitnesses are highly fallible," Caston went on. "You saw someone do a bad thing, and you're led to believe that one of the people in the lineup may be the fellow that you saw. So you look— and there's a heuristic that most people follow. They choose the one who looks most like the person they remember."

"Why's that a problem?" Laurel sounded puzzled.

"Because the closest person isn't necessarily the *same* person. 'It's Number Four,' they say. 'It's Number Two.' And sometimes Number Four or Number Two is a cop, a stand-in, and there's no harm, no foul. The investigators thank the witness and send him on his way. But, as the odds will have it, sometimes that guy is a suspect. Not the actual perp, but a suspect. He happens to look a little more like the fellow you saw than any of the others. But he's *not* the fellow you saw. All of a sudden, you're got an eyewitness testifying against the suspect: 'Can you point to the man that you saw that night?' and that whole rigamarole, and a jury imagines that nothing could be more open-and-shut than that. Now, there's a way to elicit what an eyewitness saw without that distortion: you do it seriatim. Show them photographs of people, not at the same time, but one after another. You ask: 'Is *this* the one? Yes or no?' If you switch to the seriatim method, the rate of misidentification plunges from seven percent to less than one percent. It's an outrage that people in law enforcement haven't grasped these basic statistics." He looked up, suddenly sharp. "But my point: in the real world, often enough, close gets you your goddamn cigar." He blinked rapidly. "The data are very clear on this. Ergo: we find the person who looks most like you. Fifteen hundred faces—that's a sample space we can work with."

Ambler did not reply right away.

As Caston stood near him, Ambler began to flip through the book, rapidly, methodically, a wetted forefinger whisking through almost mechanically. "I want you to look at the pictures, too," he told Laurel. "If it's close enough, you'll know it at once. Don't think about it. Just look—*experience* it. If it's workable, you'll know it in an *instant*."

The faces flew by, about two per second. "Wait," Laurel said.

Caston stuck a small, rectangular Post-it on the page and said, "Keep going."

Ambler did, whisking through the next hundred pages without interruption until he paused at one. Caston placed another adhesive flag on the page, and Ambler resumed paging through. When Ashton Palmer's face appeared, Ambler paused briefly. None of them spoke. None of them had to. It was the same when he reached Ellen Whitfield's page. She looked blandly handsome, as her mentor looked distinguished, but their coiled intelligence and ambition was filtered out of the official postage-stamp-sized photograph. At this point, their images provided nothing but distraction.

By the time Ambler had gone through the entire book, four pages had been flagged. Ambler handed the book over to Caston. "You've got the fresh eyes. Take a look."

Caston flipped to each of the four. "The third one," he said, passing it to Laurel, who did the same.

"Probably the third," she said, a little more hesitantly.

Ambler opened the book to the third Post-it flag and tore off the page, scrutinizing the man's biography. "Not the *strongest* resemblance, I wouldn't have thought," Ambler said, half to himself. "But then I have a hard time remembering what I look like these days." He glanced again at the black-and-white photograph. The man's eyes conveyed a self-regarding severity, bordering on hauteur, though it was hard to know how much of it was him, how much the particular photograph.

Jozef Vrabel was his name, and he was the president of V&S Slovakia, a Bratislava-based company that specialized in "wireless solutions, services and products, and security in access networks."

"I don't mean to puncture the mood," Laurel said. "But how are we going to get the guy's card in the first place?"

"Don't ask me," Caston said, shrugging. "Ask Mr. Human Factor over here."

"Can we find him?" Ambler looked at Caston and then peered out of the window again. On the roof, two stories above him, a pair of sharpshooters were on patrol, he knew. Yet what good were weapons without a target? How ironic that he had first to outwit those who sought, as he did, to ensure security. The enemies of his enemies were his enemies.

Now his gaze settled on a long dark blue wall—a solid but movable barrier—that stood in front of the Congress Center's poured-concrete exterior. Along its length was a series of large white rectangles with a blue logo: WORLD ECONOMIC FORUM, each word stacked on top of one another, with a thin crescent curling through the *o*'s. To the left, there was a sign with the same logo, and arrows directing MEDIA/STAFF to a different entrance than the "middle entry" meant for participants.

Fear, hopelessness, and sheer rage swirled within him, and the result, somehow, was to form an alloy stronger than any of its components: an alloy of sheer resolve.

It took him a few moments before he realized that Caston had been speaking. "Wonders of technology," the numbers maven was saying. "There's a computer intranet at the conference center and a lot of the hotels here, too. It's all designed so that you can find people. The networking aspect is pretty key to the Davos experience."

"You do any networking when you were there, Caston?"

"I don't network" was the peevish response. "I *analyze* networks. Point is, if I go to the lobby, they'll have a terminal there. I can type in this name, and it'll say what programs he's signed up to attend. Because you have to sign up, you see. Then . . ."

"Then you find him, and tell him that there's an emergency, and bring him outside the center."

Caston coughed. "Me?"

"How are you at lying?"

Caston reflected for a moment. "Mediocre."

"Mediocre will be good enough," Ambler said. He reached over and gave Caston an encouraging squeeze on the shoulder. Caston squirmed at his touch. "Sometimes, if it's worth doing, it's worth doing badly."

"If I can help . . ." Laurel began.

"I'm going to need you on the logistics front," Ambler told her. He started to explain. "I'll need binoculars or some high-powered device for vision enhancement. There are more than a thousand people at the center. According to the printed agenda, the president of China is scheduled to speak at the Congress Hall."

"That's the biggest hall in the place," Caston said. "Seats a thousand, easily. Maybe more."

"That's a lot of faces, and I'm not going to be able to get near them all."

"You're going to stick out if you start walking around with a pair of binocs around your neck," Laurel cautioned. "You could attract the wrong kind of attention."

"You're talking about security surveillance."

"That place is camera central," Laurel said, "with all the broadcast cameramen around."

"How's that?"

"I had a chat with one of the camera guys," Laurel replied. "Thought it might turn up something useful. Turns out that the WEF records a lot of events for its own purposes, but more than that, the major events—plenary sessions and a few open forums— are taped by some of the major broadcast media. The BBC, CNN International, Sky TV, SBC, like that. Amazing lenses on those cameras—I took a peak through the viewfinder of one."

Ambler tilted his head.

"So I was thinking—you could use one of those, just for the zoom. Those television cameras—they're portable but bulky, and they have a powerful optical zoom. That's better than any binocular. And they're nothing that would attract a second look."

Ambler felt a tiny flutter within him. "My God, Laurel," he said.

"Don't look so shocked that I had a good idea," she joshed. "Only thing I'm wondering is, why would the head of V&S Slovakia be toting a camera through the convention hall?"

"It's not an issue when you're inside," Caston said. "You need the badge to enter. Once you're in, nobody's going to be paying that much attention. The badge itself doesn't display your affiliation, just your name. Once you're inside, it's a whole different ball game."

"What about getting hold of a camera?" Ambler asked.

"Not a problem—I know just how to pick up a couple," Laurel said. "The guys I spoke to showed me a storeroom full of them."

"Listen, Laurel, you're not trained for operational—"

"You're in a life raft and you want to check whether someone has a boater license?" Caston scoffed. "I thought I was supposed to be the rule stickler here."

"Fact is, it's gonna be easier for me than for 'Jozef Vrabel' to get into that storeroom," Laurel said. "And I've already had friendly chats with the boys who go in and out of it." In a mock-vampish tone, she added, "I may not have 'skills,' but I do have . . . assets."

Ambler looked at her. "I just don't see a way—"

Laurel gave a half smile. "I do."

The funny thing, Adrian Choi reflected as he sat at Clayton Caston's wonderfully tidy desk, was that his boss managed to create as much work for him when he was away as when he was in the office. Caston's recent telephone calls had been abrupt, hurried, and *cryptic*. Lots of urgent requests, no explanations. It was all very mysterious.

Adrian was loving it.

He was even enjoying his slight hangover this morning—a hangover! An unaccustomed sensation for him. It seemed so very . . . Derek St. John. In those Clive McCarthy page-turners, Derek St. John was always prone to overindulgence. "Too much is never enough" was among his signature lines; another was "Instant gratification tries my patience." In the line of duty, he was regularly obliged to spend long evenings seducing beautiful women, ordering costly champagnes with French names that Adrian couldn't pronounce,

followed by a morning hangover. "It's pronounced 'Sin-jin,'" the su-
perspy would suavely, waggishly, explain to those women who mis-
pronounced his surname. "With the stress falling on *sin*." Derek St.
John even had a special hangover recipe, detailed in Clive Mc-
Carthy's *Operation Atlantis*, but it contained raw eggs, and Adrian
didn't think it was a good idea to eat raw eggs.

Not that Adrian had spent the evening with a long-legged super-
model known to be an associate of a villainous quadriplegic who
lived in a special zero-gravity satellite circling the earth, which is
what had happened in *Operation Atlantis*. Adrian's evening was definitely more earthbound. When he thought about it, actually, he had
a twinge of guilt, which wasn't very Derek St. John at all.

Her name was Caitlin Easton, and she was an administrative assistant at the Joint Facilities Center. On the phone her voice had become giggly and appealing once he had warmed her up. Adrian had
to hide his disappointment when they finally met, at Grenville's
Grill. She was just a little *heavier* than he had imagined, and he noticed the beginnings of a pimple near one corner of her nose. Not
that the place he'd brought her to was any great shakes: Grenville's
Grill was a self-styled "eatery" in Tysons Corner where the staff
slapped down oversize laminated menus, served potato chips in an-
noying little napkin-lined baskets, and put toothpicks in its club
sandwiches; it just happened to be on the way home for both of
them. Still, the more they spoke, the more he saw that she had a lively
sense of humor, and he'd had a pretty decent time. When he told her
his full name, saying, "It's Adrian Choi, with the stress falling on *oy*,"
she laughed, though she couldn't have caught the reference. She
laughed at a lot of things he said, even when they weren't especially
funny, and that gave him a real high. She was *fun*.

So why the *twinge*? Well, he had been using her, hadn't he? He'd
said, "Hey, if you're not doing anything after work, maybe we could
have a drink, grab a bite?" He hadn't said, "You guys have something
my boss needs." So in a way the whole operation was a little under-

cover. And Caitlin Easton wasn't an enemy agent, after all; she was just—well, a file clerk, in plain English.

The phone purred, an inside call. Caitlin?

Yes, it was Caitlin.

He took a deep breath. "Hey you," he said, surprising himself; he sounded more relaxed than he'd felt.

"Hey you," she said.

"That was fun last night."

"Yeah," she said. "Yeah, it was." She lowered her voice. "Hey listen, I think I've got something for you."

"Really?"

"I don't want you to get into any more hot water with your boss is all."

"You're talking about . . . ?"

"Uh-huh."

"Caitlin, I don't know how to thank you."

"You'll think of a way." Caitlin giggled.

Adrian blushed.

Ambler's first glimpse of Jozef Vrabel in the flesh was disheartening: the person he had chosen for a doppelgänger was an unimpressive man, barely five foot five, with a small head, narrow shoulders, and a round, protruding belly over wide hips; he looked like a human top. If Caston was right, though, all that had to match was the face; and the face was—well, close enough for a quick glance by someone who was looking for similarities rather than differences.

"I don't understand," the Slovak businessman, drably garbed in a suit of taupe gabardine, was repeating as Caston led him from the Congress Center. The heavy clouds transformed the street into a grisailles version of itself, a picture done in shades of gray.

"It's crazy, I know," Caston was saying. "But the agency has already negotiated a deal with Slovakia Telecom, and it's our last chance to reconsider. We're almost out of the due diligence period. Otherwise, contractually it takes effect by the end of the day."

"But why were we never contacted about this? This is ridiculously last minute." The Slovak's English was accented but fluent.

"You're surprised that the United States government mishandled an RFP? You're asking how it could possibly *be* that our federal government could mishandle the bidding process?"

The Slovak snorted. "When you put it that way . . ."

Ambler, who had stationed himself across the street, strode swiftly toward him. "Mr. Vrabel? I'm Andy Halverson, with the U.S. General Services Administration. Clay here says we're about to make a pretty costly mistake. I need to know if he's right."

Caston cleared his throat. "The current offering costs out at a twenty percent premium over our existing telephony arrangement. Even with embedded security features, it seems to me that we're not getting the best possible value for the annualized expenditures."

"That's a preposterous deal!" the squat Slovak said. "You should have been talking to *us*."

Caston turned to Ambler with an elaborate I-told-you-so shrug.

Ambler's manner was that of a bureaucrat who was fearful of future reprisals but determined to avert a crisis while it was still possible. "We've got an office filled with people whose job that is," he said steadily. "Guess they never bothered to learn their way around Bratislava. Thing is, we were told Slovakia Telecom had the market to themselves."

"Two years ago, maybe," Caston said, as Vrabel started to splutter with disbelief. "You're about to sign a two-hundred-million-dollar contract, Andy, and your guys are relying on two-year-old market analyses? Glad *I'm* not the one whose job it is to explain that to Congress."

Bit by bit, Ambler noticed, Vrabel began standing a little straighter; the human top was squaring his shoulders. His annoyance at being dragged from the "Two Economies, One Alliance" ses-

sion gave way to a certain pleasure at witnessing the mutual recriminations between two powerful American officials, and the prospect
of a highly lucrative American contract.

The Slovak's face relaxed into a genial smile. "Gentlemen—the
hour is late, but it is not *too* late, I trust. I think we can do business
together."

The two Americans brought him to a small second-floor conference room at the Belvedere, one they had ascertained would be unoccupied until an ASEAN "working group" arrived an hour from
then. Ambler knew that the conference room would be theirs, if only
briefly, so long as they simply looked as if they belonged. Hotel
staffers, puzzled by their appearance, would assume the mistake was
their own, and, given the density of VIPs in residence, their main
priority would be to avoid causing offense.

Laurel, dressed severely in a gray skirt and white blouse, met the
two inside the small conference room and approached Jozef Vrabel
with a black, wand-like device.

Ambler made apologetic noises. "Just a formality. Technically,
when we're having an offsite discussion of what's officially classified
information, we're got to do a scan for listening devices."

Laurel waved the device—a thing fashioned out of two television
remote controls—along the man's extremities, then his torso. When
she approached the badge, she paused and said, "If you'll let me remove that name tag, sir . . . I'm afraid the chip inside creates interference."

Vrabel did so with a complaisant nod, and she stepped behind
him, pretending to scan his back. "All right," she said presently. She
replaced nylon rope around his neck, tucking the card inside his
lapel; since nobody ever looked at his own badge while it was on,
Vrabel would have no occasion to notice that his conference badge
had been replaced by a Triple-A membership card.

"Please, sit," Ambler said, gesturing. "Can we get you some coffee?"

"Tea, please," the Slovak said.

"Tea it is." Then Ambler turned to Caston and said, "You've got the terms of offering?"

"You mean here? We can download the encrypted files, but we'd have to use one of our machines." Caston spoke his lines a little stiffly, but it passed as the awkwardness of embarrassment. "The station boys have the clear-connect."

"Jesus Christ," Ambler said. "At the Schatzalp? You can't expect Mr. Vrabel here to ride the funicular up the mountain to the Schatzalp. That's just too far. He's a busy man. We're all busy. Forget about it. Just forget about it."

"But it's a bad deal," Caston said. "You can't just—"

"Then I'll face the music." He turned to the Slovak. "Sorry to waste your time."

Vrabel broke in with a tone of lordly magnanimity. "Gentlemen, please," he said. "Your country *deserves* the highest consideration, not to be shaken down by a bunch of scheming *zeks*. My own shareholders have interests aligned with yours. Put me in the funicular. In truth, I was rather hoping for a chance to visit the Schatzalp. I'm told it's not to be missed."

"Are you sure you want to take the time?"

"Absolutely," said the Slovak, with a $200 million smile. "*Absolutely.*"

At the main entrance to the Congress Center, the fast-moving queue sluiced between two movable steel fences and a no less formidable human cordon of military policemen, their cheeks pink from the cold, their breath forming sfumato puffs of smoke in the chilled air. Immediately past the entrance, at the left, was a series of efficiently manned coat-check stations. Then came the security area, staffed by half a dozen guards. Ambler took his time removing his coat, patting himself down as if fearful of forgetting something in his coat. He wanted to time his entrance, to be certain there were plenty of people ahead of him and behind him. He now wore a blazer without a tie; the ID badge hung from his neck, near the shirt's third button.

Finally he saw a crowd of men and women pushing through the entrance and he nimbly stepped into line at the security desk.

"Cold outside!" he said to the man seated by the computer monitor with what he told himself was a passable tinge of a Mitteleuropan accent. "But I guess you're used to it!" He pressed his card to the card reader and patted his cheeks, as if they were frozen. The man at the monitor glanced at the screen and at him. A light at the turnstile pulsed green, and Ambler pushed his way through a gate bar.

He was in.

He felt something flutter inside him, something tiny and bird-like, and he realized that it was hope.

Hope. Perhaps the most dangerous of all emotions, and perhaps the most necessary.

CHAPTER THIRTY-TWO

Inside felt like the outside; passing from the Davos gloom into the vast arena of the Congress Center was like walking from a darkened theater into blazing day. Every corner was brightly lit, the walls and floors all warm, glowing shades of cream, tan, ocher. Stenciled on the wall to the left of the first big atrium were various panels of the globe—continents or parts of continents—in shades of brown, criss-crossed with curved lines of latitude and longitude, as if projected from a globe. Ambler strolled farther into the buzzing space, almost preternaturally alert to his surroundings. The ceiling, twenty feet above, was a curving expanse of narrow wooden planks, giving the sense that one was inside an enormous ark. He paused at a seating area where coffee was served on small, round glass-topped tables. Banks of orchids in heavy brown planters were interspersed among them. Raised lettering on an umber wall declared the area to be a WORLD CAFÉ. The wall was decorated with the horizontal names of countries intersected by vertically arrayed capitals, like some sort of acrostic. The capitals were in white, the country names in dark brown, except for the overlapping letter. The *a* in *Poland* provided the *a* in *Warsaw;* the *o* in *Mozambique* was the *o* in *Maputo;* the *I* in *India* held up the stacked letters of *New Delhi*. Ambler wondered about complaints from countries like Peru and Italy.

Still, he could not help but be impressed with the amount of sheer attention that had gone into every incidental detail. The forum's an-nual meeting took place during six days in January, and then all the walls would be repainted, all the sculptures and decorative elements would be warehoused—and yet the décor displayed a level of care and attention that even permanent structures rarely received. Maybe twenty people were at the World Café, mainly seated in clear Plexiglas chairs. There was the handsome, if slightly mannish, woman with a navy skirt-suit, a heavy ring on one finger, and what looked at first like a scarf around her neck; as he approached, he saw that her name card was not white, like the others, but blue, and that the scarf was in fact a Trimline headset in repose. Farther away, he saw a man with a friendly, square, soon-to-be-jowly face, heavy-framed glasses with amber-tinted lenses, a buttoned jacket strained by the convexity of his belly—a German or Austrian, Ambler guessed—speaking with a man whose back was to Ambler, a man with fluffy white hair and a dark blue suit. Investment bankers, a bit too pleased to be here: "guests," rather than "participants," in the ironclad hierarchy of the conference. At another table, a prosperous-looking man with spare, tidily combed salt-and-pepper hair was shuffling papers; his eyes were impassive behind his steel-rimmed glasses. He had the air of someone who knew the rules of the road and never broke them; a man with a lighter suit and graying brown hair was speaking to him with greater animation than was returned, obviously the conversational suitor. A third man with a spread collar and a pink-blue patterned shirt, a polka-dotted tie—a Brit, by nationality or aspiration—was leaning toward the other two, openly listening and reserving the right to contribute. There was unease beneath his beaming bonhomie: that of someone who was neither definitely part of a conversation nor yet definitely excluded from it.

Nobody here was his man.

At the end of a long corridor on the lower level of the Congress Center, Caston pressed his cell phone to his ear, straining to hear Adrian's instructions. From time to time, the auditor glumly broke in with questions of his own.

It wasn't what Adrian had signed up for when he joined the Office of Internal Review, but somehow his dewy assistant did not seem to mind. Indeed, if Caston was not very much mistaken, Adrian seemed to be *enjoying* his turn as *shifu*.

Ambler walked down a broad red-granite stairway to a sort of mezzanine, like the dress circle of an opera house. Along a corridor snaking off behind the stairs was a blue sign that read TV STUDIO; evidently it was reserved for broadcast journalists to conduct interviews with some of the luminaries in attendance. A sign at another alcove advertised BILATERAL ROOMS, presumably reserved for small private discussions. The main flow of traffic on the mezzanine was to the left, toward another gathering spot: an area with wicker chairs and a bar on which were arrayed various small bottles and cans, mainly sodas and fruit juices and beverages that were in-between. A couple of high-mounted television monitors displayed scheduling updates and what looked to be video excerpts from some of the high-profile "briefings." As he got closer, he saw that the beverages came from around the world: Fruksoda, a lemon-lime drink from Sweden; Appletize, a fizzy apple juice from South Africa; Mazaa, a mango-flavored beverage from India; even Titán, a gooseberry-flavored soda from Mexico. It was a model UN of soft drinks, Ambler thought mordantly.

Even more popular was the adjoining computer bay: radial clusters of chairs and intranet-linked computers, decoratively partitioned by thin rectangular tanks of clear liquid through which a slow and steady stream of bubbles rose. Dozens of fingers clicking at dozens of keyboards; visages of boredom, satisfaction, uncertainty, aggression. But nothing to detain him. He peered down from the balcony and saw the much larger space below, a terrarium of power. On a vast brick wall opposite him were enormous African and Polynesian sculptures, which consorted oddly with the array of World Economic Forum flags along the balcony's five-foot inside rim.

Ambler descended the flight of stairs to the babbling crowd beneath him, checked his watch, and pushed through the throngs. A midafternoon crowd of people, between sessions, grabbing canapés that were whisked through on silver trays, or crystal glasses of conference-approved beverages. The air was fragrant with expensive colognes, aftershave, and hair pomades, not to mention the trays of *Bündnerfleisch* on pumpernickel triangles, a regional specialty. Ambler slowed and began to take in his human surroundings.

A youngish, thickset man in an unfashionable but well-tailored suit—its quality evidenced by the fact that his avoirdupois was well concealed at first glance—was surrounded by members of a slightly frumpy entourage; the man's gaze swiveled around him, taking in everyone but those closest to him. Occasionally he murmured something Slavic-sounding to a waistless black-haired woman nearby. He was probably a new head of state from one of the Baltic republics, on the lookout for foreign investment. The man's gaze paused at one point, and Ambler followed the sight line: a young, curvy blonde across the room, clearly the trophy wife of the small, withered plutocrat beside her. Ambler nodded at the Slav, and the man nodded back, half warmly, half warily: it was a look that said, *Are you somebody?* The look of someone who did not trust himself to know. Ambler sensed, too, that the man's entourage was simultaneously a source of comfort and humiliation to him. He was used to being the most important man in the room. Here, at Davos, he was strictly minor-league—and there was some discomfiture to have his entourage witness the evident fact. A couple of yards away from him, an older, rangy American billionaire—someone whose "enterprise software" was an industry standard across the globe—was surrounded by people seeking a word with him, attempting, like whistling, chirping modems, to establish a connection. He was like a massive planet drawing in satellites. By contrast, few seemed interested in catching the Baltic politician's eye. At Davos, the heads of small states were further down the pecking order than the heads of

large multinationals. Globalization, like business-process reengi-
neering, did not "flatten hierarchies," as its boosters proclaimed; it
merely established new ones.

As Ambler continued his way, he noticed the pattern continuing:
Some figures swelled, inflated by the attention they gathered; some
shrank, deflated by the scarcity of it. Yet others seemed jubilant
merely to breathe the same air as the giants among them. Tray after
tray of canapés disappeared into yearning gullets, though Ambler
doubted whether anyone really tasted them. Attention was elsewhere. The "social entrepreneurs"—as the savvier heads of charities
and NGOs now styled themselves, effectively conceding that only the
vocabulary of business had any traction in the new era—chatted energetically with one another and even more energetically with bona
fide entrepreneurs, the sort whose checkbooks could underwrite
their programs.

A handsome young Indian man was speaking animatedly to a
Western businessman with thatchy, shelf-like white eyebrows and
whiskered ears. "We're all about figuring out what's not working
and then fixing it," the young man was saying. "Find out what's stuck
and get it unstuck. You must do a lot of that at Royal Goldfields."

"In a sense," the older man allowed in a rumble.

"You know the saying: Give a man a fish and he'll eat for a day.
Teach a man to fish—"

"And he'll just go into competition with you," the old man—the
head of some mining consortium, obviously—drawled in a voice
buzzy with phlegm.

A brief flash of teeth, white against the Indian's dark brown skin;
Ambler doubted whether the man's interlocutor saw the annoyance
that was so obvious to him. "But the real challenge is to transform
the whole fishing industry. Put it on a rational footing. Make sure it
pays for itself. Speaking metaphorically, of course. We're all about
sustainable solutions. Not the quick fix."

As Ambler zigzagged through the crowd, he picked up snatches of

conversation—"Were you at the attorney general's breakfast thing?";
"You could call us a mezzanine fund, sure, but we'll go in earlier if
we're really confident about the risk metrics"; "I figured out why it's
always easier to understand the francophone African ministers than
their French counterparts: they always speak slowly and clearly, just
the way they were instructed to in grade school"—and glanced at
dozens of faces, many glimpsed partially, crescents glinting through
occluding bodies.

From a cluster nearer the bar he saw a pair of eyes radiating
malevolence, and decided to move in for a closer look. As he got
there, he saw that the man was being badgered by another, someone
in an off-the-rack worsted and a poorly knotted tie. An academic, no
doubt, though probably one at a high-powered institution and with
a high-powered reputation of his own. "With respect, I don't think
you really grasp what's happening here," the academic was saying.
With respect was one of those phrases that signified the opposite of
their literal meaning, rather like *perfectly good*, as when used of milk
that had passed its expiration date. "I mean—with respect—maybe
there's a reason you haven't been in government since the Carter administration, Stu!"

The other man's eyes narrowed; he smiled to suggest amusement
and disguise his profound annoyance. "Nobody's disputing that
China's growth rate has been impressive, but the question is whether
that's sustainable, and what the global consequences are, and
whether we're not seeing the beginnings of a bubble, as far as foreign
investment goes."

"Wake up and smell the jasmine!" the academic retorted. "It's not
a bubble. It's a big tidal wave and sooner than you think it's gonna
wash away your little sand castles." The nasal hectoring tone was his
default way of speaking, Ambler suspected. He probably prided
himself on his candor and, cushioned by tenure, had little idea how
grating others could find him.

Ambler turned around and moved toward an arbitrary point in

the crowd with a spurious but attention-deflecting air of purpose. Suddenly a man stepped in front of his path and looked at him with an expression of bewilderment. He spoke to him rapidly in a language Ambler did not understand. Something Slavic again, but different from the language muttered by the politician.

"I'm sorry?" Ambler placed a finger on his ear, miming incomprehension.

The man—red-faced, burly, and nearly bald—now spoke in laborious English. "I said, I don't know who you are, but you are not who your badge says." He pointed to it. "I know Jozef Vrabel. You're not him."

At the other end of the hall, Clayton Caston was quailing beneath his icy smile. "Undersecretary Whitfield?" he asked.

Undersecretary Ellen Whitfield turned to him. "I'm sorry?" She adjusted her gaze downward in more ways than one as she took in the diminutive auditor.

"My name is Clayton Caston. I'm with the CIA, Office of Internal Review." Whitfield seemed distinctly unimpressed. "I'm really here with an urgent message from the DCI."

Whitfield turned to the African dignitary with whom she had been speaking. "Will you excuse me?" she said apologetically. To Caston, she said, "How's Owen doing?"

"I think we've all been better," Caston replied tightly. "Would you come with me. It's *very* important."

She tilted her head. "Certainly."

The auditor took her swiftly to down a rear hallway to a room by a sign that read BILATERAL ROOM 2.

When Whitfield entered and saw that Ashton Palmer was already seated in one of the room's white leather chairs, she turned to Caston. "What's this about?" she asked evenly.

Caston closed the door and gestured for her to have a seat. "I'll explain."

He took a deep breath before joining them. "Undersecretary Whitfield, Professor Palmer, let me make a long story short—well, not so long, and not so much of a story. From time to time, a specialist in forensic and investigative auditing turns up things he wished he hadn't."

"I'm sorry—did I take an unwarranted home-office deduction?" said the silver-haired scholar with the high, distinguished forehead.

Caston colored slightly. "The intelligence communities in the United States are, as you know, something of a patchwork quilt. One division may be utterly oblivious of an operation authorized by another. So long as legitimate procedures have been followed, the nature of these operations is not my concern. The point about the clandestine services is that their work is—"

"Clandestine." Whitfield nodded primly.

"Exactly. Including, often, to other clandestine services. But imagine that an analysis of open-source data points leads you to uncover an operation that is potentially explosive in its consequences—especially if the operation should come to be exposed." He paused briefly.

"Then I'd think the person who exposed that operation should consider himself to be responsible for those explosive consequences," Whitfield replied smoothly. Her lips were pressed tightly together. "That's logical, isn't it?" She was an elegant woman, but there was something deathly about her, too, Caston thought. Her chestnut hair softened her strong features; her dark blue eyes looked like pools of infinite depth.

"Is this something you've discussed with the DCI?" asked Palmer.

"I wanted to talk to you first," the auditor said.

"That's wise," said Palmer. His eyes were watchful but unintimidated. "That's very wise."

"But you're not getting me," Caston went on. "My point is that if I have been able to connect the dots—align the data points—then so will others."

"Data points?" Palmer blinked.

"They run the gamut, from—I'm speaking hypothetically here, you understand—airplane tickets purchased and trips made to payments routed to foreign officials. They include accounting irregularities to do with the use of PSU resources—and many, many other items, which I'd prefer not to get into."

Palmer and Whitfield looked at each other.

"Mr. Caston," the professor began, "we both appreciate your concern, and your caution. But I fear you've become involved in matters that are rather above your head."

"Top-level command tier decisions," Whitfield put in.

"You continue to miss my concern."

"*Your* concern?" Whitfield's gaze was level, her smile disdainful.

"Which will be shared by the DCI, I have no doubt."

Her smile faded.

"Quite simply, you've been *sloppy*. You've left a trail of digital spoor. What I have been able to find out, others will be able to find out. Such as any investigating domestic or international commission. And I wonder whether you factored that into your equations when you devised this harebrained operation in the first place."

Whitfield bristled. "I don't know what you're talking about, and I very much doubt you do, either. All this indirection is getting tiresome."

"I'm talking about the termination of President Liu Ang. Is that direct enough for you?"

Palmer blanched. "You're not making any sense—"

"Come off it. What I found out is what *any* competent investigation is going to uncover. You complete the operation, and our government is going to get blamed. Sure as shooting."

"Quintilian, the Roman rhetorician, tells us that the unintended pun is a solecism," Palmer said, with a hint of a smirk.

"God*dammit*!" Caston snapped. "You rogue warriors are all the same. You never think ahead. You're so caught up in your scams and gambits and subterfuges that the *blowback* always takes you by surprise. I've respected the interorganizational partitions, kept quiet to give you the benefit of the doubt. Now I see I was mistaken. I'm going to file my report with the DCI immediately."

"Mr. Caston, I'm impressed by the seriousness with which you take your work," Whitfield said, suddenly cordial. "Let me apologize if I've offended you. The operation you're discussing is an Omega-level special-access program. Of course we trust your discretion and your judgment—your reputation quite precedes you. But we need you to trust ours as well."

"You're not helping me to. You talk as if you've been caught smoking in a no-smoking area. Fact is, your 'special-access program' is about as private as a Liz Taylor wedding. And my question to you is: What the hell are you going to do about it? Because I can't help you unless you help me—help me make sense of this goddamn ball of wax."

"Please don't underestimate the level of calculation and planning that has gone into this," the undersecretary said. "And please don't underestimate the benefits to be secured by it."

"Which are?"

She turned to the man seated beside her. "We're talking about history, Mr. Caston," said the silver-haired scholar. "We're talking about history, and the making of it."

"You're a *historian*," Caston growled. "That's the study of the past. What do you know about the future?"

"That's a very good question," Palmer said with a genial if fast-fading grin, "but my studies do tell me this much. The only thing more hazardous than trying to change the course of history is *not* doing so."

"That doesn't add up."

"History, especially these days, is like a race car. Dangerous to drive."

"I'll say."

Palmer smiled again. "But even more dangerous if you don't. We simply choose not to be a passenger in a driverless vehicle."

"Enough with the abstractions. We're talking about a head of state. One revered the world over."

"Men must be judged by their consequences, not their intentions," Palmer said. "And consequences must be assessed by the techniques of historical analysis and projection."

"You're saying you prefer a Chinese despot to a Chinese democrat?" Caston asked, swallowing hard.

"From the viewpoint of the world, there's hardly any question about it. Despotism—the traditions of autocracy, whether monarchical or totalitarian in form—has kept the lid on Pandora's box. Weren't you ever told, as a child, that if everyone in China jumped at the same time, the world would be shaken from its axis? Despotism, as you term it, is what has kept the Chinese nation from jumping. *Despotism* is what has kept the Chinese foot bound."

Caston's heart was racing. "What you two are doing—"

"Please note," Whitfield said brightly, "*we're* not doing anything. Oh no. Do you see us in that hall? We're not even present at the scene of the prospective . . . incident. We're *here*. As plenty of people can vouch for, we're here with *you*, Mr. Caston."

"*Huddled* in conference," Palmer picked up, a small, steely smile playing on his lips. "With a senior officer of the CIA."

"Again, that's something plenty of people can vouch for." The undersecretary flashed a brief, perfect smile. "So if we *were* up to something, the natural inference would be that *you* were up to the same thing."

"Not that we expect anyone to be making such inferences at all," Palmer said. "They'll be making other inferences."

"That's what I'm trying to tell you," Caston started. "The U.S. government is going to be suspected immediately."

"Exactly. We're counting on it," Whitfield said. "I'm sorry, these geopolitical calculations aren't the usual province of an auditor. All we require is your discretion. You're not paid to have opinions about events of this complexity. But all the eventualities have been explored by our finest minds—or perhaps I should say our finest mind." She gave Palmer an admiring glance.

"Wait a minute. If the U.S. is suspected—"

"Suspected, yes, but *only* suspected," Palmer explained to the auditor. "The State Department used to call its two-China policy one of 'constructive ambiguity.' Well, constructive ambiguity is exactly what we're aiming for here. Blame but not absolute knowledge, suspicion without hard evidence. Guesses piled upon guesses—but mortared by suspicion into a very strong wall."

"Like the Great Wall of China?"

Palmer and Whitfield exchanged glances again. "Nicely put, Mr. Caston," said the silver-haired scholar with the high, distinguished forehead. "Another Great Wall of China—yes, that's what we're talking about. It's the best way to confine a tiger. And, as history shows, there's just one way to wall China in."

"Get the Chinese to build the wall themselves," Caston said slowly.

"Why, Mr. Caston," the scholar said, "it seems you're of our party without knowing it. We both understand the ascendancy of logic, don't we? We both appreciate that ordinary intuitions, including moral intuitions, must capitulate before the clean force of *reason*. Not a bad place to start, I'd say."

"You still don't convince me," the auditor said. "Maybe the world is messier and less controllable than you know. You think you're the masters of history. From where I sit, you're a couple of kids playing with matches. And it's a goddamn flammable world out there."

"Trust me, Ashton and I have done a very thorough risk assessment of the whole situation."

"This isn't about *risk*," Caston said levelly. "That's what people like you never understand. It's about *uncertainty*. You think you can assign a probability metric to future events like this. For technical reasons, we do that all the time. But it's bullshit—nothing more than a convention, an accounting conceit. *Risk* suggests measurable probability. *Uncertainty* is when likelihood of future events is simply incalculable. *Uncertainty* is when you don't even know what you don't know. *Uncertainty* is humility in the presence of ignorance. You want to talk about reason? Start with this: You've made a basic conceptual error. You've confused theory and reality, the model with the thing you're modeling. Your theories never left space for the most basic and elemental factor in the course of human events: uncertainty. That's what's going to come back and bite the whole goddamn world in the ass."

"And you state that as a certainty?" Palmer retorted. For the first time, his air of equipoise slipped, but he swiftly regained it. "Or just a risk? Perhaps you forget the Heraclitus principle: the only thing constant is change. To do nothing is to do something, too. You speak of the dangers of acting, as if there were some null-set alternative. But there is none. What if we were to decide to let Liu Ang live? Because, you see, that's an action as well. What would our responsibilities be then? Have you performed the risk assessment of *that* situation? We have. You can't step into the same river twice—nothing ever stays the same. Heraclitus understood that five hundred years before the Common Era, and it remains true in a civilizational order he couldn't have begun to conceive. In the event, I trust our logic is clear enough by now."

Caston snorted. "Your *logic* has more holes than a showerhead. The simple truth is, you're putting the nations on course for open warfare."

"The United States has always performed best when it was on a wartime footing," Palmer said, the voice of disinterested scholarship. "Panics and depressions—these things always happened in times of peace. And the Cold War—in fact, a period of endless small-scale skirmishes—was what secured our global preeminence."

"Americans do dislike the notion of dominating the globe," Undersecretary Whitfield said. "In fact, there is only one thing they like less. And that's the prospect of someone else doing it."

The auditor took a shaky breath. "But the prospect of global war—"

"You act as if any possibility of conflict is to be shunned, and yet, as a historian, I must report a paradox you seem blind to," Palmer cut in. "A nation with a habit of shunning war actually *encourages* war— encourages acts of belligerence that lead to its own defeat. Heraclitus saw that, too. He said, 'War is the father of all, king of all. Some it makes gods, some it makes men, some it makes slaves, some free.'"

"Are you hoping to be made a god, Professor Palmer?" Caston asked witheringly.

"Not at all. But as an American, I don't want to be made a slave. And slavery, in the twenty-first century, is something imposed not by manacles of steel but by economic and political disadvantages that no lock can ever open. The twentieth century was a time of American freedom. Through inaction, you would seem to prefer a new century of American servitude. You can sermonize about the unknowns. I'll *grant* the unknowns. But that doesn't justify passivity in the face of aggression. Why be overtaken by events when you could help *shape* those events?" Palmer's voice was a soothing, professorial baritone. "You see, Mr. Caston, the course of history is too important a thing ever to be left to chance."

Ambler studied the Slovak's face: confusion was steadily, irreversibly hardening into suspicion, like epoxy exposed to the air. He glanced at his badge: Jan Skodova. Who was he? A government official? A business colleague—or rival?

Now Ambler smiled broadly. "You're right about that. We were on a panel together. Switched badges as a joke." A beat. "Guess you had to be there." He thrust a hand out. "Bill Becker, from EDS, in Texas. Now, how do you know my new friend Joe?"

"I am also a businessman from Slovakia Utilities. Where is Jozef, then?" His eyes gleamed like anthracite.

Goddammit—there was no time.

"Hey, you got a card?" Ambler asked, and pretended to fumble for one of his own.

Warily the Eastern European withdrew a card from the inside breast pocket of his suit jacket.

Ambler glanced at it quickly before pocketing it. "Wait a minute—you're the cable guy from Kosice? Joe was telling me about you."

A flicker of uncertainty appeared on Skodova's face; Ambler pressed the advantage. "If you ain't busy, maybe you could come with me. Joe and I were just talking in that little private lounge out back. Had to nip out here to wet my whistle, but I ain't one for crowds. Seems to me you and I just might be able to do business. You know about Electronic Data Systems?"

"Jozef is where?" The question was polite but pointed.

"I'll bring you to him," Ambler said, "but first I promised I'd snag him a bottle of slivovitz." As Jan Skodova followed him, he borrowed a bottle of the plum brandy from a gently protesting bartender and then led the Slovak businessman through a corridor that led to a series of small rooms. Ambler stepped into the first one where the door was ajar, indicating it was unoccupied.

Jan Skodova followed Ambler in, looked around, and said testily, "Please explain."

"He was just here a moment ago," Ambler said, shutting the door behind him. "Musta had to take a piss."

Less than a minute later, he left the room alone. Skodova would be unconscious for at least an hour or two. The operative had propped him in a chair, slumped forward on the table, his shirtfront drenched with the brandy, the remains of the bottle nearby. Anyone who entered the room would draw the obvious conclusion and select another place to meet. It was not perfect, but it would do. It would have to.

Now Ambler swept through the crowd quickly, clockwise and then counterclockwise, alert to anything beyond the usual range of human anxiety, resentment, envy, vanity, and pique. He glanced at his watch. It was now a quarter to five—fifteen minutes before the president's big speech at the conference's plenary session. Already, Ambler saw, people were beginning to file into the Congress Hall, whose doors were along the wall opposite the stairway. At a doorway to the rear of the hall, cameramen—dressed far more casually than the conference participants—began entering with their outsized equipment. His heart began to race. He caught a glimpse of a woman in a simple button-down shirt and jeans, her auburn hair tousled, and again he felt that tiny, fluttering bird within his breast. *Hope.*

This time, it almost took wing.

It was Laurel. She had done exactly what she said she would do, had arrived on schedule and secured the equipment. *You'll need me,* she had said. Christ, that was an understatement. He needed her in so many ways.

Moments later, the two of them had ducked into the still-deserted balcony above the seating area.

"The camera crews are going to be arriving in just a couple of minutes—lose the jacket, lose the tie, and you'll blend right in." They were the first words she spoke to him; her eyes, alive with love and devotion, spoke to him of things no words could convey.

He quickly stuffed his blazer and tie into one of the equipment boxes that were lying around. Now Laurel reached over and mussed his hair; the grooming appropriate for a Forum participant was not appropriate for a cameraman.

"Looking good," she finally said. "Any leads yet?"

"Not yet," Ambler said, feeling an upwelling of despair that he quickly tried to purge, both from his voice and from his heart. "Where's Caston?"

"He's probably off talking to his assistant—he's been on the phone with him a lot."

Ambler nodded but said nothing; the simple act of speaking was now an effort. In the next small sliver of time, he would succeed or he would fail. It was as simple as that.

"We've got two cameras here. Got you one with a 48X optical zoom." She handed him the bulky camera, which was secured to a folding tripod. Both were a sort of drab green.

"Thanks," he said. He meant, *I love you more than life itself.*

"Think he'll be seated in front?"

"Could be," Ambler said hoarsely. He cleared his throat. "Could be seated further back, too. Too many possibilities."

"Well, you're here. Just do what you do." Bravely she was maintaining a bluff, almost jovial tone. Yet Ambler could tell that, like him, she was terrified.

The effects of stress could be paradoxical and unpredictable, like fueling an engine. Sometimes it provided a surge of power. Sometimes a flooded engine would stall. So much depended on the next several minutes. *Just do what you do,* she had said. What if he didn't? What if he *couldn't*?

Liu Ang was the beloved leader of the world's most populous nation. He was not just the hope of his people—he was the hope of the world. With the squeeze of a trigger, that hope would be extinguished. China would be derailed from the carefully laid tracks of peaceful evolution and pushed onto a collision course—and the results would surely be nothing short of cataclysmic. An outraged, seething population of billions would clamor for revenge. A blind fury, multiplied by sheer mass, could pose a peril greater than any the planet had ever confronted.

In the artificial "courtyard" adjacent to them, the great and the good—and the not very good at all—chewed on canapés, checked their costly watches, and, wafting the fragrance of power, began to fill the Congress Hall. They were excited, of course, though many of them were too grand to let on. Liu Ang was arguably the most important statesman on the planet and quite possibly the most effective. Visionaries were plentiful, but Liu Ang had so far shown the ability to translate vision into reality. These thoughts raised dust storms within Ambler's head; he had to banish them—had to banish thinking itself—if he was to see clearly.

The stakes had never been higher. They could scarcely *be* higher.

The hall itself was larger than it seemed at first. Simply arranging the chairs—each chair was separate, its chrome frame in contact with its neighbors but not physically connected to them—must have taken hours. At each seat was a plastic-wrapped RF headset, which would receive and transmit a simultaneous translation in one of ten languages, depending on the channel selected.

As the crowd drifted into the hall, Ambler decided to make a first pass through the floor without the camera's zoom lens; he'd be relying on what his naked eyes could take in but would enjoy greater mobility. His eyes swept toward the front of the hall. Two immense blue panels on either side of the stage bore the familiar World Economic Forum logo. At the rear of the stage was a backdrop like a checkerboard, with tiers of smaller blue rectangles, emblazoned with the same white logo, the effect like that of a Chuck Close portrait. A large screen hung two-thirds of the way down the central section of the stage; the video feed from the official WEF camera would be projected upon it, for those who were seated in the rear of the plenary hall and could not see the figure at the lectern.

Ambler checked his watch again and then looked around him; the seats were nearly all filled now—it was astonishing how quickly it had happened—and the Chinese leader would be making his appearance in a matter of minutes.

Ambler paced across the front row, as if looking for a vacant seat. His eyes darted from face to face, and he detected . . . only the banal sentiments of the self-important. A pudgy man with a narrow stenographer's notebook exuded the sort of anxiety appropriate to a journalist with an impending deadline; a lean man in a loud Glenurquhart plaid gave off the buzzy exhilaration of a self-made hedge-fund manager who was about to see a great man in the flesh. Another audience member—a woman Ambler vaguely recognized from pictures, a CEO of a tech company, blond and perfectly coiffed—looked distracted, as if rehearsing talking points for an up-coming interview. A silver-haired man with wire-rim bifocals, a forehead speckled with liver spots, and eyebrows you could pull a brush through was scrutinizing the small page of instructions that accompanied the headset and looking faintly dispirited, as if he had recently got word of a fall in stock prices. Ambler walked slowly along the rightmost aisle, carefully looking at a photographer carry-ing an outsized SLR camera equipped with an enormous lens. The man looked affable and simple, pleased, perhaps, with the position he had staked out by the wall and ready to defend it against any rival who staked a claim to it. At his feet was a hard-sided photographer's case, on which countless travel stickers had been attached and care-lessly ripped off.

Ambler's eyes swept down the rows. There were so many people—Christ, there were *too* many people. Why did he think he could . . . He reeled himself in, shut down that line of thought. Thinking was the enemy. He cleared his mind again, tried to achieve a state of pure receptivity, drifting through the hall like an invisible cloud. Like a shadow, seeing all, seen by none.

A kaleidoscope of human emotion lay before him. The man with the fixed grin who—Ambler would have sworn to it—was desperate to go to the bathroom and equally desperate not to lose his seat. The woman who was trying to make conversation with the stranger next to her, a man who had sized her up and dismissed her in a single numbing look, leaving her fearful that she had been insulted, hopeful that it was a simple linguistic misunderstanding. A flush-cheeked jowly man with a comb-over who seemed disgruntled that he had not had time to down a proper highball. The know-it-all who, teetering past the edge of his knowledge, was discoursing about contemporary Chinese politics to his companions—employees?—who politely disguised their resentment.

There were hundreds just like them, all with their peculiar patterns of fascination, boredom, peevishness, and anticipation—daubs from the palette of ordinary human emotion. None of them was the person Ambler was looking for. He knew the type. He couldn't analyze it; he just recognized it when he saw it or, really, *felt* it, like the wave of cold you feel when opening a freezer on a warm day. It was the glacial deliberateness of the professional killer, the man who was too alert to his surroundings, the man whose anticipation was not simply of what he would witness but of what he would do. Ambler could feel it, always could.

But now—when it mattered most—nothing. *Nothing.* Panic swelled inside his chest, and, again, he pushed it down. He race-walked to the rear of the long hall and mounted the narrow terrazzo stairs to the balcony. In the center, he saw a battery of three stationary cameras and half a dozen irregulars, from media companies across the world. The balcony would be an ideal site for a gunman; it would take relatively little skill to hit the target from such an elevated perch. Ambler met Laurel's eyes—a parched man taking a quick sip from a desert oasis—and then glanced at the others, his eyes seeking out each strange visage. *Nothing.* No twitch on the dowsing rod, no click on the Geiger counter—nothing.

The camera eye could prove his salvation. Wordlessly, he came over to Laurel and took the camera she had prepared for him, the one with the 48X zoom lens. For purposes of show, she had stationed herself at an older twin-lens camera, even more dinged and dented than his. Struggling for calm, he angled the camera head downward

with the knobbed level and took in the members of the audience below; the nature of the sight lines meant that an assassin in the audience would have to position himself in the front half of the seating
section. This still left five hundred candidates. How had he ever
imagined he would have a chance? He felt as if a band were tightening around his chest, as if he were breathing against resistance. To
think of the odds—but *no*, such things were best left to the likes of
Clayton Caston. Ambler breathed a different atmosphere. He had to
banish self-consciousness, banish rationality.

He could not fail.

If he had been faltering, at least the camera was working just as
they had hoped. Its automatic focus provided almost immediate
clarity of field. *Don't think. See.* The faces were sometimes in silhou-
ette, often at odd angles, but the camera electronics were sophisticated enough to compensate swiftly for variations in light level, and
the level of detail was astonishing. He studied face after face in the
viewfinder, waiting for the prickling that would tell him to pause, to
look again.

Laurel, standing close behind him, murmured something encouraging at him. "It'll come, my dear," she said softly.

He could feel the warmth of her breath against his neck, and it was
the only thing that kept the black miasma of despair from engulfing
him. In a world of falsity and pretense, she was the one true thing,
his polestar, his lodestone.

It was his belief in himself that was unsustainable. He had peered
at row after row, and he could only conclude that his instincts, at last,
had failed him. Would someone dart in from the entrance doors at
the last moment? Was there a face he had somehow not seen?

Presently a rustle went through the crowd, and he heard the sound
of the side doors shutting, locked now to outsiders. The guards
would not open them again until after the speech was concluded.

Briskly the founder and director of the World Economic Forum, a tall, nearly bald man with steel-rimmed glasses, strode across the stage to make a few introductory remarks. He wore a dark blue suit and a blue and white tie, the colors of his organization.

Ambler turned around and glanced behind him, where Laurel was standing, tousle haired and beautiful and alert, peering through the eyecup of her own bulky, long-lensed television camera; and he tried to conceal the abyss that he felt in his own soul.

He knew she was not fooled. She mouthed the words *I love you,* and it was as if a glimmer of light appeared in a long, dark tunnel.

He could not give up. He must not give up.

The killer was *here,* ready to derail human history with a single squeeze of the trigger.

It was up to Ambler to find him, and the Ambler who could do so was the Ambler who was Tarquin.

He was Tarquin now.

He squinted once more at the viewfinder. Sound disappeared for him, save only for the slow thudding of his own heart.

The sound of seconds ticking past.

Adrian Choi shuffled through the dossiers that Caitlin had given him. Those personnel records from the psychiatric facility that Caston had been so intent on getting his hands on. Personnel records, for crying out loud—a bunch of goddamn résumés, for the most part. It should not have been so hard to get hold of them.

But it had been. That was why he'd figured he might as well go through them with a goddamn magnifying glass.

Boring as shit, most of them. A whole lot of technical schools and community colleges and military tours—for the orderlies, anyway. Psychiatrists with degrees from Case Western Reserve or the University of Miami medical school, nurses with diplomas from the Naval School of Health Sciences and other places with similar names, guards with backgrounds in the 6th MP Group, or the 202nd, whatever the hell that meant, with the initials *CID* in parentheses. Like that.

Except there was one—what would Caston call it?—*anomaly*.

Yes, it was definitely an anomaly.

Someone was knocking on his door, loudly. Adrian sat up with a jerk. Nobody knocked that loudly on Clayton Caston's door, for Chrisssakes.

Operating on some dim intuition, Adrian decided not to answer it. A few moments later, he heard departing footsteps. *That's right—nobody here but us chickens.* Maybe it was some jackass who thought it was the storage room with the printer cartridges. Or maybe it was something else. Adrian didn't feel like dealing with it, either way.

He started dialing Caston's cell phone; it was one of those international kinds, which rang wherever the user was in the world, and it would be their fourth conversation within the hour.

Caston answered immediately. Adrian briefly gave him the update. Caston had him repeat certain details, not testily but with an air of urgency.

"And when you cross-check," Adrian said, "the Social Security numbers don't match." Adrian listened to Caston's reply; he had never heard him sound so breathless.

"That's what I thought," Adrian put in. "Anomalous, huh?"

A study in expensively attired gravitas, the director of the World Economic Forum concluded his slightly grandiloquent remarks, received a warm hand of applause, and took a seat to the right of the stage. Then the applause began to grow as Liu Ang himself walked onstage, with a gentle, loping gait, and took his own place before the lectern.

He was—well, physically smaller than Ambler had expected, somehow. Yet there was something large about him as well: his mien

conveyed an almost bigger-than-life serenity, a sense of great patience, even wisdom, a gentleness that knew itself to be stronger than
brutality. He thanked the director of the World Economic Forum in
a lilting, melodic English and then began to speak in Chinese. He
was addressing the world—but his own countrymen were a large
part of the world, too, and when his speech was broadcast to them he
wanted them to know he had spoken his native tongue with pride
and eloquence. He wanted them to know he was no returning sea
turtle—no *hai gui*—but a citizen of China as authentic as any of
them. Ambler could understand nothing of what the man said but a
great deal from the way he said it. So often, the propositional content
of language was mere distraction from the subtleties of tone and intonation. Simple emotions were coated by a lacquer of complex
ideas.

Liu Ang was wry and funny—the headset-equipped audience guf-
fawed at just the moment Ambler would have guessed—and then
was somber and impassioned. He understood a truth that he wanted
others to understand as well. He was not *selling* them; he was telling
them. It was not the usual politician's voice. It was the voice of a genuine statesman, the voice of somebody who envisaged a future of
peace and prosperity and wanted to invite the rest of the world to
join that future. A man who saw that cooperation could be as powerful, and powerfully productive, as competition. A man who was
helping to bring tolerance and enlightenment not only to the Middle
Kingdom but to the world at large.

A man who was slated for death at any moment.

Somewhere in the hall, the assassin was biding his time, and Ambler's instincts, his peculiar gift, had failed him, failed him utterly.
Again, Ambler scanned the rows beneath him, gazing so intently into
the viewfinder that his vision began to blur, his neck to stiffen. Now,
abruptly, almost involuntarily, he looked up and craned his head
around him, his gaze taking in the camera operators and coming to
rest on Laurel's face.

She had been peering through her camera at the man at the lectern, clearly as mesmerized by the statesman as he had been, and it was a moment before she realized Ambler was watching her. Something rippled through her face and then she turned to him with an expression of shaky resolve, an expression that was also brimming with love and loyalty and devotion. Ambler blinked hard. He felt as if there were a sty in his eye. No, not a sty but—*what had he just seen?*

The temperature of the room plummeted, it seemed to him; he felt as if he had been whipped by an Arctic blast.

Yet it was *madness*—he could not have seen what he thought he had seen.

He replayed it in his mind. Laurel, his beloved Laurel, studying the scene through the camera calmly—no, *stonily,* could it be?—and then the look on her face, a moment before it was wreathed in a loving smile. Again, he replayed that fraction of a second in his mind, and he saw another expression on her face, as fleeting as a firefly's glow, and as unmistakable.

It was an expression of pure and crystalline contempt.

CHAPTER THIRTY-THREE

Ambler stole another look at Laurel and saw her right finger on what looked like a brace beneath the camera lens—in fact, he now realized, a trigger. A lightning bolt of comprehension struck him with devastating force.

How could he have been so blind?

All along, there had been a missing piece to the puzzle, hadn't there? Caston's voice: *There's always got to be a fall guy*. A scheme of this sort always demanded one. The realization staggered Ambler like a body blow. He was not meant to prevent the assassination.

He was meant to take the blame for it.

The cameras—Laurel's idea. Her "inspiration." The old models were steel-clad contraptions, and dozens of them went through the X-ray detectors every day. But the rays could not penetrate the metal. Laurel's camera didn't conceal a weapon; it *was* a weapon.

It *couldn't* be—yet it *was*. His mind lurched and reeled.

The twin-lens model was a ruse: protruding from the top hole was the bore end of a rifle. As a piece of engineering it was elementary: the long camera body and two-foot zoom served as a barrel; the functioning lens could double as the sights. And the trigger, of course, was exactly . . . where her finger was now.

Indeed, she was fingering the trigger with the assurance of experience. It had to have been she who had killed Benoit Deschesnes, in the Luxembourg Gardens: the Chinese marksman must have seen her do it, had seen through her deadly ruse and recognized the true threat to his people.

How slow Ambler had been to see what was before his very eyes!

Yet now, with dizzying immediacy, he saw what would ensue. The shots would come from almost the precise area where Ambler was standing. Security would tackle him: his adversaries would have found that part easy to arrange. Circumstantial evidence would suggest that he was an American—but it would be impossible to prove. Nothing would connect him with any identity.

Because his identity had been erased.

Suspicion without proof would be the most explosive thing of all. Beijing had broken out in riots when the United States accidentally bombed a Chinese embassy in Belgrade, as Ashton Palmer had noted. The loss of the beloved Liu Ang to a suspected U.S. agent would produce an instant conflagration. And the United States could not apologize, could not acknowledge what the rest of the world would suspect: because Harrison Ambler did not exist.

> *As I was going up the stair*
> *I met a man who wasn't there.*
> *He wasn't there again today.*
> *I wish, I wish he'd stay away.*

Riots—on a scale without precedent—would overrun the People's Republic; the PLA would be forced to step in. But the sleeping giant would not return to its slumbers: not before wreaking havoc on a sleeping world.

The thoughts filled his mind like a deepening shadow, yet all the while he and Laurel maintained eye contact. *I know that you know that I know that you know . . .* the childish regress came to mind now, too.

Time slowed to syrup.

Yes, security had no doubt already been primed to look for him; his enemies were more than capable of that.

He had been wrong about so much but right about some things as well. Liu Ang would die; fire would sweep a nation; the PLA would step in, cracking down, imposing the yoke of an old-style Maoist regime. But the sequence of events would not come to a halt there: fanaticism had blinded the conspirators to the true consequences of their machinations. Once the clamor mounted and the outrage spread, the world would be plunged into war. Events of this sort could never be contained. The puppet masters never understand that. They played with fire and were consumed by it, too, in the end.

What Ambler felt was anguish and rage and regret, twined together like strands of a steel cable.

All of it—starting with his "escape," and everything that followed—was according to plan. Their plan. Like a child in possession of a treasure map, he had been following the course laid out for him. A course that led to Davos, and to death.

For a moment, shock rendered him insensate, made him feel like a thing of wood and cloth—and why not?

He had been nothing more than a puppet.

On a small closed-circuit monitor in the bilateral room, the Chinese leader was shown speaking, captioned with an English translation. Neither Palmer nor Whitfield paid more than casual attention. It was as if, having rehearsed the event thoroughly in their heads, they found its realization was of only secondary interest.

Caston flipped his cell phone shut. "Sorry. I need to pop out for a sec." He stood up, shakily, and started for the door. It was locked—from the inside. *Impossible!*

Now Ellen Whitfield flipped off her own cell phone. "I'm sorry," she said. "Given the *delicacy* of our conversation, I just thought it would be best if we weren't disturbed. You'd been worrying about our precautions. As I've been explaining, they're far more extensive than you seem to have realized."

"I see." Caston felt winded.

Her mouth formed a small moue. "Mr. Caston, you *worry* too

much. What we've arranged is a tidy little bank shot, strategically speaking. Liu Ang is assassinated. The U.S. government, inevitably, is suspected. And yet plausible deniability is maintained."

"Because, after all, the assassin doesn't exist." Palmer's expression remained self-amused.

"You're talking about . . . Tarquin." Caston watched them carefully as he said the name. "You're talking about . . . Harrison Ambler."

"Harrison *who*?" Whitfield asked lightly.

The auditor stared straight ahead. "You *programmed* him."

"Someone had to." There was no trace of self-doubt in Whitfield's dark blue eyes. "Let's give the man his due, though. He's done a magnificent job. We'd set a difficult course for him. Few could have navigated it. Though we *did* think it prudent to give him a heads-up about the Cons Ops sanction. I'd asked our principal to commission Tarquin to take out one Harrison Ambler. I'm almost sorry I wasn't around for that conversation. But that's a detail."

"How did you set Ambler up, then?" Caston asked, his voice neutral.

"That's the beauty part," Ashton Palmer said sagely. "So to speak. '*Und es neigen die Weisen / Oft am Ende zu Schönem sich*,' as Hölderlin once wrote. 'And in the end, the wise often succumb to the beautiful.'"

Caston tilted his head. "I've seen the payment records," he bluffed, "but they don't tell me how you found her. Laurel Holland."

Whitfield's countenance remained sunny. "Yes, that's how Tarquin knows her. And she really played her part to perfection. She's a true prodigy, Lorna Sanderson is. I suppose you could say it was really a matter of matching one extraordinary talent with another, reciprocal one. As you probably know, there isn't a person in ten thousand who could fool a man like Harrison Ambler."

Caston's eyes narrowed. "But Lorna Sanderson is one in a million."

"You got it. A hugely talented actress. Won the top drama prizes in college. She was the star protégée of a disciple of Stanislavsky, who said he'd never seen such raw talent."

"Stanislavsky?"

"Legendary acting coach—devised the concept of the Method. Method actors train themselves to experience the very emotions they're projecting. That way they're not, in a sense, really acting. Quite a skill, if you can master it. And she did. She was extremely well trained, extremely promising. Right after she left Julliard, she played the lead in an off-Broadway production of *Hedda Gabler*, got raves for her performance. Truth is, if she'd caught the right breaks, she could have been another Meryl Streep."

"So what happened?" And what was happening outside the door? As sturdy as it was, Caston was seated close enough to it that he could detect the vibrations from some sort of—well, scuffle.

"Unfortunately for her, she had a problem. Lorna was a junkie. Speed, then heroin. Then she started to deal, mainly to be sure of having a steady supply for her own use. When she was arrested, well, her life was effectively over. New York has those Rockefeller drug laws, of course. Sell two ounces of heroin, and it's a Class A felony, a sentence of fifteen to life. And fifteen's the *minimum*. That's where we stepped in. Because a talent like that doesn't come along every day. Through a PSU liaison officer, we had a federal prosecutor broker a deal with the local DA's office. After that, we owned her. She was a special project of ours—and she proved an awfully apt pupil. Really grasped the vision."

"And so everything has unfolded according to plan," Caston said heavily; his eyes darted from one to the other. Two infuriatingly smug faces, one shared vision. *Madness!* What frightened him most, he realized, was how unfrightened they were.

Abruptly the door burst open. A burly, barrel-chested man loomed in the door frame; others were crowded immediately behind him.

Caston turned and looked at the man. "Don't you ever knock?"

"Evening, Clay." His hands on his hips, the ADDI stared at Whitfield and Palmer with recognition but without surprise. "Wondering how I figured out what you were up to?" he asked the auditor.

"What I'm actually wondering, Cal," said Caston mirthlessly, "is what side you're on."

Norris nodded gravely. "I guess you're about to find out."

Time and space, the *here* and *now,* all seemed transformed to Ambler. The Congress Hall felt as airless and as cold as outer space, and time ticked by in slow, thudding seconds, keeping rhythm with his own pumping heart.

Harrison Ambler. How hard he had worked to reclaim that name—a name that would soon be nothing other than a byword for infamy. He felt sickened, battered by nausea and self-disgust, and still he would not stand down.

She must have seen that in him, for while eye contact between them remained unbroken, he detected—saw or sensed—the faintest movement, some muscle contraction preparatory to the squeezing of a trigger, or perhaps he simply *knew* it without seeing or sensing at all, because for just that split second he was she and she was he, the two sharing an instant of transparency that was an instant of identity, a connection no longer of love but of loathing, and—

Ambler *threw* himself at her even before he realized what he had done, threw himself at her at the very moment she squeezed the trigger.

The weapon's loud report pulled him back into himself. An explosion overhead a microsecond later—a popping noise, the shattering of brilliant, tiny fragments of glass, a faint but perceptible diminishment of illumination—told him that the bullet had gone awry, had struck one of the tank lamps racked at the ceiling. Even as that thought sunk in, he felt a searing pain at his midriff, felt the pain even before he registered the flashing motion of her hand, the shiny steel of the blade it held. Some part of his mind reeled, baffled—*it made no sense*. It took another split second before he realized that she was stabbing him now for a *second* time, that she had slashed at him first unseen, was slashing at him—yes, slashing and *plunging*, again and again, *penetrating* him in a spasmodic frenzy.

Blood poured from him, like wine from an overfilled goblet, and none of it mattered, for he had to stop her or he would lose everything—his name, his soul, his being. With all his remaining strength, he *lunged* at her, even as the long blade plunged once more into his entrails. His hands formed grappling hooks that wrested her arms up and to her sides, pinning them to the floor. The screams and shrieks around him sounded as if they were coming from miles away. He was conscious of nothing other than her, the woman he had loved—the killer he had never known at all—thrashing and struggling beneath him, a grotesque parody of lovemaking that was fueled by the opposite of love. Her face, inches from his, showed nothing other than fury and the pure vicious determination of a jungle predator. The loss of blood began to cloud his mind, even as he relied on his own body weight to supplement his ebbing strength and prevent her escape.

A distant voice, emerging from the hiss of white noise like an AM radio station bounced by sunspots from another continent. *Recall the man, of ancient times, who set up shop in a village selling both a spear he said would penetrate anything and a shield he claimed nothing could penetrate.*

The spear. The shield.

A man who saw through everybody. A woman whom nobody could see through.

The spear. The shield.

Fragments of time past flashed through his head, dimly, as through a malfunctioning slide projector. In Parrish Island, the quietly murmured words of encouragement: it was she who had planted the notion of his escaping in the first place, even the exact date—he realized that now. It was Laurel who, at every juncture, had kept him both off balance and on track. Tarquin, the *Menschenkenner,* had met his match. It was Laurel all along.

The realization pierced and transfixed him, opened a wound more painful than those she had inflicted with her blade.

He closed his eyes briefly and then opened them, and the opening of them felt as arduous as any physical task he had ever done.

He peered into her eyes, searching out the woman he had thought he knew. Before he lost consciousness, he saw only blackness and defeat and a snarling antagonism, and, then, in that blackness—faintly, flickeringly reflected—he saw himself.

EPILOGUE

Harrison Ambler closed his eyes and felt the gentle glow of the March sun. Lying on the deck-top chaise lounge, he could hear sounds. Soothing ones. The water lapping gently against the hull of the fishing boat. The sound of a spinning reel, as a fishing line was cast. Other sounds, too.

He finally knew what it felt like to be a family man, and contentment welled up within him. On the other side of the boat, the son and daughter, bickering playfully as they baited a fishing hook. The mother, reading the newspaper, casting a rod of her own, and intervening with a wry, loving look when the kids got too rambunctious.

He yawned, felt a slight twinge of pain, and adjusted his loose-fitting T-shirt. Bandages still ridged his midriff, but after two operations he was healing up; he could feel it, could feel his strength starting to return. The sun glittered off the lake, a small one in the Shenandoah Valley region, and though it was not yet spring, the weather was balmy, in the mid-fifties. He decided that he would probably never return to the Sourlands, but he still loved boats, and lakes, and fishing, and he was glad to be with others with whom he could share his expertise. The scene was not as tranquil as it looked, to be sure: not with the demons that still chased themselves inside him. Not with two rambunctious teenagers and their tart-tongued, attractive mother. But somehow it was better this way. More real.

"Hey, daddy-o," the boy said. At seventeen, he was already broad shouldered and deep chested. "Got you a ginger ale from the cooler. It's still cold." He handed Ambler the can.

Ambler opened his eyes and smiled at him. "Thanks," he said.

"You sure you don't want a beer?" asked the woman—not young but elegant and very funny. "There's a Guinness somewhere. Breakfast of Champions."

"Nah," Ambler said. "Got to start slow."

Yes, it felt good being a family man. He could get used to this.

Not that it was *his* family, exactly.

As a gentle, barely detectable ripple moved the boat ever so slightly, Clayton Caston clambered up from below deck, sweating and green at the gills. He leveled a baleful, reproachful gaze at Ambler and dry-swallowed another Dramamine.

Linda, anyway, knew a thing or two about fishing, and the kids were an easy sell. Getting Clay to come along was more of a struggle. Clay was right to have been skeptical of the promised tranquillity, though only a high-grade hypochondriac like him could have convinced himself that he was suffering from seasickness on the nearly motionless lake.

"How I ever allowed myself to be talked into coming aboard this vomit-inducing vessel . . ." Caston began.

"I envy you, Clay," Ambler said simply.

"Do you realize that the actuarial odds of drowning in a domestic body of freshwater are actually greater than the odds of drowning while at sea?"

"Aw, come on. Fishing is one of the great American leisure time activities. Like I told you, it's the most fun you can have without a spreadsheet. Just give it a chance. You might even turn out to be good at it."

"I know what I'm good at," Caston groused.

"You're full of surprises—bet you even surprise yourself sometimes. Who knew you were such an ace with the AV equipment?"

"I told you," Caston said. "My assistant walked me through all that stuff. All I know about coaxial cables otherwise is their purchase price per meter and the recommended amortization table." But from the self-satisfied look on Caston's face, Ambler could tell he was remembering what happened after Whitfield and Palmer discovered that the bilateral room had discreetly been turned into a closed-circuit TV studio and that their entire conversation had been fed to the Congress Center's media center. Both the scholar and the political official were mesmerizing in their sheer fanaticism—hundreds of Davos participants could agree about that as they watched their faces on the video monitors that were mounted throughout the conference center.

It took Palmer and his protégée little time to realize the implications—not merely for their own futures but for their plan. Like many a dark venture, the one thing it could not survive was exposure to light.

As Caston recounted to Ambler during one of a number of hospital visits, Caleb Norris was the one who directed the Swiss military policemen to the bilateral room and made sure that the conspirators were taken into joint-service custody. He had been alerted, as it turned out, by an emergency message that a Chinese spymaster named Chao Tang had arranged to have delivered to him personally. It was an unusual step, to say the least, but top-level spy officials often made a study of their opposite numbers. The two men had never met, but each had a distinct sense of the other. In a situation of extremity, Chao decided to enlist the personal assistance of an American. Then, too, the fact that the Chinese spymaster was reported dead soon thereafter served as powerful authentication. As a heavily sedated Ambler had drifted in and out of consciousness during the first weeks he spent in the hospital, Caston had to tell him what happened several times before he understood it wasn't just a dream, an artifact of the narcotics.

Later, when he was mentally alert, if still physically debilitated, other visitors arrived, some visits organized by Caston, some not. A fellow from State named Ethan Zackheim dropped by twice, with lots of questions. There were a couple of visits from Caston's assistant—who thought Ambler was *super* and kept making comparisons to Derek somebody or other. There was even a visit from Dylan Sutcliffe—the *real* Dylan Sutcliffe, although, given the fifty pounds he'd put on since Carlyle College, it took Ambler a moment to recognize him—and as they paged through the college yearbook, he had lots of fun stories about college hijinks, most of which Ambler remembered just a little differently. Caston himself had spent a fair amount of time figuring out the methods by which calls had been rerouted and the aberrations in service billings that resulted.

"Well," Ambler said after a while, shifting slightly on the deck-top chaise lounge, "your broadcast career might have been brief, but it was mighty effective. Sunshine is the best disinfectant, right?"

Caston suddenly blinked. "Did the kids put on sunblock?" he asked his wife.

"It's *March,* Clay," Linda replied, amused. "March. Nobody's exactly sunbathing here."

A delighted squeal and a shout from the other end of the fishing boat: "I caught it. *I* caught—it's *mine.*" Andrea's voice: prideful and emphatic.

"Yours?" Max's voice, a teenager's not-quite-convincing baritone. "*Yours?* Excuse me, but who cast the line in the first place? Who baited the hook? I just asked you to hold on to the goddamn rod while I got some—"

"*Language,*" Linda interjected warningly. She went over to the squabbling pair.

"Language? What, *English*?" Max balked.

"Anyway, that fish is too small," their mother went on. "You kids better throw it back."

"You heard what Mom said," Andrea said gleefully. "Throw your teensy-weensy fish back in the water."

"Oh, so it's *my* fish now?" Max's voice broke in a squawk of indignation.

Ambler turned to Clay Caston. "They always like this?"

"Afraid so," Caston said happily.

Caston sneaked a glance at his wife and kids across the deck, and Ambler could see the pride and devotion that pulsed through him, his lifeblood. But the auditor was not distracted for long. A few minutes later, when another gentle ripple moved through the craft, he plopped himself down on the canvas chair next to Ambler, readying himself for a serious entreaty.

"Listen, can we just turn the boat around and get back onshore?" Caston was almost pleading.

"Why would we want to do that? It's a beautiful day, the water's lovely, we've rented this incredible boat—how could we be doing better?"

"Yeah, but this was supposed to be a *fishing* trip, right? See, I think you'll find that all the fish are lurking around the dock. In fact, I'm *sure.*"

"Come on, Clay," Ambler said. "That doesn't stand to reason." He arched an eyebrow. "The most probable distribution of fish this time of the year—"

"Trust me," Caston implored, cutting him off. "The dock's the place to be. I've got a *good feeling* about this."

700043524757

LABYRINTHS

Also by Catrine Clay

Trautmann's Journey:
From Hitler Youth to FA Cup Legend

King, Kaiser, Tsar:
Three Royal Cousins Who Led the World to War

Princess to Queen

Master Race:
The Lebensborn Experiment in Nazi Germany

LABYRINTHS

Emma Jung, Her Marriage to Carl
and the Early Years of Psychoanalysis

CATRINE CLAY

WILLIAM
COLLINS

William Collins
An imprint of HarperCollins*Publishers*
1 London Bridge Street
London SE1 9GF
www.WilliamCollinsBooks.com

First published in Great Britain by William Collins in 2016

1 3 5 7 9 8 6 4 2

A catalogue record for this book is
available from the British Library.

ISBN 978-0-00-751066-5

Printed and bound in Great Britain by
Clays Ltd, St Ives plc

MIX
Paper from
responsible sources
FSC® C007454

FSC™ is a non-profit international organisation established to promote
the responsible management of the world's forests. Products carrying the
FSC label are independently certified to assure consumers that they come
from forests that are managed to meet the social, economic and
ecological needs of present and future generations,
and other controlled sources.

Find out more about HarperCollins and the environment at
www.harpercollins.co.uk/green

For Gaby

Mini liebe Cousine und Helferin

Contents

'Their [marriage] partners can easily lose themselves in such a labyrinthine nature, sometimes in a not very agreeable way, since their sole occupation then consists in tracking the other through all the twists and turns of his character.'

Carl Jung

1

A Visit to Vienna

On Saturday 2 March 1907 Carl and Emma Jung arrived in Vienna for a five-day visit. They stayed at the Grand, the city's most fashionable hotel, just a few minutes' walk from the Opera and the famous Ringstrasse. Accompanying them was Ludwig Binswanger, an assistant at the Burghölzli lunatic asylum in Zürich, where Carl Jung worked as a doctor and first assistant to the director Eugen Bleuler. At ten the next morning the threesome waited to be collected by Sigmund Freud, who had invited them to Sunday luncheon at his family home, a short walk away at 19 Berggasse. None had met the Herr Professor before, though Jung and Freud had been corresponding for over a year.

Emma Jung was twenty-four, attractive – her wavy brown hair pinned up under a large hat – and very wealthy. But although her outfit was expensive, with its long skirts and furs against the March cold, it was not showy, because Emma herself was not showy. Carl was strikingly good-looking in a Teutonic sort of way – light brown hair, small moustache, dark eyes behind gold-rimmed spectacles, over six foot tall and powerfully built, with an imposing presence: a brilliant and ambitious young man just beginning to make his mark on the new and as yet not very scientific field of 'Psychoanalysis', of which Professor Freud, twenty years his senior, was already the acknowledged master. Anyone observing Emma and Carl Jung seated on the plush velvet canapé in the elegant foyer of the Grand Hotel – with its chandeliers, ornate galleries, steam-powered elevator and liveried footmen and porters – would have seen a couple perfectly fitted to their surroundings: rich, handsome, young, and, by all appearances, happy.

But appearances can be deceptive. Some time before the Jungs left their home town of Zürich for Vienna, Emma had considered delivering her husband an ultimatum: either change his ways or she would divorce him – a shocking and rare thing at the beginning of the twentieth century, and one utterly alien to the retiring character of Emma Jung. She felt lost in the labyrinth of her marriage to Carl, beset with problems. Life could not go on the way it was.

By 1907 the Jungs had been married for four years and had two young daughters – Agathe, aged three, and Gretli, almost two – who were being cared for back in Zürich by the children's maid, helped by Carl's mother and his unmarried sister Trudi. Four years might not be long, but it was long enough for Emma to discover the extent and complexity of her situation, though not long enough to know what to do about it. The problem was twofold: Carl's outward manner, so confident he could come across as arrogant, concealed a very different and infinitely more complicated interior, one which constantly eluded Emma, however hard she tried to understand it. The second problem was no easier to solve: Carl was always flirting with other women, and they with him, provoking in Emma emotions she had never even known she possessed: storms of jealousy and fury followed by terrible feelings of self-doubt and recrimination. On top of all this Carl was extremely ambitious, working day and night at the asylum like a man possessed, driven by a conviction that he had a special understanding of the insane, because in many ways he was so like them. One way or another, it left almost no time for family life. Emma would spend hour upon hour in the Jungs' apartment on the second floor of the Burghölzli asylum waiting for her husband to return.

There were further complicating factors. Emma came from a well-known family of wealthy industrialists, the Rauschenbachs of Schaffhausen, making her one of the richest heiresses in Switzerland. Carl on the other hand was the son of a poor pastor of the Swiss Protestant Reformed Church. In fact, he was in debt when he first met Emma to the tune of 3,000 Swiss francs, which at a time when a working man might earn thirty francs a week was a very large sum indeed. It was a humiliation for Carl, this poverty, because the Jung family was respected in his home town of Basel and most of them were not poor at all. But his father, for reasons best known to himself, chose to work in remote parishes which barely offered a living. So they were the poor relations and Carl hated it. On marrying Emma he inherited all his wife's money and possessions, and became not only debt-free but a man of independent means in his own right, and able to support his impoverished mother and sister. Uncertain whether the young, ambitious Herr Doktor Jung was not just a plain old-fashioned fortune-hunter, Emma's family allotted her an additional monthly allowance of her own. In the event of a divorce everything each partner brought to the marriage reverted to them – a useful tool when delivering an ultimatum.

This is how things stood between the couple waiting for Herr Professor Freud in the foyer of the Grand Hotel in March 1907. One thing, however, was clear: Emma loved Carl fiercely and was prepared to fight to the bitter end to keep him. Carl, for his part, may or may not have married his wife for her money. But it certainly was not his only reason. The deeper reasons, true to his character, were infinitely more complicated.

The Jungs' spring break was a useful distraction, travelling to three countries over a period of three weeks, just the two of them, and staying at the very best hotels. Their tour would take them to Budapest, then Fiume and Abbazia in northern Italy, but their first stop was Vienna, where Carl had already made arrangements. 'I shall be in Vienna next Saturday evening, and hope I may call upon you on Sunday morning at 10 o'clock,' Carl had written to the *Hochverehrter* – highly esteemed – Professor Freud on 26 February. 'My wife has relieved me of all obligations while I am in Vienna,' he added, and 'I shall take leave, before my departure, to let you know at what hotel I am staying, so that you could if necessary send word there. Most truly yours, Dr Jung.'

Who knows what Freud made of Jung's repeated use of the first-person pronoun, as though he were coming on his own, but he must have understood because when he arrived at the Grand Hotel that March morning, Freud was bearing some flowers for Frau Doktor Jung. As he presented them to her, with a formal bow, Emma saw a small dapper man with a neatly clipped moustache and beard, dressed in his winter best: a worsted overcoat in the English style; a suit, waistcoat, floppy bow tie, homburg hat, spats over boots, and a cane. His hair, inclined to be unruly, was combed down with his usual pomade supplied by the local barber he frequented every morning.

Originally the Jungs were meant to visit over Easter when Professor Freud had time to spare, but this was not possible for Carl and Emma who always spent Easter with their children. This presented a problem for Freud, who worked from eight in the morning till eight at night, apart from a break for the midday meal followed by a walk round the district for some air and a visit to the cigar shop. Unlike Carl Jung, Freud had not married into money and had to earn a living to support his large and extended family. 'But Sundays I am free, so I must ask you to arrange your visit to Vienna in such a way as to have a Sunday available for me,' he had written to Jung on 21 February. 'If possible I would like to introduce you to a small circle of followers on a Wednesday evening. I further assume you will be willing to forgo the theatre on the few evenings you will be spending in Vienna, and instead to dine with me and my family and spend the rest of the evening with me. I am looking forward to your acceptance and the announcement of your arrival.' Forgo the theatre? Jung had absolutely no intention of going. He hated the theatre. That was what Ludwig Binswanger was there for, to chaperone and entertain Emma. He himself wanted to spend every available minute with the Herr Professor.

As the four of them walked along, Freud smoking his third or fourth cigar of the day, the conversation remained on the formal level: the journey, the weather, their hotel accommodation – polite talk, just filling in. They must have made a comic sight – the two men who would become the two giants of psychoanalysis, walking side by side: Jung over six foot, Freud five foot seven, and Jung already talking his head off, loudly, as he always did.

Berggasse may have been only a short walk from the Ringstrasse, but it was far enough to leave the grandeur of the Ring district behind and enter the more modest, cobbled streets surrounding Vienna University. And it was long enough for a small misunderstanding to occur, seemingly insignificant at the time, but in hindsight very significant indeed. Freud, trying to put the visitors at their ease, joked that he was happy to be receiving them as guests to his home, but warned that it was a very modest place and had little to offer, just his *alte* (old woman) – nothing much else. Emma was shocked. So was Carl. What a way to talk about your wife, the mother of your children! Swiss haute bourgeoisie as they were, Freud's self-deprecating Jewish humour was completely lost on them. Emma, usually blessed with a healthy sense of fun, was puzzled.

Frau Professor Freud was there to greet the guests from Zürich as they mounted the stone steps of 19 Berggasse, and then up the stairs to the apartment. Emma, shaking Martha Freud formally by the hand – '*guten Tag, guten Tag*' – observed an older woman in a long-skirted, high-necked Sunday dress, stylish in its way, with a simple brooch at the neck, her dark hair pinned up neatly with combs. Behind her stood a younger woman, Martha's unmarried younger sister Minna who lived with them – an interesting set-up which caused plenty of gossip and speculation over the years. Herr Professor Freud and his two women. Apparently Minna sometimes answered the telephone calling herself 'Frau Professor'! Freud himself did not like the newfangled telephone and always left it to one of the women of the house to answer. In 1907 Sigmund Freud was fifty-one, Martha forty-six. They had been married for twenty-one years and had six children ranging from Mathilde twenty, Martin eighteen, Ernst sixteen, Oliver fifteen, Sophie fourteen, down to Anna, twelve. Freud called them his 'rabble' and his 'rascals' with affection and some pride.

Martha, greeting Emma Jung, observed a formal, reticent young woman, dressed with an understated style, and only a few years older than her daughter Mathilde. She already knew about the Frau Doktor's wealth. Everyone knew. But what she could not fail to notice was that Frau Doktor Jung did not act wealthy. As the two women exchanged greetings, Jung was shaking hands in the formal Swiss way. No fancy Viennese kissing of ladies' hands for Carl.

On special occasions such as this Martha would cook a chicken for the midday meal, though her husband was not keen. 'Let them live,' he always said. 'Let them lay eggs.' But his wife made all the household decisions, it had been that way from the start: he earned the money, she ran the house. It suited them both and Freud never interfered and never complained. So there they sat, twelve of them, round the dinner table having their meal, served from the kitchen by the maid, with the men at one end and the women and children at the other. Emma was surprised by all the talk – the Freud children expressed themselves easily and cheerfully. 'Our upbringing might be called liberal,' Martin Freud later wrote, reflecting on his 'gay and generous' father. 'We were never ordered to do this, or not to do that; we were never told not to ask questions.' For their part, Martha and Minna, the two sisters, could not fail to notice that the Jungs both had strong Swiss accents, making them seem more provincial than they were. Apparently, Frau Doktor Jung had wanted to attend

Zürich University to study the natural sciences but her father wouldn't let her. Understandably. The only women who attended university were rich foreigners – Russians and the like.

Looking back, Martin Freud, as an observant eighteen-year-old, remembers Herr Doktor Jung having a 'commanding presence': 'He was very tall and broad-shouldered, holding himself more like a soldier than a man of science and medicine. His head was purely Teutonic with a strong chin, a small moustache, blue eyes, and thin closely cropped hair.' In fact, Jung's eyes were brown not blue, but in the almost entirely Jewish environment inhabited by the Freud family the Teutonic aspect was unusual and rather interesting. Still, Martin took a dislike to Jung: 'He never made the slightest attempt to make polite conversation with mother or us children but pursued the debate which had been interrupted by the call to luncheon. Jung on these occasions did all the talking and father with unconcealed delight did all the listening,' he wrote, still irked by the memory. Martin was doubly surprised because normally his father strongly disapproved of visitors ignoring his family and he would deliberately change the conversation to include them, making it clear that this was not how things went in the Freud household. But not with Herr Doktor Jung, who talked throughout the meal exclusively to his father, showing no awareness of or concern for anyone else. Emma might have told them this was typical of her husband, who had gained some enemies amongst his colleagues at the Burghölzli asylum because of it, though never amongst his patients who all revered him.

After the meal there was coffee and then Emma and Binswanger took their leave, as arranged, so Carl could spend more time with Freud. The two men swiftly retired to Freud's consulting rooms on the mezzanine floor below, which looked out over a small garden with a single chestnut tree. They talked for thirteen hours without a break. It was love at first sight, a mutual enchantment accompanied by every high hope. Freud had read this brilliant young doctor's papers on *dementia praecox* – or 'schizophrenia' as Bleuler of the Burghölzli asylum had coined it – as well as Jung's 'Experiments in Word Association', and now, to his delight, he found that the man in conversation was as brilliant and challenging as the writer on the page.

As for Carl Jung's first impressions of Freud: 'In my experience, up to that time, no one else could compare with him,' he wrote later. 'There was nothing the least trivial in his attitude. I found him extremely intelligent, shrewd, and altogether remarkable.' Carl did not get back to the hotel until two in the morning, having to call out the night porter, by which time Emma was fast asleep.

Over the next five days a routine was established: the visitors would be picked up from the hotel every morning by one of the Freud family to be shown around the city. By the end of each day's sightseeing everyone was exhausted, everyone except Jung, who enjoyed a rude energy throughout his life, and who would hurry along to 19 Berggasse for his late-night sessions with Freud, talking psychoanalysis, the new and shocking movement that the Herr Professor was leading with missionary zeal, and which, it soon transpired, he meant to bequeath to this brilliant young doctor from the Burghölzli asylum, naming him his 'crown prince and heir' with typical impulsiveness, and much to the annoyance of his Viennese colleagues.

The reasons were obvious: not only was Carl Jung brilliant, young and energetic, he was charismatic – an essential prerequisite for a leader. In addition, all the other men in the Viennese group were Jewish, whereas Jung was a Gentile, an Aryan from Switzerland. Freud knew this was the only way psychoanalysis could reach a wider, international public, transforming it into a world movement. He knew it because he had lived with anti-Semitism all his life. As much as he tried to ignore it he knew he could never overcome it. As he wrote to one of his most loyal followers, Karl Abraham, in December 1908: 'Our Aryan comrades are really completely indispensable to us, otherwise Psycho-Analysis would succumb to anti-Semitism.'

The Vienna Emma and Carl Jung visited at the beginning of the twentieth century was a great cosmopolitan city of 2 million inhabitants, only half of whom had *Heimatberechtigung*, that is, were legally domiciled Viennese German-speaking Austrians. The rest came from the four corners of the Austro-Hungarian Empire: Bohemians, Moravians, Hungarians, Poles, Czechs, Croats, all bringing different languages and embracing different religions. And Jews, many Jews. These ranged from Vienna's poorest inhabitants living in the slums of Leopoldstadt to the new professional classes, lawyers, writers, journalists, artists and doctors like Freud, and the very richest: the fabulously wealthy merchants and bankers who lived in the nouveau riche Ring district in houses so large they were referred to as *palais*, often built in the neo-Renaissance style with columns, loggias and caryatids. It was these wealthy Jews who had helped finance Emperor Franz Joseph's transformation of Vienna from the walled medieval city it once was to the capital of imperial grandeur which Emma and Carl saw all about them.

The sheer scale of it all was staggering. The grand boulevard of the Ring offered a dramatic setting for the Rathaus and

Reichsrat, the city hall and parliament, as well as the Opera, the Burgtheater, the churches of St Stephen and the Votivkirche, the stock exchange, and, leading to the Heldenplatz, a vast columned piazza in front of Kaiser Franz Joseph's Hofburg palace adorned with two massive equestrian statues, one of Prince Eugene of Savoy, the other of Archduke Charles of Austria. Then there were the museums – the one dedicated to natural history being of particular interest to Emma – and the many parks where you could wander up statue-lined avenues, sit by fountains or listen to one of the military bands playing Viennese waltzes and marches or melodies from the latest operetta. Everywhere you looked there were uniforms, army officers of the empire in red or pale blue, with sashes, epaulettes, gold braid, plumed helmets, swords, sabres, and highly polished boots. Every official appeared to have a uniform too, even the tram drivers, and little boys were often dressed in miniature military uniforms for their Sunday best.

The Hungarian court put on frequent displays of imperial pomp and power, such as the City Regiment's daily march. On one occasion when Martin Freud was with Carl and Emma in the Ring district, Emperor Franz Joseph's coach drove past, resplendent in red and gold with liveried coachmen and postilion. The Jungs had never seen such a thing and Martin was amazed to see the Herr Doktor, usually so superior, pushing to the front of the crowd, 'like a small boy' thrilled to catch a glimpse of the emperor with his companion, the former actress Katharine Schratt, seated at his side. For the Jungs, from small, republican Switzerland, it was the stuff of fairy tales. Whether visiting the famed Schiffmann's department store, illuminated with the latest forms of electric lighting, or Demel's, where the cakes and the *Sachertorte* were the best in the world, or joining the daily *Corso* along the Kärntner Ring, where Viennese society paraded in the latest fashions, everything dazzled. The Baedeker travel guide put it nicely: 'With limited time, a week would suffice for a superficial overview of everything worth seeing.'

In the evenings after Carl had left for 19 Berggasse, Emma rested in the hotel before venturing out into the city – to the Burg Theatre or the Opera or to one of the famous Viennese operettas, perhaps with Binswanger, perhaps with one of the Freud ladies. Or she might stay in the hotel and dine in their *Salle de Diner* and later sit in one of their more intimate *salons* to read before retiring to her bedroom. She was surrounded by opulence, the Grand being the very first of the fashionable hotels of Vienna, built in the 1870s, with 300 bedrooms, half of which had ensuite bathrooms – a luxury as yet unheard of in Zürich. It had central heating and electric lighting, its own telegraph office in the foyer from which guests could send telegrams and make telephone calls with the assistance of well-trained telegraphists, and a private fiacre carriage service to take them anywhere they wished. So Emma could not have been better cared for whilst her husband was with Professor Freud. But she might have been happier if Carl had whiled away some of those evening hours with her.

Aside from psychoanalysis and the campaign to conquer the world, Freud and Jung talked about themselves – a natural transition since psychoanalysis dealt with neuroses and psychoses and all manner of obsessive behaviours, most of which appeared to have their roots in childhood, including their own. The subject they discussed most was sex: specifically, Freud's theory that sexual trauma in childhood was the root cause of later neuroses and hysteria. It might be sexual abuse by a stranger or a family friend, or by a family member in which case it was incest. Freud had many examples from his own patients who came to him in the first instance because they were unaccountably paralysed, or suffering from chronic anxiety, depression, physical pain, sleeplessness, paranoias. Time and again it transpired that they were repressing early sexual experiences, though by 1907 Freud had modified his earlier view that all cases of hysteria had a sexual origin. He and his colleague and teacher Professor Breuer had published their *Studies on Hysteria* in 1895, by which time some doctors were diagnosing their female hysterics with sexual dysfunction and treating them with hypnosis or various forms of massage, including that of their genitals to bring about orgasm. But these were not subjects spoken about openly, except by Freud, who made sexual repression the linchpin of his work, shocking the general public and plenty of his medical colleagues in the process. His 'cure' was revolutionary: the 'talking cure' of psychoanalysis, designed to uncover the origin of the neuroses rather than merely treating them. The unconscious, Jung and Freud agreed, was the key to everything. And the key to the unconscious was the dream.

Carl had been conducting a good deal of research into the unconscious himself, especially the 'Word Association' tests he carried out in his laboratory at the Burghölzli on both 'normal' and 'abnormal' subjects – using a galvanometer to measure the patients' reactions by applying a weak electric current to the subject which measured the fluctuations in the skin with each association, the reaction recorded on a graph. He had also read Freud's most famous work *The Interpretation of Dreams*, published in 1900, which boldly stated: 'In the following pages, I shall demonstrate that there exists a psychological technique by which dreams may be interpreted and that upon the application of this method every dream will show itself to be a senseful psychological structure which may be introduced into an assignable place in the psychic activity of the waking state.' So the two men were in agreement about the powers of the unconscious. What Carl Jung could not agree with, however, even before he met Freud in person, was the central role played by childhood sexual trauma. 'It seems to me,' he wrote to Freud on 5 October 1906, six months before his visit to Vienna, 'that though the genesis of hysteria is predominantly, it is not exclusively, sexual.' He thought this might be because 'I: my material is totally different from yours [working mostly with uneducated insane patients], II: my upbringing, my milieu, and my scientific premises are in any case utterly different from your own, III: my experience compared to yours is extremely small.' Freud, superior in age and experience, was happy to bide his time. Sooner or later the crown prince would see the light. He could not know that Jung had personal as well as professional reasons for believing what he did.

As Freud had mentioned in his letter to Jung, on Wednesdays there was always a meeting at 19 Berggasse of his Viennese colleagues, including Alfred Adler, Rudolf Reitler, Max Kahane and Wilhelm Stekel – later joined by Paul Federn and Eduard Hitschmann and occasionally Sandor Ferenczi and Otto Rank. On that particular Wednesday in March 1907, Binswanger, attending with Carl Jung, remembered there were only five or six others present.

They assembled in Freud's consulting room as usual – a room filled with cigar, pipe and cigarette smoke, dimly lit with gas lamps and surrounded by Freud's growing collection of antique and oriental art – with wine brought to them by Martha Freud. The atmosphere was relaxed, with no etiquette and plenty of humour. Binswanger was amazed how Freud could dominate the evening so completely after a long day's work. The subject was exclusively psychoanalysis: the interpretation of dreams, neuroses, paranoias, childhood sexuality and so on – Freud offering detailed examples from his cases, then listening care- fully, answering questions with gestures of the hand, sometimes holding one of his smaller antiques, and always the cigar. His manner was simple and filled with charm, Binswanger recalled, but you could never forget you were in the presence of greatness.

Jung took part in the discussion, but less loudly than usual. The evening left him perplexed. 'I felt so foreign before this Jewish intellectual society. That was something completely new to me. I had never experienced that before,' he told his friend Kurt Eissler some years later. 'I found it very difficult to adjust, to adopt the right tone.' Their conversation had 'a certain cyni- cism', he said, and it made him feel 'like a country bumpkin'. When Freud joked: 'You wouldn't be an anti-Semite now, would you?' Jung took it seriously, answering: 'No, no. Anti- Semitism is out of the question,' which must have amused Freud quite a bit.

At the end of the evening the Herr Professor turned to his Swiss guests and said: 'Now you've seen the whole *Bande*, the whole gang.' That shocked Binswanger; it seemed so dismissive. Something else shocked him too. Earlier in the week he, Freud and Carl Jung had been analysing one another's dreams. In later life he recalled Freud's interpretation of Jung's dream, though not the dream itself: apparently Jung had a hidden wish to dethrone Herr Professor Freud and place the 'Crown of Psycho-Analysis' on his own head. It was that Jewish–Viennese humour again. Binswanger's own dream was of arriving at 19 Berggasse to find it was the old, not the newly renovated entrance, with two ancient gas lamps hanging outside. That, announced Freud, revealed Binswanger's wish to marry Mathilde, his eldest daughter – and then his deciding against it because the place was too shabby. But it was said with a laugh, and even Binswanger got the joke.

When the five-day visit was up the Jungs took their leave with many heartfelt thanks, and travelled on to Budapest by the Continental Express sleeper, in the comfort of a first-class carriage. Binswanger stayed behind for another week with Freud, establishing a friendship that would last a lifetime. On the train, looking out at the passing hamlets and farms and the Alps beyond, Emma had no idea how deeply her husband had been affected by his encounter with Freud. And if she had, she could hardly have guessed the reason why.

The idea of visiting Budapest originally came from Emma's wish to see the city where her father had established a branch of the Rauschenbach family business in agricultural machinery. She wanted to go to the premises and perhaps meet some of the employees her father had known when he was there back in the

1880s. But if Emma hoped for some time sightseeing with Carl she was mistaken. He showed little interest in it, preferring to spend his time with a colleague, Philip Stein, discussing medical cases and his own recent experiments in word association, so Emma was forced to do most of her sightseeing on her own.

Worse was to come when they arrived in Abbazia, a fashionable resort on the Adriatic coast. A woman staying at their hotel struck up a conversation with them at dinner on their first evening. She was attractive, intelligent, Jewish – a lady of independent means with progressive opinions and quite fascinated by the new and daring science of psychoanalysis. And even more fascinated by the charismatic and handsome Herr Doktor, as most women were. And Carl, in the wake of his infatuation with Freud and all things Jewish, was a willing partner. Every evening he and the woman retreated to a sofa in the corner of the drawing room to discuss psychoanalysis. If Emma joined them the woman talked down to her as the mere wife. Emma, jealous and humiliated, complained to Carl, but he told her there was nothing to it – their discussions were purely professional. It took him two years before he could admit the truth: that this was another of his 'infatuations'.

2

Two Childhoods

Emma Rauschenbach first met Carl properly when she was seventeen. She had just returned home to Schaffhausen in eastern Switzerland from Paris where she had been staying with friends of the family, being 'finished off' in preparation for marriage to a suitable young man from a similar haut-bourgeois Swiss background to her own. She was shy and quiet, but clever, always top of her class at the *Mädchenrealschule*, the local school for girls from every kind of background, rich and poor alike. She had not wanted to go to Paris; she had wanted to continue her education and go to university to study the natural sciences, a subject which had fascinated her since childhood, but it was not considered the right path for young Swiss women like Emma, and her father would not hear of it. Instead she went to Paris to perfect her French and acquaint herself with La Civilisation Française. Serious young woman that she was, Emma spent hour upon hour in the museums and began to learn Old French and Provençal in order to read the legend of the Holy Grail in the original – the twelfth-century romance about Perceval, a knight in the Arthurian legends, that would fascinate her for the rest of her life. By the time Carl Jung came to pay a visit she was informally engaged to the son of one of her father's wealthy Schaffhausen business colleagues, and her future lay predictably before her.

Emma's childhood home, the Haus zum Rosengarten (the House of the Rose Garden), was an elegant seventeenth-century mansion situated on the banks of the Rhine. It had been bought by Emma's grandfather Johannes Rauschenbach with the fortune he made from his factory producing agricultural machinery, exported worldwide, and the iron foundry next to it, both within walking distance of the house. Later he augmented his fortune by buying the Internazionale Uhren Fabrik (the International Watch Company, IWC), an American firm producing the first machine-made fob and wrist watches. Emma's grandfather died young in 1881 and her father Jean, aged twenty-five, took over the running of both factories and moved into the house, still lived in by his mother, with his young wife Bertha. Their daughters, Emma and Marguerite, were both born there: Emma on 30 March 1882, and Marguerite fifteen months later.

Emma recalled her childhood as being idyllic, combining untroubled happiness and privilege in equal parts. Her nickname was 'Sunny' and her life at that time gave her no reason to feel otherwise. The house itself, large, square, solid, was separated from the banks of the Rhine by a formal rose garden, laid out by her uncle Evariste Mertens, a landscape designer, and which gave the house its name. Schaffhausen itself was a prosperous town of fine Renaissance buildings with stuccoed and frescoed façades adorned with high-minded words exhorting the good burghers to lead virtuous lives. In the back streets and away from the grandeur stood the many factories, small industries and workshops which were the foundation of its wealth, a tribute to the Swiss tradition of hard work, and to the benefits of hydroelectricity, derived from the power of the massive Rhine Falls nearby. 'Standing in the window,' recalled Gertrud Henne, Emma and Marguerite's cousin who came to the house to play with the sisters, 'I liked to watch the big "Transmissions": pillars standing in the Rhine with giant wheels that conducted hydropower via cables to the various factories along the Rhine.' Anyone with ambition might make themselves a fortune in those heady early industrial days in Schaffhausen, and Johannes Rauschenbach, who started with nothing more than a machine repair shop, then a pin factory supplying the local cotton industry, and finally the world-renowned agricultural machinery factory, became the wealthiest of them all, and one of the richest men in Switzerland.

When Jean Rauschenbach took over the business, with factories at home and abroad, Emma's mother and grandmother took over the running of the house. Grossmutter Barbara lived in rooms upstairs and liked to sit in a fauteuil by the window overlooking the Rhine, reading her *Gazette* with her lorgnon, wearing a large bonnet with ribbons and surrounded by her collection of dolls, kept in a large old wall bed, and which the girls were sometimes allowed to play with. Having started life modestly, Grossmutter Barbara never fully accustomed herself to the great wealth the family came to enjoy. 'If only you'd remained a mechanic,' she used to tell her husband.

The two sisters were very different but they were close and remained so all their lives. Emma could spend hours on her own, reading, writing, thinking. Marguerite was less the thinker, more the sporty, outward-going type, and moodier. Both sisters played the piano well, but Marguerite liked to sing too, and play-act, and she swam in the Rhine in all weathers, right into old age. They shared a private tutor before moving up to the local school for girls, and their upbringing was conventional Swiss haut bourgeois, instilling the values of a Protestant work ethic, social conformity, and feminine grace and good manners, so they knew how to behave when Herr Direktor Rauschenbach and his wife gave one of their grand receptions required of the foremost family of Schaffhausen.

Emma at school, third row, third from right.

Both girls adored their mother, Bertha, who allowed her daughters plenty of freedom. For this the Haus zum Rosengarten was perfect, with its large cobbled courtyard, extensive outhouses, and the stables where the girls kept their horses, Lori and Ceda, looked after by Reeper, the groom, an ex-cavalry officer in the Austro-Hungarian Army. If it was raining there were plenty of toys to play with inside; if it was snowing there was sledging and ice-skating; if it was one of those heatwave summers there was swimming in the Rhine, and all year round Reeper took them out riding to villages and castles and other local landmarks.

The question of Carl and Emma's first meeting is a moot one: was it in 1896 when he was still a student or was it three years later, when he was poised to take his first job working as a lowly assistant physician at the Burghölzli asylum and Emma had just returned from Paris? If it was in 1896, then it was at the Haus zum Rosengarten and it was an event hardly even remembered by Emma. But if it was in 1899 it was at Ölberg, the Mount of Olives, an ancient property like a small castle, square and thick-walled, with its own medieval chapel, the St Wolfgangs Kapelle, high on the slopes overlooking Schaffhausen with a drive so long and steep you could not see from one end to the other. The family had spent every summer there since the girls were small. But by 1899 Jean Rauschenbach had decided to sell the Haus zum Rosengarten and make Ölberg their family home, replacing the beautiful little castle with a *Jugendstil* mansion, a vast stone pile in the heavily ornate style of the time, with turrets and gables and oriels, high-ceilinged reception rooms, and a grand stairway leading up to a wide landing with bedrooms and bathrooms off.

One entire floor was set aside for Emma and Marguerite, then in their teens, and the whole house was lit by electricity, heated by central heating, and served by a raft of servants inside and out. The architect was Ernst Jung of Winterthur, by chance one of Carl Jung's uncles, who had already renovated the Sonnenburg property next door which belonged to Emma's landscape architect uncle Evariste Mertens, who now proceeded to design

22

the far grander gardens at Ölberg. According to his own account, as soon as Carl first set eyes on Emma, in the half-light, coming down the grand stairway into the hall, he decided this was the girl he would marry. If it was 1899 then Emma would have been seventeen, just back from Paris, more self-assured than before but still shy and retiring, poised on the edge of adulthood. If it was 1896, as Carl described in *Memories, Dreams, Reflections*, that would make Emma just fourteen.

How an impoverished medical student came to be visiting this prominent and unimaginably wealthy family in the first place is down to Emma's mother. Bertha was the beautiful daughter of Schenk, patron of the local *Gasthof*, a successful family business, providing rooms as well as excellent food – but still a *Gasthof*. So when Bertha married Jean, the son and heir to the Rauschenbach fortune, she married well above her station. But, rather like her mother-in-law, she never forgot her humble origins. Bertha knew the Jung family because she and Carl's mother, Emilie Preiswerk, had attended the same school, and the Schenk *Gasthof* was in Uhwiesen, one of three villages in the parish of Laufen by the Rhine Falls where Carl's father was pastor. The living at Laufen was poor: only enough to employ one maid-of-all-work, which included looking after infant Carl when his mother was not 'well', which was often. Bertha Schenk was one of Pastor Jung's parishioners and she helped him out from time to time, taking the baby for walks along the Rhine in his pram. Years later Carl still remembered her as she was then: 'the young, very pretty and charming girl with blue eyes and fair hair' who 'admired my father'.

Now, encouraged by his mother, who had remained in touch with Bertha, he decided to pay Frau Rauschenbach a visit, and there saw the daughter Emma coming down the stairs. Even if Carl first clapped eyes on Emma when she was fourteen, she herself first knowingly met Carl in 1899 when she was seventeen. And the first correspondence between them dates from this year, when Emma returned from Paris. It was a one-way sort, that is, mostly from Carl, starting with picture postcards addressed formally to '*Sehr geehrtes Fräulein!*' – most esteemed young lady, always ending in an exclamation mark.

It took Carl many months before he could summon up the courage to ask Emma to marry him, and when he did she refused him. 'For various reasons I was turned down when I first proposed,' he wrote to Freud in 1906: 'later I was accepted, and I married.' Various reasons, plural. One was that Emma was already engaged, albeit informally, to the son of one of her father's business colleagues. Another: Carl's loud and rumbustious personality was utterly overwhelming for a young woman such as Emma. Another: Carl Jung did not have a penny to his name, nor was he ever likely to have, since by then he had decided to be an *Irrenarzt* – a doctor of the insane – the most lowly of professions. This presented a serious social barrier and was so shocking that Emma's father could not be told. Their engagement, when it finally occurred, was a secret one.

What changed Emma's mind? The short answer is probably Carl himself. It took him a while but he was utterly determined and marshalled everything he had to win her hand, starting with certain natural advantages: his good looks, his imposing presence, his challenging conversation, his intelligence, his lively humour, and what he himself called his 'intuition'.

Carl's intuition told him that beneath her reticent, formal manner Emma was yearning for something less conventional, more intellectually satisfying, more adventurous – an outlet for her cleverness which she could not have if she married her haut-bourgeois beau. So he embarked on his campaign, bombarding her with letters filled with fascinating ideas and amusing self-deprecating comments. He told her about his favourite writers and philosophers, his love of mythology, his work, and he confided in her about his ambitions, his hopes and his fears. And he gave her lists of books to read for discussion next time they met. A seduction by intellect.

Even so, Emma still refused him. Everything about Carl, his physical size, his huge personality, his brilliance, was too powerful for her. How was she to know that Carl had another self, well hidden, full of doubt and complexes and feelings of social inferiority? One refusal was enough for 'other Carl'. 'Father would never have asked her again,' their son Franz confirmed years later. 'He was crushed. He was poor, and not on the same social level as Emma, and so he thought he didn't have a chance.' Carl thanked Emma for her honesty and withdrew. These were his early months working at Burghölzli asylum and he became so plagued with insecurity that he hid himself behind the high walls of the institution. By his own account, he never went out for six months, causing colleagues to think he was behaving more like an inmate than a doctor. As for Emma: 'My mother was very shy then, and introverted,' said Franz. 'She was afraid to move ahead, to say yes.'

But Carl had a key ally within the Rauschenbach family. Intelligent, modern in outlook, and coming from modest beginnings herself, Emma's mother Bertha saw nothing wrong with Carl Jung, the lowly assistant physician now employed in a lunatic asylum. Money? Emma had plenty of money. Bertha remembered the little boy she had pushed alongside the Rhine in his pram, now grown into a fine young man, and here was her daughter Emma, the clever, studious one – and what did it matter that she was engaged to another young man? It was hardly an engagement at all, nothing fixed, nothing formal.

Emma adored her mother and without her encouragement she would probably never have found the courage to marry Carl. After some months Frau Rauschenbach contacted Carl, arranged to meet him in a restaurant in Zürich, and urged him not to be put off and try asking Emma once more. She even invited him back to Ölberg, sending her own green carriage and coachman to collect him from Schaffhausen station. And this time, in October 1901, Emma said yes. Once decided, she never wavered. He need not worry, she assured him: she knew exactly what she was doing.

But Emma said yes to the Carl she knew: the extrovert, clever, handsome Carl with his earthy energy and loud exuberant laugh, not the 'other' Carl, the hidden one. Had she known the strangeness and complexity of the 'other' Carl – had she been able to see what lay ahead – she might have answered differently. Or not. Over the weeks till their secret engagement she caught glimpses of this 'other' Carl. To her surprise, it was she who had to reassure him, again and again, of her love. She thought it would be the other way round.

'My situation is mirrored in my dreams,' Carl wrote in his 'secret diary' in December 1898, whilst still a medical student:

Often glorious, portentous glimpses of flowery landscapes, infinite blue seas, sunny coasts, but often too, images of unknown roads shrouded in night, of friends who take leave of me to stride towards a brighter fate, of myself alone on barren paths facing impenetrable darkness. 'Oh fling yourself into a positive faith,' my grandfather Jung writes. Yes, I would be glad to fling myself if I could, if that depended only on the uppermost me. But an inexplicable heavy something, a listlessness and numbness, weariness and weakness, always prevents the final step. I have already taken many steps, but I am still a long way from the final one. The greater the certainty, the more superhuman the doubts . . .

This was and always would be the crux of the matter for Carl: he had a personality which was split: sure and unsure, optimistic and pessimistic, introverted and extroverted, sensitive and insensitive, brilliant yet obtuse; genial yet given to violent rages; cold under warm, dark under light – always split, and that split always hidden. Secret.

Later he called them 'Personality No. 1' and 'Personality No. 2', but growing up he hardly knew the difference. At the parsonage of Klein-Hüningen near Basel, where the Jung family moved when Carl was five, there was an old wall in the garden made of large blocks of stone and in the gaps between the stones he lit small fires which had an 'unmistakable aura of sanctity' about them and had to burn 'for ever'. One stone jutted out of the wall. 'My stone,' he called it:

Often, when I was alone, I sat down on this stone, and then began an imaginary game that went something like this: 'I am sitting on top of this stone and it is underneath.' But the stone could also say 'I' and think: 'I am lying here on this slope and he is sitting on top of me.' The question then arose: 'Am I the one who is sitting on the stone, or am I the stone on which *he* is sitting?' This question always perplexed me, and I would stand up, wondering who was what now. The answer remained totally unclear, and my uncertainty was accompanied by a feeling of curious and fascinating darkness. But there was no doubt whatsoever that this stone stood in some secret relationship to me. I could sit on it for hours, fascinated by the puzzle it set me.

He sat on that stone for hours, trying to work out whether it was him, or he was it. This was how Carl Jung described it to his assistant, the analyst Aniela Jaffé, when he was eighty and finally agreed to recount his life. Thinking about it then, he added:

Thirty years later I again stood on that slope. I was a married man, had children, a house, a place in the world, and a head full of ideas and plans, and suddenly I was again the child who had kindled that fire full of secret significance and sat down on a stone without knowing whether it was I or I it. I thought suddenly of my life in Zürich, and it seemed alien to me, like news from some remote world and time. This was frightening, for the world of my childhood in which I had just become absorbed was *eternal*, and I had been wrenched away from it and had fallen into a time that continued to roll onwards, moving further and further away. The pull of that other world was so strong that I had to tear myself away violently from the spot in order not to lose hold of my future.

A strange child and a strange childhood. When the young Bertha Schenk came to take the infant Carl for walks along the Rhine,

Pastor Jung had often been looking after his son on his own, the mother, Emilie, being 'away' in some unknown place for people suffering from unknown ills. 'Dim intimations of trouble in my parents' marriage hovered around me,' Carl later recalled. As a child he fell ill with fever and suffered horribly from eczema. 'My illness, in 1878, must have been connected with a temporary separation of my parents. My mother spent several months in a hospital in Basel, and presumably her illness had something to do with the difficulty in the marriage.' Usually the maid looked after him, but often it was his father. 'I was deeply troubled by my mother's being away. From then on, I always felt mistrustful when the word "love" was spoken.' Whilst Emilie was 'away' Carl slept in his father's room. He remembered his father carrying him in his arms, trying to get him to sleep, pacing up and down, singing his old fraternity student songs. When Carl's mother finally came back home his parents no longer shared a bedroom. Frightening things emanated from her room, indefinite figures, floating, headless, luminous. Carl had 'vague fears' and heard strange things in the night, all mixed up with the muted roar of the Rhine Falls nearby. He could not breathe and thought he would suffocate. 'I see this as a psychogenic factor,' he later told Aniela Jaffé; 'the atmosphere of the house was beginning to be unbearable.' He went on sleeping in his father's room throughout childhood. In fact, until he was eighteen and preparing to go to Basel University.

'I had never come across such an asocial monster before,' recalled Albert Oeri, one of Carl's few playmates during those early years. Albert had been brought to the parsonage by his father, an old student friend of Pastor Jung's, to play with Carl. 'But nothing could be done. Carl sat in the middle of the room, occupied himself with a little bowling game, and didn't pay the slightest attention to me.' Carl was not used to playing with other children, not even the village children who were anyway mostly out in the fields helping their parents with haymaking or herding the cows. When the Jung family moved to Klein-Hüningen, Albert's family still sometimes visited on a Sunday afternoon. By now a different Carl had made an appearance: extrovert Carl, boisterous Carl, the one who did not like weaklings, especially one of his cousins whom he teased mercilessly. 'He asked this boy to sit down on a bench in the entrance way,' recalled Oeri. 'When the boy complied, Carl burst into whoops of wild Red Indian laughter, an art he retained all his life. The sole reason for his satisfaction was that an old souse had been sitting on the bench a short time before and Carl hoped that his sissy cousin would thus stink of a little schnapps.' But the moment he had done it he regretted it. Introvert Carl did not want to hurt anyone.

Under the loud whooping lurked the other Carl, the one with secrets to hide. The first of these was a dream he had when he was four, one so significant and so terrible he never told anyone about it until he was sixty-five: 'A dream which was to preoccupy me all my life.' He was in a meadow when he discovered a dark hole which he had never seen before, stone-lined, with a stone stairway leading far down. Fearfully he descended. At the bottom there was a doorway with a round arch and a heavy green curtain, brocade, leading through to a rectangular chamber with an arched ceiling, again of stone. A blood-red carpet ran from the entrance to a low platform on which stood a golden throne and on this throne stood something which he first took to be a tree trunk, twelve to fifteen feet high and two feet thick: a huge thing, reaching almost to the ceiling and made, he then realised, of skin and naked flesh. On the top was a rounded head with no face or hair, only a single eye. An aura of brightness wafted above it. Carl was paralysed with terror, believing it might at any moment crawl off the throne like a worm towards him. At that moment he heard his mother calling from above: 'Yes, just look at him. That is the man-eater!' and he woke sweating and scared to death. 'This dream haunted me for years.' Much later he realised it was an anatomically accurate phallus.

When the family moved to the old parsonage at Klein-Hüningen, Pastor Jung became chaplain at the local lunatic asylum as an additional role and Carl started going to school. Academic work was easy for him, but not the social side – he was not used to other children and they were not used to a child as strange as him. In time he learned to join in but he always felt it alienated him from his true self. At home he played alone for hours, hating to be watched, building high towers with wooden bricks, making drawings of battles and sieges, lighting fires in the garden. When he was ten he did something which was totally incomprehensible to him, even then: he had a ruler in his pencil case, of yellow unvarnished wood, and out of it he carved 'a little manikin about 2" long, with a frock coat, top hat, and shiny black boots. I coloured him black with ink, sawed him off the ruler, and put him in the pencil case, where I made him a little bed. I even made a coat for him out of a bit of wool.'

He also put a smooth blackish stone from the Rhine in the pencil case, painted to divide it into an upper and lower half. This was *his* stone. 'All this was a great secret. Secretly I took the case to the forbidden attic at the top of the house [forbidden because the floorboards were worm-eaten and rotten] and hid it with great satisfaction on one of the beams under the roof – for no one must ever see it! I knew that not a soul would ever find it there. No one could discover my secret and destroy it.' He used to go up there to visit the manikin, always surreptitiously, and deposit tiny scrolls in the pencil box for him, written in a secret language. Like sitting on the stone, it always made him feel better, bringing him back to his true self. This ritual lasted for about a year. Then he forgot all about it till he was thirty-five and writing *Wandlungen und Symbole der Libido*, later translated as *Transformations and Symbols of the Libido*, the book which would signify his final break with Sigmund Freud.

Apart from arithmetic, which always remained a terrifying mystery to him, Carl was clever and when he was eleven he easily gained a place at the *Gymnasium*, the grammar school, which was situated in the precincts of Basel cathedral. The work, classics-based, was no problem – he already knew Latin which his father had taught him since the age of six, and he was already widely read, especially the Bible. If anything, boredom was the problem. But social life was another matter. Here came Carl, the poor parson's son, walking from his village far out in the countryside, through meadows and woods and fields, in his bumpkin clothes and holes in his shoes so he had to sit for the rest of the school day in wet socks, talking in his broad yokel Basel dialect. And there came the well-dressed sons of the foremost families of Basel in horse-drawn carriages, with fine manners, plenty of pocket money, talking in refined High German or French about their holidays in the Alps, and Carl, having no holidays, felt an envy he had never felt amongst the poor farmers' sons who had been his classmates at his local school.

Now, for the first time, he realised that his family was poor, and when any of his classmates invited him to their grand houses he felt 'as timid and craven as a stray dog'. His feelings of inferiority, fatefully accompanied by equally powerful feelings of superiority, were exposed to the world: 'My shoes are filthy, so are my hands; I have no handkerchief and my neck is black with dirt.' His first year was completely ruined, he said, because he had the 'disagreeable, rather uncanny feeling' that he had 'repulsive traits' which caused the teachers and pupils to shun him, and it is true – many pupils did shun him, even at times Albert Oeri who was in the same class, because Carl was just too strange, too uncouth, too different. The only boys he spent his time with, if at all, were the sons of farmers, the poor ones who spoke the same local dialect. It did not help that he was clever, thirsty for knowledge, arrogant. On one occasion a teacher accused him of cheating because he could not believe this boy could write such an essay on his own. Carl was mortified. He had spent hours of hard work on it. Grown big by now, he got into plenty of fights and brawls. But he always felt 'a certain physical timidity' – a feeling that he was somehow repulsive.

In his twelfth year he had what appears to have been a breakdown. As he described it, he was standing in Basel cathedral precinct one day in early summer, waiting for a classmate before setting off on the long trek home, when another boy from the *Gymnasium* knocked him over and as he fell he struck his head against the kerbstone. He lay there, half-unconscious, but only half. The other half saw the advantage: if he lay there a little longer he might not have to go to school. From then on he had regular fainting fits, half real, half not, causing his parents so much worry that he was finally allowed to stay away from school for six months. 'A picnic,' he called it. But he also pitied his poor parents who were consulting many doctors, all in vain. No one could work out what was wrong with the boy. Finally it was decided he needed a change and he was sent off to stay with his architect uncle Ernst Jung in Winterthur. Carl loved it, spending hours at the town's railway station watching the steam trains come and go. But when he returned home to Klein-Hüningen he found his parents more worried than ever: he might have epilepsy, he overheard, and what were they to do, with no money and a boy who could not look after himself? 'I was thunderstruck. This was the collision with reality.' That same day he went to his father's library and started cramming. He had only one more fainting fit after that but did not let it master him, and soon he was back at school. 'That was when I learned what a neurosis is.'

From then on he got up at five every morning to study before setting off for school at seven. Sometimes it was 3 a.m. He felt he was himself for the first time. 'Previously I had existed too, but everything had merely happened to me. Now I happened to myself. Now I knew: I am myself now, now I exist.' In this elevated state he went to stay with a school friend who had a house on Lake Lucerne. How lucky the boy was, thought Carl, and how lucky they were to be allowed to use the *Waidling*, the punt, plunging the pole into the water as they manoeuvred out of the boathouse and into the blue. But when Carl started doing some fancy tricks, showing off, the boy's father whistled them back to shore and gave Carl a dressing down. Carl was seized with rage 'that this fat, ignorant boor should dare to insult ME'. But just as quickly he realised it was another conflict with reality: the father was right, he was wrong. It occurred to him that he might be two different people, the unsure boy and the 'other', the sure and powerful one. Not only did this other Carl exist, he was an old man, wore buckled shoes and a white wig and drove about in a fly with high wheels and a box suspended on springs with leather straps: a man living in the eighteenth century. The one as real as the other.

Around this time Carl was giving much thought to the idea of God. Not necessarily the God of his father's Protestant Reformed Church, but 'God the Creator', 'God of all Things'. One summer's day he came out of school and was again standing in the precincts of the cathedral – blue sky, radiant sunshine, gazing in awe at the pitched roof which had recently been retiled and glittered in the bright light – and thinking 'the world is beautiful and the church is beautiful, and God made all this and sits above it far away in the blue sky on a golden throne and . . . Here came a great hole in my thoughts and a choking sensation. I felt numbed, and only knew: Don't go on thinking now! Something terrible is happening, something I do not want to think, something I dare not even approach. Why not? Because I would be committing the most frightful of sins . . .' And on it went, all the way on the long walk home, all through that night, and the next. By the third night the feeling had become unbearable. 'Now it is coming, now it's serious,' he thought. *I must think.*' The thinking brought him to the idea that it was God, the creator of this beautiful world, who wanted him to think, and, what's more, to think of something inconceivably wicked. In a way it had very little to do with him, he had no choice. Adam and Eve had been perfect creatures before they sinned, *'Therefore it was God's intention that they should sin.'*

35

That thought liberated him and he gathered all his courage to think about the cathedral, the clear sky, and God sitting high above it on His golden throne, 'and from under the throne an enormous turd falls upon the sparkling new roof, shatters it, and breaks the walls of the Cathedral asunder'. To his own amazement he felt an indescribable relief; and instead of damnation he felt grace had come down on him 'and with it an unutterable bliss such as I had never known'.

He never spoke about this to anyone, or about the other two secrets of the phallus dream and the manikin, until, finally, many years later, he told Emma. 'My entire youth can be understood in terms of this secret. It induced in me an almost unbearable loneliness. My one great achievement during those years was that I resisted the temptation to talk about it with anyone.'

His mother reminded him he had often been depressed as a boy, but by his mid-teens Carl's depressions gradually lifted. He read voraciously: Plato, Socrates, Hegel, Schopenhauer, Kant, Goethe, all the writers he would later introduce to Emma. His school friends started calling him 'Father Abraham'. Personality No. 1 was to the fore and he lived more in the present, active at school and out and about in Basel. But Personality No. 2 was never far away. One day, walking along the banks of the Rhine on his way home from school, he saw a sailing ship. A storm was blowing up and the mainsail was running before it. The sight propelled him into a detailed fantasy which would stay with him for the rest of his life: the river became a great lake with a high rock rising out of it, only connected to the mainland by a narrow causeway. A wooden bridge led to a gate flanked by towers opening into a little medieval town, and on the rock stood a castle: 'This was my house.' The rooms were panelled and simple, a fine library held everything worth knowing, and there were weapons and canons for protection as well as a garrison of fifty men at arms. The little town had several hundred inhabitants and Carl was the mayor, the justice of the peace, and general adviser. There was a small port on the landward side of the town where he kept his two-masted schooner. 'The raison d'être of this whole arrangement was the secret of the keep, which I alone knew. The thought had come to me like a shock. For, inside the tower, extending from the battlements to the vaulted cellar, was a copper column.' It was as thick as a man's arm and it stood like a tree, upside down with rootlets reaching into the air. These roots drew something from the air and conducted it down the column into the cellar where there was a laboratory in which Carl made gold out of the mysterious substance.

From this point on, Carl's long, boring walk home from school became a short, delightful one, lost in the fantasy, making structural alterations to the buildings, holding council sessions, sentencing evil-doers, firing canons. Alternatively he might go for a sail in his schooner, and before he knew it he was standing on the parsonage doorstep. The fantasy lasted several months before he bored of it. Thereafter he started building with mud and stones in the garden of the parsonage, he studied fortifications, collected fossils, learnt about plants and read numerous scientific periodicals. Building miniature castles and towns is what he used to do as a young boy to bring him back to himself, and he would do it for the rest of his life.

Carl passed his matriculation examinations with ease and went on to study medicine at the University of Basel. Originally he, like Emma, wanted to study the natural sciences, but he knew he needed to earn a proper living, and, deep down, he knew where he was going. After all, six of his mother's relations were pastors, healers of the spirit, and his Grandfather Jung, arriving in Basel from Germany, was a doctor of medicine with progressive views, believing that the insane should be given treatment, not incarcerated. Grossvater Jung was a well-known and respected figure around Basel – the kind called 'larger than life', a democrat and a liberal, somewhat eccentric, with a pink pig for a pet – in a word, just the kind of man Carl would wish to emulate. He never knew his grandfather but he shared his name: Carl Gustav, except his own spelling was with a K. He changed it to a C once he left university, embarking on his own life.

If Grossvater Jung was a liberal in public, at home he was authoritarian. His son, Paul Achilles Jung, Carl's father, found he could never live up to his expectations. Though Paul was a fine scholar, studying oriental languages and Hebrew at Göttingen, writing his dissertation on the Arabic version of the 'Song of Songs', when it came to choosing a profession he decided to become a pastor in the Protestant Reformed Church, a modest, retiring life, with a poor living. Perhaps he was encouraged in this by his future father-in-law, Samuel Preiswerk. Paul was Preiswerk's student and they spent many happy hours in his library going over ancient Hebrew texts. But something caused Paul Jung to always be racked with doubts. Most summers he went, alone, to stay with a Catholic priest in Sachseln. It was odd behaviour for a pastor of the Protestant Reformed Church, and no one knew why he went. In a way, Carl respected him for it.

But his respect for his father was ebbing away. By the time of his confirmation Carl was completely alienated from the

Church, bored and sceptical, arguing vehemently with his father about the hypocrisy of it all, and, worse still, his father's own hypocrisy. He watched his father go through the motions day after day, knowing what doubts and torments he suffered privately in the dark hours of the night. 'I was seized with the most vehement pity for my father,' he remembered in old age. 'An abyss had opened between him and me, and I saw no possibility of ever bridging it, for it was infinite in extent.' He was still his 'dear and generous father', but Carl could do nothing for him. He searched the Bible for answers but found none. Surely the devil was God's creature too? But of that the Bible gave no sign. It was nothing but 'fancy drivel'. In a letter of 13 June 1955, Jung admitted the tragedy of his youth had been to see his father 'cracking up' before his eyes.

Carl's mother, Emilie, came from a long line of seers. Her own mother had two personalities: a good monk and a bad monk, and she had visions and saw ghosts. The occult was part of everyday life for many of the Preiswerks and once Carl's mother came back home after being 'away', the occult became part of his everyday life too, or more often his night life when alarming 'atmospheres' emanated from her bedroom. 'I was sure she consisted of two personalities, one innocuous and human, the other uncanny,' he wrote. In her Personality No. 1 she was a good mother: warm, pleasant, with a good sense of humour, and a fine cook, and inclined to look up to her son as he grew older, confiding in him instead of in his father. But her Personality No. 2 was a different matter: 'a sombre, imposing figure possessed of unassailable authority – and no bones about it'. She was also very large and overweight. Later he realised this was due to her depression and the bad state of the marriage, but as a boy he did not understand, and his deep, complicated ties were to his clever, tormented father. 'The feeling I associated with "woman" was for a long time that of innate unreliability. "Father", on the other hand, meant reliability and – powerlessness. This is the handicap I started off with. Later these early impressions were revised: I have trusted men friends and been disappointed by them, and I have mistrusted women and was not disappointed.'

By the time Carl enrolled in Basel University in early 1895 his father had become, in his eyes, like the Fisher King from the Grail legend 'whose wound would not heal', and had begun to show signs of a real wound which would not heal. He had been depressed and tormented for years but now the family doctor found serious physical symptoms which he could not diagnose, but which were nevertheless killing him. By the end of the year he was bedridden. Carl carried him from room to room like a bag of bones. Within months he was dead. 'The following days were gloomy and painful,' wrote Carl. 'Little of them has remained in my memory.'

Before he died Carl's father had applied to the canton of Basel for a stipend to help fund his son's studies. The request was granted, but instead of being pleased Carl was mortified at having to resort to charity. He also had to borrow money from his wealthy Jung relations and he bought and sold antiques for one of his aunts to make ends meet. As to his mother, Emilie: 'Once my mother spoke to me or to the surrounding air in her "second" voice, and remarked: "He died just in time for you."'

At the time Carl was not sure what she meant, but his father's death certainly freed Carl: his student years were a good time, full of energy, friendship and intellectual activity, fuelled, as he himself recognised, by a 'vaulting ambition'. Soon he was dominating the discussions at his Zofingia fraternity, challenging the others with brilliant forays into the ideas of Schopenhauer and Nietzsche and talking about things unknown: dreams, visions, and the occult. His friend, Albert Oeri, progressing with him from the *Gymnasium* to Basel University, remembered discussions on subjects such as: 'The Limits of Exact Science' and 'Some Reflections on the Nature and Value of Speculative Research' and 'Some Thoughts on Psychology', and that Carl easily succeeded in 'intellectually dominating an unruly chorus of fifty or sixty students from different branches of learning, and luring them into highly speculative branches of thought'. He quickly acquired the nickname Walze – 'the Steam-Roller' – and looking at fraternity photographs of Carl at the time, anyone can see why: large and round, he has an overbearing presence and a less than charming, closed expression. His vaulting ambition and superior manner did not endear him to everyone. As to women, there weren't any.

When his father died, Carl and his mother and his sister Trudi, nine years his junior, had to leave the parsonage. They had no money and nowhere to go so they moved in with the Preiswerk family in an old, dilapidated mill, the Bottminger Mill, in a run-down district on the outskirts of Basel. Moving into the mill brought Carl into direct contact with spiritualism and the occult because this was the branch of the family who were seers, had visions, heard voices and held seances. 'He was appalled that the official scientific position of the day towards occult phenomena was simply to deny their existence,' wrote Oeri, 'rather than investigate and explain them.' Consequently

Carl decided to investigate them, regularly attending seances at the mill led by his cousin Helly, and subsequently basing his doctoral dissertation on them, entitled 'On the Psychology and Pathology of So-Called Occult Phenomena'.

So this was the man Emma met, or became reacquainted with, in 1899 on her return from Paris, aged seventeen. He was twenty-four, just starting work at the Burghölzli asylum, a complex man with many secrets. In fact there was one further secret Emma did not know about the 'other' Carl. It was one he himself no longer 'knew', having repressed it deep in his unconscious where it safely remained until that wizard of the unconscious, Sigmund Freud, uncovered it during one of those long, intense evenings the two men shared in March 1907.

It threw Carl right off balance, as Emma cannot have failed to notice. Especially in the way he behaved with the Jewish woman they met in the hotel in Abbazia. He did not admit it to Emma then, or for many years. At the time he did not even admit it to himself – not until the crisis had become so unmanageable that he could no longer avoid it: Carl had been sexually abused when he was a boy and the only way he could deal with it was to repress the memory. But in October 1907, a good seven months after the discussions with Freud had forced the memories to the surface, and after his life had been thrown into further confusion, he had to confront it. His answers to Freud's letters had been more and more delayed, and finally Freud, usually so tolerant and indulgent of his crown prince, voiced his objections and Carl came clean. 'Your last two letters contain references to my laziness in writing. I certainly owe you an explanation,' he wrote on 28 October, first blaming his workload but then admitting that it was actually what Freud had termed his 'self-preservation complex' which often bedevilled his pen, preventing him from writing.

> Actually – and I confess this to you with a struggle – I have a boundless admiration for you both as a man and a researcher, and I bear you no conscious grudge. So the self-preservation complex does not come from there; it is rather that my veneration for you has something of the character of a 'religious' crush. Though it does not really bother me, I still feel it is disgusting and ridiculous because of its undeniable erotic undertone. This abominable feeling comes from the fact that as a boy I was the victim of a sexual assault by a man I once worshipped. Even in Vienna the remarks of the ladies ('*enfin seuls*' etc.) sickened me, although the reason for it was not clear to me at the time. This feeling, which I have still not quite got rid of, hampers me considerably.

He goes on to explain that this has made close friendships with male colleagues 'downright disgusting', and ends the letter abruptly, saying: 'I think I owe you this explanation. I would rather not have said it.'

All these secrets, and Emma knew none of them.

3

A Secret Betrothal

Emma and Carl were betrothed on 6 October 1901, in secret, at the family's Ölberg estate in Schaffhausen. The only other guests apart from Emma's mother and sister were Carl's mother and sister and the only record of the event are a few out-of-focus snapshots, probably taken by Marguerite, in the garden, where the couple appear to be walking away from the camera as often as towards it, as though trying to avoid it. By the time of the betrothal they had been courting for eighteen months and Emma was nineteen. She looks younger, almost a schoolgirl, and Carl still has the look of the Steam-Roller about him, not yet the confident man of the world he would become. They agreed to wait until Emma was twenty-one before getting married.

Jung had been assistant physician at the Burghölzli asylum for almost a year by then, having moved to Zürich straight after his medical examinations, taking a temporary job in a doctor's practice to fill in time before starting at the Burghölzli in December 1900. The move puzzled his colleagues and upset his mother. Why would anyone want to leave cosmopolitan Basel for dull, commercial Zürich, and how could he abandon his impoverished mother and sister like that? Part of the reason was that Carl had fallen foul of Herr Professor Wille, the first in a long line of senior men Jung would quarrel with in his working life. Ludwig Wille was the new professor of psychiatry at the University of Basel, the discipline of psychiatry itself dating no further back than the 1880s. In deciding to specialise in it, Jung embarked on the least fashionable and least remunerated branch of the medical profession, seen as another odd decision by his colleagues, given he was one of their best with the brightest of futures. They could not know that psychiatry spoke deeply to the 'other' Carl who had had, ever since he could remember, the kind of dreams and visions some people might deem insane. When he read Krafft-Ebing's 1890 work on 'diseases of the personality' in the *Lehrbuch der Psychiatrie*, he recognised it immediately. 'My heart suddenly began to pound. I had to stand up and draw a deep breath. My excitement was intense . . . Here was the empirical field common to biological and spiritual facts, which I had everywhere sought and nowhere found.' Professor Wille, however, was firmly of the old school, seeing all mental illness as the result of a physical deterioration of the brain. Sooner or later Jung was bound to take issue with that, the net result being that he decided to present his doctoral dissertation to the medical faculty of the University of Zürich, not Basel. The city had the added advantage of being closer than Basel to Schaffhausen and Emma.

There were around 400 patients at the Burghölzli asylum when Jung arrived to take up his position, but apart from Bleuler there was only one other qualified doctor, Ludwig von Muralt, the day-to-day care being carried out by unqualified helpers, male and female. This meant an extremely heavy workload for Carl, who also lived on the premises. The only time he had off was Sundays, when he was able to visit Emma, first walking fifteen minutes down the hill to the tram station which in those days did not reach as far as the Burghölzli, then taking the recently electrified tram to Zürich's Central Station, then the steam train to Schaffhausen, speeding northwards leaving lake and alps behind and into a landscape of farmland, meadows and scattered villages, past the crashing Rhine Falls, finally pulling in to Schaffhausen railway station where he was met by coachman Braun in the green Rauschenbach carriage and conveyed up the hill to the Ölberg estate – thereby travelling from the lowest to the highest *niveau* of Swiss society all in the course of two hours, a journey which never failed to delight.

And there in the grand front hall waiting expectantly for him was Emma, eager to listen, eager to learn, eager to help. She had started taking Latin lessons in order to read Carl's medical texts, and maths lessons to discipline her mind, and she was practising her handwriting to help Carl with the daily reports which Bleuler was most particular about, regardless of how many hours it took to write them up. Boring for Carl, but thrilling for Emma. As to her general knowledge: as with Carl, the natural sciences were her enthusiasm; so too her interest in the Legend of the Holy Grail, which had likewise been Carl's for many years. Emma meant to help Carl with his work, if only in small ways, and Carl was only too happy to oblige.

In many ways Emma was preparing to be 'the good wife' in similar vein to those recommended to young ladies by the weekly magazines. 'The ideal wife,' wrote Rudolf von Tavel in the monthly *Wissen und Leben*, 'should live and act entirely in her husband's spirit. She must support him in his task, softening him, warming him, and praising him in golden terms, convincing her children of the same, so that the way of life in the family is the right one, fostering the right social attitudes for the upholding of the Vaterland.' Rosa Dahinden-Pfyl agreed, writing in *Die Kunst mit Männern Glücklich zu Sein* (*The Art of Being Happy with a Man*): 'The happiness and lasting power of married love relies largely on the good and clever ways of the woman.' She should never complain about the husband's coldness towards her, whether real or imagined. She should take a gentle interest in everything which concerns him, always showing her appreciation, and make his home comfortable, never tiring him with needless chatter. She should avoid becoming bitter about his weaknesses, and never meddle in his business affairs. To remain attractive to him she should always be sweet-tempered, dress nicely and with good taste; in fact, always take care of her appearance but also her health, her character and her soul. 'Should her physical charms fade, she should retain her husband's interest by her sympathy, her learning, her heart and spirit, but never by showing a knowledge greater than his.'

Had Emma married her haut-bourgeois beau this would surely have been her whole life, and nothing more. But not with Carl. His own childhood had nothing bourgeois about it and his own character was not suited to fitting in with convention. His requirements of Emma would be infinitely more complex and challenging than any handbook on marriage could encompass. But all that came later. For the time being it was simply exhilarating for Emma to be with someone who brought her books and scientific articles to read and was happy to discuss his plans and ideas with her.

Carl and Emma easily fell into the roles of teacher and student. Carl had already completed five years of medical studies and embarked on the work and profession that would occupy him for the rest of his life. At this time he was working on his doctoral dissertation, 'On the Psychology and Pathology of So-called Occult Phenomena', investigating the uncharted world of the unconscious through the evidence he had gathered during Helly's seances at Bottminger Mill. Herr Professor Freud in Vienna had just published a book called *The Interpretation of Dreams*, which investigated the unconscious from a different angle, the hidden meaning of dreams, which had often filled the pages of literature but had never yet been scientifically investigated, and Carl had been deputed by Bleuler to read it and present his findings to the Burghölzli staff at one of their evening meetings. As if he didn't already have enough paperwork to do. But this was different. This was the new world, just waiting to be discovered.

To Emma, Carl was worldly and sophisticated and, as his friend Albert Oeri described, he was a mesmerising talker. So Emma might have been surprised to discover that her fiancé had absolutely no experience of women. 'He didn't think much of fraternity dances, romancing the housemaids, and similar gallantries,' recalled Oeri, making Carl sound like a bit of a prig. He did bring Luggi, Helly's older sister, to some dances, but Oeri only remembered one occasion when Carl was really smitten, at another fraternity dance, with a young woman from French-speaking Switzerland, at which point he began to behave very oddly indeed. In fact, if Oeri had not been such a reliable witness, one would wonder at the veracity of the story. 'One morning soon after,' Oeri wrote, 'he entered a shop, asked for and received two wedding rings, put twenty centimes on the counter, and started for the door.' Presumably the twenty centimes were by way of a deposit. When the owner objected,

Carl gave back the rings, took his money and left the shop 'cursing the owner, who, just because Carl happened to possess absolutely nothing but twenty centimes, dared to interfere with his engagement'.

With anyone else you might think this was some kind of student prank, but not with Carl, hovering precariously between two personalities and having no idea how to handle such a situation. Afterwards 'Carl was very depressed,' said Oeri. 'He never tackled the matter again, and so the Steam-Roller remained unaffianced for quite a number of years.' Until he met Emma, in fact, and persuaded her to marry him.

But Emma had a secret of her own. When she was twelve her father started to lose his sight. Soon he could no longer read for himself, and Emma, the studious one, was deputed to sit and read out loud to him: newspapers, magazines, books, business matters brought over from the factory and foundry nearby, so she became quite knowledgeable in financial matters and the handling of accounts. Later, as his condition worsened, plans for the redevelopment of the Ölberg estate were made for him in Braille. It was hard for Emma, not least because her father was a difficult, sarcastic man – a trait which got worse with age and the advance of his illness. Harder still was the fact that the cause of his blindness had to be kept secret, such was the shame and stigma attached to it: Herr Rauschenbach had syphilis. According to the family, he had caught the disease after a business trip to Budapest, presumably from a prostitute. Bertha had decided not to go with him on that occasion because she felt the two little girls were too young to be left alone with the children's maid. Had she gone, everything might have been different. It was a tragedy for the family, and photographs of

Emma during her teens show a shy, round-faced, podgy girl, surely feeling the stress of the family secret. She was trying her best to help her mother with this awful burden as her father became more and more bitter and desperate, shut away from the world in his room upstairs. It robbed Emma of her sunny nature, making her too serious for her age.

Albert Oeri remembered visiting the Jung household not long before Pastor Jung died and described how Carl, aged twenty, carried his father 'who had once been so strong and erect' around from room to room 'like a heap of bones in an anatomy class'. Emma sat at her father's side reading to him as he went blind, bitter and half mad. There was not much to choose between them.

By the end of the nineteenth century doctors were finally on the verge of finding a cure for syphilis, but not soon enough for Herr Rauschenbach. By 1905 Fritz Schaudinn and Erich Hoffmann in Berlin had identified the causative organism, the microbe *Treponema pallidum*, and by 1910 Dr Paul Ehrlich, director of the Royal Prussian Institute of Experimental Therapy in Frankfurt, developed the first modestly effective treatment, Salvarsan, though it was not until the discovery of penicillin in the 1940s that a cure was certain. In the 1890s the treatment still relied on the use of mercury, which could alleviate the condition if caught early enough though the side effects were extremely unpleasant, and it was not a cure. Syphilis, highly infectious and primarily transmitted through sexual contact, had stalked Europe for centuries, causing fear and dread and giving rise to a great deal of moralising about the virtues of marriage. The symptoms were horrible, the first signs being rashes and pustules over the body and face, then open suppurating lesions in the skin, disfiguring tumours and terrible pain, only alleviated by regular doses of morphine. Some of the most tragic cases were those of unsuspecting wives infected by their husbands, in turn infecting the unborn child. Wet nurses were vulnerable, either catching it from the child, or, already infected themselves, passing it on to the child instead. To make matters worse for families like the Rauschenbachs, society was hypocritical about syphilis. Everyone knew about the disease but it was not talked about, except in the medical pamphlets read in the privacy of a doctor's surgery: 'The woman must submit to her husband – consequently, whereas he catches it when he wants, she also catches it when he wants! The woman is ignorant . . . particularly in matters of this sort. So she is generally unaware of where and how she might catch it, and when she has caught it she is for a long time unaware of what she has got.' Another pamphlet concentrated on women of the lower classes, unwittingly revealing a further hypocrisy of the times: whilst the bourgeois woman was seen as the victim, the working-class woman, not her seducer, or client if she was a prostitute, was to blame: 'The woman must be told . . . Every factory girl, peasant and maid must be told that if she abandons herself to the seducer then not only does she run the risk of having to bring up the child which might result from her transgression, but also that of catching the disease whose consequences can make her suffer for the rest of her life.'

In Vienna, Sigmund Freud was investigating the psychological effects of syphilis on the next generation, finding that many of his cases of hysteria and obsessional neurosis, such as his patients 'Dora' and 'Rat Man', had fathers who had been treated for syphilis in their youth. It is possible that Bertha

Rauschenbach was keen on Carl Jung as a suitor for Emma not only because she could see how well suited they were, but because Carl had just completed his medical studies and could help with the treatment of her husband's illness, in secret, in the privacy of their own home. And she was no doubt relieved to realise how little experience her future son-in-law had had with women.

Meanwhile Carl was working at the Burghölzli, putting his father, who had died 'just in time' as his mother said, behind him. But he could not leave Personality No. 2 behind. Years later his friend and colleague Ludwig von Muralt, the other doctor at the Burghölzli when Carl arrived, told him that the way he behaved during those first months was so odd people thought he might be 'psychologically abnormal'. Jung himself described experiencing feelings of such inferiority and tension at the time that it was only by 'the utmost concentration on the essential' that he managed not to 'explode'. The problem was partly that Bleuler and Von Muralt seemed to be so confident in their roles, whereas he was completely at sea in this strange new world of the institution, and partly because he felt deeply humiliated by his poverty. He had only one pair of trousers and two shirts to his name and he had to send all his meagre wages back to his mother and sister, still living on charity at the Bottminger Mill. The humiliation was accompanied by a general feeling of social inferiority, heightened by the fact that Von Muralt came from one of the oldest and wealthiest families of Zürich.

They were the same feelings which had often plagued Carl in the past and his solution was the same: to withdraw into himself and become what he called a 'hermit', locking himself away from the world. When he was not working, he read all fifty volumes of the journal *Allgemeine Zeitschrift für Psychiatrie*, cover to cover. He said he wanted to know 'how the human mind reacted to the sight of its own destruction'. He might have used his own father as an illustration. Or himself during those first months of 1901 after Emma had refused his hand in marriage, perhaps the real reason why he was so distressed, when his confident Personality No. 1 disappeared into thin air along with all his hopes and dreams, and he was close to a mental and emotional breakdown, as he had been in the past and would be again in the future.

The crisis was extreme. But then, quite suddenly, at the end of six months, he recovered. In fact, he swung completely the other way, the inferior wretch replaced almost overnight by the loud, opinionated, energetic Steam-Roller of old. Once betrothed and sure of Emma's love, Carl was able to take life at the Burghölzli at full tilt, with the kind of energy which left others breathless. No one could fail to notice it, but no one knew the reason why, because no one knew where he went every Sunday on his day off.

Not knowing of Carl's extreme crisis of confidence, Emma remained dazzled by his love, hardly able to believe it was true. She worried that she was a boring companion as she recounted small details about her mundane week – the riding, the walks by the Rhine, the family visits, her father's deteriorating health, the musical evenings which her mother liked to host at Ölberg. The best moments were when they discussed the books she'd been reading, which gave her week its shape and purpose, enabling her to be 'herself' in a way which would otherwise have eluded her. To her joy Carl was delighted by her progress, always encouraging her to do more. And to her relief she soon the time for hysteria were 'animal magnetism' and hypnotism, each requiring a doctor with special 'intuition'. In animal magnetism the doctor passed his hands over the patient to release the vital fluid or energy which had supposedly become blocked. In hypnotism the doctor took control of the mind, providing the most dramatic demonstrations as patients fell into trances and spoke in strange voices. When Eugen Bleuler continued his training under Auguste Forel at the Burghölzli in the early 1880s, hypnotism was one of the main treatments and Forel had his own '*Hypnosestab*', a wand with a silver tip which he used with some success on obsessives and neurotics as well as hysterics. But his greatest success was with alcoholics. The Burghölzli was then, and remained when Bleuler took over from Forel, an institution which held strictly to the virtues of abstinence. Drink was one of the worst afflictions of the age and asylums were full of chronic cases who were contained whilst 'inside', but, without a vow of abstinence, soon reverted to old habits once they left.

All this Carl explained to Emma in his letters, or on their Sundays in the drawing room at Ölberg, or on their afternoon walks high up in the meadows above the house, up to 'their' bench by the edge of the forest beyond. Later Emma confessed she only understood half of it at the time. Apparently Bleuler was continuing the progressive methods he had started to develop at Reichenau: staff lived amongst the inmates, eating with them at the same tables and socialising with them in their spare time. His theory of *affektiver Rapport*, listening with empathy, was the guiding principle. There was also a great emphasis put on cleanliness. Inmates were helped to wash thoroughly, in spite of a shortage of baths and bathrooms, and to keep their clothes in good order; likewise their beds, a dozen on each side of a ward, which were kept neat, the heavy feather covers hung out of the windows every morning to air and the mattresses regularly turned. The patients were kept occupied, Herr Direktor Bleuler believing that physical activity was good for the distraught mind. The kitchen gardens lay beyond the walls of the asylum extending down the slopes and provided all their vegetables and fruit, which were brought fresh to the kitchens every day. The dairy produced the milk and cheese. Hens provided the eggs. The laundry kept inmates busy washing and starching and ironing. The *Hausordnung* kept the building spick and span, smelling of floor polish and soap. There were workshops: woodwork and wood-chopping for the tiled stoves in winter, sack-making, silk-plucking, sewing, mending, knitting. The place was to all intents and purposes self-sufficient and the food, for an institution, was good: always a soup for the midday meal followed by meat and vegetables, with soup and bread again for the evening meal along with a piece of cheese or sausage. The patients were divided into three categories and while third-class patients did not eat as well as the first-class (private) ones, it was still a better standard than at most asylums. In the evenings there were card games, reading, concerts; sometimes the patients produced an entertainment, sometimes lectures were put on, and at the weekends there were occasional fetes and dances for those willing and able. Jung was put in charge of social events as soon as he arrived. He hated it.

To keep things going day to day there were seventy *Wärters*, male and female helpers in long white aprons and starched white collars, the men in trousers, shirt and tie, the women in long dark skirts and starched white caps. Like the doctors they lived on the premises, but unlike the doctors they had no quarters of their own. They slept on the wards or in the corridors, on wooden camp beds put up for the night, the women in the women's section, the men in the men's. The only exception was the *Wärter*s in charge of the 'first-class' patients, who would sleep in the patient's private room. This was a great privilege because not only was there some peace and quiet but the private patient was allowed candles in the room at night, or even an oil lamp if their behaviour was good enough and they were no danger to themselves or others. It was an eighty-hour week and the pay was low: 600 Swiss francs per annum for the male *Wärter*s, a hundred francs less for the women. But board and lodging was all found, so the rest could be saved.

Carl's day started at 6 a.m. and rarely finished before 8 p.m., after which he would go up to his room to write his daily reports, work on his dissertation, and compose his daily letter to Emma. There was a staff meeting every morning, after a breakfast of bread and a bowl of coffee, ward rounds morning and evening, an additional general meeting three times a week to consider every aspect of the running of the institution, and at least once a week a discussion evening, which, by the time Carl joined, was already well versed in the writings of Freud. Once into his stride there was no stopping Herr Doktor Jung, and his sheer brilliance soon singled him out. Bleuler's *affektiver Rapport* was exactly the kind of treatment he himself believed in: listening acutely and with empathy to the apparent babblings of inmates with *dementia praecox*, or the outbursts of hysterics and the circular repetitions of obsessive neurotics. Carl was fascinated by the chronic catatonics who had been at the Burghölzli for as long as anyone could remember, including the old women incarcerated since they were young girls for having illegitimate children, who no longer knew who they'd once been.

Carl could listen to his patients for hours, taking notes, catching clues, watching how the mind worked. The Burghölzli was known for its progressive research, and inmates demonstrating interesting symptoms were the willing, and unwilling, guinea pigs – ushered into the room or lecture theatre for the doctor to examine, question and offer a diagnosis. It was a fine apprenticeship for Carl, as he himself admitted. He had little interest in the patients who were there with TB or typhus, and he could not bear the routine work, the meetings and the administration, to which he rarely gave any proper attention. But the old lady who stood by the window all day waiting for her long-lost lover, or the schizophrenic who talked crazily about God – that was a different matter altogether. Here his Personality No. 2 came into its own, working hand in hand with No. 1. 'It was as though two rivers had united and in one grand torrent were bearing me inexorably towards distant goals,' he later wrote. Bleuler soon saw that Herr Doktor Jung, with his fine intuition on the one hand and his brilliant mind on the other, understood the inmates like no one else.

Carl's listening was made more effective by Bleuler's insistence that everything be conducted in Swiss dialect, not the High German which doctors normally used, and which effectively meant no communication since most inmates could not understand High German, and even if they could, it caused such a social gulf between doctor and patient that the patient felt browbeaten. When speaking High German, Carl retained his broad Basel accent, something which had humiliated him at grammar school, but no longer. Now he learnt all the other regional Swiss dialects as well because at the Burghölzli it was expected that the doctor should adapt to the patient, not the other way round, an idea generally held as odd and even dangerous by the vast majority of the medical profession. Besides, without it Jung could do no useful research.

On Sundays he retold the patients' stories to Emma, shocking her, entertaining her, keeping her spellbound. Stories about women in the asylum held a special fascination for her, such as the woman in Carl's section who had been diagnosed with schizophrenia. Jung disagreed with the diagnosis, thinking it was more like ordinary depression, so he started, *à la Freud*, to ask the woman about her dreams, probing her unconscious. It turned out that when she was a young girl she had fallen in love with 'Mr X', the son of a wealthy industrialist. She hoped they would marry, but he did not appear to care for her, so in time she wed someone else and had two children. Five years later a friend visited and told her that her marriage had come as quite a shock to Mr X. 'That was the moment!' as Jung wrote in his account of it. The woman became deeply depressed and one day, bathing her two small children, she let them drink the contaminated river water. Spring water was used only for drinking, not bathing, in those days. Shortly afterwards her little girl came down with typhoid fever and died. The woman's depression became acute and finally she was sent to the Burghölzli asylum. Jung knew the narcotics for her *dementia praecox* were doing her no good. Should he tell her the truth or not? He pondered for days, worried that it might tip her further into madness. Then he made his decision: to confront her, telling no one else. 'To accuse a person point-blank of murder is no small matter,' he wrote later. 'And it was tragic for the patient to have to listen to it and accept it. But the result was that in two weeks it proved possible to discharge her, and she was never again institutionalised.'

Love, murder, guilt, madness. Emma had never heard stories like it. Nor had she ever considered the powerful workings of the 'unconscious'. But she was intelligent and well read. She knew all about Faust's pact with Mephistopheles, Lady Macbeth's guilty sleepwalking, and Siegfried, the mythical hero. Now she was beginning to realise that this 'unconscious' was the key to the hidden workings of the mind and could be accessed in various ways, then used as a tool to cure the patient. By the time of their secret betrothal Emma was helping to write up Carl's daily reports, learning all the time. If these years were the beginning of Carl Jung's career, they were the beginning of something for Emma too.

Meanwhile Jung was trying, between his eighty-hour week and his social duties, to finish his dissertation on the 'So-called Occult Phenomena'. There had been a revival of interest in the occult at the end of the nineteenth century, people using Ouija boards and horoscopes, having seances, delving into magic and the ancient arts, and reporting strange paranormal occurrences. Carl was used to such things from his mother's 'seer' side of the family, like the time when a knife in the drawer of their kitchen cupboard unaccountably split in two, or the times when his mother spoke with a strange, prophetic voice. But what interested Jung the doctor was the way the occult provided another route to the hidden world of the unconscious, more psychological than spiritual. Cousin Helly was probably a hysteric, he now concluded, a young girl falling into trances to get attention.

In fact Helly's mother had become so worried about the way the trances and the voices were dominating her life that she had packed her off to Marseilles to study dress-making, at which point Helly's trances stopped, and she became a fine seamstress.

Jung presented his dissertation to the faculty of medicine at the University of Zürich in 1901 and it was published the following year. The Preiswerk family, reading it on publication, were distressed. After a general introduction about current research on the subject, Jung concentrated on one case history: Helly Preiswerk and her seances at Bottminger Mill, referring to her, by way of thin disguise, as Miss S. W., a medium, fifteen and a half years old, Protestant – that is, instantly recognisable by anyone who knew the family. She was described as 'a girl with poor inheritance' and 'of mediocre intelligence, with no special gifts, neither musical nor fond of books'. She had a second personality called Ivenes. One sister was a hysteric, the other had 'nervous heart attacks'. The family were described as 'people with very limited interests' – and this of a family who had come to the rescue of his impoverished mother and sister. It showed a side of Carl which Emma would have to deal with often in the future: a callous insensitivity, driven perhaps by what he himself admitted was his 'vaulting ambition'. But as far as the faculty of medicine at the University of Zürich was concerned, it was a perfectly good piece of research, fulfilling the aims Jung expressed in his clever conclusion: that it would contribute to 'the progressive elucidation and assimilation of the as yet extremely controversial psychology of the unconscious'.

The most telling thing about the dissertation is the dedication on the title page. It reads: 'to his wife Emma Jung-Rauschenbach'.

Given the dissertation was completed in 1901 and published in 1902, the dedication precedes the event of the marriage by a good year. Whatever was Carl thinking? What is the difference between 'my wife', which Emma was not, and 'my betrothed', which she was. It suggests Carl was desperate to claim Emma for himself, fully and legally, a situation which mere betrothal could not achieve. Emma was the answer to all Carl's problems: financial – certainly – but equally his emotional and psychological ones. He needed Emma for his stability in every sense, and he knew it.

Carl and Emma's wedding was set for 14 February 1903, St Valentine's Day. Buoyed up and boisterous, Carl became increasingly impatient and intolerant of the 'unending desert of routine' at the Burghölzli. Now he saw it as 'a submission to the vow to believe only in what was probable, average, commonplace, barren of meaning, to renounce everything strange and significant, and reduce anything extraordinary to the banal'. Given Bleuler's achievements at the asylum this was high-handed Carl at his worst. The fact is, he was fed up. He wanted to take a sabbatical, to travel, to do things he had never been able to do before. And he wanted to do it before he married Emma. Because he had no money of his own, his future mother-in-law happily offered to fund it. In July 1902 Jung submitted his resignation to Bleuler and the Zürich authorities, and by the beginning of October he was off, first to Paris, then London, for a four-month pre-wedding jaunt. Bleuler, knowing nothing of Jung's secret betrothal to Fräulein Rauschenbach, must have been angry and non-plussed. How would Herr Doktor Jung afford it? How could he manage without a salary? And what about his poor mother and sister?

Emma and her mother meanwhile started the lengthy process of preparing for the wedding – the dress itself, the veil, shoes, bouquet, trousseau, church service, flowers, guest list, menu for the wedding banquet, and the travel arrangements for the couple's honeymoon. Emma's father's health must have caused some heartache: already parlous, it had taken a turn for the worse. He knew about his daughter's betrothal to Carl now, but what to do about the wedding? It was a terrible dilemma for Emma who had, over the years, watched her father's decline in horror and shame, and now he would not be able to attend the ceremony, or walk her up the aisle, or give her away.

Before leaving the country Carl had to complete his Swiss army military service, an annual duty for all Swiss males between the ages of twenty and fifty, in his case as a lieutenant in the medical corps. But then he was off, first paying a visit to his mother and sister in Basel on his way to France. From Paris he wrote daily letters to Emma, and separately to her mother too, giving them all the news: he lived cheaply in a hotel for one franc a day and worked in Pierre Janet's laboratory at the Salpêtrière, attending all the eminent psychologist's lectures. He had enrolled at the Berlitz School to improve his English and started reading English newspapers, a habit he retained all his life. He went to the Louvre most days, fell in love with Holbein, the Dutch Masters and the *Mona Lisa*, and spent hours watching the copyists make their living selling their work to tourists like himself. He walked everywhere, through Les Halles, the Jardin du Luxembourg and the Bois de Boulogne, sitting in cafés and bistros watching the world, rich and poor, go by, and in the evenings he read French and English novels, the classic ones, never the modern. He also saw Helly and her sister Vally, both now working as seamstresses for a Paris fashion house, and he was grateful for their company, not only because he knew no one else in Paris, but because Helly was generous enough to forgive him his past sins. When the weather turned cold Bertha Rauschenbach posted off a winter coat to keep him warm. It wasn't the only thing she sent him: when he expressed a longing to commission a copy of a Frans Hals painting of a mother and her children, the money was quickly dispatched.

By January Carl was in London, visiting the sights and the museums and taking more English lessons. It must have been his English tutor, recently down from Oxford, who delighted Carl by taking him back to dine at his college high table with the dons in their academic gowns – a fine dinner, as he wrote to Emma, followed by cigars, liqueurs and snuff. The conversation was 'in the style of the 18th century' – and men only, 'because we wanted to talk exclusively at an intellectual level'. In 1903 it was still common for men to be seen as more intellectual than women, and there were no women at high table to disagree. It was Jung's first brush with the English 'gentleman' and he never forgot it, the word often appearing in his letters as a mark of the highest praise.

In Schaffhausen, Emma received a present. It was a painting. In between all his other activities Carl took the time in Paris to travel out into the flat countryside with his easel and paints. He had always loved painting, even as a child, and in future it would go hand in hand with his writing, offering a poetic and spiritual dimension to his words. He found a spot on a far bank of the River Seine, looking across at a hamlet of pitched-roof houses, a church with a high spire, and trees all along. But the real subject of the painting was the clouds, which took up three-quarters of the canvas: light and shining below, dark and dramatic above. The inscription read: 'Seine landscape with clouds, for my dearest fiancée at Christmas, 1902. Paris, December 1902. Painted by C. G. Jung.'

It might have been a premonition of their marriage.

The painting Carl sent Emma for Christmas 1902.

4

A Rich Marriage

Emma and Carl got married twice: first the civil ceremony on 14 February, with just a few family members in attendance – Carl's mother and sister, and Emma's sister Marguerite but not her mother or father – followed by an evening wedding ball at the Hotel Bellevue Neuhausen overlooking the Rhine Falls. Then, two days later, a church wedding in the Steigkirche, the Protestant Reformed Church in Schaffhausen, at which both mothers were present, but not Emma's father. The bridal couple arrived at the church in the high Rauschenbach carriage used only for weddings, decorated with winter flowers and driven by coachman Braun: Carl in his newly acquired silk top hat and tails, Emma in her white gown, veil and fur cape against the cold – luckily there was no snow that February – waving and smiling at well-wishers left and right. The service was followed by a wedding banquet at Ölberg. Later, on 1 March, there was a further festivity at the Hotel Schiff for the employees of the Rauschenbach factories and foundry.

The wedding banquet was grand, as expected for the eldest daughter of a family of such wealth and high standing: twelve courses, starting with lobster bisque, followed by local river trout, toast and foie gras, a sorbet to precede the main course of pheasant with artichoke hearts accompanied by a variety of salads. The dessert course offered puddings, patisserie, cakes, ice creams and fruit, and each course was accompanied by a selection of wines, ending with a choice of liqueurs, sherry, port or champagne, and finally, coffee, cigars and cigarettes. The bridal couple sat side by side at a long table covered in white damask, decorated with wedding flowers, the family silver, china and glass; the servants of the house in their starched uniforms running to and fro, augmented by extra waiters from the town, each guest assigned their placement. The couple were flanked by their relations and facing the guests: Emma with her veil off her face now, her hair coiled up in the style of the times, Carl in his wedding fraque with a stiff white collar and fancy waistcoat, listening to a long list of toasts and speeches, everything as it should be, at least on the surface.

Except that the father of the bride was not present, a fact which did not escape the guests. Nor, of course, was the father of the groom, Pastor Jung – how to put it – having died some years previously. Then there was the fact that the mother of the groom was extremely large. And the puzzle that Frau Rauschenbach apparently was not present at the civil wedding, only the church wedding two days later. Above all there was the fact that the groom was a penniless doctor, not even a regular one but an *Irrenarzt*, a doctor of the insane, working in a Zürich lunatic asylum, marrying Emma Rauschenbach, one of the richest and most desirable young women in Switzerland.

Emma's wedding present to Carl was a gold fob watch and chain from the Rauschenbach factory, a magnificent piece of Swiss craftsmanship engraved around the upper inside rim with the words 'Fräulein Emma Rauschenbach' and 'Dr C. G. Jung' around the lower, with a charming design of lilies-of-the-valley at the centre, encircling two hands joined in matrimony, the date inscribed on a ribbon below: 16 February 1903. Not the 14th, then, but the 16th. Not the day of the civil wedding but of the church wedding. For Carl the church wedding was of little concern: he had rejected formal religion a long way back, during his battles with his father. 'The further away from church I was, the better I felt,' he wrote of his teenage self. 'All religion bored me to death.' But to Emma, raised in a conventional haut-bourgeois Swiss family, it was the church wedding that counted.

They spent the days before setting off on their honeymoon on 2 March at Ölberg. Early that morning they were borne away in the green everyday Rauschenbach carriage piled high with labelled trunks and hat boxes, Emma's mother and sister and the full complement of servants ranged on either side of the grand entrance, waving them off down the hill – '*Wünsch Glück! Wünsch Glück!*' – past the fountain and the vineyards and on to Schaffhausen railway station and the start of their journey – Emma in her travelling outfit and furs, Carl with his new set of tailored clothes and plenty of books.

After a short visit to Carl's mother and sister at the Bottminger Mill in Basel they travelled by Continental Express to Paris. The first-class carriages were arranged much like a drawing room, with heavily upholstered seats, writing tables and lamps for reading and curtains at the windows. The restaurant car was elegant, the menus all in French and the food excellent. The night was spent in lavishly adorned *salons lits*, with hand basin and mirror in the corner and the two bunks made up with fine bedlinen. Stewards in smart uniforms appeared at any time of day or night at the ring of a bell, and there was a quiet deference to all the proceedings. From Paris they travelled by train and boat to London, and thence down to Southampton to board the ocean liner taking them to Madeira, Las Palmas and Tenerife, always staying in the best hotels, then back via Barcelona, Genoa and Milan, arriving back at Schaffhausen on 16 April.

For Carl it was the start of a new life of considerable luxury; for Emma it was the beginning of getting to know the man she had married. He certainly looked the part: tall, handsome, beautifully attired. But at some stage during the honeymoon there was a quarrel about money. Swiss law gave the husband, as head of household, ownership of all his wife's possessions, and the power to make all final decisions in matters pertaining to family life, including the education of the children. Accordingly, the first thing Carl had done once they were married was to pay off his 3,000-franc debt to the Jung uncles. The amount of the debt tells you something about Carl's incipient taste for good living, a side of his character Emma was now discovering for herself. 'Honeymoons are tricky things,' Jung admitted to a friend years later. 'I was lucky. My wife was apprehensive – but all went well. We got into an argument about the rights and wrongs of distributing money between husbands and wives. Trust a Swiss bank to break into a honeymoon!' He laughed at the memory. But Emma had seen Carl's temper and how it could flare up out of nowhere. Ever since he was a boy Carl had flown into rages. In time Emma learnt that the rages soon passed. But for now it was distressing.

Then there was the question of sex. Was Emma surprised to discover that her husband was still a virgin? Two years earlier his mother had commented, on one of her visits to the Burghölzli and before he became engaged to Emma, that Carl knew too few women. Almost none, in fact. Jung himself later admitted he had not had 'an adventure before marriage, so to speak' and until his marriage he was 'timidly proper with women'. In one way this may have been a relief to Emma, given the terrible fate of her father. But she would not have been the only 'apprehensive' one, as Carl suggested. And now she knew Carl was not quite the man of the world he presented on the surface.

Then there was also the evident difference in their personalities. Quiet and studious as a child, as an adult Emma came across as shy and reticent, sometimes hiding behind the formality of her social background. With marriage she happily took her place in the background, giving those who did not know her the impression that she was, if not the *Hausfrau*, then just the wife. Carl was the extroverted one, the one everyone wanted to talk to. But it was only half the story, as Emma was finding out. The 'other' Carl, the hidden one, was unsure, introverted, plagued by a deep sense of social inferiority, and much in need of Emma's quiet support. Whilst Carl's childhood had been strange and lonely, Emma's had been safe, loving and happy, protected from the ills of the world at the Haus zum Rosengarten, overprotected perhaps. That world did not begin to break up until she was twelve, when her father first became ill with syphilis, and by then the confidence bestowed by a happy childhood was deeply embedded. She also had the confidence which came from belonging to the privileged *niveau* of society. It was a feeling Emma carried with her all her life, allowing her to behave in the quiet, modest manner noted by everyone who met her. A double confidence. Her new husband had neither.

On 24 April, shortly after returning from honeymoon, the Jungs moved into a rented apartment in Zürich, on

Zollikerstrasse, the road leading up to the Burghölzli asylum. Here, south of the city, the houses were solid rather than grand, the apartments spacious and the countryside within easy reach for afternoon walks. Unlike the eastern slopes of Zürich, which lay in the shade with damp air and bad soil, the southern slopes were on the sunny side, with good soil and little fog. Carl had taken up Bleuler's offer of a temporary post at the asylum, acting as his deputy whilst others were on leave, just filling in time whilst he looked for a better job elsewhere. It was a typically generous gesture from Bleuler who had already suffered Carl's precipitate resignation six months earlier, and it was received with a typically grudging gratitude by Carl.

With Carl back at work, Emma took stock of her married state. She started to set up home, arranging for furniture and fine antique pieces to be brought over by horse and cart from the Ölberg estate. Her mother came to help, plus a live-in maid, also from Schaffhausen, and gradually the apartment took shape. It was not the kind of living Emma was used to but it was only temporary after all. In many ways it was refreshing. From her bedroom window in the mornings she watched as bare-footed farm boys in short trousers and braces led cows down the hill to the slaughter-house, and smallholders from the neighbouring village of Forch came down in their wooden farm carts to sell their vegetables at the market, the husband in front driving the horse, the wife and children behind among the laden wicker baskets. Given Zollikon's proximity to the Burghölzli asylum, quite a few of the villagers worked there as helpers, the low wages still better than they could earn as farm labourers or domestic servants.

Carl left for work early every morning, walking up the hill through farmland and meadow, past the Burghölzli kitchen gardens where inmates in overalls were already hoeing and digging, watched over by the *Wärters* in their long green garden aprons – then on through the gates of the asylum, up the front steps and straight into the early morning meeting. These days he was always smartly dressed in a suit and tie, waistcoat, and his gold fob watch and chain, which he wore till the day he died. But once on the wards he donned the doctor's white coat like the rest of the medical team and his daily routine began. He rarely got back before eight because Bleuler insisted Burghölzli staff eat their meals with the inmates, and the days were long for Emma left sitting in their apartment with nothing much to do and hardly any friends.

Some days she would make her way into the centre of town, walking down Zollikerstrasse, then taking the tram to Stadelhofen, where she joined a crowded, busy, modern city. Zürich was so much larger, noisier, and more commercial than Schaffhausen. Everything seemed so much faster. Trams could travel at fifteen kilometres an hour, conveying shop girls, hairdressers, waiters, bank clerks and office workers from the outskirts into the business district and back out again after a long ten-hour day. The tram drivers and conductors sported military-style uniforms and handlebar moustaches, as did the captains of the paddle steamers which plied their way across the lake, bearing freight as well as passengers.

By 1903 Zürich was a city on the make. Its population had doubled since 1890 to over 162,000 and was growing by the day. The unification of the outlying districts under one 'City Administration' in 1893 had propelled it into an era of thrusting capitalism and commercial activity, quickly followed by a property boom which led to massive land and building speculation, which in turn led to a financial crisis. But by the turn of the century the recovery was in full swing. Everything relied on Zürich's geographical position on the Limmat and the Sihl rivers flowing from Lake Zürich, their bridges linking the two parts of the town, with a chain of Alps beyond, each peak with a *Gasthof* or hotel on the summit. Zürich was postcard-pretty and good for business: commerce and finance, banks, a stock exchange, import and export, construction and engineering, heavy and light industry, all thrived on the shores of the lake. Further out in the industrial district of Sihl factories and sweatshops produced silk, cotton, lace and embroidery and bit machinery of every sort, all stored in warehouses on the bank of the Limmat beyond the Bahnhof Brücke, the bridge leading off Bahnhofstrasse. Rich foreigners were beginning to flock to Zürich for the Alps, the air, the shops and the lake. Fashionable hotels catered for this early tourist industry, none grander than the Baur-au-Lac, with gardens leading down to the lake. 'Hotel-keepers who wish to commend their houses to British and American travellers are reminded of the desirability of provid-ing the bedrooms with large basins, foot baths, plenty of water, and an adequate supply of towels,' advised the Baedeker guide. Thomas Cook & Son had a bureau in the *Hauptbahnhof*, the central station, if further guidance were needed; they reminded travellers that no servants were allowed on the platforms: luggage had to be conveyed by the uniformed porters.

As spring gave way to a hot summer and she got used to her new surroundings, Emma found there was plenty to do in Zürich, quite apart from her usual reading, writing, needlework or knitting, and helping Carl to write up his daily reports and research. There were plenty of museums: the Ethnographical

Museum, the Municipal Museum of 'Stuffed Wild Animals', the Landesmuseum, a massive building in the neo-Gothic style recently opened in celebration of Zürich's increasing importance, housing an extensive collection of Swiss artefacts from prehistoric to modern times – bridal coffers, carved altars, old sleighs, tapestries, a distillery from the ancient Benedictine monastery of Muri, musical instruments, local Swiss *Trachts* (each canton having its own costume), china from the old factory at Schoren, banners and ducal hats and military uniforms of every kind, plus an entire Zürich house from the fourteenth century. But as far as Emma was concerned there was nothing more important than the Zürich Central Library with its collection of 160,000 books and its large, high-ceilinged, silent reading room – open in the morning from ten until twelve, and again after lunch from two till six, entry costing 60 rappen – ideal for her research into the Legend of the Holy Grail, which she now returned to with joy, like greeting an old friend.

Emma found a pleasing anonymity in Zürich: whilst the Rauschenbachs were the foremost family of Schaffhausen, known and respected by everyone, here Emma was mostly unknown and unregarded, in spite of her great wealth. The old ruling families of Zürich kept very much to themselves, entertaining one another in their villas in quiet, prosperous districts such as Seefeld, or meeting for private luncheons in fine restaurants, or at one of their many *Verein*s: the Yacht Club, the Rifle Club, the Rowing Club, the Riding Club, and the recently founded Automobile Club. Who among them would want to pass the time of day with the wife of an *Irrenarzt* employed at the Burghölzli asylum – an institution which had, after all, been built high up on the Zollikon hill, well away from the town, for a reason? This snobbery bothered neither Emma nor Carl, who were content, each for their own reasons, to be outsiders: Carl because he was born that way, Emma because society never held much importance for her, preferring as she did the company of close friends and family.

Marguerite often came to visit during that first year and the sisters would wander up and down the Bahnhofstrasse or the Parade Platz, though Emma bored of it quickly, one shop being much like the next. With the exception of the fashion houses. Both sisters were interested in the latest fashions, noting they were distinctly more modern in Zürich than sleepy Schaffhausen. Day wear was much the same: long-skirted and high-necked, worn with hats and button boots, but evening gowns were very décolleté, set off by heavy strings of pearls. The waists seemed narrower in Zürich, fishbone corsets pulled tight every morning by the maid, and the hats seemed larger, decorated with plumes and bows and veils, the hair curled with heated irons and pinned up with combs and grips. Feather boas and tassels were the fashion that year, and no lady went about without gloves, short for the day, long for the evenings. In the summer months the dark patterns gave way to white – long white skirts, high-necked white blouses, white stockings, white shoes. Swiss lace and embroidery came into their own then, along with parasols and wide straw hats decorated with ribbons and cherries and artificial flowers. Perfumes of violets, lilies-of-the-valley or eau de cologne were especially popular. On the Bahnhofstrasse in the recently opened *Salon de Beauté* there were boxes of rice powder, pots of white and rose creams, tiny bottles of nail polish and glass balls of bath salts displayed in discreetly half-netted windows, offering manicures and pedicures and other beauty treatments in the privacy of curtained-off niches, administered by trained young ladies in white overalls with their hair tightly pulled back.

After their shopping exertions Emma and Marguerite usually went to a café for *kaffee* or *thé citron* and *pâtisserie*. Other days they might take the cable tram up to the Grand Hotel Dolder, with its wide terrace and Zeiss telescope to better appreciate the view of the Alps. There were two picture houses showing news-reels and new features like *The Great Train Robbery*, jerky and silent except for the piano accompaniment, though good bour-geois people rarely visited them other than incognito, via a private side door. Emma and Marguerite preferred to promen-ade along the many *quais* which bordered the lake, or sit in the gardens of the Tonhalle – the grand concert hall built in 1895 in imitation of the Trocadero in Paris – listening to one of the mili-tary bands and talking about Marguerite's fiancé, Ernst Homberger, the son of another of their father's former business associates in Schaffhausen. One thing they did not do was visit the Panoptikum on the seamier side of the Bahnhof Bridge, with curtains drawn and dimly lit by gaslight, where men could, by looking through small panes, view a tiger hunt in the Sudan, or the 'Rape of the Sabines', or a wax Sarah Bernhardt in a negligee, or the 'medical' exhibition with lifesize models of naked women.

Sunday was Carl's day off. In the morning all the church bells, Protestant and Catholic, rang out across Zürich and families put on their Sunday best to attend the services, prayer books in hand, little girls with hair done up Heidi-style, boys in matelot suits. Not the Jungs, however. Carl had vowed never to set foot in a church again, other than on unavoidable occasions such as his own wedding, and he was determined not to have any of his children confirmed, remembering the debilitating boredom and depression which overcame him during the instruction given him by his father, who was all the while denying his own religious doubts, battling with his unnamed torments. Emma accepted Carl's rejection of formal religion without much trouble, not least because by Sunday they were often on the train to Schaffhausen, to be met at the railway station by coachman Braun as usual, then up the hill to Ölberg where Emma's mother and Marguerite and the servants waited, and Emma was back to the world she knew and loved.

Their first years of married life were happy for them both. A studio portrait taken at that time shows the couple side by side and close, looking into the lens of the camera with confidence and ease. Emma's wavy brown hair is done simply in a modern style – softly off the face. Her expression is shy but calm and direct, and quite determined. She is wearing a blouse in the Grecian style, high-necked, modern again. The skirt is long, simple and elegant, very unlike the elaborate outfits displayed in most of the fashion magazines. She may be standing on a box – the custom for studio photographs if the difference in height was too great – but she still looks half Carl's size. He stands there solid, with his hand nonchalantly in his pocket – dark suit, light waistcoat, a stiff-collared white shirt and small bow tie – a confident man of the world with no trace of the pompous and rather unhappy student of earlier photographs. His gold-rimmed spectacles glint in the studio lights and it is just possible to see the gold chain of his wedding present from Emma. His small moustache is trimmed the way it will be for the rest of his

life. In another take of the pose, Emma is smiling more, probably encouraged by the photographer, but Carl is just the same.
He looks – there is no other way to put it – like the cat that got
the cream.

'I'm sitting here in the Burghölzli and for a month I've been
playing the part of the Director, Senior Physician and First
Assistant,' Carl wrote on 22 August 1904 to Andreas Vischer, an
old friend from university days. It was summer, and everyone
else was away on holiday. 'So almost every day I'm writing
twenty letters, giving twenty interviews, running all over the
place and getting very annoyed. I have even lost another fourteen pounds in the last year as a result of this change of life,
which otherwise is not a bad thing of course. On the contrary,
all that would be fine (for what do we want from life more than
real work?) if the public uncertainty of existence were not so
great.' He might claim it annoyed him, but his tone is buoyant,
optimistic. There was nothing Carl loved more, he admitted,
than work – at least work that made sense to him: investigating
the dark corners of the mind. Emma was getting used to the idea
that she hardly ever saw him.

By the end of the year it was becoming clear that Jung was
not going to find another job elsewhere, certainly not in his
home town of Basel, which had been his plan. Apparently his
falling-out with Professor Wille had well and truly ruined his
chances: the job of director at the Basel asylum, which Carl had
applied for, was given to one of Wille's German colleagues, a
man named Wolff. Swinging from high spirits to low, Carl called
it the 'Basel calamity', which had 'wrecked for ever' his academic

career in Switzerland. Now he had to consider remaining in Zürich and at the Burghölzli. 'I might as well sit under a mill-stone as under Wolff,' he wrote to Vischer, 'who will stay up there immovably enthroned for thirty years until he is as old as Wille. For no one in Germany is stupid enough to take Wolff seriously, as Kraepelin has appropriately said, he is not even a psychiatrist. I have been robbed of any possibility of advance-ment in Basel now.'

Carl did not want to stay in Zürich nor take on a permanent post at the Burghölzli. He had no wish to do endless ward rounds, attend endless staff meetings, write up endless daily reports. He wanted to continue his research into the workings of the unconscious. He wanted to bring scientific proof to this new field and write scientific papers about his findings to be published in medical journals like the *Journal für Psychologie und Neurologie*. He wanted to make his name. But he had been rejected for the post in Basel and now he didn't know what to do. His crisis confronted Emma with the other Carl again, the one who fell out with colleagues through arrogance and an unshakeable conviction in his superior intelligence, but then became cast down and plagued with doubts when things went wrong. There was no steadiness in Carl, she discovered. And yet to the outside world he appeared his usual loud, confident, char-ismatic self. It was as though he were two different people.

The one thing which never left him was his vaulting ambition. 'As usual you have hit the nail on the head with your accusation that my ambition is the agent provocateur of my fits of despair,' Jung wrote to Freud some years later. He could admit it, but he could do little about it. Because the ambition was not just to gain worldly acclaim; it was in order to understand the complex workings of the unconscious because he suffered so much from it himself.

Bleuler again came to the rescue. He wasn't a crafty Swiss peasant for nothing and he wanted to keep his exceptional young colleague at the Burghölzli. So he made Jung an offer he couldn't refuse: he could continue the word association research he had begun with his Burghölzli colleague Franz Riklin, but more systematically, in a laboratory with proper equipment, and, under Bleuler's own supervision, write papers to be published in the medical journals. These could later be gathered into a book on this important new field of scientific research. Carl accepted. Bleuler and Jung shared an interest in the paranormal as a means of accessing the unconscious, and the Burghölzli already enjoyed an international reputation as great and controversial in its way as Freud had acquired after the publication of *The Interpretation of Dreams* in 1900. Everyone in the field, it seemed, wanted to research the unconscious, whether through dreams, hypnosis, the paranormal, or word association tests. Jung needed a base from which to launch himself. Bleuler needed the best doctors specialising in diseases of the mind, both for the sake of his patients and the reputation of the Burghölzli. Where else, after all, could Carl find so many guinea pigs to experiment on? Discussing it with Emma, Carl could see there was no better solution.

However, Carl was now tied to doing all the routine work as well – a twelve-hour day at least – and being completely teetotal, and, above all, having to move back and live on site. Nevertheless, by October 1904 Jung had exchanged the part-time for the full-time position, and he and Emma moved into an apartment in the main building of the Burghölzli, on the floor above Bleuler and his wife Hedwig and their children, bringing Emma's maid and the beautiful furniture with them. The only concession made to Herr and Frau Doktor Jung was that Carl was allowed to miss the midday meal with patients and staff and return to the apartment to have lunch with his wife. So began Emma's new life as the wife of an *Irrenarzt*, living amongst hysterics, schizophrenics, catatonics, alcoholics, addicts, chronic neurotics and suicidal depressives – people who had lost their minds for one reason or another, and who spat and screamed and paced the wards, up and down, shouting obscenities, tearing at their hair, breaking the furniture. The contrast with her former life was complete.

Now she had to find a way of relating to the kind of people she had never expected to meet: inmates and staff alike.

It is telling that Emma was able to do it quickly and naturally, as testified by everyone who met her. Of course they knew Herr Doktor Jung had married a wealthy wife, but it was soon noticed that the Frau Doktor did not 'act wealthy', dressed simply, and was friendly to everyone equally, regardless of position. She was quite reserved, it was true, but she was liked. For Emma the problem was more the question of how to fill her days. The maid did the cooking and the cleaning, and, unlike Hedwig Bleuler as the wife of the Herr Direktor, she did not have a formal role in the institution. She still helped Carl privately with his research and reports, and she continued to go to the library in Zürich and research the Legend of the Holy Grail, but it still left her with many hours alone. There were just two people nearby who she could visit regularly – a duty or a pleasure, depending on how you looked at it: Carl's mother and his sister Trudi, because once it became clear that Jung was staying in Zürich he swiftly moved them out of the Bottminger Mill and into an apartment in nearby Zollikon. He did not have much time to see them himself so the visits naturally fell to Emma, the wife and daughter-in-law. It can't have been easy: most of the time her mother-in-law was normal and good company, but she still heard voices, had visions, and made sudden prophetic announcements. Her second personality always hovered in the background, and you never knew when it might emerge.

Soon Emma found a role to play at the Burghölzli after all, because Eugen Bleuler believed women and wives should be included as much as possible in the daily life of the institution – another of his progressive ideas, quite alien to other lunatic asylums where all women other than the female *Wärter*s were kept well away. Emma was encouraged to join in, participate in social events, and sit at the same tables as the patients as long as there was no danger. There were also regular evening discussion 'circles' to which all doctors and their wives were invited. And if a patient was in the rehabilitation phase of their treatment and they were allowed out of the asylum grounds, it was as likely to be Frau Jung or Frau Direktor Bleuler as much as it was one of the *Wärter*s who accompanied them on walks, or even on a short shopping trip. 'The years at Burghölzli were the years of my apprenticeship,' Jung acknowledged later. But in a smaller way they were Emma's too. 'Dominating my interests and research was the burning question, "What actually takes place inside the mentally ill?"' Jung wrote. Now, almost by osmosis, it came to interest Emma too.

The other plus for Emma at the Burghölzli was Hedwig, who was a remarkable woman and an early feminist. Eugen Bleuler was already forty-four when he married her in 1901; Hedwig was then a history teacher, twenty-four years old, clever, elegant, charming. They met at one of Bleuler's lectures at Zürich University, and wed within the year. Hedwig's ambition had been to become a lecturer herself but it was not possible in Switzerland at that time, it being the preserve of men. And once she was pregnant she could not continue her studies anyway, so her life centred round her role as Frau Direktor Bleuler, and she made very good use of it, supporting her husband in every way she could. Their apartment was large enough to accommodate two maids, had bedrooms enough for their growing family, and a large, sunny room for Bleuler's schizophrenic sister Pauline. There was a library and a stairway which led directly down to the wards, so Bleuler could be there at any time of day or night if there was a crisis. Hedwig's special interests were the abstinence movement and women's position in a modern society. Years later she travelled throughout Switzerland lecturing on both, but whilst the children were growing up she limited herself to helping her husband at the Burghölzli and editing his lectures and published papers. It was a happy marriage but she always regretted having to give up her own career. 'The woman is always the one who has to make the sacrifices,' she said. Another clever woman, then, who had to find her intellectual satisfaction through her husband's work.

Once back full time at the Burghölzli, Jung was soon dominating the place with his energy and booming laugh. He was happy to spend hours with a patient listening to their strange utterances, finding meaning in their madness. While he was liked by many, some of his colleagues found his presence irritating, accusing him of throwing his weight around, doing just what he wanted and not bothering with the dull administrative work. The *Wärter*s, who did all the day-to-day caring and were only allowed home one afternoon a week, claimed the doctors spent more time on their research than on routine ward rounds, especially Herr Doktor Jung. But Bleuler let him get away with it. Auguste Forel, the former director who still liked to wander about the institution, was soon asking: 'Who's running this place, Bleuler or Jung?'

The reason was simple: Bleuler did not want to lose Jung. So he allowed Jung and his 'esteemed colleague Herr Doktor Riklin' to spend hours pursuing their word association tests in a laboratory at the back of the main building, near both the laundry and the dairy, wafts of steam emanating from the one and the moos of cows from the other. Riklin was the junior partner in the venture but he had worked on word association tests before, in Germany with Gustav Aschaffenburg who followed Dr Wundt, who in turn referred back to the first tests conducted by Galton in England in the 1880s, each contributing to the growing body of evidence about the unconscious. All over Europe doctors in asylums were experimenting on their patients, and Jung's papers on the word association tests are filled with references to others already embarked on the same track. The difference was that Jung and Riklin's methodology was far more systematic, more scientific. They published their findings in the *Journal für Psychologie und Neurologie*, and Bleuler wrote the introduction when the book was published in 1905 as *Studies in Word Association*.

The method was described as 'the uttering of the first word which "occurs" to the subject after hearing the stimulus-word', and suggested that it would help in the diagnoses and classification of *dementia praecox*, epilepsy, various forms of imbecility, some forms of paranoia, and the diseases grouped under hysteria, neurasthenia and psychasthenia, 'not to speak of manic depression with its well-known flight of ideas'. Jung and Riklin went about it systematically and scientifically, by using a much larger pool of guinea pigs and by increasing the number of stimulus words from 100 to 400 – nouns, adjectives, verbs, adverbs and numerals, using the Swiss dialect form when necessary – and timing the reactions with the greatest possible accuracy using the 'one-fifth-second stop watch', the very latest model from the Rauschenbach factory in Schaffhausen. The reaction times varied considerably, sometimes taking up to 6 seconds. Galton had found that the average time was 1.3 seconds. Jung with his modern stopwatch found it was 1.8 seconds, women subjects taking slightly longer. To distract the conscious mind a metronome was used. Other researchers used whistles, trumpets or darkened rooms. At times the tests were done when the subject was 'in a state of obvious fatigue', and once 'in a state of morning drowsiness' (Jung himself). One important innovative decision of Jung's was to test 'normal' as well as 'abnormal' people, and the groups were divided into male and female, 'educated' and 'uneducated'. Everything had to be written up, by hand, night after night. Emma was kept busy, and she was happy to do it.

In those early years of psychoanalysis it was common and considered perfectly acceptable to use friends and relatives as well as patients as subjects for scientific research. Jung and Riklin's first test was on 'Normal Subjects': thirty-eight persons in all, nine men and fourteen women of whom were classified as 'educated'. The rest were mostly male and female *Wärter*s at the Burghölzli, who, Jung declared, were not so much 'uneducated' as 'half-educated'. The tests were often repeated so that in the end they had 12,400 associations and timings on which to base their conclusions. There were statistics and tables and graphs, and a complicated list of different types of reaction, including those which showed evidence of 'repression', a term made familiar in the writings of Sigmund Freud. As with Freud, there was often enough of a description of the person to make an enticing story. Thus 'Uneducated Woman, Subject No. 1: she is of country origin and became an asylum nurse at the age of seventeen, after having brooded at home for over a year over the unhappy ending of a love affair'. This subject would not or could not understand the stimulus words 'hate, love, remorse, rattle glass, hammer ears . . . because they intimately touched the complex which she was trying to repress'. The term 'complex' was coined by Jung and Riklin to denote 'personal matter . . . with an emotional tone'. It could be spotted by a significantly longer reaction time and the peculiarly forced nature of the reaction.

Then there were *clang* associations – that is, based upon sound rather than on concepts: simple, thoughtless, sound similarities – and interesting 'preservation' ones, first noted by Aschaffenburg, where 'the current association revealed nothing, but the succeeding one bears an abnormal character'. There was also the egocentric reaction: grandmother/me; dancing/I don't like; wrong/I was not, and so on. 'If we ask patients directly as to the cause of their illness we always receive incorrect, or at least imperfect information,' explains Jung. 'If we did receive correct information as in other (physical) illnesses, we should have known long ago about the psychogenic nature of hysteria. But it is just the point of hysteria that it represses the real cause, the psychic trauma, forgets it and replaces it by superficial "cover causes". That is why hysterics ceaselessly tell us that their illness arose from a cold, from over-work, from real organic disorders.' He compared their method with Freud's 'free association' and reminded the reader that a 'delicate psychological intuition in the doctor is as much a requisite as [is] technique for a Psycho-Analysis'. If this all sounds familiar now, it was not then, back in 1904.

Emma appears as 'Subject no. I, aged twenty-two, very intelligent', in the 'educated' category. By way of introduction Jung wrote: 'No. I is a married woman who placed herself in the readiest way at my disposal for the experiment and gave me every possible information. I report the experiment in as detailed a way as possible so that the reader may receive as complete a picture as possible. The probable mean of the experiment amounts to 1 second.'

The first five word associations were: head/cloth, 1 second; green/grass, 0.8 seconds; water/fall, 1 sec; prick/cut, 0.8 seconds; angel/heart, 0.8 seconds. So far so good, but reaction 5 was deemed striking because 'the subject cannot explain to herself how she comes to *heart* . . .'. Emma denied it was the result of any disturbance from without, and could not find any inner one either. Jung concluded it might therefore be some unconscious stimulus, very likely one of Aschaffenburg's 'preservation' reactions, carried over from the previous prick/cut, which caused 'a certain slight shade of anxiety, and image of blood'.

'The subject is pregnant,' Jung noted with scientific detachment, 'and has now and then feelings of anxious expectancy.'

There followed a sequence of stimulus words which were not especially memorable, except that 'to cook' endearingly elicited 'to learn', as did 'to swim' – because it was her sister Marguerite who was the swimmer, whereas Emma was apparently still learning. Only Carl could know why 28: lamp/green took 1.4 seconds. It followed threaten/fist, and he noted it was clearly another case of 'preservation' and that lamp/green denoted her home life (the colour of the lampshades). He does not say which home, Zürich or Schaffhausen, but it was most likely Schaffhausen and the fist her father's as he became more and more ill and desperate.

Further associations offered little which was significant for the test but tell us something of Emma's outlook on life: evil/good; pity/have; people/faithful; law/follow; rich/poor; quiet/peaceful; moderate/drink; confidence/me; lover/faithful; change/false; duty/faithful; serpent/false. And then we come, in no particular order, to: family/father and mother/tell and dear/husband. Father is still the head of the family. Her mother is the one to whom she tells almost everything. Her husband, she loves.

Using his intuition, and inevitably his personal knowledge of Subject No. I, Jung focused on a sequence of associations, nos 70–73: blossom/red; hit/prick; box/bed; bright/brighter. The first pair only took 0.6 seconds. 'She explains this short reaction by saying that the first syllable of the stimulus-word Blo-ssom brought up the presentation of blood. Here we have a kind of assimilation of the stimulus-word to the highly accentuated pregnancy complex . . . It will be remembered that in the association Prick/Cut (no 4) the pregnancy complex was first encountered,' yet:

Box/Bed which followed Hit/Prick went quite smoothly without any tinge of emotion. But the reaction is curious. This subject has now and then paid a visit to our asylum and was alluding to the deep beds used there, the so-called 'box-beds'. But the explanation rather surprised her, for the term 'box-bed' was not very familiar to her. This rather peculiar association was followed by a clang-association (Bright/Brighter) with a relatively long time . . . The supposition that the clang-reaction is connected with the previous curious reaction does not, therefore, seem quite baseless . . . assuming a clang-alteration at the suppressed pregnancy complex, the complex becomes very sensible.

By Association 83 we come to injure/avoid. The German for 'injure' is *schaden*. As Jung explains, the word is very like and easily confused with *scheiden* – divorce. Luckily, apart from these, there were plenty of happy associations too.

So the main complex which emerged from the test was Emma's fear of the pain of childbirth. Association 43, despise/*mépriser*, reminds us how well Emma spoke French, but this, it turns out, was not the point. The reaction took 1.8 seconds. Why so, Jung wondered? 'Despise is accompanied by an unpleasant emotional tone. Immediately after the reaction it came to her that she had had a passing fear that her pregnancy might in different ways decrease her attractiveness in the eyes of her husband. She immediately afterwards thought of a married couple who were at first happy and then separated – the married couple in Zola's novel *Vérité* [Truth]. Hence the French form of the reaction.' Poor Emma.

In his summing up of 'Subject No. I', Jung commented:

In reality our experiment shows beautifully, the conscious self is merely the marionette dancing on the stage to a hidden automatic impulse . . . In our subject we find a series of intimate secrets given away by the associations . . . We find her strongest actual complex to be bound up with thoughts about her pregnancy, her rather anxious expectancy, and love of her husband with jealous fears. This is a complex of an erotic kind which has just become acute; that is why it is so much to the front. No less than 18% of the associations can certainly be referred to it. In addition there are a few complexes of considerably less intensity: loss of her former position, a few deficiencies which she regards as unpleasant (singing, swimming, cooking) and finally an erotic complex which occurred many years back in her youth and which only shows itself in one association (out of regard for the subject of the experiment I must, unfortunately, omit a report on this).

Jung ended the German text of *Studies in Word-Association* giving 'special thanks to Frau Emma Jung for her active assistance with the repeated revision of the voluminous material'.

5

Tricky Times

Agathe Regina was born at Emma's family home in Schaffhausen on 26 December 1904, a Christmas child. Emma was twenty-two, had been married for a year and ten months, and now she was a mother. Overnight, it seemed, her life had changed again, this time for ever.

It was common for mothers of Emma's social class to use a wet nurse to still their babies. But Emma breastfed hers herself. She did not want to hand her baby over to a stranger and deprive herself and the child of this pleasure, as Carl later described it to Freud. Nevertheless, a first baby is a strange and unknown experience. Emma had plenty of help with 'Agathli' – little Agathe – whilst she was still at Ölberg with her mother and sister Marguerite, but when she moved back to Zürich and the Burghölzli, keen not to be away from her husband for too long, she largely looked after the baby herself. Feeding took many hours. Waking through the night disturbed sleep. Changing the thick towelling nappies was onerous, though it was the maid's job to soak them in a pail before washing them by hand, then through the wringer, then hanging them out on a wooden horse by the tiled stove to dry. It was a winter with deep snow, white pitched roofs with icicles hanging from the eves and the window sills, and no hope of using the washing line in the garden. There were coughs and colds and nappy rashes to deal with, and the terrible responsibility of a new life. For a young mother who had shown such anxiety about the pain of giving birth and the fear that having a baby might affect the feelings her husband had for her, Emma was having to grow up very fast indeed.

In addition, Emma had just started what she had longed to do since leaving school: furthering her education. Though it was done circuitously, by helping her husband with his work, it was certainly an education. And she was still going down to Zürich Central Library to pursue her own research into the Grail legend. But now Carl and Emma slipped back into more conventional roles: she as wife and mother; he as husband, breadwinner and authoritative head of house. Carl did not subscribe to '*Das Weib sei dem Mann untertan*', 'The woman shall be subservient to the man', as a popular book, *The Way to the Altar*, quoting the Bible, reminded, but once Agathe was born things changed in the Jung household. Carl was conventional when it came to parenthood: he saw children largely as the responsibility of the mother. Now his sister Trudi came to help with the secretarial work and Emma found herself more and more on the sidelines. If she hoped it was merely temporary until she found her feet, it didn't work out that way: within six months she was pregnant again. Anna Margaretha, known as Gretli, and later Gret, was born on 8 February 1906.

Emma's story was typical enough of the times. Many women were frightened of getting pregnant, either because they already had too large a family or because they were not married, which was worse. There was no safe method of birth control, and a reliance on coitus interruptus had limited success. In 1909

Richard Richter, a German doctor, would develop an early form of an interuterine device using the gut of the silkworm, but it was not marketed until the 1920s, by which time Marie Stopes had opened the first birth control clinic in England, and there were similar initiatives in America and France and Germany. The Catholic Church, however, forbade any form of contraception and the Protestant Church did not look on it with favour either, believing that it was the duty of Christian marriage to 'increase and multiply and fill the earth'. It all came too late for Emma and Carl anyway.

Sigmund Freud could have told them. His letters to his doctor friend Wilhelm Fliess are full of pleas that he come up with a reliable form of contraception. Every month he and Martha worried she might be pregnant again. Fliess looked into the 'rhythm method', making calculations and trying to work out a safe period during Martha's monthly cycle; he even tried to come up with a similar cycle for Freud himself. Evidently it was not successful: Martha became pregnant six times in ten years. For the first three months of her sixth pregnancy she insisted it was the start of the menopause, not another pregnancy. She couldn't face it. She had never wanted more than four children. Once the baby, Anna, was born, Martha went to her mother's in Wandsbek for several weeks of recuperation and there developed 'a writing paralysis': she found she literally could not form the words to write Sigmund a letter. Her face was puffy and her teeth hurt. She was only thirty-four and she was exhausted. After that they stopped having sex, that side of their marriage becoming 'amortised', as Freud later confided to Emma.

* * *

In March 1905 Emma Jung's father Jean Rauschenbach died. Marguerite and Ernst Homberger, who had married a year earlier, now moved in with Bertha whilst they built a house of their own. Ernst took over the running of the Rauschenbach business from Bertha and Jean's sister, though the two women had managed it all splendidly during the last years of Jean Rauschenbach's decline. But custom had it that if there was a man in the family there was no need for the women to carry on working. Ernst, a quiet, ambitious, tough man twenty years his wife's senior, ran the business for the rest of his working life.

The immediate reaction to Herr Rauschenbach's death was relief as well as sorrow, his last years being so terrible, shut away from the world. 'A poor rich man finally closed his eyes last night, but their light had already gone out a long time ago,' stated the obituary in the *Schaffhausen Tagesblatt* on 3 March 1905, written by an old friend. 'Herr Johannes Rauschenbach, manufacturer, died at his country seat at Ölberg, aged 48. He saw nothing of his beautiful new home, being already fully blind by the time work on it was begun . . . He was no longer able to see his two young daughters grow into lovely young women, nor was he able to lead them up the altar into married life, because by then he had already been leading the life of a hermit for many years, shut away in his upstairs room.' He was described as the son of a simple locksmith who became the founder and owner of the world-famous machine factory and foundry, after the early death of his father. After fetching himself 'a beautiful young bride from Uhwiesen . . . the world stood gloriously before him. He threw himself into the business which his father had built up, having been underestimated like the sons of all self-made men. And he felt it, resulting in a certain disdainful sarcasm.' But he did well, overcoming a financial crisis in the Budapest branch of the family business. Then 'the most terrible bad luck overcame him'. At first, when he started to go blind, 'he was almost totally cast down. In vain was the loving care of his wife! Heart-breaking was his despair.' Over the years he became calmer, and finally he was at peace from his suffering. 'His life was like a glorious morning, a sunny midday, but a heavy, rainy evening. Let us remember him as he was in the morning and midday. Rest in peace.'

Herr Rauschenbach left all his worldly goods and his vast fortune to his wife and his two daughters – in effect, to his two sons-in-law. From now on Ernst remitted an annual sum from the profits of the business to Carl, who duly sent an annual letter of thanks. It made Emma and Carl even wealthier, so wealthy in fact that Carl would never need to work again. He could leave the Burghölzli any time he wished.

But he didn't wish. His 'real creative work', as he put it, was at the Burghölzli, doing research on word association in the laboratory. There was an outpatients' clinic now too, so his subjects, 'normal' and 'abnormal', could be drawn from these as well as from the inmates and the staff of the asylum. Where else could Carl find such a pool of 'volunteers'? Bleuler allowed him private patients as well, another concession which annoyed some of his colleagues. When in 1905 Karl Abraham arrived from Germany to join the staff, together with assistants Hans Maier and Emma Furst, Jung was appointed senior physician. He also became a guest lecturer in psychiatry at Zürich University, following in Bleuler's footsteps.

From the start Jung knew how to attract an audience to his lectures, avoiding the dry academic style of most professors, including Bleuler, and instead peppering his presentations with dramatic stories, instructive case details and sharp insights. 'My aim was to show that delusions and hallucinations were not just specific symptoms of a mental disease but also had a human meaning,' he said. 'To my mind, therapy only really begins after the investigation of that wholly personal story. It is the patient's secret, the rock against which he is shattered. If I know his secret story, I have a key to the treatment. The doctor's task is to find out how to gain that knowledge. In most cases exploration of the conscious mind is insufficient. Sometimes an association test can open the way; so can the interpretation of dreams, or long and patient human contact with the individual.' Secrets and rocks. Rocks and secrets. Jung knew it all from personal experience. But for those who came to his lectures it was all thrillingly new.

There was no shortage of stories: the seventy-year-old female inmate of the Burghölzli who had been there for fifty years, bedridden for the past forty. She couldn't speak. She ate with her fingers. She made curious rhythmic motions with her hands. At Burghölzli demonstrations she was presented as a hopeless case of catatonic *dementia praecox*. But one day a female *Wärter*, who had worked at the Burghölzli for decades, told Jung that in the early years the woman had been put to work by Bleuler making shoes, which kept her busy and her mind occupied. Not long after Jung arrived at the asylum the woman died. A brother came to the funeral. He told Jung his sister had once been in love with a shoemaker but it had not worked out. Now Jung understood the rhythmic motions with her hands. 'That case gave me my first inkling of the psychic origins of *dementia praecox*,' he wrote.

Another case: a female doctor, who was one of Jung's private patients, had murdered her best friend out of jealousy because she wanted to marry the husband. She was never found out and she married the widower, but he died young. She had little contact with their only daughter. People and even animals seemed to turn away from her. She lived 'plunged into unbearable loneliness'. Finally she came to see Jung, to 'confess'. He did not give her secret away and she left to carry on her life, but he dreaded what fate held in store for her.

'He kept his students spellbound by his temperament and the wealth of his ideas,' recalled Ludwig Binswanger, who came as a volunteer to the Burghölzli in 1906 and to write his dissertation under Jung's supervision. But it was not only Jung's students who were spellbound: the lectures were open to the public and soon he had a large following of wealthy Zürich women who had too much leisure on their hands. Here they found an outlet for their underused intellects and often for their underused emotions too, what with talk of erotic complexes, repression, and this new world of the unconscious, illustrated with fascinating references to literature, mythology, art and plenty of real-life stories. Carl's lectures were soon the best act in town and the medical students complained that they often could not find a seat in the lecture theatre, so popular were they with the so-called *Pelzmäntel* – fur-coat – brigade.

For Carl it was a revelation. He had never been a 'ladies' man'; he had, in fact, held himself somewhat aloof from that kind of thing, mostly in self-defence, lacking the confidence and the know-how to woo a young woman. He never thought of himself as handsome, and in truth the 'Steam-Roller' was not very handsome, nor confident, nor charming, being too loud and brash, peasant-crude at times, and suffering from a keen sense of social inferiority. But now, three years into marriage with Emma and approaching thirty, everything was changing. His new wealth made him confident, he had lost some weight and he looked handsome in his expensive clothes worn casually *à l'anglaise* like the gentlemen he had met in Oxford. His position at the Burghölzli was a good one, his research was consuming, his lectures a sell-out, and he was doing court work too – giving expert psychiatric evidence in legal cases, which allowed him to take time off and go down to Zürich, lunch in a restaurant or go for a walk along one of the *quais* before taking the tram back up the hill again. Underpinning it all was his domestic life – a happy one, from his side anyway – with Emma and their two little girls.

For Emma things were not so good. Where Carl's life was full of variety, hers was limited. Where he was getting on with his career, she, the 'very intelligent' subject of the word association tests, felt stuck. Where he was free to come and go, she felt trapped. It was not that Emma was unhappy to be a mother, just held back. And in fact there were always happy times too. They talked together. They laughed together. They enjoyed their children together. A series of charming, fuzzy snapshots taken with a box camera in the Jungs' apartment at the Burghölzli shows Carl seated on the canapé with Agathli and Gretli, happy in the role of Papa, clothes awry. Another is of Emma, on the same canapé, holding Gretli, smiling and demure. Jung took the one of her, she took the one of him. They are informal and domestic in a way rarely seen in photographs of the time, and they show a very different side of Carl. Emma loved her children. It was just that, as Hedwig

Bleuler said, it was always the woman who had to make the sacrifices. Never the man.

Underlying everything was Emma's anxiety that her husband was beginning to attract so much female attention. Rumours of the admiring *Pelzmäntel* ladies at the university lectures did not take long to reach the Burghölzli. And Carl himself told Emma about some of his female patients who were caught in an 'erotic complex', falling in love with their doctor, a common hazard of the profession.

He had been treating two female inmates, both aged twenty-four, both diagnosed as 'hysterics'. The first had been institutionalised because she was overcome by a debilitating exhaustion, lying in the house all day or down in the cellar if it got too hot in the summer. Her symptoms had started when she was still a schoolgirl, with attacks of tremors in her right arm which spread to the whole body, accompanied by tics and shrieks. By the time she came to the Burghölzli she thought she was going mad. Applying his word association test and analysing her dreams using Sigmund Freud's methods, Jung uncovered a sexual complex and suspected sexual abuse, probably incest. Gradually her symptoms improved. She was enjoying the one-to-one attention she got from Herr Doktor Jung and as time went on she became more and more demanding. Finally, Carl found he had to 'pitilessly disturb her illusions' about himself. 'It is to no purpose that she seeks to still her craving for love by falling in love with her doctor,' he wrote, 'for he is already married.'

Her friend, 'Miss L' in Room 7, had become ill through an unhappy love affair and was another 'who gushes about the writer. Like the patient, she has become ill through an erotic complex.' Transference was not well understood in the early years of psychoanalysis, nor the position of women in a society where marriage was virtually their only outlet, and doctors like Jung and Freud often encountered such fixations. Carl had first come across it with his cousin Helly: 'The girl had of course fallen hopelessly in love with me,' as Carl later wrote. 'But I paid very little attention to it and none at all to the role I was playing in her psychology.'

Jung, previously so awkward with women, was beginning to enjoy the attention. Gossip and rumour, so much part of institution life, abounded, and Emma could not fail to hear it, though she probably knew most of the talk was tittle-tattle not to be taken seriously. However, on the night of 17 August 1904 a young woman had been admitted to the Burghölzli as a case of emergency, and this one would be serious.

It was 10.30 p.m. and Jung was the doctor on duty, so he was the one to write the admission notes. A medical police officer and an uncle had brought the young woman in, having taken her by force from the Hotel Baur-en-Ville, where she had been staying with her mother. She had already been thrown out of the Heller Sanatorium at Interlaken because of her behaviour. Jung noted that she was laughing one moment, crying the next, 'in a strangely mixed compulsive manner', and that she had numerous tics, rotated her head in a jerky fashion, stuck out her tongue, and that her legs were twitching. She kept insisting she was not mad, she just had a terrible headache and got 'upset' at the hotel. Jung recorded the uncle's statements as 'meagre and evasive', partly because his command of the German language was not good, being 'an old Russian Jew'. Apparently Fräulein Spielrein had always been 'rather hysterical', and had been 'ill' for the past three years. When she was thrown out of the Heller Sanatorium she was meant to go to the Monakow clinic but they refused to take her 'because she was too disturbed'.

Jung's report was detailed, to the high standards required by Bleuler, and he did not get back to the apartment until close on midnight.

The next day Jung carried out a full anamnesis. The young woman was Sabina Spielrein, the nineteen-year-old daughter of wealthy Russian Jews from Rostov-on-Don. The female *Wärter* who had spent the night in her room reported that the new patient had been anxious in the dark and wanted a light, that she said she had two heads and her body felt foreign, but otherwise it had been a quiet night. The examination was difficult – 'like walking on eggshells' – and it became 'a powerful battle' between doctor and patient. When Jung pointed out that she would have to divulge 'everything' if she wanted to get better, Fräulein Spielrein replied 'she would and could never talk about it, and in any case does not want to be cured at all'. Jung noted 'stomach pains, angina a thousand times, precocious, sensitive'.

Sabina Spielrein was the eldest of five children. Her only sister, whom she had loved 'more than everything in the world', had died aged six of a stomach complaint. Her father was a successful businessman. At the age of five Sabina had unaccountably been sent to a school over a thousand kilometres away in Warsaw; Jung's report did not say if her mother went with her. By the age of six she already spoke German and French. Later she was taught at home until she entered the *Gymnasium*, where she was considered 'intellectually very advanced'. She complained that the teachers were 'very stupid'. She played the piano and sang. She was interested in the natural sciences and wanted to study medicine at Zürich University, which already had some wealthy Russian female students, part of a Russian colony in Zürich which included Jews escaping the pogroms.

Jung arranged for Fräulein Spielrein to be accommodated in the women's section with a female *Wärter* and a private room to herself, costing 1,250 Swiss francs a quarter, a sum roughly equivalent to Jung's salary for a year. He wrote to Fräulein Spielrein's mother at the Hotel Baur-en-Ville, requesting Sabina's belongings to be sent over, and signing it 'Doktor Jung, Senior Physician'. For now, the mother remained at the hotel and the father returned to Rostov.

Over the next few days Emma noticed that her husband seemed even busier and absorbed than usual. He spent several long sessions with Fräulein Spielrein, battling to get what he called a 'confession' out of her. Spielrein admitted that her father hit her several times on her bare buttocks, sometimes in front of her siblings, and when he hit her she had to kiss his hand afterwards. When she talked about this, 'innumerable tics and gestures of abhorrence occurred ... which have a certain connexion with her complexes'. Jung noted that her father was always threatening suicide while at the same time tyrannising the family. One brother had hysterical fits of weeping, another suffered from tics; the last was described as a 'melancholic'. Fräulein Spielrein said she loved her father 'painfully', but she could not turn to him. 'The peak of the experience,' wrote Carl, 'was that her father was a *man*.' Her mother also beat her, in front of her brothers and even their friends.

Sabina Spielrein's reaction to all this was to chastise herself, and fall in love with her uncle, and later with an assistant doctor at the Heller Sanatorium. When she was fifteen she tried to starve herself to death 'because she had made her mother angry'. Aged seven, she had become very pious and started to talk 'with a spirit'. God spoke to her in German. She felt she was 'an extraordinary person'. All this was a bit too close to the bone for the 'other' Carl, the one who had heard voices, had visions, and knew he was 'extraordinary'.

Whilst her husband worked all hours, Emma's life gradually settled into a pattern. During the week she spent time with Hedwig Bleuler and her children, and helped her with social events for the asylum inmates. In the evenings, once the baby slept, she worked on Carl's research and daily reports. Weekends were often spent in Schaffhausen with her mother and Marguerite and Ernst, where Agathli received the happy attention Emma herself had enjoyed as a child. But she did not like to be away from Carl for too long. There were growing rumours about Fräulein Spielrein, and Emma could not fail to notice that this private patient was more demanding than all the rest. Still, that spring, Carl and Emma were able to go for a short holiday to Berlin, leaving the baby in the care of the children's maid, again helped by Groma Jung and Trudi. For once Emma had Carl to herself, in the great city: the palaces, art collections, the avenue of Unter den Linden, the Brandenburg Tor, the cafés and the restaurants, the theatres, the opera, though Carl spent much of the time in bookshops and visiting hospital laboratories. But, perhaps at Emma's insistence, it began a ritual which lasted for the rest of their lives: an annual spring holiday on their own, just the two of them.

It would have been easy to feel cut off from the rest of the world, living behind the high walls of an institution like the Burghölzli, but Carl and Emma were both minded to keep abreast of events. They took three newspapers: the Swiss *Neue Zürcher Zeitung*, the French *Le Monde* and the English *Daily Telegraph*, to be well informed internationally as well as locally, and to practise their languages. They also took the *Schweizer Illustrierte* magazine and *Nebelspalter*, a Swiss satirical publication; and *Punch*, the *Illustrated London News* and *L'Illustration* – all passed on from Bertha via the Lesezirkel Hottingen, the fashionable reading circle in Zürich.

The *Neue Zürcher Zeitung* felt there was too great an appetite for change and everything was going too fast. Every week there was a report about some tram or train accident, and did the telephone and telegraph systems really improve the average Zürich burgher's life? The rich were merely getting richer. 'An automobilist is a capitalist gone mad,' agreed the editor of *Der Bund*. 'Who sits at the wheel of this appalling vehicle? A speed fanatic, an addict of self-indulgence, and a show-off!' Internationally the talk was all about revolution and Russia: the peasants were starving, workers were striking, anarchists and socialists agitating against a dictatorial Tsar. Now the strikes were spreading across Europe, even reaching Zürich where the workers, usually so docile, demanded a nine-hour day and better working conditions. At the Arbenz automobile factory there was a strike after one of the workers was dismissed for 'sabotage'. The employers got rid of the 'trouble-makers' and advertised for replacements, adding: 'Only hard-working, quiet and solid workers will find full employment,' When the unrest in the streets got out of hand the military was called in to help the city police and many arrests followed. The good burghers of Zürich had never seen such a thing. Worse was to follow: the San Francisco earthquake of spring 1906 would almost ruin the Swiss insurance business, and the New York stock exchange crisis would do the same for the banks.

At the Burghölzli, Carl acquired another private patient: an American, Elizabeth Shepley Sergeant. She arrived at the asylum after suffering a breakdown whilst travelling in Europe with an aunt, becoming the first in a long line of wealthy Americans to cross the ocean to be treated by Herr Doktor Jung. The Burghölzli up on Zollikon hill might seem cut off from the rest of the world behind its high walls, but it was getting better and better known in the wider world. At the same time as Jung was attracting attention, a book by the Burghölzli's previous direc-tor, Auguste Forel, was causing quite a stir. *The Sexual Question* was 600 pages of shocking 'progressive' ideas, championing the equality of the sexes and advocating no punishment for 'mutu-ally consensual homosexuality', as well as promoting teetotal abstinence. The Churches – Protestant and Catholic alike – were up in arms and the book was banned in parts of Switzerland. Internationally, however, it was a runaway success.

Meanwhile Fräulein Spielrein had been formally diagnosed with 'hysteria', and her treatment was taking up even more of Jung's time, with sessions lasting up to three hours. He noted that Fräulein Spielrein 'felt as if someone were pressing in upon her, as if [someone], something was creeping around in her bed, something human. At the same time she felt as if someone were shouting in her ear.' It made her feel repulsive, 'like a dog or a devil'. Oddly, Jung made no further comment about this, merely stated the facts, a strange decision which may have had something to do with the fact that he himself knew what it was like to feel repulsive and plagued by the devil. One day Fräulein Spielrein did a drawing relating to her time in Interlaken which showed Dr Heller giving a patient electrical treatment. 'The position is a remarkably sexual one,' Jung noted, leaving it at that. Fräulein Spielrein meanwhile was becoming more and more obsessed with her Herr Doktor.

At first Emma may have thought Fräulein Spielrein, who was neither particularly attractive nor well dressed, was just another of those tragic young women made hysterical by their family circumstances. And normally she would have felt sorry for a young woman so burdened by such a traumatic childhood that a full 'cure' was unlikely. But Fräulein Spielrein was turning out to be trouble. Emma already knew something of Sabina Spielrein. She had even spent time with her in Carl's laboratory where Fräulein Spielrein was helping him collate the word association tests as part of her occupational therapy. 'Patience, calm, and inner goodwill towards the patients' were Bleuler's method 'to remove the basis of hysterical outbursts, and other symptoms, which have merely an attention-seeking nature, by deliberately ignoring them'. Thereafter, as their health and behaviour recovered, the patient needed to be given a purpose in life. In Fräulein Spielrein's case this had started with letting her accompany doctors on ward rounds, because it was known that she wanted to study medicine. Later she was allowed to eat with the assistant doctors and help Herr Doktor Jung collate his word association test results. Emma saw Carl less and less and Fräulein Spielrein saw him more and more. It was all the wrong way round.

Gradually Fräulein Spielrein grew calmer and her behaviour improved, with everyone but the poor female *Wärters* who had charge of her when she was not with her Herr Doktor. 'Suicide attempts to frighten the nurses,' Jung noted; 'running away, giving people scares, transgressing prohibitions'. And if he went away for a few days, perhaps to Schaffhausen with his family, she 'used' his return 'to produce a few scenes': climbing up on the window grille in the corridor, forcing him to pay her an evening visit, or sitting in the doorway of her room in her night-dress wrapped in a blanket, and when no one took any notice, falling into a convulsive fit.

When Carl had to go away for his annual three weeks of military service Direktor Bleuler took over the Spielrein notes: 'Owing to the absence of the Senior Physician pat.[ient] left almost entirely to herself for the last week, and much worse.' One night at 1 a.m. after making a 'scene', she kicked the nurse who was trying to get her back into bed. The next day she was found clinging to the wall until Bleuler came to talk to her. She hid knives, left 'farewell letters', threatened to starve herself to death, stole the gas worker's ladder from the ward and put benches in the corridor for him to 'jump over'. She demonstrated how she would strangle herself with the curtain cords, and she composed 'songs' about the doctors which she found so funny she could not sing them for hysterical laughing. When Herr Doktor Jung returned there were 'all kinds of pranks': she 'torments the nurse so horribly that she has to be withdrawn'; she 'kicks the stepladder around the corridor' and 'scratches the floor'. She refused to go into town, even though it was part of her rehabilitation programme in preparation for leaving the asylum. She again threatened to starve herself to death. 'She insists that every evening she travels to Mars,' wrote Jung, 'on to which she projects all her contra sexual fantasies.' When she complained of pains in her feet, Jung noted: 'She is afraid of going out and of the future, so she tries to postpone going out as long as possible through the pain in her feet.'

It is not hard to imagine how Emma reacted to all these endless 'pranks' and 'scenes'. Carl had always discussed his work and his cases with her, so she knew what was going on, and she could see for herself how Fräulein Spielrein manipulated events to spend all her time with Carl. So it must have been a relief to Emma when it was decided that Fräulein Spielrein was well enough to leave the Burghölzli and attend as an outpatient instead. But, as Jung had divined, Fräulein Spielrein did not want to leave. The lengthy sessions continued, and she began telling Herr Doktor Jung new and distressing stories about her father: how 'he took her into a special room and ordered her: "lie down"; she implored him not to beat her (he was trying to lift her skirt from behind). Finally he gave in, but he forced her to kneel down and kiss the picture of her grandfather and to swear always to be a good child. After this humiliating scene the boys (her brothers) were waiting outside to greet her.' She admitted to Jung that 'since her fourth year she had experienced sexual arousal'. She had 'orgasmic discharge' and eventually she only had to see or hear one of her brothers being beaten for her to 'want to masturbate'. Even a threat was enough for her to lie on her bed and masturbate. Someone only had to laugh at her, inducing a feeling of humiliation, 'to cause her to have an orgasm'. Jung's notes added: 'during the act, pat. wishes on herself all manner of torments; she pictures these as vividly as possible, in particular being beaten on her bare bottom and, in order to increase her arousal, she imagines that it is taking place in front of a large audience'.

Bleuler wrote to the woman's father in Rostov: 'As her memories of you agitate her greatly, we are of the opinion that Fräulein Spielrein should not write to you directly over the next few months,' and ended the letter: 'Fräulein Spielrein now occupies herself almost daily with scientific reading and she has also commenced practical scientific study in the anatomy laboratory. She wishes to convey her fond greetings. Yours faithfully, the Direktor, Bleuler.'

Sabina Spielrein was finally discharged from the Burghölzli on 1 June 1905, to attend college in preparation for her medical studies at the University of Zürich. 'In the last few weeks distinctly improved,' wrote Jung, 'and increasingly calm. Now listens to lectures conscientiously and with interest.' The treatment could be counted as a success. But if Emma hoped that Fräulein Spielrein would now exit their lives, she was wrong. Soon she was turning up at the Burghölzli for her private outpatient sessions with Jung, fashionably dressed and newly independent, embarked on just the kind of studies Emma herself would have dearly loved to pursue. Worse still, she took to telling anyone who would listen that she was in love with Herr Doktor Jung. And that he loved her. Instead of trying to extricate himself from this highly charged relationship, Jung wrote to Herr Spielrein suggesting he channel the money for his daughter's allowance through himself. Emma was angry, jealous, distressed. But what could she do?

By the autumn Fräulein Spielrein's mother had discovered what was going on. She demanded that Jung write a report on her daughter's treatment for Herr Professor Freud in Vienna, in case her daughter needed to be removed from Zürich for further treatment. Her daughter had already fallen in love with an uncle, and with one of the doctors at the Heller Sanatorium, and she did not want it to happen all over again. She needed to have the report in her possession 'to use if the occasion arises'.

Jung's report, dated 25 September 1905, written on official Burghölzli notepaper, begins with a brief summary of Fräulein Spielrein's history and then continues:

Masturbation always occurred after she underwent punishment from her father. After a while the beatings were no longer necessary to initiate sexual arousal; it came to be triggered through mere threats and other situations implying violence, such as verbal abuse, threatening hand movements, etc. After a time she could not even look at her father's hands without becoming sexually aroused, or watch him eat without imagining how the food was ejected, and then being thrashed on the buttocks, etc. These associations extended to the younger brother too, who also masturbated frequently from an early age. Threats to the boy or ill-treatment of him aroused her and she had to masturbate whenever she saw him being punished.

It goes on to describe how at the Burghölzli, Fräulein Spielrein 'initially harassed everybody, tormenting the nurses to the limits of their endurance. As the analysis progressed, her condition noticeably improved and she finally revealed herself to be a highly intelligent and talented person of great sensibility. There is a certain callousness and unreasonableness in her character and she lacks any kind of feeling for situation and for external propriety, but much of this must be put down to Russian peculiarities.' Her mother, Jung added, could 'not quite comprehend' why Fräulein Spielrein suffered enormously whenever she met any member of her family, even though she knew about the 'most important part' of her daughter's complex.

Up to this point the report gave an account of a case which Jung had handled professionally and with some success. But the last paragraph reads: 'During treatment the patient had the misfortune to fall in love with me. She raves on to her mother about her love in an ostentatious manner, and a secret perverse enjoyment of her mother's dismay seems to play a not inconsiderable part in this. In view of this situation her mother therefore wishes, if the worst comes to the worst, to place her elsewhere for treatment, with which I am naturally in agreement.'

6

Dreams and Tests

One day during the summer of 1905 Emma sat down at her desk in their apartment on the upper floor of the Burghölzli, and, with Carl at her side, dipped the nib of her pen in the inkwell and began to write. Jung was dictating a dream he had had, and his interpretation of it. Emma was pregnant with their second child. The dream was long and detailed:

> I saw horses being hoisted by thick cables to a great height. One of them, a powerful brown horse which was tied up with straps and was hoisted aloft like a package, struck me particularly. Suddenly the cable broke and the horse crashed to the street. I thought it must be dead. But it immediately leapt up again and galloped away. I noticed that the horse was dragging a heavy log along with it, and I wondered how it could advance so quickly. It was obviously frightened and could easily cause an accident. Then a rider came up on a little horse and rode along slowly in front of the frightened horse, which moderated its pace somewhat. I still feared that the horse might run over the rider, when a cab came along and drove in front of the rider at the same pace, thus bringing the horse to a still slower gait. I then thought now all is well, the danger is over.

Carl went on to dictate a detailed interpretation of the dream, which he would include in his next book, *Über die Psychologie der Dementia Praecox*, which he had been working on since 1903 and would complete in July 1906. The book was, as he explained in the foreword, based on his clinical experiments and researches, so combining 'all the disadvantages of eclecticism, which to many a reader may seem so striking that he will call my work a confession of faith rather than a scientific treatise. *Peu Importe*! The important thing is that I should be able to show the reader how, through psychological investigation, I have been led to certain views which I think will provoke new and fruitful questions concerning the individual psychological basis of *dementia praecox*.' He went on to acknowledge his debt to Herr Professor Bleuler and 'my friend Dr Riklin' and – significantly – to Sigmund Freud in Vienna, a man he had not yet met: 'Even a superficial glance at my work will show how much I am indebted to the brilliant discoveries of Freud.' In Part One he gave a summary of work which was currently being done in the field: by Pierre Janet, Kraepelin, Aschaffenburg, Ziehen, Tschisch, Freusberg, Sommer, Clemens Neisser and Otto Gross – a brilliant doctor who would soon become Jung's patient at the Burghölzli.

The dream came in Part Two. Carl did not admit to it being his own dream but ascribed it to a 'friend', adding that 'the personal and family circumstances of the subject are well known to me'. The analysis took the form of Jung asking the friend what he made of each point of the dream, then offering his own interpretation based on his theory of associations. 'It seemed to him that the horses were being hoisted onto a skyscraper,' Emma wrote, to Carl's dictation; 'X had recently seen in a periodical the picture of a skyscraper being built.' Horses working in the mines were tied with straps in the same manner, his 'friend' recalled, before being lowered down. These 'dizzy heights' brought to mind mountains and the friend admitted that he was a passionate mountain climber, and that:

> just about the time of the dream, [he] had had a great desire to make a high ascent and also to travel. But his wife felt very uneasy about it and would not allow him to go alone. She could not accompany him, as she was pregnant. For this reason they had been obliged to give up the idea of a journey to America [skyscrapers], where they had planned to go together. They realised that as soon as there are children in the family it becomes much more difficult to move about and one cannot go everywhere. [Both were very fond of travelling and had travelled a good deal.] Having to give up the trip to America was particularly disagreeable to him, as he had business dealings with that country and always hoped that by a personal visit he would be able to establish new and important connexions. On this hope he had built vague plans for the future, rather lofty and flattering to his ambition.

He went on to point out some further associations: 'to work like a horse' and 'to be in harness' leading to the meaning 'by labour one gets to the top'. On the other hand, being 'hoisted like a package' reminded X of tourists who he had always despised for getting themselves hoisted up to the highest alpine peaks 'like sacks of flour'. Not something he himself ever required, and there was an element of contempt here. So where was the dreamer in all this? Because, as Jung reminded the reader, Freud said the dreamer was usually the chief actor. Surely his 'friend' was the 'powerful brown horse'. But what about the log he was dragging along? Now the 'friend' recalled that 'Log' (or Steam-Roller) had been his nickname when he was younger, on account of his powerful, stocky figure. But, despite the burden, it did not actually hinder the horse. On the other hand, the galloping horse was frightened, and that could easily cause an accident.

Jung had reached an impasse and needed to approach the dream from another angle. Why had the cable broken, causing the horse to fall down to the street? It seemed to associate with an earlier career ambition, which had been thwarted and others preferred over him. 'His disappointment over his failure was so great, he said, that for a moment he almost despaired of his future career. In the dream he thought the horse was dead, but soon saw with satisfaction that it got up again and galloped away.' Jung thought a new section of his 'friend's' dream began here, corresponding to a new period in his life. The friend now remembered something else about the dream: there was another horse, very indistinct, in the background: 'X was dragging the log with someone else, and this person must be his wife, with whom he is harnessed "in the yoke of matrimony",' suggested Jung to X, noting that although the encumbrance might have hindered his progress he was able to gallop away, revealing he could not be tied down. The galloping horse reminded X of a painting by Welti, *Mond Nacht* ('A Moonlit Night'), where galloping horses were shown on the cornice of a building. One of them was a lusty stallion, rearing up. In the same picture there was a married couple lying in bed. The image of the galloping horse, therefore, had led to the very suggestive painting by Welti. 'Here we get a quite unexpected glimpse into the sexual nuance of the dream, where till now we thought we could see only the complex of ambition and careerism,' concluded Jung, adding that this could easily be interpreted as 'X's own impetuous temperament which he feared might involve him in impetuous acts'.

If Emma did not know it before, she knew it now: Carl felt that marriage held him back, but, be warned, nothing would stop him from doing what he wanted to do. That there was a sexual element to it can not have come as a surprise. But did Emma agree with Carl's interpretation of the dream?

'Then a rider came up on a little horse and rode along slowly in front of the frightened horse, which moderated its pace somewhat': Jung first interpreted the 'little horse' as his 'superior', Bleuler. But he had to admit that the horse was 'small and dainty like a rocking horse', which certainly did not fit. Instead, the 'friend' recalled an incident in his childhood when he saw a pregnant woman, and this led once again to his pregnant wife. Another impasse. He turned his attention to the cab which joined the 'little horse' to slow the stallion down, and now the 'friend' saw it was full of 'a whole cartload of children', a fact which had been repressed when he first recounted the dream and only recalled in the telling.

'The meaning of the dream is now perfectly clear,' Jung concluded with a flourish. 'The wife's pregnancy and the problem of too many children impose restraints on the husband. This dream fulfils a wish, since it represents the restraint as already accomplished. Outwardly the dream, like all others, looks meaningless, but even in its top layer it shows clearly enough the hopes and disappointments of an upward-striving career.' He ended enigmatically: 'Inwardly it hides an extremely personal matter which may well have been accompanied by painful feelings.' This is as much as the interpreter of the dream is prepared to reveal about why the stallion was 'frightened'. It was not a word he cared to investigate. Nor the association with the 'little horse' coming to the stallion's rescue, which led to the last thought of the dream to be: 'I then thought now all is well, the danger is over.'

Perhaps Emma realised she was the little horse who came to the frightened stallion's rescue. But she said nothing, or if she did, Carl did not record it. As she wrote and Carl dictated, no one thought it wrong for the analyst to be both subject and interpreter. In later years it became clear that analysis required a practitioner quite separate from the subject to do the interpreting, but not in 1905.

One thing the dream reveals: in real life Carl did not always get his way. When Emma insisted he could not sail off to America or go mountain-climbing because she was pregnant he was forced to agree. After almost three years of marriage Emma was beginning to leave behind the ingénue she was when Carl first met her. In public she remained quiet and reserved, but in private some things were changing. And another thing: for all the years she had been writing down Jung's dictation, writing up reports, helping with research, she was learning first-hand how dreams and associations revealed the hidden desires of the unconscious and the secrets of repression. It was an apprenticeship by default. When the book *Dementia Praecox* was finished, Carl once more dedicated it to Emma, his wife.

Carl sent a copy to *Hochverehrter Herr Professor!* – Professor Freud in Vienna. He had previously sent him a copy of his *Diagnostic Association Studies*, thereby starting the now famous

Emma and Carl at the time of their visit to Vienna. Carl, a penniless doctor, married Emma, one of the richest heiresses in Switzerland, in 1903 – the start of a long and complex marriage.

Sigmund Freud: a photograph taken by his sons and sent as a gift to Carl after the visit to Vienna. Emma had it enlarged and framed for Carl's Christmas present.

Vienna was one of the great cosmopolitan cities of Europe. Only half the inhabitants were German-speaking Austrians; the rest came from the four corners of the Austro-Hungarian Empire, including many Jews, rich and poor.

The two sisters, Emma (*left*) and Marguerite Rauschenbach, in a setting befitting their position in society. They were close but very different: Emma clever and studious, Marguerite outward-going and sporty.

The Haus zum Rosengarten on the far bank of the Rhine was Emma's 'idyllic' childhood home. Large and square, it was the finest in Schaffhausen, with a rose garden by the river, next to the town's washing stand.

The Rhine Falls at Schaffhausen were close to Emma's home. The intrepid could hire a ferryman to row them through the roaring torrent to the rock in the middle, the Swiss flag flying high above.

When Emma was twelve the family moved to Ölberg, a vast Jugendstil mansion above Schaffhausen. By this time Emma's father was blind, so all the plans were produced in braille.

Carl as a boy. 'I had never met such an asocial monster,' recalled a friend. Carl's mother had a second personality and heard voices. His father was plagued with unnamed torments.

Early on Carl sensed problems in his parents' marriage. His mother had to go 'away' occasionally, when Carl was looked after by his father, sleeping in the same room till he went to university, aged eighteen.

Jean Rauschenbach. Emma's father was director of the internationally renowned family business in agricultural machinery until he went blind in 1894, when Emma was twelve.

Emma aged sixteen. Shy and podgy, Emma's 'idyllic' childhood was over. There was a terrible family secret: her father's blindness had been caused by syphilis.

Carl at Basel University. A complicated, ambitious young man, outwardly confident but plagued by deep feelings of inferiority, and with little experience of women.

stions in the lost letter: 'I have been unable to
fantile root anywhere.' Clever Freud had put his
orts of repressed associations, but neither Jung nor
to have considered the possibility that 'the little
ented Emma, coming to the rescue. 'The analysis
e's own dreams is a ticklish business at best,' Jung
Freud; 'one succumbs again and again to the inhibi-
ting from the dream no matter how objective one
eself to be.'

rote to his 'esteemed colleague' on 30 December,
usly giving him an example of a case of a female
his who had suffered from depression. 'She is very
ove with her husband (he is an actor) but has been
esthetic in sexual intercourse. The patient adds that it
occurred to her to blame her husband for her lack of
n, that she is convinced it is her fault.' He worded it
he was asking for Jung's opinion in a professional
ding: 'Forgive me for taking up your time.' Apparently
d not believe Jung's 'no sexual failure, more likely a
e'. But then Freud knew nothing of Carl's complex
lity No. 2.

New Year's Day 1907 Professor Freud wrote again. He
ant his previous letter to be longer but: 'I broke it off
for incidental reasons and partly because my guess,
med by you, as to the identity of the dreamer, bade me
ny peace. I merely thought you might have gone so far as
ss the interpretation log = penis and the "alternative"
, horse/career, without giving yourself away.' He
nted himself with pointing out that Jung's version of the
fulfilment, to have a son, was hardly credible. After that

Carl (*middle row, third left*) dominated discussions at his Zofingia fraternity with his powerful personality, superior intellect and lively humour. His nickname was Walze, 'Steam-Roller' or 'Barrel'.

Emma (*left*) and Marguerite (*centre*) in Canton of Schaffhausen costume. Back from Paris, Emma had turned into a slim, attractive young woman with plenty of admirers.

The Burghölzli was the vast Zürich lunatic asylum where Carl worked from 1900. Under the directorship of Dr Bleuler it was gaining an international reputation for its progressive methods of treatment.

Carl at the Burghölzli. Other staff thought he might have some psychical disturbance because he seemed so alienated. He didn't leave the asylum precincts for his first six months.

One of the men's wards at the Burghölzli. Patients, if not bedridden, were encouraged to take part in the many activities provided under the Bleuler regime.

correspondence of 3! The letter Freud wrot *Praecox* is lost, but i offered a somewhat diff suggesting it related to ' rumbled that the drea himself.

'You have put your fir analysis,' Jung wrote in December 1906:

> I do in fact know the drear
> much better than I have sai
> he is myself. The 'failure o
> thing essential that is undo
> though not in the way you th
> reasons I was turned down w
> accepted, and I married. I am
> way (not merely from optimisi
> nothing to prevent such dream:
> failure, more likely a social one.
> 'sexual restraint' is, as I have said
> pushed into the foreground and l
> wish that had better not see the lig

Jung then offered another interpret the wish for a son, adding 'we have tv having been born on 8 February 1906

It would be surprising if this expla Jung also insisted, presumably with

Freud's sugge discover an in finger on all s Freud appear horse' repres and use of o admitted to tions emana believes on

Freud w disingenuo patient of much in l totally ana has never satisfactio as thoug matter, er Freud di social o Persona On l had me partly confiri hold to str gallo conte wish he concentrated on their hoped-for future partnership. 'The "leading lights" of psychiatry really don't amount to much,' he told him, 'the future belongs to us and our views, and the younger men – everywhere most likely – side actively with us. I see this in Vienna, where, as you know, I am systematically ignored by my colleagues and periodically annihilated by some hack, but where my lectures nevertheless draw forty attentive listeners, coming from every faculty.' He hoped Jung would come to Vienna soon, 'before you go to America (it is nearer).' Still, he could not end the letter without some further reference to his usual topic: 'I should like to observe that you omit a factor to which, I am aware, I attribute far more importance than you do at the present time; as you know, I am referring to xxx sexuality.' Three crosses meant danger. They used to be chalked on the inside of doors in peasant houses to ward it off.

Jung did not answer for a week, and when he did he apologised for not writing sooner. Presumably Freud's letter had given him plenty to think about and he took his time. 'Afterwards I was rather embarrassed at having played hide and seek with my dream,' he admitted, adding: 'There are special reasons why I did not bring in the interpretation log = penis, the chief of which was that I was not in a position to present my dream impersonally: my wife wrote the whole description (!!).' Perhaps Emma was doing more than merely taking down Carl's dictation by offering interpretations of her own. After this admission his letter quickly reverted to professional talk and the hope that he might visit Freud in Vienna during their forthcoming spring holiday.

Emma was meanwhile beginning to take a more active role at the Burghölzli asylum. In 1907 Dr Abraham Brill (known as A.

A. Brill) arrived from America to join the staff, replacing Karl Abraham who returned to Germany. Brill's account of the way Bleuler's 'active community' involved everyone, each to their own capacity, is full of the atmosphere of those heady times. He points out that the community included the wives:

> In the hospital the spirit of Freud hovered over everything. Our conversation at meals was frequently punctuated by the word 'complex', the special meaning of which was created at the time. No one could make a slip of any kind without immediately being called upon to evoke free associations to explain it. It did not matter that women were present – wives and female voluntary interns – who might have curbed the frankness usually produced by free associations. The women were just as keen to discover the concealed mechanisms as their husbands. There was also a Psychoanalytic Circle which met every month. Some of those who attended were far from agreeing with our views; but despite Jung's occasional impulsive intolerance, the meetings were very fruitful and successful in disseminating Freud's theories.

Whatever else Emma's life in Schaffhausen might have provided, it could never have competed with the fevered atmosphere at the Burghölzli asylum in those early years. 'Jung brooked no disagreement with Freud's views,' Brill added, 'impulsive and bright, he refused to see the other side. Anyone who dared doubt what was certainly then new and revolutionary immediately aroused his anger.'

Auguste Forel, the former Herr Direktor still wandering around the corridors of the Burghölzli, was distinctly fed up about it. 'This Freud cult disgusts me,' he wrote to his friend Ludwig Frank. 'I leave open the question if the famous discovery of Freud is really his and doesn't rather belong to Bleuler but it is certain that in Vienna, where people aren't prudish, Freud has a very bad reputation which is not unfounded ... It appears to me as if Bleuler is no longer the Director of the Burghölzli, but Jung, and I am sorry.'

Jung was certainly getting into his stride. 'It is amusing to see how the female outpatients go about diagnosing each other's erotic complexes although they have no insight into their own,' he wrote to Professor Freud in June, quite forgetting the trouble he had with his own. Ten days later he went on a trip to Paris and London, furthering his career and leaving Emma back at the Burghölzli with the two little girls. Once he was back home he wrote to Freud about 'a German-American woman who made a pleasant impression on me – a Mrs St, aged about 35', whom he had met in Paris. They were at a party, chatting about landscapes, when 'Mrs St' declined the offer of black coffee saying she could not tolerate even one mouthful. Impetuous Carl plunged in with an unasked-for interpretation: this was a nervous symptom, he suggested, and would only apply when she was at home; elsewhere she would tolerate the coffee better. 'Scarcely had this unfortunate phrase left my mouth than I felt enormously embarrassed,' he admitted to Freud, 'but rapidly discovered – luckily – it had "slipped by" her.'

In the same letter Jung wrote: 'My wife, who knows a thing or two, said recently: "I am going to write a psychotherapeutic handbook for gentlemen."' Having attended all the meetings, with their talk of erotic complexes, repressions and slips of the tongue, and participated in research and the word association tests, Emma, on the eve of their first visit to Freud in Vienna, was learning fast.

At 19 Berggasse that March, 1907, Freud watched Emma Jung: the reserved but friendly way she behaved at that midday Sunday meal – intelligent, interested, talking to Martha and Minna and the children at one end of the table whilst her husband talked his head off down the other. So when Freud received Jung's letter in July he probably was not surprised to hear that Emma Jung 'knew a thing or two' about psycho-analysis.

For Jung the Vienna visit had been thrilling, talking with Freud late into the night. But the after-effects were traumatic. Too much had been stirred up with all the talk and the flattering admiration, and above all Freud's implacable insistence that sexuality was the root cause of all neurosis, which Jung struggled to accept. 'But don't you think that a number of borderline phenomena might be considered more appropriately in terms of the other basic drive, *hunger*; for instance, eating, sucking (predominantly hunger), kissing (predominantly sexuality)?' Jung had written in October 1906, even before meeting Freud in person.

Growing up in a poor, isolated Swiss peasant village he knew all about hunger. And not only hunger. 'I had grown up in the country, among peasants, and what I was unable to learn in the stables I found out from the Rabelaisian wit and the untrammelled fantasies of our peasant folklore,' Jung wrote years later. 'Incest and perversions were no remarkable novelties to me, and did not call for any special explanation. That cabbages thrive in dung was something I had always taken for granted.' The trouble was, he himself had been sexually abused as a boy, so, ironically, he was an example of Freud's theory. And with all this talk about sex he was no longer able to repress it. It was another two years before he could admit to Freud that the Vienna visit had culminated in an obsession with the lady in Abbazia. 'As I have indicated before, my first visit to Vienna had a very long unconscious aftermath, first the compulsive infatuation in Abbazia, then the Jewess popped up in another form, in the shape of my patient. Now of course the whole bag of tricks lies there quite clearly before my eyes.'

In fact Freud had recently shifted his views on childhood sexuality, deciding that some patients who claimed to have been sexually abused were, in fact, fantasising. Karl Abraham agreed with Freud: one of the reasons there appeared to be so many cases of child sexual abuse was that 'the trauma [was] wished for in the unconscious, so we have here a glimpse of a form of infantile sexuality'. The child was fantasising, or, if a real act, was to some extent a willing participant. Why, otherwise, did the child not call for help? Or run away? Thence the feeling of guilt in the child, suggested Abraham. But Jung knew he was not fantasising. And he knew that in isolated villages, where families were already too large, there were plenty of cases of incest. And he knew from personal experience that abused children do not always run away, or tell anyone about it. They repress it. 'You will doubtless have drawn your own conclusions from the prolongation of my reaction-time,' he told Freud. 'Up till now I have had a strong resistance to writing because until recently the complexes aroused in Vienna were still in an uproar. Only now have things settled down a bit, so that I hope to be able to write you a more or less sensible letter.'

In August, Jung was again apologising to Freud for his 'long silence'. He had been away on his annual three weeks' army military service: 'at it from 5 in the morning till 8 at night' and then, dog-tired, back to the Burghölzli where he was over-worked, with never enough time to do his own research. 'Often I want to give up in sheer despair,' he wrote. By September he was at a congress in Amsterdam defending Freud's reputation. He spoke without his usual clarity and confidence and had to be called off the podium for overrunning, 'refusing to obey the chairman's repeated signal to finish. Ultimately he was compelled to, whereupon with a flushed angry face he strode out of the room,' as Ernest Jones, a young Welshman and a keen disciple of Freud, later described. When Jones had first met Jung, during a visit to the Burghölzli to observe the Herr Doktor's methods, he noted his 'formidable presence', but now, seeing this lamen-table performance, he was not so sure. Jung knew it. Writing to Freud afterwards, still smarting from the humiliation, he described the crowd as 'ghastly, reeking of vanity' and the discussions 'a morass of nonsense and stupidity!'

By the end of September, Carl was in bed with severe gastro-enteritis, requiring Emma's nursing and stabilising. A new voluntary assistant at the Burghölzli, Max Eitingon, was getting under his skin but it took Jung a while to admit why. 'I consider Eitingon a totally impotent gasbag,' he wrote to Freud. 'Scarcely has this uncharitable judgement left my lips than it occurs to me that I envy him his uninhibited abreaction to the polygamous instinct.' Eitingon had many affairs quite openly, and Jung envied him.

Emma and Carl spent Christmas and the New Year, 1908, with Emma's mother at Ölberg, whence Emma sent Freud and his family a New Year's greeting. Though she had not spent a great deal of time with Freud in Vienna, it had been enough to appreciate his charm and the cleverness with which he handled her ebullient husband. This Christmas, Emma had a surprise present for Carl: an enlarged and beautifully framed photograph of the Herr Professor. Jung had been asking Freud to fulfil 'a long-cherished and constantly repressed wish' for a photograph, and Freud had finally sent one – taken informally by 'my boys', using a roughly hung curtain as backdrop. On 25 January, Jung wrote to thank him in terms which might have surprised the Herr Professor: 'I have a sin to confess: I have had your photograph enlarged. It looks marvellous.' A sin? What Emma thought of Carl's claim to have done it himself is not recorded. Freud forbore to comment on the photograph in his reply, telling Jung about his health instead: he had recovered from his bout of influenza which had lasted long enough: 'For six long weeks the frog was ill/But now he's smoking with a will,' he wrote, quoting his favourite Wilhelm Busch, and taking no notice of the doctor's warnings about what might happen to him if he did not give up smoking those cigars.

Carl had also been ill again, but by the beginning of January he was already back at the Burghölzli leaving Emma and the girls behind in Schaffhausen. 'At the moment I am treating another case of severe hysteria with twilight states. It's going well,' he wrote to Freud with evident relish. Originally Hans Maier, the first assistant, was meant to conduct the analysis with the patient, but the woman resisted, having already 'set her cap' at Herr Doktor Jung. Doctors and nurses clustered round when the patient was in one of her twilight states, full of wonderment at the dramatic beauty of her utterances. 'At present she is expecting a visit from her lover, but is afflicted with a ructus [burping]. She is always standing at the window looking out to see if he is coming.' Two weeks later Jung was wowing a mesmerised public in the auditorium of the Zürich city hall. Up one minute, down the next, was the pattern: by February he was ill again, this time with 'a beastly attack of influenza'. He felt run down and listless and Emma had to steady him once more. His scientific work had come to a total stop. He needed a holiday.

'All sorts of psychogenic complications insinuated themselves into my influenza, and this has had a bad effect on my convalescence,' wailed Jung. 'First of all a complex connected with my family played the very devil with me, then I got disheartened by the negotiations over the journal.' The journal – *Jahrbuch für psychoanalytische und psychopathologische Forschungen* – was close to Freud's heart, the means by which Freudian psychoanalysis could reach an international public, and he was determined that Jung should be the editor. As to the 'complex connected with my family', we can only guess what it was about: maybe his age-old feelings of social inferiority, his 'vaulting ambition' which led him again and again to overwork and exhaustion. But the most likely reason was quarrels with Emma over his continued involvement with Fräulein Spielrein. Emma probably knew it was not a fully sexual relationship, but it was a highly charged emotional one – much more than the usual 'infatuations' – and Carl seemed quite unable or unwilling to break it off.

Emma was at her wits' end, mortified and jealous. At some point she threatened Carl with divorce, either before or after their visit to Vienna, but certainly once she realised Fräulein

Spielrein was still making trouble, spreading rumours. Emma knew Carl. She knew that the last thing on earth he wanted was divorce. Now she summoned all her courage to have it out with him. Her own childhood had not prepared her for a husband with 'polygamous instincts'. Her father had been a good husband to Bertha, caught out by a transgression on a business trip to Budapest. It is not known how Emma handled the showdown with Carl. She was not used to making scenes. It was not in her nature and it was humiliating. But scenes she made. 'It seems a very long time since I last wrote to you,' Jung wrote to Freud from the Grand Hotel Bellevue, Buvento, on 11 April 1908. 'All sorts of things have played the devil with me, for instance a hideous bout of influenza that left me so debilitated that I had to take thermal baths at Baden. Now I'm setting about recovering as thoroughly as possible on Lago Maggiore.' He would write again once he was back home. 'At present I am too dissociated.'

'Divorce/force' was one of the word associations in the long series of tests Jung underwent for Ludwig Binswanger, spread across several weeks. Binswanger's family ran the Bellevue Sanatorium at Kreuzlingen and he came to the Burghölzli asylum like so many others, attracted by its international reputation and that of Herr Doktor Jung. Jung, always generous to students with his time, agreed to be Binswanger's supervisor and offered himself as one of the 'educated subjects' for the tests. This came a month or two before the Jungs' second visit to Vienna, otherwise Carl might well have refused, because the word associations turned out to be much more revealing and unsettling than he had anticipated.

Binswanger's dissertation was titled 'On the Psychogalvanic Phenomenon in Association Experiments'. He used twenty-three subjects in all, taken from the usual source: educated and uneducated, some patients, some doctors, some *Wärters*, male and female. He made use of the galvanometer again. 'I will begin with an experiment on a subject remarkable for penetrating and reliable self-analysis – a married doctor well acquainted with the association experiment,' he wrote.

The galvanonmeter – a scientific technique.

Using the Rauschenbach stopwatch he noted that the subject's mean time for a reaction was 1.8 seconds. 'Head/band' it started, followed by 'blue/sea'. But then came 'wall/star', an odd association which Binswanger asked the subject to explain. Apparently the subject meant to say 'stone' but deviated from it. There followed a long explanation of the deviation, none of which mentioned the fact that a stone in the garden wall of the parsonage where Jung lived as a child had played such a vital part in his young life, when he had tried to decide whether he was the stone or the stone was himself.

Then Binswanger, seeing Jung was too well prepared, changed the stimulus word from 'angel' to 'devil'. That took Carl by surprise. The devil played a critical part in the secret life of the 'other Carl', as did religion in general, albeit in an unconventional way.

'My veneration for you has something of a "religious" crush,' Jung had confessed to Freud in the letter in which he also disclosed he had been sexually assaulted by someone he had 'worshipped' as a boy. Five days later, waiting for Freud's reply which was unusually long in coming, he wrote again: 'I am suffering all the agonies of a patient in analysis, riddling myself with every conceivable fear about the possible consequences of my confession.' Freud's reply is missing but it evidently managed to calm Jung about his 'confession'. It worked wonders for him, he said, and you can hear the relief: 'You are absolutely right to extol humour as the only decent reaction to the inevitable. This was also my principle until the repressed material got the better of me, luckily only at odd moments. My old religiosity had secretly found in you a compensating factor which I had to come to terms with eventually, and I was able to do so only by telling you about it. In this way I hoped to prevent it from interfering with my behaviour in general.' Freud answered this one in typical fashion, combining good advice with humour: 'A transference on a religious basis would strike me as most disastrous; it could end only in apostasy, thanks to the universal human tendency to keep making new prints out of the clichés we bear within us. I shall do my best to show you that I am unfit to be an object of worship. You probably think I have already begun.'

When Binswanger got to 'will/strive' there was a long deviation because 'the subject has a strongly pronounced striving for knowledge, work and recognition. A strong complex.' This was followed by 'friendly/hateful', to which Binswanger comments: 'Wanted to say *hate*. Constellated by a dream of the previous night which referred to an old complex not recently revised and which will be dealt with later. So far there has been a rapid rise of the whole curve.' To 'thorn' Jung responded 'flesh'. 'It at once occurs to him that *thorn* signifies a sexual symbol and has replaced the similar *stalk*. During the reaction he is thinking that [Saint] Paul says of himself he has a thorn in his flesh.'

'Dance/joyous' was accompanied by a big increase in the curve on the graph, because, said Jung, he was annoyed that he had to accompany his wife to a ball the next day. 'Sea/lake' came next: he had a journey to England planned. 'Proud/eminent' elicited the comment: 'he is often reproached by his family with being too proud! He has, in general, a strongly developed conscience.' It was followed by a rise in the curve for 'oil': '*öl/berg*', the name of Emma's family estate in Schaffhausen. 'Threaten/hit' aroused the same complex as an earlier association 'on account of which he was for a time threatened'. 'Rich/poor' caused the biggest deviation so far: 'Money complex plays a large part in this subject and is closely connected with his love of travelling, his salary at the asylum, and his future way of living.' The same applied to 'money/have'. With 'play/cards' the subject thought of his wife and children. Then came 'repent/spent' and another rise of the curve denoting 'a rising emotional tone' and referring back to the same old 'not gone into' complex.

A footnote comments: 'For personal reasons this complex was not analysed more fully.'

From Association 51 onwards 'the subject admits he experienced distinct excitation'. This followed 'belly/lie' and 'wrong/right', so it was back to the same old complex again. It is at this point that 'divorce/force' was introduced, followed by 'child/have' where Binswanger, alerted to Jung's deviations, comments: 'He thinks that his youngest child is slightly unwell. But there seems to be some stronger complex behind this apparently "innocent" reaction.' He goes on to quote Freud's *Interpretation of Dreams*, that superficial reactions often hide 'a real and deeper link' – a complex and the resistance to it. 'It is as if the barricade, e.g. an inundation in the mountains, had made the large and best road impassable,' wrote Freud, 'transport then becomes restricted to the inconvenient and steep bridle-paths, which are otherwise only used by the hunter.'

In Jung's case these steep paths often led to his father, the pastor, and to his own 'religiosity', Binswanger noted, adding that 'the subject was very religious in childhood'.

The climax came in a series of tests conducted about a month later during which Binswanger used further methods of distraction to penetrate Jung's resistances: a metronome set fast at ninety-four beats a minute, electrodes on the soles of the feet, and a beam of light shone in the eyes. The subject is described as the married doctor again, but from Binswanger's point of view we are told: 'He is also reserved in ordinary conversation. This reserve is a defence measure against his extreme sensibility, but it is not so much inherited as acquired from various events which have acted upon him as boy and youth, which even today are still to some extent active . . . The bright, careless boy early became a very serious man who has developed, as compensation, a most unusual zeal for duty, and anxiety about work.' Apparently the subject was now 'in a state of active opposition to the analysis'.

It had begun happily enough with 'head/beautiful', apparently an association to the subject's wife. For 'friendly/beloved' the subject commented that 'beloved' was always a word that stood for his wife, and he thought of his wife again with 'dance/much' and with 'housekeeping/wife', followed by 'wicked/good', both 'strongly emotionally toned'. Likewise 'child/mother'. To 'people/state' he commented: 'the State makes such demands upon him that he has little time to devote to his wife', the state in this case being the Canton of Zürich. Other insights into the subject's preoccupations included 'ride/well': 'During his military service he would like to have learnt to ride well, but an illness prevented his riding.' Since Emma was a fine horsewoman perhaps it is not surprising that this comment is followed by: 'He admits that this worried him afterwards. We see that everything that hinders him in his ambition provokes vivid emotional expressions.' Glass/drink 'reminds him of the teetotal movement, of which he is a fervid partisan'.

But there is an undercurrent running along which Jung was trying hard to avoid. Binswanger noted that the subject's whole upper body and legs were moving about. Certain sounds agitated him, he noted, especially: 'Shortly before the experiment the subject had been informed that a former female patient, whose name begins with this sound, had slandered him.' The sound was an 'S': Sabina Spielrein. At the end of the test Binswanger made Jung calm down and rest quietly, whereupon he fell fast asleep.

7

A Home of Their Own

Apart from threatening divorce, Emma now insisted on moving out of the Burghölzli and having a house of her own. The rumours flying about the place were too hurtful. Apparently Herr Doktor Jung was on the verge of leaving her to marry Sabina Spielrein. Emma knew it was not true and that most of the rumours emanated from Fräulein Spielrein herself. But no smoke without fire. It was mortifying, knowing people were talking about you, feeling sorry for you, wondering how you put up with it. People whispered about her wealth too, and the fact that Carl had not had a penny when they married – the inference being obvious. She had had enough. She wanted to have a home of their own where they could lead a proper, private family life.

It didn't take much insistence on Emma's part. All his life Jung had longed for such a family house, dreamed of it, had visions of it. Money not being an object, they decided to build their own. They purchased a plot of land at Kusnacht, a village on the right bank of the Lake of Zürich some fifteen kilometres from Zürich itself, which could be reached by paddle steamer or the local railway. There was a country road along the lake, which would later become the busy Seestrasse, but in 1908 the village was just a small farming community with orchards, meadows for the cows, vineyards rising on the slopes and heavy beds of reeds all along the waterfront. There was an orphanage, a poor-house, a church, a schoolhouse, and a few scattered villas which had been built in the 1890s when the railway network reached Kusnacht, bringing the wealthy of Zürich who were looking for a pleasant spot to build their homes away from the increasing noise and bustle of city life. The plot Carl and Emma bought was right on the lake, next to the poorhouse: 5,000 square metres at eleven francs a metre – a great deal of money in the days when the average office worker was lucky to earn 800 francs a year. Their neighbour was a farmer called Hermann Stahli, who lived in a typical vintner's farmhouse, solid and rectangular, dating from the seventeenth century, with a steeply pitched saddle roof and elevated ground floor, a wine cellar, barns and stables. Further along the lake the reeds had been cleared for a small communal bathing station.

Emma knew how much such a house would mean for Carl and no doubt she hoped it would have a steadying, grounding effect on him. But she probably did not realise how profoundly significant it was to Carl's Personality No. 2, a personality she lived with day by day, without understanding or even completely recognising it.

Carl's Personality No. 2 had already seen his 'house' when he was a twelve-year-old schoolboy in Basel, suffering from depression, and 'No. 1 wanted to free himself from the pressure or melancholy of No. 2. It was not No. 2 who was depressed, but No. 1 when he remembered No. 2.' That day a wild wind had lashed the Rhine and during his long walk home from school he had seen a ship with a great mainsail running up river before the storm. The sight thrilled Carl and set off his vivid imagination. He saw water all around, like the sea or a lake, with a rock rising up out of it. 'And on the rock stood a well-fortified castle with a tall keep, a watch-tower,' he wrote. 'This was my house. In it there were no fine halls or any signs of magnificence. The rooms were simple, panelled, and rather small. There was an uncommonly attractive library where you could find everything worth knowing. There was also a collection of weapons, and the bastions were mounted with heavy cannon.' The vision was so vivid he indulged in it for several months, making his long walk home so short he would suddenly find himself in his village. There was a two-masted schooner in the harbour because ever since Carl could remember he had longed for a sailing boat. But 'the nerve centre' and main significance of it all was 'the secret of the keep, which I alone knew'. It was hidden inside the tower: a copper column as thick as a man's arm with 'a certain inconceivable something' down in the cellar where there was a laboratory in which Carl made gold. The castle came from another era and another world where there would be 'no *Gymnasium*, no long walk to school, and I would be grown up and be able to arrange my life as I wished'. From then on he had started building miniature castles and fortifications in the garden of the parsonage using stones and mud, and did so for the rest of his life, whenever he needed to calm his mind. But it was the secret of the keep which held the key, mirroring the phallus dream he'd had when he was four years old.

Within a month of buying the plot Carl had already drawn a rough sketch of the property and worked out some of the details of the house. The sketch is done in pencil on a piece of brown paper, indicating the shape of the property, the country road behind the house and the lake in front. The boathouse for a future sailing boat is already there, the word 'boat' written boldly in blue, as is the word 'lake', with 'natural bank with reeds' also marked. The house itself is to the left and rectangular with a tower at the front entrance and a veranda at the side, surrounded by a garden with a pavilion by the lake in the style of the local vintners' huts. Orchard, vines, garden wall and small gate are all included, as they soon would be in reality. There are three plans showing the three floors, all small rooms as in his schoolboy fantasy, except for the main room on the ground floor which was as large as a medieval hall. The drawings were enclosed in a letter sent to Ernst Fiechter, an architect and cousin of Carl's. He may also have included some drawings of houses he had done earlier, all looking like small castles, always with towers, built of the local Bollenstein stone, with crenellations, high saddle roofs, rusticated ground floors, small grilled windows to keep the house safe from the outside world, and walled gardens – like buildings from another era, medieval or Renaissance, and quite unlike the large villas built on the shores of the lake by wealthy Zürich burghers at the beginning of the twentieth century.

'You can get an approximate idea of the external character from my ever-so imperfect sketch,' he wrote in the accompanying letter to Fiechter. 'Rough ashlar below; plasterwork and splatter-dash above. It is to have stepped gables with small steps . . . All windows on the raised ground floor are to have grates (*sic volo, sic jubeo*, thus I will, thus I command)' and so on for a good two pages, the pronoun always 'I', never 'we'. The hall should have simple brown wainscoting to head height and a large fireplace of red brick. The ceiling wooden, the floor red-tiled. This was the *Stube*, the main family room, in white stucco, where the tapestries Emma brought from Schaffhausen would be hung, with decoration on the doors and ceiling in the rococo style, and the floor to be raised by one step. There should be one other large room, on the upper floor: the library, separated from Carl's 'workroom' by double doors. All the small rooms to be wallpapered quite simply, the floors simple parquet, the windows with small leaded panes. Downstairs the windows high and narrow, the hall ones of a Renaissance character, again leaded, some heraldic. Kitchen and bathroom: all simple and functional, with an additional bathroom for the servants in the basement. The veranda: white and rococo. Plus a wooden boat-house up to four metres in length. The small yard by the lake to be surrounded by a wall and symmetrically laid out with country flowers; the rest of the garden like a meadow with apple and pear trees. There would be a simple balcony with iron railings for the library on the second floor. On and on it went, down to the last detail. He signed off with the hope of hearing from Fiechter soon, with an approximate estimate, reminding him that the furnishings of the house 'are to be as simple as possible. (With the exception of the reception room and hall.)' The words 'small' and 'simple' pepper the letter without the slightest regard for reality.

Emma was the one concerned with reality. 'Much of it struck us as laboured and strange, not beautiful,' she wrote to her mother about an exhibition of modern villas they were visiting at Darmstadt on one of their holidays without the children. 'Moreover, the houses seemed to be somewhat light in construction and in some cases already looked rather *passé*. The gardens by contrast were charming; it would be nice if Uncle

Mertens could have a look at them sometime.' Uncle Evariste Mertens was their next-door neighbour at Ölberg and the one who had designed the gardens for her parents, even the gardens along the Rhine for the Haus zum Rosengarten, all those years ago. Unlike Carl's letter, Emma's is full of 'us' and it sounds as though the two of them, Emma and Carl, walking around the exhibition arm in arm, were in complete agreement about what they considered 'beautiful': nothing too modern or self-conscious which would soon look *passé*, and something solid and well built. Later, on their next spring holiday on Lake Maggiore, Emma again wrote to her mother: 'On our morning walk we saw many fine villas with splendid southern gardens and have observed with satisfaction that there are still many people who spoil themselves even more than we do.' Emma, modest by temperament, was feeling uneasy as the budget for the house rose higher and higher.

Bertha Rauschenbach was taking a keen interest in the project. 'View received with thanks,' Jung wrote to Fiechter on 14 March 1908, shortly before he and Emma set off on the holiday. 'My mother-in-law will certainly take pleasure in a copy. She was always delighted with your plans.' If Ernst Fiechter was alarmed at Carl's overly detailed plans he did not show it; he just went ahead and produced a charming set of sketches and drawings of houses firmly in the local Lake of Zürich style. Emma must have had a hand in this – they certainly do not look the least bit medieval. They do not even include a tower. At which point Carl put his foot down. How could he live in a house without a tower? He had the boathouse, he had the lake, he had the large hall, he had the veranda and the garden pavilion, but where was his tower?

It appeared in the next set of drawings, a month later, at the front entrance: a large double tower. Two weeks later came the final design: with a single tower, functioning as a stairwell. It came with an update of the budget. The 'garden hall': 4,600 francs; 'courtyard, driveway, and enclosure toward street': 2,500 francs; 'garden by the lake': 4,000 francs; 'boathouse with landing stage': 1,600 francs.

Jung replied that 'we' would like 'to dispense with the garden hall for the moment', but 'we' would like the garden pavilion enlarged instead 'so that a little table and a few chairs can be placed inside'. The 'we' was Emma insisting on some savings: 4,600 francs for a garden hall was just too much. Thereafter Carl reverted to the more typical first person. 'After that, my desire is to have an iron harmonica shutter on the three-part window in the study,' followed by detailed instructions about all the other shutters on all the other windows. 'The little garden gate can stay right next to the house, but best to run the garden wall directly from the corner of the house to the neighbouring property. Likewise, I would like a wall from the house to the lake running along the neighbour's property to the north, thus creating a proper termination there (see sketch 3). A gateway at the house large enough that a carriage can be driven in comfortably. As for the rest, nothing has changed.' Carl, so progressive in his treatment of patients, was in many ways a typical husband of the times: as head of house he expected to take all the decisions. And Emma did as the books on how to be a good wife advised: she submitted to her husband, but learnt to quietly circumvent him when he wasn't looking.

Imagine the hours and hours Emma and Carl spent poring over plans – the discussions, the excitement. Somehow Carl managed to fit it all in: his job at the Burghölzli, writing academic papers in the evenings, the constant correspondence with Herr Professor Freud, and the work involved in founding the journal. Plus 'The Psychology of *Dementia Praecox*', 'On Disturbances in Reproduction in Association Experiments', 'Association, Dream, and Hysterical Symptoms', 'Further Investigations on the Galvanic Phenomenon and Respirations in Normal and Insane Individuals', 'The Content of the Psychoses', 'The Freudian Theory of Hysteria', 'The Analysis of Dreams' – all written during this period, at a time when psychoanalysis was taking its first shaky steps. On top of which came his lectures. The one he gave on 16 January 1908 on 'The Content of the Psychoses' was so oversubscribed they had to move it from the university's main lecture hall to the auditorium in the city hall.

The plans for the house continued apace. By 1 May 1908 Carl was able to write to Fiechter: 'We are in complete agreement with the design and no longer wish to anticipate fate any further. The solution is, as I have said, very satisfying! Even the veranda promises to be most handsome.' The 'solution' is telling: less a medieval castle, more a building in the Zürich style, the *Heimatstil*, fitting in nicely with its Kusnacht neighbours, but with a tower at the front entrance: a happy compromise. Emma had managed to hold her own. There only remained the small matter of the builder's shockingly high estimate: 156,000 Swiss francs. 'I believe a series of cuts still have to be made,' Carl wrote to Fiechter a few days later – 'Ugh!' But none were implemented.

By 4 July 1908 Fiechter wrote to say that work would begin the following Monday.

Now Carl turned his attention to words to adorn the building. The entrance was in the neo-baroque style with a broken
pediment, decorated with garlands and fruit above, laurel wreath
below, encircling an inscription. 'What will the inscription and
decoration over the entrance be like?' he wondered in a letter to
Fiechter on 18 September, before giving him the answer: 'I
would like to propose the following, deferring to you: *Carol.
Gust. Jung et uxor ejus Emma Rauschenbach hanc villam ridenti
in loco otioso erigere iusserunt anno domini MCMVIII.* [Carl
Gustav Jung and his wife Emma Rauschenbach built this house
in a cheerful, tranquil place in 1908] . . . This way the inscription
is quite long, as is befitting the style. The house already looks
very good.' And beneath it, on the lintel, in larger Roman lettering: '*Vocatus Atque Non Vocatus Deus Aderit*': Summoned or
Unsummoned, God Will Be Present. It was the Oracle of
Delphi, which Jung knew from a volume of classical sayings and
proverbs published by Erasmus of Rotterdam, which he had
bought when he was nineteen, presumably adding to his even-
tual 3,000-franc debt.

By March 1909 the building of the house was finished. One
last message to posterity was added, in the ball beneath the
weathervane which crowns the stairwell tower. It contains a lead
box with a page from a newspaper dated 12 March 1909 and a
card in Jung's hand, written on both sides in blue, a colour he
reserved for the most important matters. On one side, all in
English: '1908–1909. Carl Gustav Jung, med Dr, and his wife
Emma had this house built in 1908', followed by a quote in
English from Shakespeare's *Twelfth Night*: 'Fate, show thy
force – ourselves we do not owe; what is decreed must be, and
be this so.' On the other side of the card, in German: 'You who

will read this in a later age will perhaps not know my name, and my fates are unknown to you. When I wrote this, I was in the middle of life, perhaps as you are, and did not know the fates of the future. You and I will both succumb to transience. I will simply precede you.'

The master plumber, August Keller of Kusnacht, who installed the lead box, was not impressed. 'Opening this will not be worth the effort. The plumber Aug. Keller. Anno 1909' was inscribed on the outside. Inside he added more, dated 23 March 1909: 'To the openers! The master plumber to whom the execution of this metalwork was entrusted has also taken the liberty of enclosing a few lines in haste. My wish would have been for the builder Dr Jung-Rauschenbach, doctor at Burghölzli in Zürich, to have placed important documents and coins inside this ball, but it seemed to me he prefers to use the coins for something else . . .' and ended: 'I send my best compliments to the openers of this lead box, I will have long since ceased to be among the mortal, to any descendants I may have, I send regards. Aug Keller Jr. master plumber, born 1881. Citizen of Kusnacht.' Both messages were discovered in October 2005 when the stairwell tower was being repaired.

The finishing touch was the weathervane high above, crowning the tower, turned this way and that by the winds which blew down from the Alps or across the Lake of Zürich with the early morning mists, shining golden in the summers, covered in icicles and snow in the winters. 'CJ ER – AEDIFIC – Ao 1908' it announced to the world, as if the world did not already know it.

* * *

Before CJ and ER moved to the house there was another trip for the Jungs to see Freud and his family in Vienna. Again the girls were left in the care of the maid and Carl's mother and sister, who had already moved out of Zürich and into an apartment in one of the Kusnacht houses further along the lake. This time Jung wrote to Freud to say they preferred to stay at the Hotel Regina, the Grand Hotel being a bit too grand for them. In reality it was not, accustomed as they were to staying in such hotels, but it was too extravagant for the occasion. As Carl and Emma knew, Freud had to earn every penny he spent providing for his large family. Besides, as Jung pointed out, the Regina was much closer – just round the corner from Berggasse.

This second visit to Vienna had undercurrents. Freud was still determined that Jung would be his crown prince, now replacing his usual *'Lieber Herr Kollege'* with *'Lieber Freund'*, a most informal address for those formal times. On other occasions it was even 'Dear Friend and Heir'. Jung progressed from *'Hochverehrter Herr Professor'* – most highly esteemed – to plain *Lieber Herr Professor*. But Jung still had his doubts. Ernest Jones, recalling Freud's failure to see this at the time, decided it was because Freud was so fixed on Jung becoming his 'heir' plus editor of their journal and president of the planned International Association, that he was blind to his doubts. This was only natural, Jones suggested, because:

> to begin with, Jung, with his commanding presence and soldierly bearing looked the part of a leader. With his psychiatric training and position, his excellent intellect and his evident devotion to work, he seemed far better qualified for the post than anyone else. Yet he had two serious

disqualifications for it. It was not a position that accorded with his own feelings, which were those of a rebel, a heretic, in short a 'son', rather than those of a leader, and this consideration soon became manifest in his failure of interest in pursuing his duties. Then his mentality had the serious flaw of lacking lucidity.

Jones – who would become an ardent follower of Freud, not averse to orchestrating oblique attacks on Jung – was at this early stage an astute observer. 'It was natural that Freud should make much of his new Swiss adherents, his first foreign ones and, incidentally, his first Gentile ones,' he wrote. 'After so many years of being cold-shouldered, ridiculed, and abused it would have needed an exceptional philosophical disposition not to have been elated when well-known University teachers from a famous Psychiatric Clinic abroad appeared on the scene in whole-hearted support of his work.' Freud was quite straight-forward about it: 'My selfish purpose, which I frankly confess, is to persuade you to continue and complete my work by apply-ing to psychoses what I have begun with neuroses. With your strong and independent character, with your Germanic blood which enables you to command the sympathies of the public more readily than I, you seem better fitted than anyone else I know to carry out this mission.' But Jung did not want to complete Freud's work. He wanted to complete his own.

The signs were already there six months earlier, in September 1908, when Freud came to visit Jung for four days at the Burghölzli. Emma was not there for most of it: she was preg-nant with their third child and spent the summer at Schaffhausen, not returning to Zürich until October.

Freud arrived at the Burghölzli in high good humour. He had been to Manchester to visit his half-brother Emmanuel, then on to London where he bought a fine new pipe, some excellent cigars, visited the National Gallery and the British Museum with its incomparable collection of antiquities. He sailed from Harwich via the Hook of Holland, stopping off in The Hague to see the Rembrandts. In Zürich he and Jung walked and talked for hours as usual, observed some of Jung's patients, and went climbing in the Alps – Mount Pilatus and the Rigi – each man clad in alpine boots and knickerbockers with their walking sticks and alpine hats. There was little sign of the illnesses which had been plaguing Jung that year, nor of the earlier tensions between Carl and Emma which were surely the cause. Freud said he was looking forward to visiting them in their new house; Jung said nothing could delight them more. It is likely that Emma was present for a day or two because, along with a thankyou letter, Freud sent her 'a surprise package of books', which suggests a conversation. 'Please tell your wife that one passage in her letter gave me particular pleasure,' he wrote to Jung after receiving Emma's letter. Later, during a short stay in Venice, he sent her a postcard. It marks the start of a relationship between the wise old Viennese professor and the young Frau Doktor Jung, who was just beginning to assert herself against an overpowering husband. And it sent a message to Jung: value her.

But for most of Professor Freud's visit Emma stayed with her mother at Ölberg. The weather that summer was exceptionally warm, with temperatures regularly reaching the mid-thirties. Luncheon was often served under the shade of one of the trees, afternoon tea on the veranda. The children played in the garden for hours, watched over by Emma and her mother knitting or doing their needlework. In the afternoons there was usually a walk through the meadow and up the hill behind the house into the forests beyond. Sometimes Marguerite joined them. She was also pregnant and living not far away in her own home – a house she and Ernst had commissioned in the latest modern style, in the sharpest contrast to Emma and Carl's traditional house at Kusnacht. Towards evening the hot weather could turn heavy at Ölberg, only broken by violent thunder storms when the maids ran about the house closing the windows and fastening all the shutters.

Before dressing for dinner, there was bedtime for the little girls, which Emma liked to do herself with the help of the children's maid. If Bertha was hosting one of her receptions, inviting all sorts of interesting people from the town and further afield – writers, astrologers, artists, often including the musicians from the town orchestra who performed a musical entertainment after the dinner – then Emma put on her jewels – pearls, rubies, diamonds – the ones she would show to her wide-eyed grandchildren years later. Emma always loved being in her mother's company. As the word association tests revealed, she could talk to her about anything, even some of the problems in her marriage. After all, it was Bertha who had encouraged her to marry Carl in the first place. Her mother, modern and broadminded in outlook, knew the rumours about Carl's infatuations and flirtations and she knew what a complicated man he was, but she counselled fortitude. Her own marriage had not been easy, and Marguerite did not have an easy marriage either. Ernst Homberger had a reputation as a harsh, ambitious man who brought up his children with military discipline.

Carl only visited at the weekends, sometimes only on Sunday, as he was working his usual long hours. But he and Emma wrote to each other most days, a habit they maintained for the rest of their lives whenever they were apart. That summer he was preparing the first edition of the *Jahrbuch* and his own paper for it, 'The Significance of the Father in the Destiny of the Individual', as well as standing in for Bleuler during his summer vacation, attending court once a week to give psychiatric evidence, and receiving visits of doctors from foreign parts, including one from the president of the 'Lunacy Commission of New York State'. He also had to complete his military service, which ran to five weeks that year. His own holidays began on 21 August and he decided to spend the first part on his own 'fleeing into the inaccessible solitude of a little Alpine cabin on Mount Santis', as he put it to Freud. For just these few days the fine weather broke, the mornings so dense with fog there were no Alps to be seen and it rained for part of every day. But Carl had not come for the weather; he'd come for the climbing and the solitude. Emma was well enough acquainted with the 'other Carl' by now to know that solitude was indispensable to him. By the time he got to Schaffhausen there were only six days of his holiday left.

At the Burghölzli, one of the patients Freud and Jung observed was 'Babette S'. As Emma could have told Professor Freud, Babette S – old and demented as she was – was extremely important to Carl. He spent hours with her trying to discover meaning in her ramblings. She was the subject of his over-subscribed city hall lecture and she appeared in his *Psychology of Dementia Praecox*. 'She came out of the Old Town of Zürich, out of narrow, dirty streets where she had been born in poverty-stricken circumstances and had grown up in a mean environment,' he wrote. 'Her sister was a prostitute, her father a drunkard. At the age of thirty-nine she succumbed to a paranoid form of *dementia praecox*, with characteristic megalomania. When I saw her, she had been in the institution for twenty years.' Babette uttered and wailed the most extraordinary things. 'I am the Lorelei'; 'I am unjustly accused like Socrates'; 'I am the double polytechnic irreplaceable'; 'I am plum cake on a cornmeal bottom'; 'I am Germania and Helvetia of exclusively sweet butter'; 'Naples and I must supply the world with noodles'.

The reason for Jung's dedicated interest, as well as his evident compassion, was clear: 'My preoccupation with Babette and other such cases convinced me that much of what we had hitherto regarded as senseless was not as crazy as it seemed. More than once I have seen that even with such patients there remains in the background a personality which must be called normal. It stands looking on, so to speak. Occasionally, too, this personality – usually by way of voices or dreams – can make altogether sensible remarks and objections.' He knew from his own experience how thin the line between sanity and insanity could be. But all Freud had to say after the observation was: 'You know, Jung, what you have found out about this patient is certainly interesting. But how in the world were you able to bear spending hours and days with this phenomenally ugly female?' It was a double miss. Freud missed the reason why Jung spent all those hours with his schizophrenic patients; Jung completely missed his friend's Jewish humour.

There was another double miss on one of the evenings during the Jungs' second visit to Vienna. Emma had returned to the

Hotel Regina, alone as usual, whilst the two men sat talking late into the night in Freud's small study crammed with books and antiquities he had collected on his travels. On this occasion the conversation turned to the occult, precognition and parapsychology. The occult was still a live subject in Switzerland and Bleuler at the Burghölzli did not exclude it as a valid area of scientific investigation, even dispatching Jung to observe seances. However, Freud, Jewish, urbane and determinedly rational, rejected it out of hand. At this rejection, Jung felt a pressure in his diaphragm like red-hot iron, whereupon there was a loud 'report' from the bookcase, leaving both men shocked. Jung told Freud it was a 'catalytic exteriorisation phenomena'. 'That is sheer bosh,' replied Freud, whereupon an offended Jung predicted there would soon be another, which there was. Later Freud accounted for it in a rational way but at the time he was visibly shaken.

By the time Emma and Carl got back from Vienna the house at Kusnacht was almost ready, but not quite. They gathered up their children and the maid and went to stay at Schaffhausen again for the duration, Carl taking the opportunity to go off on a bicycle tour of northern Italy with an old friend. He had just done what he had been talking about for a long time: handed in his Burghölzli resignation to the Zürich authorities, which had been accepted, and now he felt free as air.

Things were not as they seemed, however. In fact Bleuler had dismissed Carl from his post the previous October, finally fed up with his arrogant behaviour and increasingly critical attitude, especially of Bleuler himself. Jung could spend hours with his patients, but still could not be bothered with the day-to-day administrative side of his job. Jung was shocked by his dismissal. That was not the way things were meant to be and it was not the way he meant to leave. He wanted to be affiliated to the Burghölzli so he could continue seeing his private patients and continue his lectureship at the university. Bleuler, ever generous, agreed to a compromise: Jung could stay in his post until the house at Kusnacht was ready, but then he had to go. They would put out a formal statement saying Herr Doktor Jung was leaving by mutual consent to pursue his private practice.

The intervening months were not a problem for Carl, but they were very difficult for Emma. She and Hedwig Bleuler had been friends since Emma first arrived at the Burghölzli in 1904. They had spent many hours together watching over the children and talking, and they had much in common: both married to men who had chosen to make psychiatry their lives, both mothers of growing families, both intelligent, keen to further their education. They had attended the Burghölzli meetings together and, as A. A. Brill described, were just as keen as the men to interpret dreams, analyse complexes, describe fantasies. The older woman had become something of a role model for Emma, introducing her to the idea that women could be ambitious, all the while supporting their husbands as society required. Emma helped Hedwig with the asylum's social events, and Hedwig's boys often ran upstairs to the Jungs' apartment to play with Agathli and Gretli. There is a charming out-of-focus photograph of Emma in the snow outside the front entrance of the Burghölzli with the children, perhaps Hedwig's, perhaps her own. Her skirts are long and dark and she is wearing a large hat, even though it is no more than an ordinary day. When the Jungs left the Burghölzli, the boy, Manfred, stood by the window of the Bleuler apartment with tears running down his face: he loved Frau Doktor Jung. But now Hedwig turned cold. She disapproved of Carl's treatment of her husband and she was not inclined to indulge Emma either. Gossip about Carl's flirtations did not help, nor the fact that the Jungs were so wealthy he did not have to work another day if he did not want to. Try as she might, there was nothing Emma could do. Her friendship with Hedwig was lost.

By the end of May 1909 Carl and Emma were finally able to move into the new house. 'This last miserable week should now be followed by festive days, for it really was a bad week, only my wife has kept her head above water,' Jung wrote to Freud from Kusnacht on 2 June. 'I am just beginning to guide my thoughts back into rectilinear channels, until now I haven't been able to concentrate on a thing. Although we began the move last Tuesday, only four rooms are really finished today. In the dining room, for instance, not even the floor is ready.' It did not stop him working though. 'Out here my practice is picking up again – something I hadn't expected.' By 12 June he was able to write: 'Today my children have moved into the new house. Everything is going well, including my practice, which makes me very happy.'

One of his new private patients was Joseph Medill McCormick, scion of the wealthy and powerful American newspaper proprietors of the *Chicago Tribune*. Medill was an alcoholic who had experienced a breakdown whilst travelling in Europe. Jung saw it as a providential act of fate that he landed on his doorstep at just the moment when he needed him most, setting up his private practice. But as so often with Jung, things were not what they seemed; in fact it was another reason Bleuler was fed up with him. Medill had ended up at the Burghölzli because it was an institution of international repute, not specifically for Herr Doktor Jung. But Carl bagged him before anyone else could get a look-in. Medill's problem, he quickly divined, was a powerfully dominating mother. When Medill returned to Chicago apparently 'cured', word went round about the remarkable Swiss doctor, and Medill joined the long line of wealthy Americans crossing the Atlantic to be treated by Jung.

In the intervening days, Emma and her newly engaged staff – a cook, a kitchen maid, two housemaids, the children's maid, one handy-man-cum-gardener – worked hard arranging all the furniture from the apartment at the Burghölzli, including the beautiful walnut desk, the tapestries and the paintings, and bringing some extra pieces from Ölberg as well. Everything again had to be moved by horse and cart, and the chaos was indescribable. The weather was unusually hot for that time of year, with the bluest skies and the Alps so clear you could almost touch them. That was at the beginning of the ten days' move. But then it turned to rain and thunderstorms. By the time the good weather came back the move was done and only the mess and muddle in the unfinished rooms remained.

On the ground floor the large tiled entrance hall was ready, the garderobe to the left for coats and hats, outdoor shoes and boots and a large collection of umbrellas and walking sticks, with a downstairs toilet next to it, modern and self-flushing, not like the majority of toilets in Switzerland at that time, which consisted of nothing more than a hole in a plank of wood and a deep shaft. A small salon led off to the left, a cosy room with dark wallpaper and a high tiled stove, bright blue, beyond which a heavily bolted door led out to the garden room, the one which had briefly seemed too expensive. The wooden stairs which led up to the next floor were wide and gracious befitting the tower which contained them. The kitchen to the right of the entrance was ready with a fine cooking range and a large pantry off, but the children's room next to it was not ready, nor, as Jung noted, was the pièce de résistance, the *Stube*, the long family room, with a brown marble fireplace flanked by two tapestry-covered chairs and the Frans Hals copy above, the one commissioned by Jung with a loan from his future mother-in-law when he was living in Paris. The alcove next to the fireplace was lit by two panes of stained glass, reproductions of medieval ones in Zürich's Landesmuseum: one commemorating Carl and Emma's marriage, the other Agathe and Gretli's births. One of Emma's large tapestries was hung at the other end, above a canapé with an antique dresser alongside. And her beautiful writing desk. In time Emma's piano came from Ölberg. Three long, deep-set windows overlooked the lake, glass cabinets in between with decorative landscape paintings above. Not so charming was the dark painting of John the Baptist's dripping head held by some unknown hand, which came from Jung's old parsonage home. A dining table and six chairs stood in the middle of the room on a Persian rug. From then on everything happened around that table: mealtimes, homework, drawing and model-making, knitting and stitching, and endless games of cards and mahjong.

Upstairs there was a spacious landing leading to the library, with Carl's *Cabinet* (study) and a small waiting room for the patients to the right, already finished so he could continue working undisturbed by all the surrounding chaos. The library is much the same today as it was then, Jung's books back in their original place on the shelves. One glance is enough to confirm Emma's hand: no dark wood, nothing medieval or eighteenth-century in the decor, but a spacious, light room overlooking the lake, the woodwork painted pale green with a white-and-green-tiled stove by the door. Like the family room it was parquet-floored. One wall was papered orange-brown, with a canapé and table below and a large painting of a young boy, naked, riding a white stallion bareback, above. The boy has his back to us, his arm raised in greeting to an unseen person out of frame, a poetic image probably painted by local artist Rudolf Koller. There is a communal vestibule between the library and Jung's *Cabinet*, with heavy double doors to shut out any noise and all connection to the outside world. Inside, the *Cabinet* has the feel of a chapel, small and dimly lit by three narrow, leaded windows each with a stained-glass panel representing the most Christian of iconographies: 'the Flagellation of Christ', 'the Crucifixion of Christ' and 'the Entombment'. No one could enter this sanctum without knocking, not even Emma.

The mood of the reception rooms might be traditional, but the rest of the house was thoroughly functional and modern, lit by electricity and heated by a central heating system fed by a huge wood- and coal-fired boiler in the cellar, installed by Gebrüder Sulzer of Winterthur. To the left of the upstairs land-ing beyond a glass door were three bedrooms, the one belonging to Emma and Carl having an en-suite bathroom. From the small corridor between the parents' and the children's bedrooms there was an exit to the roof of the veranda where the maids hung out the washing on washing days. One floor further up in the attic were the maids' and guest rooms.

Once the house was finished and everything in its place, Carl and Emma commissioned a local photographer to take pictures of the main rooms and the garden. You have to look closely at a small photo, also of 1909, taken of the terrace at the back of the house overlooking the lake, to discover the figures of two women. They are standing at the south corner of the terrace, one looking out, the other across, together but alone, posing for the camera. Emma and Trudi, Carl's sister. Trudi is wearing a long white dress, with her hair loosely rolled up. Emma wears her dark hair in a soft chignon at the nape of her neck, lovely in a quiet sort of way, as she was herself.

The terrace, 228 Seestrasse, 1909.

8

A Vile Scandal

Before they moved into the new house there were two events which took up a great deal of Emma's time and concern, the one happy, the other quite the opposite.

To start with happiness: Franz Karl Jung was born on 28 November 1908, their third child. Although Emma had spent the four months before the birth at Ölberg she was determined to have her baby at home, with Carl in attendance. It was six months before they could move into the house at Kusnacht, so back to the Burghölzli she came, together with the two little girls and the maid. And this time, to Emma's joy, it was a boy. 'Having dropped all my duties today because my wife is about to be confined, I at last have time to write to you,' Jung wrote to Freud on 27 November, to which clever Freud answered: 'Fate has made you a father again, and perhaps the star you spoke of on our long walk has risen for you. The transfer of one's hopes to one's children is certainly an excellent way of appeasing one's unresolved complexes, though for you it is too soon. Let me hear from you; until then I assume that the valiant mother is well; to her husband she must indeed be more precious than all her children, just as the method must be valued more highly than the results obtained by it.' Bertha was evidently not the only one who had heard rumours of Carl's flirtations.

'Heartiest thanks for your congratulatory telegram!' Jung responded. 'You can imagine our joy. The birth went off normally, mother and child are doing well. Too bad we aren't peasants anymore, otherwise I could say: now that I have a son, I can depart in peace.' And in a later letter: 'Everything is fine here. My wife is, of course, nursing the child herself, a pleasure for both of them.'

A month later he was writing about four-year-old Agathli's reaction to her baby brother's birth. When Jung asked her what she would say if the stork brought her a little brother, she replied: 'Then I shall kill it.' 'Franzli' had been born in the middle of the night. The next morning Jung carried Agathli to her mother's bedside. Emma naturally looked tired and pale, which alarmed the child, who said nothing and showed no joy. Later that morning she flung her arms round Emma: 'But, Mama, you don't have to die, do you?' A day later the two little girls went back to Schaffhausen to stay with their grandmother for several weeks. When they got back Agathli at first acted shy and suspicious of Emma, but once she had regained her confidence she became very fractious, asking endless questions: 'Shall I become a woman like you? Shall I then still talk to you?' 'Do you still love me too, not just Franzli?' 'Is that true? You're quite sure it's true? You're not lying? I just don't believe it.' Emma tried to distract her: 'Come, we'll go into the garden.' Agathli had become obsessed with news of an earthquake at Messina in Italy, '75,000 dead', demanding to be told about it again and again. Emma had to reassure her 'hourly' that there were no earthquakes in Zürich. Her father did the same.

Outside heavy snow fell. Emma was up and about again, finding books with pictures of earthquakes and volcanoes for Agathli, who pored over them, examining every detail. But she would not let it go. Finally Carl suggested that Emma tell Agathli how babies are made. Children grow in the mother like flowers on plants she explained, the days of sex education lying far in the future. It seemed to do the trick. 'Have you a plant in your tummy too?' she asked Carl and skipped off merrily when he said no. The next day she announced: 'My brother is also in Italy and has a house made of glass and cloth and it doesn't fall down.' When female guests came to the house she surprised them by asking whether they had a child or whether they had been to Messina. Then she invented a new game with her doll, sticking it between her legs under her skirt so only the head showed: 'Look, a baby is coming!' she cried, pulling it out slowly: 'And now it's all out!' One morning she insisted on coming into her parents' bedroom and created a scene when she was not allowed. Once Emma and Carl got up she hopped into the bed, lay flat on her stomach, and flailed about, kicking her legs like a horse: 'Is that what Papa does? That's what Papa does, isn't it?'

Meanwhile Gretli, aged three, was quite unperturbed by the birth and ridiculed the stork theory because the stork had not just brought Franzli, it had brought the children's nurse as well.

From all this one might assume that Carl was as happy to have a son as Emma. Not so. Six days after the birth he wrote a letter in sharp contrast to those he wrote to Freud, revealing a man in turmoil. 'I regret so much; I regret my weakness and curse the fate that is threatening me. I fear for my work, for my life's task, for all the lofty perspectives that are being revealed to me by this new *Weltanschauung* [world view] as it evolves,' he wrote on 4 December. 'You will laugh when I tell you that recently *earlier and earlier childhood memories have been surfacing*, from a time (*3rd to 4th year*) when I often hurt myself badly, and when, for example, I was once only just rescued from certain death by a maid. My mind is torn to its very depths, I who have to be a tower of strength for many weak people, am the weakest of all. Will you forgive me for being as I am? For offending you by being like this, and forgetting my duties as a doctor towards you? Will you understand that I am one of the weakest and most unstable of human beings?'

The recipient of this letter was Sabina Spielrein, she having made contact with Carl again in June of that year, and it became the prelude to the second event, the unhappy one, which eventually forced Emma to take the kind of action which would normally have horrified her. Ostensibly Fräulein Spielrein had written to Herr Doktor Jung to commiserate when she heard about the dramatic failure of his treatment of Otto Gross, the patient who had been a psychiatrist himself and had helped Jung with his paper about the 'Significance of the Father', suffering from a father complex himself, just like Jung. It did not take much to work out that Fräulein Spielrein, now completing her medical exams at the University of Zürich, was still obsessed with her former doctor.

Otto Gross had been passed to Jung by Freud in the hope that he could cure him of his opium and cocaine addiction before Freud took over further treatment, admitting to Jung that he himself had been dangerously addicted to cocaine as a young man, which, 'as I well know, produces a toxic paranoia'. In Freud's view Gross was the only other member of the psychoanalytic fraternity who could rival Jung in brilliance. But Jung soon discovered that Gross's problems extended beyond his addictions; he was suffering from a form of schizophrenia as well. He was anarchic and charismatic and before Jung knew it he was completely caught up in the case, spending hour upon hour analysing him. And when that did not work, he decided to reverse the roles, allowing the patient to analyse the doctor. This was dangerous territory for Jung – with his split personality and instability – and it made him vulnerable to all sorts of doubts and confusions.

Gross's schizophrenia stemmed from his childhood and a homosexual fixation on his father, which had led to obsessive masturbation from an early age. For Jung it was too close for comfort. 'In Gross I experienced all too many aspects of my own nature, so that he often seemed like my twin brother,' he later admitted to Freud, adding 'but for the *dementia praecox*' almost as an afterthought. Gross was serially unfaithful to his wife and as a self-proclaimed revolutionary, argued that political and sexual freedom went hand in hand, preaching polygamy as the only solution to marriage. Jung, who less than a year earlier had insisted to Freud that sexual repression was 'a very important and indispensable civilising factor', was soon sucked into this *Weltanschauung*. Heady with the thrill of their marathon conversations, and convinced of the apparent success of the treatment, Jung gradually reduced Gross's medication. It took a few weeks to realise that this was a disastrous mistake, by which time it was too late. One day in June, Jung had to admit to Freud that Gross had absconded over the Burghölzli's walls and disappeared, declaring himself 'cured'. Jung was left feeling guilty and confused, all sorts of demons reawakened. And, with

Emma away during the summer and then taken up with the birth of Franz, he was open to all sorts of temptations.

Which is when Sabina Spielrein wrote her letter to Carl, making contact again.

'My dear Fräulein Spielrein,' he replied. 'You have managed well and truly to grasp my unconscious with your sharp letter,' referring bitterly to the Gross debacle. 'Such a thing can only happen to me.' He suggested they meet at the paddle steamer landing stage on the Bahnhofstrasse at 11 a.m. the following Tuesday: 'So we can be alone and able to speak undisturbed, we'll take a boat on the lake. In the sunshine, and on the open water, it will be easier to find a clear direction out of this turmoil of feelings. With affectionate greetings from your friend.'

What was Carl thinking? He knew better than anyone how vulnerable Fräulein Spielrein was and how dangerous it was to take up contact again, but the 'other' Carl needed someone to talk to, and Emma was not the one. The birth of Franz, a son and heir, only made matters worse. Now 'The Significance of the Father in the Destiny of the Individual', based on his experiences as a son, referred to him as a father as well. Carl, 'other' Carl, felt no joy, only regret and fear of instability, his mind 'torn to its very depths'.

Seventy-five years later a suitcase belonging to Sabina Spielrein was found in an attic in Geneva. It contained twenty-one yellowing double pages of small black handwriting – a journal, undated, sometimes coherent, often rambling and opaque, the outpourings of a desperate young woman in a foreign land still traumatised by her father's sexual abuse and still obsessed with her one-time doctor, Jung. In addition, there are letters, undated and not always complete, which Spielrein later sent to Freud describing and sometimes quoting from letters Jung wrote to her. And some dated letters from Jung and Freud. There is also a diary from 1909 to 1912. The problem this material presents is that, apart from the Jung and Freud letters, all the evidence comes from Spielrein herself, with no one to corroborate it. The journal is so rambling and oblique that it is impossible to work out what is fact, what is wish-fulfilment or fantasy, leaving others to interpret it as they may.

Jung's letter to Fräulein Spielrein six days after Franz's birth was confused and desperate. Apart from memories of childhood which kept coming back to him unbidden, he was paranoid, fearing Fräulein Spielrein would take revenge on him once she discovered how unstable he was. He was looking for someone 'as yet unrealised' who would love him with no strings attached, social or other. And no punishment. 'It is my misfortune that I cannot live without the joy of love, of tempestuous, ever-changing love. This daemon stands as an unholy contradiction to my compassion and my sensitivity. When love for a woman awakens in me, the first thing I feel is regret, pity for the poor woman who dreams of eternal faithfulness and other impossibilities, and is destined for a painful awakening out of all these dreams.' As the months passed Spielrein became even more obsessed with Jung. She knew he would never leave Emma, but she held fast to the idea that he loved her. Then she had decided she wanted a child by him. That brought Carl sharply back to reality. The last thing he wanted was a child by Spielrein. He wanted an infatuation. And someone to talk to about his torments.

At some point in early 1909 Emma realised Carl was seeing Fräulein Spielrein again and it confronted her with the greatest dilemma of her life so far. Married for six years, the mother of three children and in love with a husband who could not stop flirting with other women, she was still too young and inexperienced to see the situation for what it was, still dreaming of 'eternal faithfulness and other impossibilities'. She became so desperate she took an action utterly alien, even repugnant, to her: she wrote an anonymous letter to Fräulein Spielrein's mother, warning her to 'rescue' her daughter before Doktor Jung 'ruined' her. We know about it because of a letter Fräulein Spielrein wrote to Freud in June 1909: 'Four and a half years ago Dr Jung was my doctor, then he became my friend and finally my "poet", i.e. my beloved,' she wrote. 'Eventually he came to me and things went as they usually do with "poetry". He preached polygamy; his wife was supposed to have no objection, etc. etc. Now my mother receives an anonymous letter that minces no words, saying she should rescue her daughter, since otherwise she would be ruined by Dr Jung. The letter could not have been written by one of my friends, since I kept absolutely mum, and always lived far away from all the other students. There is reason to suspect his wife (?)' she wrote.

In fact rumours of Jung's relationship with a young lady had already reached Freud. He sent Jung a telegram which put him 'in a fluster'. Jung replied that he had not written for such a long time because he had been 'under terrific strain day and night', blaming a mass of correspondence every evening, plus invitations, concerts, three lectures, and all the while the new house. 'The last and worst straw' he wrote:

is that a complex is playing Old Harry with me: a woman patient, whom years ago I pulled out of a very tricky neurosis with unstinting effort, has violated my confidence and friend-

165

ship in the most mortifying way imaginable. She has kicked up a vile scandal solely because I denied myself the pleasure of giving her a child. I have always acted the gentleman towards her, but before the bar of my rather too sensitive conscience I nevertheless don't feel clean and that is what hurts the most because my intentions were always honourable. But you know how it is – the devil can use even the best of things for the fabrication of filth.

This is surely Jung at his worst, spouting excuses, feeling sorry for himself, indignant even. Reading between the lines it sounds as though Jung went much further with the relationship than was 'proper', but not so far as to become what Fräulein Spielrein enigmatically called her 'poet'. A case of the spirit if not the letter of the law. 'I have always told your daughter a sexual relationship was out of the question,' Jung wrote to Fräulein Spielrein's mother after she had received the anonymous letter, leaving the question of 'poetry' up in the air.

There had been a row with Emma. 'Meanwhile I have learnt an unspeakable amount of marital wisdom,' his letter to Freud continued, 'for until now I had a totally inadequate idea of my polygamous components despite all self-analysis. Now I know how and where the devil can be laid by the heels. These painful yet extremely salutary insights have churned me up hellishly inside, but for that very reason, I hope, have secured me moral qualities which will be of the greatest advantage to me in later life. The relationship with my wife has gained enormously in assurance and depth.' Characteristically he failed to praise Emma for her part in it, though he knew well enough how much courage it must have taken for her to confront him, rescuing him from himself. Instead he talked on about his own part in it: he did not yet possess Freud's assurance and composure, he explained: 'Countless things that are commonplace for you are still brand new experiences for me, which I have to relive in myself until they tear me to pieces. This urge for identification (at the age of eleven I went through a so-called traumatic neurosis) has abated considerably of late, though it still bothers me from time to time.' He turned quickly to other matters, the journal, Ernest Jones who had lately become sexually involved with Otto Gross's wife, and finally: 'My small son is flourishing, my wife is in good shape.'

Jung need not have worried about Freud, who wrote back happily about an invitation he had received from America to give a series of lectures at Clark University in Worcester, Massachusetts, and telling Jung that he had already heard about the young woman who was going about introducing herself as the mistress, which he did not believe and put down to the neurosis of the woman in question. 'To be slandered and scorched by the love with which we operate – such are the perils of our trade, which we are certainly not going to abandon on their account.' There was no chance that Freud, still determined to have Jung as his crown prince, would side with the unknown woman, an ex-patient to boot. He was more bothered by Jung's talk of the devil and filth. 'You definitely lapse into the theological style in relating this experience,' he wrote, obliquely alluding to Jung's father, the pastor of the Protestant Reformed Church. Jung, usually so dilatory, replied immediately: 'I must answer you at once. Your kind words have relieved and comforted me.' He reassured Freud about his 'theological' style, not noticing Freud's warning: that Jung was still labouring under a father complex, an opinion Freud never altered, believing it lay at the heart of Jung's neuroses. 'Now and then, I admit, the devil does strike a chill into my – on the whole – blameless heart,' Jung wrote shiftily. But he denied the rumour outright: 'I've never really had a mistress and am the most innocent of spouses.' He simply could not imagine who the woman might be. And that, he hoped, was that.

By June, the Jungs had settled into their house at Kusnacht – 228 Seestrasse – and a new era began. It was part of the agreement Emma reached with Carl after the showdown: new house, new life. On one level it worked beautifully: this was a place they had created together and they both loved. Emma knew this was one thing Carl would never want to give up: this home, this stability.

'Hurrah for your new house!' wrote Freud on 3 June 1909. But in the same letter he enclosed another, from Fräulein Spielrein. 'Weird! What is she? A busybody, a chatterbox, or a paranoiac? If you know anything about the writer or have some opinion in the matter, would you kindly send me a short wire, but otherwise you must *not* go to any trouble.' Jung shot off a telegram, immediately followed by a letter. 'Spielrein was the person I wrote you about,' he finally admitted, explaining that he had prolonged the relationship because he felt indebted to her for being the most important of his early 'test-cases' and because he was worried that she was not fully cured and might relapse. 'She was, of course, systematically planning my seduction, which I considered inopportune. Now she is seeking revenge. Lately she has been spreading a rumour that I shall soon get a divorce from my wife and marry a certain girl student, which has thrown not a few of my colleagues into a flutter. What she is now planning is unknown to me. Nothing good, I suspect.' Hers was a case of 'fight-the-father', just like Gross, he explained, which he had been trying to cure with 'untold tons of patience, even abusing our friendship for that purpose', and the whole thing had set off a complex in him like his 'compulsive infatuation' with the Jewish woman in Abbazia after their fist visit to Vienna.

Freud wrote to Fräulein Spielrein making it clear whose side he was on. To Jung he wrote: 'Such experiences, though painful, are necessary and hard to avoid. Without them we cannot really know life and what we are dealing with. I myself have never been taken in quite so badly, but I have come close to it a number of times and had *a narrow escape*.' The fact that he was older than Jung helped and no lasting harm had been done. 'They help us to develop the thick skin we need and to dominate "countertransference" which is after all a permanent problem for us; they teach us to displace our own affects to best advantage.' They are a *'blessing in disguise'*. Both 'narrow escape' and 'blessing in disguise' are written in English. The fact is, for both Freud and Jung nothing mattered so much as their pioneering work and assuring the place of psychoanalysis in the future. And if it required a thick skin, well, so be it.

But Fräulein Spielrein was not quite done. She was too intelligent and resourceful, in spite of her emotional difficulties, to let the two men gang up against her in that way. On 19 June she turned up at the Jung house in Kusnacht insisting on talking things through. Emma had little choice but to let her in, and Carl had little choice but to come to terms. She insisted he write a letter to Freud. 'Although not succumbing to helpless remorse, I nevertheless deplore the sins I have committed, for I am largely to blame for the high-flying hopes of my former patient,' he duly wrote, describing Fräulein Spielrein as having freed herself from the transference 'in the best and nicest way' and admitting he had written letters to her mother Frau Spielrein, which he called a 'piece of knavery', all of which he 'confessed' to Freud 'as my father'. Freud cannot have relished the role of Jung's 'Father Confessor' and what it told him about Carl's continuing complexes.

But he did as Jung requested – 'a great favour' – he wrote to Fräulein Spielrein, confirming that Jung had written to him about the whole thing 'in perfect honesty' (this in English again). As for Jung, after asking Freud to 'pardon' him once again, he was breezily off on another matter: he too had now been invited to America to speak at Clark University, and he was happy to confirm he had managed to book a cabin on the same transatlantic liner as Freud and his colleague the Hungarian psychoanalyst Sandor Ferenczi, but 'a very expensive cabin, however', there being nothing else available at this late stage.

Life at 228 Seestrasse fell into place again. The Jungs' summers assumed a pattern which would last through the years: home-based, with Carl working all hours and only taking odd breaks for a bicycle tour or an Alpine hike with a friend. And sailing, now that he had his longed-for boat happily moored in his boat-house, fulfilling all his boyhood dreams and visions. Emma meanwhile ran the house, supervising the maids, the children's nurse, the cook and the gardener. She saw Carl's mother and sister often, since they lived nearby, and took the children off to Schaffhausen whenever possible.

On 13 July 1909 Jung wrote to Freud listing everything he had to do before leaving on the trip to America: the *Jahrbuch*, six private patients, the lectures for America, and writing up two reports for the courts – all of which cannot have left much time for Emma and the family. Freud replied from Ammerwald in the Austrian Alps, where the Freud family liked to spend their summers, and making a point of signing off with kind regards to Jung's 'charming' wife.

By 18 August, Carl was bound for Bremen to meet Freud and Ferenczi and embark on the liner the *George Washington*, briefly stopping off en route in Basel to visit old friends and family. Emma was probably relieved to see him go after the dramas with Fräulein Spielrein. But Carl's long letters kept her fully up to date throughout his seven-week absence. Keen psychoanalysts as they were, the men took the opportunity of analysing each other's dreams during the nine-day sea voyage, whiling away the time in the luxury of Jung's first-class cabin, or seated in a corner of the fine library or one of the plush salons. When Jung asked Freud for more detail from his private life to help with the interpretation of one of his more intractable dreams, Freud refused, saying he could not 'risk his authority!' That did it for black-and-white Carl: 'Freud was placing personal authority over truth.' Later he considered this refusal as a turning point, foreshadowing the break-up of their relationship. 'Father was very disappointed in his own father; and after that dream on the ship, he became very critical of everything that Freud said,' was Jung's son Franz's opinion years later, with the benefit of hindsight. 'He had a negative-father-complex, and he brought it to his relationship with Freud.'

On the voyage Jung recounted one of his 'house' dreams, the kind he had had ever since he was a child. It started on the top floor in the rococo style, then descended, the floors getting more and more ancient until he arrived at a heavy door to a vaulted cellar with a stone floor, where he discovered an old ring which he pulled to reveal some narrow stone steps leading down even further to a low cave cut into the rocks, with thick dust, scattered bones and broken pottery on the ground, the remains, he presumed, of a primitive culture. And two skulls. Jung later described it as one of his most important dreams, presaging his theory about the 'collective unconscious', but Freud focused exclusively on the two skulls, suspecting Jung of death-wishes against him – the father – and wanting to replace him. 'I knew perfectly well, of course, what he was driving at: that secret death-wishes were concealed in the dream,' wrote Jung later, admitting that he decided to go for the easy solution: he lied. He said they were the skulls of his wife and sister-in-law. 'After all, I had to name someone whose death was worth wishing! I was newly married at the time and knew perfectly well there was nothing within myself which pointed to such wishes . . . And so I told him a lie. I was quite aware that my conduct was not above reproach, but "*à la guerre, comme à la guerre!*"'

'*Liebste Frau!*', Dearest wife, Carl wrote to Emma from New York on 31 August 1909. 'When did I last write? I think it was yesterday. Time here is so frightfully filled up. Yesterday Freud and I spent several hours walking in Central Park and talked at length about the sociological problems of psychoanalysis. He is as clever as ever and extremely touchy; he does not like other sorts of ideas to come up, and, I might add, he is usually right.' Their relationship had evidently weathered the storms of the two dreams. After the walk they were invited to Dr Abraham Brill's home for supper. 'The meal was remarkable for the unbelievable, wildly imaginative dishes,' wrote Carl, wide-eyed:

> Picture a salad made of apples, head lettuce, celery root, nuts etc. etc. But otherwise the meal was good. Afterwards, between 10 and 12 pm, we drove down to Chinatown, the most dangerous part of New York, accompanied by three sturdy rascals. The Chinese all wear dark blue clothing and have their hair in long braids. We went into a Chinese temple, located in a frightful den called a joss house. Around every corner a murder might be taking place. Then we went into a Chinese teahouse, where we had really excellent tea, and along with it they served us rice and an incredible dish with chopped meat, apparently smothered in earth worms and onions. It looked ghastly. But the worms turned out to be Chinese potato, whereupon I tasted some, and it was not at all bad.

There were 'hoodlums' hanging about – 9,000 'Chinamen' to only twenty-eight women – and scores of white prostitutes, who had just been cleared out by the police. Next they went to 'a real Apache music hall . . . a rather gloomy place' where the audience threw money at the feet of the singer to show their appreciation. 'Everything most odd and terribly discomfiting, but interesting,' he confided to Emma. 'I should mention that Dr Brill's wife was along for the whole expedition, like the good American she is. We finally got to bed at midnight.'

The next morning, with his usual boundless energy, Jung was up at seven and off to visit Ward Island, the home of the New

York State Psychiatric Institute, then on to the Metropolitan Museum looking at the Egyptian, Cypriot and Cretan antiquities collections, as well as the 'wonderful' tapestries of the Pierpont Morgan Collection. He went alone because Freud and Ferenczi were probably still recovering from the journey and the exertions of the night before, and as the day went on he started to feel lonely and adrift in this strange land, telling Emma: 'Today there's some homesickness floating on the surface, sometimes no slight amount. I long for you and keep thinking whether you would like it here.' By the evening he had cheered up again. They were going out to Coney Island, the largest marine amusement park on the Atlantic coast, and he was also going to do a bit more work on his Worcester lectures, though it was impossible to concentrate in such a place and in such heat. Freud found the same, he said. After Worcester he planned to visit Niagara Falls, and perhaps travel some way into Canada but he thought he would skip Chicago for lack of time, 'because I want to be back on 21st September at the very latest. This can not go on too long. Give my best to everyone, and many kisses from your Carl.'

His host at Clark University was its president, the distinguished scholar G. Stanley Hall. Once settled in Professor Hall's house, Jung wrote to Emma describing their journey from New York. All three visitors had been suffering from diarrhoea and stomach pains, no doubt those Chinese 'worms'. They had taken the 'elevated' from 42nd Street to the piers, joined by Ernest Jones who had just arrived from Europe, and boarded 'a fantastically huge structure of a steamer that had some five white decks', sailing from the West River round the point of Manhattan with its 'tremendous skyscrapers' up the East River under Brooklyn and Manhattan Bridges and through the Sound behind Long Island. They arrived in Fall River City the next morning and took the train to Boston and thence to Worcester. The countryside was 'utterly charming, low hills, a great deal of forest, swamp, small lakes, innumerable huge erratic rocks, tiny villages with wooden houses, painted red, green or grey, with windows framed in white (Holland!)'. The happy reference was to one of their annual spring holidays together.

Dinner at the Halls' on that first evening was full of interest. Professor Hall himself was a 'refined', 'distinguished' old gentleman, his wife 'plump, jolly, good-natured, and extremely ugly'. You can almost hear Emma laughing as she read it. There were books everywhere and many boxes of cigars, which surely lightened Freud's heart. Freud suffered from a travel phobia, fretting about this and that – even wetting himself in agitation on one occasion – so arriving at the Halls' comfortable New England home must have come as some relief. 'Two pitch-black Negroes in dinner jackets, the extreme of grotesque solemnity, perform as servants. Carpets everywhere, all the doors open, even the bathroom door and the front door; people going in and out all over the place; all the windows extend down to the floor,' wrote Carl, knowing how interested Emma was in house details, especially now they had their own.

Two days later he wrote again. Freud had begun his lectures to great applause. 'We are gaining ground here, and our following is growing slowly but surely.' Solid Swiss Carl was surprised to find the American ladies were cultivated, well informed and free-thinking. He was happy to admit to Emma that he had been surrounded by five of them at a garden party. 'I was even able to make jokes in English – though what English!' One can imagine it: this large, brash, charismatic man, ruddy with alpine health, roaring with laughter at his own jokes and his awful English, with Freud nearby, small, dapperly dressed, just beginning to find his form in the new world, surrounded by other admirers, seducing them with his quieter, subtle Jewish–Viennese humour. They were causing quite a stir, were older Freud and young Jung, both of them interviewed by the *Boston Evening Transcript*. Things were going well. 'In fact we are the men of the hour here,' Carl declared. 'It is very good to be able to spread oneself in this way once in a while. I can feel my libido is gulping it in with vast enjoyment . . .'

Emma certainly knew what that meant. But out of sight was out of mind. Before he left Zürich, Carl had been in a parlous state: depressed, ill, falling into rages which he seemed unable to control. Along with everything else, he had been bypassed for a professorship at the University of Zürich for the second time. He blamed Bleuler, apparently not realising the faculty had its own reasons: Herr Doktor Jung's reputation with women went before him. But now he wrote: 'I have, thank God, completely regained my capacity for enjoyment, so that I can look forward to everything with zest. Now I am going to take everything that comes along by storm, and then I shall settle down again, satiated.'

The main thing both Jung and Freud meant to take by storm was America itself. In Carl's case, he had already treated some American patients in Zürich, and a handful of early practitioners of psychoanalysis in the United States, such as Abraham Brill, had made their way to the Burghölzli to observe him at his work and work there themselves for a time. Now he meant to build on his growing reputation, lecturing, giving interviews, writing papers, meeting distinguished Americans, and acquiring influential patients. One of these was Joseph Medill McCormick, whom Jung had first treated in Zürich earlier that year. 'Fate, which evidently loves crazy games, has just at this time deposited on my doorstep a well-known American (friend of Roosevelt and Taft, proprietor of several big newspapers etc.),' as he had written to Freud on 7 March 1909, right in the middle of the Spielrein drama.

Medill, as he was mostly known, was the grandson of Joseph Medill, publisher of the *Chicago Tribune*, the great-nephew of Cyrus Hall McCormick, founder of the International Harvester Company, and cousin of Harold Fowler McCormick, married to Edith Rockefeller. When Medill married Ruth Hanna, daughter of Mark Hanna, one of the Republican Party's big hitters, President Theodore Roosevelt himself travelled to Cleveland for the wedding, bearing a gold coffee set as a present. Medill was the manager and assistant editor-in-chief at the *Tribune*, but known mainly as a dedicated party-goer and an alcoholic. When he came to see Jung in Zürich it was the second of Medill's leaves of absence from the *Tribune*. Jung's treatment worked for a time, mainly because he insisted Medill quit his job, thereby escaping the clutches of his 'daemon' mother, who was a powerful figure on the *Tribune* board and the dominating force in his life. On this trip to America Jung saw Medill once, in New York. 'Jung was pleased with me apparently,' Medill wrote to his wife Ruth. 'He rejoiced that the savage in me looked out of my eye . . . and warned me against being too good . . . He said he quite permitted flirtations and had had one himself in this country.'

Medill also told Ruth that 'the doctor' had had the same 'conflicts' with his wife as himself: apparently Emma Jung used to think 'she could not understand his science and paid no attention to it. Now she is his partner in his work.'

1909 is the year Emma began to move from being little more than Carl's occasional assistant to being more of a partner in his work, not that they shared the work equally, but in the sense that Emma now knew enough about psychoanalysis to offer suggestions and criticisms, and enough to pursue her own interest in the field. The day Fräulein Spielrein turned up at their home had been a watershed. Emma finally found the courage to put her foot down: she would no longer be the mere wife and mother. They would work together again, as they had in the early days of their marriage. Other husbands might have demurred, but not Carl. He was always encouraging Emma to do more for herself, develop her own work and her own life.

Carl's letters to Emma from America show the closeness of their relationship and how far their partnership had come. He wanted to tell her everything. '*Mein liebster Schatz*', my darling treasure, he wrote from a camp in the Adirondacks, where he had been invited by James Jackson Putnam, one of the guests at Clark University, on 16 September at 8.30 in the morning. 'You would be absolutely amazed if you could see where I have ended up this time in this land of truly boundless opportunities':

I am sitting in a large one-room wooden cabin looking into a massive fireplace of rough brick with mighty logs on the hearth. The walls are crowded with china, books, and the like. Around the cabin runs a covered porch, and when you step out the first thing that meets your eye is a sea of trees – beech, fir, pine, cedar, everything slightly eerie in the gentle rustling rain. Through the trees you can glimpse a mountainous landscape, all of it forested. The cabin stands on a slope, and somewhat further down you can see about ten other wooden cabins. Over here the women live, and over there the men; that is the kitchen, there you see the dining hall, and cows and horses are grazing among the buildings. I must explain that two Putnam families live here, and a Bowdrich family, complete with servants.

He describes primeval forests, glacial boulders, moss and fern, blackberry and raspberry bushes, wild, 'and a curious cross between the two'. Climbing to the top of a 3,500-foot bluff, he describes looking out over:

a wild glacial landscape of fields and lakes covered since the time of the glaciers with virgin forest . . . The area still has bears, wolves, deer, elk, porcupines. Snakes also abound. Yesterday when we arrived a two-footer was waiting to welcome us. My last letter was written to you in the railway station at Lake Placid, at the end of the line. From there we continued on to here, travelling for more than five hours in a curious two-horse conveyance over deeply rutted roads. All the Gerstacker memories [a German writer of American West stories] of my boyhood came rushing back. In what seemed like a completely desolate area we saw metal boxes nailed to trees so the mailman could drop off the letters for the farmers. Then came the little wooden shack by the road which housed the 'store', carrying every conceivable line of merchandise, then the 'hotel', where for lunch we were served 'brown bread' and 'corn on the cob' with salted butter and crisp bacon. A fire was lit. The Putnams have a harmonium; we sang German folk songs to it! They are terribly nice people. The hospitality is downright Indian. Except for train tickets I hardly need money. We really must come back here together some time; it is just too good to be missed . . .

A couple of days later he wrote again:

Two more days before departure! Everything is taking place in a whirl. Yesterday I stood upon a bare rocky peak nearly 5,600 feet high, in the midst of tremendous virgin forests, looking far out into the blue infinities of America and shivering to the bone in the icy wind, and today I am in the midst of the metropolitan bustle of Albany, the capital of the State of New York! The hundred thousand enormously deep impressions I am taking back with me from this wonderland cannot be described with the pen. Everything is too big, too immeasurable. Something that has been gradually dawning on me in the past few days is the recognition that here an ideal potentiality of life has become reality. Men are as well off here as the culture permits; women badly off. We have seen things here that inspire enthusiastic admiration, and things that make one ponder social evolution deeply. As far as technological culture is concerned, we lag miles behind America. But all that is frightfully costly and already carries the germ of the end in itself. I must tell you a great, great deal. I shall never forget the experiences of this journey. Now we are tired of America. Tomorrow morning we are off to New York, and on September 21 we sail!

9

Emma Moves Ahead

Carl arrived back from America in the highest spirits. There had been a storm lasting a day and half the night during their sea passage from New York to Bremen and he had spent much of it in a protected spot under the bridge of the *Kaiser Wilhelm der Grosse*, admiring the mountainous waves rolling over the deck until he got soaked through. When he went below decks for a cup of tea he immediately felt sick and quickly retired to his cabin, where he found all the objects had come to life, as he described in a letter to Emma the next day:

The sofa cushion crawled about on the floor in the semidarkness; a recumbent shoe sat up, looked around in astonishment, and then shuffled off quietly under the sofa; a standing shoe turned wearily on its side and followed its mate. Now the scene changed. I realised that the shoes had gone under the sofa to fetch my bag and briefcase. The whole company paraded over to join the big trunk under the bed. One sleeve of my shirt waved longingly after them, and from inside the chests and drawers came rumbles and rattles. Suddenly there was a terrible crash under my floor, a rattling, clattering, and tinkling. One of the kitchens is underneath me. There, at one

I in my turn have learnt a great deal. The main point always comes last: my wife is pregnant again, by design and after mature reflection.

Jung appears to have come out of the quarrels with Emma unbowed, holding fast to his new conviction that he should have a 'licence to be unfaithful'. Freud, answering the letter, made no comment about Jung's prerequisite of a good marriage, contenting himself with: 'I should have thought it quite impossible to analyse one's own wife.'

There was no lack of women to trigger Emma's 'number of jealous scenes': Fräulein Aptekmann, Maria Moltzer, Martha Boeddinghaus, all independent women connected with the Burghölzli, all vying for Carl's attention if not his love. And then there were the wealthy ladies of Zürich's *Pelzmäntel* brigade, who still thronged to his lectures. And Fräulein Spielrein. Emma probably thought the worst was behind her, but it was still worrying when, throughout the summer, Sabina Spielrein appeared at the house, ostensibly to ask for Carl's help with her dissertation, in fact trying to rekindle the flames of their relationship. How must it have felt for Emma to watch Fräulein Spielrein go up the stairs to Carl's *Cabinet* and not emerge for the next hour? Who knew what was happening behind those closed doors.

But Emma knew Carl and his 'infatuations'. As did Fräulein Spielrein. 'My friend said we would always have to be careful not to fall in love again; we would always be dangerous to each other,' Spielrein wrote ecstatically in her journal on a good day when the Herr Doktor 'pressed my hands to his heart several times and said this should mark the beginning of a new era'. But this was quickly followed by despair. 'My heart contracts painfully, for the main thing is missing, and this main thing is love. Oh, again this "What to do?" I hardly believe that I could love anyone the way I love my friend. I fear my life is ruined.' And a few days later: 'To be one among the many who languish for him, and in return receive his kind gaze, a few friendly words . . . fulfil his every wish . . . his vanity. He assumes a frigid, official tone, and who suffers from that? Not he, of course.' Out walking one day she bumped into Fräulein Aptekmann, another of Herr Doktor Jung's students, also besotted with him. 'She loves him and believes that he loves her,' wrote Spielrein that evening in her journal. 'She was so happy about it – her eyes gleamed, her cheeks glowed.' Emma could only watch as all these young women competed for Carl's attention and love, interpreting his flirtations as something more.

Using 'poetry' again to describe in typically enigmatic terms the 'more' in their relationship, Fräulein Spielrein wrote: 'Yes, the stronger poetry probably occurred a week ago. He said then that he loves me because of the remarkable parallelism in our thoughts . . . he told me he loves me more for my magnificent proud character, but he also told me that he would never marry me because he harbours within himself a great philistine who craves narrow limits and the typical Swiss style.' One day, Carl showed her sections of the secret diary he had kept until he married Emma, after which he had put it away in a drawer:

When he gave me his diary to read, he said in a very soft, hoarse voice, 'Only my wife has read this . . . and you.' And yet his wife, who, as his diary makes clear, hesitated for a long time before marrying him, because in spite of her love she gave thought to her own comfort and did not want any wild-eyed 'slave to an ideology'; his wife is protected by the law, respected by all, and I, who wanted to give him everything I possessed, without the slightest regard for myself, I am called immoral in the language of society – lover, maybe maîtresse! He can appear anywhere in public with his wife, and I have to skulk in dark corners . . . True, he wanted to introduce me in his house, make me his wife's friend, but understandably his wife wanted no part of this business.

When Fräulein Spielrein turned up at the house for her appointment on 20 September 1910 she was turned away by a maid without an explanation. Upstairs, in the bedroom overlooking the garden, Emma had that morning given birth to a baby girl, Marianne, their fourth child.

For Carl it was a repeat of his experience after the birth of Franz: happiness closely followed by distress. Split Carl. When she came for her postponed appointment two days later Fräulein Spielrein found him in the kind of mood which gave her hope: 'Yes, my dear good friend, I love you and you love me. The thing I was longing for only recently has been fulfilled: he revealed his love almost too clearly . . . We were supposed to sit down and work . . . So I am not one among the many . . . He resisted, he did not want to love me. Now he must, because our souls are deeply akin.' How could she know it was not about her but all about Jung's own complex psychology? As he put it, remembering how he had carried his own once powerful father, now dying, from room to room: 'To be fruitful means, indeed, to destroy one's self, because with the rise of the succeeding generation the previous one has passed beyond its highest point.

Thus our descendants are our most dangerous enemies, whom we cannot overcome, for they will outlive us, and therefore, without fail, will take the power from our enfeebled hands.'

Carl needed to get away. Less than a week after Emma gave birth to their baby daughter he was off on a two-week cycling tour of northern Italy with his friend Wolf Stockmayer, a doctor from Munich. But things did not work out as planned. On their way home they spent a night in Arona on Lake Maggiore, intending to set off along the lakeshore the next morning and on through Tessin as far as Faido, where they planned to take the train back to Zürich. However, that night Jung had a dream which blew him right off course. He found himself in an 'assemblage of distinguished spirits of earlier centuries', the conversation conducted in Latin. Amongst them was a gentleman with a long, curly wig who addressed him and asked a difficult question. Carl understood the question but did not have sufficient command of the language to answer in Latin. He woke with a start, feeling 'such intense inferiority feelings about the unanswered question that I immediately took the train home in order to get back to work. It would have been impossible for me to continue the bicycle trip and lose another three days. I had to work, to find the answer.' It was the same old thing: a dream which took him back to his boyhood and those terrible feelings. Work was the only solution. Work and home. Emma must have been surprised when he arrived back three days early. Or maybe not. These days she knew how much Carl needed her for his emotional stability. Probably better than he did.

* * *

Earlier that year, in March 1910, Emma had taken a more direct role in Carl's work. The Second International Psychoanalytic Congress was taking place on 30 and 31 March in Nuremberg, but on 8 March, Carl unexpectedly left for America: his old patient Medill McCormick had had a relapse with manic episodes and all the signs of another breakdown. Medill's desperate wife begged Jung to come and attend to him. Carl did not need much persuading, even though the length of the sea passage meant he would be hard pressed to get to Chicago and back in time for the congress.

'*Sehr Geehrter Herr Professor!*' Emma wrote to Freud that same day from Kusnacht, 'I am writing to you in the name of my husband, who suddenly left for Chicago today, where his former patient, McCormick, is seriously ill.' She assured Freud that Jung would be at Nuremberg by 29 March, or the 30th at 5 a.m. at the very latest, and might she meanwhile ask whether Freud would mind being the first speaker and what title he wanted for his lecture? All this in her husband's name, exercising the side of herself as she had done all along, assisting Carl as she had assisted her father with his accounts and business correspondence. But the letter carries on, first mentioning a paper on neurosis theory, then passing on a bit of gossip about someone whom Jung had refused attendance at the congress. Emma was going beyond her normal role and involving herself actively. Stepping out. Cautiously. She wrote again on 16 March, thanking the Herr Professor for his kind letter and offer of help, saying that her husband's assistant Dr Honegger was 'deputising with the patients and looking after the Nuremberg business with me, otherwise I would be rather nervous about everything turning out all right'.

'Now don't get cross with me for my pranks!' Jung wrote to
Freud the next day from the Grand Hotel Terminus in Paris.
'You will already have heard from my wife that I am on my way
to America. *I have arranged everything so as to be back in time
for Nuremberg.* Everything else is so arranged that it will function automatically, i.e. with the help of my wife and the assistance of Honegger, to whom I have entrusted my patients.'
Honegger was Carl's most promising student and assistant, so
the patients were deemed to be in good hands. But Freud was
put in a fluster by all this uncertainty. 'Bleuler is not coming
either, and Jung is in America, so that I am trembling about his
return,' he wrote to Oscar Pfister, another of the Zürich group
who could not attend. 'What will happen if my Zürichers desert
me?' But Jung came in time, having rescued Medill once again
from his self-destructive urges, chasing him all the way to
Chattanooga in Tennessee and back. And the congress was a
success too, founding the International Psychoanalytic
Association, a key step towards establishing the pre-eminence
of the Freudian school of psychoanalysis. At a private meeting
of the Viennese group of analysts at the congress, Freud
announced: 'Most of you are Jews, and therefore incompetent
to win friends for the new teaching. Jews must be content with
the modest role of preparing the ground . . . The Swiss will save
us – will save me, and all of you as well.'

Emma had now met Freud twice in Vienna and once in Kusnacht.
She liked and admired him and sensed he was an ally who
understood the dilemmas she faced in her marriage. She wanted
to keep in touch with the Herr Professor on her own behalf. So

when he answered her letter about the Nuremberg arrangements she wrote back, confiding in him the fears she had had about her husband's enthusiasm for America. For a while she had worried Carl might want to emigrate and, good Swiss woman that she was, the thought horrified her. But now she realised 'America no longer has the same attraction for him as before, and this has taken a stone from my heart. It is just enough to satisfy [his] desire for travel and adventure, but no more than that.' And indeed, Jung wrote to Freud that when he got home he was pleased to find 'wife, children, and house in good shape, and work aplenty'.

As for Emma, having once tasted the pleasures of connecting with the exciting new world of psychoanalysis, she was not about to give it up. When preparations were being made for the next congress, at Weimar the following autumn, she was determined to be part of it.

From now on Emma stepped in for her husband every time he went away, and he seemed to be away more and more. In April he was in Berlin, then home for two days before going to Stuttgart for the annual meeting of the German Society for Psychiatry, then 'working like mad' until July, when he set off on a two-week sailing holiday on the Lake of Constance, the Bodensee, sending his boat ahead; then three weeks' military service, then a trip to London for a consultation at the beginning of September, and so on into 1911, 'gadding about like mad' as he admitted to Freud. When Honegger left to work at another asylum, causing one of Carl's furious outbursts – 'How could he do this to me?' – Emma stepped in again.

* * *

Respite came with the annual spring holiday. This time they took a sixteen-day motoring tour to the South of France, complete with chauffeur, staying in the grandest hotels. These holidays were always the best of times for Emma and Carl, sharing their love of travel, history and books, just the two of them.

At the beginning of July a heatwave hit the Continent that lasted right through the summer and into September. In Zürich people walked in the shade of the chestnut trees, the ladies in white ankle-length cotton dresses, white shoes and stockings, wide straw hats and parasols, the men in waistcoats and shirt sleeves with the open-necked Schiller collars normally only worn to the bowling alley. The heat changed the whole atmosphere of the city: the gardens of the Wirtschaften always crowded, waitresses in long skirts and starched white aprons carrying jugs of Hürlimann beer from table to table, and the lidos on the lake full to bursting. Apparently the supply of lemonade ran out at the annual Cantonal Gymnastics Fest at Winterthur. In the evenings people promenaded along the *quais* until the light faded, listening to the military bands in the pavilions.

Still, the heat did not stop some antimilitarists demonstrating in front of the Italian embassy against the war with Turkey, a few communists and anarchists telling the crowd it was an imperialist war, Italy helped by the British colonialist pirates and French finance. 'Italy has her right for a place in the sun like anyone else,' shouted back Benito Mussolini, the fiery young editor of *Avanti!*, who was in the crowd. The city police had to be called in to calm things down.

On the morning of 16 September, Jung took the paddle steamer from Kusnacht to the Bellvue landing stage and then the tram to Central Station, to meet Freud who was arriving from Bolzano, where he had been spending his annual summer holiday with Martha and the family. Jung had invited him a day earlier but Freud answered that this was 'unfulfillable, and has been for twenty-five years': it was the date of his and Martha's wedding anniversary. In the end Freud stayed with the Jungs for four days before they all set off for the Weimar Congress. Emma, in happy anticipation of Freud's visit, made sure the room on the second floor with a view of the lake was beautifully prepared for their honoured guest: fine bedlinen, a table for work, flowers for decoration, and plenty of books.

The days in Zürich were packed with activity, as Ernest Jones, joining them from Toronto, recalled: 'There were of course seminars, visitors and receptions, so it was by no means a pure holiday. Putnam who was staying in Zürich not Kusnacht, participated in all these activities.' Apparently Freud found time in the packed schedule to give Putnam, their new friend from America, six hours of analysis. He also found time to spend a morning alone with Emma whilst Carl was busy with other matters. They talked mostly about family, his and hers. It is clear from letters written later that Emma confided in Freud about some of the dilemmas in her life, seeing in the Herr Professor something of a father figure, perhaps a replacement for her own father who had failed her so badly. Freud in turn confided more to Emma about his private life than he had to almost anyone else, admitting that his relationship with Martha was 'amortised' as he put it – surely in response to Emma's revelations about the difficulties in her own marriage. But it also reveals how relaxed Freud felt in the presence of this 'charming, clever and ambitious' young woman, as he later described her to Jung.

Charming? Clever? Ambitious? Modest Emma did not see herself in those terms.

Conversation continued as they travelled together to Weimar, Emma included for the first time in the exalted company of Freud, Ernest Jones and James Putnam, though once Carl was present she soon slipped into the background. He was telling them, with his usual energy and relish, about a pedagogic congress in Brussels he had attended, where he spoke on the psychoanalysis of children, a provocative subject at the best of times. When he delivered his bombshell of theories, a few people had left the hall in protest muttering, 'Oh, c'est un homme odieux!' – an odious man – and 'Vous avez déchaîné un orage' – you've let loose a storm. It could not have been better. After the Brussels congress, and in triumphant mood, he'd collected Emma from Kusnacht and they'd set off on a mountain tour of the Bernese Oberland. And now here they were speeding through the German countryside at twenty miles an hour, the train belching out steam, on their way to Weimar. To Emma, it seemed, life was looking up.

The formal photograph taken of the attendees at the Third International Psychoanalytic Congress in September 1911, on the steps of the Erbprinz Hotel in Weimar, marks an important moment in the history of the early psychoanalytic movement – and a key moment in Emma's life. There she sits in the front row looking elegant in a dark two-piece suit with a high collar and long skirts – remarkably trim in spite of her four pregnancies – hands in lap, composed, hair nicely but not extravagantly coiffed, a small smile on her lips as she looks straight into the camera, attractive and alert with the pleasure of being part of the company. Beside her, along the front row, sit the other women, the independent ones Emma must until recently have envied. They are nearly all from the Zürich group, Vienna lagging far behind as far as accepting women into the fold. On the far left of the picture sits Maria Moltzer, a nursing sister from the Burghölzli and another of Carl's female admirers; two down is Lou Andreas-Salomé from Germany, sporting a flamboyant fur stole in spite of the warm weather; next to her, with Emma on her other side, sits Beatrice Hinkle from New York in a smart American two-piece with striped collar and cuffs; a lady from Berlin in an enormous hat sits on Emma's other side, flanked by Antonia Wolff, a young woman who had until recently been Carl's patient, looking rather cross and unsure in a girlish dress and hair done up in rolls. Lastly, Martha Boeddinghaus, another of Carl's admirers. Noticeably absent was Fräulein Spielrein, who had taken her final exams in January, passing them with top honours; she hadn't been able to make up her mind whether to attend or not, feeling that Herr Doktor Jung had not given her any real encouragement to do so. A relief no doubt to Emma.

'This time the feminine element will have conspicuous representatives from Zürich,' Jung had written to Freud on 29 August 1911: 'Sister Moltzer, Dr Hinkle-Eastwick (an American charmer), Frl Spielrein (!) then a new discovery of mine, Frl Antonia Wolff, a remarkable intellect with an excellent feeling for religion and philosophy, and last but not least my wife.' The 'last but not least' was written in English, everything else in German.

'Dear friend,' Freud replied. 'We Viennese have nothing to compare with the charming ladies you are bringing from Zürich,' adding: 'I am glad to release you as well as your dear wife, well known to me as a solver of riddles, from the darkness by informing you that my work in these last few weeks has dealt with the same theme as yours, to wit, the origin of religion.' The reference to Emma as solver of riddles is praise indeed from the old wizard of psychoanalysis, and references a comment Jung made about Freud's enigmatic way of expressing himself: 'together with my wife I have tried to unriddle your words'. But clever Freud was surely alluding to this talent of Emma's in a more general sense as well, knowing how much riddle-solving life with Jung involved.

Behind the women seated in the front row of the photograph, and all around them, stand most of the male representatives of the Freudian school of psychoanalysis as it was in 1911: Professor Eugen Bleuler, Ludwig Binswanger and Franz Riklin, Alphonse Maeder, Adolf Keller, Oscar Pfister, all from Zürich; then Otto Rank, Wilhelm Stekel, Paul Federn and Isidor Sadger from Vienna; Sandor Ferenczi from Budapest, Ernest Jones from Toronto, originally of Wales, Max Eitingon, Karl Abraham, Leonard Seif and one or two others from Germany; and finally the Americans: Abraham Brill and James J. Putnam. Everyone dressed in dark three-piece suits with stiff collars, cravat or tie and gold watch chains, over forty attendees, all gathered round the two principal participants: Herr Professor Freud and Herr Doktor Jung. The photograph is artfully arranged, an early example of media management: Jung, the only one in a stylish floppy bow tie, standing behind his wife Emma, leaning forward, his arms resting on the back of her chair, thereby minimising his great bulk and height; Freud next to him, formal in tails, standing a good deal higher thanks to a stool, commanding the company with his presence, making Ferenczi on his right, who was the same height, look tiny by comparison.

Emma spent the two days of the congress listening with keen interest to Professor Putnam of Boston 'On the Significance of Philosophy for the Further Development of Psychoanalysis', Professor Bleuler of Zürich 'On the Theory of Autism', Dr Sadger of Vienna 'On Masturbation', Dr Abraham of Berlin on 'The Psychosexual Foundation of States of Depression and Exaltation', Sandor Ferenczi of Budapest 'On Homosexuality', Professor Freud of Vienna on 'Postscript to the Analysis of Schreiber', her own husband on 'Contributions on Symbolism', and many more. She knew most of the speakers, either from the Burghölzli, or from their visits to Seestrasse. When Professor Putnam visited from Boston, for instance, Jung had picked him up from his Zürich hotel and brought him back to the house for a meal and to meet Emma and the children. To think she might have been married to a Schaffhausen businessman, taking afternoon *kaffee kuchen* with their wives and entertaining dull business colleagues in the evenings.

A bonus for Emma was meeting Beatrice Hinkle, the 'American charmer'. She was exactly the kind of woman Emma liked. Seated side by side in the front row of the photograph, it is easy to see why: each had a quiet composed elegance – two intelligent women in the company of some of the most advanced thinkers of the age. Emma found she had much to learn from Hinkle, who was an early feminist. Like Emma she came from a wealthy family, but unlike Emma she had been allowed to further her education, studying medicine at the Cooper Medical College in San Francisco. In 1892 she married attorney Walter S. Hinkle and by 1899 she had gained her doctorate with a thesis entitled 'Enuresis in Children'. In 1905 she was appointed San Francisco's city physician, the first woman in the United States to hold a public health position. Later, moving to New York, she founded the first therapeutic clinic in America. By 1909 she was travelling to Vienna to study under Freud, later moving to Jung because she found Freud's rigid sexual theories – male-dominated in her opinion – hard to accept. And now she was here in Weimar, taking an active part in all the discussions and, during the recesses, talking advanced ideas about the place of women in society. What with the congress and the feminist ideas, Emma came home dizzy with a new confidence.

After Weimar, Jung immediately set off for St Gallen and three weeks' military service and Emma took the children to stay with her mother in Schaffhausen. On 30 October, in her new confidence, she did an extraordinary thing. She wrote to Herr Professor Freud – whilst Carl was away and without telling him. During the four days of Freud's visit to Kusnacht, and beneath the friendly collaboration of Weimar, she had detected a certain unease between the two men. Carl had previously sent Freud the first part of a paper he was writing, later to be published as *Transformations and Symbols of the Libido*, and he was waiting anxiously for Freud's reaction, knowing that the ideas expressed in it would not please him.

'Dear Professor Freud,' Emma began:

I really don't know how I am summoning the courage to write you this letter, but am certain it is not from presumption; rather I am following the voice of my unconscious, which I have so often found was right and which I hope will not lead me astray this time. Since your visit I have been tormented by the idea that your relation with my husband is not altogether what it should be, and since it definitely ought not to be like this I want to do whatever is in my power. I do not know whether I am deceiving myself when I think you are somehow not quite in agreement with 'Transformations of the Libido'. You didn't speak of it at all and yet I think it would do you both so much good if you got down to a thorough discussion of it.

It is an astonishing letter, courageous, and perhaps a little rash. Whatever would Carl say if he found out? The letter shows how much Emma has absorbed of the language and methods of psychoanalysis. She talks of 'following the voice of my unconscious', having picked up an incipient rift between the pair. Emma the peacemaker, Emma the defender of her husband.

'Or is it something else?' she intuits, perhaps referring to Freud's admission that his own marriage was 'amortised', as well as his concerns about his children:

If so, please tell me what, dear Herr Professor; for I cannot bear to see you so resigned and I even believe your resignation relates not only to your real children (it made a quite special impression on me when you spoke of it) but also to your spiritual sons; otherwise you would have so little need to be resigned. Please do not take my action as officiousness and do not count me among the women who, you once told me, always spoil your friendships. My husband naturally knows nothing of this letter and I beg you not to hold him responsible for it or let any kind of unpleasant effects it may have on you glance off on him. I hope nevertheless that you will not be angry with your very admiring

Emma Jung.

On the same day Carl sent Freud a postcard from his military barracks in St Gallen. The last ten days had completely worn him out, he said, having suddenly been detailed for a mountain exercise in the back of beyond where he was quite out of touch with the rest of humanity. He was returning home from these brutalities the next day. 'I am glad you are home again and no longer playing soldiers, which is after all a silly occupation,' replied Freud, never mentioning Emma's letter. Nor the fact that he had answered it.

'My dear Professor Freud,' Emma wrote back, presumably hiding away in her room so Carl did not find out what she was up to. Freud's letter is lost, but it is not hard to work out what it contained. 'Your nice kind letter has relieved me of anxious doubts, for I was afraid that in the end I had done something stupid. Now I am naturally very glad and thank you with all my heart for your friendly reception of my letter, and particularly for the goodwill you show to all of us.' Freud must have remonstrated that he was not really resigned, as she put it, nor defensive, but Emma was not minded to accept it: he had not even let them sympathise with his toothache, she pointed out, versed as she now was in repression, projection, resistances, the unconscious and so forth. She also explained why she had mentioned 'Symbols': because she knew how eagerly Carl was waiting for the Herr Professor's opinion, having often said he was sure 'you would not approve of it', and was thus 'waiting with some trepidation'. She reckoned it was a residue of Carl's father (or mother) complex, which was probably being resolved in the book, 'for actually Carl, if he holds something to be right, would have no need to worry about anyone else's opinion'. Not content to let sleeping dogs lie, she reminded Freud of the conversation on that first morning when he told her about his family: 'You said then that your marriage had long been "amortised", now there was nothing more to do except – die. And the children were growing up and then they become a real worry, and yet this is the only true joy.' This comment of his had seemed so significant to her, she had to think of it again and again. She fancied it was intended for her private information, and not for Carl, because Herr Professor's comments likely referred 'symbolically' to her husband at the same time.

She moved boldly on, oblivious to the likely reaction of the venerable old man who was, after all, the founder of the Viennese school of psychoanalysis. This was so unlike the normally reserved Emma, so alien, it suggests the heady experience of Weimar had temporarily sent her off beam: 'I wanted to ask then if you are sure that your children would not be helped by analysis. One certainly cannot be the child of a great man with impunity, considering the trouble one has in getting away from ordinary fathers. And when this distinguished father also has a streak of paternalism in him, as you yourself said!'

On she went, in full swing: 'You said you didn't have time to analyse your children's dreams because you had to earn money so that they could go on dreaming. Do you think this attitude is right? I would prefer to think one *should not* dream at all, one should live.' This was an extraordinary statement to make to the father of psychoanalysis. Then she returned to the subject of her own life: 'I have found with Carl also that the imperative "earn money" is only an evasion of something else to which he has resistances.' How hard she is trying to understand it, to explain it all to herself. 'Please forgive me this candour, it may strike you as brazen; but it disturbs my image of you because I somehow cannot bring it into harmony with the other side of your nature, and this matters so much to me.' The Protestant Swiss young woman might have misunderstood the Jewish Viennese professor's quirky comments about his children, but she was spot on about her own Swiss husband.

'You may imagine how overjoyed and honoured I am by the confidence you have in Carl, but it almost seems to me as though you were sometimes giving too much – do you not see in him the follower and fulfiller more than you need?' she carried on, quite oblivious that she was going too far. 'Doesn't one often give much because one wants to keep much? Why are you thinking of giving up already instead of enjoying your well-earned fame and success? Perhaps for fear of letting the right moment for it pass you by? Surely this will never happen to *you*. After all, you are not so old that you could speak now of the "way of regression", what with all these splendid and fruitful ideas you have in your head! Besides, the man who has discovered the living fountain of ps.A.[psychoanalysis] (or don't you believe it is one?) will not grow old so quickly.'

She signed off with a final flourish: 'And do not think of Carl with a father's feeling: "he will grow, but I must dwindle", but rather as one human being thinks of another, who like you has his own law to fulfil. Don't be angry with me. With warm love and veneration, Emma Jung.'

When Freud wrote to Jung on 12 November he made a point of praising *Transformations and Symbols of the Libido*, but added: 'Sometimes I have a feeling that [your] horizon has been too narrowed by Christianity.' Again Freud never mentioned Emma's letters, only sent a 'heartfelt to your wife and children'. But he'd had enough.

'You were really annoyed by my letter, weren't you?' Emma wrote back to Freud on 14 November:

I was too, and now I am cured of my megalomania and am wondering why the devil the unconscious had to make you, of all people, the victim of this madness. And here I must confess, very reluctantly, that you are right: my last letter, especially the tone of it, was really directed to the father-imago, which should of course be faced without fear. This thought never entered my head; I thought that, knowing the transference side of my father-attitude towards you, it would all be quite clear and do me no harm. After I had thought so long before writing to you and had, so I believed, fully under-stood my own motives, the unconscious has now played another trick on me, with particular finesse: for you can imagine how delighted I am to have made a fool of myself in front of you. I can only pray and hope that your judgement will not prove too severe.

Once again Freud's letter is lost but Emma's response makes it quite clear how sharp it was. There was one thing she neverthe-less wanted to vigorously defend herself against: the way the Herr Professor reacted to her 'amiable carpings', as he put it. She had not suggested Carl should set no store by Freud's opin-ion, she protested, it went without saying that one recognised authority. It was just that her husband had been so anxious and uncertain, which had seemed superfluous to her. But now she saw that she had got it wrong: Carl had not been worried about what Freud would say, he had just been analysing his attitude to his work and discovered some resistances to it. The worry about

Freud was really only a pretext for not going on with the self-analysis. She realised now that she had projected something 'from my immediate neighbourhood into distant Vienna and am vexed that it is always the nearest thing that one sees worst'.

'You have also completely misunderstood my admittedly uncalled-for meddling in your family affairs,' she went on, showing that she was quite up to defending herself:

> Truthfully I didn't mean to cast a shadow on your children. I know they have turned out well and have never doubted it in the least. I hope you don't seriously believe that I wanted to say they were 'doomed to be degenerate'. I have written nothing that could even remotely mean anything of the sort. I know that with your children it is a matter of physical illness, but just wanted to raise the question whether these physical symptoms might not be somehow psychically conditioned, so that there might for instance be a reduced power of resistance. Since I have made some very astonishing discoveries in myself in this respect and do not consider myself excessively degenerate or markedly hysterical, I thought similar phenomena possible with other people too. I shall be grateful for enlightenment.

This is Emma at her best: lucid, honest, open, and quite assertive. She continues:

> That you think it worthwhile to discuss your most personal affairs with me is something for which I thank you with all my heart. What you tell me sounds so convincing that I simply have to believe it, although much in me struggles

against it. But I must admit you have the experience and I do not, consequently I am unable to make any convincing rejoinders. You are quite right about one thing, though: despite everything and everybody, the whole affair is only a blessing in clumsy disguise which I beg you to forgive. Please write nothing of this to Carl; things are going badly enough with me as it is.

Emma Jung.

No one could have guessed that things were going 'badly enough' for Emma. So generous towards her husband, there was no sign of the struggle going on within. Not until she had to explain herself to Freud.

Freud wrote back quickly and sympathetically. 'Heartfelt thanks for your letter,' she replied on 24 November 1911:

Please don't worry. I am not always as despondent as I was in my last letter. I was afraid you were angry with me or had a bad opinion of me; that was what made me so downhearted, especially because my main complex was hit. Usually I am quite at one with my fate and see very well how lucky I am, but from time to time I am tormented by the conflict about how I am to hold my own against Carl. I find I have no friends, all the people who associate with us really only want to see Carl, except for a few boring and to me quite uninteresting persons. Naturally the women are all in love with him, and with the men I am instantly cordoned off as the wife of the father or friend.

Here was Emma's dilemma in a nutshell, expressed with courageous honesty – or, more accurately, her many dilemmas, all connected to the central one: Carl.

Yet I have a strong need for people and Carl too says I should stop concentrating on him and the children, but what on earth am I to do? What with my strong tendency to autoeroticism it is very difficult, but also objectively it is difficult because I can never compete with Carl. In order to emphasise this I usually have to talk extra stupidly when in company. I do my best to get transferences and if they don't turn out as I wished I am always very depressed. You will now understand why I felt so bad at the thought that I had lost your favour, and I was also afraid Carl might notice something. At any rate he now knows about the exchange of letters, as he was astonished to see one of your letters addressed to me; but I have revealed only a little of their content. Will you advise me, dear Herr Professor, and if necessary dress me down a bit? I am ever so grateful to you for your sympathy.

With warmest greetings to you and yours, Emma Jung

Imagine Carl's surprise when he found a letter in Freud's hand on the hall table one morning – addressed to his wife, not himself. Emma's private correspondence with Herr Professor Freud ceased forthwith.

10

A Difficult Year

1912 was a difficult year in the Jung house. A crisis was looming, provoked by Carl's split from Freud. Emma had sensed it coming, but she had no idea it would be so bad, no idea it would bring her husband close to a complete emotional breakdown.

It was a difficult year for Zürich too, plagued by a series of strikes which disrupted the usually peaceful and orderly way people went about their business. The *Neue Zürcher Zeitung* reported that the strike at the automobile factory at Schlieren was quickly followed by one at the Firma Gauger in the Unterstrasse. The city police intervened to protect the strike-breakers, good family men as the newspaper described them, who were beaten up as they went to work. Finally, the local military were called in. One striker was fatally wounded in the fray and his funeral on 24 April became the occasion for a noisy demonstration. The strike leaders accused the military of being the 'lapdog of Capitalism'. Activists and revolutionaries, some from Russia and Germany, told demonstrators to 'Stop work! It's the only way the Capitalists will recognise that they belong to you, not you to them!' People marched through the streets, banners waving, distributing flyers: 'Down with the military! Swiss soldiers, don't shoot your brothers! Long live the International Revolution!' There were 60,000 foreign workers in Zürich: Germans, Austrians, Czechs, Italians, most anti-militarists. The younger generation from the Yiddish-speaking Jewish community joined the protests whilst their elders worked day and night in small factories making buttons and ribbons and trimmings for the clothing industry. There were instances of sabotage and in the 'red' working-class district of Ausser Sihl, a bomb-making factory was found, stocked with tin boxes, nitroglycerine and fuses.

Neither Emma nor Carl was especially political, but this was shocking. The class war appeared to be entering new territory: it was not just the anarchists and revolutionaries creating the unrest now, but regular social democrats too. It was all the odder since the financial pages of the newspapers showed that everything else seemed to be going so well: millions invested in stocks and shares, post office traffic of letters, telegrams, telephone calls all growing exponentially. A glance through the newspaper advertisements showed you could buy everything in Zürich: the new Waterman fountain pen from America, beer from Bavaria, Indian teas directly from Fortnum & Mason department store in London. Over 3,000 Swiss owned an automobile, the majority living in Zürich. Trade was thriving thanks to the efficiency of the new railway system, with wheat arriving from Russia and machinery of all sorts from America. Locally the watch industry, the chocolate factories, the embroidery business, the tourist and hotel trade – all thriving. Add to this the recognised fact that Switzerland had the finest sanatoriums and offered a humane refuge to those fleeing political repression and religious intolerance, and you have Helvetia, proud and independent. The burghers had their rights, could read and write; they were not beaten, or hanged; they elected their administrators, and could marry whom they wished. It was amusing to Carl to find that a new word had entered the vocabulary: psychoanalysis, though not everyone knew what it meant, or even how to spell it.

In January 1912, an unusually mild month with clear blue skies, the citizens of Zürich had woken up to psychoanalysis. Carl was obliged to go public and defend it in the pages of the *Neue Zürcher Zeitung*, writing to Freud that there were 'mighty rumblings in Zürich over Psycho-Analysis. The Keplerbund is sponsoring a public lecture against this abomination. Protest meetings are afoot!' In the evening edition of 5 January, amongst articles about the invention of the electric iron, central heating, the typewriter and the latest craze for winter sports – which was 'only for Englishmen and women and our rich who like to imitate them' – came a sharp attack on this 'Psycho-Analysis', which pretended to be scientific but was nothing more than dubious hypotheses. Rumours spread about strange goings-on and loose morals. 'Zürich is seething,' Jung wrote. 'Psycho-Analysis the talk of the town. One can see here how worked up people can get . . . These people are vermin that shun the light.' He needed a break. He went to Lugano on his own for a week at the end of March. Then Emma joined him and they toured northern Italy together.

When Emma took the paddle steamer into town to meet Marguerite that summer, she found a city in buoyant mood: ladies' fashions more modern, corsets less restrictive, the skirts shorter, showing an ankle. Some ladies even rode bicycles now, braving the traffic and the danger of the wheels getting stuck in the tramlines. As ever, the sisters would make for the fashion house Grieder on the Bahnhofstrasse, with its wondrous variety of silks and fine cottons, embroidery, lace and ribbons laid out for them on wide wooden counters by deferential assistants. Further down the street were the new travel agents advertising exotic destinations. Marguerite and Ernst were keen travellers and sometimes Emma joined them on short trips when Carl was too busy or too distracted to get away. After shopping, the sisters might sit on the terrace of the Hotel Baur-au-Lac or if the weather was inclement, in one of the fashionable cafés – the Sprüngli or the Wiener – taking coffee with a slice of Schwartzwalder Torte or millefeuilles, two young women in elegant day wear, hats and gloves, talking about their children and their husbands.

Equally they might browse the newspapers and talk about the worsening international situation: there was trouble in the Balkans, France wanted Alsace Lorraine back, the Germans wanted a bigger fleet to match the British, the socialists wanted to be rid of the monarchies. One in five of all Zürich workers were German, and some warned that social discontent still lay not far below the surface. On 12 July there was a general strike. The City Fathers blamed those 'other Germans': the activists, socialists and anarchists from Berlin who came to do mischief in Zürich because they could not get away with it in the Reich. Shopkeepers pulled down their blinds again as strikers ran through the streets waving flags and shouting slogans through megaphones en route to the Volkshaus, where a large demon-stration was taking place. Smallholders from Forch coming down the hill in their wooden carts for the weekly market were told to go back whence they came. The city police had to be reinforced by the canton military again, Battalions 62, 64 and 67 standing guard in front of city hall, rifles at the ready. But you could see their hearts were not in it, most of them being the sons of local farmers or factory workers. Several arrests were made, including Fritz Brupbacher, the proto-communist doctor and known associate of Russian 'agents provocateurs'. By 13 July the strike was officially over, but on the 15th, after another demonstration outside the Tonhalle, over 700 workers were fired or had their wages docked. Some German members of the workers' unions were deported under emergency legislation passed on 18 July, implemented with immediate effect.

Then everything went back to normal. The *Neue Zürcher Zeitung* reported that on a sunny Sunday a large crowd gathered in Sihl Tal to watch a flying machine display by the glamorous pilot Maffei, who liked to sport his leather cap back to front. Faces turned skywards as he circled above before landing bumpily on the grass. The organisers had to rope off an area round the plane to stop spectators crowding in as Maffei posed beside it, smiling for the cameras. Other photographs showed fathers and small sons gazing at the plane in wonderment whilst mothers and daughters sat on rugs further off. Stalls selling bratwurst were doing brisk business, and there was beer for the men, apple juice or lemonade for the women and children. Later in the afternoon Maffei climbed back into his flying machine, reversed his cap, his assistant turned the propellers, and the flying machine bumped and hopped a few feet along the grass before rising unsteadily in the air, turning in the direction of Leimbach, the red and white Swiss flag fluttering gaily behind.

In September there was an event of far greater significance: the state visit by Kaiser Wilhelm II. Besides the growing

German population of Zürich, there were plenty of burghers who saw the visit as historic and an honour, possibly including Carl, who had been so excited to catch a glimpse of the Emperor Franz Joseph in Vienna. Others were indifferent, some actively opposed. Whilst grand ladies ordered their day and evening gowns from their favourite fashion houses and practised their curtsies and their best High German, others muttered dissent. The old Swiss song 'Wir Brauchen Keine Schwaben in Der Schweiz' ('We Don't Need Any Germans in Switzerland') was whistled by workers in the streets. The anarchists were crueller, chanting: *'Alle Raeder stehen still, wenn mein starker Arm es will'* ('All the wheels will stop turning if my strong arm wants it'), a reference to the Kaiser's withered left arm. The Kaiser's days were filled with receptions, presentations and entertainments, all amply covered by the newspapers. But everyone knew that his real interest was the military manoeuvres and his inspections of the Swiss Army. What no one knew, not even the Swiss President Herr Doktor Ludwig Forrer, was that in the same month, September 1912, the Kaiser had held his first *Kriegsrat*, war council, in preparation for a war which he and his advisers already considered inevitable. Nor did they know that in London, King George V's advisers were doing the same.

There were pictures of President Forrer and selected members of the Swiss government in top hats and tails, standing on the red-carpeted platform of Zürich Central Station awaiting the imperial train, with an honour guard in full dress uniform and a military band at the ready. As the state carriage proceeded down Bahnhofstrasse, outriders clattering alongside, the Kaiser apparently told President Forrer how pleased he was to be in Zürich, a city close to his heart, and congratulated him on his iron-fisted suppression of the strikers. To which Forrer responded by reminding the Kaiser that unfortunately there were many Germans amongst the red agitators. 'Quite so! Quite so!' replied the Kaiser, rather missing the point.

By November there were more demonstrations, by the unemployed of Zürich at the Volkshaus, and later that month by the ordinary *Hausfraus* – hatless, wrapped in black woollen shawls. Emma felt for them: the price of everything had gone up, but not their husbands' wages: eggs were 11 rappen each now, milk up by 2 rappen, cheese up by 10 rappen, stewing beef 2 francs 10 rappen a kilo, which was more than their men earned in a day. Bread up, flour up, oats, briquettes for the stove, sugar, and rents as well. The weather report that day predicted rain. Black umbrellas went up as the crowd dispersed.

At 228 Seestrasse, Kusnacht, half an hour along Lake Zürich by paddle steamer, the strikes, the Kaiser's state visit, the sinking of the *Titanic* in April, revolution in China and unrest in Persia, all remained no more than a backdrop to the dramas taking place in Carl and Emma's own lives – private dramas, hidden away from public view. It was like an island, that house, during 1912, surrounded by the garden with its long yew-lined drive, lawns, terraces, rose bower, boat house and summer pavilion looking out across the lake, cut off from the rest of the world, intro-verted, battling with itself, all the optimism of the previous year and the Weimar Congress forgotten.

The problem lay with Carl. Split Carl. Personality No. 2 was back in the ascendant, bringing him close to an emotional breakdown. Day after day he locked himself away in his *Cabinet*, writing, delving into his unconscious, dicing with madness. He called it his experiment. 'It is of course ironical that I, as a psychiatrist, should at almost every step of my experiment have run into the same psychic material, which is the stuff of psychosis and is found in the insane,' he wrote later.

The crisis was brought about, as Emma had divined, by his imminent break with Freud following the publication of his *Transformations and Symbols of the Libido*, written in two parts during 1911 and 1912 and presenting Jung's own highly personal theory about the libido. 'When working on my book about the libido and approaching the end of the chapter "The Sacrifice" I knew in advance that its publication would cost me my friendship with Freud,' Jung recollected in the tranquillity of old age, years after the drama of the falling-out had subsided into psychoanalytic history. 'For I planned to set down in it my own conception of incest, the decisive transformation of the concept of libido, and various other ideas in which I differed from Freud.' He was turning Freud's theory of the libido and the oedipal complex of the child's repressed incestuous wish towards the parent on its head. 'To me incest signified a personal complication only in the rarest cases,' Jung wrote:

> Usually incest has a highly religious aspect, for which reason
> the incest theme plays a decisive part in almost all cosmogo-
> nies and in numerous myths. But Freud clung to the literal
> interpretation of it and could not grasp the spiritual signifi-
> cance of incest as a symbol. I knew that he would never be
> able to accept any of my ideas on this subject. I spoke to my
> wife about this, and told her my fears. She attempted to reas-

sure me, for she thought Freud would magnanimously raise no objections, although he might not accept my views.

Emma was wrong. Carl was right. Freud was profoundly angry and felt betrayed. He had deceived himself on one point and one point only, as he wrote to Sandor Ferenczi on 26 November 1912: that Jung was 'a born leader', where in fact he was 'immature himself and in need of supervision'.

Emma had seen it coming. She had been 'tormented by the idea' that Carl and Freud's relationship was in trouble when she had written in secret to Freud on 30 October the previous year. She sensed Freud was not in agreement with 'Transformations of the Libido': 'You didn't speak of it at all and yet I think it would do you both so much good if you got down to a thorough discussion of it.' She was not deceiving herself, but she was on the wrong track if she thought Freud would be prepared to discuss it. Carl knew Freud would not compromise. He knew it, but he did not know the break would send him almost insane.

Now Carl was assailed by all the old horrors from his unconscious. Without Emma keeping the steady rhythm of family life going he might have cracked. 'The unconscious contents could have driven me out of my wits,' he wrote. 'But for my family, and the knowledge: I have a medical diploma from a Swiss university, I must help my patients, I have a wife and [five] children, I live at 228 Seestrasse in Kusnacht – these were the actualities which made demands upon me and proved to me again and again that I really existed, that I was not a blank page whirling about in the winds of the spirit, like Nietzsche.' Here he was again, as he had been in the garden of his father's parsonage, staring at the stone jutting out from the wall, asking himself: am

I the stone or is the stone me? 'Whenever I thought that I was the stone, the conflict ceased.'

There had been early signs of friction with Freud, when Jung began to take his first steps on the path to his own theory about the libido. In June 1910, Jung had written to Freud about a talk he had given on 'Symbolism' to a group of Swiss psychiatrists in Appenzell – the most traditional of Swiss cantons, still deeply embroiled in the superstitions and occult of Alpine people cut off from the more modern ways of the towns. His lecture had been received with enthusiasm, he told Freud, and he promised to send him a copy. Apart from the logical, he posited, there was another language based on symbols and images. Logical thinking was thinking in words. Analogical or fantasy thinking was emotionally toned, pictorial and wordless, a rumination on materials belonging to the past – archaic and unconscious. Jung spent every evening immersed in 'the overflowing delights of mythology'.

'I read your essay with pleasure the day it arrived,' replied Freud, taking his time, promising to respond to it soon. His response, when it arrived, caused dismay in the Jung household. The letter only exists in copy form, the original being lost or destroyed. Freud suggested Jung's use of the word 'symbolical' was vague and not really correct when formulated in such general terms, and noted that Jung had 'wholly overlooked' the customary symbolism of the wedding ceremonial, wreaths, rings, and so on. But what Freud really disliked was the sentence: 'Sexuality destroys itself', which, he said, had provoked 'a vigorous shaking of the head'. Further, he did not like Jung's idea that modern dreams were a residue of the ancients: 'This would be more apt if the ancients, who lived in mythology, had not also had dreams.' As to myths, they were originally psychological, later overlaid by adaption to the calendar and thence projected into the realm of natural phenomena. In other words, there was not much in the essay Freud could agree with. 'As usual, I have mentioned only objections and made no comments on many things I liked very much,' he added by way of encouragement, but ending with the comment: 'Despite all its beauty, I think, the essay lacks ultimate clarity.'

It was the beginning of the parting of the ways, though neither man could yet admit it. Freud was for the knowable, based on scientific 'proof'; Jung was increasingly for the unknowable, where no final 'proof' could exist. In his reply to Freud he admitted the essay was just a 'rough sketch', but he held fast to the basics, so fast that it had to be expressed in italics: 'What it boils down to is a *conflict at the heart of sexuality itself*. The only possible reason for this conflict seems to be the *incest prohibition* which struck at the root of primitive sexuality.' Freud, still hoping his brilliant colleague would become his heir, answered with careful conciliation: he saw now that his criticism was quite premature but he warned that proof was nevertheless needed. He threw in another of his Wilhelm Busch humorous couplets, by way of apology: 'The ass is stupid, thence his name/The elephant is not to blame.'

Jung had managed to write Part One of *Transformations and Symbols of the Libido* without too much difficulty, but Part Two confronted him with appalling problems, plunging him into the nightmare of his own fantasies – pages and pages of rambling, incoherent material, embracing parapsychology, spiritualism, the occult and his new investigations into archaic symbols and rituals and myths. 'It seemed to me I was living in an insane asylum of my own making. I went about with all these fantastic figures: centaurs, nymphs, satyrs, gods and goddesses, as though they were patients and I was analysing them.' And astrology, for without astrology how could one understand mythology? 'I make horoscope calculations in order to find a clue to the core of psychological truth,' he wrote to Freud. He was like a detective, hunting for clues. He remembered the Burghölzli patient Emile Schweizer, the schizophrenic who thought he was God and that the sun had a penis. Was this not also archaic symbolism and myth? He remembered his assistant Honegger, who had worked on Schweizer's fantasies. After leaving the Burghölzli, Honegger had committed suicide, taking an overdose of morphine. Jung saw too late that Honegger had himself been suffering from incipient schizophrenia. He re-examined the theory of the death wish which he had first discovered with Fräulein Spielrein. Round and round he went, lost in his own labyrinth behind the doors of his *Cabinet*. 'I have tried to put the "symbolic" on a psychogenetic foundation, i.e., to show that in individual fantasy the *primum movens*, the individual conflict, material or form (whichever you prefer) is mythic, or mythologically typical,' he wrote to Freud, still trying to explain.

But that was all over now. Effectively, he was plunging into his own unconscious fantasies, back to the exalted and terrifying images of his childhood and adolescent dreams and visions. To his first biographer, Barbara Hannah, he admitted that he was in a deep depression the whole time he was writing *Transformations and Symbols of the Libido*: 'While working on the book I was haunted by bad dreams,' he admitted. 'It took me a long time to see that a painter could paint a picture and think the matter ended there and had nothing whatever to do with himself. And in the same way it took me several years to see that it, the *Psychology of the Unconscious* [i.e. *Transformations and Symbols*], can be taken as myself and that an analysis of it leads inevitably into an analysis of my own unconscious processes.' It went against everything he had learnt during his medical training about the need for scientific objectivity, but he could not stop. He heard voices dictating to him, and he had to obey. 'They would have torn me up, or I could have been split off,' he admitted years later. 'I had known that everything was at stake and that I had to take a stand for my convictions. I realised that the chapter 'The Sacrifice" meant my own sacrifice.'

Why was the break with Freud so bad? Emma thought she knew: she had touched on it in her letter to Freud of 6 November 1911. She thought Carl was so anxious waiting for the Herr Professor's opinion on 'Symbols' because it was a residue of the father (or mother) complex which was probably being resolved in the book. 'So perhaps it is all to the good that you did not react at once so as not to reinforce this father–son relationship,' she added, revealing how much she had learnt about psycho-analysis in general and her husband in particular over the years. Nor did Carl disagree, at least not in the early days. In 1909 he had been so grateful for Freud's support in the Fräulein Spielrein crisis that he had to keep telling himself he would have done the same for a friend: 'I had to tell myself this because my father-complex kept on insinuating that you would not take it as you did but would give me a dressing down more or less disguised in the mantle of brotherly love.' A year later he was still able to admit why he struggled to write to Freud: 'The reason for my resistance is my father-complex, my inability to come up to expectations (one's own work is garbage, says the devil) . . .'

Now he also recalled his first year at grammar school, when he had his vision of God sitting high above Basel cathedral and the wicked thought, the 'enormous turd falls upon the sparkling new roof, shatters it, and breaks the walls of the cathedral asunder', leaving him with 'an enormous, indescribable relief', so that he wept for happiness and gratitude. It was then that it dawned on him for the first time that God could also be something terrible, not only good, and split Carl embraced the idea: 'I am a devil or a swine,' he thought. 'I am infinitely depraved.' He never spoke about it, nor the phallus dream, nor his carved manikin, but kept everything hidden away. 'My entire youth can be understood in terms of this secret.' It was his great achievement, he felt, not to disclose the secret to anyone, but it induced 'an almost unendurable loneliness'. In time he would tell Emma. Finally, when he was sixty-five, he wrote it down in the 'Protocols' which became the basis of *Memories, Dreams, Reflections*.

Jung held his secret so close that few people noticed any difference in him, seeing only Personality No. 1. He was always busy, always on the move. By August he was away on military service again, quickly followed by another of his trips to America, leaving Emma to placate his patients and see to all his correspondence as usual. He did not get back until the beginning of November. Away from home he was released from his demons. His letters to Emma are full of vitality, with no sign of Personality No. 2. First he gave a series of lectures in New York on 'The Theory of Psychoanalysis'. This covered many of the same ideas as *Transformations and Symbols*, but the style was quite different, clear and lucid with no ramblings or confusions. Speaking with impressive fluency in English, albeit with a strong Swiss accent, he pinpointed the differences between his own and Freud's approach fairly, describing Freud's concept of the libido as 'an exclusively sexual need' whereas he saw it 'in the more general sense of passionate desire'. It was only in his lecture on the Oedipus complex that he described Freud's definition as 'too narrowly restrictive'. He also gave two-hour-long seminars every day, addressing scores of psychiatrists and neurologists, and clinical lectures at Bellevue Hospital and the New York Psychiatric Institute on Ward Island, and he spoke at the New York Academy of Medicine. After New York he travelled to Chicago to check on his old patient Medill McCormick and treat some new ones, many of whom later became his patients in Kusnacht. Then he travelled on to Baltimore and thence to Washington where he met Medill's cousin, Theodore Roosevelt, but also visited the other district of Washington – black Washington, where the poverty was in shocking contrast to rich white Washington. He was keen to treat and analyse the 'Negro' patients in a local asylum, which he did, using them as research material in much the same way as he had used the inmates of the Burghölzli asylum.

Throughout his tour of America, Personality No. 1 prevailed, with Carl exuding energy, charm and charisma. To catch a glimpse of Personality No. 2 you have to look elsewhere, to the black-and-white studio portrait photograph which accompanied an article and long interview in the *New York Times* on Sunday 29 September. Here Jung looks very different: eyes hard and dark behind his gold-rimmed spectacles, mouth shut tight beneath the small moustache; no smiles, no charm, and none of his usual robust humour.

Carl Jung, New York, 1912.

'America Facing its Most Tragic Moment' ran the alarming headline, followed by a series of equally alarming thoughts about the current state of America, a country Jung had visited three times, none for more than a few weeks. The interviewer set out Dr Jung of Switzerland's theory of the unconscious: 'He believes that, if a man can understand his hidden motives and impulses, he comes into a new power.' The word 'unconscious' signified 'all the facts we refuse to face'. Jung's classrooms and clinics were constantly crowded, wrote the reporter, baffling other doctors.

Jung was well on the way to becoming a *succès fou*, and this was only increased by the combative nature of his comments. 'When I see so much refinement and sentiment as I see in America I look always for an equal amount of brutality. The pair of opposites – you find them everywhere,' he opened, firing on all cylinders. He found a lot of prudery in the United States, he wrote, which was always the cover for brutality. This is what America needed to address. 'It seems to me you are about to discover yourselves.' Listing the country's past achievements he noted that in the present era America did not appear to know it was in danger. A choice had to be made. Americans had built their big cities with their theatres and clubs and cathedrals, all ready and waiting to be used to some great end once they discovered themselves. They should stop hiding from themselves. Then their success in the big achievements of art and literature would astound Europe as their big business and philanthropy did now. Conquerors descend to the level of those they conquer, he suggested. 'I notice that your Southerners speak with the Negro accent,' he continued, apparently oblivious to overstepping the line, and then, right over the top now: 'your women are coming to walk more and more like the Negro.'

Allowing for some deliberate exaggeration for effect, this was still wild and provocative, crazy stuff. Carl was letting Personality No. 2 freewheel, and once he was in his stride there was no stopping him. Had Emma been with him it might have been different. But she wasn't. 'In America,' he preached:

your women rule their homes because the men have not yet learned to love them, it takes much vital energy to be in love . . . The American husband is very indignant when he comes to me for treatment . . . and I tell him it's because he is brutal on one hand and prudish on the other . . . You think your young girls marry European husbands because they are ambitious for titles . . . I say, they like the way European men make love, and they like to feel we are a little dangerous. They are not happy with their American husbands because they are not afraid of them.'

Jung himself later said of this period of his life: 'The journey from cloud-cuckoo-land back to reality lasted a long time . . . Pilgrim's Progress.'

At home in Kusnacht, Emma waited for Carl's return. 'Dear Professor Freud,' she wrote on 10 September 1912, unaware of how grave the situation between her husband and Freud would shortly become. 'The offprints of Part II of "Transformations and Symbols" have just come out and you must be the first to receive one.' She went on with 'heartfelt sympathy' to share the worry and the hope that Freud's daughter Mathilde, who had been very ill, would soon recover. 'We had a dismal summer too, the children had whooping cough and now measles; Carl was away nearly all summer; since Saturday he has been on to America after spending only one day here between military service and departure. I have so much to do now that I don't let too much libido travel after him to America, it might so easily get lost on the way. Please greet all your dear ones from me and give my best wishes to your daughter. With kindest regards, Emma Jung.' The letter was full of warmth, reaching out to Freud and his family. She also confided in him about her 'libido', which she says she has to protect. Libido was still a term in transition then, everyone using it for their own purposes. For Emma it sounds more like 'out of sight, out of mind': that is, do not think too much about what Carl was up to in America. Reserve your energy for your own life.

Once Carl was back from America all Emma's diplomacy was undone. Carl turned against Freud with a vengeance, unable to come to terms with his rejection of *Transformations and Symbols of the Libido* – that is, Freud's rejection of Carl's very self. He saw through his little tricks, he wrote in a furious letter on 18 December, using the French word *truc*: 'You go around sniffing out all the symptomatic actions in your vicinity, thus reducing everyone to the level of sons and daughters who blushingly admit the existence of their faults. Meanwhile you remain on top as the father, sitting pretty. For sheer obsequiousness nobody dares to pluck the prophet by the beard and inquire for once what you would say to a patient with a tendency to analyse the analyst instead of himself. You would certainly ask him: "*Who's* got the neurosis?"'

Freud knew the answer. 'As regards Jung,' he wrote to Ernest Jones, 'he seems all out of his wits, he is behaving quite crazy. After some tender letters he wrote me one of utter insolence . . .' To Ferenczi he wrote that Jung was 'behaving like a florid fool and a brutal fellow, which he certainly is'. The love affair between Freud and Jung was well and truly over.

* * *

Around Christmas, Carl had another significant dream. He was in a magnificent Italian loggia, high in the tower of a castle, with pillars, marble floor and balustrade, sitting on a gold Renaissance chair in front of a table of rare beauty made of an emerald-like green stone. His children were sitting at the table too. Suddenly a white bird like a dove descended and came to rest on the table. He signed to the children to be still so as not to frighten the bird away, whereupon it transformed into a little girl, about eight years old, with golden blonde hair. She ran off with the children to play amongst the colonnades of the castle. When she came back she put her arms tenderly round his neck, then transformed back into the dove, which then spoke to him in a human voice: 'Only in the first hours of the night can I transform myself into a human being, while the male dove is busy with the twelve dead.' Then it flew off into the blue air and Carl awoke.

What could it signify, this dream? He thought of the twelve apostles, the twelve months of the year, the signs of the zodiac, but he found no solution. More dreams followed, all echoing the kind of dreams he had had when he was a boy, taking him back through the layers of time, to ancient castles and tombs and burial vaults, down, down, deeper and deeper into his unconscious. But they were unable to relieve his conscious mind, which remained disorientated 'as if under constant inner pressure. At times this became so strong that I suspected there was some psychic disturbance in myself.' Finally, he decided the only solution was to submit himself consciously to his own unconscious.

First, a memory from his eleventh year surfaced, the time when he had gone through an extreme crisis and started to build houses and castles with gates and vaults, 'passionately' at first with building blocks, then outside in the garden with stones and mud. 'To my astonishment, this memory was accompanied by a good deal of emotion.' He realised he had to re-establish contact with that period and that self. He had to overcome endless resistances but finally he resigned himself: he went out into the garden and started looking for suitable stones along the lake shore and in the shallow water, building 'cottages, a castle, whole villages, a church. But the altar was missing.' He didn't know what to do about that, till, one day, walking along the shore, he caught sight of a red stone, a four-sided pyramid about an inch and a half high. 'I placed it in the middle under the dome, and as I did so, I recalled the underground phallus of my childhood dream. This connexion gave me a feeling of satisfaction.'

Every day now, after taking his midday meal with Emma and the children in the *Stube* with its long windows looking out over the lake, Carl would go out into the garden, weather permitting, to build and play like the child he once was, till the first of his afternoon patients arrived. And he went back to it every evening, day after day. He asked himself: 'Now, really, what are you about? You are building a small town, and doing it as if it were a rite!' There was no answer to the question, only an inner certainty that he was discovering his own myth. The activity released a stream of fantasies which he later wrote down and illustrated, much like a medieval manuscript. From then on, every time he came to a blank wall in his life, he painted a picture or hewed a stone. 'Father would be down there fitting rocks together,' Franz remembered. 'He was a genius at that. He would build towers and houses and churches until he had whole villages. I would cut reeds for the roof beams and fill the little houses with sand so they wouldn't fall down.'

'My father says he chose. I do not believe he chose,' said Franz. 'I believe he had no choice. Can you imagine what it must be to think that you might be going mad? That you might fall for ever into the void?' It was a crisis which his father could no longer avoid. 'For years after he and Freud parted, my father could do no work,' said Franz. 'He placed a gun in his night-stand, and said that when he could bear it no longer he would shoot himself. Other people fell away, and he was alone . . . Think of my mother. Think of her. Can you imagine living with a man who slept with a gun by his bed and painted pictures of circles all day?'

What indeed was Emma to make of it? In 1912 she was thirty, married for nine years, the mother of four young children and the wife of a man who locked himself away in his *Cabinet* for hours on end, or played in the garden, building stone and mud villages, castles and churches. How could she tell anyone about it? Who would understand? In the old days she could have confided in Freud, but no longer.

It was all the more puzzling because outwardly so much carried on as normal. Patients came and went, the children played in the garden alongside their father, the housemaids went about their work cleaning and dusting, the cook cooked, the gardener gardened. Emma oversaw it all, giving everyone their daily duties, helping the children with their homework, and disciplining them, because Carl had no wish to do so, had no wish, really, to act as a father at all. But she also carved out time for herself, reading and writing at her desk by the window over-looking the lake, continuing her own researches. Because, as

227

Freud noted, Emma was not only charming, but clever and ambitious too.

All the while Carl's Personality No. 1 functioned alongside Personality No. 2 with no outward sign of conflict. 'It was most essential for me to have a normal life in the real world as a counterpoise to that inner world. My family and my profession remained the base to which I could always return, assuring me that I was an actually existing, ordinary person,' he wrote, again and again. Years later he acknowledged it was only Emma and the children who had got him through this period of semi-madness after the split with Freud: 'My family and my profession always remained a joyful reality and a guarantee that I also had a normal existence.' By his own account it was not until the end of the First World War that he emerged from the darkness and confusion.

11

Ménage à Trois

Besides her husband's fragile mental state, Emma had another recurring problem. As early as January 1910, just seven years into their marriage, Carl had written to Freud airily declaring he had decided the prerequisite of a good marriage was the licence to be unfaithful. There must have been a row with Emma about it, because she 'staged a number of jealous scenes, groundlessly', as Carl had put it. 'At first my objectivity got out of joint (rule 1 of psychoanalysis: principles of Freudian psychology apply to everyone except the analyser) but afterwards snapped back again, whereupon my wife also straightened herself out brilliantly.' The two sentences follow on, one from the other, but there appears to be no connexion between the two in Carl's mind. Emma, usually so contained, beside herself with jealousy, humiliated, making 'scenes'; Carl denying everything, protesting his innocence. It was happening all over again.

Polygamy had been on Jung's mind for some time. At first he could only envy cheerful polygamists such as Max Eitingon, the doctor at the Burghölzli, or Otto Gross, Jung's one-time patient with the wife who let him do pretty much as he pleased. 'I've never really had a mistress and am the most innocent of spouses,' as he'd written to Freud in March 1909. But Emma already had her suspicions because in another letter to Freud in the same month Jung admitted: 'the devil can use even the best of things for the fabrication of filth. Meanwhile I have learnt an unspeakable amount of marital wisdom, for until now I had a totally inadequate idea of my polygamous components despite all self-analysis.' He knew how to lay that devil now, he wrote, but he had been 'churned up hellishly inside'. Through all the drama and pain, his relationship with his wife had 'gained enormously in assurance and depth'.

But, as Emma knew, the problem was not only Carl. Women seemed to find Herr Doktor Jung irresistible. 'I really cannot remember whether I have already told you that Sister Moltzer is reproaching herself for having painted too black a picture of Fräulein Boeddinghaus,' a disingenuous Jung wrote to Freud in September 1910. 'Between the two ladies there is naturally a loving jealousy over me.' Naturally. Both women were volunteer nurses at the Burghölzli, where Jung still treated some patients. Sister Moltzer assisted Jung in his work while training to be a psychoanalyst herself.

Jung knew that many men in his circle kept mistresses, most of them in secret. In addition to Eitingon and Gross, there was Ernest Jones, who ended up being blackmailed, Ferenczi, who even had an affair with the daughter of the woman who was his mistress, and later Oscar Pfister, one of the Zürich Protestant pastors connected to the Burghölzli. Often, in those early days of the psychoanalytic movement, the mistresses were patients or former patients. Only Freud seems to have steered more or less clear, in spite of the gossip about his unmarried sister-in-law, Minna. To his American friend, James Putnam, Freud explained in 1915: 'I stand for an infinitely freer sexual life, although I myself have made very little use of such freedom.' And to Jung: 'My Indian summer of eroticism that we spoke of on our trip has withered lamentably under the pressure of work. I am resigned to being old and no longer even think continually of growing old.'

An underlying problem was the fear of pregnancy. 'All is well with us, except for the worry (another false alarm, fortunately) about the blessing of too many children,' Jung had written to Freud in May 1911. 'One tries every conceivable trick to stem the tide of these little blessings, but without much confidence. One scrapes along, one might say, from one menstruation to the next. The life of civilised man certainly does have its quaint side.' He didn't need to tell Freud, who, after fathering six children with Martha, had decided the only solution was abstinence. A subject rarely discussed was prostitution. The old town of Zürich was teeming with prostitutes, the sordid underbelly of a clean, prosperous, upright society. And God's punishment? The scourge of syphilis. If Carl watched his father crack up and die an early death from an unnamed torment, Emma watched her father die in terrible pain from syphilis, blind, shunned and shamed. It bound them deeply together, Emma and Carl, the horror of their two fathers' deaths.

By 1912 rumours were rife that Jung was having an affair with the volunteer nurse Maria Moltzer, who had come to the Burghölzli to get away from her family in Holland, rebelling against her father, the powerful proprietor of the Bols gin family business. Even Freud in Vienna had heard the rumours. Members of Emma's family and close friends have said that in the course of their long marriage Emma threatened divorce three times. The Maria Moltzer 'infatuation' may have been one time, not because Emma wanted to end her marriage, but to give Carl a fright – bring him into line – because deep down she knew he loved her. The last thing Carl wanted was divorce. Whenever Emma threatened to leave him he fell ill with stomach cramps, influenza, bouts of depression. And whenever one of the women started making demands, seriously threatening their marriage, he fell into a panic. Infatuation was Carl's problem, not discontent with his marriage. 'Except for moments of infatuation my affection is lasting and reliable,' he explained to Freud.

But now Emma was confronted not only with the Maria Moltzer affair. There was another relationship too, one quite different from the rest. With the sure instinct of a worried wife Emma sensed this was much more than the usual infatuation. Jung, already teetering on madness, seemed to be losing his wits.

The woman in question was Antonia Wolff, the same Fräulein Wolff who had only recently attended the Weimar Congress, with apparently no threat to Emma. There she sits in the front row of the famous photograph, a thin, intense, frowning, unconfident young woman, two seats away from Emma, who is smiling, elegant, more confident now that the threat of Sabina Spielrein has passed, with Maria Moltzer four places to her right and Martha Boeddinghaus – that other admirer of Carl's – three to her left. And behind them stands Carl, bending solicitously over Emma as though to say: 'You are mine, and I am yours.'

'A new discovery of mine,' was how Carl had described Wolff to Freud in his letter to finalise the Weimar conference arrangements: 'a remarkable intellect with an excellent feeling for religion and philosophy'. Knowing the significance of Jung's shift away from the 'provable' science of psychoanalysis to the unprovable, transcendental realms of myth and religion, and knowing Jung's weakness for such women, Freud no doubt foresaw the dangers. But not Emma. Not yet. Unsure of herself, so serious she 'never laughed', and not obviously attractive, Fräulein Wolff was probably the last of those women in the front row Emma felt she had cause to worry about.

Antonia – Toni – Wolff had started out as one of Carl's patients. Her mother had brought her to see Jung in the summer of 1910, on the recommendation of friends, and having consulted various other doctors about her profoundly depressed daughter. The problem had begun some six months earlier after the death of Toni's father on Christmas Eve 1909, probably from cancer. Toni was twenty-one, the eldest of three daughters, and no one knew why she had fallen into such a deep, inconsolable state. The family lived on the Zürich Berg, the exclusive enclave where many of Jung's admiring *Pelzmäntel* ladies lived. The Wolffs were leading members of old wealthy Zürich, Herr Wolff having made a great deal of money importing silks from the Far East, where he had lived for many years. When he finally came back to Switzerland he was in his early forties and soon married Toni's mother, twenty-year-old Anna Elizabeth Sutz. Their villa on Freiestrasse was filled with Japanese antiques and beautiful paintings and a fine library.

Toni and her sisters, Erna and Susi, had a childhood in Zürich as privileged as Emma Rauschenbach's in Schaffhausen. Toni was academic, highly intelligent, interested in philosophy, mythology and religion, but emotionally fragile, even as a girl.

Erna wanted nothing more than a good marriage, a good house and children; and Susi was unconventional, temperamental and artistic. Toni was her father's favourite, permitted to spend evenings with him in his *Herrenzimmer*, the room in fine villas reserved exclusively for the men. Like Emma, Toni had been prevented from continuing her studies at university in favour of the traditional path of a good marriage. To that purpose her father sent her off to one of Switzerland's many housekeeping schools for young ladies, and for some further months in England. But this was not to interfere with the main task. 'A woman who does not have the household completely under control and in all details is a failed creature; yet her whole life does not have to revolve around it,' Herr Wolff wrote to his daughter by way of loving explanation. 'It is self-evident that in addition to this you are free to pursue more serious intellectual and aesthetic studies, but not to the exclusion of practical ones.'

By the time her mother brought her to Herr Doktor Jung at 228 Seestrasse, Toni Wolff's depression was entrenched. The chasm left by her father's death could not be filled and her unofficial studies in philosophy and theology at the university, which is all her father had finally permitted, had led to nothing substantial. She was lost and disturbed. Even so, the extent of it was hard to understand. What was it about her favoured relationship with her father that had so derailed her? At first Jung made no headway. But once they talked mythology and symbolism, the subject currently obsessing Jung, embroiled in writing *Transformations and Symbols of the Libido*, they found their common ground and her depression began to lift. To Jung's pleasure Fräulein Wolff was also interested in astrology, and they spent many hours drawing up astrological charts. Carl

Meier, a young doctor who later left the Burghölzli to become Jung's assistant, described Jung at this time as being 'very near psychosis' himself, his crisis resembling 'a schizophrenic episode'. Jung used to say Toni Wolff was the one case of schizophrenia he had been able to cure.

Unlike Sabina Spielrein, who had been an official patient at the Burghölzli asylum, Toni Wolff was Jung's private patient so there are no proper case notes to record her treatment, only a general sense that by September 1911 she was essentially 'cured' – and well enough to attend the Weimar Congress. By then the treatment had moved to its next stage, just as Eugen Bleuler at the Burghölzli always advised, and the patient was set to work: in this case going to Zürich Central Library to help Jung with his research. Not long after the congress Jung had written to Freud about his ill-humour: 'I was furious because of something that happened in my working arrangements. But I won't bother you with that . . .' Then in a later letter: 'With us everything is peaceful and serene and my wife is working conscientiously at etymology.' There are many references to etymology in *Transformations and Symbols of the Libido*. Seeing the dangers, Emma must have insisted on helping Carl with the research herself.

Toni Wolff was a strange, other-worldly being. 'Intense' is the word most often used to describe her. She rarely laughed, hardly ever smiled, though when she did it lit up her face. Her sister Susi, the lively one who married Hans Trüb, another of the Zürich group of psychoanalysts, described Toni as 'never totally in life', and never coming fully alive except through Jung. 'Toni was all spirit. It was almost as if she *had* no body,' Franz Jung recalled. 'A ghost-like figure, haughty and forbidding' was how another contemporary described her. 'She had very changeable looks, sometimes beautiful and sometimes quite plain,' said another: 'Her extraordinarily brilliant eyes – mystic's eyes – were always expressive.' These days Toni dressed more elegantly, in the wealthy Swiss bourgeois style: hats and gloves, expensive shoes, a long black cigarette-holder in her hand because she was an inveterate smoker. She lived with her mother at the family villa on Freiestrasse until her mother died in 1940, at which point she moved into an apartment in her sister Erna's house, taking her personal maid with her. She had few real friends, and if at all, she was the kind of woman who preferred men. 'If you were a woman she had to lord it over you. If you were a man it was peaches and cream.' Many found her unapproachable, but she had a great gift. 'In her presence, inner pressure became images,' said Tina Keller, another of the Zürich group around Carl and Emma. 'She helped Jung see his images and talk with them.'

The relationship with Fräulein Wolff started at a time of crisis for Jung, battling with the loss of Sigmund Freud, his father figure, stirring up all the old feelings about his own father: 'After the parting of ways with Freud, a period of inner uncertainty began for me. It would be no exaggeration to call it a state of disorientation. I felt totally suspended in mid-air, for I had not yet found my own footing.' He started to develop a new method with his patients, not guiding them with psychoanalytic theory but waiting to see what they would tell him of their own accord – a conversation between two equals, sitting facing one another; the kind of approach that Freud, seated formally in a chair behind the analysand's couch, preserving professional objectivity, would disapprove of. Just at this jagged point in his life, entered Toni with her gift of seeing images and talking to them.

'Please write nothing of this to Carl,' as Emma had said to Freud, without mentioning Fräulein Wolff, and more likely thinking of Maria Moltzer.

At home, Carl's odd behaviour continued. He was frequently so overwrought he had to do yoga exercises to hold his emotions in check. At the midday meal with Emma and the children he might be completely silent and distracted, lost in his own thoughts, and the children had to sit quietly and stop fidgeting. Equally he might talk his head off, enchanting them with his stories, throwing his head back, laughing 'down to his shoes', as Franz put it. Then it was back to his *Cabinet* again. Or out into the garden, walking up and down, talking away to Philemon, one of the mythological figures from his unconscious who had first appeared to him in a dream representing superior insight. 'He [Philemon] was a mysterious figure to me. At times he seemed to me quite real, as if he were a living personality. I went walking up and down the garden with him, and to me he was what Indians call a guru,' Carl wrote later. But the guru is a separate person from the seeker of wisdom, whereas Philemon was all Carl.

By autumn 1913 Jung feared he had a psychic disturbance. He knew there had been some mental illness in earlier generations of his family, and that his mother heard voices and had to go 'away' when he was a child. 'Then I came to this. "Perhaps my unconscious is forming a personality that is not me, but which is insisting on coming through to expression." I don't know why exactly, but I knew to a certainty that the voice that had said my writing was art had come from a woman . . . Well I said very emphatically to this voice that what I was doing was not art, and I felt a great resistance grow up within me . . .' If it was merely art, then it was not symbolic. Years later he wrote: 'I knew for a certainty that the voice had come from a woman, a talented psychopath who had a strong transference to me.' It was Maria Moltzer's.

In September there was another Psychoanalytic Congress, this time in Munich. Jung's talk was about 'Psychological Types' and the idea that people could be divided into extroverts or introverts, terms which were quite new at that time. It was an important, imaginative insight – Carl at his best. But his emotional state was not good. 'Two years ago there was robust gaiety and exuberant vitality in Jung's booming laughter,' said one attendee, 'but his seriousness now is made up of pure aggression, ambition and intellectual brutality.' Freud and Jung talked politely, but it was all over between them.

A month later Jung was on the train to join Emma and the children for a weekend in Schaffhausen, to celebrate his mother-in-law Bertha's fifty-seventh birthday, when he had what he called an overpowering vision: a monstrous flood covered all the land between the North Sea and the Alps. He realised it represented a frightful catastrophe, the whole sea turning to blood and thousands of bodies drowned. The Alps of Switzerland grew higher and higher to avoid the flood. What could it mean? In October he wrote to Freud, finally breaking off relations completely and resigning his position as editor of the *Jahrbuch*. He also started to write his secret diary again, the one he had abandoned when he became engaged to Emma. His last entry then had been: 'I am no longer alone with myself, and I can only artificially recall the scary and beautiful feeling of solitude. This is the shadow side of the fortune of love.'

In November 1913 Ernest Jones reported to Freud from America that an acquaintance of theirs 'considers Jung to be mentally disordered'. Jung saw it differently:

When I had the vision of the flood in October of that year 1913, it happened at a time that was significant for me as a man. At that time, in the fortieth year of my life, I had achieved everything that I had wished for myself. I had achieved honour, power, wealth, knowledge, and every human happiness. Then my desire for the increase of these trappings ceased, the desire ebbed and horror came over me. The vision of the flood seized me and I felt the spirit of the depths, but I did not understand him. Yet he drove me with unbearable inner longing and I said: My soul, where are you? Do you hear me? I speak, I call you – are you there? I have returned. I am here again.

This is the beginning of chapter one of Jung's visionary *Liber Novus – The Red Book* as it is now known – a work of extraordinary creative imagination which he began at this time of crisis and continued to work on for the next sixteen years, leaving it unfinished. The theme of the book is how Jung regains his soul which he felt he had lost during the years since giving up his secret diary and his marriage to Emma. It takes the form of conversations with various biblical, mythological and symbolic figures Jung encounters along the way. First he wrote the encounters in a series of notebooks bound in black leather, the 'Black Books'; later he transcribed them into a massive red leather-bound tome, 189 pages of Old Italic script, sometimes Latin, mostly German, accompanied by brilliantly coloured manuscript illuminations, the translation of his emotions into symbolic images, in the style of a medieval Bible. The first initial of the first page, the 'D' of *Der Weg des Kommenden*, 'The Way of What Is to Come', is quite beautiful, reminding one that the landscape paintings Jung did in Paris as a young man already had an otherworldliness to them. The 'D' is red, a snake wearing a crown rising from a black cauldron of fire on the stem. It is set in a Swiss landscape, a lake with a sailing boat, a green fish and plants in the foreground, village with church spire in the middle ground, chain of Alps in the background, the whole dominated by a luminous blue. The text is in Latin, from Luther's Bible: 'Isaiah said: Who hath believed our report? And to whom is the arm of the Lord revealed?'

When Jung finally put the *Liber Novus* to one side it lay undisturbed in his *Cabinet* for the next twenty years, and would not be published until 2009. It comes from the period Jung described as 'the most important time in my life. Everything else is to be derived from this.' The only people he shared these inner experiences with at the time were a few 'close associates'. And Emma, and Toni Wolff.

On 12 December 1913 Jung was sitting alone at his desk in his *Cabinet* in the dim light of the stained-glass windows depicting the Crucifixion and Passion of Christ, 'thinking over his fears', and he resolved to again let himself drop, deep down into his unconscious. 'It was as though the ground literally gave way beneath my feet, and I plunged down into dark depths. I could not fend off a feeling of panic.' He landed in a soft, sticky mass, in complete darkness, but with a feeling of relief at having landed. Once his eyes got used to the gloom, a deep twilight, he saw the entrance to a dark cave, guarded by a dwarf with leathery, mummified skin:

> I squeezed past him through the narrow entrance and waded knee deep through icy water to the other end of the cave where, on a projecting rock, I saw a glowing red crystal. I grasped the stone, lifted it, and discovered a hollow underneath. At first I could make nothing out, but then I saw that there was running water. In it a corpse floated by, a youth with blond hair and a wound in the head. He was followed by a gigantic black scarab and then by a red, newborn sun, rising up out of the depths of the water.

He tried to replace the stone, but a fluid welled out. It was blood. 'A thick jet of it leaped up, and I felt nauseated. It seemed to me the blood continued to spurt for an unendurably long time. At last it ceased and the vision came to an end.' Dark caves and projecting rocks and precious stones – just like the dreams and visions of his childhood.

He realised it was a hero-myth, a drama of death and renewal. Six days later he had a dream: he was with an unknown brown-skinned man, a savage, in a lonely rocky landscape. It was before dawn and the eastern sky was bright, the stars fading. 'Then I heard Siegfried's horn sounding over the mountains and I knew we had to kill him.' Siegfried appeared high on the crest of a mountain, the first rays of the rising sun behind him. He drove with furious speed down the precipitous slope, in a chariot made of the bones of the dead. 'When he turned the corner, we shot at him, and he plunged down, struck dead.' Now Carl, the dreamer, fled, filled with disgust and remorse at having killed something so great and beautiful, and frightened that the murder might be discovered. But then there was a tremendous downfall of rain and he knew it would wipe out all the traces. 'I had escaped the danger of discovery; life could go on, but an unendurable feeling of guilt remained.' As he tried to go to sleep the voice spoke again: 'If you do not understand the dream you must shoot yourself,' it said. He thought of his military service revolver in the drawer of his night table, loaded, and felt very frightened.

Emma, understanding more about Carl's complex personality now, and fearing for his emotional stability, saw to it that everyday life at Seestrasse carried on as normal. The children, Aggi aged ten, Gret eight, Franz six and Marianne (known as Nannerl) aged three, still noticed nothing unusual: their father saw patients, as many as seven a day five days a week, he gave lectures, kept up a lively correspondence, went on his travels and Alpine hikes, took friends sailing on Lake Zürich, and every day if the weather was fine he took coffee with their mother on the terrace after the midday meal, often with visitors, because there were always visitors. The only difference was that Fräulein Wolff seemed to be around more and more. The children were told to call her Tante Toni and be nice to her, and to include her in family life. They resented it deeply and couldn't understand it. They didn't know that a year earlier their father had had the dream which caused him to embark on a relationship with a woman he had known for three years – the dream of the dove that turned into a little girl with golden hair – and that he had almost let himself drown in despair one day, swimming in the lake, trying to work it all out.

The children didn't like Tante Toni. She wasn't good with children, didn't know how to speak to them, and she didn't care for card games. They took to playing pranks on her when their father was absent. Or their mother. Because although it was an agony for Emma to have to bear what was fast becoming a *ménage à trois*, she never allowed the children to be impolite to Tante Toni. She knew Carl was in a desperate state, despite outward appearances, and she decided that somehow or other she was going to have to come to terms with it.

On 18 March 1914 Emma and Carl's fifth child, Emma Helene, known as Helene, or 'Lil', was born. The baby was another of what Carl called their 'little blessings', but this would be the last. The family say Emma was angry to find herself pregnant again – angry with her fate as a woman, and angry with Carl who did not have to endure the pain of labour or the restrictions of motherhood. Only two weeks after the birth at home in Seestrasse, Carl left for Ravenna on a bicycle tour with his friend Hans Schmid. Emma and the baby went to stay with her mother at Schaffhausen, where she was the unhappy recipient of cheerful postcards telling her all about the beauty of the Ravenna mosaics. Carl's mother and Trudi moved into the house to help the children's maid look after the other four. When Carl returned he and Emma moved into separate bedrooms. There were to be no more children. Emma was thirty-two.

That spring, Jung embarked on a flurry of resignations and withdrawals. On 20 April 1914 he resigned as president of the International Psychoanalytic Association, along with fifteen other Swiss members, all rejecting 'the papal policies of the

Viennese', to which Freud reacted, writing to Karl Abraham: 'So we are rid of them at last, the brutal holy Jung and his pious parrots.' Ten days later Jung resigned as lecturer in the medical faculty of the University of Zürich, though no great effort was made to persuade him to stay. By 24 July he was in London at the Psycho-Medical Society giving a talk, 'On Psychological Understanding', describing Freud's methodology as reductive, comparing it to someone who tried to understand a Gothic cathedral through its mineralogical aspect. On the 28th he was in Aberdeen addressing the British Medical Association on 'The Importance of the Unconscious in Psychopathology'. Outwardly confident and combative, inwardly fragile, Jung could not stop working. 'As a psychiatrist I became worried, wondering if I was not on the way to "doing a schizophrenia" as we said in the language of those days,' he admitted years later to a friend. 'I was just preparing a lecture on schizophrenia to be delivered at a congress in Aberdeen, and I kept saying to myself: "I'll be speaking of myself! Very likely I'll go mad after reading out this paper."'

Meanwhile the world itself was going mad. On 28 July, Austria declared war on Serbia. The following day the Tsar of Russia, Serbia's ally, mobilised his army along the Austrian border. On 1 August, Germany declared war on Russia. On the 2nd the Tsar signed a declaration of war. Three days later Britain declared war on Germany.

The sequence of events was so quick that many people found themselves in the wrong place and the wrong country. Prince Heinrich of Germany, the Kaiser's younger brother, was visiting his cousin Georgie, George V, at Buckingham Palace. The Dowager Tsarina of Russia was also in England, on her way to

Sandringham with her sister Alexandra, the Dowager Queen of Britain. All over Europe nannies and governesses, tutors, valets and ladies' maids, businessmen and diplomats, husbands and wives, raced for home. In Zürich a French theatre troupe had to cut short their stay. Italian bricklayers downed tools and made their way to Zürich Central Station, along with 42,000 German factory workers, waiters and hotel employees, some singing the patriotic 'Wacht am Rhein' as they marched up the Bahnhofstrasse with the Slavs and Russians, the Poles and Bohemians, carrying their small suitcases and cardboard boxes done up with string, making for the third-class carriages.

Carl wrote a hasty letter to Emma on 1 August: he had heard news that Switzerland was mobilising and had left Scotland immediately in order to get a place on a boat to Holland, since it was more likely he could get a train through Holland and Germany than through France. There was an enormous fleet under steam on the Firth of Forth. If Maria Moltzer was in Holland, he would bring her with him. 'Greet the children from me,' he ended his letter. 'And be kissed by me, my darling, your Carl.'

All the apocalyptic dreams and visions he had been experiencing were not signs of incipient schizophrenia, he decided, but premonitions of war from his subconscious. 'Finally I understood. And when I disembarked in Holland on the next day, nobody was happier than I.'

Cabaret Voltaire in the Niederdorfstrasse – 'an International Cabaret', as Ball described it. They opened their doors to a bemused public with an evening of 'Negro music', Tristan Tzara, the Rumanian poet, chanting *'Boum, boum boum – drabafja mo gere drabatja mo bonoooo'*, costumed in a cardboard suit of armour, his head covered by a cardboard box, robot-like. Emmy Hemmings appeared from behind a makeshift green curtain, lips bright red, kohl-black eyes, bright green pullover, standing in the spotlight beside the piano singing: 'This is how we live, this is how we live, this is how we die, this is how we murder our Kamaraden in the Dance of Death. Sleep on.' At the end of the evening she sold the song lyrics written on postcards to members of the public, collecting money, and thanking their friends in Russia and France, announcing that Dada stood for 'a rejection of War Fever and a disgust at petty-minded Bourgeois values – a new beginning and a return to the primitive'. The press was scathing. 'We reject this Bolshevism in art, as we do Bolshevism proper,' announced the *Winterthur Tageblatt*. The audience, mostly enthusiastic supporters from the Café Odeon, stamped their feet, shouted, threw orange peel and coins. A few students and passers-by in evening clothes joined in, but the orderly bourgeois of Zürich kept away. They had better things to do than watch *so en Schmarre* – such rubbish.

Vladimir Ilyich Ulyanov – Lenin – was able to enter Switzerland via Bern without even a passport in those early days of 1914, before suspicion of foreigners took hold. All he had to do was mention the highly respected socialist politician Hermann Greulich, who had worked with Marx and Engels on the First International, and he was in. He was not the only one. Soon Switzerland was awash with anarchists and leftists from all the surrounding countries, enthusiastically welcomed by the Swiss socialists but increasingly viewed with alarm by the rest. By September 1915 Robert Grimm, leading member of the Social Democrat Party, was organising a conference at Zimmerwald attended by Lenin and a contingent of communists and pacifists as well as socialists. Their call was for a new International and a reawakening of the class struggle. They were in little doubt that this war, dragging on for over a year now, was a capitalist imperialist war, setting worker against worker, when what they needed was unity to fight the real war: the class war.

Lenin and his wife Nadya stayed in Bern till February 1916 when they moved to Zürich. One of the main reasons was Zürich Central Library, much superior to the one in Bern, and the very same library Emma attended to pursue her studies whenever time and family permitted. Mostly Lenin worked on his thesis 'Imperialism, the Highest Stage of Capitalism', in which he argued that imperialism was the product of capitalism, capitalists being bound to extend their search for profit into territories where labour and raw materials were cheaper, with war the inevitable result. On Sundays when the library was shut, Lenin and his wife liked to walk up the Zürich Berg, finding a spot with a good view of the Alps and the lake, lying in the grass, both reading. First they lived at Geigerstrasse, but it was next to the Ruff sausage factory and the smell was awful. So they moved to Spiegel Gasse, not far from the Cabaret Voltaire, where they remained for the rest of their stay in Zürich, waiting for the call to return to Russia. They preferred the local Sussihof restaurant to the Café Odeon or the Kronenhalle, and Lenin loved his local bowling alley where he became a keen member of the club. The Swiss socialists were generous in their financial support of the couple, but the Lenins found they weren't very revolutionary. In April 1917 they suddenly disappeared, back to Russia and some real revolution.

During the early days of the war everyday life in Zürich went on much as before, only the gas lamps were turned low, making the streets more hazardous as night fell. The trams still ran, ringing their bells at bicyclists and automobilists, the *Droschken* drivers still stood by their stamping horses outside Central Station waiting for custom, the market gardeners still came down from the uplands of Forch on their farm carts every Tuesday and Thursday. The fowl market in Augustiner Platz was still as busy as ever. The commodities agents were quick to adjust to war, selling their stocks in Schneider-Creusot and Standard Oil in favour of General Motors, Baltimore and Ohio and Royal Dutch – American stocks, not European. Neutral Zürich thrived as a commercial and financial centre, with the tiny kiosk of the telegraph office at Central Station busy day and night.

But once it was realised the war would last longer than six months, agents switched to raw materials and foodstuffs, shifting goods out of the warehouses as fast as possible before all the borders were completely shut – the Basel frontier already gone but Geneva still open for the time being – buying sugar and coffee, cotton and coal, flour, rice, raisins, oats, noodles, tins of sardines, cocoa beans, condensed milk. *Hausfraus* who could afford it started to stockpile, dragging the food home with the help of their maids and storing it in the cellar. Shop windows started to empty. The Jelmoli department store ran out of rayon stockings, lampshades and perfumes. There were queues everywhere. The black market boomed. Gold was the answer, not paper money, which was useless.

At the city hall emergency measures were brought in: a strengthening of police powers and a limit to personal freedoms. Street demonstrations were banned. Everyone had to pull together, it was said. *Gasthofs* and hotel restaurants were henceforth to close by 11 p.m. Landsturm Battalions 54 and 57 and 58 stood at the ready in preparation for general mobilisation. New recruits assembled ramshackle in school yards across Zürich in the shade of the chestnut trees; young lads with woollen vests knitted by their mothers under their shirts; farm boys, office workers, shop assistants, tradesmen, apprentices, fitted out in caps and uniforms with red collars, heavy leather belts and sabres, not yet a military unit but getting there – set up not to fight the war, but to patrol the borders, to keep Switzerland safe. Whole divisions marched out of the yards and into the streets, officers on horseback keeping up the pace, flags flying, military bands playing, housewives in aprons waving from their doors, on their way to the barracks at Winterthur.

Carl was hardly back from his travels before he was called up to the Army Medical Corps, taking his rifle out of the cupboard in the front hall at Seestrasse, and donning his old uniform, ready to vaccinate hundreds of new recruits. Later he tended to the sick and occasional wounded. Later still he was deputed to the POW camps set up in neutral Switzerland, serving all sides in the war though mostly the officers, not the men. It was a shock for the good ladies of Zürich gathered in their starched Red Cross uniforms at Central Station, military band playing, waiting for the first train of French wounded from the Battle of the Marne, bunches of alpine roses in hand by way of welcome, to see half-dead soldiers carried off the train on stretchers or limping down the platform on crutches, or led along, eyes bandaged, blind. And these no older than their own sons and brothers and husbands patrolling the Swiss borders.

Military service for Jung never lasted more than a few weeks at a time. He wrote to Emma from one billet or another – describing his work, asking her to visit, send him fresh clothes, and bring him more books as his new work 'Psychological Types' began to take shape – signing off with his usual *Küsst Dich Dein Carl*, 'with kisses from your Carl'. But Emma could rarely visit, what with the demands of a new baby and four other children, and the house to keep going. Unlike Toni Wolff or Maria Moltzer, who could get away easily.

Carl loved Emma. But at the same time he held fast to his ideas on polygamy, assuring her it made no difference to the way he felt about her. As far as Carl was concerned, men and women were different: 'In a man this relationship is not exclusive. When the average man permits comparison of his wife to other women he says, "She is my wife among women." To the woman, though, the object that personifies the world to her is *my* husband, *my* children, in the midst of a relatively uninteresting world.' The man was free to have a family, pursue a career, have affairs; the woman remained confined to the home with little chance of a life outside – views not unusual for the times. Less usual was that Carl conducted his affairs openly, not in secret. Emma, meanwhile, remained monogamous and devoted. 'I think she had many admirers,' a friend of the Jungs later recalled. 'She was very beautiful.' But she would never have had an affair, thought the friend, because of her background and the type of person she was.

Inveterately fair-minded, Emma tried to do right by Toni Wolff, even by Maria Moltzer, but seemed unable to do right by herself, hardly recognising herself any more. In her distress she turned to Carl, as she always did, describing her predicament and her feelings of dissociation. He told her these feelings were a necessary outcome of the development of the personality. He had had them himself, so he understood. But all the promises and understanding in the world could not make up for the fact that she, still young, was now living the life of a celibate, standing by as other women enjoyed her husband's attentions. A photograph taken of Carl, Emma and the children on one of the rare occasions the family were able to visit him during the war, when he was at the Château d'Oex in Vaud overseeing British POWs, catches this moment in Emma's life painfully well. There stands Jung, large, vigorous, the confident pater familias dressed English-style in plus-fours and tweed jacket, arm round his son Franz, now aged nine, with three of his daughters ranged alongside, each one as interesting and characterful as the next, looking direct and unsmiling at the camera, with Lil off camera, presumably in the care of the children's nurse as she was only two. And there sits Emma, quietly elegant in long dark skirts, a white broderie anglaise blouse and dark jacket, brooch at the neck, feet neatly crossed, head bowed, her face in shadow hidden by the rim of her wide straw hat, almost invisible, hating to be photographed – a picture of misery.

'Dear Gretli,' Carl wrote cheerfully to his second daughter, in the Basel dialect:

Many thanks for your sweet letter. I have a lot to do. Today I have to go back up to the Bernese Oberland, way high up to the glacier. There are lots of Englishmen there. Tell Agathli that we have only two Gurkha officers left. They are all brown and have heads wrapped round with a turban. Yesterday I was up on a high mountain and we got horribly rained on. I was with an Englishman who had been imprisoned in Germany for almost three years. While we were climbing the mountain we saw hundreds of black salamanders. They all sat there on the path and looked at us as if we had lost our wits to be out walking in weather where only salamanders are out.

Many kisses from Papa

Carl seemed to be having a fine time at Château d'Oex, living in a comfortable hotel, in charge of the kind of English he liked – officers and gentlemen – far from the horrors of war. The food was not bad, the company agreeable, conversation being in English, and there was even free time for reading and cycling and hiking in the Alps. But Personality No. 2 was never far away.

'While I was there I sketched every morning in a notebook a small circular drawing, a mandala, which seemed to correspond to my inner situation at the time. With the help of these drawings I could observe my psychic transformations from day to day,' he wrote later, recalling his inner struggle to understand what was happening to him at the time. Day after day he drew his mandalas, dozens of them. 'My mandalas were cryptograms concerning the state of the self which were presented to me anew each day. In them I saw the self – that is, my whole being – actively at work. To be sure, at first I could only dimly understand them; but they seemed to me highly significant, and I guarded them like precious pearls.'

Toni Wolff was a frequent visitor at the Château d'Oex. Of all the people surrounding Jung at that time only Toni was able to follow him into his symbol-laden unconscious. Emma tried, but found it impossible. She was less 'spiritual' than Toni, less intellectual perhaps. 'Toni was so important for him; she had an understanding for it,' said Toni's sister Susi. 'She perhaps was able to encourage him and so gave him the faith in himself. Frau Jung wasn't able to do it.' It was Toni he needed when, battling with his unconscious, teetering on the edge, he worked on 'Transformations of the Libido' and *Liber Novus*. 'Phenomenologically one might classify it as a schizophrenic episode,' thought Carl Meier. 'But it was voluntary. He simply had the guts and courage to deal with these contents which nobody has experienced except schizophrenics.' In Meier's opinion, this was Jung's real pioneering work. And living proof of Jung's theory that crisis need not be negative, might in fact be the very thing which led to development and healing: 'creative illness' as it was later described. And it was Toni Wolff who was his confidante then, not Emma. 'Going into the depths, no, that wasn't her kind of fish,' according to Meier.

Though still living at her mother's, Toni now seemed to be at Seestrasse all the time, helping Carl with his research, joining the family for meals and teas, followed by long private walks and talks with Carl in the garden during the summer months, long hours shut away with Carl in his *Cabinet* during the winter. Carl and Emma and Toni. Toni and Emma and Carl. The children hated it more than ever. Tante Toni appeared in their home as if by right, interfering in their private family life, taking their father away from them, making their mother unhappy. And their mother did nothing about it. It was beyond belief.

The only meal Emma managed to keep sacrosanct was the midday meal, when Carl would emerge from seeing his patients in his *Cabinet* and take his place at the head of the table in the *Stube* overlooking the lake. As usual, he was sometimes totally silent, lost in his own thoughts, when the children had to sit quiet and stop fidgeting; or at other times loud and exuberant, full of stories and jokes and tricks, making everyone laugh, causing havoc. He might tease the maid, flick peas and meat across the table with his fork, or shout at the cook if he felt the food wasn't hot enough, the meat too tough, the vegetables overcooked, leaving the cook in tears. It was like having a sixth child. '*Also, hör uf Carl!*' Emma would remonstrate: 'Stop it, Carl!' whilst the children fell about laughing. They soon knew when there was licence for bad behaviour and when not: if they had guests and they were getting bored they might squabble, or tell silly jokes or start to sing. Or if it was their favourite chocolate pudding for dessert, perform their 'party trick', taught to them by their father: pick up your bowl, hold it close to the lips, and blow the chocolate across the table, all over the crisp white tablecloth. Carl or Emma might admonish them for these misdemeanours but they were rarely punished, neither parent having the inclination to do much about it. The most that happened was a threat, rarely carried out, to be locked for a while in the small room under the cellar stairs.

But it was no laughing matter when their father got into one of his rages. These came out of nowhere like an Alpine storm, terrifying the children. Only their mother seemed unperturbed. 'He doesn't mean it. He can't help it,' she explained to Agathe when she was old enough to understand. It was true: the storms did pass, but it was hard for the children to understand. It just depended which Papa you had at any one time. It was the same in the evenings. If their father was in an introverted mood he might just go back into his *Cabinet*, or he might stay in the *Stube* – there but not there, reading one of his books, smoking his pipe, oblivious, whilst they sat at the table doing their home-work or playing quietly at one of their board games. If on the other hand he was in an exuberant mood everyone was ener-gised, up for some fun, whilst their mother, the only grown-up in the room, did her knitting or needlework, overseeing the chaos till bedtime.

Emma was always busy. First thing every morning, once the children set off for school after a rushed breakfast – 6.15 in summer, 7.15 in winter, Swiss style – she dealt with the servants, formally, as was the custom: the cook, the three maids, and the gardener-cum-handyman who brought in the daily vegetables and flowers and went shopping with his wooden cart into Kusnacht village for groceries or fresh fish and Herr Doktor's tobacco, but never the meat which came by post from the family butcher in Schaffhausen. Then it was a long morning of corre-spondence, mostly business for Carl, often interrupted by one of his patients – placating them if he was running late, arranging their next appointment; then checking up on the midday meal before the children came running back from school, wanting to tell their mother about their morning, followed by the meal itself which might run this way or that, depending on Carl's mood. During the hot summer months it was often taken outside in the garden under the rose bower, but it was always rushed, the maids hurrying in and out with the dishes, because the children had hardly an hour. Then off they went again, along the country road, leather satchels on backs, past the farm through the meadow with the cows and along the lake to the village school, the girls in their pinafores and pigtails, Franz in short trousers and leather braces, barefoot in the summer.

Once a week a seamstress came to the house who sewed the 'whites' – underclothing – and twice a year a tailor arrived from London to keep Carl attired in the English style, though naturally not during wartime. For Carl, it was either his Swiss peasant clothes – dungarees or shorts, or baggy old trousers, and green gardening apron – or those of an English gentleman: tweed or linen jackets, shirts and ties, corduroy trousers and woollen cardigans straight from St James's. 'How lucky you English are because you have these aristocrats and we in Switzerland don't know whether to wear yellow boots with top hats,' as Jung once wrote to his English friend Maurice Nicoll.

Emma's afternoons were more of the same, mostly revolving around Carl: the appointments diary, the social diary for visits, receptions, lunches, relations, family friends, unexpected guests from abroad – everything passed through her hands as she sat at her writing desk by the window in the *Stube*. And always Carl himself, bursting out of his *Cabinet* between appointments, wanting to know what she thought of his draft article, his chapter, his latest idea. 'Papa was always full of ideas and they talked and talked and we weren't allowed to go with them into the garden or library. We stayed downstairs,' remembered Agathe. 'She was not neglecting us, but her chief interest was Papa. She was there for Papa.' Their mother was very intelligent, Agathe thought, and should have gone to university. 'I think she was very good for Papa because she helped him, and was terribly interested.' Franz agreed: 'My father always kept her in play.' The world might not know it, but the family knew: their father couldn't manage without their mother. He was always demanding her attention: where was his favourite pipe, he'd put it down somewhere, and where was yesterday's newspaper, and had she answered so-and-so yet? And tell Toni to come straight up when she arrives.

At Seestrasse the *ménage à trois* became a permanent fixture. Susi Trüb saw how hard it was for Emma: 'She tried very hard to accept it and to understand it. But it was impossible.' When the Jungs were invited anywhere Carl arrived with both Emma and Toni. It did not do his reputation locally much good, though what did he care – these narrow-minded Swiss. The Jung family didn't go to church either, though churchgoing was part of the very fabric of Swiss life, everyone dressed in their Sunday best, the church bells pealing out across lake and Alps. Carl held strongly to his own private, symbolic religion, but gave a wide berth to the official Protestant Reformed Church which had caused his father so much anguish. There was no grace before mealtimes either, the only prayers being said by Emma at bedtime, when she came to say goodnight and the children put their hands together and shut their eyes, asking their guardian angel to protect them through the night. It all added to the rumours about the strange goings-on at Seestrasse, and the children found that some of their school friends were not allowed to visit the house. The walk to and from school could be hazardous too, especially for Franz, because the two Morell boys from the farm next door often lay in wait with sticks and stones. Aggi and Gret were safer because they were girls. Not that Gret cared. She was the rebel of the family and whenever there was discord amongst the children you could be sure Gret was behind it.

On the way home from school they would drop in on Groma Jung. Groma Jung was always there, ready with a drink of milk and a bun. In fact she never went anywhere except to visit Seestrasse. It was one of the best things about her, especially as the parents were always so busy. Tante Trudi was there too, but one hardly noticed her because she was so quiet, almost invisible really. If it was cold or raining Groma Jung would be inside by the tiled stove, doing some knitting or darning. If it was warm she would be out in the garden, tending her flowers and vegetables. She was always full of talk, telling stories from the Bible, or ghost stories on dark winter nights that were so real they were frightening. She had plenty of visitors, mainly her Preiswerk relations from Basel, but the only time she left her home was when she came to look after the children during one of Carl and Emma's holidays, when she and Trudi moved into one of the upstairs guest rooms. Apart from that there was Saturday bath night at Seestrasse, when the gardener fired up the big boiler in the cellar, or bathing in the lake in the summer, and the occasional Sunday lunch. Otherwise Groma Jung was happy not to budge.

Emma's central dilemma – how to manage life with her husband and how to find her own way through it – remained. Whenever she talked to Carl about it he always said the same thing: she had to shape her own life, develop her own way, stop relying so heavily on him and the children, analyse her dreams and her feelings, and pursue her studies. *Individuate*, as he termed it, summing up. It was Carl's suggestion that Emma start an analysis with Toni's brother-in-law Hans Trüb, Susi's husband, who had become one of Carl's students after training as a doctor. And so she did. The analysis covered many things: the problems in Emma's life and marriage certainly, but also their mutual interests in literature, mythology, religion, history. Emma and Hans found they had much in common, not least because they were both married to errant spouses. Susi Trüb was wild and sexually free, way beyond the norms of the times and in sharp contrast to her sister Toni. She was having an affair with a wealthy Russian émigré in Zürich named Emilii Medtner, who was one of the Jung circle. But he was by no means the only one.

Carl was often a guest for lunch or dinner at the Wolff house in Zürich, usually following a seminar or lecture, after which he would retire with Toni to her room. Whether it was a full sexual relationship remains a moot point, but the spiritual side of the relationship was what mattered most to Carl. Their mother knew about the relationship, said Susi, and it troubled her: 'But I think perhaps she was more troubled for Emma. Perhaps she thought it was good for Toni to have a "friend". But for Emma . . . She felt for Emma. All those difficulties!' Everyone in their circle knew about it. 'This was an exceptional relationship, because of the quality of the three persons involved,' thought Tina Keller, wife of Adolf Keller, pastor of St Peter's Church in Zürich. 'As a spectator I felt it was very different from an "affair" as I saw them around. There was responsibility and a common task which was beyond but included the love relationship.' The Kellers never invited the Jungs for supper without inviting Toni as well. When Tina arrived for an analytical session one day at Seestrasse, Jung said: 'This is how we three struggle with this problem.' He was at his desk in his *Cabinet* painting a manuscript illumination for his *Liber Novus* of three snakes intertwined.

Others in their circle saw Emma's distress: 'There isn't the slightest doubt in my mind that this relationship was a torture and a painful thing for Frau Jung to bear,' recalled one friend. 'He was so powerful.' When Carl and Emma entered a room everyone turned to Jung, drawn like a magnet, whilst Emma stood quietly in the background, saying little. One friend called Emma 'Mona Lisa' because of her quiet beauty and slow, knowing smile. Everyone liked and admired her for the dignified, intelligent and courageous way she handled herself. The only people who could have told you different were her maids. Every now and again Emma blew, and when she blew it was a flame of fury out of control and way beyond the misdemeanour which occasioned it.

The Jungs had a close-knit group of friends, built up over the years of their marriage. Many had children the same age and they all shared an interest in psychoanalysis. During the early years of the war, stranded as they were in neutral Switzerland, they spent many evenings together in each other's houses: the Trübs, the Kellers, the Pfisters, the Riklins, the Siggs (Martha Boeddinghaus, Carl's old admirer, had married a successful local businessman named Sigg), the Maeders, Maria Moltzer, Emilii Medtner, and of course Toni Wolff, with Seestrasse always at the heart of things. It was an interesting group: liberal, well educated, combative. Here women were included in the conversation as equals, not left behind in the drawing room whilst the gentlemen retreated to the *Herrenzimmer* to drink their wine and smoke their cigars. Tina Keller recalled that in the early days Frau Jung would sit quietly on the sidelines, but as time went on and she saw how forthright the women could be, as much as the men sometimes, she joined in more and more, gaining confidence and finding she had opinions as strong as anyone else.

Tina Keller first heard about psychoanalysis through her husband Adolf, who had already been a member of Bleuler's study evenings at the Burghölzli, discussing the new ideas emanating from Professor Freud in Vienna. Tina's parents had warned her about the 'dangerous' company Adolf kept: 'in 1912 Psycho-Analysis was [regarded as] a very controversial issue', but that only interested Tina more, and the pair were married in 1912. Tina's upbringing had been similar to Emma's, with the limited education routinely offered to girls, except for a stimulating period attending Cheltenham Ladies' College in England, where the headmistress encouraged her young ladies to aim high. The suffragists were grabbing the headlines, marching with banners for women's rights, a movement which the *Neue Zürcher Zeitung* described as 'ridiculous'. Tina came home fired up, but soon found there was nothing more for a woman in Switzerland to do – but perhaps become a nurse and then marry, which she duly did. But like Emma she married contrary to expectation, determined not to lead a life of stifling leisure. Adolf, almost twenty years her senior, came from modest peasant stock: a good, straightforward, open man in contrast to her much more complicated self. She was soon pregnant with their first child, and had four more children in quick succession, like Emma. After her third child she suddenly and unaccountably became profoundly depressed, filled with irrational fears and anxieties. Adolf worried that his wife had gone crazy and in 1915 brought her to see Jung for what would turn out to be a prolonged spell of analysis.

Jung told Frau Keller what he told so many of the intelligent, frustrated women who came to see him: she wasn't ill, she just needed to get away from her restrictions, have the courage to live her life more fully, more creatively, to individuate. Note all your dreams, he told her, and write down your thoughts in letters to me – not to send, just to express them fully. Jung was always good on practical advice like that, well ahead of his times in this as in other ways. She was to embrace her dark side too: 'God has a dark side,' he assured her. It was a good thing, not a bad. When Tina found the effects of the analysis were causing trouble in her marriage he told her it had little to do with the analysis; her depression showed she was already embarked on change.

It was during Frau Keller's visits to 228 Seestrasse for her sessions with Jung that she and Emma became friends. As the two women talked, they discovered they were both keen to further their education and make something more of themselves. Soon they had decided, with Carl's active encouragement, to employ the services of a professor to teach them maths, physics, and in Emma's case, more Latin and Greek. Emma was changing. Forced by difficult circumstances, trying to come to terms with the realities of her marriage, she finally began to take her life into her own hands.

13

The Americans

America and Americans had played an important part in Jung's working life ever since his first visit to Worcester with Freud and Ferenczi back in 1909. He had fallen in love with the place, the energy, the sheer newness and vastness of it all, and America in her turn had fallen for Dr Jung of Switzerland, the coming man, with his own brand of vitality and a bagful of challenging views, not all of them congenial. As a result there had been a stream of American physicians and patients crossing the Atlantic on the great ocean liners, making their way to Jung's door, first to the Burghölzli, then to Seestrasse. None spoke Swiss German but both Carl and Emma spoke English well enough, so conversation could still flow around the table over lunches and suppers or tea on the terrace, everyone throwing in their penny's worth, but dominated as ever by Jung.

One couple who became key figures in Carl and Emma's circle of friends was Edith and Harold McCormick. Edith was the daughter of John D. Rockefeller, the Standard Oil baron, reputedly the richest man in America. Edith was headstrong and outspoken, a keen reader with intellectual aspirations. In 1895 she married Harold McCormick, scion of the International Harvester family, thereby joining two of the wealthiest dynasties in the United States. Harold was a Princeton man, more sporty than intellectual, a clubbable genial sort, good-looking and a bit of a dandy. They lived in Chicago in a vast lakeshore mansion where they entertained lavishly, American style. On Chicago opera gala night Edith would arrive bedecked in the Rockefeller pearls, which the newspapers assured their readers were worth $2 million. Their opera dinner which followed made even splashier headlines than the pearls. They were the golden couple, but three years into their marriage they were hit by tragedy: their baby daughter died, aged one. A few years later their three-year-old son John died of scarlet fever, for which there was still no cure, all the money in the world unable to save him. Edith plunged into a depression with bouts of agoraphobia. There followed years of traipsing about the world to see the best medical specialists, but nothing helped – until they met Dr Jung of Switzerland on his trip to America in 1912.

The introduction came through Harold's cousin Medill McCormick, from the *Chicago Tribune* side of the family – the one who had been a patient of Jung's since 1908, suffering from alcoholism brought on, Jung suggested, by a domineering mother. Jung thought it had driven him to 'a wild and immoral life', as Medill wrote to his wife Ruth, and had warned him against being 'too good', recommending a little flirtation. He had just had one himself. But Jung also suggested that in a marriage 'love could suppress the former immoral tendencies'. So Medill recommended Jung to his cousin.

Edith had just finished another treatment, a fresh-air 'cure' in the Catskill Mountains. Jung found her lively and mentally alert but emotionally fragile. For her part, Edith was soon convinced that Jung was the man to save her and, accustomed to buying everything she desired, offered to set him up in America, including bringing his family over to live nearby. It must have come as a surprise that Jung refused her offer – not only refused, but insisted that if she wanted to be treated by him it was she, not he, who had to up sticks. Jung saw her again during his next trip to America in 1913, and this time she accompanied him back to Europe, together with her three surviving children, Muriel, Matilda and Fowler, and mountains of travelling trunks and hat boxes. Harold stayed behind in Chicago working in the family business. Edith set herself up in a large suite at the Baur-au-Lac, the grandest hotel in Zürich, ostensibly for a few months. She stayed for eight years.

By October 1913 it was clear to Harold that Edith was not coming back, so he too embarked for Zürich, to check on his wife's progress. 'Edith is becoming very *real* and *true to herself*,' he wrote to his father-in-law Rockefeller in December, 'and is seeking and I am sure will find her path . . . At any rate, she is in absolutely safe and trustworthy hands for no finer man ever breathed than Dr Jung. He has an intense admiration for Edith and yet recognises she is the toughest problem he ever had to deal with.' One of Jung's approaches was to encourage Edith to lead a more 'normal' life. Edith had a travel phobia and usually went everywhere in the safe confines of her chauffeur-driven automobile. Now she agreed to take the train from Zürich for her analytical sessions in Kusnacht – even buy her own ticket – but only if her chauffeur drove the car alongside the tracks so she could abandon the task if her panic grew too severe. Jung offered practical advice again: walk more, he told her, preferably hatless to abandon formality, and learn to knit (she never mastered it) and tidy your own room, which Mrs McCormick duly did, even helping the hotel chamber maid to clean the floor, which must have come as a shock to the maid.

Edith found 'normal' family life difficult. To simplify matters, Muriel and Matilda were each given twelve identical outfits, one set in pink the other in blue. By 1914 they were enrolled in local schools while Fowler plied back and forth to America, where he attended Groton prep school in Massachusetts. Years later Fowler still remembered Herr and Frau Doktor Jung coming to dine with his parents at the Hotel Baur-au-Lac and Jung teasing his wife when she, newly liberated, smoked a cigarette after the meal. Beaming, Jung invited everyone present: 'Now please look at Mrs Jung – how she is working with this new toy she has.'

Harold returned to Chicago and the family business but came back to Zürich in September 1914, by which time war had broken out. He kept the family in America up to date with Edith's progress in his chatty letters. 'Her step is springy and she walks with her arms free and swinging. She notices all things of nature and dresses simply and in very artistic taste,' he wrote to his mother. 'In the mornings we usually take a walk before lunch and in the afternoon also. Then in the evening we sit around the hotel or go to some moving picture show.' By October, Edith was deemed cured and able to turn her attention to other matters: astrology, biology, history and music – and training to be an analyst. Harold meanwhile entered analysis with Jung, as did Muriel, who had already spent some time in local sanatoriums. And the McCormicks joined Carl and Emma's circle of personal friends. They had a lot in common, especially with Emma, whose family had made their fortune in agricultural machinery just like Harold's. In August 1915

Harold joined Carl on a walking tour through the Swiss Alps, but only for a few days because Carl said he needed solitude and time to meditate.

Even the Jung children could see that Mrs McCormick was eccentric. But her hats were marvellous. As soon as she disappeared upstairs to see their father or into the *Stube* for one of their parents' receptions, they raced to the garderobe in the front hall and tried them on – huge hats decorated with all manner of feathers and veils. Papa's hats were there too: his flat straw hat, battered, his old grey Filtz, the black melon bowler hat, a sou'wester from America, a black silk top hat, and later, when he came back from Africa, a sola topi which he liked to wear on their Sunday afternoon walks. Mama had plenty of hats too, since women never went anywhere without a hat, but none as dramatic as Mrs McCormick's. Apparently Mrs McCormick was not the only eccentric in the family. When Papa came back from America he told them that her father had a bodyguard who followed him everywhere, because the tycoon had hurt so many people in business he had to be careful. All the gold in the world could not stop Mr Rockefeller being a lonely, suspicious old man, said Papa.

It soon came to the McCormicks' attention that Jung needed a proper place to give his talks and seminars, which usually took place, somewhat impromptu, in the private rooms of the Seidenhof restaurant in Zürich. They suggested establishing a club, which Edith was more than happy to fund. A substantial property was found in the centre of town at 1 Löwenstrasse, and by early 1916 it was set up. 'I am enclosing a photo of the Psychological Club which I founded on 26th of January this year,' Edith wrote to her mother-in-law. 'The house I have rented for two and a half years. It makes a centre for analysed people where they can be in *pension*, or come in for meals, or come for the evenings for lectures, discussions and study, all of which teaches collectively. Any new movement has a slow growth, but this assures a lasting quality.' To fund it further she asked her father to increase her allowance, currently at $2,500 a month. Whatever he gave her was not enough, apparently, as she subsequently took out a bank loan of $80,000. 'Pfister writes that Rockefeller's daughter presented Jung with a gift of $360,000 for the construction of a casino, analytic institute etc.,' Freud wrote sourly to Sandor Ferenczi on 29 April 1916: 'So Swiss ethics have finally made their sought-after contact with American money. I think not without bitterness about the pitiful situations of the members of our Association.' No wonder he was bitter. Times were hard, not only for Viennese psychoanalysts. Austria was at war. All three of Freud's sons were enlisted, fighting for their country.

Despite the lavish funding, there was trouble at the Psychological Club from the start. First it was Alphonse Maeder, a colleague of Jung's since early days at the Burghölzli who had become the first president of the Swiss Gesellschaft für Psychoanalyse when the Zürich group split from the Viennese in 1913, but who now refused the post of president of the new club, protesting he would be no more than a mouthpiece for Jung. 'He was too strong and dominant,' Maeder said later. 'He was a man of great stature, surely a genius personality, but strong and a bit massively Swiss German.' Maeder knew he couldn't stand up to him. Meier noted: 'Jung was very critical of men. It was frightening almost. There was something odd about it.' Maeder agreed: 'He was not able to maintain a real friendship among men. He had some, but rather weak ones. Those were men who admired and followed him. He had intelligent women, crowds of women, around him, but with men he could not really get along.'

It was true: there were few men of real stature in Jung's group, and he was not above bullying them either when the mood took him. Tina Keller came to hate the way Jung could behave in company, magnetically charismatic one minute, 'vulgar and repellent' the next, making fun of someone sarcastically and unfeelingly, picking on the weaker ones, and swearing as crudely as a Swiss peasant. In that mood split Carl could frighten people and Emma often had to step in to console and conciliate. Maria Schmid, the wife of Jung's friend and colleague Hans, with whom he often went bicycling, remembered Emma Jung saying she was rather sorry that her husband had no real friends; Hans was one of the few people Jung addressed as *Du* rather than the more normal and formal *Sie*. Alphonse Maeder decided to protect himself and ducked out. But who should take on the job instead? The answer was Emma.

The timing could not have been better: Lil was nearly three, the other four children were out at school most of the day. Emma was just beginning to develop her own life and here was the perfect opportunity. Encouraged by Carl, she decided to take it on. It was something of a turning point, even though most members thought, like Maeder, she would be little more than a mouthpiece for her husband. The first meeting was held on 26 February 1916 with forty people present, twenty-four of whom were women. Emma was approved as president, their friend Hermann Sigg, with his business experience, was appointed treasurer, and Irma Oczeret, a Hungarian who was part of their analytic circle, secretary. The second meeting was held on 15 March, when fifteen further members joined. Almost immediately, however, there was more trouble.

It lay in the fact that the club did not really know what it was. The McCormicks saw it as a club along American lines, social as much as a place of study, with rooms for *pension* on the upper floors, and on the lower floors a dining room, billiard room, games room including a table-tennis table, library, lecture room and big reception room, with a variety of smaller withdrawing rooms where analysts could see their patients. The Swiss on the other hand saw it essentially as a serious meeting place for talks, lectures, analytic sessions, and relevant social functions; a place for an informal exchange of views, certainly, but hardly a place to attend in order to play ping-pong. The club was serviced by a staff of three servants, a cook, maintenance men and a concierge, all overseen by a Fräulein Teuscher. Toni Wolff was one of the first to point out that it was too luxurious for their local members, the restaurant too expensive, and likewise the accommodation. As a result it was rarely used during the week unless there was a talk by a club member or one of Jung's sell-out lectures or seminars. By July 1916 the club was in financial trouble, only solved by Edith McCormick pressing her father for more funds. There was also the problem of rank: who was a full member, who an associate. Analysts formed one group, analysands the other. Harold McCormick, the sociable club-bable man who once entertained the assembled with a whistling serenade, noted that 'unconsciously there is too much atmos-phere of rank in the Club ... the mantle of "caste" should be laid aside at the threshold of the Club and the Natural Simple Human Relation assumed in its real aspect'. His private view was that the Swiss did not know how to have some plain good fun. But some of the plain good fun – the jolly Christmas party and the fancy dress balls, some of the evenings of games and the summer excursions to the Swiss Alps and lakes – was open exclusively to full members, leaving associate members out in the cold.

Jokey Harold McCormick with his daughters in Zürich during the First World War.

Jung himself was clear about the essential purpose of the Psychological Club: to overcome the limitations imposed by one-to-one analysis, another forward-looking view anticipating later developments in group therapy. He thought both aspects of club life, intellectual and social, could contribute to this – in fact it rather neatly fed into his new concept of introvert and extrovert, which he liked to try out on members by way of research for his book on psychological types. But the rows and disagreements would not go away, bedevilled as they were by jealousies and rivalries, everyone competing for Jung's attention. It was the first test of Emma's leadership, and in October 1916 she issued a circular letter about 'the Club problem' to all members. In her role as conciliator she asked all 'who have a real interest in the development of our Club' for their 'impressions, encouragement and criticisms both in matters of principle and practical'.

If anyone thought the letter had been dictated by Jung they only had to look at the language to see that it was pure Emma. 'If the Club hasn't as yet become as great a boon as we hoped, this doesn't mean it won't become one in the future. In my view it takes time to establish a thing . . .' Emma was liked and respected by everyone. Most members responded to her appeal, though not everyone in the same spirit of optimism. 'My suggestion would be: an absolute reorganisation of the Club,' wrote Maria Moltzer, now a practising analyst, but disconsolate that she had been given no formal role to play, 'since it seems to me that the present club is incurably ill.' It was her view that the organisation, financially supported by Edith McCormick, was parasitic. Fanny Bowditch, an American who came to Zürich to be analysed by Jung after she had fallen into a deep depression following the death of her father, wrote to 'My dear Mrs Jung' saying she was interested in the club's welfare but she found herself unable to take an active part because she needed solitude more than collectivity. Used to having Jung to herself in their private sessions, and half in love with him, she later admitted to Herr Doktor that seeing him in a group was not to her liking: 'my eyes were opened to the reality of things and I saw you in a new light – for the first time, in the grip of your own complexes'. She was not the only one. No wonder Jung wanted a club 'to overcome the limitations of one-to-one analysis'. No wonder Emma did too. Jung soon passed Fanny Bowditch over to Maria Moltzer. Emma's efforts prevailed: within three years the Psychological Club had moved to a more modest house in Gemeindestrasse, where it still functions to this day.

When it was Emma's turn to give a lecture at the club it required courage to overcome her natural shyness. As her subject she chose 'Guilt'. Even in the English language this is a challenging word, but in German '*Schuld*' has several meanings: guilt, blame/fault, debt. Everyone in the room knew about the *ménage à trois*. Once, when Alphonse Maeder slighted Toni Wolff at the club, Jung stormed out of the room, furious, red-faced and shouting: 'I'll take her on my knee and hold her there throughout every meeting till they stop hounding her.' So now here was Emma standing at the lectern, facing the members, speaking about guilt, with Carl and Toni in the front row in the armchairs always reserved for them.

She began with etymology, an interest she had pursued from the early years when she had first helped Carl with his work: in French there's '*devoir*' and '*conscience*', in English there's 'should', in German '*Pflicht*', duty. Already in mythology the word 'guilt' is linked to suffering, she said. But without suffering there could be no development, no growth. 'I myself have had to grapple with this,' she added, surprising everyone in the room with her boldness. The feeling associated with guilt was often fear, she went on, bolder and bolder. But the main interest in the word 'guilt' was psychological, which in turn depended on the context, the time and the place. She offered some history, starting with the cleansing ceremonies in primitive cultures, warding off evil. The feeling of guilt could come when a person was not 'at one with himself'. Was she looking at her husband when she said it? By his own admission Jung suffered from a 'constant feeling of guilt'. On Emma went, addressing the Christian concept of 'sin', a word which cropped up again and again in Jung's writings: the forbidden fruit of Adam and Eve; Pandora opening her dreaded box. She ended with the central message of the lecture: we have to take responsibility for the sufferings in our own lives and solve our dilemmas for ourselves. You can almost hear the clapping.

Emma's friendship with Tina Keller was put to the test during this time when, in a classic case of transference, Tina fell passionately in love with Carl during her analysis. But Emma stayed steady and Jung handled the situation with 'respect, tact and sincerity', telling Tina: 'You must be quite clear that you are alone in this experience.' Always believing that analysis was an equal give-and-take between the analyst and the analysand, Jung admitted to her how he sometimes felt close to insanity. And Tina could see for herself how deeply he was still affected by his split from Freud because he could never talk about Freud without his face suffusing with emotion. 'My father would not confess it,' his son Franz later reflected, 'but he probably never got over Freud in all those years.' Alphonse Maeder thought it went back to Jung's own father. 'Jung [was] religiously interested. But religious in a somewhat other sense than Christian or ecclesiastical religion . . . Even up to his last day he had a complex against the Church and her mission. He would never use the word "Church" without swearing: it remained a real father complex.'

Emma knew her husband teetered on insanity at times and that he needed Toni Wolff to help him through his struggles. She was what the Jung circle of analysts came to term an 'anima' figure, a sort of muse to the unconscious. 'She had an extraordinary genius for accompanying men – and sometimes women too, in a different way – whose destiny it was to enter the unconscious,' recalled Barbara Hannah, the Englishwoman and member of the Jung circle who later wrote a biography of him. 'Toni Wolff was perhaps – of all the "anima" types I have known – the most suited to carry the projection of this figure.' Hannah saw how hard this was for Emma. 'What saved the situation was that there was no lack of love in any of the three. Jung was able to give both his wife and Toni a most satisfactory amount, and *both* women *really* loved him. Therefore, although for a long time they were most painfully jealous of each other, love always won out in the end and prevented any destructive action on either side.' Emma even said years later: 'You see, he never took anything from me to give to Toni, but the more he gave her, the more he seemed able to give to me.' Hannah doubted Jung could have survived this time of inner crisis alone.

Jung himself put it more breezily: 'It is unfortunately true that when you are a wife and mother you can hardly be the *hetaira* too, just as it is the secret suffering of the *hetaira* that she is not a mother.' The *hetairai* were the courtesans of ancient Greece, respected for their learning and beauty, and afforded greater freedom than married women. 'There are women who are not meant to bear physical children,' Jung went on, 'but they are those that give rebirth to a man in a spiritual sense, which is a highly important function.' Susi Trüb agreed: 'She wasn't at all practical,' she said of her sister Toni. 'She would never have been able to lead a married life.'

* * *

Jung's Personality No. 2 often caused havoc at at 228 Seestrasse. One day in 1916 everything came to a head. 'It began with restlessness, but I did not know what it meant or what "they" wanted of me. There was an ominous atmosphere all around me. I had the strange feeling that the air was filled with ghostly entities. Then it was as if my house began to be haunted.' Aggi saw a white figure passing through the room. Gret said her feather bedcover was snatched in the night. Franz had a nightmare. In the morning when Emma gave him some crayons he drew a picture of his dream: a fisherman on the banks of a river with a chimney on his head belching flames and smoke, landing a fish. From the other bank the devil came flying through the air, cursing because the fish had been stolen. An angel hovered above the fisherman, saying: 'You cannot do anything to him; he only catches the bad fish.' Franz called it: 'The Picture of the Fisherman'. Perhaps he knew about the story of the Fisher King his father had illustrated in the *Liber Novus*.

The next day at 5 p.m. the doorbell at 228 Seestrasse began clanging frantically. It was a bright summer's day and the two maids were in the kitchen which overlooked the front entrance. There was no one there. Everyone raced to look, but there was nothing. 'The atmosphere was thick, believe me! Then I knew that something had to happen. The whole house was filled as if there were a crowd present, crammed full of spirits,' wrote Jung. 'They were packed deep right up to the door, and the air was so thick it was scarcely possible to breathe. As for myself, I was all aquiver with the question: "For God's sake, what in the world is this?" Then they cried out in chorus: "We have come back from Jerusalem where we found not what we sought."'

The engagement. A few out-of-focus snapshots taken at Ölberg are the only record of Emma and Carl's secret engagement in October 1901. *Verlobung*, 'engagement', is written faintly on the reverse.

Emma on her wedding day, 14 February 1903, St Valentine's Day. There was a ball and a grand banquet, but Emma's father was too ill to attend either of these, or even the church ceremony.

Zürich c. 1905. Once married, Emma joined Carl in Zürich. While he worked a twelve-hour day, Emma ventured into the city, much more modern and busy than sleepy Schaffhausen.

Carl and Emma with Aggie and Gretli. Emma took the photograph of Carl, and Carl took that of Emma. These early years were happy ones for them both. Married for four years, Emma was already the mother of two. Within a year she would be pregnant again, with Franz.

Emma with Aggie and Gretli outside the Burghölzli. By now she was taking an active part in the life of the asylum. Bleuler thought it a good idea to involve the wives.

A rare studio portrait of Emma, who hated having her photograph taken, preferring to stay in the background. It was Carl who enjoyed the limelight.

The Weimar Congress, 1911. All the leading lights of the early psychoanalytic movement were present, with Freud standing on a stool in the middle row, dominant. In the front row are Maria Moltzer (*third from left*) and Toni Wolff (*third from right*).

Emma (*front row, centre*) was encouraged to attend by Carl, who bends solicitously over her. More confident now, she was beginning to engage in the exciting new world of psychoanalysis.

Seestrasse 228, Küsnacht.
Emma and Carl finally
built their own home,
on Lake Zürich, in 1909,
when these photographs
were taken. Carl oversaw
every last detail of the
building, but Emma quietly
got her way too, and the
final result is a pleasing
compromise between
husband and wife.

Toni Wolff. Originally a patient of Carl's, she soon became indispensable to him. She had 'seer's eyes', and understood Carl's 'other' personality – the hidden, complex one.

Carl and Toni in England, 1922. Soon they were a *ménage à trois*, but Carl did it openly, flaunting bourgeois conventions. Emma was left to come to terms with it.

Emma (*left*) and Toni (*right*) at the Psychological Club, Zürich. By the 1930s Emma was practising as an analyst in her own right, and Toni Wolff no longer caused her the same anguish.

The Jung family in 1917 – only baby Hélène is missing. At this point in their marriage Emma was still having a difficult time.

Emma and Carl in the 1930s. By now they had come through their turbulent times to emerge triumphant. They could always laugh together, said their grandchildren, and 'both learned from each other all their lives'.

Jung went to his *Cabinet* and began writing *Septem Sermones ad Mortuos* (*Seven Sermons to the Dead*). 'It began to flow out of me, and in the course of three evenings the thing was written.' As soon as he started to write the whole ghostly assemblage evaporated, the room quieted and the atmosphere cleared. 'As day fades the unconscious is activated, and by midnight the censer is full blaze, but lighting up the past,' Jung said in one of his 1925 talks to the Psychological Club. 'As the dynamic principle increases in power, and the further back we go, the more we are overcome by the unconscious. Lunatics go further back to a strange psychological state where they cannot understand their ideas, nor are they able to make them understood by others.'

In a sense *Septem Sermones* is the distillation of everything Jung had been battling over the years: the spirits had not found what they sought. Now it had to be found: the integration of the personality, both good and evil, including the 'daemon of sexuality'. No more splitting. In the seventh and last sermon there is a star, shedding light. Later Jung conceded: 'No doubt it was connected with the state of emotion I was in at the time, and which was favourable to para-psychological phenomena. It was an unconscious constellation whose peculiar atmosphere I recognised as the *numen* of an archetype.' It was the same territory as his 1902 dissertation 'On the Psychology and Pathology of So-Called Occult Phenomena'. 'The intellect, of course, would like to arrogate to itself some scientific, physical knowledge of the affair, or, preferably, to write the whole thing off as a violation of the rules,' he wrote, back to his confident self. 'But what a dreary world it would be if the rules were not violated sometimes!' Are you listening, Freud? he might as well have

written. He showed the text to only a few people, including
Emma and Toni Wolff and Edith McCormick, and he did not
publish it till a year before his death.

The place the Jung family spent most of their free time during
those war years was at Ölberg, with Emma's mother, Bertha.
Many weekends and Easters and the long summer holidays
were whiled away there, and even if it had not been wartime and
they'd been free to travel elsewhere it would still have been their
favourite place. 'All summer long we played Indians against the
English with my cousins. Papa was the leader,' remembered
Franz. 'He wore a Canadian Mountie's hat and a pair of cowboy
boots from his visit to America with Freud. He looked like a
sheriff. We built teepees and huts big enough to sleep in, and
each side had a horse. We would light fires and burn down each
other's teepees and steal the horses. This was Papa's idea. He
played with us all the time, although his brother-in-law did not
approve.' Ernst Homberger, married to Emma's sister
Marguerite, the hard, ambitious man running the family business, found Carl a complete anathema, hardly a man at all really:
playing like a child, and always talking about something called
'the unconscious'.

The Hombergers had five children and the cousins,
Homberger and Henne alike, joined in the wild games. Mostly
Emma let them be – '*heb die Daumen*', fingers crossed that no
one got badly hurt. Bertha Rauschenbach never worried: she
loved adventure and thought it was good for the children. Every
year she booked the ferryman to row the cousins, screaming
with excitement and fear, to the rock in the middle of the hazard-

ous Rhine Falls, or took them on steep single-track mountain railways high into the Alps, or more sedately on carriage drives with faithful Braun the coachman, to places of local interest. Marie always came too. Her father had been Jean Rauschenbach's carer during the last years of his life, and Marie herself had started as a housemaid aged seventeen. Now, thirty years later, she was Bertha Rauschenbach's faithful companion. They never quarrelled and they agreed on everything. But even they were alarmed when Carl got the cousins digging tunnels in the sandy soil, crawling through them by way of a daring escape from the enemy.

Summer weekends were often spent by the lake at Seestrasse. Everything centred on it: swimming, sailing the *Pelican*, Carl's yawl with red sails; rowing, digging dams and channels down to the lake from the stream by the vegetable patch, or making fires on the lakeshore to roast *Cervelat* sausages. And there it was always Carl who played with the children, never Emma. She preferred to sit on the terrace reading or doing her needlework, keeping an eye on things. If she was reading her *Nebelspalter*, the satirical weekly magazine, it could make her laugh out loud. Occasionally she took a swim, though rarely further than their own small harbour walls, whereas Marguerite swam far out. A wondrous event occurred on Saturdays when Groma Jung and Tante Trudi would arrive to bathe in the lake, swathed in voluminous bathing dresses, bearing bars of soap and flannels, because during the hot summers they preferred to wash there, not in the bathroom tub. And once every summer an old *Tante* arrived on a visit, one of Emma's many distant Schaffhausen relatives, and Carl would often take her back to Kusnacht by sailboat to catch the local train to Zürich and thence back to

Schaffhausen. One year, as the aunt stood balanced between jetty and boat, Carl offered a helping hand but she lost her footing and in she went, hat and all. Judging by his bellowing laughter it was one of Carl's little 'tricks'. The children howled with delight. Even Emma found it hard not to laugh. Luckily the old aunt was happy to share the joke.

In the evenings the family, like many Swiss, played *Jass* cards, and if not cards, then mahjong. They sat round the big table and played, fiendishly and noisily, till bedtime. The children knew from experience that when Papa was losing he was not above cheating. It was the same with badminton, where he unashamedly toed his opponent's shuttlecock outside the line when necessary. He always had to win. Once the children were in bed and if Carl wasn't working, he and Emma might settle down to one of their marathon games of patience, which ran not just for one evening but over many, pitting themselves furiously against one another. Or billiards in the veranda room which could, likewise, run for days. And somehow Carl always won in the end. Because, cheating or not, Emma always let him.

Christmases were spent at Ölberg or at home. Either way it was in the deepest snow, the garden, trees, lake, meadows, Alps, all white. At Seestrasse the Christmas tree stood in the far corner by the big fireplace, high as the *Stube* ceiling, lit only by candles and hung with stars and hearts baked by the cook. The crib with baby Jesus, Mary and Joseph, the three kings and the shepherds, stood on a table between the fireplace and the alcove with the two stained-glass windows commemorating Emma and Carl's wedding and the birth of Aggi and Gret. On Christmas Eve everyone dressed for dinner, Carl in black tie, Emma in evening gown and jewels, with the children, Emilie Jung and Trudi and sometimes Bertha Rauschenbach, all grouped round the tree singing 'Stille Nacht, Heilige Nacht'.

Groma Rauschenbach sitting at her usual table at Ölberg.

Then the servants, standing in a row at the back, were given their presents before returning to their work. The Christmas feast was followed by rowdy games such as musical chairs, led, as ever, by Carl. The next day the gardener Herr Müller's children would arrive to present themselves in the front hall, standing in a row from the oldest to the youngest, waiting for Frau Doktor Jung to come down the stairs and present them, formally, with their gifts. Then the children would curtsey and bow: '*Danke Frau Doktor, danke Frau Doktor*', before walking back home along the country road to Kusnacht village.

As the war entered its fourth year even safe little Switzerland was feeling the deprivations. Coal was so scarce the Jung house could no longer be heated by the boiler in the cellar. With his usual enthusiasm for camping and the outdoors, Carl fixed up a tent-like construction round the big marble fireplace and every-one crowded in there for warmth. As everything with Carl, it became an exciting thing to do. Petrol had run out long ago, for everyone but the McCormicks who did a deal with the American armed forces in Europe. But the Jungs were hardly struggling: the hens still laid their eggs, the lake still had its fish, Bertha Rauschenbach still sent the occasional joint of meat in the post from her butcher in Schaffhausen, and there was never a lack of vegetables because the lawn to the left of the drive with the swings and sandpits had been dug over to augment the vegetable patch, supplying the cook with all the fresh produce she required. Carl was in charge of the potatoes. Wearing his old gardener's overalls, he planted them, dug them up, kicked the earth off them and washed them in the stream before dumping them on the kitchen table like the good Swiss peasant he was at heart.

It was a different story for the Zürich poor. By 1917 they were close to starving. In November there were the first signs of unrest: *Hausfraus* in slippers and aprons queued outside shops complaining about the exorbitant rise in prices: bread up 19 rappen the kilo, milk up 6 rappen, flour up 20, sugar doubled in price, even potatoes cost 15 rappen a kilo more than in 1915. Forget coal, meat and wood. And all the while their husbands and sons stood at the Swiss borders doing their guard duty for 2 francs a day, with no assurance that their factory jobs would still be waiting for them when they returned. But up the Bahnhofstrasse, the cafés and restaurants remained busy, full of the idle rich, the ladies dripping with jewels. Life went on as usual in the Kronenhalle and the Odeon with those crazy expatriates. The rich of Europe and America still lived it up in the Hotel Baur-au-Lac, war profiteers among them. It wan't right. The political activists reminded them that Switzerland was still producing armaments for anyone who would pay. Down with war! Down with Capitalism! Workers of the World Unite! Look at Russia – do as they do!

On 17 November 1917 there was a demonstration in the Helvetia Platz. Barricades went up on the Badenerstrasse. The city police and then the military arrived. Shots were fired, resulting in four dead and seventeen wounded, scattering the protestors. And nothing changed. The following year, in September and with the end of war in sight, there were more strikes. In November there was a general strike. The country was hit by Spanish influenza, from the soldiers in the trenches they said. All schools, theatres, churches and public gatherings were shut down, but after more than four years of war the population had little resistance: 200,000 stricken in Switzerland, 900 died. The City Fathers, terrified by the spectre of revolution in Russia and now in Germany too, accepted that reforms were necessary. A forty-eight-hour week was agreed before the end of the year. But the following spring, once the immediate threat was over, the strike leaders were arrested.

Most of Zürich could not wait to get back to normal. Fashion was always of interest. 'The longer the war, the shorter the skirts,' quipped the *Neue Zürcher Zeitung*. Gerhart Hauptmann arrived to give a reading of his *Versunkene Glocke* in the Tonhalle; Herr Professor Einstein joined the University of Zürich; women's rights and the vote were discussed in the chamber. 'We know bayonets are not the solution,' said *Wissen und Leben* magazine. 'Zürich, the largest Swiss city, stands in a crisis of European origin. We stand on the edge of an era of social fairness, on the edge of a new Switzerland. Zürich is suffering, but has faith. And faith will triumph.'

At Seestrasse they had their own renewed faith, out of times of war into times of peace. Carl had spent 117 days on active military service in 1917, but now it was over. And so, more or less, was his inner crisis. As was one of his long-running infatuations. 'It was only towards the end of the First World War that I gradually began to emerge from the darkness,' he wrote. 'Two events contributed to this. The first was that I broke with the woman who was determined to convince me that my fantasies had artistic value; the second and principal event was that I began to understand mandala drawings.' Emerging from his darkness, he saw their true significance: the way they expressed 'wholeness'. As to 'the woman' he broke with: that was Maria Moltzer. The two events went hand in hand. Because Maria Moltzer failed to understand that his paintings were not aesthetic but symbolic – a route to the unconscious. That is, she failed to understand the core of his being. It was the end of things between them. Soon she had resigned from the Psychological Club and was effectively gone from Carl and Emma's life.

14

Into the Twenties

'London, 1 July 1919. Dear Marianne. It was sweet of you to write me a letter. It has made me so happy that I am writing a letter to you too. If you can't read it, Mama will read it to you. I have bought a doll here. It is carved from brown wood and comes from India. But it is for Mama,' wrote Carl to his eight-year-old daughter. In Switzerland children did not go to school till they were seven, so perhaps Marianne's reading was not yet good enough, but Carl's handwriting was more likely the problem.

As soon as possible, once the war was over, Jung had escaped the enclosed world of Zürich and made his way to London, where he had been invited to lecture to the Royal Society of Medicine and the Society for Psychical Research. He was staying near the King's 'Castle', he told Marianne, and there was a Tower where the Crown Jewels were kept. 'London lies on a big river where the seaships go,' he continued. 'Every day the river flows downwards for 6 hours and then upwards for 6 hours. Just think, more than twice as many people live in London as in the whole of Switzerland. Chinamen live here too. Many loving greetings to you and Lilli, from your Papa.'

Marianne was the musical one in the family: like her mother, she played the piano and the guitar too, and she had a fine voice.

When she left school she did a course of bookbinding in Paris and took some music and language courses in London. Later she was the one to show an interest in her father's work and acted as his secretary for some years. Aggi hated school and couldn't wait to leave. She resented her mother's decision to send her to the 'horrible' *Mädchenschule* in Zürich, the private young ladies' school, rather than the *Gymnasium* which was co-educational, with Emma concerned that her daughter was more interested in boys than her studies. Considering the unconventional way their parents chose to lead their lives, it is striking that the way they brought up their daughters was so conventional. All four daughters were sent to French-speaking Switzerland for a year when they left school, to improve their French and learn something of the 'art of housekeeping', because their parents thought their daughters' futures lay in being good wives and mothers. Further education could come later, if at all, as it had with Emma.

In 1919, aged fifteen, Aggi had already met the man she would marry, Kurt Niehus, a friend of one of the Preiswerk cousins and an engineering student at Zürich's famous ETH, the Federal Institute of Technology. They married when she was nineteen. Meanwhile she settled down to life at home because young women of her background rarely went out to work. Instead she helped with the younger children, attended some courses at the university, and spent time with her grandmothers in Kusnacht and Schaffhausen, filling in time until she could marry Kurt and lead her own life. Marianne and Lil were thrilled. Aggi was sweet-natured and happy to play with them, giving them rides on the back of her bicycle, swimming with them in the lake, taking them for walks, or if it was raining, sitting round the large table in the *Stube* pressing flowers or drawing or playing with their set of wooden animals, whilst Franz raced around playing with his train set. In the evenings, if her parents were engaged in one of their marathon card games, Aggi might help the children's maid get the younger ones ready for bed, brushing their hair and reading them bedtime stories.

Gret's memory of their parents was different to Aggi's because she was closer to their mother and never really got on with their father. It annoyed her that her mother always defended him, even when he got into one of his rages, saying he didn't mean it, he couldn't help it, and it would soon pass. Once the girls were married and had homes of their own it was always Aggi their father liked to see, rarely Gret. She irritated him too much. Ever since she was small they had rubbed each other up the wrong way because Gretli was strong and wilful and moody, much like Carl himself. She was interested in astrology and said she wanted to go to university to study psychology, but she wasn't allowed. Perhaps she should have been the boy. Franz was the 'soft' one, the one who took after his mother's side of the family, as Carl often pointed out. Being the only son, Franz found himself in a difficult position: on the one hand his father spent much more time with him than the girls, taking him on Alpine hikes, or sailing, or even letting him sit and draw beside him whilst he worked on his *Liber Novus*. On the other, he felt awed and dominated by his father and had to find ways of holding his own. By the 1920s Carl had acquired a collection of boats: the *Pelican*, two smaller sailing boats, as well as a rowing boat and a canoe. Franz refused point blank to crew for his father in the yawl, preferring to take the helm of one of the smaller boats. It was no fun sailing with Papa, who shouted orders at everyone and raged if someone did something wrong – until they were out into the lake at which point he relaxed, filled his pipe, and started telling his magical stories. But as far as Franz was concerned it wasn't worth it. He left crewing for his father to his Preiswerk cousins and the Niehus boys, Kurt and his brother Walter, who later married Marianne.

Perhaps Lil was the lucky one. Youngest of the five, she had what she remembered as a happy childhood in the safety of their home in Seestrasse, surrounded by the big garden, playing with the dogs – because Papa always had dogs – swimming in the lake, and going for visits to Groma Jung or Groma Rauschenbach in Schaffhausen. Lil spent a lot of time with Müller, helping him in the garden, collecting the eggs from the henhouse or accompanying him on shopping trips to Kusnacht village, pulling the little wooden cart behind them. Müller had been with the Jung family for ever, having started as 'young Müller' and ending as 'old Müller' forty years later. Looking back, Lil recalled that though their mother never kissed them, except on birthdays or at Christmas and Easter (few Swiss mothers did in those days), Emma was a warm-hearted and thoughtful mother. But busy, always busy, with the large house to run and countless visitors to entertain, including those coming from England and America. Famous ones too sometimes, such as Albert Einstein, Hermann Hesse and James Joyce, who came to see Jung about his daughter Lucia's troubles. But Emma still found time to listen to her children's problems and questions, sitting at her desk in a corner of the *Stube*, which was her base, the heart of the house. Any subject was allowed. 'She had a natural authority,' remembered Lil. And a good sense of humour too, laughing easily, especially when Papa told one of his outlandish stories. But when she was discussing work with their father she could be quite critical, observed Lil, which other people never dared. So her mother's occasional uncertainty came as a surprise. It was the same old uncertainty Emma had to deal with all her life: with strangers she was reserved and quiet, appearing a bit grand, 'always the lady', preferring to stay in the background. So many people got the wrong impression of Frau Doktor Jung, seeing her as little more than the wife and mother. But none who knew her well.

Aggi and Lil both remembered animated mealtimes, lively family festivities, and lots of card-playing in the evenings. If their father was in one of his good moods, full of vitality, trans-forming everything, then the fun would begin. 'Father was often terribly funny. We used to talk silly things and laugh like anything – terribly silly things sometimes,' Aggi said about the midday meal. Their mother didn't like it, but the children would repeat the silly words again and again, 'until we finally nearly rolled on the floor with laughter. Father loved such things. I can still remember mother saying: "It's really too stupid."' She did not like it either when Carl started feeding one of the dogs under the table, teasing them and working them up into a state. Even worse were his eating habits, because Carl had not been brought up with the same manners as Emma, and he had no intention of changing either. Swiss peasant was his style. 'The way he used to sip or eat his soup or soft boiled eggs was simply disgusting, one of the most disgusting things you could see in your life,' one of Jung's grandchildren later recalled. 'He made such horrible noises when he ate. Many times my appetite was completely spoiled. Of course nobody dared to say a word of criticism. When you saw him and my grandmother eating – she was such a gracious and refined lady – it was the most grotesque contrast.

He was aware of this and he just used to say "one has to eat one's food the way one enjoys it most".'

Jung was not home for long after his 1919 trip to England before he was off again. Over the next five years he went to England three times, America twice, Germany, France and Holland, and now, in the spring of 1920, he went to North Africa, invited by his friend Hermann Sigg, who had to go there on business, the business being oil. Jung called it his 'syndrome ambulatoire', explaining that 'in such cases people are seized with something like an urge to travel, have an amnesia concerning the past and just travel or run away'. Partly it was wanting to get away from the pressure of work. There were now so many patients arriving from England and America to add to his local ones that he often started work at 7 a.m. The patients stayed at the Hotel Sonne in Kusnacht village, sitting on the terrace overlooking the lake every morning, writing out their dreams of the night before. 'Jung unfortunately had a great success in his London lecture,' Ernest Jones had written to Freud in the summer of 1914 – and the price of that success, now that the war was over, was an endless succession of patients, and with them more and more doctors who wanted to be analysed and trained by Jung, so that they too could practise the new psychoanalysis.

So when Hermann Sigg suggested the trip to North Africa, Carl jumped at the chance. As he recounted to Emma in his letters, he and Sigg boarded the steamer at Marseilles, landing in Algiers and thence by train to Tunis, a journey of thirty hours followed by a further twenty-four to Sousse in central Tunisia. It was the first time Jung had come into contact with a civilisation utterly unlike his own. 'This Africa is incredible,' he wrote to *Mein liebster Schatz*, 'my darling treasure', from the Grand Hotel Sousse on 15 March 1920. 'Unfortunately I cannot write coherently to you, for it is all too much.' Algiers was 'bright houses and streets, dark green clumps of trees, tall palm crowns rising above them. White burnooses, red fezzes, and among these the yellow uniforms of the Tirailleurs d'Afrique, the red of the Spahis, the Botanical gardens, and an enchanted tropical forest . . .'. Carl the artist described 'A patch of deep blue sky, a snow-white mosque dome; a shoemaker busily stitching away at shoes in a small vaulted niche, with a hot, dazzling patch of sunlight on the mat before him'. Back on the train he gazed out of his carriage window hour after hour, mesmerised. 'Between Algiers and Tunis lie 550 miles of African soil . . . whole Roman cities, small flocks of black goats grazing around them, nearby a Bedouin camp with black tents, camels, and donkeys.' At one point the train ran down a camel, and always the deep blue sea, glittering, and the olive groves and the palms: 'Then comes Sousse, with white walls and towers, the harbour below; beyond the harbour wall the deep blue sea, and in the port lies the sailing ship with two lateen sails which I once painted!!!!' So there it was, his dream from long, long ago, when he had painted his longed-for vision of a town, with a tower by the sea and a harbour with a sailing ship. And now he had the tower, and the sailing ship, and everything.

Two days later he wrote again from the Grand Hotel Sousse, having 'blown the desert sand off my table, which stands in the columned courtyard of an Arab house'. He had been woken early that morning by a great commotion. 'At the crack of dawn the grunting and groaning of camels, many running footsteps, sheep bleating, men shouting, then muffled drumbeats, the sky grows red in the East.' He got up and looked out of the window at the fabulous scene unfolding below:

> The square in front of the Hotel full of sitting camels, great numbers of black bearded faces in snow-white burnooses, shouts echoing back and forth . . . Three fellows with tremendous drums are drumming incessantly, along with them a sort of clarinet – flute-oboe, sounds like bagpipes – rapid rhythm, some men dance with arms outstretched – a caravan from the Sahara has arrived, about 150 men with many camels, to do one day of holy work for the Marabout, the holy man, who lives here – he feeds the poor from his garden – now the sun is rising majestically from the red and purple haze of the vast desert – three large flags of green silk with golden crescents unfurl . . .

He ended, breathless: 'I am having a shamelessly good time. I hope all is well with you, too. With loving greetings, your Carl' – adding by way of a postscript: 'I have been collecting some desert flora for Aggi.'

'At last I was where I longed to be: in a non-European country where no European language was spoken and no Christian conceptions prevailed,' he wrote in *Memories, Dreams, Reflections*. 'Where a different race lived and a different historical tradition and philosophy had set its stamp upon the face of the crowd.' He sat for hours in an Arab coffee house listening to the conversations, understanding not a word but studying the men's gestures and expressions of emotion. He reminded himself that this strip of land had already borne the brunt of three civilisations: Carthaginian, Roman and Christian. He could smell the blood. He wondered what effect the coming of Western technology would have on Islam.

After Sousse he and Sigg travelled further south to the oasis city of Tozeur. 'Towering date palms form a green, shady roof overhead, under which peach, apricot, and fig trees flourished, and beneath these alfalfa of an unbelievable green. Several king-fishers, shining like jewels, flitted through the foliage. In the comparative coolness of this green shade strolled figures clad in white, among them a great number of affectionate couples hold-ing one another in close embrace – obviously homosexual friendships.' The women were heavily veiled. If not, they were prostitutes, Jung's dragoman had explained to him. All this he relayed to Emma, back at home in Kusnacht.

Over the next few years there was a shift in Emma's life as her three eldest children grew up and left home. In September 1923 Agathe and Kurt were married at Seestrasse, without fuss – Agathe, beautiful in her wedding gown of cream silk and veil, Lil and Marianne, now nine and thirteen, their bridesmaids. But no fancy church wedding, just pastor Adolf Keller, Tina's husband, to officiate. Two years later Gret married Fritz Baumann, another ETH student – furious that her wedding day had to be postponed from an auspicious date in March, accord-ing to her astrological charts, to an average day in April, just because her father was away on his travels again.

Agathe had to leave almost immediately for Augsburg in Germany where Kurt had an engineering job, and by the time Gret got married Carl and Emma were already grandparents. In all, Agathe and Kurt had three children, two girls and a boy. Gret and Fritz had five, all boys. Franz was still at home but having difficulties, unsure what to do with his life. His father was no help, unwilling to offer any guidance, expecting him to find his own way. Confused, he started to study medicine but it did not suit him and he failed his exams. His impatient father gave him some money and told him to go off travelling until he found something he could do. It was Groma Rauschenbach who, typically, came to the rescue and suggested architecture. Franz ended up in Stuttgart with Ernst Fichter, the relation who designed Seestrasse, and an architect he became. When Fowler McCormick came back on a visit to Zürich after studying in America he saw for himself how it was with Carl: 'I remember him saying way back that really, if a family is healthy, the children grow up by themselves, you don't need to do much about the children then. Of course I always thought it was fine to say that, but Mrs Jung did a lot of valuable work with the children, there is no doubt about that at all. They did not grow up just by themselves. Most of the credit for the condition of the children should go to Mrs Jung.'

With Carl frequently away, and just Lil and Marianne at home, Emma had more time to pursue her own interests. Throughout the 1920s she began to shape her lifelong research into the Grail legend into a book. The twelfth-century romance by Chrétien de Troyes about Perceval, a knight in the Arthurian legends, which had fascinated her since her days in Paris, ran like a thread through her own life: Perceval is born in a forest, in twilight and only half conscious, protected from all dangers by his mother. His father is absent, killed in battle. One day he sees five knights in the forest, and he leaves his mother and childhood behind to follow them. It is his odyssey, and each adventure brings him further into the world of consciousness. Finding the castle of the Grail he meets the Fisher King and embarks on his quest for the Holy Grail, described as a cup or vessel possessed of symbolic and magical powers – in later Christian texts transformed into the Holy Chalice which Joseph of Arimathea was said to have brought to Britain after the Last Supper, containing the blood of Jesus from the Crucifixion

The book, *Die Graalslegende in psychologischer Sicht* (*The Legend of the Grail from a Psychological Standpoint*), was a scholarly work with an extensive bibliography, ranging from classical derivations and Eastern parallels to etymology. 'The Grail Legend is an especially stimulating subject for psychological consideration because it contains so many features that are also found in myths and fairy-tales,' Emma writes in her introduction. The story was known to everyone, she explained: a mysterious vessel guarded by a king who is ailing in his castle – a place which is difficult to find. The king can only be restored to health if a knight 'of conspicuous excellence' finds the castle and then asks a certain question. This is the quest with its symbolic meaning: the quest of every individual for psychic health and wholeness achieved by asking the right questions and freeing themselves from the dark forces of the unconscious, symbolised by the forest where Perceval was born and spent his childhood. 'Moreover, it has lost far less fascination for contemporary men and women than have the latter [fairy-tales] which may indicate that it still embodies a living myth.'

Respecting Emma's prior interest in the Grail, Carl left the subject to her, though he himself had had a profound interest in it from an early age. It was one of the first things he and Emma shared when they were courting, talking like-minded as they walked high on the slopes above Ölberg to 'their' bench at the edge of the wood. And in fact Carl is never far away in Emma's text. His ideas on symbolism run right through it, above all Perceval's odyssey and his individuation from unconscious to consciousness. Every now and again Emma interprets a passage with specific, if unnamed, reference to Carl: 'a man naturally has the tendency to identify with his masculinity, and, as is well known, the acceptance of his feminine side is a severe problem for him. He is therefore inclined to act unjustly towards the feminine. Historically the woman was stigmatised as the devil,' and this followed shortly by: 'It often happens that people who behave in a markedly egocentric way are basically in constant danger of being absorbed by other people or situations, so that in such cases the egocentricity may be looked upon as a kind of bulwark against this tendency.' It is as though Emma, grappling with the labyrinth of her life with Carl, trying to understand him, uses the book as her own quest. She continued to work on the book for the rest of her life, leaving it unfinished when she died. It was Carl who made sure it was completed after her death, by one of their colleagues, Marie-Louise von Franz, and Carl who had it published.

These days Emma also had more time with her circle of female friends – Martha Sigg, Johanna Meier, Tina Keller, Susi Trüb. And Toni Wolff, always Toni. They spent evenings together, often discussing women's matters: their problems, their place in society, the social changes in Switzerland as a result of the war, their work, their hopes, their ambitions. And Emma was still the president of the Psychological Club, more established now after her diplomatic manoeuvres, though as troubled as ever with rivalries and jealousies. But now, finally feeling confident enough, and encouraged by Carl, she took the decisive step to train as an analyst herself, with their friend Hans Trüb. From Carl's point of view it was a perfect solution. Every time he went away he would be able to hand over his patients to Emma. Or to Toni Wolff, who was already training to be an analyst. A *ménage à trois* of a different sort.

The other *ménage à trois* carried on as before, the two women sharing Carl more or less equably these days, each with their own role. Emma at Seestrasse represented stable, everyday life. 'Her influence brought him every moment back to the normality of a normal Swiss. Whenever he was with her, he was just a normal Mr Jung living in Kusnacht and was in no danger of running away with his fantasies,' recalled Heinrich Fierz, the son of good friends of Emma and Carl. 'This is a very important function of a wife, and Toni Wolff had, of course, the function of the anima figure. It is always a fault [mistake] if the wife tries to play the role of the anima. This gives a terrific cocktail.' Carl Meier's wife Johanna remembered it in much the same way: 'It wasn't just a triangle situation like it is for most people.' At one point Emma and Toni shared an analysis with Meier, but nothing changed. Because there was no getting away from it: Carl needed both of them, for his sanity – Emma wife of Personality No. 1, Toni wife of Personality No. 2. 'Mrs Jung was more extroverted than Toni Wolff,' said Johanna. 'She could sit after lunch in the afternoon with her comic magazine . . . and just sit there and laugh and laugh. She had a great sense of humour. Both were strong women, but it was easier with Emma. 'She was his partner,' said Tina. 'They were equals. She could stand up to him.' And they could laugh together, as they always had.

By September 1920 Jung was in Cornwall for a series of talks organised by Constance Long. She had been introduced to Jung by her friends Dr David Eder and his wife Edith who had gone to Zurich before the war to be analysed by him. Long was one of a handful of impressive female doctors, English and American, including Beatrice Hinkle, who gathered round Jung. In Cornwall, about a dozen people attended the two-week session, everyone staying in the same boarding house: the Eders, Maurice Nicoll, Peter Baynes, an English doctor who had served with the Army Medical Service during the war and was now turning to Jung and psychoanalysis, and Esther Harding, who had graduated from the London School of Medicine for Women in 1914 and was a friend of Constance Long. This time Carl took both Emma and Toni with him. But at the end of the fortnight Toni went to London alone, and thence back to Zürich, whilst Carl and Emma travelled to Glastonbury, where Emma wanted to pursue her researches into the Holy Grail.

One day at Easter, 1922, a boy was standing on the shore of Lake Zürich, at the upper, isolated end, by a village called Bollingen. Hans Kuhn was twelve and lived in the village, no more than a hamlet, with his parents and siblings. As he stood there throwing sticks and skimming stones he saw a boat, a fine yawl with red sails containing a man and a woman and two children, making for the shore, and as the man steered it to the shore he called out to the boy to lend a hand. This was Herr Doktor Jung, it turned out, and he wanted to know if there was land to be bought along that shore. He had already tried to buy up one of the small islands on the upper lake where he often took his children camping, but the owner was not prepared to sell. Hans could have told the Herr Doktor that a purchase at Bollingen would not be popular either, it being the village bathing place, but he went to fetch his father as bidden. The Herr Doktor, a man who seemed used to getting his own way, came back at Whitsun and managed to make a deal with the owner and by the autumn he had engaged the mason from Schmerikon, who owned the quarry on the opposite shore of the lake, to ferry stones across and start building what would become the famous Tower at Bollingen.

Bollingen Tower – Carl's spiritual home.

The property consisted of a stretch of shore with a large meadow to one side. At first Carl wanted to build the tower himself, with help from the Niehus and Preiswerk boys and Franz, arriving by boat and camping in the tents he had brought back from Château d'Oex at the end of the war. But the stones were massive and the work too hard, even for him, and he was soon obliged to ask the mason from Schmerikon to engage some men to do the heavy work. Still Carl helped with the stones and oversaw every last detail, just as he had with the building of 228 Seestrasse.

The design was for a simple single-storeyed round tower in the medieval style, with a hearth at the centre and bunks for sleeping round the edge, and small windows in the thick walls piercing the darkness, creating a powerful, spiritual atmosphere, just like the towers in his dreams. Emma and the girls stayed away until the weather got warmer but then they came too, bringing provisions to cook on the open fire. There was no running water and no lighting other than oil lamps. Hans Kuhn brought milk from the farm every morning and water from the village well, and bread. It was a primitive life, exactly as Carl liked it, and an adventure. Soon he had dug a garden at the far side of the tower where he planted potatoes and maize, a favourite of his for breakfast. He did most of the cooking, because he liked it, and he liked it just so: if someone was helping him and they got it wrong he shouted at them, so mostly they just let him get on with it, dressed in his old gardener's apron and shorts and his battered straw hat.

After a big breakfast, it was bread and a piece of sausage or cheese in the middle of the day and a big meal in the evening, sitting round the hearth inside the tower if the weather was bad or outside round the campfire if it was good, Carl smoking his pipe and telling stories late into the night. Sometimes he would go into the village for a cheese and onion tart; once, when the tart wasn't to his liking, he swore at the baker and threw it in the air so it hit the ceiling. 'Odd, that Herr Doktor', is how the villagers described him. But once they got talking to him they usually changed their minds. He was so full of information and spellbinding stories, so interested in their lives, as happy to spend time with them as with the 'grand people' at Kusnacht. He was simple in his manner, often arriving at the village on his bicycle with a knapsack on his back, and content to spend long evenings playing games of *Zweierli*, two-handed cards, with Hans: at heart a peasant just like them. Later, when he was abroad, he wrote long letters to Hans, which the boy read out loud to his family, and thence to the whole village – marvellous letters full of unimaginable things.

As the tower grew larger and life there became more routine, Carl liked to sail to Schmerikon to visit the wine merchant and sit on his cellar steps tasting a good local Riesling or a fine Italian Chianti. Often he went to Bollingen on his own for days at a time, either sailing there or taking the local train and walking the rest, rucksack on back. Storms could blow up suddenly on the lake, and then the boats had to be battened down and the heavy doors of the tower bolted, and he would stay inside, reading and writing. But in summer Carl lived and worked mostly out of doors, sitting for hours at a time on the shore, digging his channels and dams, thinking things out, giving full rein to his unconscious. Often he was joined by one of his two 'wives'. When Emma came she set herself up at a small table a short distance from the tower to read or do her needlework. Toni Wolff didn't know how to cook and she didn't like camping or any kind of physical discomfort, so she didn't come to the tower till it had an upper floor with proper sleeping quarters. But then she too came, sometimes with Emma as a threesome, mostly alone with Carl.

In February 1923, shortly after the Jungs had bought the land at Bollingen, Carl's mother died unexpectedly after a short illness. It was from Emilie that Carl had inherited his sixth sense, his visions and voices and a respect for the occult which never left him. Her death brought up all sorts of spookery from his unconscious, though he recovered sooner than he would have done during his years of crisis. Ever since the end of the war Carl's inner life had steadied. Bollingen, the true home of Jung's Personality No. 2, felt like fate, a favourite word of Jung's. 'Gradually, through my scientific work, I was able to put my fantasies and the contents of the unconscious on a solid footing,' he wrote. 'Words and paper, however, did not seem real enough to me; something more was needed. I had to achieve a kind of representation in stone of my innermost thoughts and of the knowledge I had acquired. Or, to put it another way, I had to make a confession of faith in stone. That was the beginning of the "Tower", the house which I built for myself at Bollingen.' Stone had always held an almost magical power for Jung – the boy who sat on the stone in his garden wondering whether he was the stone or the stone was him. Bollingen was 'for myself' and no one else.

Carl's wanderings continued. It was Fowler McCormick who first suggested a trip to East Africa in the summer of 1925, an 'Expedition into Interior Africa', as the *Milwaukee Journal* would describe it, for research into 'the psychology of savage peoples'. Carl was only too happy to leave the house and patients at Seestrasse to Emma and Toni Wolff. The previous autumn he had gone to America at the urgent request of Fowler's parents, Harold and Edith McCormick. They had been divorced not long after their return to America after the war and Harold had remarried, but now they joined forces, begging Carl to come and give Fowler a good talking to. Fowler, their only son, was threatening to marry Anne Stillman, known as Fifi, the mother of his room mate at Princeton. Carl did his best, but to no avail. Instead he and Fowler took a long trip round America and New Mexico, including the Grand Canyon, Arizona, New Orleans, Washington, where Jung studied 'Negro patients' at St Elizabeth's Hospital, and Taos for two weeks, where Jung met Native Americans, in particular Ochwiay Biano, or Mountain Lake, an elder of the Hopi tribe, who talked to him about their rituals and the mythology of the sun. Christmas was spent in Chicago with George Porter, heir to a vast railway fortune and old friend of the McCormicks. Left to her own devices, Emma took her younger children off to Schaffhausen to spend Christmas with her mother in the comfort of Ölberg, as much a pleasure for her as for the children. Toni Wolff spent Christmas alone with her mother at Freiestrasse.

In the event Fowler did not accompany Jung to East Africa, but Jung's new friend, the Englishman Peter Baynes, did, plus George Beckwith, another wealthy American who was prepared to foot the bill. Unfortunately Baynes and Beckwith didn't get on, even though Baynes, who had moved to Zürich to become Jung's assistant, had been Beckwith's analyst off and on for some years. Matters were made infinitely worse by the fact that Baynes's wife, Hilda, had committed suicide in London on the eve of their departure. Baynes was guilt-ridden and morose throughout the journey. Beckwith turned out to be a champion sulker.

They sailed from Southampton for Mombasa in Kenya in October 1925. On board the ship was a group of young women travelling out to be married to officers in the Colonial Service. Among them was Miss Ruth Bailey, the sister of a bride-to-be. She was thirty-three years old and had been engaged herself, twice, but both men had been killed in the war. Miss Bailey hailed from Cheshire, one of those straightforward, adventurous, hearty and jovial Englishwomen from a good family who did not let life get her down. She did not meet Jung on board because he was not much in evidence, spending the six weeks avoiding his two travelling companions as much as possible, and learning Swahili from an old colonial officer. But they ended up at the same New Stanley Hotel in Nairobi, and during one of the fancy dress parties which the hotel laid on for their guests Ruth took herself off to a small drawing room to get away from all the noise and merriment and there she found Jung poring over a map of Kenya. He did not look up so she just sat there, passing the time. After about an hour he asked if she was interested in maps. She was. The following day he invited her to join them for breakfast, then a shopping trip to the bazaar. There was nothing sexual about it, she noted, he merely wanted a buffer between himself and his two awkward companions. Miss Bailey was underestimating herself. Jung immediately enjoyed her no-nonsense, direct and humorous ways and especially the fact that she had absolutely no interest in psychoanalysis. By the time the three men set off on their expedition, Ruth was on her way to Turbo in the Rift Valley Province with her sister and future brother-in-law, rather dreading the boring months of expatriate life which lay ahead. Jung had probably already made up his mind to ask her to join them.

Two months later a runner turned up at the bungalow in Turbo with an invitation for Ruth to come to Mount Elgon on the border region between Kenya and Uganda. The three men had embarked on what they called their 'Bugishu Psychological Expedition', with a large contingent of bearers and plenty of supplies, but they had had a tricky time getting there, as Francis Daniel Hislop, a junior colonial officer in a remote up-country station, discovered when he saw a large safari box-body car pulled up on the side of the track near his bungalow in the Nandi District. 'Good afternoon,' he said. 'Can I help you in any way?' To Hislop's surprise one of the men turned out to be Dr Jung of Zürich. Jung was delighted that young Hislop had heard of him. They wanted to get to Mount Elgon, he explained over tea in Hislop's bungalow. Hislop had to inform them they were on the wrong road and he wondered how they were going to communicate with the Karamojong and the Sabei, who did not in fact speak Swahili.

By the time Ruth Bailey arrived from Turbo, resisting all attempts to stop her embarking on this foolish and dangerous escapade, 250 miles of it, the three men had found Mount Elgon and Jung had found a man amongst the bearers who could communicate with the elders of the tribe, and spoke some pidgin English too. Fascinated by the three white men, the tribal people were happy to talk about their rituals and beliefs, and especially their dreams, to which they attached profound meanings, just as the white doctor did.

The postal service was hit and miss in those regions, but Carl managed to write to Emma his usual vivid accounts, and even sent a long letter to young Hans Kuhn. A snake had attacked Herr Beckwith, he wrote, and one evening he had been infected by sand-fly fever and dreamt that he was 'going black'. They would be home by the beginning of April. Franz recalled that this was the one and only time he ever witnessed a jealous scene between his mother and Toni Wolff: they fought over who should go and meet Carl at Marseilles. His mother settled it: neither of them. Franz, now eighteen, would go.

Perhaps Emma was anxious when she heard about the intrepid young Englishwoman who acted as a buffer between the three men and was able to make Carl laugh out loud. She need not have worried. Not long after Carl's return, Emma wrote to Miss Bailey inviting her to stay at Seestrasse. When Ruth arrived she found Emma sitting on the landing of the stairs having her portrait painted. Apparently George Beckwith, who adored Emma, had commissioned the painting as a gift for Carl, but the artist was having trouble making her smile. 'I remember this man saying to me "Come Miss Bailey, and amuse her. Tell her funny stories. She is much too serious. Much too serious." So Ruth quickly settled into her usual role and soon had Emma laughing and giggling like a schoolgirl at her stories of Kenya. Emma was beautiful, Ruth noted, but not happy. 'Her eyes were very sad,' she remembered, 'and I sat on the stairs below telling her all these daft things about Africa.'

Ruth hardly saw Jung except at mealtimes, spending all her time with Emma and the children. They went for walks, stayed with Emma's mother in Schaffhausen and her sister Marguerite living nearby, visited the galleries and theatres in Zürich, including a picture house where they watched an English comedy which made Emma laugh until she cried. Another time they went to a fancy dress party at the Psychological Club, to which Toni Wolff turned up as Queen Nefertiti, chain-smoking her cigarettes in her long cigarette holder. But though Ruth and Emma talked about many things, they never discussed Emma's marriage. After that first visit Ruth came to Kusnacht every summer, and the Jung girls went to stay with Ruth in Cheshire, as did Emma. After Emma's death Ruth was the one to come to look after Carl, staying with him till the end, as friend and carer, loved by the whole family.

Why was Emma so 'sad' in 1925? A clue lies in something Jung wrote about his obsessive travels at that time: to his own astonishment he realised it was partly to avoid 'personal problems', and the suspicion dawned on him that he had undertaken his African adventure 'with the secret purpose of escaping from Europe and its complex of problems'. He admitted to himself that this was not so much 'an objective scientific project as an intensely personal one, and that any attempt to go deeper into it touched every possible sore spot in my own psychology'. The atmosphere had become too 'highly charged' at home. In *Memories, Dreams, Reflections* he uses the word 'Europe' not 'home', which only appears in the 'Protocols'. But the sense of it is clear; juggling his life between two women was difficult. There were rumours of another 'infatuation' too. And his mother's death had brought up all sorts of buried memories. Split Carl concluded: 'My European personality must under all circumstances be preserved intact.' Split, or wanting everything both ways? Jung by his own admission was a trickster: 'I can let myself be deceived from here to Tipperary when I don't want to recognise something, and yet at bottom I know quite well how matters really stand.' As Fowler McCormick put it: 'For Mrs Jung it was a rough time, for she was a very lovely woman, a gentle woman, a good mother, and she loved Dr Jung.'

* * *

By now Emma had handed over the role of president of the Psychological Club to Hans Trüb, and it was as Alphonse Maeder predicted: Jung and Hans soon fell out because Hans began challenging Jung's theories. Jung resigned from the club, taking Toni and Emma with him, though it was the last thing Emma wanted to do, but she felt she had to stand by Carl. She tried again and again to reconcile the two men but the rift could not be healed. Perhaps she suspected that it was not only a professional disagreement but also a certain jealousy on Jung's part: Emma had become very close to Hans and Susi Trüb. When life got too difficult at Seestrasse she would sometimes decamp to their holiday home in Ticino in southern Switzerland. Both the Trübs were distressed by the rift, but Susi understood that Emma 'had to be on her husband's side. But I only saw that later; and then I never blamed her for it, because I too had to support my husband.' It was doubly upsetting because the two women were very close: 'With my sister [Toni] I only related as a sister. The personal relation was with Emma,' said Susi. 'She was truly and completely a woman.' It was Susi who knew Emma had considered divorcing Carl three times. There was something innately brutal about Carl, she felt, certainly in his dealings with Hans. 'People just came into conflict around him.' Soon enough it was Hans Trüb who had resigned from the club, and the holy trinity of Emma, Carl and Toni, as some members liked to jest, returned.

From March to July 1925, shortly before his extended trip to East Africa, Jung gave a series of seminars at the Psychological Club in Zürich charting the development of his ideas from the early days of his cousin Helly's seances, to his work at the Burghölzli, to Freud, and on to the sinologist Richard Wilhelm, whom Jung had met in 1923 and who had now a profound influence on his thinking. Jung spoke in English at these seminars, many of the twenty-seven people who attended being either English or American, including Esther Harding, who he knew from England, and two impressive American doctors now training to be Jungian analysts, Kristine Mann and Eleanor Bertine. Their friend Cary Fink, another trained doctor, took the notes. She had come to Zürich with her daughter, Ximena, in 1923 after getting divorced, and was soon part of the Jung circle of friends. After the seminars Jung liked to repair to a local café, everyone vying to walk with him, sit next to him, talk to him, grab a piece of his magnetic self. Emma preferred to go home alone.

Over the next few years Emma gave several talks to the Psychological Club, some on the Legend of the Holy Grail, others on the Jungian theme of animus/anima, which were later published in a slim volume. These turned out to be highly personal and revealing, rather as her talk on 'Guilt' had been. With her usual modesty Emma admitted she could not claim a complete understanding of the terms and would therefore limit herself to an examination of the animus and anima in relation to the individual and to consciousness. She began with a brief definition: animus was the masculine principle, anima the feminine, a man having some feminine characteristics, a woman some masculine ones. Normally both were present to a degree, but often hidden, conditioned by latent sexual characteristics and a person's experiences in life with the opposite sex. Being unconscious these could interfere in an individual's life, sometimes in a disturbing, even destructive way. So they had to be understood.

For a young woman, a man of physical power could easily become an animus figure, she suggested: heroes of legend and so forth. For an older and more exacting woman a man who had accomplished things, or offered spiritual guidance, would be a more likely focus. Each could be problematic because of the danger of projecting the image on the man. Some women, the active, energetic, brave and forceful ones, already had the masculine aspect harmoniously integrated, but if it was not properly integrated it could overrun the feminine aspect and result in brutal, aggressive behaviour, including in the sexual domain. Then the animus could be destructive to the woman and her relationships, leading to depression or general dissatisfaction with life. It had something to do with the modern times they lived in: the women's movement, advances in birth control, technological advances, psychology's discovery of the unconscious, and the law which still gave the man greater privileges. The result was a lack of self-confidence in women and a resistance to becoming conscious. In many ways it was like a household budget, declared Emma, the practical wife and mother: women had a finite amount of psychic energy, and it had to be well spent.

The lines between professional and personal were often blurred in those early days of psychoanalysis. Even so, Emma sailed close to the wind, barely bothering to disguise references to her own life and marriage. Women often fell back on a projection of their hopes and ambitions, she suggested, but that could rarely be successful for long, especially if the woman was in a close relationship with the man in question. Then the incongruity between the idealised image and the image-bearer often became all too obvious: 'We become aware, to our great confusion and disappointment, that the man who seemed to embody our image does not correspond to it in the least, but continually behaves quite differently from the way we think he should. At first, perhaps, we try to deceive ourselves about this and often succeed relatively easily, thanks to an aptitude for effacing differences, which we owe to blurred powers of discrimination. Often we try with real cunning to make the man be what we think he ought to represent.' That was not easy for the man either, who already had his own problems discovering his 'anima'. 'When a man discovers the anima figure, image or human, he finds it fascinatingly attractive and hence it appears valuable.' Everyone in the audience at the Psychological Club must have known whose animus and anima Emma was talking about.

Jung put in his pennyworth too, writing his paper titled 'Marriage as a Psychological Relationship'. Setting out boldly, he stated: 'There is no such thing as a psychological relationship between two people who are in a state of unconsciousness.' The bond to the parents unconsciously influenced the choice of husband or wife in the first place, either positively or negatively, compensating for everything which was left unfulfilled in the parents' lives. In a typical marriage, one partner is usually the 'contained', the other the 'container'. The 'contained' partner was the simpler case, 'grounded on a positive relationship to the parents', whilst the more complex partner was hindered by a deep-seated unconscious tie to parents and 'burdened with hereditary traits that are sometimes very difficult to reconcile'. These people, 'having a certain tendency to dissociation, generally have the capacity to split off irreconcilable traits of character for considerable periods, thus passing themselves off as much simpler than they are. Their partners can easily lose themselves in such a labyrinthine nature, sometimes in a not very agreeable way, since their sole occupation then consists in tracking the other through all the twists and turns of his character.'

It was rare to have a smooth, crisisless marriage, he said. It was not possible to become conscious without pain, and usually that transformation began in the second half of life when the passion of the early years gave way to duty and the feeling of a burden, like a vampire, creating disunity with the self. 'This disunity with oneself begets discontent, and since one is not conscious of the real state of things, one generally projects the reason for it upon one's partner. A critical atmosphere thus develops, the necessary prelude to conscious realisation.' It was at that very moment of crisis that everything could begin. This was one of Jung's most important and practical insights: crisis may feel intolerable at the time, but it was only through crisis that development of the personality occurred. As for the partner: she had to give up that *he* belonged to *her*, and stop looking for her security in him but find it in herself, at which point she became valuable again.

Did Emma manage it? It would seem so. In 1927 Jung was asked to lecture at the Kulturbund in Vienna. He took Emma with him, and they were met at the station by the vice-president of the association, Jolande Jacobi. 'I went to the train to fetch him and his wife and I met two wonderful people, looking marvellous, very alert, very jolly, and not at all [as expected].' Jacobi had evidently been forewarned. 'I was absolutely impressed when a beautiful tall, handsome man with beautiful white teeth, laughing, arrived with a charming woman with dark hair and light blue eyes. Like a saint, she looked, Mrs Jung.'

Jacobi was a thirty-eight-year-old good-looking, extroverted, charming Jewish Hungarian. She lived in an elegant apartment with her two young sons, her husband having returned to Budapest for unspecified reasons, possibly because his wife had a longstanding lover. Perhaps Jung hesitated before accepting the invitation to Vienna because of Freud; there had been no rapprochement between them since the final breakdown in their relationship in 1914. By all accounts Freud had not found a crown prince to replace him and he still maintained that Jung had broken away from him and betrayed him, rather than admitting that Jung might have been on a different tack from the start. Freud told Ernest Jones he would not be attending the lecture, pleased to miss 'an excellent opportunity of hearing about the Structure of the Soul from a first-rate source'. However, over a thousand people did turn up to the lecture, which was unheard of at the association, but it turned out to be a disappointing event, the shadow of Freud probably damping Jung's style.

Yet here they were in Vienna again, Emma and Carl, after all this time. They spent the next five days with Jolande Jacobi, who was as enchanted with Emma as she was with Carl. One evening they went to the theatre to see the musical comedy *No, No Nanette!*, during which Carl laughed 'so terribly loud and yelled so that the performance was stopped and the prima donnas greeted him with their hands, and he threw kisses, and they threw kisses, and there was quite an upheaval in the theatre'. Jacobi had never seen anything like it, but Emma was used to it. 'She was the most generous wife you can imagine,' recalled Jacobi. 'Mrs Jung was always tactful and wanted to leave her husband alone with the person he was interested in. She said she would like to see the town and left him alone with me.' The three became firm friends. There was no need for Emma to worry: sophisticated Jolande Jacobi was never going to fall in love with Jung. For one thing he had 'dirty fingers' and he was *schlampig*, a bit messy, whereas Jacobi had fine manners. 'He was somewhat heavy,' she concluded, 'a peasant-like Swiss who did not know how to deal with ladies of high society who flirted with him.' By the end of February they were home again.

In the winter of 1928 the Lake of Zürich froze over. People walked and sledged across it to visit friends, wrapped in furs and hats and muffs, quite dazzled by the whiteness and the magic. To her children's surprise, Emma strapped her skates onto her boots, a thing they had never seen, and took off into the ice-blue.

15

Coming Through

We were *jung* [young]
We were called Jung
To eternal youth
We belong

Lines carved in the terrace wall at Seestrasse

In 1929 Emma was forty-eight. Two daughters, Agathe and Gret, were married, and she had become a grandmother. Franz, twenty-one, had left home for Stuttgart to study architecture. Her two youngest daughters, Marianne and Lil, were nineteen and fifteen respectively. She felt more self-assured these days, though plenty of difficulties still lay ahead. But her central dilemma – how to manage life with her husband Carl and how to find her way through it all, the dilemma she had been grappling with ever since her marriage in 1903 – that was behind her. Or if not exactly behind her, then beside her, flowing along more like a stream than a torrent, winding its way towards the open sea. Perhaps most important of all: she was past the age of menopause, past the danger of having too many 'little blessings'.

She had taken her decisive step: to work as an analyst in her own right. In a sense she had been training for it ever since the early years at the Burghölzli, unwittingly at first. But as the years passed and she became increasingly involved in Carl's work, she found she knew more about it than she realised, not least because of living with split Carl. By the time of the Weimar Congress in 1911 she was acquainted with many of the leading lights of psychoanalysis, including Professor Freud of Vienna, and she had met some forward-thinking women too – Hedwig Bleuler and Beatrice Hinkle among them – who had introduced her to new and challenging ideas about women in society. Encouraged by Carl, Emma had become the first president of the Psychological Club of Zürich, where she discovered she could hold her own and rise above the jealousies and rivalries which somehow always surrounded her husband. Her own jealousies were harder to resolve, but now, helped by embarking on her own working life, she found she could contain them if not actually banish them.

As though to celebrate, Emma learnt to drive a motor car in 1929, taught by faithful Müller, who these days functioned as chauffeur and general handyman as well as gardener, and bought herself a Dodge Sedan. Carl learnt to drive at the same time, buying himself a red Chrysler Convertible, which he called the 'Red Darling' and which he parked outside Toni Wolff's house on Freiestrasse every Wednesday for all the world to see, like a red rag to a bull.

Emma's first analysand was the young Englishwoman Barbara Hannah, who later wrote the first biography of Jung. Hannah's father was Dean of Chichester Cathedral, and she had so far led the kind of life typical of people from her background:

Church of England, conventional middle class. But one way or another she had reached a point of crisis in her life. She came to Zürich hoping to be analysed by Herr Doktor Jung, but just then he was in a phase of trying to extricate himself from the demands of so many patients, all craving his attention. 'Oh my God, you bore me!' he announced, and promptly passed her over to Emma. Later she was passed on to Toni Wolff. That was how the threesome worked those days, passing patients on from one to another. When she came back to Jung he had changed his tune: 'Ah, you've ditched both of them, and now, you hellcat, you want to get me in the ditch,' he roared at her. Jung loved American slang. Hellcat was good. 'I knew you were a hellcat from the start. That's why I passed you on. But I tell you what I will do. I will take you on again on the understanding that, if you get me in the ditch too, it's up to you to get me out again.'

But Hannah started with Emma. 'She was just beginning. It was all very much like going to tea with a lovely and gracious lady, and only afterwards did one realise that she was an excellent analyst,' she recalled. 'She used to give you two hours instead of an hour. She did a tremendous amount for me.' Another analysand put Emma's method this way: 'She approached the problem you brought to her quietly, even tentatively, but there was no fumbling. To be "right" did not appear to interest her. She met you where you were at.'

At the Psychological Club, Emma was known as 'the unofficial authority of the Club', not because she was the wife of Jung but because of her 'strength and serenity'. When Carl offended people with his sudden rages or rudeness or sarcasm, Emma appeased them. When he became too boisterous playing games such as 'Alleluia' – where people threw a ball at one another shouting *Alleluia!* as a means of accessing their unconscious, and which could quickly descend into chaos – she kept him in check. She never joined the Wednesday lunches where he was surrounded by 'those fawning women, hanging on every word and fighting among themselves to get into his graces', as the forthright American Jane Wheelwright described, preferring to go home alone.

One afternoon in March 1931, Peter Baynes arrived at Seestrasse unannounced and in a state of high tension. Carl was away lecturing. Emma invited him in and they settled down to tea and talk. 'Emma was just lovely,' Baynes wrote to his future wife, Anne Leay, back in London. 'We just seemed to get to a calm leisurely mood like a broad river where we found the most human understanding. She told me lots of things about herself and her deep feeling conclusions seem to me ever so true. So you see I was able to tell her about you and me.' Baynes was in a difficult situation: since his return from the Africa trip, and in the wake of his wife's suicide, he had married – against Jung's advice – Cary Fink, newly divorced and living permanently in Zürich with her daughter. But the marriage was not working out, and now he had met and fallen in love with Anne in London and was stuck between the two women, unable to move forwards or backwards.

Emma calmed him. 'She got your spirit, as a woman I felt, and she said: "You see Peter, I would never say that the way things are in our lives [meaning Toni and C.G.] is in any way a solution ..."' Emma was warning against a love triangle. 'She let me know how she had suffered and how she still suffers.' Her advice must have helped: Baynes married Anne that same year, and it turned out a happy and successful marriage which lasted for the rest of their lives.

In March 1932 Emma's mother Bertha Rauschenbach died. Emma was profoundly affected. She adored her mother and loved spending time in her company. Whenever she was getting lost in the labyrinthine problems of her marriage, it was in her mother she confided. After all, it was Bertha who had brought Carl and Emma together again after Emma refused Carl's proposal of marriage. Summer holidays, Christmases, weekends, so much of Jung family life had taken place at Ölberg. Now Marguerite and Ernst moved in to take over the house, but it wasn't the same.

Within months came word of another death. 'Dear Mr McCormick,' Emma wrote to Harold McCormick on 1 September 1932, having just heard of Edith's death. 'The news of Mrs McCormick's death was a great shock to me, and thinking of her brought up so many reminiscences that I must send you a word of sympathy.'

After the McCormicks' divorce Edith had retreated to her vast mansion on Lake Michigan, no longer taking part in the high life, in fact not taking part in anything very much at all. 'A tragic fate', as Emma put it. Harold had been a frequent visitor when Edith was ill, which Emma suggested must have been a great relief to Edith but perhaps also to Harold: 'In my thoughts she will always, as you too, be linked with a very intense and important phase in my life, and I shall always be grateful to have had the privilege of coming to know her and you, and of all the stimulating and precious contributions to my own development

I got through this relation. And of course the Club will always be a living and lasting expression of her great and generous personality, to which we owe it.'

Life at Seestrasse went on as usual, wrote Emma. Jung was at Bollingen, where he spent most of the summer holidays. 'I am also doing some analytical work and I like it very much indeed. I find it most satisfactory, and am sure it does me at least as good as the analysands.' She ended with the hope that everything was well with Harold and sending her warmest regards. 'Yours very sincerely, Emma Jung.'

Edith's death had taken Emma right back to the time, twenty years earlier, when her misery and crisis about her husband's 'infatuations' had forced her to confront her own demons. Few close to Emma and Carl in 1912 thought she would ever manage to overcome the difficulties, but gradually they had changed their minds. 'I think she underwent the most spectacular transformation during their married life. More than any of the women I saw. She was quite an exceptional person,' observed Carl Meier. His wife, Johanna, who was able to observe Carl and Emma at close quarters over the years, saw that not only did Emma find a way to manage her own life, but increasingly she underpinned Carl's too. 'I think this relationship, the real marriage relationship, was carrying his life work actually, certainly you could see this when you watched them,' she said. 'When you saw this couple it was a very harmonious couple. They belonged to each other. Certainly they did. I always had the feeling that his strength, both physically and spiritually, came through this marriage. He was in the centre and carried it all. But I'm convinced that this marriage carried the load, actually, of the whole Jungian development. If this marriage hadn't been right and true, it would not have gone through the mill. I'm sure only Mrs Jung could do it.' They could see now that it was a 'joint career' in every sense, to the extent that the world would not have had the Carl Jung it knew without Emma Jung, steady in the background.

Johanna had once gone to talk to Emma about some difficulties in her own marriage. 'Well, do you want to carry on or are you going to quit it all?' Emma challenged her. Emma was no quitter evidently. 'I'm sure that each of them knew that it was worthwhile to carry through,' said Johanna. 'They belonged together.'

In September 1932 Emma was invited as guest of honour at the Analytical Psychology Club in London for a discussion of her paper on 'Animus'. She stayed with Peter and Anne Baynes, taking Franz and Lil with her. During her stay Emma and Anne became friends, later cemented by Anne travelling to Zürich to spend a month at Seestrasse being analysed by Emma. The analysis made everything extraordinarily clear, Anne said, noting a wisdom and warmth in Emma which she had not had from her own mother. 'I do love Emma. She does symbolise for me the kind of woman I want to be.' This was Emma's strength: to be simple and honest in her approach, empathetic but not directive, helping people to find their own way, as she had hers. Or, to use the Jungian term: to individuate.

And yet Toni Wolff was still there, still part of the *ménage à trois*, still claiming her share of Carl with her cleverness and spirituality, arriving at Seestrasse in her elegant outfits and big hats, puffing away at her cigarettes, wandering around the garden in deep conversation with Carl, irritating the children, causing Emma distress. 'Toni was a manipulator in a very lady-like way. She'd sure get rid of her enemies, but you never saw it happen. Emma was more forthright, less of a manipulator,' is how Jane Wheelwright remembered it. In January 1930 Carl went to Berlin to give a talk. He took Toni with him. As usual he left all the arrangements to his travelling companion. In a letter to a colleague Toni wrote asking for two single rooms in the hotel, but interconnecting, with a joint bathroom. In October 1935 he took Toni, not Emma, to London for a series of lectures he had been invited to give by the Institute of Medical Psychology at the Tavistock Clinic, introducing her to everyone as his 'colleague', though there can't have been anyone there who didn't know her true status – so unconventional, so un-Swiss, and how impressive was Miss Wolff's collection of stylish hats.

The Englishman Joseph Henderson, who first came to Zürich to be analysed by Jung in 1929 and later became a leading analyst, saw it this way: 'Jung told me personally once that the most valuable thing in his life was his marriage. He would give up anything before he would give up his marriage.' Toni Wolff knew it too. 'The thing went on for a lifetime because Toni was not married, and she was so alone and she had given her whole life to Jung,' thought Jane Wheelwright. 'She lived for him. And he could not dump her. So it was tough.' Barbara Hannah thought Toni Wolff learnt to accept it over the years: 'Toni over-came the besetting sin of so many single women, the desire to somehow destroy the marriage and marry the man herself.' In truth, Toni had little choice. 'The law Jung was faithful to was the creative instinct in him, he would abandon almost anything for that,' said Carl Meier. And Toni was still crucial to that. 'In their discussions she played an enormous role. She sometimes became quite dramatic too. Sometimes it became rough. Real rough.' Emma was no pushover either. 'She was a tremendously forceful person. She could put her foot down and attack you face to face and ask you to be really honest. She really was a forceful person, not someone who is easily pushed around.'

Toni's advice to a patient whose husband was having an affair was: ask the other woman to lunch.

You would then get to know her a bit, you might even like her . . . Sometimes if a man's wife is big enough to leap over the hurdle of self-pity, she may find that her supposed rival has even helped her marriage! This 'other woman' can some-times help a man live out certain aspects of himself that his wife either can not fulfil or else she doesn't especially want to. As a result, some of the wife's energies are now freed for her own creative interests and development, often with the result that the marriage not only survives but emerges even stronger than before!

She made it sound easy, but it was not easy for her, still living with her mother and seeing little of Carl. But she had her work, and her analysands, who appreciated her cleverness. 'She did not give herself easily to a human relation, but once the ice was broken she was loyal and steadfast', said one analysand, Gerhard Adler. Another felt the much same: 'My original image of her was of a rather tall, very serious, erect, straight-backed woman – the way she always sat in her chair. Later I saw her as a warm, comforting, gentle, relating person.' Apart from her private practice, Toni Wolff headed the lecture committee at the Psychological Club, and for over forty years she assisted Jung with his 'group psychology' experiment, another of his forward-thinking ideas, designed to overcome the transference difficulties of one-to-one analysis. Work was Toni's salvation, and her constant link to Carl.

Each year, from 1933 onwards, Carl and Emma attended the annual week-long Eranos conference at Ascona on Lake Maggiore, organised by a wealthy Anglo-Dutch woman called Olga Froebe-Kapteyn, who aimed to bring together thinkers from many disciplines, including all forms of spiritual research such as the occult and theosophy. As usual people flocked around Jung, but these days Emma held her own. A photograph taken of the Jungs at one of the conferences shows a couple married for over thirty years, relaxed and at ease with one another: Emma in a white summer dress and hat, laughing, happy, looking directly at camera, Carl beside her, leaning towards her, pipe in hand, smiling, satisfied. When Jung was invited to America in 1936 for Harvard's tercentenary, to receive an honorary doctorate and to lecture on 'Factors Determining Human Behaviour', Emma went too. She attended all of Carl's lectures and seminars, and whilst he was seeing private patients, who came from as far away as California, she went sightseeing, probably with Fowler McCormick, who seems to have accompanied them for most of the trip.

After Boston they travelled to Bailey Island in Maine at the invitation of their new friends Eleanor Bertine, Esther Harding and Kristine Mann, where Jung gave another series of lectures and Emma was able to spend time with her old friend from the Weimar congress, Beatrice Hinkle. They stayed in Kristine

Mann's large old family house overlooking the sea and whenever there was some free time, Carl went sailing. Bailey Island
was connected to the mainland by a series of wonderfully engineered bridges, but the coastline was untouched by the present
– most appealing to the Jungs. They left for home in October,
stopping off in London to catch up with more old friends and
for Jung to give a series of lectures at St Bartholomew's Hospital.
Barbara Hannah met them at Waterloo station and drove them
to a small hotel off Regent's Park where Jung again saw private
patients. By the time they got back to Kusnacht they were both
exhausted. Jung cancelled his seminars at the Psychological
Club and the lectures at the ETH to concentrate on the study of
his new enthusiasm: alchemy. Emma took up her usual pursuits:
the home and family, her research, her book, her analytical work
– and Carl.

By the spring of 1937 Carl and Emma were travelling again,
first to the Eranos conference, then back to America, this time
to Yale for Carl to give the Terry lectures on 'Psychology and
Religion'. The packed audience included Mary and Paul Mellon,
who would soon step into the Jungs' lives in much the same way
that Edith and Harold McCormick had done twenty years
earlier.

Like the McCormicks, the Mellons were fabulously rich, from
the Mellon banking family, and in time they became the founders
and funders of the Bollingen Press, publishing Jung's works in
English. Mary Mellon was lively and fun and a classy dresser, but
she suffered all her life from acute asthma attacks, and, like Edith
McCormick, she was seeking a cure. 'I was sitting directly
beneath the platform under a large black hat,' she recalled, 'and
I understood not one word, but I thought, though I don't know

what he means, this has something very much to do with me.'
When Carl and Emma went to New York the Mellons followed
to attend Jung's seminars, hoping to have a private session of
analysis with him. But Carl was too busy with the lectures and
seminars and another hectic round of social engagements, with
Esther Harding on hand to drive them about. Anyway, he and
Emma wanted some free time to visit the museums. Carl's lecture
at the Plaza Hotel was followed by a banquet in his honour. In
his impromptu speech, apparently still thinking of religion, he
said all we could do was follow Christ's example and live our
lives as fully as possible, even if it was based on a mistake. We
should go and make our mistakes, because there was no full life
without error. This was Jung at his practical best again, allowing
for mistakes, his own included. At another supper party the
guests, including the Mellons, were somewhat taken aback when
Jung took out his Swiss Army penknife to open a bottle of
Chianti, then retrieved a stick from his dinner jacket pocket and
started to do a bit of whittling, Swiss-peasant style.

Mary and Paul Mellon at Eranos, 1938, with Jung in the background.

Not everyone warmed to Jung's provocative manner, suspecting he put it on deliberately as a rejection of the decorum Americans expected from their honoured guests. He was too loud and brash, they said – he dominated dinner conversations, ignored people he did not want to talk to, and flirted with their women. Worse: there were rumours that Jung was pro-German if not actively pro-Nazi, perhaps anti-Semitic, based largely on those of his writings which addressed differences in racial and national psychologies, including 'Negroes' and American Indians, as well as Christians and Jews, and on the fact that he remained affiliated to the International Society for Analysts in Germany, accepting the editorship of their publication the *Zentralblatt* after their president, Ernst Kretschmer, a Jew, was forced to resign when the Nazis came to power. After the war these accusations were taken up again, mainly in America, quoting the article he had written for the *Zentralblatt* about racial differences, but instead of Jung's word 'differences', the word 'higher' was used, suggesting racial superiority. The rumours were also fanned by some of Sigmund Freud's more ardent followers, Ernest Jones amongst them, making it hard to distinguish fact from fiction. Freud, who had suffered true anti-Semitism all his life in Vienna and was soon to flee the city and the Nazis for London, surely knew the difference. Rumours flew about, 'cock-and-bull stories' as Jung would describe them: 'Whatever I touch and wherever I go I meet with this prejudice that I am a Nazi.' They were not persecution delusions, he said. They presented a very real difficulty.

Even with the benefit of hindsight, Jung does not come well out of this. But racial theories of the sort were common then, and no one yet knew what the Nazis were capable of. Emma's role during these visits to America was the usual one: as smoother and pacifier, keeping Carl steady. As to the Mellons, they travelled to Zürich and the Eranos conference at Ascona in order to have private sessions with Jung, which they did in 1938 and 1939, by which time another European war was once again threatening.

The Jungs arrived back in Seestrasse in late October 1938. By December Carl was already off again, this time to India with Fowler McCormick, stubbornly refusing to get inoculated before he left, trusting to fate. Emma and Toni stepped in to take over his analysands as usual. Toni went on organising the lecture committee at the Psychological Club, Emma went on giving her lectures on animus, and the Legend of the Holy Grail, and continued writing her book, her life's work, as close as she could ever get to Carl's complex inner world. When she was not working she liked to stay with Agathe and her growing family in Baden, or with Franz in Stuttgart, or Hans and Susi Trüb in Ticino.

Carl came back from India delighted to have found that in Eastern thought the concept of evil went hand in hand with the concept of good, something he had discovered for himself as a schoolboy in his vision of the turd falling on Basel cathedral. He also came back with amoebic dysentery. But it did not stop him travelling to England with Emma the following Easter, 1939. They stayed with the Bayneses again, the main purpose of the trip being for Emma to visit, or revisit, the sites connected with the Holy Grail: Glastonbury, Stonehenge, Avebury, Cerne Abbas. 'It was an extremely happy time for all of us, I think, for Emma was doing what she most wanted to do. Everybody was extremely carefree, somehow,' recalled Anne Baynes. Jung was in one of his high-jinks moods, making everyone laugh, bemusing guests in their Glastonbury hotel. 'Other people in the hotel just could not make out how four people could rock with laughter every morning at breakfast, because it isn't an Englishman's best time for laughter, as a rule. They were all having their quiet breakfasts' – shattered, no doubt, by Jung's bellows. As they drove into Salisbury they saw newspaper billboards announcing that Germany had invaded Czechoslovakia.

By the late 1930s Carl and Emma's 'joint career' was well established. He discussed all his ideas with her. She read everything he wrote. She looked after his patients when he was away, and she picked up the pieces he left in his wake. She kept him steady during his times of doubt or incipient insanity. Finally, Carl told Emma about his early traumas and his phallus dream – the great secret.

'My entire youth can be understood in terms of this secret,' he wrote. 'It induced in me an almost unendurable loneliness. My one great achievement during those years was that I resisted talking about it with anyone. Thus the pattern of my relationship to the world was already prefigured.' When he heard his pastor uncles discussing theology he thought: 'Yes, yes, that is all very well. But what about the secret?' His only consolation was the stone – the leitmotif to his secret life. 'Somehow it would free me of all my doubts. Whenever I thought that I was the stone, the conflict ceased.'

Perhaps the stone was bound to lead Jung to alchemy sooner or later. The sinologist Richard Wilhelm had sent him a Taoist alchemical text, *The Secret of the Golden Flower*, which Jung described as 'the first event which broke through my isolation. I became aware of an affinity; I could establish ties with something and someone.' Soon he was deep into the symbols and secrets of alchemy – another route to deciphering the unconscious.

But alchemy was a step too far for Toni Wolff. From the mid-1930s their relationship was on the wane, until finally it almost ceased. Most observers thought the break came from Carl. They saw how hard it was for Toni. She had met Carl when she was twenty. As her sister Susi said, she had no other partner but Jung all her life. 'She was afraid. She was a very lonely person, and in Jung she surely found the man or partner, someone who could correspond to her intellectual [spiritual] nature. And so that was the way for her, I think. This was everything for her. She had some connexions to other people; she was a very good analyst. But somehow she was never totally in life.' She still came to Seestrasse on Sundays, but it wasn't the same. Ruth Bailey, visiting, noticed how Carl would take out a book and start to read when they were all sitting on the terrace having tea. 'That was a terrible situation and I used to think: "Why do you ever come? I wouldn't come if I were you."' Reflecting on it years later Franz Jung said: 'When I was a ripe man, I felt sorry for Toni. She never knew what it was to be a wife and mother.' In contrast to his own mother who, he said, 'was sure of herself and she was sure of her femininity, so she could deal with Toni.'

Fowler McCormick, commuting between America and Zürich, noticed that Emma and Carl's relationship was getting stronger whilst the relationship with Toni became more distant, until finally in later years Carl could be openly quite cutting and hurtful to her. Often now he left the two women, Emma and

Toni, together, and took himself off to his *Cabinet* until it was time for Toni to leave. Even Emma, after all the years of tolerance, was losing her patience. Once when Jolande Jacobi was visiting from Vienna, Toni Wolff arrived and Jacobi made to leave. 'No,' protested Emma. 'This woman tries all the time to mix herself in my house. Every Sunday she must have my husband. No, you are our guest and you stay.' It was quite unlike Emma, certainly unlike the young Emma. But these days she was less accommodating. 'Well, she was a marvellous woman,' concluded Jacobi about Emma. 'She carried on during this friendship of her husband with serenity and with enormous generosity, until she won.'

When the Second World War broke out Franz and all Emma's sons-in-law – three of them as Marianne had meanwhile married – were called up for border control duties. Jung was too old, but he was drafted as a doctor and psychiatrist for the district on the west bank of Lake Zürich. The garden was once again dug up by Müller to plant potatoes and vegetables. Mary Mellon and other American friends wrote to ask how they could help, but there was nothing to be done except send food parcels. Mary sent coffee, sugar, even butter, via Macy's and the Red Cross. 'I think the night has descended upon Europe,' wrote Jung. Gret arrived from Paris, where her husband worked for a Swiss firm, bringing her five sons to live with her on the top floor of 228 Seestrasse. After the fall of France, Jung moved the entire family up to the Bernese Oberland for safety, including Franz and his new wife, Lilly, expecting their first child. Emma had wanted to leave Kusnacht for some time, but Carl had been reluctant to abandon his medical post. Then came a telephone call from an official in Bern warning Jung that he was on a Nazi 'blacklist', no doubt for his 'degenerate' writings, and would be arrested if Germany invaded Switzerland. Lilly gave birth while they were up in the Alps. But once it became clear the Germans would not invade, the family returned to Seestrasse.

Emma noticed that Carl looked exhausted, quite unlike his usual ebullient self. In fact he had not been fully well since his return from India in 1939. His work as a doctor also tired him. He looked thinner and older. In February 1944 he had a heart attack. He was already in hospital when it happened, in a private clinic near the Burghölzli, where he was being treated for a broken fibula from a fall while out walking in the snow. The leg was set and he was ordered to stay in bed, which caused embolisms in his lungs and heart, in turn causing a cardiac arrest. He remained in hospital until the end of June, and in all that time Emma never left his side. She took a room in the same corridor and rarely left the clinic, getting her daughters and daughter-in-law to bring in whatever was needed. Visitors queued up to see the patient but they were often refused, even Toni Wolff. Usually it was at Carl's bidding, but it was Emma who enforced it. Susi Trüb remembered how shocked Emma was that people who were refused entry could be so rude. They seemed to think Carl belonged to them. Susi also noticed how close Emma and Carl were, or perhaps how clear it now became that they had been all along.

By the time Carl came back home he was so weak he could not climb the stairs and had to have a daybed in the *Stube*. Gradually Jung started to walk round the room, then the garden. By the end of the summer he was almost well again, but Emma could not let her new role go, overseeing him, constantly checking for any dangerous signs. It did not always go down well.

Ruth Bailey saw how things were. 'I think one time she would almost have had him in a wheelchair as an invalid, so as to care for him, to make quite sure. She was not possessive, as such. She wanted to keep him going, keep him well, you see, and of course, he was older than she was.'

Once Jung was better, the grandchildren came and went again. The Baumanns had moved to a house in Kusnacht, but the five boys were always biking or running up Seestrasse, down the yew-lined drive and into the house. It was open house at Seestrasse, their grandmother always welcoming, ready with her bowl of Sprüngli chocolates, and often they bumped into other cousins already there. They swam, they boated, they chased around the garden, or drew, or played cards at the table in the *Stube* if it was raining. In fact, they could do pretty much as they wanted, just as the Jung children had. Their grandfather was not often around. He was either in his *Cabinet* working, or at Bollingen, or off giving a lecture somewhere. But when he was around it was wonderful. He told them stories, he took them sailing, he lost his temper, he swore like a Swiss peasant: *Hoore Verdammt! Du Loeli!* You bloody idiot! He laughed his loud laugh. And he cheated at games. But then it was time for him to go back to his work. It was their grandmother who was always there and made time for them, as much as they wanted. She never forgot a birthday, and she had a talent – they all agree – for finding just the right present. Christmas followed much the same pattern as it had when their parents were young: crackers and games and entertainments round the piano, and the tree in the corner lit up with candles and Christmas hearts and stars. When Adrian Baumann, Gret's son, was ten he asked to see his grandmother's jewels. She took him up to her room and showed them to him, one by one, each with its own story. He never forgot it. 'She was the heart of the family,' he said. 'We adored her.'

Emma and Carl had nineteen grandchildren, and as the children grew older they began to understand how it was with their grandparents. They saw how strong their grandmother was underneath her quiet exterior: never frightened, as others were, of criticising their grandfather if she thought he had said or done something wrong. 'She was strong,' says Adrian, 'but very feminine.' She was always modest, never showy, recalls his brother Dieter, the eldest grandchild, but she had great influence on their grandfather, moderating him: 'It's remarkable how she was able to steady him.' Emma was clever, thought granddaughter Brigitte, Agathe's daughter. And 'always the lady'. It was deep in Emma, this modest grandeur. 'Oh she was la Grande Dame,' one of the younger members of the Psychological Club recalled. 'She was very simple, absolutely Swiss, she was the great Bourgeois Swiss, you know. But she had something more than this. She had something absolutely superior, *une grandeuse mere*. She was the only person there [at the club] who had really individuated.' Dieter agreed: 'There was something aristocratic about her, but in a positive way.'

It was with her children and grandchildren that Emma could best be herself. 'She treated us all the same, as she did her own children. My mother really adored her,' says Adrian. She was unusually open-minded. You could talk to her about anything. But unlike their grandfather, she could not let out her feelings. That was her Achilles heel. She had deep feelings, but she could not show them. Their grandfather, on the other hand, showed everything, good and bad. In the Switzerland of those days, grandparents greeted their families with a handshake. Lil's son, Hans, remembered how warm his grandfather's handshake was. And 'the totality of his laugh'. Brigitte remembers his Basel sarcasm and being a bit frightened of him. 'Sometimes he was very loud and sarcastic, while she was very quiet,' said Jost Hoerni, another of Lil's sons. 'We loved her, really, because she was very nice with us and she spoiled us a little bit, as grand-mothers usually do. She was a very different temperament than grandfather.' Andreas Jung, Franz's son who took over the Jung house with his wife Vreni when their children were small, remembers his grandfather's large personality. 'He was so powerful,' agrees Dieter.

On Sunday afternoon walks it was clear there was no tension between their grandparents. 'Children can feel such things,' says Adrian. 'Even in Bollingen, I never felt any tension. Of course he had a temper, but it never lasted.' When he was a child he did not understand about his grandfather's flirtations, but he is sure it made no difference, at least to Carl. 'It didn't mean they didn't have a good marriage. I'm absolutely convinced that he really loved her. Even with those escapades. But it must have been difficult for her. Toni Wolff. I don't know any woman who could bear it. But I had the feeling she always loved him. I'm sure she did.' His brother Klaus agrees. 'He depended on her more than she on him.' He remembers his grandfather as a bit of a joker and a cheat. 'There was something in his trickiness which attracted her to him.' They all remember how much they laughed together. 'Oh yes! Of course! He had a great sense of humour. And so did she.' Dieter, now in his late eighties and an analyst himself, says his grandmother was aware of how much she owed their grand-father, who always encouraged her to do her own work, find her own way, individuate. 'Both learned from each other all their lives,' he says. 'They are a great example of this.'

Toni still visited on Sundays. As far as the grandchildren were concerned, all they saw was a bird-like old woman who smoked like a chimney. Klaus remembers his mother Gret saying: 'A normal person would never love such a woman like Toni Wolff.' Even their grandfather made rude comments about her sometimes these days. But she retained a key role at the Psychological Club, and once the Jung Institute was founded in 1948 she was invited to give lectures there. So was Emma. Jung himself tried as much as possible to stay in the background. 'I remember when the Institute was just being organised and there was much nervous tension and criticism to be observed, the only person who was *not* a target was Mrs Jung,' recalled one student. 'I found myself wondering what could be wrong with Mrs Jung – until in the course of several months at the Institute, it became clear to me that everything was so right with Mrs Jung that nobody felt the need to find fault. She was admired, respected, beloved.' Another student recalled the difference in style between the two women: 'Emma Jung was still teaching at the Institute and contact with her in class or in her home was always warm and cordial. She was an ample woman, with an open and accepting attitude, very much her own person, who seemed to take the complexities and difficulties of life rather as a matter of course. She was always available for counsel and made me feel genuinely welcome.' Toni Wolff, in sharp contrast, appeared gaunt, haughty and forbidding. 'No smile crossed her face in class, in fact she betrayed no emotion of any kind. Questions were answered in clipped tones which made the questioner feel small, even stupid . . . The icy impression made us ponder how she could ever have been a "femme fatale" or "femme inspiratrice" to anybody, least of all C. G. Jung.'

People respected Toni Wolff's intellect but they had to know her very well before they discovered her inner warmth. And now even Carl, her life's partner, was turning away from her. In March 1953 she died, unexpectedly. She was sixty-five. She had been suffering from crippling arthritis for many years, but the week before she died she was still seeing patients and had attended the Psychological Club. The previous week she had gone to Seestrasse, and, quite unusually, stayed for the afternoon as well as lunch with both Emma and Carl. As the news spread of her death people turned up at the Jung house, not knowing where else to go. Emma received them courteously and gave them tea. A week later she attended the funeral service in the Peterskirche in Zürich. Carl stayed away. Some thought it heartless. Others thought he could not trust himself not to break down.

Later he carved a memorial stone with Chinese letters in her memory, and placed it in the garden at Seestrasse. 'Lotus. Nun. Mysterious', it read. But the stone gives it away. Whenever Carl was 'dissociated' he found a stone, held it, carved it, placed it.

'I shall always be grateful to Toni,' Emma said later with typical generosity, 'for doing for my husband what neither I nor anyone else could have done for him at a most critical time.'

Sabi Tauber, the daughter of a member of the Psychological Club, once asked Jung what was the happiest moment in his life. He answered that it had been when he was out sailing on the lake, after finishing *Answer to Job*, and he heard his father's voice saying: 'You have done the right thing, and I thank you for that . . .' Hearing this voice, he felt that 'he redeemed his father'. It was always his father, as Freud said.

On Valentine's Day 1953, Emma and Carl celebrated their golden wedding anniversary: fifty years of marriage. Surrounded by their children and grandchildren and a few close friends, they luncheoned, listened to some heartfelt speeches, and drank a toast to their achievement. Two years later it was Carl's eightieth birthday. The Kusnacht band came to play in the garden, and Emma and Carl danced a waltz on the terrace. But as it turned out, Emma was already ill with the cancer that would kill her a few months later.

Emma had had an operation that spring, 1955, but by November the metastasis had returned. Ruth Bailey, visiting from England, found Emma bedridden and Jung taking over the running of the house. On 22 November their family doctor telephoned with the test results. The family were gathered in the *Stube*, waiting, the women knitting or reading, the men smoking and walking about. Jung went into the hall to take the call: Emma only had days to live. When he came back into the room he was distraught, 'all tense and white – and not speaking'. Everyone was frightened to say anything. He told them the news and then he went upstairs to tell Emma. She took it calmly. Death appeared not to frighten her. During those last few days Andreas Jung remembers his mother telling him to go and see his beloved grandmother for the last time, to say goodbye. He found her reading a book about Eskimos. 'She was in bed, but we had a long and wonderful talk about Eskimos and how they got their green vegetables through eating sea-lions who had in turn eaten the ice moss.' Natural history had been Emma's first love all those years ago. Half an hour before she died her daughters Gret and Marianne were with her. Emma said, 'I'm going to die now, I'm going to say goodbye to you right now.' And so she did. Only Carl, her husband of fifty-two years, was with her when she died.

'I cannot continue the letter,' Jung wrote to a friend on 28 November. 'Yesterday I lost my wife after a serious illness lasting only five days. Please excuse me.' He had started the letter a week earlier but had not managed to finish it because of 'much anxiety'. Letters of condolence poured in but he couldn't answer them. 'Many thanks for your kind letters,' he finally wrote to Professor Boehler, a colleague from the ETH, on 14 December. 'The loss of my wife has taken it out of me, and at my age it is hard to recover.' To his old friend Erich Neumann he wrote describing the moment of 'illumination' he had experienced at Emma's bedside just before she died, which he was certain came from her:

Deepest thanks for your heartfelt letter. Let me in return express my deepest condolences on the loss of your mother. I am sorry I can only set down these dry words, but the shock I have experienced is so great that I can neither concentrate nor recover my power of speech. The quick and painless end – only five days between the final diagnosis and death – and this experience [the illumination] have been a great comfort to me. But the stillness and the audible silence about me, the empty air and the infinite distance, are hard to bear.

Michael and Frieda Fordham, an English couple who were part of the Jung circle, visited Carl some days after Emma's death to offer their condolences. 'We went to see him and really he could do nothing but weep,' remembered Frieda. 'He kept saying "She was a queen. She was a queen." We went to the funeral and went to see him at home afterwards. He was so broken up. He had become quite small, as if he had shrunk. It was quite an odd impression.' Ruth Bailey felt the same: 'he was sad for a long time when Emma went. It was touch and go whether he would ever come back, in a way.' The grandchildren were amazed to see their grandfather crying. 'He was terribly upset, he was really crying. I couldn't believe it,' said Jost Hoerni. Adrian agrees. 'I know that when she died he was extremely sad. Extremely. He had the feeling that a part of him had gone. He went to Bollingen, where he was really in grief. I think he was working something in stone.' No one knew what to do, and the family turned to Ruth for help. 'Aggi called after me and said "What do you do with him, Ruth, when he is like this? What can we do with him? I would not know what to do with him. What would you do with him?" I said "Oh, love him a bit. That is what he wants you to do, show him affection." Really, no one knew what to do.' None of them had ever seen him like this before.

'Mama's death has left a gap for me that cannot be filled,' Carl wrote to his daughter Marianne. 'The stone I am working on gives an inner stability with its hardness and permanence, and its meaning governs my thoughts.' The inscription was in Latin: 'My most beloved and faithful wife . . . she lived, she died, she suffered, she is missed . . .' Later he built a third and final tower at Bollingen, needing something even larger, more solid and permanent, to keep him steady.

The funeral service took place in the Protestant Reformed Church at Kusnacht on 30 November 1955. Emma Jung-Rauschenbach 30 March 1882–27 November 1955. The church was full, with people standing at the back, waiting. Then Carl walked in from a side door, followed by members of the Jung family, and took his place in the front row. The memorial oration was delivered by the Reverend Hans Schaer. 'Let every man be fully persuaded in his own mind,' he began, quoting St Paul to the Corinthians – a sure sign that this and what was to follow came direct from Jung, who quoted St Paul all his life, as did his father who was named after him. An interpretation of St Paul's words followed: 'All the threats, dangers and abysses to which man is exposed will not succeed in overpowering him but on the contrary will lead him further, and they will work together for his good. To be sure, this is only possible when man is guided by the strongest spiritual force, love.'

Then the Reverend Schaer came to Emma: 'a woman who has had a full life and has accomplished great tasks, leaves our midst; one who was a source of sustenance and strength to many. Rich gifts of mind and spirit had been entrusted to her. Life presented her with a rich fate and she carried it with great strength and in doing so was always true to herself.' It was a painful loss even to those who paid only occasional visits to the beautiful house on Seestrasse, where her living presence in the home was like a gift to all those who came there. But how much greater the loss of those who were near to her. It was a fulfilled life, and she was permitted to carry out fine and important tasks. She saw something good in everything and she was able to bestow good because she was persuaded and convinced in her own mind. Hers had been an idyllic childhood till tragedy struck. 'When she was only twelve years old her father became blind and this saddened her childhood. For the man who had been so active till then could not reconcile himself to his fate. His suffering caused many a bitter hardship and heartache to his family. She helped her mother carry the burden which was really beyond the strength of her years,' said the Reverend Schaer. Everything that was careless or artificial and theoretical was foreign to her. She had great kindness and modesty. She was always able to hold her own as an independent, at the side of her husband. 'With her sense of humour that saw through everything that was inflated or one-sided, she resolved difficulties and tensions and helped to overcome obstacles. She was the nurturing soil in which his [Jung's] creativity took root and from which he drew essential strength. A light emanated from her . . . She was able to carry and endure life's burdens and above all she knew how to recognise and safeguard the secrets of others.' Meaning, surely, the secrets of her husband Carl.

If there was any doubt that the text had been written by Jung, it was banished now. No one in the church could be in any doubt that Carl Jung had finally made public his deep debt to his wife.

That afternoon the Jung family opened Seestrasse to the mourners. Carl did not come downstairs. He stayed up in the library, surrounded by his own thoughts.

'I saw her in a dream which was like a vision,' he wrote:

She stood at some distance from me, looking at me squarely. She was in her prime, perhaps about thirty, and wearing the dress which had been made for her many years before by my cousin the medium. Her expression was neither joyful nor sad, but, rather, objectively wise and understanding, without the slightest emotional reaction, as though she were beyond the mists of affects.

I knew that it was not she, but a portrait she had made or commissioned for me. It contained the beginning of our relationship, the events of fifty-three years of marriage, and the end of her life also.

Emma and Carl. Carl and Emma. 'Face to face with such wholeness one remains speechless, for it can scarcely be comprehended.'

Notes

Abbreviations used in the Notes

CW: C. G. Jung, *The Collected Works of C. G. Jung*, 20 vols, Bollingen Series, Princeton, NJ: Princeton University Press, 1960–90 (see Bibliography for individual volumes)

Freud/Jung Letters: Sigmund Freud and C. G. Jung, *The Freud/Jung Letters: The Correspondence between Sigmund Freud and C. G. Jung*, ed. William McGuire, tr. Ralph Manheim and R. F. C. Hull, Princeton, NJ: Princeton University Press, 1974

Interview with G. F. Nameche: the interviews conducted 1969–70 by G. F. Nameche are held at the C. G. Jung Biographical Archive, Countway Library of Medicine, Harvard Medical School

MDR: C. G. Jung and Aniela Jaffé, *Memories, Dreams, Reflections*, New York: Pantheon, 1962

Chapter 1: A Visit to Vienna

2 'Psychoanalysis': the term went through many variations during the early years.

3 3,000 Swiss francs: *MDR*, p. 101.

3 a very large sum: Swiss money value in Rolf Mösli, *Eugen Bleuler: Pionier der Psychiatrie*, Zürich: Römerhof Verlag, 2012, p. 116.

3 In the event of a divorce: with thanks to Dr Elizabeth Schlumpf in Zürich for legal details taken from Peter Tuor et

al., *Das Schweizerische Zivil-Gesetzbuch*, p. 139: 'End of Marriage and Divorce, 1905: in case of divorce, each partner takes out of the marriage what they originally brought in. Any subsequent incoming extras to be divided two-thirds to the husband, one-third to the wife.'

4 'I shall be in Vienna': *Freud/Jung Letters*, p. 24.

4 that March morning: for the first meeting see Ludwig Binswanger, *Sigmund Freud: Reminiscences of a Friendship*, tr. Norbert Guterman, New York: Grune & Stratton, 1957, p. 10; also Eva Weissweiler, *Die Freuds: Biographie einer Familie*, Cologne: Kiepenhauer & Witsch, 2006, p. 139, and C. G. Jung, *Letters of C. G. Jung*, ed. Gerhard Adler and Aniela Jaffé, tr. R. F. C. Hull, Princeton, NJ: Princeton University Press, 1973–75, Vol. 2, p. 36.

5 'Sundays I am free': *Freud/Jung Letters*, p. 23.

6 Freud's self-deprecating Jewish humour: Deirdre Bair, *Jung: A Biography*, Boston, MA: Little, Brown, 2003, p. 119.

7 On special occasions: for the Sunday lunch see Martin Freud, *Glory Reflected: Sigmund Freud – Man and Father*, London: Angus & Robertson, 1957, p. 108.

9 'In my experience': *Introduction to Jungian Psychology: Notes of the Seminar on Analytical Psychology Given in 1925*, ed. and Introduction by William McGuire, tr. R F. C. Hull, new Introduction and updates by Sonu Shamdasani, Princeton: Princeton University Press, 1989, p. 20, and *MDR*, p. 146.

10 'Our Aryan comrades': John Kerr, *A Most Dangerous Method: The Story of Jung, Freud, and Sabina Spielrein, New York: Knopf, 1993*, p. 384.

11 'like a small boy': Martin Freud, *Glory Reflected*, p. 109.

12 the Grand: for the Grand Hotel see Karl Baedeker, *Switzerland: And the Adjacent Portions of Italy, Savoy, and Tyrol*, Leipzig: Karl Baedeker, 1905.

13 female hysterics with sexual dysfunction: Maines, Rachel P., *The Technology of Orgasm: 'Hysteria', the Vibrator, and*

Women's Sexual Satisfaction, Baltimore, MD: Johns Hopkins University Press, 1999.

14 'In the following pages': Sigmund Freud, *The Interpretation of Dreams*.

14 'It seems to me': *Freud/Jung Letters*, pp. 4, 14, and as discussed in George Makari, *Revolution in Mind: The Creation of Psychoanalysis*, London: Duckworth, 2008, p. 203.

14 that particular Wednesday: for the Wednesday meeting see Binswanger, *Sigmund Freud*, p. 11.

15 'I felt so foreign': Kurt Eissler interview, 1953, Sigmund Freud Collection, Manuscript Division, Library of Congress, Washington DC, in Bair, *Jung*, p. 118.

15 'Now you've seen': Binswanger, *Sigmund Freud*, p. 11.

15 When Freud joked: for the Jewish joke see Bair, *Jung*, p. 119.

17 Worse was to come: for Carl's flirtation see *Freud/Jung Letters*, pp. 229, 24 and 25.

Chapter 2: Two Childhoods

19 Emma recalled her childhood: the description of Emma's childhood is based on interviews with the Jung grandchildren (see Chapter 15) and Beatrice Homberger; *Jugend-Erinnerungen einer Grossmutter* by Gertrud Henne, privately printed 1960, quoted in Andreas Jung, Regula Michel, Arthur Ruegg, Judith Rohrer and Daniel Ganz, *The House of C. G. Jung: The History and Restoration of the Residence of Emma and Carl Gustav Jung-Rauschenbach*, Wilmette, IL: Chiron Publications, 2008; and the family memoirs of Helene Hoerni-Jung, with thanks to Carl and Emma's grandson Adrian Baumann.

20 'If only you'd remained': *Schaffhauser Biographen*, p. 21, with thanks to the Stadtarchiv Schaffhausen.

23 'the young, very pretty': *MDR*, p. 23.

24 Carl first clapped eyes: for their first meeting see Alan C. Elms, *Uncovering Lives: The Uneasy Alliance of Biography*

and Psychology, Oxford: Oxford University Press, 1994, p. 61.

24 the first correspondence between them: with thanks to Andreas Jung, who checked this in the family archive.

25 Franz confirmed years later: the interview with Franz is in Linda Donn, *Freud and Jung: Years of Friendship, Years of Loss*, New York: Charles Scribner's Sons, 1988, pp. 61 and 62.

26 'My situation is mirrored': Aniela Jaffé, *C. G. Jung: Word and Image*, Bollingen Series XCVII, Vol. 2, Princeton, NJ: Princeton University Press, 1979, p. 27.

27 'My stone,' he called it: *MDR*, p. 33.

29 'Dim intimations of trouble': *MDR*, p. 22.

29 'I had never come across': William McGuire and R. F. C. Hull (eds), *C. G. Jung Speaking: Interviews and Encounters*, London: Picador, 1978, p. 25.

30 The first of these was a dream: *MDR*, p. 25.

31 'a little manikin': *MDR*, p. 34.

33 'as timid and craven': *MDR*, p. 39.

33 'disagreeable, rather uncanny feeling': Bair, *Jung*, p. 30.

33 As he described it: *MDR*, p. 42.

35 'The world is beautiful': *MDR*, p. 47.

36 'My entire youth': *MDR*, p. 52.

36 on the rock stood a castle: *MDR*, p. 86.

39 'I was seized with': *MDR*, p. 64.

39 the tragedy of his youth: Jaffé, *C. G. Jung*, p. 20.

39 'I was sure': *MDR*, p. 58.

40 'The feeling I associated': *MDR*, p. 23.

40 'The following days': *MDR*, p. 100.

40 a stipend to help fund: *MDR*, p. 92.

41 'intellectually dominating': McGuire and Hull (eds), *C. G. Jung Speaking*, p. 29.

41 the nickname Walze: *Walze* has often been translated as the 'barrel' or 'log', but 'Steam-Roller' is more accurate, and describes Carl's personality as well as his appearance.

11 'He was appalled': McGuire and Hull (eds), *C. G. Jung Speaking*, p. 30.

42 'Your last two letters': *Freud/Jung Letters*, p. 94.

Chapter 3: A Secret Betrothal

45 'My heart suddenly began to pound': *MDR*, p. 111.

46 'The ideal wife': Albert Tanner, *Arbeitsame Patrioten – wohlanständige Damen: Bürgertum und Bürgerlichkeit in der Schweiz, 1830–1914*, Zürich: Orell Füssli Verlag, 1995, p. 209, author's translation.

47 'The happiness and lasting power': Rosa Dahinden-Pfyl, *Die Kunst mit Männern Glücklich zu Sein*, p. 219, author's translation.

48 'He didn't think much of': McGuire and Hull (eds), *C. G. Jung Speaking*, p. 28.

49 a difficult, sarcastic man: see Jean Rauschenbach's obituary in *Tagesblatt*, with thanks to Stadtarchiv Schaffhausen.

49 Herr Rauschenbach had syphilis: this sad story is based on author interviews with the Jung family. A dramatic illustration is Rembrandt's portrait of the artist Gerard de Lairesse with his grossly deformed face, who, like Emma's father, eventually went blind.

51 in the medical pamphlets: see Claude Quétel, *History of Syphilis*, tr. Judith Braddock and Brian Pike, Cambridge: Polity Press, 1990.

52 'psychologically abnormal': Bair, *Jung*, p. 59.

52 'the utmost concentration': Jung, *Introduction to Jungian Psychology*, and Bair, *Jung*, p. 59.

53 'how the human mind reacted': *MDR*, p. 114.

53 She worried: author interviews with the Jung family.

54 '*Mein liebster Schatz!*': with thanks to Andreas Jung for confirmation of this form of address.

54 The Burghölzli at the turn of the twentieth century: with thanks to Herr Rolf Mösli, first archivist at the Burghölzli

and author of an excellent book on Bleuler (*Eugen Bleuler: Pionier der Psychiatrie*, Zürich: Römerhof Verlag, 2012), who was most generous with his time.

54 'In the medical world at the time': *MDR*, p. 111.

57 there were seventy *Wärters*: Mösli, *Eugen Bleuler*, p. 138. Mösli's book is also excellent on daily life at the Burghölzli.

59 'It was as though two rivers': *MDR*, p. 112.

60 the woman in Carl's section: for the depressive woman see *MDR*, p. 116.

62 'a girl with poor inheritance': C. G. Jung, *CW1: Psychiatric Studies*, ed. Herbert Read, Michael Fordham and Gerard Adler, tr. R. F. C. Hull, Princeton, N.J.: Princeton University Press, 1970, p. 17.

62 'vaulting ambition': *Freud/Jung Letters*, p. 78.

62 'the progressive elucidation': Jung, *CW1* (author's own translation as it appears only in the German version).

63 'a submission to the vow': *MDR*, p. 114. Jung describes this as his feelings at the start of his time at the Burghölzli but it more accurately describes how he felt later, once he had got used to the work and the routine of the institution. At first, by his own account, he was completely overwhelmed.

64 Swiss army military service: with thanks to Othmar Zeltner, who began his military service in St Gallen in 1952.

65 'in the style of the eighteenth century': Bair, *Jung*, p. 80, and Andreas Jung confirms that Carl had an English teacher in London. This is probably how Carl came to be in Oxford.

66 'Seine landscape with clouds': Jaffé, *C. G. Jung*, p. 42.

Chapter 4: A Rich Marriage

67 a church wedding in the Steigkirche: the wedding details based on author interviews with Jung grandchildren (see Chapter 15), and with thanks to David Syffer at the IWC archive, Schaffhausen.

67 luckily there was no snow: the wedding-day weather is
    thanks to Nicola Behrens at the Stadtarchiv Zürich.

67 The wedding banquet: Gerhard Wehr, *An Illustrated
    Biography of C. G. Jung*, tr. Michael Kohn, Boston:
    Shambhala Publications, 1989, p. 25.

69 'The further away from church': *MDR*, p. 81.

69 setting off on their honeymoon: With thanks to Andreas Jung
    for the details of their itinerary.

69 Continental Express to Paris: thanks to SSB Historical
    Archives in Bern for answering queries about the comforts of
    first-class travel and providing timetables and illustrations.

70 a quarrel about money: Vincent Brome, *Jung: Man and Myth*,
    London: Macmillan, 1978, p. 83.

70 Swiss law gave the husband: with thanks to Dr Elizabeth
    Schlumpf in Zürich for legal details from Dr P. Tuor, *Das
    Schweizerische Zivil Gesetzbuch*.

70 Emma had seen Carl's temper: for Carl's violent rages see
    MDR, p. 54, and Jaffé, *C. G. Jung*, p. 132.

71 'an adventure before marriage': Bair, *Jung*, p. 70, and that Carl
    was an 'absolutely reliable husband' for the first seven years
    or so of marriage.

71 a rented apartment in Zürich: for Zurich in 1903 see Kurt
    Guggenheim, *Alles in Allem, Zürich: Artemis Verlag, 1954*;
    Walter Baumann, *Zürich: La Belle Époque*, Zürich: Orell
    Füssli Verlag, 1973, and Zürcher Schlagzeilen, Zürich: Orell
    Füssli Verlag, 1981; Hanspeter Danuser, *Das Trambuch: 100
    Jahre Züri-Tram*, Zürich: Verlag Neue Zürcher Zeitung, 1982.

75 entry costing 60 rappen: There are 100 rappen to the Swiss
    franc.

77 Marguerite's fiancé, Ernst Homberger: author interview with
    Ernst and Marguerite's granddaughter Beatrice Homberger.

79 'I'm sitting here in the Burghölzli': C.G. Jung letter to
    Andreas Vischer in Angela Graf-Nold, 'The Zürich School of
    Psychiatry in Theory and Practice: Sabina Spielrein's

Treatment at the Burghölzli Clinic in Zürich', *Journal of Analytical Psychology*, Vol. 46, Issue 1, January 2001, p. 83.

80 'As usual you have hit the nail on the head': *Freud/Jung Letters*, p. 78.

83 'The years at Burghölzli were my apprenticeship': *MDR*, p. 116.

83 Hedwig, who was a remarkable woman: for Hedwig Bleuler see 'Erinnerungen an Hedwig Bleuler-Waser', *Zentralblatt* 20, April 1940; Mösli, *Eugen Bleuler*; Hedwig Bleuler-Waser, 'Aus meinem Leben', *Schweizer Frauen der Tat* 3, 1929.

86 Other researchers used whistles: C. G. Jung, *Studies in Word Association*, in *CW2: Experimental Researches*, ed. and tr. Gerhard Adler and R. F. C. Hull, Princeton, NJ: Princeton University Press, 1973, pp. 5, 228.

86 diagnoses and classification of: Jung, *Studies in Word Association*, p. 6.

86 the 'one-fifth-second stop watch': with thanks to David Syffer at IWC Schaffhausen

87 'If we ask patients directly': Jung, *Studies in Word Association*, p. 298.

88 Emma appears as 'Subject no. I': Jung, *Studies in Word Association*, p. 240.

88 'The subject is pregnant': for Emma's pregnancy complex see Jung, *Studies in Word Association*, p. 243.

Chapter 5: Tricky Times

92 Emma breastfed hers herself: see *Freud/Jung Letters*, p. 188, 'My wife is, of course, nursing the child herself, a pleasure for both of them.'

93 more conventional roles: for a woman's place in the society of the time see Tanner, *Arbeitsame Patrioten*, pp. 226 and 227.

94 Martha became pregnant six times in ten years: Katja Behling, *Martha Freud: A Biography*, Cambridge: Polity Press, 2005, p. 113.

94 their marriage becoming 'amortised': *Freud/Jung Letters*, p. 456.

95 Ernst Homberger, who had married: with thanks to Beatrice Homberger.

95 stated the obituary: in the *Schaffhausen Tagesblatt*, 3 March 1905, with thanks to the Stadtarchiv Schaffhausen.

97 'My aim was to show': *MDR*, pp. 112 and 118.

97 no shortage of stories: *MDR*, pp. 123, 124.

98 'He kept his students spellbound': Binswanger, *Sigmund Freud*, p. 1.

98 *Pelzmäntel* – fur-coat – brigade: Bair, *Jung*, pp. 98 and 109.

99 charming, fuzzy snapshots: the photographs are in the Jung family archive, with thanks to Andreas Jung.

99 Emma loved her children: based on author interviews with the Jung family.

100 two female inmates: Jung, *Studies in Word Association*, pp. 381 and 382.

101 his cousin Helly: Jung, *Introduction to Jungian Psychology*, p. 6

101 the night of 17 August 1904: Graf-Nold, 'The Zürich School of Psychiatry in Theory and Practice', p. 73.

101 Baur-en-Ville: there were two hotels: Baur-au-Lac and Baur-en-Ville.

102 The young woman was Sabina Spielrein: the Spielrein detail and her history are based on Bernard Minder, 'Sabina Spielrein: Jung's Patient at the Burghölzli', *Journal of Analytical Psychology*, Vol. 46, Issue 1, January 2001, and Graf-Nold, 'The Zürich School of Psychiatry'.

105 *Punch, the Illustrated London News*: from a family memoir, with thanks to Adrian Baumann.

105 The *Neue Zürcher Zeitung* felt: the news reports are from Baumann, *Zürcher Schlagzeilen*, p. 17.

107 leaving it at that: Graf-Nold, 'The Zürich School of Psychiatry', p. 93. Graf-Nold pointed out in an interview with the author how strange it was that Jung made no

further comment about the clear indications of sexual abuse.

111 Jung's report, dated 25 September 1905: Minder, 'Sabina Spielrein', p. 68.

Chapter 6: Dreams and Tests

113 'I saw horses': Jung *CW3*, p. 57.

119 'You have put your finger': *Freud/Jung Letters*, p. 14.

120 'I broke it off': *Freud/Jung Letters*, p. 17.

121 Three crosses meant danger: *Freud/Jung Letters*, p. 19.

122 Bleuler's 'active community': Graf-Nold, 'The Zürich School of Psychiatry', p. 90.

122 'In the hospital the spirit of Freud': Abraham Brill, *Lectures on Psychoanalytic Psychiatry*, New York: Knopf, 1946, quoted in Kerr, *A Most Dangerous Method*, p. 172.

123 'This Freud cult': Mikkel Borch-Jacobsen and Sonu Shamdasani, *The Freud Files: An Inquiry into the History of Psychoanalysis, Cambridge: Cambridge University Press, 2012*, p. 69.

123 'a German-American woman': *Freud/Jung Letters*, p. 71.

123 'My wife, who knows a thing': *Freud/Jung Letters*, p. 72.

124 'But don't you think': *Freud/Jung Letters*, p. 4.

124 'I had grown up in the country': *MDR*, p. 161.

125 'As I have indicated before': *Freud/Jung Letters*, p. 229.

125 'the trauma [was] wished for': Angela Graf-Nold, '100 Jahre Peinlichkeit – und (k)ein Ende?: Karl Abrahams frühe psychoanalytische Veröffentlichungen und die "sexuelle Frage"', *Jahrbuch der Psychoanalyse 52 (2006): 93–138*, pp. 52, 127.

125 'You will doubtless have drawn': Mc Guire, pp. 25 and 144.

126 'Often I want to give up': *Freud/Jung Letters*, pp. 75 and 89.

126 'refusing to obey the chairman's repeated signal': Borch-Jacobsen and Shamdasani, *The Freud Files*, p. 74.

127 'I have a sin to confess': *Freud/Jung Letters*, p. 115.

127 'At the moment I am treating': *Freud/Jung Letters*, p. 108.

128 she threatened Carl with divorce: Susi Trüb, interview with G. F. Nameche, and author interviews with the Jung family.

129 caught out by a transgression: author interviews with the Jung family.

129 'All sorts of things': *Freud/Jung Letters*, p. 117.

130 'I will begin with an experiment': Ludwig Binswanger, 'On the Psychogalvanic Phenomenon in Association Experiments', in Jung, *Studies in Word Association*, p. 457.

131 'My veneration for you': *Freud/Jung Letters*, p. 95.

132 'in a state of active opposition': Ludwig Binswanger, 'On the Psychogalvanic Phenomenon in Association Experiments', in Jung, *Studies in Word Association*, p. 497.

133 'He is also reserved': A better translation would be 'defensive', not 'reserved'.

Chapter 7: A Home of Their Own

135 The rumours flying about the place: *Freud/Jung Letters*, p. 207, and see Chapter 8.

135 They purchased a plot of land: Barbara Hannah, *Jung: His Life and Work*, London: Michael Joseph, 1976, p. 93: They found it 'more or less by chance' when out for a Sunday walk. They saw a land for sale sign. 'Her eyes still shone when she described the joy and excitement this aroused in them both.'

136 'No. 1 wanted to free himself': *MDR*, p. 86.

137 Within a month of buying the plot: The information about the house comes from Andreas Jung et al., *The House of C. G. Jung*. With thanks to Andreas Jung, who lives in the Jung house and showed me round on more than one occasion, and showed me the original sketches.

139 'Much of it struck us': Jung et al., *The House of C. G. Jung*, p. 20.

142 'We are in complete agreement': Jung et al., *The House of C. G. Jung*, p. 40.

145 they preferred to stay at the Hotel Regina: *Freud/Jung Letters*, p. 213.

145 'to begin with, Jung': Jones, *The Life and Work of Sigmund Freud*, Vol. 2, pp. 254 and 258.

146 'My selfish purpose': *Freud/Jung Letters*, p. 168.

146 Freud came to visit Jung: Jones, *The Life and Work of Sigmund Freud*, Vol. 2, p. 264.

147 'a surprise package of books': *Freud/Jung Letters*, p. 173.

147 Emma stayed with her mother at Ölberg: details of life at Ölberg based on author interviews with Carl and Emma's granddaughter Brigitte Merk and Beatrice Homberger, and family memoir, with thanks to Adrian Baumann.

148 the hot weather could turn heavy: with thanks to Nicola Behrens at Stadtarchiv Zürich.

148 Emma put on her jewels: author interview with Adrian Baumann.

149 Carl only visited at the weekends: for Carl's work and holiday see Graf-Nold, 'The Zürich School of Psychiatry in Theory and Practice', p. 175: Writing to Sabina Spielrein: 'First I am going for a week to Toggenburg and will be walking with Riklin, then a further six days to Schaffhausen to my wife and child(ren).'

149 'fleeing into the inaccessible solitude': *Freud/Jung Letters*, p. 171.

149 'Babette S': *MDR*, p. 126.

153 the boy, Manfred: Susi Trüb, interview with G. F. Nameche, and author interview with Rolf Mösli.

153 the new life: see McGuire's note in *Freud/Jung Letters*, p. 215. Carl continued as *Privatdozent* lecturer at Zürich University till April 1914.

153 'This last miserable week': *Freud/Jung Letters*, p. 224.

154 the majority of toilets in Switzerland: many were still that basic into the 1950s, including in the author's Swiss grandparents' house.

155 leading to the library: For Jung's collection of books see Sonu
Shamdasani, *C. G. Jung: A Biography in Books*, New York:
W. W. Norton & Company, 2012.

Chapter 8: A Vile Scandal

158 Franz Karl Jung was born: *Freud/Jung Letters*, pp. 183, 184,
188.

159 four-year-old Agathli's reaction: *Freud/Jung Letters*, pp. 199,
208 and 212.

160 'I regret so much': Graf-Nold, 'The Zürich School of
Psychiatry in Theory and Practice', p. 177.

161 his treatment of Otto Gross: Makari, *Revolution in Mind*,
p. 231, Otto Gros 'a sexual revolutionary'. Analysis sessions
lasted up to twelve hours when the tables were sometimes
turned and the patient became the doctor; and *Freud/Jung
Letters*, pp. 157, 156, 153, 155.

162 sexual repression was 'a very important': *Freud/Jung Letters*,
p. 90.

163 'My dear Fräulein Spielrein': Graf-Nold, 'The Zürich School
of Psychiatry in Theory and Practice', p. 173.

163 a suitcase belonging to Sabina Spielrein: Graf-Nold, 'The
Zürich School of Psychiatry in Theory and Practice', 155.

164 'It is my misfortune': Graf-Nold, 'The Zürich School of
Psychiatry in Theory and Practice', 177.

165 she wrote an anonymous letter: Aldo Carotenuto, *A Secret
Symmetry: Sabina Spielrein Between Jung and Freud*, New
York: Pantheon Books, 1982, p. 93. I disagree with Bair, *Jung*,
p. 191, who writes that Carl acquiesced to Emma's every
demand from that time onward: from his Burghölzli
resignation to the buying of Kusnacht house. Carl wanted
both these himself. Nor was it 'divorce proceedings' – threats,
certainly, and no evidence of the pregnancy being 'deliberate'.
My interviews with the the Jung family support this.

165 'under terrific strain': *Freud/Jung Letters*, p. 207.

166 'I have always told your daughter': for whether sexual relationship was sexual see Carotenuto, *A Secret Symmetry*, p. 95.

167 'To be slandered': *Freud/Jung Letters*, p. 210.

168 'I've never really had a mistress': *Freud/Jung Letters*, p. 212.

168 'Hurrah for your new house!': *Freud/Jung Letters*, p. 226.

168 'She was, of course, systematically planning my seduction': *Freud/Jung Letters*, p. 228.

169 'Such experiences, though painful': *Freud/Jung Letters*, p. 230.

170 'Although not succumbing': *Freud/Jung Letters*, p. 236.

171 'risk his authority!': *MDR*, p. 154.

171 'Father was very disappointed': Donn, *Freud and Jung*, p. 98.

172 '*Liebste Frau!*': Jaffé, *C. G. Jung*, p. 47.

174 They had taken the 'elevated': for the journey to Worcester see *MDR*, p. 336.

177 Joseph Medill McCormick: William McGuire, 'Firm Affinities: Jung's Relations with Britain and the United States', *Journal of Analytical Psychology*, 40.3, July 1995, pp. 307, 305.

178 '*Mein liebster Schatz*': Jaffé, *C. G. Jung*, p. 49.

180 'Two more days before departure!': *MDR*, p. 338.

Chapter 9: Emma Moves Ahead

181 'The sofa cushion crawled about': *MDR*, p. 339.

183 'In my family all is well': *Freud/Jung Letters*, p. 252.

183 Unterwasser, a secluded Alpine village: *Freud/Jung Letters*, p. 284.

183 She had a fairly objective view: Sigmund Freud and Ernest Jones, *The Complete Correspondence of Sigmund Freud and Ernest Jones, 1908–1939*, ed. R. Andrew Paskauskas, Cambridge, MA: Harvard University Press, 1993, Jones to Freud, 18 September 1912, p. 155.

184 There was no lack of women: for Carl's women see Carotenuto, *A Secret Symmetry*, p. 17, and Kerr, *A Most Dangerous Method*, p. 299.

184 on a good day: for Spielrein's ups and downs see Carotenuto, *A Secret Symmetry*, pp. 12–17.

185 the secret diary he had kept: Carotenuto, *A Secret Symmetry*, p. 12.

186 'To be fruitful': C. G. Jung, *CW5: Symbols of Transformation, ed. and tr. Gerhard Adler and R. F.C. Hull, Princeton, NJ: Princeton University Press, 1977*, and Kerr, *A Most Dangerous Method*, p. 327.

187 that night Jung had a dream: *MDR*, p. 284 and *Freud/Jung Letters*, p. 359, fn1.

188 '*Sehr Geehrter Herr Professor!*': for Emma's letters see *Freud/Jung Letters*, pp. 301 and 303.

189 'Now don't get cross': *Freud/Jung Letters*, p. 302.

189 'Bleuler is not coming': *Freud/Jung Letters*, p. 304. The notes add that the International Psychoanalytic Association was founded at the Congress, with Jung elected president.

189 the pre-eminence of the Freudian school: See Borch-Jacobsen and Shamdasani, *The Freud Files*, for an excellent analysis.

189 'Most of you are Jews': Kerr, *A Most Dangerous Method*, p. 287.

190 'gadding about like mad': *Freud/Jung Letters*, p. 341.

191 a heatwave hit the Continent: Guggenheim, *Alles in Allem*, Vol. 1, p. 229.

192 'Charming, clever and ambitious': *Freud/Jung Letters*, p. 436.

193 a pedagogic congress in Brussels … mountain tour: *Freud/Jung Letters*, p. 439.

194 'This time the feminine element': *Freud/Jung Letters*, p. 440

194 'Dear friend,' Freud replied: *Freud/Jung Letters*, p. 441.

192 'There were of course seminars': Ernest Jones quoted by McGuire in note to *Freud/Jung Letters*, p. 443.

197 'Dear Professor Freud': For Emma's letters to Freud see *Freud/Jung Letters*, pp. 452–67.

201 '"he will grow, but I must dwindle"': 'I must dwindle' suggests Emma has heard Carl's views on this too, not only Fräulein Spielrein.

205 'tendency to autoeroticism': the term 'autoeroticism' appears to have been used in various ways at the time, and it is impossible to know what exactly Emma meant by it, but most likely it was just a general concern with oneself.

Chapter 10: A Difficult Year

206 a difficult year for Zürich: for Zürich in 1912 see Guggenheim, *Alles in Allem*, Vol. 1, p. 259.

206 the automobile factory at Schlieren: for the automobile statistics see Tanner, *Arbeitsame Patrioten*, p. 399.

208 'mighty rumblings in Zürich': *Freud/Jung Letters*, p. 484.

210 the state visit by Kaiser Wilhelm II: Guggenheim, *Alles in Allem*, Vol. 1, p. 265.

211 his first *Kriegsrat*: Clay, p. 297.

213 'It is of course ironical': *MDR*, p. 181.

213 'When working on my book': *MDR*, p. 162.

214 Jung was 'a born leader': *The Correspondence of Sigmund Freud and Sándor Ferenczi*, Volume 1, *1908–1914*, ed. Eva Brabant, Ernst Falzeder and Patrizia Giampieri-Deutsch, tr. Peter T. Hoffer, Cambridge, MA: Harvard University Press, 1993, p. 434. Note: it is not clear whether Freud is quoting his conversation with Jung at Munich. But either way, this was his opinion.

214 I have a wife and [five] children': In fact, four. Helene was born in 1914.

214 'The unconscious contents': *MDR*, p. 181

215 'I read your essay': *Freud/Jung Letters*, p. 331, and fn3.

216 'It seemed to me': Jung, *Introduction to Jungian Psychology*, and C. G. Jung, *The Red Book: Liber Novus*, ed. Sonu

Shamdasani, tr. M. Kyburz, J. Peck and S. Shamdasani, New York: W. W. Norton & Company, 2009, p. 12.

217 'I make horoscope calculations': *Freud/Jung Letters*, p. 427.

217 the theory of the death wish: Kerr, *A Most Dangerous Method*, p. 403.

217 'I have tried': *Freud/Jung Letters*, p. 288.

217 deep depression: Hannah, *Jung*, p. 99.

217 'It took me a long time': Jung, *Introduction to Jungian Psychology*, p. 28.

217 'While working on the book': *MDR*, p. 162.

218 'So perhaps it is all to the good': *Freud/Jung Letters*, p. 456.

218 'I had to tell myself this': *Freud/Jung Letters*, p. 232.

219 the 'enormous turd': *MDR*, p. 50.

219 he would tell Emma: see the funeral oration in the Epilogue.

219 another of his trips to America: for Jung's 1912 trip to America see McGuire and Hull (eds), *C. G. Jung Speaking*, Introduction and pp. 29 and 39.

223 'The journey from cloud-cuckoo-land': see McGuire's Introduction to *Freud/Jung Letters*.

224 his little tricks: *Freud/Jung Letters*, p. 535.

224 'As regards Jung': Freud and Jones, *The Complete Correspondence*, p. 186.

224 'behaving like a florid fool', *The Correspondence of Sigmund Freud and Sándor Ferenczi*, p. 353.

225 another significant dream: *MDR*, p. 166.

225 a memory from his eleventh year: *MDR*, p. 168.

226 'Father would be down there': For Franz's quotes see Donn, *Freud and Jung*, pp. 160, 172 and 174.

227 my father could do no work: clearly Franz was wrong about that.

228 'It was most essential': *MDR*, pp. 181, 182.

Chapter 11: *Ménage à Trois*

229 'staged a number of jealous scenes': *Freud/Jung Letters*, p. 289.

230 'the devil can use': *Freud/Jung Letters*, p. 207.

230 'I really cannot remember': *Freud/Jung Letters*, p. 351.

230 many men in his circle kept mistresses: Kerr, p. 379.

230 his unmarried sister-in-law, Minna: this theory is discussed in Kerr, *A Most Dangerous Method*, p. 135.

230 'I stand for an infinitely freer sexual life': Lisa Appignanesi and John Forrester, *Freud's Women*, London: Weidenfeld and Nicolson, 1992, p. 51.

231 'My Indian summer': *Freud/Jung Letters*, p. 292.

231 Maria Moltzer: *The Correspondence of Sigmund Freud and Sándor Ferenczi*, p. 446, with thanks to Sonu Shamdasani for confirmation. The full quote from Freud to Ferenczi: 'The master who analysed him can only have been Fräulein Moltzer, and he is so foolish as to be proud of this work of a woman with whom he is having an affair.'

232 Emma threatened divorce three times: Susi Trüb, interview with G. F. Nameche, and Ronald Hayman, *A Life of Jung*, London: Bloomsbury, 1999, p. 126, and author interviews with the Jung family.

232 'Except for moments of infatuation': *Freud/Jung Letters*, p. 212.

232 'A new discovery of mine': *Freud/Jung Letters*, p. 440.

234 'A woman who does not have': Bair, *Jung*, p. 197.

235 'very near psychosis': Carl Meier, interview with G. F. Nameche.

235 Jung used to say: Donn, *Freud and Jung*, p. 179.

235 'I was furious': Kerr, *A Most Dangerous Method*, p. 373 and *Freud/Jung Letters*, p. 465.

235 'With us everything is peaceful': *Freud/Jung Letters*, p. 484.

235 'never totally in life': Susi Trüb, interview with G. F. Nameche.

235 'Toni was all spirit': Donn, *Freud and Jung*, p. 178; for further descriptions of Toni Wolff see Maggy Anthony, *The Valkyries: The Women Around Jung*, Longmead: Element Books, 1990, p. 33.

236 'In her presence': Tina Keller, interview with G. F. Nameche.

236 'After the parting of ways': *MDR*, p. 165.

237 feared he had a psychic disturbance: for Jung's illness see Brome, *Jung*, pp. 162, 301. D. W. Winnicott, reviewing Jung's *MDR* in the *International Journal of Psychoanalysis*, Apr–Jul 1964, describes him as a 'recovered case of infantile psychosis', giving us 'a picture of childhood schizophrenia' which settled down into a 'splitting of the personality'. Also with thanks to Sonu Shamdasani for pointing me to Henri Ellenberger's concept of Jung's 'creative illness' in *The Discovery of the Unconscious*.

237 laughing 'down to his shoes': Donn, *Freud and Jung*, p. 90.

237 talking away to Philemon: *MDR*, p. 176.

237 'Then I came to this': Jung, *Introduction to Jungian Psychology*, p. 45, with thanks to Sonu Shamdasani for confirmation that it was Moltzer's voice.

238 this time in Munich: Hayman, *A Life of Jung*, p. 169.

238 'considers Jung to be mentally disordered': Freud and Jones, *The Complete Correspondence*, p. 237, 11 November 1913. Freud writes back to Jones on 17 November: 'I have been very much amused by your good saying about Jung, but we must not forget, this is our only case of success in the campaign against him, and we are mostly dependent on him for helping us by his foolish ways' – revealing how there was now a concerted campaign to discredit Jung.

238 'When I had the vision': *MDR*, p. 169, and C. G. Jung, *Liber Novus*, Chapter 1.

239 Jung's visionary *Liber Novus*: see Shamdasani's Introduction to C. G. Jung, *Liber Novus*, pp. 48 and 127 (fn34) on the start of the writing – and a fine introduction to the whole.

240 it lay undisturbed in his *Cabinet*: in 1983 it was placed in a safe box and a year later five copies were made. Finally, in 2009, a facsimile edition was made at the behest of the Jung family, a superb achievement of labour and love by Sonu Shamdasani and the translators, and the publishers W. W. Norton and Company, handsomely supported by the Philemon Foundation.

122 And Emma: Ulrich Hoerni (Carl and Emma's grandson), in the Preface to C. G. Jung, *Liber Novus*.

240 'It was as though the ground': *MDR*, p. 172.

241 'I squeezed past him': Black Book 2, see Shamdasani's Introduction to C. G. Jung, *Liber Novus*, p. 17.

242 still noticed nothing unusual: Ulrich Hoerni in the Preface to *Liber Novus*.

243 almost let himself drown: Tina Keller, interview with G. F. Nameche.

243 The children didn't like Tante Toni: author interviews with the Jung family.

243 Carl left for Ravenna: Bair, *Jung*, suggests that Jung went with Toni Wolff, which would have been callous indeed, but the Jung family archive confirms it was Schmid.

244 'So we are rid of them at last': Kerr, *A Most Dangerous Method*, p. 471.

244 'As a psychiatrist I became worried': McGuire and Hull (eds), *C. G. Jung Speaking*, p. 226.

244 the world itself was going mad: for war fever in Zürich see Guggenheim, *Alles in Allem*, Vol. 2, p. 77.

245 'And be kissed by me': with thanks to Andreas Jung for confirmation.

245 'Finally I understood': McGuire and Hull (eds), *C. G. Jung Speaking*, p. 226.

Chapter 12: The Great War

246 during the First World War: for Zürich during wartime see Guggenhiem, *Alles in Allem*, Vol. 2, p. 84.

246 'In my memory': Baumann, *Zürich*, p. 57 (author's translation).

248 Vladimir Ilyich Ulyanov – Lenin: Baumann, *Zurcher Schlagzeilen*, p. 43.

249 the class struggle: Tanner, *Arbeitsame Patrioten*, p. 699 (author's translation).

252 the first train of French wounded: Guggenheim, *Alles in Allem*, Vol. 2, p. 141.

252 his ideas on polygamy: for Jung on marriage see 'Marriage as a Psychological Relationship' (1925) in *CW17: Development of Personality*, ed. and tr. Gerhard Adler and R. F.C. Hull, Princeton, NJ: Princeton University Press,| 1981.

252 'I think she had many admirers': for Emma's beauty see Ruth Bailey, interview with G. F. Nameche.

253 her feelings of dissociation: based on letter in the Jung family archive.

253 'Dear Gretli': Jaffé, *C. G. Jung*, p. 142.

254 'While I was there': for the mandalas see *MDR*, p. 187.

255 only Toni was able to follow him: for Wolff's importance see Susi Trüb, interview with G. F. Nameche.

255 teetering on the edge: *MDR*, p. 181, and Kerr, *A Most Dangerous Method*, p. 503 for his deterioration in 1915.

255 'Phenomenologically one might classify it': Carl Meier, interview with G. F. Nameche.

255 'creative illness': a term coined by Henri Ellenberger, *The Discovery of the Unconscious: The History and Evolution of Dynamic Psychiatry*, New York: Basic Books, 1970, p. 673; see also Murray Stein, *Jung's Treatment of Christianity: The Psychotherapy of a Religious Tradition*, Wilmette, IL: Chiron Publications, 1985, p. 204, for a pattern throughout Jung's life: 'the crisis would then be followed by an experience of

relief and restoration; and the final step would be an attempt to integrate the good and bad sides of the self, often in symbolic formulation …'.

256 He might tease the maid, flick peas: author interviews with the Jung family.

256 'He doesn't mean it': Agathe Jung, interview with G. F. Nameche.

258 a tailor arrived from London: author interviews with the Jung family.

257 First thing every morning: the details of family life are based on author interviews with the Jung family, and family memoirs, with thanks to Adrian Baumann.

258 'How lucky you English are': Beryl Pogson, *Maurice Nicoll: A Portrait, London*: Vincent Stuart, 1961

258 'Papa was always full of ideas': Agathe Jung, interview with G. F. Nameche.

259 Franz agreed: author interview with Franz's son Andreas Jung, and Donn, *Freud and Jung*, p. 132.

259 'She tried very hard': Susi Trüb, interview with G. F. Nameche.

260 Groma Jung was always there: Agathe Jung, interview with G. F. Nameche.

261 'But I think perhaps': Susi Trüb, interview with G. F. Nameche.

261 'This was an exceptional relationship': Tina Keller, interview with G. F. Nameche.

262 'There isn't the slightest doubt': Donn, *Freud and Jung*, p. 180, quoting Fowler McCormick.

262 'Mona Lisa': see McGuire's Introduction to Jung, *Introduction to Jungian Psychology*, p. xiv.

262 Every now and again Emma blew: author interviews with the Jung family.

263 'dangerous' company: Tina Keller, interview with G. F. Nameche.

Chapter 13: The Americans

265 Edith and Harold McCormick: for the McCormicks see Ron Chernow, *Titan: The Life of John D. Rockefeller, Sr.*, New York: Random House, 1998, p. 414.

266 Harold's cousin Medill: McCormick: McGuire, 'Firm Affinities', p. 305.

267 set him up in America: Shamdasani, *Cult Fictions*, p. 21, and Hannah, *Jung*, p. 109.

267 'Edith is becoming': Chernow, *Titan*, p. 599.

267 a more 'normal' life: Richard Noll, *The Jung Cult: Origins of a Charismatic Movement*, Princeton, NJ: Princeton University Presss, 1994, p. 212.

268 Muriel and Mathilda: Agathe Jung, interview with G. F. Nameche.

268 'Now please look at Mrs Jung': Fowler McCormick, interview with G. F. Nameche.

268 'Her step is springy': Noll, *The Jung Cult*, p. 211.

269 a walking tour: Noll, *The Jung Cult*, p. 216.

266 her hats were marvellous: author interviews with the Jung family, and family memoirs, with thanks to Adrian Baumann.

269 'I am enclosing': Chernow, *Titan*, p. 602.

270 'So Swiss ethics': Shamdasani, *Cult Fictions*, p. 21.

270 'He was too strong': Alphonse Maeder, interview with G. F. Nameche, and Donn, *Freud and Jung*, p. 133.

270 'Jung was very critical': Donn, *Freud and Jung*, p. 126.

271 'vulgar and repellent': Tina Keller, interview with G. F. Nameche.

271 remembered Emma Jung saying: Maria Schmid, interview with G. F. Nameche.

271 The first meeting was held: for the Psychological Club see Friedel Muser, *Zur Geschichte des Psychologischen Clubs Zürich von den Anfängen bis 1928*, Zürich: Psychologischer Club, 1984, and Shamdasani, *Cult Fictions*, p. 43.

272 it was too luxurious: Shamdasani, *Cult Fictions*, p. 43, and Hannah, *Jung*, p. 130.

272 'unconsciously there is too much': for McCorminck's view of the club see Shamdasani, *Cult Fictions*, p. 43.

273 Jung himself was clear: for Jung's view of the club see Shamdasani, *Cult Fictions*, p. 24.

274 'If the Club hasn't as yet': Imelda Gaudissart, *Emma Jung: Analyste et écrivain*, Lausanne: L'Âge d'Homme, 2010, p. 92.

274 Maria Moltzer ... Fanny Bowditch: Shamdasani, *Cult Fictions*, p. 66; Moltzer added: 'A club cannot survive unless it is financed by its members ... The present members should find it disgraceful to be parasitic.'

275 she chose 'Guilt': Gaudissart, *Emma Jung*, p. 93, and Psychological Club archive.

275 'I'll take her on my knee': Alphonse Maeder, interview with G. F. Nameche.

276 'You must be quite clear': Tina Keller, interview with G. F. Nameche.

276 'My father would not confess it': Donn, *Freud and Jung*, p. 27.

276 'Jung [was] religiously interested': Alphonse Maeder, interview with G. F. Nameche.

276 'religious in a somewhat other sense': For those interested in a summary of the debate based on Noll's *The Jung Cult*, see Bair, *Jung*, p. 741, fn 17, and for an excellent critique of Noll see Shamdasani, *Cult Fictions*.

277 'She had an extraordinary genius': Hannah, *Jung*, p. 118.

277 'It is unfortunately true': Jung, *Letters of C. G. Jung*, Vol. 2, p. 455, and Wehr, *An Illustrated Biography*, p. 189.

277 'She wasn't at all practical': Susi Trüb, interview with G. F. Nameche.

278 'It began with restlessness': *MDR*, p. 182.

279 'As day fades': Jung, *Introduction to Jungian Psychology*, p. 67.

279 'No doubt it was': *MDR*, p. 183.

280 'All summer long': Donn, *Freud and Jung*, p. 173, and author interviews with Jung and Homberger family, and family memoirs, with thanks to Adrian Baumann.

280 Bertha Rauschenbach never worried: author interview with Beatrice Homberger.

280 Many weekends and Easters: the details of the weekends and other holidays and Christmas based on author interviews with the Jung family.

284 By 1917: for Zürich in 1917 see Guggenheim, *Alles in Allem*, Vol. 2, p. 208.

285 there was a general strike: Baumann, *Zürcher Schlagzeilen*, p. 53.

286 back to normal: for the end of the war see Guggenheim, *Alles in Allem*, Vol. 2, p. 288.

286 117 days: see Shamdasani's Introduction to Jung, *Liber Novus*, p. 26.

286 Carl's emergence: *MDR*, p. 186, with thanks to Sonu Shamdasani for confirmation of identity. See Shamdasani's Introduction to Jung, *Liber Novus*, p. 44: 21 November 1918, 'M Moltzer has again disturbed me with letters.'

Chapter 14: Into the Twenties

287 'London, 1 July 1919': Jung, *Letters of C. G. Jung*, Vol. 1, p. 36.

287 Marianne was the musical one: Walter Niehus, interview with G. F. Nameche.

289 Gret's memory: the children's reminiscences of their parents based on Agathe Jung, interview with G. F. Nameche, and author interviews with the Jung family for the use of *Papa* and *Mama*.

289 he didn't mean it: author interview with Carl and Emma's grandson Dieter Baumann.

289 Franz was the 'soft' one: author interview with Franz's son Andreas Jung.

290 Perhaps Lil was the lucky one: for Hélène's memories of Emma see Gaudissart, *Emma Jung*, p. 161, and family memoirs, with thanks to Adrian Baumann.

291 'always the lady': author interview with Beatrice Merk.

291 'Father was often terribly funny': Agathe Jung, interview with G. F. Nameche.

291 'The way he used to sip': Adrian Baumann, interview with G. F. Nameche, and author interview with Adrian Baumann.

292 '*syndrome ambulatoire*': Bair, *Jung*, p. 315.

292 'Jung unfortunately had a great success': McGuire, 'Firm Affinities', p. 312.

292 recounted to Emma in his letters: *MDR*, Appendix, and Jaffé, *C. G. Jung*, p. 150.

294 'At last I was where': *MDR*, p. 225.

296 the Grail legend: see the Introduction to Emma Jung and and Marie-Louise von Franz, *The Grail Legend*, second edition, tr. Andrea Dykes, Princeton, NJ: Princeton University Press, 1998. It is possible Marie-Louise von Franz wrote the Introduction from Emma's notes when Carl asked her to finish the book after Emma's death.

299 'Her influence': Heinrich Fierz, interview with G. F. Nameche.

299 'It wasn't just a triangle situation': Johanna Meier, interview with G. F. Nameche, and Donn, *Freud and Jung*, p. 180.

299 'She was his partner': Tina Keller, interview with G. F. Nameche.

300 a boy was standing: Hans Kuhn, interview with G. F. Nameche.

300 village called Bollingen: the building of the the house at Bollingen and life there based on author interviews with the Jung family and G. F. Nameche interviews.

301 the famous Tower at Bollingen: *MDR*, p. 212.

304 the *Milwaukee Journal*: Bair, *Jung*, p. 341.

305 for Mombasa in Kenya: Ruth Bailey, interview with G. F. Nameche.

307 Daniel Hislop: McGuire and Hull (eds), *C. G. Jung Speaking*, p. 50.

307 a long letter to young Hans Kuhn: Jung, *Letters of C. G. Jung*, Vol. 1, p. 64.

308 Franz, now eighteen, would go: author interview with Franz's son Andreas Jung, and Donn, *Freud and Jung*, p. 181.

308 having her portrait painted: Ruth Bailey, interview with G. F. Nameche.

309 'highly charged': *MDR*, p. 255, and Bair, *Jung*, p. 356.

309 'I can let myself be deceived': *MDR*, p. 60.

309 'For Mrs Jung': Fowler McCormick, interview with G. F. Nameche.

310 'had to be on her husband's side': Susi Trüb, interview with G. F. Nameche.

310 From March to July 1925: Jung, *Introduction to Jungian Psychology*.

311 the Jungian theme of animus/anima: Emma Jung, *Animus and Anima*, tr. Cary F. Baynes and Hildegard Nagel, New York: Spring Publications, 1957, p. 15.

313 'There is no such thing': 'Marriage as a Psychological Relationship' (1925) in Jung, *CW17*.

314 'I went to the train': Jolande Jacobi, interview with G. F. Nameche.

315 'an excellent opportunity': Freud and Jones, *The Complete Correspondence*, p. 640.

Chapter 15: Coming Through

319 'Oh my God': Brome, *Jung*, p. 225.

319 'She was just beginning': Barbara Hannah, interview with G. F. Nameche, and Hannah, *Jung*, p. 201.

319 'She approached the problem': Eleanor Stone in *Bulletin of the Analytical Psychology Club of New York*, Vol. 17, Issue 5,

1955, courtesy of the Kristine Mann Library of the Psychological Club of New York.

320 shouting *Alleluia!*: Anthony, *The Valkyries*, p. 24.

320 'those fawning women': Hayman, *A Life of Jung*, p. 275, and Ferne Jensen (ed.), *C. G. Jung, Emma Jung, and Toni Wolff: A Collection of Remembrances*, San Francisco, CA: Analytical Psychology Club of San Francisco, 1982, p. 101.

320 'Emma was just lovely': Diana Baynes Janson, *Jung's Apprentice: A Biography of Helton Godwin Baynes*, Einsiedeln: Daimon Verlag, 2003, p. 151.

321 'Dear Mr McCormick': with thanks to the Wisconsin Historical Archive.

322 'I think she underwent': Donn, *Freud and Jung*, p. 180, and Carl Meier, interview with G. F. Nameche.

322 this marriage relationship: Joanna Meier, interview with G. F. Nameche.

323 'joint career': thanks to Sonu Shamdasani for his useful term 'joint career' to describe the extent of Carl and Emma's partnership.

323 'I do love Emma': Baynes Jansen, *Jung's Apprentice*, p. 258.

323 Toni was a manipulator': Jane Hollister Wheelwright, interview with Marion Woodman, *Jung Journal*, Volume 5, Issue 1, 2011, courtesy of the Kristine Mann Library of the Psychological Club of New York.

324 Carl went to Berlin: Thomas Kirsch, 'Toni Wolff–James Kirsch Correspondence', *Journal of Analytical Psychology*, Vol. 48, p. 501.

324 'Jung told me personally': Joseph Henderson, interview with G. F. Nameche.

324 'The thing went on': Jane Hollister Wheelwright, interview with Marion Woodman, *Jung Journal*.

324 'Toni overcame': Barbara Hannah, interview with G. F. Nameche.

324 'The law Jung': Carl Meier, interview with G. F. Nameche.

325 'You would then get to know her a bit': Jensen (ed.), *C. G. Jung, Emma Jung, and Toni Wolff*, p. 48. When *MDR* was published many were shocked to find no mention of Toni Wolff, though she was included in the 'Protocols' which form the basis of *MDR*. See Bair, *Jung*, Chapter 38, for a full discussion.

325 'She did not give herself easily': Jensen (ed.), *C. G. Jung, Emma Jung, and Toni Wolff*, p. 1.

325 'My original image': Jensen (ed.), *C. G. Jung, Emma Jung, and Toni Wolff*, p. 10.

326 America in 1936: Hannah, *Jung*, p. 237.

327 back to America: Hannah, *Jung*, p. 238, and McGuire, *Bollingen: An Adventure in Collecting the Past*, Princeton, NJ: Princeton University Press, 1982, p. 12.

327 Mary and Paul Mellon: William McGuire, *Bollingen*, p. 3, and William Schoenl, *C. G. Jung: His Friendships with Mary Mellon and J. B. Priestly*, Wilmette, IL: Chiron Press, 1998, p. 3.

329 perhaps anti-Semitic: for the accusations of anti-Semitism see Shamdasani, *Freud Files*, p. 277, and with thanks to Sonu Shamdasani for letter to Henry Murray, 19 December 1938: 'The origin of the story about myself being a frequent guest a Berchtesgaden has been traced back to Dr Hadley Cantil ... I should very much like to know what on earth prompted this man to tell such a cock-and-bull story ... there must be something behind it ... Whatever I touch and wherever I go I meet with this prejudice that I am a Nazi ... not persecution delusions ... a very real difficulty.'

330 'It was an extremely happy time': Baynes Jansen, *Jung's Apprentice*, p. 285.

331 'My entire youth': *MDR*, p. 52.

332 lead Jung to alchemy: McGuire and Hull (eds), *C. G. Jung Speaking*, p. 221, and *MDR*, p. 189.

332 'She was afraid': Susi Trüb, interview with G. F. Nameche.

332 'That was a terrible situation': Ruth Bailey, interview with G. F. Nameche.

332 'When I was a ripe man': Donn, *Freud and Jung*, p. 181.

332 Fowler McCormick … noticed: Fowler Mc Cormick, interview with G. F. Nameche.

333 'Well, she was a marvellous woman': Jolanda Jacobi, interview with G. F. Nameche.

333 'I think the night': McGuire, *Bollingen*, pp. 34, 49.

334 Emma who enforced it: for Emma's guarding of Carl see Susi Trüb, interview with G. F. Nameche, and Ruth Bailey, interview with G. F. Nameche.

336 'She was the heart': author interviews with Adrian Baumann and Andreas Jung, and Hans and Jost Horni, interview with G. F. Nameche.

336 'It's remarkable how': author interview with Dieter Baumann.

336 Emma was clever: author interview with Brigitte Merk.

336 'Oh she was la Grande Dame': Ania Teillard, interview with G. F. Nameche.

336 nineteen grandchildren: Author interviews with Adrian, Klaus and Dieter Baumann.

338 the Jung Institute was founded: Jensen (ed.), *C. G. Jung, Emma Jung, and Toni Wolff*, pp. 40–41.

339 'Lotus. Nun. Mysterious': Bair, *Jung*, p. 559; this is a loose translation, but makes the point.

339 'I shall always be grateful': Hannah, *Jung*.

340 'You have done the right thing': Sabi Tauber, interview with G. F. Nameche. See McGuire and Hull (eds), *C. G. Jung Speaking*, p. 220, for Jung's Answer to Job interpretation regarding his father.

340 danced a waltz: Jost Hoerni, interview with G. F. Nameche.

340 'all tense and white': Ruth Bailey, interview with G. F. Nameche.

340 During those last few days: author interviews with Andreas Jung and Adrian Baumann.

341 'I cannot continue': for Jung's letters following Emma's death see Jung, *Letters of C. G. Jung*, Vol. 2, pp. 279, 282, 284 and 316.

342 'We went to see him': Frieda Fordham, interview with G. F. Nameche.

342 'He was sad': Ruth Bailey, interview with G. F. Nameche.

342 'I know that when she died': author interview with Adrian Baumann.

342 'Mama's death': Jung, *Letters of C. G. Jung*, Vol. 2, p. 316.

342 'Let every man': Reverend Hans Schaer's funeral address courtesy of the Kristine Mann Library of the Psychological Club of New York.

344 'I saw her in a dream': *MDR*, p. 276.

Bibliography

Anthony, Maggy, *The Valkyries: The Women Around Jung*, Longmead: Element Books, 1990

Appignanesi, Lisa, and John Forrester, *Freud's Women*, London: Weidenfeld and Nicolson, 1992

Arp, Hans, *Zürcher Erinnerungen aus der Zeit des Ersten Weltkrieges*, Zurich: Artemis Verlag, 1954

Astor, James, 'Our Cause', *British Journal of Psychotherapy*, 11 July 2008

Bair, Deirdre, *Jung: A Biography*, Boston, MA: Little, Brown, 2003

Baumann, Walter, *Zürich: La Belle Époque*, Zürich: Orell Füssli Verlag, 1973

—, *Zürcher Schlagzeilen*, Zürich: Orell Füssli Verlag, 1981

Baynes Jansen, Diana, *Jung's Apprentice: A Biography of Helton Godwin Baynes*, Zürich: Daimon Verlag, 2003

Behling, Katja, *Martha Freud: A Biography*, Cambridge: Polity Press, 2005

Bennet, E. A., *C. G. Jung*, London: Barrie & Rockliff, 1961

—, *Meetings with Jung*, Zürich: Daimon Verlag, 1985

Bennet, Glin, 'Domestic Life with C. G. Jung: Tape-recorded Conversations with Ruth Bailey', *Spring*, 1986: pp. 177–89

Binswanger, Ludwig, *Sigmund Freud: Reminiscences of a Friendship*, tr. Norbert Guterman, New York: Grune & Stratton, 1957

Borch-Jacobsen, Mikkel, and Shamdasani, Sonu, *The Freud Files: An Inquiry into the History of Psychoanalysis*, Cambridge: Cambridge University Press, 2012

Brill, Abraham, *Lectures on Psychoanalytic Psychiatry*, New York: Knopf, 1946

Brome, Vincent, *Jung: Man and Myth*, London: Macmillan, 1978

—, *Ernest Jones: Freud's Alter Ego*, London: Caliban Books, 1982

Brown, Kevin, *The Pox: The Life and Near Death of a Very Social Disease*, Stroud: Sutton Publishing, 2006

Carotenuto, Aldo, *A Secret Symmetry: Sabina Spielrein Between Jung and Freud*, New York: Pantheon Books, 1982

Champernowne, Irene, *A Memoir of Toni Wolff*, San Francisco: C. G. Jung Institute of San Francisco, 1980

Chernow, Ron, *Titan: The Life of John D. Rockefeller, Sr.*, New York: Random House, 1998

Clay, Catrine, *King, Kaiser, Tsar: Three Royal Cousins Who Led the World to War*, London: John Murray, 2006

Covington, Coline, and Barbara Wharton (eds), *Sabina Spielrein: Forgotten Pioneer of Psychoanalysis*, London: Brunner-Routledge, 2003

Danuser, Hanspeter, *Das Trambuch: 100 Jahre Züri-Tram*, Zürich: Verlag Neue Zürcher Zeitung, 1982

Donn, Linda, *Freud and Jung: Years of Friendship, Years of Loss*, New York: Charles Scribner's Sons, 1988

Dunne, Claire, *Carl Jung: Wounded Healer of the Soul*, New York: Parabola Books, 2000

Dyer, Donald R., *Cross-Currents of Jungian Thought: An Annotated Bibliography*, Boston: Shambhala Publications, 1991

Ellenberger, Henri, *The Discovery of the Unconscious: The History and Evolution of Dynamic Psychiatry*, New York: Basic Books, 1970

Elms, Alan C., *Uncovering Lives: The Uneasy Alliance of Biography and Psychology*, Oxford: Oxford University Press, 1994

Ferris, Paul, *Dr Freud: A Life*, London: Sinclair-Stevenson, 1997

Fordham, Michael, 'Memories and Thoughts about C. G. Jung',
  Journal of Analytical Psychology, Vol. 20, Issue 2, July 1975
Freud, Ernst, Lucie Freud and Ilse Grubrich-Simitis (eds),
  Sigmund Freud: His Life in Pictures and Words, tr. Christine
  Trollope, London: André Deutsch, 1978
Freud, Martin, *Glory Reflected: Sigmund Freud – Man and Father*,
  London: Angus & Robertson, 1957
Freud, Sigmund, *The Interpretation of Dreams* in *The Standard
  Edition of the Complete Psychological Works of Sigmund Freud*,
  Vols 4–5, New York: W. W. Norton, 2000
—, *The Complete Letters of Sigmund Freud to Wilhelm Fliess,
  1887–1904*, tr. and ed. Jeffrey Moussaieff Masson, Cambridge,
  MA: Harvard University Press, 1985
—, *Unser Herz zeigt nach dem Süden. Reisebriefe 1895–1923*, ed.
  Christfried Tögel, Berlin: Aufbau Verlag, 2002
— and Karl Abraham, *Sigmund Freud–Karl Abraham: Briefe
  1907–1926*, ed. Hilda C. Abraham and Ernst L. Freud,
  Frankfurt: S. Fischer Verlag, 1965
—, *The Complete Correspondence of Sigmund Freud and Karl
  Abraham, 1907–1925*, ed. Ernst Falzeder, London: Karnac
  Books, 2002
— and Ludwig Binswanger, *Sigmund Freud–Ludwig Binswanger,
  Briefwechsel 1908–1938*, ed. Gerhard Fichtner, Frankfurt:
  S. Fischer Verlag, 1992
— and Sándor Ferenczi, *The Correspondence of Sigmund
  Freud and Sándor Ferenczi, Volume 1: 1908–1914*, ed. Eva
  Brabant, Ernst Falzeder and Patrizia Giampieri-Deutsch, tr.
  Peter T. Hoffer, Cambridge, MA: Harvard University Press,
  1993
— and Ernest Jones, *The Complete Correspondence of Sigmund
  Freud and Ernest Jones, 1908–1939*, ed. R. Andrew Paskauskas,
  Cambridge, MA: Harvard University Press, 1993
— and C. G. Jung, *The Freud/Jung Letters: The Correspondence
  between Sigmund Freud and C. G. Jung*, ed. William McGuire,

tr. Ralph Manheim and R. F. C. Hull, Princeton, NJ: Princeton University Press, 1974

Gaudissart, Imelda, *Emma Jung: Analyste et écrivain*, Lausanne: L'Âge d'Homme, 2010

Graf-Nold, Angela, 'The Zürich School of Psychiatry in Theory and Practice: Sabina Spielrein's Treatment at the Burghölzli Clinic in Zürich', *Journal of Analytical Psychology*, Vol. 46, Issue 1, January 2001

—, '100 Jahre Peinlichkeit – und (k)ein Ende?: Karl Abrahams frühe psychoanalytische Veröffentlichungen und die "sexuelle Frage"', *Jahrbuch der Psychoanalyse* 52 (2006): 93–138

Guggenheim, Kurt, *Alles in Allem*, 2 vols, Zürich: Artemis Verlag, 1954

Hannah, Barbara, *Jung: His Life and Work*, London: Michael Joseph, 1976

Hayman, Ronald, *A Life of Jung*, London: Bloomsbury, 1999

Jacobi, Jolanda, *The Psychology of C. G. Jung*, New Haven: Yale University Press, 1973

Jaffé, Aniela, *C. G. Jung: Word and Image*, Bollingen Series XCVII:2, Princeton, NJ: Princeton University Press, 1979

James, William, *The Letters of William James*, ed. Henry James, London: Longmans, Green, and Co., 1920

Janik, Allan, and Stephen Toulmin, *Wittgenstein's Vienna*, London: Weidenfeld and Nicolson, 1973

Jensen, Ferne (ed.), *C. G. Jung, Emma Jung, and Toni Wolff: A Collection of Remembrances*, San Francisco, CA: Analytical Psychology Club of San Francisco, 1982

Jones, Ernest, *The Life and Work of Sigmund Freud*, 3 vols, London: Hogarth Press, 1953–7

Jung, Andreas, Regula Michel, Arthur Ruegg, Judith Rohrer and Daniel Ganz, *The House of C. G. Jung: The History and Restoration of the Residence of Emma and Carl Gustav Jung-Rauschenbach*, Wilmette, IL: Chiron Publications, 2008

Jung, C. G., *Collected Works of C. G. Jung*, Vol. 1, *Psychiatric Studies*, ed. Herbert Read, Michael Fordham and Gerard Adler, tr. R. F. C. Hull, Princeton, NJ: Princeton University Press, 1970

—, *Studies in Word Association*, in *Collected Works of C. G. Jung*, Vol. 2, *Experimental Researches*, ed. and tr. Gerhard Adler and R. F. C. Hull, Princeton, NJ: Princeton University Press, 1973

—, *On the Psychology of Dementia Praecox*, in *Collected Works of C. G. Jung*, Vol. 3, *Psychogenesis of Mental Disease*, ed. and tr. Herbert Read, R. F. C. Hull and Gerhard Adler, Princeton, NJ: Princeton University Press, 1961

—, *Collected Works of C. G. Jung*, Vol. 5, *Symbols of Transformation*, ed. and tr. Gerhard Adler and R. F.C. Hull, Princeton, NJ: Princeton University Press, 1977

—, *Collected Works of C. G. Jung*, Vol. 17, *Development of Personality*, ed. and tr. Gerhard Adler and R. F.C. Hull, Princeton, NJ: Princeton University Press,| 1981

—, *Collected Works of C. G. Jung*, Vol. 18, *The Symbolic Life: Miscellaneous Writings*, ed. and tr. Gerhard Adler and R. F. C. Hull, Princeton, NJ: Princeton University Press, 1977

—, *Letters of C.G. Jung*, 2 vols, ed. Gerhard Adler and Aniela Jaffé, tr. R. F. C. Hull, Princeton, NJ: Princeton University Press, 1973–75

—, *Introduction to Jungian Psychology: Notes of the Seminar on Analytical Psychology Given in 1925*, ed. William McGuire, tr. R F. C. Hull, new Introduction and updates by Sonu Shamdasani, Princeton, NJ: Princeton University Press, 1989

—, *The Red Book: Liber Novus*, ed. Sonu Shamdasani, tr. M. Kyburz, J. Peck and S. Shamdasani, New York: W. W. Norton & Company, 2009

— and Jaffé, Aniela, *Memories, Dreams, Reflections*, New York: Pantheon, 1962

Jung, Emma, *Animus and Anima*, tr. Cary F. Baynes and Hildegard Nagel, New York: Spring Publications, 1957

— and Marie-Louise von Franz, *The Grail Legend*, second edition, tr. Andrea Dykes, Princeton, NJ: Princeton University Press, 1998

Kerr, John, *A Most Dangerous Method: The Story of Jung, Freud, and Sabina Spielrein*, New York: Knopf, 1993

McGuire, William, 'Firm Affinities: Jung's Relations with Britain and the United States', *Journal of Analytical Psychology*, 40.3, July 1995

—, *Bollingen: An Adventure in Collecting the Past*, Princeton, NJ: Princeton University Press, 1982

— and R. F. C. Hull (eds), *C. G. Jung Speaking: Interviews and Encounters*, London: Picador, 1978

Maines, Rachel P., *The Technology of Orgasm: 'Hyesteria', the Vibrator, and Women's Sexual Satisfaction*, Baltimore, MD: Johns Hopkins University Press, 1999

Makari, George, *Revolution in Mind: The Creation of Psychoanalysis*, London: Duckworth, 2008

Minder, Bernard, 'Sabina Spielrein: Jung's Patient at the Burghölzli', *Journal of Analytical Psychology*, Vol. 46, Issue 1, January 2001

Mösli, Rolf, *Eugen Bleuler: Pionier der Psychiatrie*, Zürich: Römerhof Verlag, 2012

Muser, Friedel, *Zur Geschichte des Psychologischen Clubs Zürich von den Anfängen bis 1928*, Zürich: Psychologischer Club, 1984

Noll, Richard, *The Jung Cult: Origins of a Charismatic Movement*, Princeton, NJ: Princeton University Presss, 1994

—, *The Aryan Christ: The Secret Life of Carl Jung*, New York: Random House, 1997

Pogson, Beryl, *Maurice Nicoll: A Portrait, London*: Vincent Stuart, 1961

Quétel, Claude, *History of Syphilis*, tr. Judith Braddock and Brian Pike, Cambridge: Polity Press, 1990

Schoenl, William, *C. G. Jung: His Friendships with Mary Mellon and J. B. Priestly*, Wilmette, IL: Chiron Press, 1998

Schorske, Carl E., *Fin-de-Siècle Vienna: Politics and Culture*, New York: Random House, 1981

Segaller, Stephen and Berger, Merrill, *Jung: The Wisdom of the Dream*, London: Weidenfeld & Nicolson, 1989

Shamdasani, Sonu, *Cult Fictions: C. G. Jung and the Founding of Analytical Psychology*, London: Routledge, 1998

—, *Jung Stripped Bare: By His Biographers, Even*, London: Karnac Books, 2005

—, *C. G. Jung: A Biography in Books*, New York: W. W. Norton & Company, 2012

Showalter, Elaine (ed.), *These Modern Women: Autobiographical Essays from the Twenties*, New York: The Feminist Press, 2003

Stein, Murray, *Jung's Treatment of Christianity: The Psychotherapy of a Religious Tradition*, Wilmette, IL: Chiron Publications, 1985

Tanner, Albert, *Arbeitsame Patrioten – wohlanständige Damen: Bürgertum und Bürgerlichkeit in der Schweiz, 1830–1914*, Zürich: Orell Füssli Verlag, 1995

Taylor, A. J. P., *The Habsburg Monarchy, 1809–1918: A History of the Austrian Empire and Austria-Hungary*, London: Hamish Hamilton, 1948

Waissenberger, Robert (ed.), *Traum und Wirklichkeit: Wien 1870–1930*, Vienna: Residenz Verlag, 1984

Wehr, Gerhard, *An Illustrated Biography of C. G. Jung*, tr. Michael Kohn, Boston: Shambhala Publications, 1989

—, *Jung: A Biography*, tr. David M. Weeks, Boston: Shambhala Publications, 1987

Weissweiler, Eva, *Die Freuds: Biographie einer Familie*, Cologne: Kiepenhauer & Witsch, 2006

Zweig, Stefan, *Die Welt von Gestern: Erinnerungen eines Europäers*, Stockholm: Bermann-Fischer Verlag, 1941

Credits

Unless otherwise stated, the images belong to the Jung Family Archive. They fall into two categories: those previously published elsewhere, and those never previously published. For the latter I wish to thank Andreas Jung for his generous help. These include: Emma aged sixteen; Emma at school; Emma in Canton of Schaffhausen costume; Emma and Carl's engagement; Emma on her wedding day; Carl with Aggie and Gretli; Emma with Gretli; Emma with Aggie and Gretli outside Burgholzli; the studio portrait of Emma; Emma and Toni at the Psychological Club; Emma and Carl at Eranos in the 1930s.

Section One

Page 2 (bottom): Vienna c. 1907, Stadtsarchiv Vienna

Page 3: Emma and Marguerite, with thanks to Beatrice Homberger

Page 4 (top left): The Haus zum Rosengarten, Staatsarchiv Schaffhausen

Page 4 (top right): The Rhine Falls, Staatsarchiv Schaffhausen/ Fotosammlung Neuhausen am Rheinfall

Page 6 (top left): Jean Rauschenbach, with thanks to Beatrice Homberger

Page 8 (top): Burghölzli Asylum, with thanks to Jorg Zemp, Burghölzli Archive

Page 8 (bottom): men's wards at Burghölzli, with thanks to Jorg Zemp, Burghölzli Archive

Section Two

Page 2 (bottom): Zürich c. 1905, Schweizerische Nationalbibliothek/Eidgenossisches Denkmalpflege

Page 7 (top): Toni Wolff, collection Jane and Joseph Wheelwright

Page 7 (bottom left): Carl and Toni Wolff in England, 1922, courtesy of the Kristine Mann Library, New York

Integrated

Page 130: the galvanometer, Aniela Jaffé, *C. G. Jung: Word and Image*

Page 273: Harold McCormick with his two daughters, Wisconsin Historical Society, WHS-114385

Page 283: Bertha Rauschenbach, with thanks to Beatrice Homberger

Page 328: Mary and Paul Mellon, Eranos Foundation

The author and publishers are committed to respecting the intellectual property rights of others and have made all reasonable efforts to trace the copyright owners of the images reproduced, and to provide appropriate acknowledgement within this book. In the event that any untraceable copyright owners come forward after the publication of this book, the author and publishers will use all reasonable endeavours to rectify the position accordingly.

Acknowledgements

When I first thought of Emma Jung as a subject for my next book, I rang my Swiss cousin Gaby in Zurich. I am half Swiss. Gaby and I spent every summer of our childhood together in the family home in St Gallen, an hour east of Zürich. I rang her from London: could she contact the Jung Institute for me and perhaps arrange a visit to the Jung house at Kusnacht on Lake Zürich? I knew it wouldn't be easy because the Jung family are very private people. But in her quiet way Gaby was persuasive. On my next trip to Zürich we were able to visit the Jung house, shown around by Andreas Jung, Emma and Carl's grandson, who lives there with his wife Vreni.

I thank Andreas and Vreni Jung for their invaluable help and their friendship. Equally, all the other surviving Jung grandchildren who trusted me with their grandmother's remarkable story, passing me from one cousin to the next. They shared one thing: they loved and admired their grandmother and felt that the Jung story, so often told, always neglected her, the key to it all. Or misrepresented her, which was worse. Without the vivid memories of the grandchildren I could not have written this family-based book. A cousin of the cousins, Beatrice Homberger, has my special thanks for furnishing me with some wonderful family photographs along with the many engaging talks we had in Schaffhausen together with Brigitte Merk, another Jung grandchild. A special thanks to Adrian Baumann, another grandchild, who gave up many hours to talk about his beloved grandmother. And to Thomas Fischer, Director of the Foundation of the Works of C. G. Jung, for proper clarification of the terms of the Jung archive.

Nicola Behrens at the Stadtarchiv Zürich helped me to locate newspapers, journals and maps of Zürich at the beginning of the twentieth century. And he was a marvel at finding out about the weather on any particular day: snow, rain, fog, hot summer sun. At Stadtarchiv Schaffhausen Frau Zimmermann and her team were equally helpful and friendly. Angela Graf-Nold, a Jungian who has worked extensively in the Burgholzli asylum archives in Zürich, was an excellent sounding board. Rolf Mosli is the man who started that archive, and he pointed me to some useful sources, not least his own excellent book on Eugen Bleuler. Murray Stein, an American Jungian living in Zürich, offered some interesting interpretations. In Vienna I had the help of a keen young researcher, Valentin Freyler. I thank Ingrid von Rosenberg for putting us in touch, and for giving me some good suggestions about women's lives in Germany and Switzerland at that time. In America I owe thanks to Jack Ebert at the Countway Library at the Harvard Medical School in Boston. Thanks also to the Kristine Mann Library in New York for stories of American friends and patients of the Jungs. And to David Williams for research into the fascinating McCormick/ Rockefeller story at the Wisconsin Historical Society.

In England, Sonu Shamdasani, the foremost Jungian scholar, offered many useful ideas, most especially that the relationship between Carl and Emma Jung was by way of a 'joint career'. Richard Cohen and James Astor each made some excellent suggestions. The staff at the London Library were as helpful as ever in locating long out-of-print books and erudite journals.

Arabella Pike at William Collins has been the kind of editor any writer might appreciate, making strong comments with a nice ease, happily supported by Stephen Guise, senior project editor, and Kate Johnson, the copy-editor. Jo Walker has designed a clever and beautiful jacket. As for my long-established literary agent, Anthony Sheil, the book would not have been written without him. 'Say what you mean, and mean what you say' is his mantra, and now mine. If thanks to my husband John comes last, that's typical of marriage, as Emma Jung could have told him. But it doesn't stop him being central to this book, helping with the research, reading every chapter, offering diplomatic criticisms.

All the time I was writing the book Gaby was suffering from cancer. She died last year. The book was almost finished by then and she'd been part of it all along, understanding exactly why I wanted to write it, because it was just the kind of thing we'd always talked about during those long summer holidays: family relationships, complicated marriages, women's lives, happiness and unhappiness, ambition, loyalty, love, laughter. The book is dedicated to her, with my deepest thanks.

Index